I0760397

THE STONE OF KNOWING COMPLETE SET

THE STONE CYCLE COMPLETE SETS BOOK 1

THE STONE CYCLE COMPLETE SETS SERIES

The Stone of Knowing Complete Set (The Stone Cycle Complete Sets Book 1), *comprising*

- The Stone of Knowing (The Stone Cycle Book 1)
- The Cost of Knowing (The Stone Cycle Book 2)
- The Seer: A Prequel to The Stone of Knowing (The Stone Cycle)

The Stone of Authority Complete Set (The Stone Cycle Complete Sets Book 2), *comprising*

- The Stone of Authority (The Stone Cycle Book 3)
- The Struggle for Authority (The Stone Cycle Book 4)

The Stone of Vitality Complete Set (The Stone Cycle Complete Sets Book 3), *comprising*

- The Stone of Vitality (The Stone Cycle Book 5)
- The Hope of Vitality (The Stone Cycle Book 6)

THE STONE OF KNOWING COMPLETE SET

THE STONE CYCLE COMPLETE SETS
BOOK 1

ALLAN N. PACKER

LUMINANT PUBLICATIONS

The Stone of Knowing Complete Set

The Stone Cycle Complete Sets Book 1

Comprising:
The Stone of Knowing (The Stone Cycle Book 1)
The Cost of Knowing (The Stone Cycle Book 2)
The Seer: A Prequel to The Stone of Knowing (The Stone Cycle)

First edition (v1.0) published in 2024
by Luminant Publications

ISBN 978-1-923218-09-3

Luminant Publications
PO Box 305
Greenacres, South Australia 5086

http://www.allanpacker.com

Cover Design by Karri Klawiter
Map illustration by Brian Plush

'The Stone of Knowing' Dedication

To James, Melanie, Stephen, and Deborah, for whom it was created. Their enthusiasm brought it to life and saw it through to its conclusion.

'The Cost of Knowing' Dedication

To Marc and Ray. I am grateful that they welcome me into their lives so willingly and unstintingly. And they keep presenting me with such delightful grandchildren!

'The Seer' Dedication

To Ali, so generous with her words, and already such an encouragement.

Baron Island
Savage Strait
Castel
Castel Citadel
Deadman's Pass
Steffan's Citadel
Maranelle
Arve
Duchy of Erestor
N
W
E
S
Arvenon
& surrounding Kingdoms

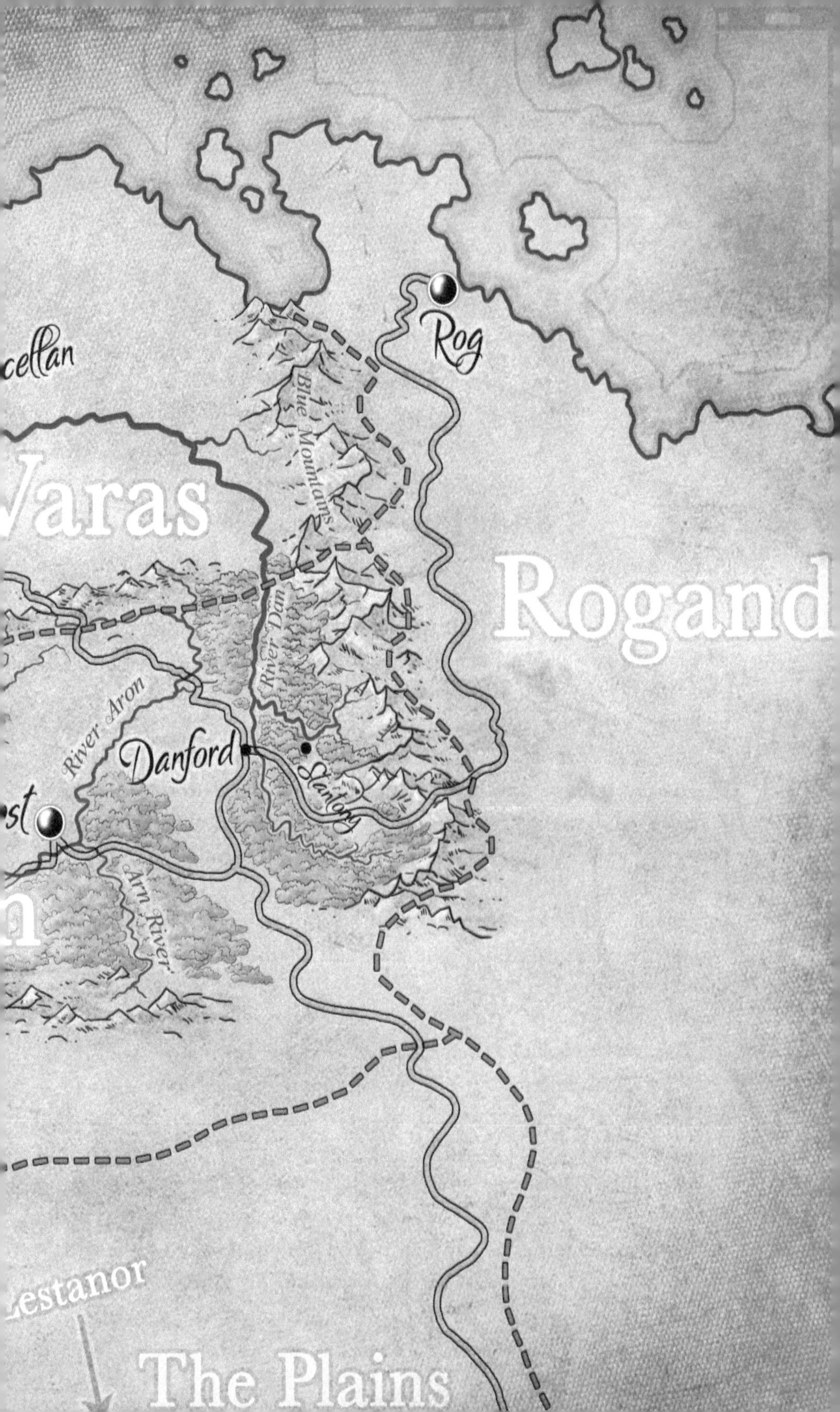
cellan
Rog
Blue Mountains
Varas
Rogand
River Dan
River Aron
Danford
Stanlong
st
Arn River
n
Lestanor
The Plains

PREFACE

The Stone of Knowing and *The Cost of Knowing* were published as separate novels, with a note in the blurb of each to indicate that together they formed a single story.

Releasing two novels had never been my intention. I always planned to publish the content as a single novel titled *The Stone of Knowing*, and the earliest cover was created with that in mind. However, with the story running to over two hundred thousand words—more than the longest book in Tolkien's *The Lord of the Rings* trilogy—I decided to revisit my plans. Splitting the content yielded two novels each exceeding one hundred thousand words, a more than respectable length for epic fantasy. *The Cost of Knowing* came into being as a result.

The Stone of Knowing Complete Set offered me the chance to deliver on my original intention by bringing both novels together in a single collection. Hopefully it will prove satisfying to read the story that way.

In addition to the two main novels, *The Stone of Knowing Complete Set* features two novelettes. The first, *The Gamble*, provides important background to the climax of the story, and it was published at the end of *The Cost of Knowing*. The second novelette, *The Seer, A Prequel to*

The Stone of Knowing, was published separately, and I have included it here for completeness. *The Seer, A Prequel to The Stone of Knowing* is also recommended pre-reading for *The Struggle for Authority, The Stone Cycle Book Four*.

The end result is *The Stone of Knowing Complete Set*.

Thanks for deciding to read it. I hope you enjoy it.

Allan Packer

PART I

THE STONE OF KNOWING

THE STONE CYCLE BOOK ONE

VOLUME 1—THE STONE

PROLOGUE

The king waited impatiently astride his horse, his thoughts dark and cold as the night that enveloped him.

For a brief moment the dazzling array of stars above captured his restless gaze, but he soon turned away. Staring at the night sky yielded no return. It wasn't worth his attention.

A torch bobbed toward him out of the darkness, the outline of an anxious servant gradually appearing beside it.

The man bowed low at his feet. "He has arrived, Your Majesty."

"Send him to me at once," growled the king.

The servant bowed again before scurrying away.

Before long a stallion pranced into view bearing a tall nobleman dressed in black.

The new arrival dipped his head as he drew closer. "The men are assembled, Your Majesty. I await only your command."

The sovereign scowled at the tall commander. "Remind me again," he demanded. "How does this plan benefit you?"

The rider barely hesitated. "Destroying our enemies and enlarging your kingdom at their expense is reward enough for me."

The king's eyes narrowed. He was well aware that the nobleman seized every opportunity to expand his own influence. This mission would be no exception. The commander had also sidestepped the question of plunder.

The evasiveness did not trouble the king. He himself would be the chief beneficiary in the end. He always made certain of that.

He studied the tall rider with a calculating eye for a long moment. Then he nodded once. "Do it."

Dipping his head once more, the commander swung his horse around and galloped away.

CRESTING THE RIDGE, the commander guided his black stallion forward until he reached the edge of the tree line. Far too many weeks had been spent moving his force into foreign territory undetected, but the time had come at last. He glanced irritably behind him as he waited for the last of the riders to take their positions in the shadow of the trees.

He stared down at the village below. The villagers had straggled home from the fields as the dusk deepened, and the laughter of children had stilled as the people disappeared into their crude dwellings.

There was nothing special about this place, no compelling reason to have lured the angel of death here rather than anywhere else that night. The slaughter simply needed to begin somewhere in Arvenon.

The tall nobleman stared out into the darkness. His presence here had a purpose, one he had carefully concealed from his scheming sovereign. The death and destruction he was about to unleash held no more interest for him than the particulars of the location. A prize beyond price lay hidden somewhere in this kingdom. His craving for it consumed him. It alone had drawn him here.

He turned to the horsemen waiting among the trees. "You all know what to do."

Dozens of torches flared into life, sending eerie shadows flickering from the horned helmets of the riders.

Rising in his stirrups, the dark leader raised a hand and thrust it toward the village.

"Destroy it all," he commanded. "Leave nothing alive."

1

Thomas found it on his way back toward the castle. The afternoon was drawing on and he was hurrying, but it caught his eye, and he quickly stopped and reached down for it. It was a small stone, almond-like in size and smooth to the touch. It lay gleaming in his palm, illuminated by the rays of the late afternoon sun.

Many times afterward he wondered how the stone came to be there and why he should have been the one to find it. But at that moment, the youth simply admired his new prize, captured by the striking swirls of blue and purple that covered its surface. He turned it over slowly in his hand. Then he tossed it into the air, once, twice, before dropping it carefully into the leather pouch at his belt. Retying the drawstring, he set off once again for home.

As the road drew him closer to the river, the orderly strips of cultivated land and clusters of cottages to his left began to fall away. Off in the distance he caught a glimpse of gray stone towers rising majestically over barren foothills. A sprawling town surrounded the castle with its lofty towers, and beyond the ford the road wound its way up to the ancient walls that encompassed the town.

To his right the last trees of the great forest advanced almost to the water's edge. Noticing the spreading gloom beneath their silent boughs, Thomas quickened his pace.

As he approached the ford, children's laughter drifted toward him from a nearby farm. A dog emerged from the forest ahead and set off slowly in the direction of the voices.

At the sight of the dog a wave of bitter memories welled up inside him. He had been up most of the previous night tending a sick greyhound and the frail litter of tiny puppies put at risk by her illness. His efforts had drawn a rare compliment from his father.

Emboldened by the unexpected response, he again asked for a dog of his own. Once more his father had refused. "There are fifteen dogs across the courtyard," he replied impatiently. "Fine animals, too —the king's own hounds. The best in all Arvenon. What do we want with another one? I'll hear no more about it!"

Thomas sensed that this time the decision was final. His father would never understand. It didn't matter if there were fifty hounds across the courtyard. They belonged to the king. They were fine animals, to be sure. But they would never compare with any one of their lesser cousins if only it belonged to Thomas Stablehand.

He grimaced and returned his attention to the animal ahead. The dog seemed unaware of his approach. In fact there was something peculiar about its gait and the way it hung its head. It wasn't unusual to see underfed and unkempt mongrels about the town. But farm dogs mostly fared better, and plenty of small game inhabited the forest at that season. The animal appeared intent on joining the children. If it was a pet someone at the farm would take care of it.

Thomas soon overtook it. As he passed by, the dog finally noticed him. It looked up at him as his hand, probing absently, chanced upon the stone hidden securely in his pouch.

He gasped with fear and amazement. How could he have thought it was a dog? He shrank back in terror from the snarling face and ravening jaws of a wolf. The wolf's eyes burned into him—hideous, unnatural, and filled with savage hate.

Nothing else mattered except to escape those eyes. Knowing it was futile, Thomas turned and ran for his life.

He sprinted down the path, heart racing. His legs, already weary, quickly began to ache. A sharp pain stabbed his side. He risked a glance behind—the wolf was almost on him. Utterly terrified, he flew blindly from it.

Once he stumbled on the rutted path and almost fell. But he recovered and flung himself forward again.

His breath rasped painfully into lungs of fire. His world narrowed to the desperate pounding of his feet and the pain in his lungs and side. Inexplicably, the wolf had not run him down, but from its snarling it was right behind.

He cast around frantically for a haven, and a rough wooden farmhouse caught his glance. Three young children chased each other nearby. Their carefree laughter snapped him out of his mindless terror.

"Run for your lives! Save yourselves," he gasped. Startled, the children stopped playing and looked up.

They were not going to move in time. For a moment, Thomas forgot his own fear. Hoping to draw the wolf away, he veered toward a small barn, shouting and waving his arms to keep its attention. At first, the wolf continued to pursue him. Then abruptly it came to a halt, turning its slavering muzzle toward the children.

The children's mother appeared from nowhere and shooed them into the house, calling urgently for her husband. As Thomas came panting up to the barn he caught a glimpse of the farmer running toward the wolf with a pitchfork, a resolute look on his face.

Not until he was safe in the hayloft did it occur to the young stable hand that the farmer might need his help. Securing the stone and quickly tying off his leather pouch, he climbed down from his perch and picked up the nearest weapon—a long-handled ax. Heart thumping, he tentatively retraced his steps.

A cacophony of loud yells and frantic snarling drew him to the battle. Thomas arrived to see the creature writhing on the ground in its death throes, its life blood drenching the soil an angry red. The farmer stood leaning on his pitchfork. He was breathing heavily, a wild look in his eyes.

When he recovered himself, he turned to face Thomas. "Thank you, son!" he said. "I owe you my children's lives. The heavens be praised that you noticed the dog was rabid."

Dog? Rabid? Thomas stared at the animal in astonishment. It was indeed a dog. And the flecks of foam around its mouth supported the alarming conclusion. The farmer, now kneeling in some grass wiping his weapon clean, appeared not to notice his confusion.

Bewildered and feeling awkward, Thomas turned away, mumbling a goodbye.

The farmer stood up quickly. "Wait!" he urged, turning to Thomas and removing his cap. "There is little I can offer you by way of thanks," he said apologetically. "But tonight we will celebrate, such as we can. You shall feast with us at least."

Thomas shook his head.

"Come, now. Look at you. Skinny as a willow branch." The farmer winked at him. "My wife can do something about that," he promised, patting his own ample stomach.

"I must go." Thomas glanced anxiously at the sun sinking low in the sky.

"Ah, of course. Well, heaven must reward you, then."

Thomas took his chance and hurried off without a backward glance.

"Hey, I don't even know your name!" the farmer shouted after him.

"Thomas Stablehand," the youth reluctantly called back over his shoulder. For the first time he discovered that he appreciated his anonymity. He little guessed how much he would miss it in the days to come.

THOMAS WOUND his way through the streets of Arnost until the walls of the castle towered above him, blotting out half the night sky. The familiar smell of horses greeted him as he pushed through some heavy wooden gates into a spacious courtyard and then into the small three-roomed stone cottage that was his home. A cheery fire crackled in the hearth. Inviting smells wafted out from the cooking pot.

His mother, Marya, a diminutive person full of nervous energy, bustled about as though she expected the king for supper. She greeted him with obvious relief. "Where have you been, Tom? I almost asked your father to call out the bloodhounds after you," she scolded. "Did you enjoy your afternoon?"

He responded with a noncommittal grunt and set to work steadily at the huge plate of steaming stew she set before him. The ups and downs of life might shatter his equanimity at times, but very little affected his appetite. His mother attempted for a while to draw him into conversation, then gave up and left him in peace.

THOMAS LAY awake that night unable to put the afternoon's events out of his mind. He could picture the dying animal thrashing in agony on the ground. The rabies had exacted a heavy toll and its body appeared ravaged and depleted. That explained its slow reactions. But nothing accounted for the haunting wolf-eyes, still vivid in his mind.

It was the early hours of the morning before he finally managed to get to sleep. When he did, his dreams were filled with strange foreboding. Wild and exotic creatures paraded menacingly before him, teeth flashing. Unfamiliar men appeared, their intentions for good or ill written plainly across their faces. Most enigmatic of all was a young woman, wild eyed and fiery, and impossible to comprehend.

He woke with the dawn, and stumbled out of bed bleary eyed and disoriented.

LATER THAT DAY, Thomas returned to the stables from an errand to find a scruffy lad of about fifteen years of age waiting excitedly for him. The youth, Simon, almost lived at the stables, helping out with menial tasks whenever he was allowed. Today Simon greeted him so eagerly and with such wide-eyed admiration that Thomas began to feel uncomfortable. "I wish I'd been there to see it!" Simon enthused.

"See what? What are you talking about?"

"You know! The way you saved the farmer's children. Wrestling that rabid dog to the ground. And killing it with your bare hands!" Simon illustrated his words with an energetic re-enactment of the feat, complete with grunting and scowling.

"What?! Who told you that?"

"Everybody knows about it. Even King Steffan. You're a hero!"

"That's ridiculous! I wasn't even the one who killed it."

But Simon, his face shining, was gone, no doubt to spread the story even further.

CHANCE ENCOUNTERS with acquaintances among the townsfolk the following day confirmed to Thomas his new status as a hero. He quickly discovered to his intense embarrassment that the episode was assuming almost mythical proportions. He tried to reason with them, but his protestations had the opposite effect. Modesty befits a hero, and his denials were taken as further confirmation of his worthiness.

It appeared that an account of the incident had reached the castle, too. Plans were already underway to beat the bushes. Rabies was a serious threat to the farming community, and the dog was unlikely to be the only carrier. The king intended to personally lead a sweep through the outskirts of the great forest the next weekend. All able-bodied men were expected to participate. In spite of the risk involved, excitement was building in the town, and the talk was of little else.

Fortunately, there was plenty to do about the stables to distract Thomas. Both horses and hounds were being readied for the weekend's hunt, and since King Steffan would be visiting the stables in person, the stalls had to be cleaned out thoroughly and fresh straw brought in. Memories of the encounter with the dog-wolf still baffled Thomas, but he gradually came to the conclusion that the wolf must have been a product of his imagination. As for the stone, it lay forgotten in his pouch.

A SMALL PAIR of eyes capped by an unkempt mess of dark hair peered hopefully over the wall surrounding the stable courtyard. Keen to avoid more questions about his heroism, Thomas tried to ignore them. But the round little eyes looked so pathetic that eventually he could bear it no longer.

He nodded at the half-face. "Hello."

The eyes brightened, and a mouth and chin bobbed into view. "Are you very busy?"

Thomas relaxed. He could guess what was coming next.

The little voice was trying not to be too eager. "Can I ride the big war-horse again?"

Thomas struggled to keep a grin from his face. He carefully chose the steadiest old nag in the stables for the little urchins to ride, but they didn't need to know that. "I guess you can."

"And my friend, too?"

"If you don't disturb the horses."

"Oh, we won't! We promise."

It wasn't really convenient, but he knew how much they loved it. "Come back just before the sun sets. My father won't be around then."

Later, Thomas waited behind the stables for his little horsemen to appear. An old gray mare, suitably saddled, stood patiently beside him. Presently two shining faces emerged over the top of the wall. He helped the boys down and hoisted them onto the horse.

Dwarfed by the mare, they bounced up and down proudly, each brandishing a wooden sword fiercely in one hand and hanging on precariously with the other.

Thomas knew the boys saw him as an adult. That felt good. And yet another part of him envied them, perched jubilantly up there in the saddle. Did you have to leave fun behind when you grew up?

THOMAS WAS WORKING with his father checking that the horses were properly shod. He sensed that his parents had noted his withdrawn mood and were watching for his reaction to the stories that were circulating.

"You're quiet today, son," his father ventured.

It was a fair understatement. Normally they conversed a little when they worked together, but the youth hadn't offered him a word all day. Thomas heard the comment but didn't respond. In spite of all that had happened since, he hadn't forgotten their interaction a few days earlier and was still smarting from it.

Axel Stablehand didn't pursue it, and Thomas was grateful.

In spite of the denial of his fondest hope, Thomas had to reluctantly admire his father. From what Thomas knew of family history, Axel, one of a long line of stable hands, had been blessed with more ability than his forebears. He was generally regarded as efficient, reliable, and hardworking. In recognition of his skills he had been appointed master of the stables when the previous incumbent died some years earlier.

Thomas knew that his father hoped and expected the position would stay in the family. But he wasn't certain he warranted the confidence this implied, and he resented the steady pressure to achieve that came with his father's expectations.

THOMAS WAS CORNERED by his mother later in the day. "What's on your mind, Thomas?" she asked. "Is it the gossip about the farmer and the rabid dog?"

He shrugged, and she eyed him knowingly. "No, I didn't think so. You're upset with your father, aren't you? Because he won't let you have a dog of your own."

He didn't respond, but he didn't need to. She knew him too well.

"Don't be angry with him," she said. "He isn't trying to be unkind."

A grunt was the best he could manage in reply.

She wasn't willing to give up that easily. "Don't forget your afternoon in the countryside. You were running an errand for him, but he was just as interested in giving you an outing. He didn't have to do that."

Thomas wasn't placated.

"He's a tough taskmaster," she said, "and he expects a lot from his workers. But you know he's always believed there should be more to life than just toil when you're young, and he hasn't forgotten that you've been hard at work for a few years already. How many other seventeen year olds have fathers who give them an afternoon off once in a while?"

He still said nothing.

She threw up her hands in disgust. "I give up. The two of you are as stubborn as each other!" And with that she was gone.

Thomas knew his mother was right. He couldn't honestly say that his father was unkind. And he had appreciated the afternoon off.

But his pleasant excursion hadn't turned out as he'd expected. Life was starting to feel complicated, and he wasn't quite sure how it had happened.

2

Threatening rain clouds dominated the sky on the morning of the hunt, but they did nothing to dampen the enthusiasm of the throng gathered outside the walls of Arnost. A constant buzz of excitement lent the event a carnival atmosphere.

A cheer went up from the gates, and all heads turned in that direction. A mounted party emerged, led by King Steffan. The cheering spread as he progressed through the crowd, acknowledging his subjects with a wave.

Overawed, Thomas stared at the king as he passed. He seemed so strong and sure of himself. Not even the simple and practical garb he wore for the hunt disguised his regal bearing. As always, he stood out from the men around him.

The king and his party moved on and the attention of the crowd turned elsewhere. Thomas stood behind his father trying to look inconspicuous.

Almost immediately one of the king's stewards approached them.

"Good morning, Master Axel," he said. "The king requests that you present your son to him."

Although Thomas understood royal protocol well enough to recognize a command when he heard it, he still waited irrationally for his father to decline graciously on his behalf. Surely it would be inappropriate to trouble the king at such a time.

"It would be a great honor," replied his father, smiling happily.

In his daydreams Thomas had been presented to the king many times. Usually it was on the battlefield as he lay victorious but seriously wounded, struck down at the last after single-handedly defending his sovereign against impossible odds. Always he spoke gravely and respectfully, modestly declining the king's repeated offers of lands and titles.

Now, in his hour of need, he found his courage deserting him unforgivably. He envied his father's quiet confidence. The master's work often brought him into contact with the king, and he could picture them as he had seen them from a distance, calmly discussing the condition of the horses or making plans for renovations to the stables.

Thomas dragged himself behind his father like a condemned man led to the gallows. When they arrived they found King Steffan occupied. The strain of waiting soon drained from the youth any traces of self-assurance that remained.

Eventually the king, mounted on his courser, noticed them and looked down with a welcoming smile. "Ah, yes. This must be our stable master's lad. I hear that you killed a rabid dog with your bare hands."

Thomas stood with his head bowed as if scolded. His father nudged him gently, and he blushed deeply. "No, Your Majesty. It was the farmer I killed," he finally blurted out. "I mean the farmer did it. Killed the dog, I mean."

A hint of a smile flickered across the king's face. "I see. No doubt you did well enough. I have arranged for you to accompany the hunt on horseback. My Lord Denison, see that the steward finds a mount for young Thomas."

The stable master swelled with pride at the honor. Coming to the aid of his son, he thanked the king on his behalf. Thomas was led away and soon found himself astride a frisky mare, feeling as if the whole crowd was staring at him.

He knew King Steffan had the best of intentions, but he felt like a fish out of water. He longed to be among the commoners where he felt secure. He took what comfort he could from his skill in handling horses: at least he wasn't going to complete his embarrassment by falling off in front of the crowd.

THE CLOUDS WERE CLEARING, and the sun had climbed high into the sky when the last of the townsmen crossed the ford. The king had appointed marshals to oversee the crossing, and they remained behind to ensure that the enthusiastic group of children from the town stayed on the other side of the river.

The mounted party and the hounds had been first to cross. They were met on the other side by a grim-looking band of farmers armed mostly with pitchforks. The townsmen carried heavy wooden clubs or crudely fashioned spears and wore thick leggings of cloth or leather to protect themselves against being bitten.

The farmer had apparently been watching for Thomas and called out eagerly to him in greeting. Once the hunt was underway, Thomas's earlier feelings of awkwardness had begun to subside. Seeing the farmer brought the discomfort flooding back again. What about the stories that were circulating? Would he think Thomas had started them? Fervently wishing he was somewhere else, Thomas waved back half-heartedly and urged his horse on.

Once they penetrated the forest, Thomas gradually worked his way to the edge of the main group. At first the going had been easy, the trees being scattered and the undergrowth sparse. But soon the trees crowded in on the riders, forcing the horses to pick their way slowly among the waist-high brush. The townsmen and farmers struggled along behind as best they could.

Paths were infrequent here, and most of them led nowhere. Few people had cause to venture further than the outskirts of the forest, and there were no signs of habitation. The riders were constantly forced to duck their heads to avoid low-hanging branches.

Thomas soon wearied of it. He headed his horse away from the others toward a section of the forest where the trees were less densely populated.

He found himself moving through a stand of tall pines toward the green expanse of a large natural clearing deep in the forest. The sunlight filtered softly through the branches high overhead, and a gentle breeze brushed at the hair dangling across his face. He loosened the reins to allow the horse to crop on the plentiful clumps of grass growing in the clearing.

A slight movement attracted his attention. He glanced up. A fox stood among the trees across the clearing eyeing him curiously. It might never have seen a human before, or a horse for that matter. Thomas's mount moved, searching for new patches of juicy green, and he lost sight of the fox.

He sat quietly, soaking in the tranquility of the scene and relishing the chance to sit upright again. The beauty that surrounded him brought to mind the attractive swirls of color that covered his new stone. He unfastened his pouch and fished his hand down in search of it. Yes, it was still there. He withdrew the stone and examined it carefully, again struck by its unusual beauty.

He was in the act of returning it to its home when something made him look up again. The fox was gone. In its place crouched a snarling wolf.

He stiffened and stared wide-eyed at the animal. Those eyes—he could have sworn they recognized him. But the wolf was dead. And yet there never was a wolf. He shook his head, trying to clear his confusion.

The silence in the clearing, which he had taken for tranquility, suddenly seemed oppressive. The usual background of forest sounds was absent, and the birds were hushed. The whole forest appeared to be holding its breath.

Bristling with menace, the wolf took a step toward him. Thomas sat transfixed in the saddle, his heart pumping wildly. The horse, sensing his tension, lifted its head from the grass and shifted uncomfortably. The wolf moved closer. Thomas wanted to call out for help, flee, do anything. But he could only sit rigid, his breath coming in gasps.

As if it were reading his mind, his horse spun around and bolted for the forest. Thomas, too slow to regain his wits, connected heavily with the first branch the horse passed under. Still clutching the stone tightly in his left hand, he fell senseless to the ground.

HE WOKE to find someone bending over him. An unfamiliar face, that of a young knight, swam unsteadily into focus. Thomas tried to lift his head and groaned. An unseen drummer pounded a relentless staccato in his skull. The knight looked at him with concern in his eyes. "Better lie still for a while," he said. "That's a nasty bump on your forehead."

"I'm all right," Thomas replied, trying to sit up. He almost swooned with the attempt, shafts of pain shooting up his left arm. "My arm!" he sobbed.

The knight leaned closer. "I think you've broken it," he said, probing the arm gently. "What's that in your hand?" he asked with sudden interest. Thomas, uncomprehending, made no reply. He gasped in protest when the knight moved his hand, working the stone from his grasp.

Thomas was totally unprepared for what followed. As the stone left his hand, the knight was transformed into a very ordinary looking man-at-arms. He must have been in his early twenties, with a shock of red hair protruding from beneath his small iron helmet. The young man held the stone up and gave a low whistle. "Very pretty," he said admiringly. "What is it?"

Seeing the stone in another's hand brought a sudden rush of energy to Thomas. "It's mine!" he exclaimed in anger. "Give it back!"

"No harm intended," replied the young man defensively. "I'll put it in your pouch," he volunteered, moving toward Thomas's uninjured side.

"Make sure it's tied properly," snapped Thomas.

The soldier obligingly put it in the pouch and tied it very firmly, carefully avoiding the bad arm.

"What is it?" he repeated.

"A good-luck charm. A family heirloom," replied Thomas testily, surprising himself with the lie.

The soldier snorted ironically. "You can keep it!" he said with feeling, looking down at Thomas spread out helpless on the ground. He patted his sword. "This is the only good luck charm I'm prepared to trust."

Thomas groaned again and closed his eyes. The exchange had exhausted him and pain once again engulfed his senses. A dull ache had started in his arm, competing with the drummer for attention. Tears of self-pity welled in his eyes. How did he get himself into this mess?

Belatedly, he remembered the wolf coming for him. "What happened to the wolf?" he asked weakly.

The young soldier stood up and moved to his horse. "If you mean the fox," he replied, "I killed it. You appear to have an attraction for rabid animals," he added dryly.

Thomas frowned. Dogs which were wolves which were dogs. Knights who were ordinary men-at-arms. Wolves which were foxes. Was he going mad? A sudden fear pushed its way through his pain. Did he have rabies himself? Had he been bitten by the dog after all?

The young man noticed his agitation. "You needn't worry," he said, as though reading Thomas's thoughts. "I killed the fox before it got to you. Your horse alerted me. It came crashing through the trees and almost collided with my own horse. I decided to find out what spooked it and what had become of its rider. The fox found out what lances are used for," he concluded with satisfaction.

"I'm going to get help." He swung himself into the saddle and leaned forward, speaking softly to his mount. They moved off toward the trees.

"I won't be long. Keep your chin up," the soldier called back as he disappeared into the forest.

. . .

THE REST of the day was a nightmare Thomas hoped he would quickly forget. Olaf, captain of the King's Guard, was among the first to reach him. The captain decided Thomas's arm needed immediate attention. Ordering two of his men to hold Thomas down, he quickly reset the arm, immobilizing it with a splint made of hastily cut branches.

The fact that Thomas vociferously disapproved of the operation seemed to worry him not a whit. He wore the air of a man who had dealt with far worse. And Thomas, who felt roughly handled, received little sympathy. All who examined his arm remarked on how grateful he must be feeling toward the old captain for the fine job he had done.

They carried Thomas out of the forest on a crudely built stretcher. The going proved very difficult, and his bearers tipped him out twice before reaching open ground. It was late at night before he finally sank onto his bed in his own home, utterly weary and miserable beyond words.

THE AFTERNOON after the hunt Thomas's mother bustled into his room announcing a visitor. Thomas, moody and still in pain, was not inclined to be welcoming. To his surprise the young soldier appeared grinning in the doorway.

"May I come in?"

"Yes, of course. I…I'm Thomas," he replied awkwardly.

"I know. My name is William Prentis, but everyone calls me Will."

There was something infectious about his cheerfulness, and Thomas's spirits began to lift. "I never thanked you for rescuing me," he said.

"No need. Actually, I should thank you."

"Why?" asked Thomas, incredulous.

"Well, it's hard for a soldier to be noticed these days. There hasn't even been a decent border skirmish for years," Will said with disgust.

"Thanks to your escapade with the fox I managed to catch the attention of Captain Olaf."

Thomas grimaced at the mention of the old captain. "He's the one who nearly ripped my arm off!"

Will chuckled. "I guess it must have hurt. But you were in capable hands. The captain may not be gentle, but he's very experienced. I'd trust him to set my arm ahead of any of Arnost's so-called doctors.

"He's appointed me to the King's Guard." Will indicated the falcon crest, the royal insignia, on his new vest. "One day I'm going to be the captain."

The claim did not seem idle or boastful. Will's words were matter-of-fact. Seeing the intensity in the young soldier's eyes, Thomas believed it. He momentarily remembered his first impression of Will, that of a young knight, strong and self-assured, and found himself thinking that one day this man would make a fearsome enemy.

"My guess is we've seen the last of rabies for a while," Will ventured.

"Were any other rabid animals found?"

"No, only the two you came across. You seem to have a knack for finding them! How do you do it?"

Thomas blushed a little. "I don't know. I don't understand it myself."

Will stood up. "I must go. I have my first duty with the Guard soon. I'll come and visit again when I can."

With that he was gone.

During his convalescence Thomas began to realize that the stone had something to do with his changes in perception. The realization first came to him in a thunderstorm.

A couple of days after the visit of Will Prentis, a storm rolled in from the west, and booming thunderclaps were soon spooking the horses. The night was pitch black; clouds blotted out the sky and neither the stars nor the moon were visible. Thomas was groping his way toward the stables when a huge sheet of lightning lit up the sky.

For a brief moment, every detail around him was plainly revealed to his sight. Then the lightning was gone, and his vision again went dark.

He remembered the image of the young knight, instantly replaced by the ordinary face of a young soldier. The transformation had occurred when the stone had been pulled from his hand. Could the stone have changed his vision, just as the lightning had done?

The stone lay securely in his pouch. That much he could tell with his right hand. Further investigation was impossible until his left arm became mobile again: Will had tied the pouch too tightly to undo it with one hand.

But how could a stone change what he saw? And where could such a talisman have come from?

A priest might know of such things. Thomas wondered uneasily, though, whether the church might regard it as black magic. He didn't like to think where that might lead.

No, he would keep it to himself for the moment. Only Will knew of its existence, and he seemed unaware of its significance. Indeed, although the two of them saw each other frequently in the weeks that followed the hunt, neither ever referred to it.

ONE MORE SURPRISE lay in store. A few days later his father, looking uncomfortable, came to his room. "Come outside, Thomas. There's something there for you."

Thomas followed him into the courtyard to find a small wicker basket on the cobblestones. Inside he saw a dark brown bundle of fur and an eager little face turned to him. He stared in disbelief.

"It's for you," repeated his father. Thomas, blinking back tears, turned to him, incapable of speech. "He'll be hungry. You'd better find him some milk," his father offered gruffly and moved off quickly toward the stables.

Thomas reached out his good arm to the puppy. The little mastiff whelp, probably no more than seven or eight weeks old, licked his hand, wagging its tiny tail frantically.

Overcome by a surge of joy, Thomas glanced up at his father's retreating form. Maybe his father cared about him after all. For as long as he could remember, his father had been quick to correct and rebuke, and slow to praise. He could not remember his father ever saying he was proud of him or pleased with him. He had certainly never expressed affection. He always felt a disappointment to his father, never able to measure up to the high standards a man had a right to expect of his only son.

In any event, being an invalid had its compensations: a broken arm and a lump on the head had achieved more in a few days than years of argument and pleading.

He smiled down at the puppy, which had curled itself into a little ball and closed its eyes. "Hello, Ben," he said quietly. "We're going to be good friends."

3

Having come off duty with time on his hands, Will decided to visit Thomas. The young stable hand might be unassuming, but the guardsman had quickly discovered that his new friend had some unexpected skills.

Will arrived in time to witness a vigorous assault by Thomas's mother on a broad expanse of dangling spiderwebs that had dared to appear above her doorway.

"Hello, Will." Marya beamed him a welcoming smile. "Thomas will be pleased to see you."

She grounded her broom. "It's nice that you've been taking such an interest in him. He's never had a chance to get to know any soldiers before."

"It's their loss, then," Will exclaimed. "Did you know he can mount a moving horse bareback, even with only one good arm?" He shook his head in wonder.

Her eyes went wide for a moment. Then a resigned look appeared on her face. "It doesn't surprise me," she said with a sigh. "He's always been good with horses."

"Where is he now?"

"At the stables. With the horses, of course." She rolled her eyes.

Will thanked her and headed toward the cluster of barns and stables that lay behind the house.

As he neared his destination, his attention was drawn to a small stockaded enclosure adjacent to the stables. A large bay stallion was screaming shrilly, rearing and flailing about with its forelegs. As Will watched, the middle-aged man hanging on grimly to its halter dropped the rope and fled the enclosure in terror. He escaped unscathed, but only barely.

Thomas emerged from a barn, and a disconcerted look appeared on his face as he took in the scene.

Curious to see what his friend might do, Will stepped quietly back out of sight.

Ignoring the man, Thomas slipped between the railings and entered the enclosure. The stallion neighed and watched him wide-eyed, its ears pinned back. Thomas approached the horse slowly, speaking to it soothingly until it gradually settled and allowed him to approach. He held up a small carrot and the horse nickered, peeling back its lips and accepting the treat.

The man looked on nervously. "Be careful!" he warned Thomas. "That animal just attacked me." He appeared thoroughly downcast. "I've never had a horse before. I was hoping to take this one back to the farm today, but it's completely unpredictable! Sometimes it lets me approach it, just like it did with you then. Other times it's totally wild."

He shook his head in dismay. "The animal is dangerous! I should never have let your father talk me into buying it."

"It's only dangerous because it's terrified," Thomas told him bluntly.

"What do you mean?"

"Which direction did you approach the horse from?"

"From behind, of course. If it sees me coming, there's no telling what it might do."

"And how are you planning to handle it when the horse behaves like it did earlier?"

"I yell at my children when they misbehave, and I'm not going to treat a horse any differently. I'd take a stick to it if it wasn't so savage."

Thomas shook his head. "You're doing everything wrong. It's not wild, and it's not unpredictable. It's scared. You're teaching it to be scared."

Thomas left the horse and returned to the railing. "Can I explain it to you?" he asked.

The older man looked uncertain, but he nodded slowly.

"Don't approach a horse from any of its blind spots," Thomas told him patiently. "If it can see what you're doing, it won't be so anxious. And you should never get angry with it. That will only scare it even more. You'll lose any trust you've built."

He paused, and peered at the man. Apparently satisfied that his words were being understood, Thomas beckoned to him. "Come with me, and I'll show you."

The man hesitated for a long moment, but then he took a deep breath and stepped back into the enclosure.

"Here," said Thomas. "You'll need this." He handed the man another small carrot. "Now, follow me."

The man trailed behind cautiously as Thomas once again advanced to the horse. Seeing their approach, the horse became restless again. Thomas spoke to it soothingly, motioning with his good hand for his companion to move more slowly.

When the man reached the horse, he tentatively offered it the carrot. He was even able to pat its neck. He still looked nervous but seemed much happier.

"Stay with it for a while," Thomas suggested. "Talk to it, but make sure you keep your voice calm and quiet. You can come back tomorrow and do the same thing. Let the horse get used to you."

Thomas turned to go, and the man thanked him gratefully.

After Thomas had left the enclosure behind, Will stepped forward and joined him. "That was nicely done, Thomas," he said with a smile. "You were kinder to the fellow than he deserved."

"I wasn't doing it for his sake," Thomas replied. "I was thinking of the horse."

Will grinned. "Either way, you did a good job." He pointed to the enclosure. "The two of them seem to be getting along like old friends."

Thomas shrugged. "I know what to do with horses. It's people I have trouble figuring out."

That drew a chuckle from Will. "How's your arm?" he asked.

"It's still sore." Thomas looked at him sheepishly. "Jumping onto moving horses doesn't seem to help it heal for some reason."

Will laughed. "We need to take your mind off it. Your mother's an outstanding cook—let's go see what we can wheedle out of her."

"I WON'T BE SEEING you for a while, Thomas. We move out in two days."

Will looked grave, but Thomas knew his friend had been longing for this. The whole of Arnost buzzed with excitement, and Thomas was caught up in it, too. "I heard some people arrived in wagons last night. Who were they? Many of them were wounded."

"Survivors from Danlenet. That's a small town near the Rogandan border. They say the whole border region is in turmoil. It was bad enough when the nomad tribes were plundering the outlying farms, but the attack on Danlenet must have been very well planned. The town was defended, but the townsmen never stood a chance."

Will lowered his voice. "One of the guardsmen overheard the captain talking to the king. They're wondering if King Agon of Rogand is behind this. King Steffan wants to find out what's going on. And he's going to teach the nomads a lesson they won't forget," he added with satisfaction.

Thomas gazed admiringly at Will. He looked every inch a soldier. "Will you be wearing armor into battle?"

"Me? Not yet." Will laughed. "The captain is the only guardsman with armor, and that's just a chain-mail shirt. Only the nobles and knights wear armor. It's too expensive.

"The King's Guardsmen are issued with thick buff leather jackets.

They'll protect against a sword cut, and they're much lighter and more flexible than armor. And we do have shields and helmets."

"I wish my arm was healed properly. I could come with you!"

Will looked startled. "You? You're a bit young. Besides, you'll never make a soldier; you're too gentle." Thomas, cut to the quick, felt his cheeks flame, but the young guardsman seemed not to notice. "And you're needed here. The King's Guard would be helpless without good horses, and you have a way with them."

The conversation sputtered on, but Thomas was far away. Long after Will had left he was still thinking up injured retorts to his friend's assertions. *Of course I can't fight! That's men's work. I'm needed to shovel manure.*

So that's all I'm good for. Well, they needn't think I'll be there to cheer them off when they leave. I'll be far too busy doing important work: mucking out the stables.

That night Thomas lay in bed tossing fitfully. He had no great ambition to be a soldier; for him the idea of battlefield glory was little more than an idle daydream. Nevertheless, he knew that few able-bodied males made it through life without being called upon, sooner or later, to defend the interests of king and country. Now, the only soldier he could call his friend—a soldier marked for greatness in the vision from the stone—had summarily dismissed him as unsuitable. He could still hear Will's words: "You'll never make a soldier; you're too gentle."

Grimly he vowed to himself that people would begin to see a new Thomas.

THOMAS PICKED at his evening meal, bone weary from the long hours of work. His arm, still not healed, had proven a frustrating restriction, and now it was throbbing painfully.

"Tarkess was still feisty when I left the stables," his father said.

At the mention of the war-horse, Thomas felt the blood drain from his face. A tight fist began to clench inside his stomach.

"Did the blacksmith have trouble with him?"

Thomas didn't answer.

"Well?" his father repeated, glancing up sharply.

Things deteriorated quickly after that. "You did take him to the blacksmith, didn't you?"

Again Thomas didn't answer.

"Do you have a tongue in your head? Answer me, boy!" his father raged.

"I started to take him, but he wouldn't settle down. You know what it was like in the stables. The horses can tell when something's about to happen, and a lot of them were restless. I couldn't manage him with only one arm."

"Did it occur to you to ask for help?"

"No one else was available."

"And so you forgot. One day, Thomas, you'll stretch me to my limit!"

Thomas squirmed uncomfortably, stung by the harshness of his father's reaction. He had worked as hard as anyone. His father had no idea how much his arm had ached all day.

The stable master pushed himself up from the table.

"Where are you going?" Thomas's mother asked anxiously.

"To get the blacksmith out of bed, Marya, where else? The king's destrier needs to be reshod, and I gave the job to your son. Only he forgot. I'm sure the blacksmith must be longing to reheat his forge." The sarcasm in his voice made Thomas cringe. "And who's going to pump the bellows?" The look he fired at Thomas felt like a physical blow.

"I'll do it!" he replied desperately.

"Do what, blow into it? Or wave your splint at it?"

With that, his father left. And with him went any opportunity for Thomas to make amends for his mistake. But it was no use anyway. His father was right—with one arm he was useless.

His father would pump the bellows himself, of course. The blacksmith's apprentice lived away on a farm somewhere; calling him was out of the question.

He longed to wait up for his father, to have some normal contact with him, even to apologize. But he went to bed. His mind was still churning restlessly when his father returned hours later, and dawn was lightening the sky before Thomas finally managed to get to sleep.

SWINGING his pitchfork ferociously with one arm, Thomas laid waste a pile of hay as the soldiers set out for the border.

The stable had been the scene of frenetic activity during the previous forty-eight hours as the stable hands prepared the horses for an extended period in the field. Now the stables were almost empty.

Ben lay quietly to one side, his little head resting on his paws and his eyes fixed on his master. No one else was anywhere in sight. Thomas might have been the only person in the whole of Arnost not at the muster.

His heart lay with the townsfolk cheering them off. But he had worked himself into a mood that reopened the wounds of his conversation with Will.

Thomas settled into a half-hearted rhythm, trying to persuade himself that his labors were essential.

Eventually he was joined by Simon. “Wasn’t that amazing?” the younger boy gushed. “There were so many soldiers. Someone said there were five thousand!”

Thomas snorted derisively. “Five thousand? I hope they’re in no hurry, then. Each horse will have to carry ten soldiers.”

Simon was unabashed. “And did you see the king? His destrier was prancing around like it was standing on hot coals!”

Thomas grunted, his eyes narrowing. Obviously nothing had changed since the previous day, then.

“And did you see the way old Olaf’s wife was carrying on?” Simon still babbled on excitedly. “Anyone would think it was his funeral. They say it’ll be his last campaign.”

Embittered by his thoughts, Thomas began to find Simon’s chatter unbearable. “Simon, go away!”

Simon looked startled. "Why?"

"Because I have work to do."

"That's all right, I'll help you."

Thomas could see the eagerness in Simon's eyes. He knew how much the younger boy admired him. But then he pictured himself with Will and thought of the bitter medicine served him by his own hero. Maybe Simon needed some of it, too. It was about time he was toughened up to the harsh realities of life.

"Look, Simon," he said with exaggerated kindness. "A boy like you is just in the way around here. And anyway, you simply aren't cut out for this kind of work."

Even as the words left his lips he regretted them. He could see the hurt and bewilderment on Simon's face. But it was too late to turn back now. "You haven't got what it takes to be successful around animals. You're too...too scatterbrained."

His barb found its mark. Simon stared wide-eyed at him in disbelief, then turned and fled, his eyes flooding with tears.

Having attained his objective, Thomas found it brought him no pleasure at all. He tried to adopt an air of detached superiority. *Children*, he told himself. *They're so immature. Why do they have to take it so personally?* But it didn't help. He felt more wretched as time went on.

He was so lost in his thoughts he didn't hear his father approach. "Thomas, where have you been?"

He turned without answering.

"Your friend Will Prentis looked for you everywhere. He wanted you to take care of this for him."

His father held out a small necklace. Thomas stared at it stupidly. "Take it!" his father insisted.

Thomas took the necklace and examined it. He recognized it at once. It was Will's most treasured possession. It consisted of an ordinary-looking chain of fine but tough metal, securing a small ring of gold. Will had told him the ring was his only memento of his parents, both of whom had died when he was a small child.

"He asked me to tell you that if anything happened to him, he wanted you to have it." Thomas's father turned on his heel and left him to his musing.

He slipped the chain over his head numbly. An hour earlier he would have received it as a portent of hope, an unlooked-for affirmation of his value in Will's eyes. Now it hung heavy around his neck with accusation.

He headed off across the courtyard, kicking irritably at the loose cobblestones that lay in his path. The church bells in the town below began to clang their monotonous refrain, marking the departure of the king and speeding him on his way with the blessings of the church, such as they were, to encourage and comfort him. Thomas decided that if there was a God in heaven who ever deigned to notice him at all, it was probably only with contempt.

He was intercepted in his progress by an energetic ball of fur, tumbling enthusiastically about his feet. He reached down and gathered up the wriggling bundle, holding it to his breast. "Ben," he said unhappily, "you're my only friend in the world."

4

Steffan the Second, High King of Arvenon and until-now unchallenged overlord of the extensive kingdom won by his namesake five generations earlier, galloped over the crest of the hill, reined in his destrier, and called down a bitter curse upon his as yet unseen enemies. Will, riding behind the king in the vanguard of the troop, guided his horse alongside and angrily surveyed the devastation below them. Along the far bank of a small river were the charred remains of a village, still smoking.

Will already knew what they would find down there. They had seen it too many times in the weeks of frustration that lay behind them. Every living creature would have been slaughtered and many of the bodies horribly mutilated. Anything of value would be gone and the rest put to the torch. Yesterday a glance beyond the river would have revealed a golden sea of waving corn, almost ready for harvest. Today ash and blackened stubble choked the fields.

Following the lead of the king, the soldiers dismounted and rested their horses at the top of the hill. The need for urgency was past, and none of them showed any eagerness to explore the wasteland awaiting them.

Scouts were sent to examine the approaches to the village before the troop's horses confused the evidence. Will watched them go dispassionately. Nothing he had seen so far suggested their efforts would lead to anything useful.

Even attempts to determine the size of the raiding parties had been largely unsuccessful. There were few clues as to their numbers or identity. It seemed they were not only ruthless but well-disciplined. And so the rage and frustration had grown in Will and his friends until they were barely able to keep their anger in check. If ever they managed to draw their foes into open battle it promised to be bitter and furious.

They were not without eyewitnesses, though. Incredibly, there were often survivors, people away from the villages when the attacks began or a lucky few who somehow concealed themselves. But the survivors offered few insights. Naturally, their reports were exaggerated—horsemen everywhere, invincible and unstoppable, crushing all resistance with contemptuous ease. Depending on the witness, there were hundreds or even thousands of them.

All were agreed on one point, though: the raiders were plains nomads.

And yet it didn't make sense. Will had grown up in the southern border region and knew something of the nomad clans. The nomads proved ferocious enemies, to be sure, but somehow these raids seemed out of character with their peculiar code of courage. Surprise attacks, yes, but these continual furtive raids against almost defenseless villages?

Will expected the nomads would view such behavior as cowardly. Long before now they ought to have been demonstrating their prowess openly in battle. No, something didn't add up.

The scouts returned and reported to the king, and the soldiers were ordered to remount. They headed down the hill, forded the river and began to pick their way through the ruins.

The wattle and daub dwellings of the peasants had been almost totally destroyed. Sections of the manor house and church remained standing, having been solidly built of stone. In time, they could be rebuilt; except that the region was being steadily depopulated. Depopulated. Might that be the nomads' intention? And if so, why?

An urgent call from away to Will's left interrupted his thoughts. Along with a number of others, including the king, he headed in that direction.

One of the soldiers had discovered a small boy, perhaps four or five years of age, huddled in the remains of a building. The lad clutched something tightly to his chest.

He didn't seem frightened by them; he was quite unresponsive. Will thought him an appealing child, with his fair curls hanging softly about his head. He was plainly but adequately clothed, although his trousers were now filthy and his little jacket scorched. He had probably been his mother's pride and joy.

Then Will caught a glimpse of his eyes and shuddered. They stared vacantly, fixed on nothing. It was as though the boy had departed but somehow his body lived on. Will decided not to think about what he must have witnessed.

A friend of Will's from the King's Guard named Rufe Sarjant dismounted and approached the boy with a gentleness that belied his fierce demeanor. The giant guardsman spoke to him quietly, offering him food and drink from his saddlebags.

Although his efforts bore no immediate fruit, he was not deterred. He persisted patiently, attempting to coax a response from the lad. Will watched tensely, compelled by his friend's refusal to accept defeat. He longed for even a symbolic victory over their elusive foes.

After what seemed an age the boy began to stir as though waking from a dream. He looked about him, his interest slowly dawning. Will's spirits soared. Audible sighs escaped from others of the onlookers.

The boy searched the face of the soldier, his eyes coming to life. Apparently not finding whatever or whoever he was looking for, he shifted his quest to the faces around him.

But the awakening proved short lived. Slowly the light died from the boy's eyes. His face again became blank and lifeless. His spirit seemed to have retreated to some distant inner sanctuary, and he gave no further response.

Rufe, his face betraying his disappointment, picked the lad up and seated him on his horse. The motion knocked from the boy's grasp the object he had clasped so tightly. As it tumbled to the ground Will caught a glimpse of a small horse, delicately fashioned from wood. The force of the impact snapped off its head.

On losing the toy, the boy let out a haunting wail that sent a shiver up Will's spine. Rufe quickly retrieved the pieces. He returned them to the boy, who clutched them protectively and fell silent again, resuming his vacant stare.

Something snapped in the guardsman. "Why are we here, poking around in burned-out villages?" he asked loudly, trembling with anger. "We should be doing some burning and pillaging ourselves—out on the plains! It's time the nomads were taught a lesson." His stirring words drew grunts of assent from many of the soldiers.

Will shot an anxious glance toward the sovereign, who sat astride his horse nearby. It was immediately obvious to him that the king had heard Rufe's comments. Will was even close enough to catch a murmured response: "Yes, I think they're expecting us to do that."

He frowned, puzzled. What did the king mean?

King Steffan faced the soldier imperiously. "It's not your job to determine our strategy," he said sharply.

Rufe subsided immediately, a flush of embarrassment covering his face. He bowed his head in shame.

The king stood up in his stirrups and addressed his troops loudly. "I understand your frustration, men. Indeed, I share it. But hasty plans bring disaster more often than success.

"There will be a Council of War tonight. We will drag these barbarians into the open, I promise you. Then we will test their courage against soldiers instead of women and children!"

The king's ringing words were met with a few half-hearted cheers, but mostly silence. Will sensed that some kind of crossroads had been reached. The sullen looks worn openly by many of the men presaged trouble if something decisive didn't happen soon.

The troop rode wearily through the gates of Danford. Will rode alongside Rufe. The boy from the village was perched securely in front of his friend in the saddle. The lad, surrounded by the new sights and sounds of a large and prosperous town, stared impassively straight ahead.

"Look at 'em," Rufe tilted his head toward a group of townsfolk who eyed the soldiers disapprovingly. "We were conquering heroes when we first got here."

It was true. They had arrived to universal acclamation. With the marauders growing daily in boldness, trade had begun to slump disastrously.

"Yes," Will responded, "they expected a quick and easy victory."

At first the good citizens of Danford proved very willing to suffer the expense and inconvenience of billeting and feeding the soldiers. Now, nearly three months later, with no easy victories and not even a fight worth speaking of, the townsfolk showed signs of impatience. There was plenty of grumbling, although no open hostility. Not yet. But the mood of their hosts affected the soldiers' morale.

"I wonder which of this fine lot will care for our little friend here?" Rufe aimed a disparaging glance at the townspeople.

Will raised his eyebrows. "You're hopeful, aren't you?"

"Well, they'll have to. I can't look after him."

It touched on another sore point. The townsfolk were becoming alarmed at the steady trickle of refugees that threatened to become a flood if the raiding continued.

Danford was large, well-situated on the banks of the Dan, and protected by a centuries-old stone wall that encircled the entire town. It sat astride the main trading routes through the Blue Mountains to Rogand in the east, and south across the vast expanse of the Plains to distant Lestanor.

Danford had prospered in recent years. But these were uncertain times, and the wealthy rarely slept easily without the comfort of thick walls and well armed soldiers to guard them. Will guessed they would put up with the soldiers for a little while longer.

WILL STRODE through the darkening streets of the town heading for the Council of War. Receiving a summons had taken him completely by surprise, and he was working hard at suppressing his excitement.

He arrived to find the king already conferring with Captain Olaf and the captain of the cavalry reserves levied by the town authorities. Two of the king's knights arrived at the same time. One of them smiled welcomingly at Will and beckoned him over to a seat beside him. "Don't be nervous," he whispered sympathetically. "The king is not at all frightening to talk to."

Will nodded, hoping he appeared suitably overawed. What the knight couldn't know, though, was that the prospect of the evening filled him with eager anticipation.

"Let's get straight to the point," King Steffan began. "We will be talking tonight about a major change of strategy. I have invited one of our men to join us briefly." He acknowledged Will with a nod. "I understand he has considerable knowledge of both the nomad tribes and the Rogandans."

Will dipped his head respectfully in response. So that was it. Clearly the king kept his ear to the ground. He wondered how he had learned of his background.

"You have lived among the nomads and speak their tongue, I'm told."

"Not exactly, Your Majesty. After my parents died my uncle adopted me. He was a trader and we traveled across the Great Plains many times. Sometimes we stayed with the nomads. Communicating with them isn't easy: the clans speak many dialects, and some of them amount to totally different languages."

"Tell us something of these nomads. Can you give us any insight into them?"

Will's mind whirled. How could he capture in a few words the spirit of these remarkable people? Even here, in a cold room dimly lit by candles and the glow from the hearth, he could summon a picture of the sun beating down on the endless grassland, and the nomads, wild and free, galloping after the vast gianhi herds. He remembered sharing the jubilation of a kill with the hunters. And the wind blowing the dark tresses of a certain lithe nomad maiden...

He checked himself. "They are fierce, proud people, but generous, too, and bound by complex codes of honor. Raiding is not foreign to them—they're very practiced at it. They treat it as a game. Or maybe more a battle of wits.

"But this raiding seems different. I don't believe they would lightly begin hostilities on this scale; not without good cause."

The king pondered Will's words before responding. "The raiding is so...so systematic. And so far from their own territory. I've never heard of the nomads behaving this way before. Can you make any sense of it?"

Will frowned. "It's strange, Your Majesty. For one thing, the raiding parties must be reasonably large, possibly as many as a hundred men. Yet most of the clans are small. Very few could put fifty warriors into the field. And they rarely unite except in times of great peril. Or perhaps great opportunity..." He trailed off and became thoughtful.

The king's eyes narrowed. "What of Rogand? Do the nomads have dealings with the Rogandans?"

"Only with traders, Your Majesty. My uncle married a Rogandan, and the nomads treated her no differently from us. They see all of us as barbarians." His remark was greeted with snorts of incredulity.

The king waited for silence again. "And your aunt taught you to speak Rogandan?"

"Yes."

"You speak it fluently?"

"Yes, Your Majesty." Will had learned to be fluent, and the lesson had been bitter indeed. Never would he forget his aunt's hand reaching with malicious delight for the willow switch when he stumbled over his grammar, nor her mocking imitations of his accent.

King Steffan smiled at Will. “You have been very helpful. We may have need of your services again.” And with that Will was dismissed.

Keenly disappointed, he headed back to his barracks. He’d hoped for much more. He couldn’t even see he’d been of much use. Yet the king seemed satisfied.

It was a start. Three months in the field had not lessened his ambitions a whit. He felt brim-full of life and energy: young, strong, capable, and eager to demonstrate it.

One day his opportunity would arrive. He would grasp it with both hands.

WILL STOOD DESPONDENTLY among some trees on a hillside overlooking a small hamlet. He was beginning to wish he’d kept his mouth shut.

The morning after the Council of War King Steffan had called for volunteers. When it was made clear it would be a crucial and dangerous assignment, Will wasted no time in responding.

The king intended to split his force into three and station them strategically around the countryside. The King’s Guard, the elite soldiers of the force, were to be split evenly among the three. Two volunteers would be sent to each major village and hamlet. At the first hint of trouble, they would race to the nearest soldiers and guide them back by the fastest route. Maybe, just maybe, they would get there before the raiders had left.

Will approved of the plan. He hoped it would offer him the chance to do something significant, and he sought out his assigned location eagerly.

That was a week ago. Now, watching the sun set lazily behind the treetops, he felt sure any exploits would be done a long way from this tranquil spot. He decided ruefully that staying with one of the main forces would have increased his chances of seeing action.

The temperature dropped quickly once the sun set. There was no cloud cover, and a full moon provided remarkably good visibility.

The dull clang of the church bell sounded across the valley, directing the villagers to their beds. In the half light Will could just see wisps of smoke coming from the chimneys of the cottages below. The villagers would be banking up their fires before settling down for the evening. It promised to be a cold and cheerless night up on the hill.

His partner, a wiry soldier named Garth, was nowhere in sight. A taciturn fellow, he obviously preferred his own company. They had agreed to take turns patrolling the main approaches to the hamlet. Garth had taken the first shift. If an enemy approached it should give them a little extra warning. If not, it might help them battle the boredom and the cold. Later they would keep alternate watches throughout the night.

Will suddenly thought of Thomas. It had been disappointing to leave without saying goodbye, and he wondered why Thomas had not been there to see him off. He reflected somewhat abstractedly that he had scarcely thought of his friend in the intervening weeks. He tried briefly to imagine life back in Arnost, but the pervasive chill pulled him relentlessly back to his dismal hillside. Hoping to prevent his feet from turning completely numb, he stamped them slowly and wriggled his toes inside his boots.

A movement away to his left stirred his alertness. Garth must be returning for some reason. Nevertheless he drew his horse further into the shadow of the trees and waited quietly, all his senses alert. A horseman moved quickly and silently in his direction.

As he drew closer, Will recognized the lean figure of his partner outlined in the moonlight, crouched forward slightly over his distinctive black roan. Will relaxed and moved into the open to be more easily seen.

When Garth spotted him, he spurred his horse on urgently. As he approached Will could see the tension in his face. “Horsemen!” he hissed frantically, “Scores of them! Massing on the spur behind us.”

Will leaped into the saddle. “Get going! I’ll try to warn the villagers, then follow you.”

Neither waited for further discussion. Will raced headlong down the hill. He glanced back over his shoulder once, but Garth was already out of sight.

The king had made it clear that they should not attempt to defend the villagers—their role was to fetch the soldiers. But nothing had been said against warning the unprotected inhabitants, and Will meant to try.

Galloping into the village, he drew his sword and banged the flat of it hard against a large iron tub lying against one of the cottages. The noise was deafening in the quietness. Almost at once, cottage doors began to open.

"Fly! Enemies are upon you!" he bellowed, then spurred his horse through the village and up a slope into a stand of trees beyond. His route now lay back through the village unless he made a wide detour to skirt it. He decided to wait a few minutes, then slip through the village in the confusion.

Looking toward the hill opposite he saw dark figures, some carrying torches, moving swiftly toward the village. There were so many of them! He quickly tried to estimate their numbers—six score at least.

He looked down at the village again. The villagers were moving too slowly. A few hurried along the stream toward the edge of the woods, and a couple had escaped on horseback. But many of them still bustled about organizing children or possessions.

"Hurry, you fools!" he groaned in exasperation.

The first of the horsemen reached the village. At once flames sprang up from the thatch on the nearest houses. He saw one or two brave villagers confront the invaders. They were quickly overwhelmed.

Fires flared everywhere now. He watched in silent horror as a chilling drama unfolded below him, illuminated by the light of the spreading flames. The slaughter being visited on the villagers so appalled Will that his stomach began to churn. He bent forward over his horse and retched violently. Then a cold fury rose slowly within him, pushing from his mind his mission and his responsibility.

A heavily pregnant woman struggled up the hill toward him,

desperately trying to reach the safety of the trees. Before Will could move to help her, a nomad rode her down, decapitating her with one fell blow of his ax.

With a wild cry Will broke from his cover and swept down upon the raider. Startled, the man tried to defend himself. But Will hacked at him so violently he was forced from the saddle, bleeding freely from multiple wounds. Will leaped from his horse and fell upon him in a frenzy, venting all his pent-up rage over the ruined villages and wasted lives.

When he came to his senses, he looked around and saw that the raiders, their work completed, were withdrawing from the village. Heedless of his own safety he mounted his horse and charged after them, a fierce battle cry on his lips. But the roar of the flames drowned him out, and his approach went unnoticed. Riding up behind one of the last nomads left in the village he dispatched him with a mighty thrust and looked around for another.

Then abruptly he hesitated. Having slaked his immediate thirst for vengeance, his wrath began to abate, and his mind again became clear. Realizing with a start how close he had come to throwing his life away, he broke into a cold sweat.

There was little time to ponder his next move. It was clear now that King Steffan's new plan was doomed. Garth had not yet been gone an hour; the nomads would be far away before he even reached the nearest troopers.

Will rapidly weighed his options. They were few indeed, but one of them stood out with awful clarity. Destiny beckoned. Calmly and without hesitation he chose the path of peril.

Jumping from the saddle, he quickly stripped from the slain nomad his gianhi-skin cloak and rawhide leggings. After placing them over his own clothes, he jammed the grotesque horned helmet tightly onto his head. He looked up just in time to see the last of the nomads disappearing over the crest of the hill. Remounting his horse, he thundered off after them into the darkness.

5

Thomas flexed his arm and grimaced as the atrophied muscles contracted painfully. It was good to be free of the splint at last, though, and everything appeared to be functioning normally. The silky voice of Medlen, the town's senior doctor, flowed smoothly on behind him. Thomas turned to observe him with some distaste.

"Hmm. Yes." The doctor was nodding sagely. "I, too, greatly regret the inconvenience of the long recovery period, Ma'am." He bowed deferentially to Thomas's mother, who seemed flustered in his presence as always. "Had the injury been treated properly from the beginning..."

This theme had become boringly predictable over the course of Medlen's visits. Captain Olaf not being there to defend himself, the doctor seemed determined to squeeze the last drop from the old campaigner's supposed mishandling of the fracture. "...But I dare to hope that my careful treatment since will have proven efficacious." He lowered his eyes humbly.

Catching a glance from his mother, Thomas rolled his eyes heavenward and shook his head hopelessly. His mother, horrified, darted an anxious look toward the doctor and fixed Thomas with a threatening frown. The doctor appeared not to have noticed. Smirking unrepentantly, Thomas turned away again and began gingerly massaging his sore muscles.

Thomas couldn't wait to see the last of the opinionated physic. He saw little evidence that the man had contributed anything of substance to his recovery, though his mother set great store by the fellow and insisted Thomas follow his instructions to the letter. Even the messy sight of Medlen bleeding her son had not shaken her resolve.

Thomas had long since tired of the doctor's visits. He would have taken matters into his own hands had it not been for an incident involving his father.

He had been working late and didn't join his parents until some time after they had begun their evening meal. As soon as he arrived he could tell his parents had been arguing. And something in his father's manner warned him that more trouble was brewing. He waited nervously for the storm to break.

Axel had motioned toward Thomas's bad arm. "Isn't it about time you took that splint off, Thomas? How much longer are you going to persist with this idiocy?"

His mother had hastened to Thomas's defense. "The doctor gave strict instructions that the splint was to stay on until he is certain the arm is mended."

"Ha! That old fraud? The only thing he's qualified for is relieving people of their hard-earned money." He frowned at his son. "It's up to you, Thomas. He'll keep coming back, like a vulture to a carcass, as long as you let him. It's time you stood up to him. Are you a man or are you still a baby?"

Thomas, provoked by his father's challenge, had dug his heels in. He stabbed a finger angrily at the splint. "Do you think I want to put up with this a minute longer than I need to? It's easy for you to criticize the doctor. But I'm the one who will suffer, and for the rest of my life, if my arm doesn't heal properly!"

His father snorted. "Looks like you two and the leech have a very cozy arrangement going. All right then, have it your own way. But let me tell you, Thomas, you'll get nowhere until you face life like a man." He had plenty more to say, too, much of it hurtful and condescending, before he finally redirected his attack to the food.

Thomas had lost interest in the meal after that. As he sat there, angry and humiliated, he decided that the splint could stay for as long as the doctor wanted it to. Even if it meant being bled regularly. It seemed his only way of hitting back. Why did his father have to be so hard on him? These interchanges were always the same: Thomas's views and feelings didn't matter. And true to form his father had once again insisted on having the last word.

But now the day had finally arrived—the doctor had announced airily that Thomas's splint could come off. Perhaps the doctor had sensed that even his mother's credulity could not be stretched much further. Thomas was simply relieved that the charade was over.

"The voice of duty calls insistently. Others also await my ministrations, sadly not always with patience." The doctor exhaled softly, sighing his regret that business must so soon take precedence over pleasure.

But he did not move. He stood solemnly with hands clasped before him and head bowed slightly.

Thomas's mother stared at him blankly for a moment, then finally grasped what was required of her. "Oh, yes, Doctor. Your fee." At her words he bowed his head further as though such crass necessities were abhorrent to him. She reached hastily into a fold of her skirt, and a small leather purse appeared in her hand.

On impulse, Thomas fumbled with the drawstring of his pouch, freed it at last and reached in to grasp the stone. It felt cold to the touch as his fingers gently caressed its smooth surface.

He fixed his attention on Medlen and stifled a gasp. It was as though he had been wandering in a fog and the mists had thinned, offering a fleeting glimpse of an unexpected and foreign landscape. He felt certain that Medlen's mind had been laid bare before him for an instant. He glimpsed sights he knew he had never witnessed himself. Unfamiliar faces and scenes flashed by in his mind, and with a clarity never surpassed in his own memory. Insistent whispers in the doctor's own voice flooded his consciousness, and audible murmurings revealed secret musings and schemes. But Thomas realized he was not hearing these sounds with his ears. He sensed that Medlen's thoughts were somehow being exposed to his awareness.

Tantalizing as these impressions were, they were eclipsed by Medlen's absorption in the little drama he was acting out. Thomas saw the physic licking his lips slightly. He wondered how he had failed to notice the predatory set of the man's features.

Medlen stood silent and unmoving, and Thomas was sure that the doctor was responding instinctively to a familiar ritual. The man watched the coins being counted from the purse as a spider might lovingly anticipate the erratic progress of a small fly toward the web so patiently and tenderly prepared against such a visitation.

Coins changed hands. But still the doctor hovered. He cleared his throat significantly, and Thomas's mother awkwardly spilled a few more coins into his outstretched hands. Abruptly the ritual was over.

Thomas was suffused with a sudden shame. His parents' money had been squandered to gratify the swollen appetite of this calculating creature. He had blamed his father's goading, but he knew it was his own fault. It had been his decision to prolong the farce.

"Thomas! What are you staring at?"

He snatched his hand from the pouch as though stung and turned guiltily away from Medlen. But the man had lost interest in them and moved toward the door, a faint smile playing across his lips.

Thomas hurried outside, eager to avoid conversation with his mother. The glittering intensity of the stone's power had begun to dazzle him, and his shame already seemed as pale and insubstantial as a shadow before the sun. He needed privacy, a quiet opportunity to explore the stone's potential unobserved.

Heading for the stables, with Ben trailing along behind, he caught sight of his father talking to Simon, who was mounting one of the horses. Thomas had seen little of the boy since the day of King Steffan's departure. Although he still came to the stables, he had made a point of avoiding Thomas, transferring his attention instead to the stable master.

Thomas noted enviously that the two of them appeared to be sharing some joke. His father appeared relaxed and happy. And, Thomas reflected bitterly, why wouldn't he be? Simon was not his son. There was no mountain of expectation for him to scale before they could enjoy one another's company.

Simon sat bolt upright in the saddle, a small figure against the gray bulk of the horse. A picture flashed into Thomas's mind of a young boy, proud and excited, atop a horse for the first time. He had been the one, Thomas remembered with a pang, who offered Simon his first ride.

Thomas's father disappeared into one of the stables. Thomas stood silently beside a tree, hoping he wouldn't be noticed. He took hold of the stone and focused his attention totally on Simon, who appeared quite unaware of his presence.

The effect was again startling, but completely different. This time he was unable to discern a dominant thought process. Instead, a restless and jumbled mass of emotions churned around him, like the turbulence where the thrusting spears of a waterfall cast themselves into the smooth surface of a lake.

But there were distinct patterns visible among the confusion of Simon's feelings. To Thomas's astonishment, the dominant underlying reality of Simon's life appeared to be deep unhappiness.

He had never thought of Simon as unhappy. Could it be that he was imagining it all? But the boy's misery washed over and through him, raw and painful. It called to his own inner gloom, pulling at him until he began to fear he would be engulfed by it.

He shut his eyes instinctively to block it out, and immediately it was gone. Relieved and startled, he kept his eyes closed until he had recovered himself. Then he tentatively reopened them. There it all was again, just as before. This time, though, he knew how to detach himself. He cautiously resumed his scrutiny, considerably sobered.

Somehow he sensed that Simon's home life lay at the heart of his distress. Thomas realized that he knew almost nothing about the boy's background. But he felt like he was staring into festering wounds of anger, fear, and despair—the merciless handiwork of other people.

Although he did not understand how, it became clear to him that Simon was an orphan. And that he lived with an old uncle, who provided him with food and shelter and plentiful cruelty and abuse as well. He sensed, too, with guilty recognition the scars of his own callous barbs. And he knew that his assertions had been far from the truth. Not only was Simon well suited to working with animals, his sojourns at the stables provided almost the only light in an otherwise dark and cheerless life.

Thomas closed his eyes again, seeking release from the intensity of Simon's inner turmoil and the unsteadiness of his own response.

The boy's plight evoked in him a strong response of sympathy, at the same time reawakening his own conscience. He knew he needed to make it right with Simon, to apologize for what he had said. He promised himself he would do it, and soon.

At the same time, a whole new world had opened before him, and it was hard to think about anything else. These new insights were unfamiliar, even threatening. Yet they were wildly alluring.

He opened his eyes to discover that Simon had finally noticed him.

A wave of emotion assaulted Thomas. The younger boy glared at him, radiating hostility, reproach, and envy. And there was something else Thomas could not readily identify, but which filled him with apprehension. It hinted at revenge, driven by the eager anticipation of spiteful satisfaction. The contact faded as Simon urged his mount forward and was lost to sight.

What was Simon up to? Having previously felt nothing but sympathy, Thomas now felt uneasy, and he struggled to untangle his own conflicting feelings. Simon had already become a rival for the attention and affections of Thomas's father. Could he somehow develop into a threat, as well? Thomas promised himself he would watch Simon more closely in future.

Noticing that Ben was distracted elsewhere, he set off walking, wanting to be alone for a while. Evidently the stone's gift might prove a mixed blessing. Thomas felt exhausted by its revelations and the questions they raised.

Again he wondered about the stone and its strange power. Where did it come from? What if it was evil? He dismissed the thought, unwilling to accept it. But he could not shake off the feeling that great evil might come of it. He wandered on aimlessly, lost in his thoughts.

The sun was slipping below the horizon when he finally turned toward home. He had decided he needed a rest from the stone for a while.

But not for too long. What incredible experiences! It was astonishing! Elation bubbled up inside him, and he let out an exultant whoop. What would people say if they knew he could see into their thoughts?

Yes, further investigation was clearly necessary. But more cautiously and discreetly next time. And some place where he would not be disturbed.

THE SUN ROSE SLOWLY over Arnost, touching the rooftops with its golden glory. Thomas, sitting alone on the edge of the market square, felt the caress of its first rays with their promise of warmth and new life. But the warmth could not penetrate deeply enough to banish the chill from his heart.

He thought of the occasion, almost three months previously, when he had first come to the square with the stone.

It was the second day after his splint had come off. His working day began soon after dawn, so he had arrived an hour earlier, knowing he would find others already there. He was filled with expectant curiosity. And he was not disappointed.

The stone had revealed more than he dreamed possible. He had heard of sailors happening upon strange lands, and he felt like an explorer stumbling upon a continent filled with astonishing wonders. He could not even begin to imagine all that had been waiting for him. Soon he was coming regularly, spurred on by the thrill of discovery.

As the weeks went by, he could sense he was adapting to the stone, or else it was adapting to him. Eventually he suspected he could almost read the thoughts of some as he observed them. He didn't understand how it worked, but thanks to the stone he somehow knew things, things that shouldn't have been possible for him to know. It was as if the knowledge, thoughts, and experiences of the people he observed had been transferred to him. These impressions could scarcely have felt more familiar to him if he had lived the experiences himself.

But his eagerness for secret knowledge diminished as inquisitiveness gradually turned to satiation. Yet he seemed powerless to stop. In recent days, as he left the square at sunrise he vowed to himself that he would not return. But each new dawn found him sitting in his accustomed position, shivering a little in the cool air and tightly clutching the stone in his hand.

What's happening to me?

He got up and set off with dragging steps back to the stables, putting the stone back in his pouch. His departure was not acknowledged by any of the merchants whose shops fringed the square. At first, the shopkeepers, bustling about in the pre-dawn half light, had eyed him curiously. One or two had even recognized him from the hunt and made friendly attempts to draw him out. He was determined, though, that his observations would not be disturbed, and his unresponsiveness had eventually defeated all comers. They soon learned to ignore him. Now, if anyone noticed his daily arrival and departure, they gave no sign of it.

Thomas walked slowly along the edge of the square, darting sidelong glances at the shopkeepers as he passed them. He caught a glimpse of Alf, the loud and bombastic butcher. His huge belly swayed from side to side as he waddled along. His face glistened with perspiration as he regaled some person unwise or unlucky enough to engage his attention.

Thomas passed the stall of Joe, the fuller. Joe was nowhere in sight, but Thomas could picture the old miser wearing his characteristic sour expression.

Next in line was a tiny stall run by Mother Joan, a snowy haired woman in the twilight of life who somehow eked out an existence selling pieces of embroidery. She sat in her usual position, her feeble fingers painstakingly stitching away the long hours in the market square. She always had a smile and a gentle word for everybody. Precious few repaid her in kind.

Lastly, he passed Frank, the flashy and extroverted cloth merchant. Frank appeared more interested in his customers than in his trade, especially the young, attractive women who frequented his stall, drawn as much by his eager flatteries as by his wares.

There were others, too. They had all become part of Thomas's world in a strangely disconnected way.

When he neared home, his mother spotted him and called him over. "Your father is looking for you. He's over in the kennels." She could not hide the concern in her eyes. "You don't look well, Tom. You need more sleep." He caught a tone of pleading in her voice.

He shrugged and headed off to the kennels. Although outwardly he made light of his mother's disquiet, her motherly attentions seemed his last link with normality. Will was far away and Simon was closed to him now, so he was grateful for her solicitude. Once again he was glad he had never tried to find out what the stone might tell him about his mother. It would have felt too much like a betrayal to pry into her secret thoughts.

He had never tested the stone on his father, either. The distance in their relationship had become a settled coolness since the king's departure, and Thomas wasn't sure he could cope with knowing his father's private thoughts about him.

His mother had good reason to worry.

What's happening to me?

He used to be happy once, before he found the stone.

At times he dreamed of being rid of it. Once he had even taken it to the river, searching out a place where the current flowed swiftly. He had toyed with the notion of casting it far out into the torrent so it would be swept from his life forever. But as he held it in his hand he was again entranced by its unusual beauty and sensed its latent power. It was the most precious thing in the world! He slipped it back into his pouch and hurried away. He hadn't repeated the attempt.

Thomas's father left him working alone in the kennels. Normally Thomas found his greatest contentment among the hounds, but today he was too troubled to enjoy it.

Only Ben was able to briefly distract him. Ben, well on his way to becoming a large and powerful mastiff, was utterly devoted to Thomas. Rolling around on the stable floor locked in a wrestle with the fawn colored ball of muscle, Thomas forgot his cares for a time.

As he lay resting afterward, he glanced affectionately at the dog. Ben had become Thomas's shadow. Thomas felt confident the animal would follow him almost anywhere; it was only with great difficulty he prevented the dog accompanying him on his daily pilgrimage to the market square.

He sighed deeply. Once again his thoughts had turned inexorably back to the square. Why couldn't he stay away? Going there afforded him little pleasure. Yet when he was honest he knew it gave him a sense of power and superiority. But although he fed off it greedily, it never satisfied him.

Before long he had begun to look condescendingly upon the vendors in the square. Fortunately they left him alone; he was not sure he could conceal his contempt for them otherwise. With the stone in his hand he felt he knew them better than they knew themselves. And he saw little that was worthy of admiration.

He knew that Frank was a lecher and an adulterer. And that Alf the butcher was barely more enlightened than the steers he carved up for his customers. Joe reminded him of a snake, coiled and ready to strike, lying in wait to poison and devour the unwary. The old man would sooner gain one coin by cheating than earn two by honest means.

Only Joan was the person she appeared to be: honest and cheerful. Yet he could not fully respect a person so poor who allowed herself to be consistently defrauded.

For the rest of the day Thomas worked half-heartedly at the menial tasks set him by his father.

Once he was interrupted by two small boys. He didn't need the stone to tell him why they were there. But he was unable to stop himself from using it.

Their shy faces gave little clue to the eager anticipation that flooded their minds. But their daydreams of horses and soldiers held no appeal for Thomas.

"Go away. I'm busy."

He relinquished the stone as he said it, unwilling to share in their disappointment.

THOMAS COULD NOT PUSH the boys from his mind. He had paid a price, too, in denying them their innocent pleasure. He faced at last the unpalatable truth: he had changed, and it wasn't for the better. The mysterious power of the stone had hopelessly ensnared him.

Yet he was so weary of it all. He had found himself immersed in an adult world he was not prepared for and did not understand. The motivations and passions of the people he observed often bewildered him.

Growing up had always seemed distant and hazy. Now it felt repulsive.

At first, stunned by the insight granted by the stone, he anticipated great revelations. But much of what he glimpsed was as trivial, selfish, and ordinary as the people he observed. So he came to see them as petty and hateful. At times, when he became party to little intimacies that he had no business knowing, he despised himself, too. He was becoming the worst kind of voyeur, peeping into people's minds.

What's happening to me?

THOMAS SAT UP WITH A START, waking from a nightmare that hovered just out of reach of his conscious mind. Dawn was still far off, but he had been waking earlier each morning, as though terrified of missing his distasteful appointment in the square.

He dragged himself out of bed and stretched his aching muscles. His head sagged wearily on his shoulders.

Seeking the reassuring feel of the stone, Thomas patted his pouch instinctively. His heart skipped a beat. The stone was not there! He clutched at the soft leather at the base of the pouch. The stitching had torn—his fingers poked through the gaping edges of a brand new hole.

Frantically he groped around his bed and under the blankets. There was no sign of the stone. He sent trembling fingers snaking over the rough flagstone floor and under the bed. It was nowhere to be found.

Fighting down his panic, he stumbled into the main room of the house and felt around until he found a torch. He lit it in the embers of the fire. Returning to his room, he began searching feverishly in its feeble light.

Before the sun rose he had turned his room upside down without success. Forcing himself to stay calm, he reviewed the previous day in his mind. He had spent time in the kennels and the stables and briefly visited the castle. And yes! He had exercised one of the mares in the grassy meadow beside the castle. And his father had sent him on an errand to the blacksmith in the town.

His heart sank. He could have lost the stone anywhere. But he had to start looking. Praying fervently for the dawn, he rushed from the house and headed for the kennels.

Seeing his master running past, Ben took off after him with a joyous bark, gamboling in front of him and leaping up excitedly. Thomas had to slow almost to a walk to avoid tripping over him. Fairly dancing with frustration, Thomas cuffed the dog hard across the ears and ran on. Ben's bewildered yelp of pain pursued him fruitlessly across the courtyard.

Thomas searched all morning, refusing to entertain the possibility that his precious treasure was gone. His desire to be rid of the stone was forgotten, his whole being focused on reclaiming it. His parents might be wondering where he was, but that thought scarcely occurred to him.

As the day wore on, he realized he might have lost it forever. Reckless of the consequences, he cursed God bitterly. But the heavens were silent, and in time his anger passed.

As he retraced his steps from the blacksmith's, Thomas came to Arnost's small cathedral. Overcome with anguish he dropped to his knees by the roadside, ignoring the stares of the passers-by.

In the extremity of his torment he was confronted with his own motives. He saw that from the beginning he had used the stone irresponsibly. He had acted as if its powers were his by right and used them for his own selfish ends. He had distanced himself, too, from anyone who might have helped him escape the snare into which he had fallen.

Perhaps God was angry and punishing him. He begged and pleaded for a second chance. Everything would change if only the stone was returned. But still the heavens were silent. In time his remorse faded also.

Hours had passed before Thomas finally returned home. He arrived to an eager welcome from Ben, and the ready forgiveness of his faithful mastiff undid him completely. Too choked up to speak, he drew his dog close, making little effort to resist as the animal reached up energetically to lick his face. In receiving a generous love he didn't deserve, he found himself overwhelmed by his own selfishness. Filled with shame, he dragged himself away and went to bed.

THE DAYS TURNED to weeks and still Thomas searched everywhere for the stone. But there came a time when, almost against his will, his loss no longer consumed him.

His thoughts turned to other things. He acknowledged at last that he would probably never recover his treasure. It was, in fact, no longer his in any meaningful sense at all. Whether he accepted it or not, the stone was gone.

6

Will leaned forward in the saddle and urged his mount up the hill toward the place where he had last seen the nomads. He topped the rise almost at a gallop, straining his eyes to see ahead in the gloom.

He could find no sign of the raiders. But his horse, no doubt alerted by its keener senses, abruptly swerved to one side and reared, almost throwing Will from the saddle. For a few moments the whinnying of horses and the angry curses of their riders filled the darkness. Will realized with alarm that he had almost charged directly into a large group of mounted nomads waiting silently just beyond the crest of the ridge.

Even before order had been fully restored, a harsh voice cut through the clamor. "It is Hocveg, I presume, who thus honors us with his presence." A sudden silence settled over both men and beasts. Something about the voice chilled Will to the marrow. He felt as though a cold blade had been passed across his flesh, setting his skin creeping.

"What have you found this time?" the cold voice mocked. "Some new toy to play with?"

The horsemen in front of him seemed to melt away. In the moonlight which filtered dimly through the trees he could make out a tall figure on a black stallion not twenty yards away. The man's horned helmet gave his silhouette an eerie appearance.

Although a response was apparently required of him, Will remained silent. He dared not speak lest he be discovered. He kept his head down, praying that he would appear either chastened or sullen, whichever best suited the character of the late Hocveg.

There was a long pause. "Bring me his helmet!"

A rider spurred his horse toward the astonished Will and snatched the nomad helmet from his head. Feeling naked and exposed he bent his head still lower, expecting every minute to be detected. But it seemed that all eyes were on the dark leader. The tall horseman seized the helmet from the rider, snapped off the two horns and flung them to the ground. The once-proud emblem appeared pathetic and emasculated as he held it aloft in the dim moonlight.

"Now put it back." He threw it dismissively to the rider.

The rider returned and thrust the broken helmet roughly onto Will's bowed head.

"He has been marked! Let him be spurned. He will be dealt with later," the voice promised with casual malice. The riders backed their horses away from Will as though he had the plague.

Will shuddered. Here was a very different kind of leader from either his own captain or king. But he had no intention of staying around long enough to find out what the tall Rogandan had in mind. For Rogandan he certainly was, nomad garb or not. Every word he had spoken was in that language. And it was his native tongue; his accent betrayed him to Will's practiced ear.

So the nomads were being directed by a Rogandan. And the man obviously expected to be understood, so at least some of them must have learned the language. What could it mean?

"How many are missing now?" The cold voice had resumed.

"Only one, Lord Drettroth," a rough voice answered in Rogandan.

"Find him and bring him back. And do not bring him back alive. His indolence has cost us precious time."

"Yes, Lord."

Three men rode back over the crest, toward the strange glow in the night sky that marked the passing of a village.

While the nomads waited, Will's mind raced as he assessed his situation. He shifted restlessly in his saddle. Then, with a sick feeling in his stomach, he remembered that nomads did not use saddles. They regarded them with contempt, learning to ride bareback almost as soon as they could run. Not only that, he wore a sword. The nomads rarely used swords, preferring axes and knives for close fighting.

He glanced about him furtively, feeling suddenly conspicuous again. But he saw to his surprise that the horses around him were saddled as well. And many of the nomads openly wore swords. He listened with new interest to the snatches of conversation going on around him. As far as he could tell, all were in Rogandan. The suspicion began to dawn on him that he and Lord Drettroth were not the only ones posing as nomads.

But before he could think this new information through, he was struck by another more disturbing thought. The search party was looking for a missing raider—what if they found Hocveg? And the bodies of two raiders were lying out there. What if they found them both?

Hocveg apparently had a reputation for looting; he would have been one of the last to leave the village. So it was probably Hocveg's clothing he was wearing now. But how had he left the body? Face down, it might be mistaken for a villager. But face up... He simply couldn't remember.

Will waited with growing tension for the raiders to return. He wondered if he could make a break for it if he was discovered. A quick glance revealed that he was now completely surrounded by riders, even though they were keeping their distance. His chances would be impossibly slim.

But with his acknowledgment of the apparent hopelessness of his situation was born a new determination. If he was going to die, he might as well make it worthwhile. His path to the tall leader was almost clear. If he was swift and lucky, he might just catch the Rogandan unprepared.

He carefully reached for the hilt of his sword and grasped it lightly, reassured by its solid familiarity. Twice tonight it had served him well. Ahead of it was the most important task of all.

Strangely, he found that his new resolve calmed him. As he waited he thought briefly of his hopes and dreams. Another would have to aspire to be captain of the Guard now. He thought, too, of Garth. He should have almost reached King Steffan's troops by now. But they would be too late. Will wondered if they would even know of his sacrifice. Perhaps a soldier would find his body up on the hill.

The horses stirred; the searchers were returning. He half lifted his sword free of its scabbard.

"Well?"

"We found him, Lord. He was dead already. Hacked almost beyond recognition. Malzakh has him now."

They had found the first one! He carefully eased his sword back into place.

"No villager could have done that." Will noted with satisfaction the apprehension in the man's tone. Let them sweat for once, the baby killers.

The dark leader must have noticed the man's tone, too. "Silence! The fool is dead as he deserves. May Malzakh bite him. Let us be gone." The riders, restless to be off, set off into the night, taking with them the body of their fallen comrade.

WILL and the raiders had been steadily riding for what seemed like hours. At first they had covered their tracks by riding single file until they reached a stream. They rode upstream for some time until they could leave the water without making tracks. The corpse of the raider was stripped and hidden in some bushes. Then they headed east toward the Blue Mountains. Will kept careful track of their bearings using the stars, a skill he had acquired while traveling with his uncle.

The extended period in the saddle offered Will an opportunity for reflection. The immediate danger had passed, and his spirits quickly rebounded. His current circumstances, while fraught with deadly peril, scarcely distressed him at all.

He had always been adventurous—foolhardy according to his uncle. He felt certain he had survived more life-threatening situations in his youth than half a dozen normal people might face collectively in their entire lifetimes. But rather than sobering him, it had given him a taste for the hazardous.

Even among the nomads he had been recognized as reckless. One of the clans gave him a name which meant "Lightning Rider." This time, though, he decided wryly, the lightning might fry him at last.

Will had wanted to be a soldier for as long as he could remember. He concluded early in life that it offered the best chance for someone in his position to make a mark in the world. Now he had what he wanted. And tonight he had killed for the first time—not once, but twice. It had been remarkably easy. He had expected that taking another's life would seem more difficult.

He even knew the name of one of his victims. Unexpectedly he found himself curious about Hocveg. Someone had invested years of time and energy, and perhaps love and affection, into raising him. Yet Will had snuffed out his life in a moment. It was so out of proportion. Were there parents or a wife somewhere praying to their Dark Gods for his safe return? Maybe even some children eagerly looking forward to the arrival of their father?

He pushed the thought from his mind. These men were barbarians, killers of the defenseless. They offered no consideration to their victims. They deserved none themselves.

He wondered what the men around him were thinking about at that moment. Were they, too, recalling their grim harvest at the village? Or were they simply anticipating a warm bed and a cup of ale? He fervently hoped their dreams tonight would be haunted by the screams of the dying.

No, these men deserved no mercy. If he could achieve it, he would cheerfully bring about the deaths of the lot of them. And he meant to try.

"RUFE, Edgar wants to speak with you."

Rufe grunted noncommittally; he knew Edgar by reputation. Edgar might have been a relatively recent addition to the king's army, but he was already well known among his fellow soldiers, and for all the wrong reasons. "What does that troublemaker want?"

The soldier's eyes were alight, and he moved around impatiently. "It's important," he protested. "He'll tell you what it's about."

Rufe hesitated a moment, then shrugged and got up to follow the man. Why not? Any diversion would be welcome; there was precious little else to get excited about.

Rufe thought he could guess a little of what Edgar might be up to. They were stationed with one of the king's three forces in a small town called Stantony. In the previous week the soldiers had been summoned into battle only once, and the action had long been finished before they arrived. They were reduced once again to the infuriating role of inspecting the destruction.

Grumbling about King Steffan's new plan and the policy toward the nomads in general had not been long in breaking out. Inaction and frustration proved a volatile mixture. Lord Gramm, the commander appointed by the king, was reputed to be reliable and fearless, but he apparently lacked the skill to deal effectively with the restlessness.

The soldier led Rufe to a barn on the outskirts of the town. Edgar was relaxing in a comfortable armchair he had commandeered from somewhere, surrounded by as likely a band of cut-throats as Rufe had seen. Rufe's guide stationed himself watchfully at the barn door.

"Ah, Rufe Sarjant. Welcome." Edgar flashed him a charming smile. "No doubt you're curious about my invitation."

"You're brewing trouble, I don't doubt." Rufe spoke curtly, unimpressed by the ingratiation he thought he could detect in Edgar's manner.

"Not at all. Why would we want to involve you if we were planning trouble?" Edgar asked reasonably. "We're hoping to benefit from your advice. Maybe even your support."

"I'm flattered," Rufe replied coldly.

Edgar apparently decided to ignore Rufe's unsympathetic demeanor. "Will you hear us out?"

"I'm listening."

"Then I'll come straight to the point. A number of us witnessed your conversation with the king at the village."

So Rufe's suspicions were confirmed. It only remained to see where Edgar was leading.

"We agree wholeheartedly with what you said. It's time the fight was taken to the nomads. On their home territory for once. A force like ours could turn this whole campaign around in a week, maybe ten days."

Edgar paused, perhaps expecting a reaction from Rufe. Since there was none he pressed on. "If we took provisions with us we could move fast, sack a few nomad encampments, and return in time to trap the raiders on their way back to defend their own women and children."

"Why talk to me about it? Lord Gramm is the one you should be speaking to."

"Ah, Lord Gramm. Yes, a trustworthy soldier, to be sure. But entirely uninspiring. He isn't a strategist's armpit. He has enough trouble figuring out which day of the week tomorrow is. A more energetic man would have done something useful for his king by now."

Rufe wondered how far Edgar was prepared to go. "And where do I fit into all of this?"

"We wanted your opinion. You have a reputation as an intelligent man."

Out of the corner of his eye Rufe caught two of the men exchanging a smirk. So Edgar's flattery amused them, did it? Well, Rufe was no more taken in by it than they were. He might never match Edgar's animal cunning or Will's natural decisiveness. But he was no man's fool, either.

Edgar lowered his voice conspiratorially. "If we all give a strong lead together we can set things to right. The men respect you, Rufe." This was closer to the mark. Rufe was no natural leader, and Edgar undoubtedly knew it. But the men respected him, both because he was physically imposing and because they trusted him. It seemed that Edgar needed him for his credibility. "All we need is to borrow Gramm's force for a short time. He'll thank us when it's all finished."

Rufe Sarjant's credibility and Lord Gramm's troops; it appeared that Edgar had it all worked out. "And what would Lord Gramm be doing in the meantime?"

"Well, it might be possible to arrange for him to become, er, temporarily indisposed, let's say for a week or two."

"And what about his knights?"

"Leave it to us. We'll arrange something suitable."

This was treason. Rufe wondered if they were all rogues or if some of them were merely fools. Even if they succeeded, did any of them seriously believe King Steffan would thank them for taking matters into their own hands?

He had a feeling that Edgar's main interest was in looting. What a surprise it would be when Edgar and his cronies disappeared with the plunder sometime during the journey back. Some other dupe would be left to face the consequences. Someone like Rufe Sarjant, no doubt. They probably had the lead role in their little drama reserved for him.

Rufe would have liked nothing better than to expose the plotters. Without hard evidence, though, he was going to be running a big risk trying to outmaneuver treacherous men like these.

He wished Will Prentis was there. Will would know how to handle them. But he was far away in some backwater, most likely longing for some action. If only Will had listened to him. Anyone could see that the important events would happen here with the main forces.

"Can we count on you?"

For now, Rufe decided to keep Edgar on the hook while he tried to figure out what to do. "I'll think about it. But until I know exactly what you have in mind for Lord Gramm, you can count me out."

"Excellent! We'll let you know when our plans are in place." Edgar was grinning triumphantly. Clearly he thought Rufe was as good as in the bag.

Rufe left the barn aware that he was playing a very dangerous game. If he put a step wrong the consequences might be catastrophic.

WILL SENSED that the riders were nearing their home base. The men seemed to be sitting a little taller in the saddle and the pace had definitely picked up, even though they were now climbing steadily.

Their path soon took them into the foothills of the Blue Mountains and eventually onto a trail that had obviously seen considerable use in recent times. The trail was narrow, and the trees clustered thickly. They were soon forced to travel single file, relying on the horses to find the way since no moonlight penetrated the forest at all.

Will planned to follow the nomads to their base and then slip away unnoticed. One day the nomads would return to find King Steffan's soldiers waiting for them.

Clearly the time had arrived to start moving toward the back of the troop before it was too late. He decided to make his move as soon as they spread out again.

Abruptly he found himself out of the trees. The riders were spilling into a large clearing bounded by the forest on one side and on two sides by a broad sweep of a river which wound its way through the upper foothills. On the other side of the clearing, readily visible in the moonlight, lay a large wooden fortress. It was tucked into a bend of the river and surrounded on three sides by water. The clearing apparently resulted from the felling of the trees used in the construction of the stronghold. The site had been cleverly selected; the fortress had been invisible among the trees until he was upon it.

It appeared well enough constructed that a few determined men could hold off a small army for some time. Will was certain that no nomad would ever have built such a structure.

A command rang out. Two great gates opened, and the riders pressed toward the opening. Will was caught, unable to turn away.

As the riders milled around the entrance waiting to get inside, he found himself jostled among the rider-less horses led back from the village as spoil. He was startled to see a horse that he recognized, though at first he was unable to place it. Then with a thrill of horror he knew: it was Garth's black roan. And there was blood on the saddle.

For a moment Will was overcome by his aloneness. No one knew where he was; no one even knew he was missing. But there was no chance to dwell on it. Carried along by a tide of men and horses, he was swept through the gates and into the stronghold. The gates were bolted shut behind them. Will was trapped inside the fortress.

7

The last armful of planks landed with a clatter as Thomas dropped them onto the now-sizable pile. A large number of small sharpened hardwood plugs lay beside them; they would be driven through holes in the planks to secure them in place onto the crossbeams.

Thomas leaned back and surveyed his work with satisfaction, letting the sweat trickle freely down his face. He had been hard at it for two days now, and the end was in sight at last.

Seeing his master taking a brief break from his work, Ben trotted up with tail wagging, looking for attention. Thomas bent down and stroked him behind the ears. The dog grunted his appreciation.

The bent figure of Jeb lumbered into sight around a building, struggling with a handcart laden with steaming horse manure. He paused to catch his breath and nodded toward the barn. "Ah, looks a bit different now! What was it—a month ago? When it was knocked down by that wagon? Can't tell it's the same building."

Thomas had removed much of the roof thatch, dug out and replaced the damaged support posts, and attached new architraves and crossbeams. "My missus says you was up early this morning, young Tom." The old man's eyes twinkled in his weathered brow.

"There are other jobs that still need to be done."

"Ahh." Jeb nodded wisely. "Yes, always something more." He paused, his eyes patiently assessing the completed frame. "Well, it's a fine job, young Tom," he finally offered. He looked at the youth knowingly. "Did yer father set you to work at this?"

"No, it was my idea."

"Ahh. It'll be a fine surprise fer him, then. Yer father'll be proud of you when 'e gets back."

To his vexation, Thomas could feel himself betrayed by the spreading warmth of a deep blush. "It's nothing much really," he replied emphatically, "nothing much at all," hoping vehemence might override the contradictory message of his face.

A gentle smile creased Jeb's wrinkled features as he slowly bent to his handcart and resumed his labored progress.

Thomas turned back to the barn with Jeb's words echoing in his mind. `Yer father'll be proud of you.' He eyed his handiwork again, more critically this time. The sun, still low in the sky, dazzled him for a moment as it peeped through the clouds. He closed his eyes and let his thoughts drift...

"Hello, son, I'm back early." He imagined himself looking up to find his father beside him. Normally an unexpected appearance by his father would be unsettling, but this time a warm shiver of pleasure traveled down his spine. "By the Saints! Did you do this, Thomas? I know I've said often enough that you lack initiative, but I'm man enough to admit it when I'm wrong."

"It's nothing," he protested mildly. This time his face behaved itself perfectly. His father surveyed the almost-completed barn with a delighted smile, pulling at the posts and nodding with satisfaction as they firmly resisted the motion. The stable master looked down at his son with new respect in his eyes.

A breeze sprang up abruptly, chilling Thomas's sweat-soaked skin, and shattering the daydream of his father's return. A cloud moved across the sun, veiling it once more. Proud of him? Maybe there was a first time for everything.

But what difference did it make? Thomas faced the bare outline of the barn—another solid day's work would complete the task. He reached down for the first plank with a sigh. He was tired.

THE MORNING WAS ALMOST SPENT and only the roof remained to be done when Simon sauntered casually into view, an open smirk on his face. Ben leaped up to greet the newcomer, his tail wagging eagerly. Simon ignored the dog.

The sight of the youth raised a familiar set of uncomfortable questions for Thomas. He had promised himself he would make things right with Simon, but he'd never made the attempt. What could he do to mend things? Would it even be possible now?

The coward in him insisted it would be wiser to just keep his distance. He knew that wasn't right.

As he wrestled with his conflicting feelings, Thomas couldn't escape the simple fact that he should have spoken to Simon long ago. So much damage had been done when he allowed himself to be dazzled and distracted by the stone. He hadn't been the only one who paid a price for his foolishness.

He remembered his earliest experiences with the stone. The depth of Simon's pain had been one of its first revelations. He had glimpsed the bitter legacy of other people, and seen that he himself had intensified Simon's misery with his cruel and thoughtless words.

Thomas took a deep breath. "Simon, I've been wanting to talk to you," he said awkwardly. "I wanted to...I wanted to say I'm sorry."

"Sorry for what?"

"For the way I spoke to you. Back when the soldiers left for Danford."

Simon's face was an impassive mask.

Thomas remembered again the rawness of Simon's pain. "I didn't mean it," he added. "What I said back then."

Simon immediately snorted in disbelief. "You said what you were thinking. Don't try to pretend now that you didn't mean it!"

Thomas's heart sank. He was telling the truth, but how could he convince his former friend?

An unyielding expression came over Simon's face. "I didn't come here to argue," he said. "Your father gave me a message for you. He couldn't find you when he was leaving."

"What message?" Thomas asked in surprise.

"He wanted you to knock down this barn and clear the site before he gets back tomorrow. He doesn't want a barn here anymore."

Thomas frowned. "Surely you're not serious."

Simon shrugged indifferently. "Believe it or disbelieve it. It's your choice. But don't say I didn't tell you."

Thomas furrowed his brows. "If he gave you that message, why wait until now to deliver it?"

"I saw you pulling down the roof and timbers a couple of days ago and assumed he must have seen you after all and told you himself," Simon answered innocently. "It only just occurred to me that you didn't know."

Thomas looked at the younger boy uncertainly, suddenly doubting himself. What if the message was genuine, and Simon had deliberately withheld it until the work was nearly finished? Over the last couple of days Thomas had occasionally noticed him watching from a distance. His behavior now made sense.

"Anyway, you still have plenty of time," the youth continued. "This scrap heap shouldn't take long to clear away." Simon sniffed contemptuously at the fruit of Thomas's prodigious labors.

With great difficulty, Thomas held his peace.

The smirk returned to the younger boy's face. He turned his back on Thomas and ambled off.

After a time Thomas sat down, head in his hands, miserable and disheartened. He had made an attempt—finally—to fix his mistake, but it had been too late. It was abundantly clear that Simon had no interest in reconciliation. He wasn't going to forgive him.

Thomas hadn't forgotten, either, that the stone showed him more than just Simon's distress. It had also revealed that Simon was actively seeking revenge.

Where would it lead? Thomas could no more avoid Simon than he could avoid the stables. Both of their lives were centered there.

And now a new decision had been forced upon him. A crucial decision. What should he do about the barn? He had to assume that Simon was telling the truth, even if his timing had been motivated only by spite.

With an effort, he put Simon from his mind. He needed to think clearly about the problem before him.

He could understand his father wanting to remove the barn three days ago—it had been a useless eyesore. But would his father want him to demolish it now? Surely that would be pointless and wasteful. His father might even accuse him of lacking initiative again if he simply obeyed blindly.

What should he do?

He turned it over and over in his head, struggling to reach a conclusion. Finally, knowing he needed to settle it, he called an end to his agonizing and made his choice. Picking up a bundle of thatch, he headed for the ladder.

THOMAS'S FATHER discovered the barn soon after his return late the next afternoon. Thomas, walking behind him, saw him stiffen abruptly and stare at the structure standing bright and renewed in the sunlight.

Seeing it again brought a thrill of pride to Thomas. Breathless, he waited for his father's response. After a time his father turned to him, and Thomas, smiling expectantly, was stunned to see his face white with anger.

"What is the meaning of this?"

"I, I..."

"Did you do this?"

"Yes. I thought I would surprise you."

"Surprise me? Well, you have succeeded beyond your wildest hopes!" Eyes flashing, the stable master bent toward him and spoke slowly and distinctly. "Perhaps you didn't get my message." Thomas recognized a dangerous tone in his father's voice.

"Yes, I did. But..."

"Including the part about not wanting a barn here anymore?"

"Yes." Thomas felt physically sick. He forced out a response. "I thought you'd be pleased."

"Pleased?" his father shouted. "How could I possibly be pleased? You ignored my instructions and did exactly the opposite!"

Thomas could not manage a reply.

"This will have to be removed. You realize that, don't you? And since you built it, you can pull it down. Is that clear?"

Thomas, his head bowed, could only nod. He turned to go. In doing so he noticed a familiar figure disappearing behind a nearby building. His humiliation was complete: Simon had witnessed the whole interaction.

THAT NIGHT THOMAS did not appear for the evening meal. Marya, normally talkative, had very little to say. But she bustled about so relentlessly that Axel was finally driven to exasperation. "What on earth is wrong with you, woman?"

"Thomas is what's wrong with me." She turned on him like a hen cornered in defense of her chicks. "What did you say to him?"

"Nothing he didn't deserve. I left a message for him to pull down that damaged barn. But no, he had his own ideas. He rebuilt it instead."

"Maybe he didn't get your message."

"He got it all right. He admitted as much."

"Maybe he got it after he'd already started."

"Maybe. But that hardly excuses him."

The stable master's wife had found her voice at last. "You don't know how hard he worked while you were away. Up well before dawn, and barely pausing for breath all day. It was all he could do to raise the food to his mouth each night." She pointed an accusing finger at him. "And he was doing it for you! Can't you see that?"

"Well, he has a strange way of being helpful."

"What did you say to him about the barn?"

"I told him to pull it down." Axel refused to meet his wife's eyes.

She stared at him in disbelief. "Pull it down! You can't be serious! Why can't you think of him for once? How do you think he's feeling right now?"

"How should I know?" he replied obstinately.

But Marya knew her man, and she pressed home the attack. "Are you telling me you can't find a use for a solid little storage barn?" she asked incredulously.

"I don't know. Well, maybe. Perhaps I could." He still would not meet her eyes. "It appeared solid enough," he finally muttered.

"Go and tell him, then!"

"All right, all right. I'll tell him first thing in the morning."

His wife softened, like a flower blooming with the melting of the snow in spring. She came to him and draped her arms about his neck, cooing happily in his ear.

"By the Saints, Marya, will you stop fussing?"

Grinning at his discomfort, she left him to finish his meal in peace.

EARLY THE NEXT morning Axel appeared grim faced in the doorway.

"Did you speak to Thomas?" Marya's face was eager.

"No, I couldn't find him. But there's no longer any point."

Her face clouded. "Why not?"

"The barn is gone. He must have pulled it down during the night." The stable master raised his arms heavenward in hopeless appeal. "The senseless stupidity of it! Why can't he think for once instead of just reacting?"

He glanced once at his wife, then turned and hurried outside, away from the grief in her eyes.

THOMAS WANDERED AIMLESSLY through the town, letting his feet take him where they would, but carefully avoiding people.

After a time he found himself in the oldest part of the city. Dilapidated houses crowded into narrow streets fouled with rubbish and effluent. Repelled by the place, he steered a course away from the sights and smells assaulting his senses. His instincts told him, too, that this was not a place to be found alone. Not even in the daytime.

He did not welcome the return to reality. He preferred the empty numbness that had pervaded him since the previous night. Soon after dark he had set upon the barn, almost blinded by tears that flowed uncontrollably. When there were no more tears he attacked it with a savage energy fueled by bitterness and anger. In time that passed, too, and his nerveless fingers completed the destruction mechanically. Then he sat down inside one of the stables, the faithful head of Ben cradled in his lap. At dawn he had stolen away, knowing only that he wanted to be alone.

Although Thomas was unfamiliar with this part of the city he was confident he was heading in the right direction. Thankfully, there were few people about, just a few children playing amidst the reeking muck. As he passed a particularly ill-favored residence, a figure detached itself from the doorway and stepped directly into his path. He froze.

A gaunt and wizened face thrust expectantly toward him and yellow eyes, gleaming with a mad light, peered intently into his. A thin arm shot out, and a bony hand grasped him by the wrist.

"It's him, it's him! At last!" The old man danced and capered about in triumph, never for an instant letting go his grip on Thomas's arm.

Thomas tried to pull free. But the old man was remarkably strong for one who appeared so frail. The wrinkled face drew nearer. A hoarse cackle sounded from the grinning lips, and Thomas, disgusted, noticed saliva running freely down his unkempt beard and onto his filthy tunic.

A child appeared in the doorway and ran back inside crying, "Mama, Mama! Grampaw's got out again."

The old man looked at Thomas shrewdly. "He'll try to make you give it to him, he will." He pulled at Thomas's arm urgently. "You mustn't let him have it. Not for anything!" Thomas stared back wide-eyed, wanting to escape yet gripped by a strange fascination.

A large woman bustled into the street, jaw set grimly, and waddled determinedly toward the old figure. She grabbed him firmly by both shoulders and pulled him bodily away from Thomas.

"Get back inside," she yelled. Then, with forced politeness, "Please pay him no heed, young man. He's always trying to accost people in the street." She tapped her forehead significantly as she shoved him back into the house.

"No! No!" shrieked the old man. "This is him, I tell you! He's the one from my dreams. There's more. I've got to tell him..."

The voice trailed off as the door slammed shut behind him. The sound of blows and more yelling carried into the street. Thomas turned away in revulsion. Shaken and confused, he hurried toward home.

8

Will sat with his back to the wall of the stockade, enviously watching the raiders feasting heartily around a huge fire. He was cold and hungry and his eyes drooped with weariness, but he was determined he would not remain idle in whatever remained of the night.

The small garrison had evidently made preparations against the return of the raiders for there was ale and freshly roasted meat in plenty as soon as the horses had been attended to.

Will kept his distance from the others and was relieved to find they continued to avoid him. Indeed he was beginning to think they had forgotten him entirely when someone tossed a hunk of roast meat in his direction. He retrieved it gratefully, brushing resolutely at the dirt that covered it when it landed. The flesh was only partially cooked, and the best meat had apparently been eaten already, but he bit into it hungrily, pausing only to lick off the juices freed by his exertions.

No one offered him any ale, and he tried to convince himself it was a good thing. Certainly he needed a clear head tonight.

. . .

HUNCHED up against the cold watching the revelers, Will found himself becoming impatient. They had long since tired of eating, but the ale still flowed freely, and they showed no signs of moving away from the fire, which had begun to die down. He guessed they wouldn't be sleeping in the open tonight; not when there were buildings at hand to offer shelter from the cold. Even though he knew it was irrational, he found himself frequently glancing at the sky, watching anxiously for any lightening of the darkness. But it had to be at least four hours before dawn.

His restless mind had already come up with a scheme. It was daring and risky, and he needed darkness to give it the best chance of success. If only the Rogandans would move off to sleep.

There was no longer any question that they were all Rogandans. Will had not heard any other language used since joining them, and any remaining doubt was dispelled as they feasted: their bawdy songs branded them more effectively than any coat-of-arms could have done.

Will's thoughts were interrupted by the appearance of Lord Drettroth. There had been no sign of the tall leader since they entered the stockade. Perhaps the Rogandan lord was above feasting with lesser mortals. Or maybe he knew his presence would inhibit the revelry, for a hush came over the scene as soon as the soldiers registered his arrival.

One man, too drunk to notice what was happening, lifted a wobbly voice in a crude tavern song. His solo might have been amusing had it not attracted the deadly gaze of Lord Drettroth. The man's companions, at first nudging him frantically, backed away from the hapless soldier. At last he realized his peril. He looked around expectantly as though hoping for a miraculous deliverance. Finding no help in sight, he sank to his knees as if to plead for mercy. But the excitement along with his drunken stupor must have been too much, and he finally pitched forward, senseless, landing flat on his face.

It probably saved him. The Rogandan lord, after regarding him icily for a moment, turned his attention to the others. They were now as silent and attentive as mice watching a barn owl.

"You have feasted well, men." It was a statement rather than a question. "Now you must rest, for tomorrow night we set out for the town of Danford." A murmur arose at his words, but the men were quieted by an imperious flick of his hand.

"Yes, their king has been slow to take our bait. So we must send a message that even a simpleton like him can understand. He seems reluctant to ride south against the clans. Nomad raiders in the streets of Danford might help make up his mind." A rumble of approval broke out from the assembled soldiers.

"We must be fast and efficient. Some of our men posing as merchants are already in the town. They will overwhelm the guards and open the city gates.

"You know what to do! But there will be no plundering. Kill and burn, but do not plunder, on pain of death. As always, there is to be no speaking at all, except for the nomad battle cries you have learned.

"Once the streets are flowing with blood we will leave as quickly as we came. No one must be left behind.

"If you are foolish enough to fail, you will taste my wrath." He stretched out a finger toward them and slowly swung it around, fixing the men huddled before him with an unearthly glare that shone with a terrible light of its own.

A tremor passed through the assembly like a ripple spreading over the surface of a lake. Then his voice dropped almost to a whisper which carried clearly in the stillness. "If you do well, you will be rewarded."

The gathered throng was silent. None dared to stir or speak. But more was required of them, for thunder gathered slowly on the brow of their master, exaggerated by the flickering firelight which played strangely across his angular features.

Then one or two cheers broke out, breaking the silence and charming away the growing storm. Scattered at first, the sound quickly swelled to a crescendo, an awful paean of praise for the terrible overlord. Their leader raised his arms exultantly as though invoking the affirmation of his Dark Gods, too.

Will sat numbed and unable to move. The scene he had just

witnessed unnerved him. The horror in store for the comfortable citizens of Danford appalled him. And yet the nightmare would be only just beginning. So much depended on him.

"Go now. Rebuild your strength. Tomorrow there will be entertainment. And then there will be glory."

At the mention of entertainment a number of heads turned in Will's direction. For an instant, panic threatened to engulf him. He barely checked himself from leaping up and dashing blindly for the gates. Instead he lowered his head between his knees to fight off his dizziness.

Then the moment passed, and he mastered himself again, grim and more determined than ever in his resolve.

When he looked up again Lord Drettroth was gone, back into the darkness from which he had come. The men jumped up and scurried off like frightened sheep to their shelters. Soon only Will remained, staring fixedly into the glowing embers of the dying fire. His hope flickered like its last flames, but his spirit was unbowed and unbroken still.

No one had stayed to guard the outcast Hocveg. After all, what could he do? Even if he escaped, how could he survive in the wilderness without a horse or hunting weapons? Apparently Hocveg was fully expected to take his chances with tomorrow's entertainment.

Well, they were in for a surprise. He pulled the broken helmet from his head, stood up, and threw it high over the wall. The sound of a splash carried to him faintly on the night air. Looking around he selected another from among those abandoned by the men in their haste and planted it defiantly on his head.

Will swayed unsteadily atop the stockade walls for a moment, then with a sharp intake of breath he jumped. He hit the ground hard, tumbled forward, and lay motionless, listening for the footfall of the guard patrolling on the wall above. When the guard had passed he moved stealthily to the river. After hesitating briefly he eased his body into its icy waters and struck out confidently for the other bank. After reaching it he disappeared into the trees on the other side.

HALDEK GOT up and reluctantly dragged himself away from the fire and his cup of ale. The guardhouse at the gates was hardly comfortable, but at that moment it seemed very appealing.

He had to check on those fool guards once in a while, though. Otherwise one of them would find a quiet corner and put his feet up. If Lord Drettroth ever caught a guard asleep on the job there would be no second chances for the half-wit. That would be bad. But he, Haldek, would be held responsible. The consequences of that didn't bear thinking about.

Life would have been much easier if Lord Drettroth would only stop turning up unexpectedly at odd times of the night. In fact the later and the darker it was, the better he seemed to like it. But no one in his right mind inquired too closely into the habits of their strange master.

Haldek sighed and clumped slowly up the ladder onto the walkway circling the top of the walls. He paused at the top and glanced down into the stockade. The great fire was little more than glowing embers now. All was quiet. The soldiers were no doubt sleeping soundly after their earlier carousals. He turned back to the wall and decided to stay put. If the guards were doing their job they would be along soon enough.

He gazed out over the wall into a sky brilliant with stars. The full moon, low in the sky now, illuminated the open space beyond the walls, picking out the stumps of the felled trees. The clearing appeared to be populated with tiny standing stones, silently watching and waiting.

Often, on lonely nights on the wall he found himself half-expecting to witness some dark and sinister ceremony. He shuddered, only partly from the cold. What in the name of the Dark Gods had he done to warrant being banished to this forsaken hole? He rubbed his hands together vigorously, trying to restore the feeling that yielded slowly to a creeping numbness.

Where were those guards? He turned and glared along the walls, finally making out a figure moving toward him.

Haldek noticed the man's shoulders drooped despondently. A wave of irritation washed over him. These men didn't know what sentry duty was. Compared to his years on the battlements of Agon's castle in Rog, this was a carnival. Apart from the isolation, anyway. And the primitive quarters. And the eeriness of the clearing in the moonlight.

He softened a little in spite of himself and greeted the sentry almost warmly. "Anything happening?"

"No." The sentry yawned hugely and tightened his shoulders against the chill. "I thought I heard something in the river earlier, but it must have been fish. Or maybe a bear."

Shortly the other sentry joined them, and all three leaned over the wall without speaking. Banished from home and familiar routine by his circumstances, Haldek allowed his imagination to carry him away.

But a startled gasp from the second sentry interrupted his reverie. "What's that moving over there?"

"Where?"

"Over there, by the trees!" The man pointed away toward the edge of the clearing.

Something was moving. The standing stones were coming to life. Gripped by an awful fascination, Haldek stared fixedly, unable to tear his eyes away. He couldn't tell what it was in the moonlight, but it was definitely coming toward them.

Haldek squinted, trying to identify it in the gloom. It was walking upright. But it appeared to have horns. A horrible thought came to him—could it be a demon?

The horned silhouette moved into the shadow of the walls and disappeared from sight. Haldek and the sentries stood motionless, holding their breaths to catch the slightest sound. Then, from before the great gates, they heard a voice: "Open, in the name of Agon!"

Haldek stood dumbfounded. After a pause the voice called again. "By the Dark Ones, is no one awake in this place?" It was definitely a human voice, weary and with an edge of desperation. And the words were Rogandan.

Haldek found his voice at last. "Go on, you fools! Don't just stand there!"

The men burst into life and hurried down off the wall to the gate. Haldek roused two other guards from the guardhouse. Together they took up positions inside the gate, weapons and burning torches in their hands.

"Open it!" Haldek commanded. The men unbarred the gates and swung them slowly inward.

A young man dressed as a nomad stumbled inside. He stood shivering before them, and Haldek saw that his clothing was soaked through.

"Who are you and what is your business?"

"I have come with an urgent message for Lord Drettroth."

Haldek glared at him suspiciously. "What is this message and who sends it?" he challenged.

The stranger bristled. "My message is for the ears of Lord Drettroth alone," he snapped, "as is the identity of the sender. I would not pry too closely into Lord Drettroth's business if I were you. He is not known to be a forgiving man."

Haldek could find no argument with that. "Where, then, is your horse?"

The man's face was grim. "My horse went lame two days ago. I have been forced to walk through this accursed wilderness. It was many leagues before I found a suitable ford across the river, and even then I became soaked." He paused, his chattering teeth emphasizing his plight. "Haven't you got a fire somewhere?"

Haldek hesitated. The fellow's accent was unfamiliar; he couldn't identify it. But he seemed genuine. And if Lord Drettroth learned that an important messenger, already delayed, had been hindered by Haldek...

He nodded to the guards. "Close the gates." He gestured toward the guardhouse. "Come with me."

Once inside, the stranger rushed to the fire with all the desperation of a drowning man clutching at a floating branch. For some time he stood before it in his dripping garments. He looked more like a half-drowned animal than a human.

Finally he spoke. "Can you have a horse prepared? I expect Lord Drettroth to send me back immediately with a reply."

Haldek was aghast. "Send you back like this? You're in no condition to go anywhere!"

The man looked genuinely surprised. "Has Lord Drettroth discovered compassion during his months in the wilderness?" Haldek gave no answer, so the man went on. "I'll be fine once I get some ale into me." He looked hopefully at Haldek.

"Ale? Yes, you certainly look like you need some."

Haldek felt ashamed—only a few months in this accursed place and already he had forgotten common courtesies. He personally drew a large mug of ale from a barrel in the corner. He carried it to the man, who eagerly followed its progress across the room. He took a long pull. Then he closed his eyes and let out a deep sigh.

The recuperative effect was immediate. "The horse," he said, assuming a businesslike manner. Haldek nodded to one of his men who headed for the door. "Make sure it's a fast one. And I'll need provisions in the saddlebags," he called after the sentry's retreating form.

The resilience of the young man amazed Haldek. He had been well chosen.

"I must speak to Lord Drettroth."

"Now? It will be dawn in only an hour."

"I said my message was urgent!" The man's eyes flashed angrily. "You will answer to Lord Drettroth if you delay me."

"Of course."

Haldek did not find the idea of rousing Lord Drettroth an attractive one. He glanced at the other men and guessed from the tension in their faces they were thinking the same thing. But this was one job he was not going to delegate.

"I will take you to him now." The other guards visibly relaxed.

They set off toward the buildings on the far side of the stockade. As they drew level with the remnants of the great fire, the man turned to him and gently placed a hand, still trembling slightly from the cold, on his shoulder.

"Listen," he said, his voice softening. "Do you think Lord Drettroth will be pleased about being woken from his sleep?"

Haldek shook his head emphatically.

"Then let me do it. If he is angry I won't be here to remind him of it for long. Just take me to the guards outside his building."

There was sense in the man's words, and the sentry found the idea dangerously appealing. But he knew his duty. Surely the stranger was mad if he thought Haldek would leave him to approach Lord Drettroth alone and unannounced. He shook his head dismissively and resumed his journey.

A pair of burly guards challenged them as they approached the lord's cabin.

"This man has an urgent message for Lord Drettroth," Haldek responded importantly.

One of the guards stepped forward. "Now? You want to see him now?" he asked incredulously. "You're braver than I thought, Haldek!"

Haldek bristled. "I said it was urgent."

"He'll have your guts for bowstrings."

"Let Lord Drettroth decide that," Haldek replied confidently, feigning a self-assurance he didn't feel.

The guard shrugged. "It's your funeral. Both of you leave your swords here."

They handed the swords to the guard, and his companion ran his hands roughly over their clothing, checking for hidden weapons.

"Wait here." The first guard disappeared into the building. He returned after a seemingly interminable delay. "Lord Drettroth will see you now."

Haldek stepped into the building, trying by a supreme act of his will to stop his body from shaking. The stranger followed him, cool as ice.

Two oil lamps on a low table filled the room with a dim light. A fire in one corner sent glimmers of light chasing after the shadows on the walls. Lord Drettroth awaited them, dark and inscrutable.

"Your reason for disturbing my rest must be pressing," he growled. "I hope so, for your sake."

Haldek gave in to the tremors that shook his frame. "This m-man has come with an urgent message, L-lord," he stuttered. "He insisted it would not wait."

Lord Drettroth turned to the man and surveyed him coldly. "I am expecting no message. Who sent you?"

Instead of answering, the man glanced significantly in the direction of Haldek and the guard. Lord Drettroth gestured impatiently. "Leave us."

Haldek stepped outside, relieved to be gone from the presence of his dread master. The guards positioned themselves before the door again, and he leaned back against the wall of the building.

The shutter of the window beside him lay slightly ajar. He found he could just make out the conversation inside. After a brief struggle between fear and inquisitiveness, his natural curiosity won out. He quietly leaned closer to the window.

"I bring greetings from Agon, High King of Rogand, Overlord of the Dukedom of Nakos, Master of the Idrenian Isles, and soon-to-be Emperor of the known world. To his loyal and beloved servant, Lord Drettroth, Commander of…"

"Enough of this! Where is Agon's message, curse you!"

The messenger cleared his throat. "Due to its sensitivity, His Majesty entrusted it to my memory rather than write it down."

"Hah! So how am I to be sure that this message is from the king?"

"With respect, My Lord, who else could have directed me to your fortress in the midst of this wilderness?"

"Do not be clever with me, young fool. Were you not the king's messenger, your life would be instantly forfeit for such impertinence.

Be sure I will remember you when I return to Rog. What is this all-important message, then?"

"King Agon is concerned about the progress of the raiding."

"So he is concerned is he? Our king is concerned? I am touched. But he did not send you here to tell me that. Get to the point!" Lord Drettroth's voice had taken on a dangerous tone. Haldek held his breath.

"His Majesty gives you one month more," the messenger said bluntly. "If your mission is not accomplished within that time, he regrets that it will be necessary to replace you, or recall you and your troops."

Haldek had heard enough. He eased himself away from the window and leaned toward the guards. "I will await the messenger at the gate," he whispered. Retrieving his sword, he sped away toward the welcome glow of the guardhouse by the gates.

THE MAN RETURNED after what seemed an age. Haldek was unable to read him. "Did it go badly?" he asked, offering another cup of ale.

The man accepted it gratefully, and soon a little life returned to his face.

"I'm to leave immediately. He wants my visit to be treated with the utmost secrecy." The man hesitated. "At least I think that's all he meant."

"Meant by what? What did he say?"

"He said that if he ever hears of me again, the man who mentions it will be flayed alive."

"You'd better go, then," Haldek said anxiously. "If he finds you here at dawn there'll be hell to pay."

"You're right about that," the man replied with feeling.

"The horse is ready." Haldek clapped him on the back and propelled him to the door.

Once outside, the man moved to the horse swiftly and prepared to mount it.

"Wait," Haldek called suddenly.

The man froze, his foot in the stirrup.

Haldek approached him until he was close enough to see his face. "May the Dark Ones look kindly upon your path," he offered quietly.

The man's startled eyes stared back at him for a moment. Then a warm smile slowly softened his burdened visage, like a first glimpse of the sun after many days of storm clouds. "And also upon yours!" He swung nimbly into the saddle.

The guards opened the gate once more, and he was gone.

An awful thought thrust itself upon Haldek: no one was patrolling the walls. The visit of the messenger had absorbed him so totally he had neglected his main duty.

"You two, get that gate closed. The rest of you get up on the wall. Now! Oh, and one other thing: if there's as much as a whisper about this messenger, I'll personally roast the man responsible over a slow fire. The fellow doesn't exist, and his visit never happened. Is that clear?"

They nodded obediently and went about their tasks.

WILL HALTED his horse at the edge of the clearing and looked back. He ought to have been elated. But already his fingers and toes were numb with the cold, and a long and crucial journey lay ahead of him.

His thoughts were drawn to the gatekeeper; in another place and time they might have been friends. He raised a hand in farewell and felt sure he could dimly make out an arm raised in reply from the walls.

But there was no time to lose. He glanced up at the sky, noting the telltale signs of the approaching dawn. Digging his heels into the ribs of his horse, he set out on the ride of his life.

9

The sights and smells of the town sometimes appealed to Thomas and occasionally overwhelmed him. But every year they combined in a dizzying assault on the senses called the Feast of St. Michael.

Thomas was convinced the whole world descended on Arnost for the Feast. Stalls lined every street, and hawkers crowded the market square. Dried fruit from Lestanor, exotic spices from the distant Simion Isles, and cleverly wrought metal goods from Rogand tempted the eager throngs that engulfed the town like a human tide.

Lords and ladies pampered themselves with rare luxuries. Peasant farmers traded their produce for much-needed farm implements. And, whatever their station in life, all feasted heartily, for food and ale were plentiful and inexpensive.

Everyone was saying the crowds were smaller than usual this year. Thomas heard his father suggest that the unrest in the border region was having an effect, along with the absence of the king from Arnost with so many men. The general mood was still one of celebration, though. The trouble at the border seemed a long way off, and the king's soldiers were there to deal with it now.

Thomas hadn't noticed any difference. To him the whole experience was just as exciting as ever.

"Enjoyin' the Feast, Thomas?"

The familiar level tone of old Jeb's voice sounded through the hubbub in the market square.

Thomas swung around eagerly. "Course I am, Jeb!"

A gentle smile creased Jeb's steady face. The man seemed rooted in solid rock. Not even the excitement of a Feast penetrated his calm.

"What about you, Jeb? Don't you enjoy it, too?"

"Me?" Jeb looked mildly surprised, as if the idea hadn't occurred to him before. "Yes, lad," he replied in his deliberate way. "I'm glad of the break."

"But why does it have to be so short? Three whole days gone already. And today's all but over."

"Ah, best not to think about that," the old man replied simply.

"I try not to. But I can't help it. Only three more days and the Feast will be finished."

"Don't waste yer time talking to an old man, then, young Tom. Be off with you, and have yer fun." As if to reinforce his advice he turned and, with a single wave of his weathered hand, was gone.

MEANDERING through the hawkers in the market square, Thomas noticed a crowd gathering nearby. The banners of the cobblers' guild waved proudly above a huge decorated wagon.

As he hurried over to join them the chatter of the onlookers ceased. All eyes were on the wagon. He craned his neck hopefully but could see nothing. Bending almost double, he burrowed determinedly into the solid mass of people, ignoring the ensuing growls of disapproval. He emerged at the front in a perfect position to watch the morality play that had just begun.

Battle had already been joined. Satan, richly clad in a magnificent gown of crimson and black, was enticing a poor shepherd boy to steal from his master.

A mound of newly baked bread covered a nearby table. Satan

casually selected a loaf. He set it down within easy reach of the hungry shepherd, who eyed it nervously.

The Tempter gazed at the youth pityingly and shook his head. "You work so hard! And he gives you so little to eat." He paused to let his words sink in.

"How long since you've tasted bread like this?" He indicated the loaf. It was so fresh from the oven that steam still rose from its golden-brown crust.

His silky voice took on a wheedling tone. "It smells good, doesn't it? Why don't you try it?"

The lad stared at the loaf longingly. A trembling hand reached out uncertainly. He was almost touching it.

Satan glanced around furtively before lowering his voice. "It's only one tiny loaf. He won't miss it. Go on, take it!" he insisted.

Close by a horde of demons hovered expectantly. Gloating in their hideous masks, they stood poised to drag the fallen youth away to everlasting torment. The onlookers, thoroughly alarmed, shouted encouragement and warnings.

Just when all seemed lost, the shepherd rallied, and directed a desperate last-minute appeal heavenward. Two saints climbed into the wagon. Hands clasped, they knelt to pray.

Soon a shining Jesus-figure simply dressed in a white robe appeared and banished the demons. Satan, shaking his fists in impotent rage, turned and fled. The shepherd boy followed Jesus with eyes alight, his hunger forgotten.

The onlookers erupted in cheers. Thomas shouted with them until hoarse.

THE PLAY OVER, guild members hitched horses to the wagon and marched proudly off behind it to repeat the play elsewhere in the town.

As the crowd dispersed Thomas drifted off toward the stalls just beyond the square. On the first day of the Feast his father had given him a small handful of coins. If he intended it as a peace offering,

Thomas's non-committal grunt in response must have offered him little satisfaction. Nonetheless, Thomas was pleased with the gift. Money commanded respect, and the coins earned him the right to walk among the stalls with head held high.

All but one still lay safely in the pouch at his waist. The missing coin was now in the keeping of an old peasant woman. Thomas had exchanged it for a large piece of honeycomb dripping with sweet nectar. He had spent a whole day savoring it in anticipation before the purchase; the reality was impossibly fleeting by comparison.

He could spare no more coins, though. The rest should be just enough to buy a bolt of bright cloth for his mother. Thomas had already wandered wide-eyed for hours among the bewildering array of options, and he was no closer to a decision. But there was plenty of time.

HE WAS STILL SEARCHING, totally absorbed, when an angry yell rose above the background babble of voices.

"Stop him!"

Thomas swung around in time to see a wooden cart upended into the street. A grim-faced boy erupted from the chaos. He dodged through the crowd frantically, a large loaf of bread tucked firmly under each arm.

"Stop him! Thief!"

A burly stall-keeper stepped into the boy's path. The youth tried desperately to evade him, but the man's two powerful arms ended the flight.

The baker arrived, red faced and panting. His finger stabbed accusingly at the boy. "He stole my loaves!" he gasped indignantly. "Tipped over my cart!"

His captor wrested the loaves from his grasp and returned them to their owner. The lad's eyes glared back defiantly out of a gaunt face. But his thin body trembled in the stall-keeper's firm grip.

He was hustled away toward the market square. Shouts of "Make way! Thief!" preceded him. The crowd caught up the cry, and it spread quickly. "Thief! They've caught a thief."

The angry crowd jostled and buffeted the lad. Thomas followed, curious to see the outcome. He could not grasp why anyone would be stupid enough to steal, especially so soon after the cobblers' guild drama. Surely the lad must have been aware of it.

The inevitable punishment was well deserved. Yet the frail youth seemed so pitiable he could not help feeling sympathy for him.

Town officials readied the stocks and secured the ankles of the luckless thief. The crowd subjected him to a continual stream of jeers and occasionally blows. He bore it bravely for a time. Eventually, though, he buried his face in his hands, his bony frame wracked by heaving sobs.

Unable to witness the humiliation further, Thomas turned away in distress. Silently he vowed that he would never yield to temptation, no matter how sorely he was pressed.

HEAD HELD high and lips pursed in a cheerful whistle, Thomas pushed through the merrymakers and set off for home. The pouch at his waist no longer jingled with coins, but he had every reason to be satisfied. He had bargained a good price for the large piece of deep blue cloth now clutched possessively in his hands.

Although the vendor had grumbled, Thomas saw his coins forced into an already bulging pouch. With six good days of the Feast behind him the man could probably afford to relax his price a little.

Almost clear of the main mass of people, Thomas found a small crowd pressed into a square. A performing bear? There were certainly bears at the Feast again this year—his father had seen one. Anxious not to miss any action, he elbowed his way eagerly toward the front.

Surprisingly, the crowd readily let him through, closing silently behind him. The youth popped into the open to find himself face to face with an old friar. Deep-set and brooding eyes locked on him briefly. Then the disturbing visage turned away.

Snow-white hair and an unkempt beard flowed restlessly around the man's face, caught up in a sudden gust of wind. He fixed his gaze heavenward. So intently did he stare that Thomas followed his gaze, half-expecting to see some marvel descending on the wings of a gathering storm.

Nothing unusual appeared. Thomas creased his forehead and regarded the friar in puzzlement. Plainly dressed in rough burlap and leaning on a sturdy wooden staff, the man could have been a prophet of old. As if to complete the image, he rounded sternly on the onlookers, spreading his arms grimly over them.

"Repent of your avarice! Turn away from your licentiousness." His thin voice grew in strength, and his hands shook. "Repent! Before it is too late.

"Darkness awaits you. You call down doom upon yourselves. The Feast of St. Michael? You dishonor his sacred memory with your gluttony and drunkenness! Do you expect to answer only to yourselves?" The old man pinned the crowd with flaming eyes. No one dared move.

"Cold, hard-hearted folk! What of the widows and the orphans among you? How many of you care for them? Which of you place the Eternal God above your appetites and desires? Do not think to escape the fires of hell should death take you." Several of the bystanders trembled, eyes wide with dismay.

"Turn away from the wrath to come! Seek mercy before justice befalls you."

The prophet glared around him, and a shaking finger picked out Thomas. "Think not that you will be spared. Your hatred and rage prepare you only for damnation."

Shaken and abashed, Thomas bent his head and shuffled his feet. When he finally risked a snatched glance, the friar's attention had shifted elsewhere.

Thomas grew restless. The old man's warnings clearly applied to someone else. How could he have been foolish enough to stop here?

He stole another glance at the friar. Seeing the man looking in his direction he rapidly shifted his gaze downward again.

The dire warnings rumbled on like thunder rolling through the hills. Head down, Thomas found his mind wandering. The bare and callused feet of the old prophet captured his attention. Travel-hardened toes poked out from the hem of his tattered robe, and Thomas observed that the toenail of his right big toe was missing. The toes bobbed up and down rhythmically. He hadn't noticed before, but the man was slowly swaying backward and forward like a sapling bending in a stiff breeze.

The strident voice ceased abruptly, cutting short Thomas's investigations. He looked up. The friar leaned heavily on his staff, head bowed, his fire extinguished. He appeared frail and tired.

Along with almost everyone else, Thomas grasped his opportunity and slipped away.

Strolling home in the sunshine clasping the precious cloth to his heart Thomas found the apocalyptic warnings of the old friar gradually fading from his mind. He savored in anticipation his mother's reaction to the gift. He had never before had an opportunity to give her anything substantial. He was confident she would be delighted. There could be no doubt about her surprise.

Once he reached home he decided not to go straight inside. An occasion like this needed to be shared. Though his best friend wouldn't understand, he could still participate in Thomas's pleasure. He headed for the stables, calling for Ben.

When he found Ben he also found Simon. The dog's chin nestled appreciatively in Simon's lap while the boy's left hand deftly stroked under his muzzle and behind his ears.

Thomas had been fool enough to think nothing could mar his enjoyment of this occasion. He flashed a grim look at his rival.

With his right hand Simon tossed a small object in the air, catching it before it fell. He tossed it again, and it spun in the air, flashing in the afternoon sunlight. Thomas froze. Could it be? Surely it was impossible! Once again the tiny object sailed into the air. He peered intently, neck craned forward and eyes narrowed.

For a moment the world stopped. "You stole it!" he gasped. "You stole it from me."

Simon stared at him, uncomprehending, but unmoved. "What are you raving about?"

"How *dare* you!"

Thomas's focus narrowed to the object of his hate before him. First he had snatched away the attentions of Thomas's father. Now it was Ben.

Worst of all, he had dared to steal Thomas's precious treasure. Once Thomas had been all-seeing. Now he was blind.

He abandoned himself completely to the fury which rose within him. A red veil spread behind his eyes and briefly blinded him. Then he leaped at Simon.

Ben sprang aside with a bewildered yelp. Thomas grabbed Simon's right hand, prizing open his clenched fingers. Simon fought back savagely.

Momentarily possessed of a superhuman strength, Thomas wrested the stone from his opponent with a jubilant bellow. Grasping it triumphantly, he attacked the younger boy ferociously, desiring only to hurt him. The two rolled across the floor of the stable, striking and clawing at each other.

Bruised and bloodied, Simon tore free of Thomas. Picking up a stick he struck out at the older youth, landing a painful blow across the arm.

This was too much. Thomas snatched up a pitchfork lying nearby. Pushing aside all thought of the consequences, he raised it and lunged.

Simon barely managed to avoid it. He turned and fled. Tail between his legs, Ben slunk away.

Thomas stood still for a very long time. Eventually he moved, wincing with the pain from his arm and numerous scratches. Blood trickled down his face and dripped off his chin. He opened his hand. The stone was still there, fouled with blood.

He turned absently and noticed the bolt of cloth for his mother. It had been trampled during the fight. He bent slowly and picked it up.

Grime and fresh horse manure had changed its color from a deep blue to a speckled dirty brown. Blood stains mingled with the dirt. He regarded it numbly.

On his way to the well to clean up Thomas passed old Jeb. Ashamed, he kept his head down, hoping Jeb wouldn't speak to him or notice his appearance.

Having washed himself as best he could, he tried to restore the cloth to its original condition. His efforts were in vain. Several large stains remained, and there were two small but noticeable tears in the middle where it had apparently been ground under foot. He couldn't give it to his mother now.

Thomas wandered aimlessly into the street, trying to push from his mind a vivid image of a lunging pitchfork. He couldn't go home. Simon would have been there first, of course. His father would be furious.

There would be a heavy punishment. He could weather it. But he could imagine already the disappointment in his mother's eyes, and he knew he had no resources to deal with that.

IT DAWNED on Thomas later that the stone had revealed nothing to him, either of Simon during the fight or later Jeb.

It was the same stone. He knew it as well as his own hand. But it took only a few minutes in town among the revelers to drive home the harsh reality: the stone was utterly useless.

10

In the distance Will noticed a lone woodcutter at work among the pines on the fringes of the forest. Until now he had seen no one since leaving the forest stronghold, and the need to check his direction had become pressing. He headed toward the man eagerly.

Seeing another human lifted his spirits considerably. The journey had been demanding and uncomfortable, and he had driven himself unmercifully. People meant warmth and shelter, and both he and his horse needed rest.

As the sun rose he had gradually warmed up. Despite his sleepless night he had felt refreshed and energized. He made good progress while the sun climbed into the sky and paused briefly at noon only to rest the horse. Again he had reason to thank the Rogandan guards; his saddlebags overflowed with fresh bread, dried meat, and even a skin filled with ale.

Early in the afternoon, though, a fine rain set in, and before long it had soaked him thoroughly. Then a steady breeze sprang up out of the east and chilled him to the bone. He needed to dry out and sleep for a few hours before pressing on.

Soon the Rogandans would ride for Danford. They needed to arrive fresh enough to fight, so it did not seem possible that they could be in position in one day. Will's head start should allow him plenty of time to alert the nearest troops at Stantony and still get inside the walls of Danford first. The 'nomads' would get a taste of their own medicine.

The woodcutter spotted Will while he was still some distance away. To Will's vexation, the man dropped his ax and sprinted off into the forest before he could call out, soon disappearing among the trees. The young soldier quickly realized that following him was hopeless.

It dawned on Will that he must look like a nomad. He had kept the gianhi-skin cloak—it had a way of retaining his body heat without making him sweat. Even the horned helmet still sat in place. It had proven surprisingly effective at keeping the rain off his head.

He dismounted and pulled off the cloak and helmet, tossing them in frustration into a nearby clump of bushes. Then he thought better of it. Retrieving them, he stowed them carefully in his saddlebags, making sure they were out of sight.

As he was remounting, a hoarse cry rang out. He looked up to see two mounted men and several others on foot heading determinedly in his direction. Apparently the woodcutter had not been working alone. The men were armed and clearly meant business.

Will decided quickly that now was not the time for explanations. Trying to outrun them made even less sense. He turned his weary mount toward the forest and dug his heels into its flanks.

"Have you given our conversation any more thought, Rufe?"

Rufe had been called from his bed back to the barn commandeered by Edgar. Edgar seemed casual and relaxed. But his companions were like taut bowstrings. Something was brewing.

The small group of plotters had been conspicuous by their

absence in the last couple of days, but Rufe knew they would not have been idle. And after considering and rejecting many desperate schemes, he was no closer to blocking them. He felt hopeless and powerless and yet strangely responsible for the looming disaster.

That it would be a disaster he had no doubt. Why hadn't King Steffan dealt with the nomads more effectively? His failure had all but handed Edgar his opportunity.

Rufe decided his only option was to stall Edgar. "You haven't told me your plans for Lord Gramm and his knights."

"Trust, Rufe, trust," Edgar chided. "How can friends help each other without a little trust?"

Rufe did not reply.

"So you're still undecided?" Edgar asked.

Rufe nodded.

"Well, you can join us in a toast at least." Edgar nodded to one of his friends, and a mug of wine was thrust into Rufe's hands. "To the speedy downfall of the nomad raiders."

Rufe hesitated, unwilling to rely on Edgar even for a mug of wine. Where had it been pilfered from?

Then he shrugged and drank deeply. The wine seemed good on the way down, but left a bitter aftertaste. Just like everything about Edgar, he reflected grimly.

Rufe headed back to bed determined to find a way of stopping Edgar. But sleep overtook him before he had even begun to think about it.

THE SOUNDS of pursuit had faded away. Tall, stately oaks surrounded Will on all sides, and their leafy green canopy shut out the sky. The forest was almost completely silent. Warm drafts of air soothed his aching limbs, but he knew he could not afford to relax until he was clear of the trees.

His detour had already cost him several hours. At first he planned to hide until his pursuers had left. When it became clear they did not intend to give up the search, he decided to try to find a way around them. Now he was entirely lost.

As the daylight slowly failed Will happened upon a stream gurgling merrily along a deep gully. On the far side he could just make out a faint path in the half light. By the time he managed to find a suitable place to descend into the gully and cross the stream the path was barely visible.

No obvious token indicated which direction to take or even whether the path led anywhere at all. He debated with himself for a while then turned his horse upstream.

The path followed the stream for a while then turned away, skirting a dense tangle of fallen trees choked by thick undergrowth. The ground sloped steadily upward as the path wound its way around the hillocks. Soon the sound of the water had faded away altogether. Then the path turned sharply, and the stream abruptly reappeared. Droplets of spray danced gloomily in the fading light to the ceaseless music of a small waterfall.

Will paused beyond the waterfall and watered his horse before drinking deeply himself. Continuing in the dark seemed pointless, so he searched around for a comfortable place to lie down. Having tied up the horse to the branch of a fallen tree, he settled down for the night just off the path. His dwindling food supply he left untouched; it might need to last longer than he had expected.

A succession of attractive scenarios had paraded irresistibly before Will since leaving the Rogandan stronghold. All of them strongly featured honors and rewards for the man who so bravely saved the great town of Danford.

Now he berated himself for his foolishness. Never before had reality seemed to smile so intimately on his idle fantasies. And never before had his need for clear headedness been so urgent. He resolved henceforth to shun daydreams as a luxury that a man of action could ill afford.

The darkness was almost complete. Will sighed and closed his eyes, determined to rest.

A slight movement of air past his cheek roused him. His horse nickered loudly. A pale flash of white disappeared up the path as he looked up.

It seemed so insubstantial he wondered at first if he had imagined it. But his horse had sensed it, too.

Could it have been an apparition? A nameless dread worked its way up his spine, making his scalp crawl. Suddenly he felt vulnerable.

Will sat without moving for a long time. At last he could bear it no longer. Taking on an army would be better than waiting for a phantom to reappear. He untied the horse and set off up the path.

Negotiating the path in the dark took all his concentration. It continued to wind its way about, sometimes near the stream and sometimes away from it.

He would have missed the house but for the familiar smell of smoke from a wood fire. The dwelling had been built only a short distance from the path, but hidden from direct sight among the trees. All was silent apart from the quiet gurgle of the water and the throaty 'ribbit' of frogs, which faded away behind him as he moved further from the stream.

Still leading his horse, Will blundered around the rough wooden walls of the cabin, blindly searching for a way in. His fears had receded into the background with the anticipation of hot food, companionship, and a place by the fire.

An ominous voice from within the cabin stopped him cold. "Trespass in the haunted wood at your peril. Worse things than death may await you."

For a moment Will's fear welled up again. Then he called out boldly. "You will not readily drive me away from a warm fire with such words. I am cold and weary and need shelter for the night. I'll take my chances." It didn't hurt to be prepared, though. He quietly drew his sword.

An urgent mumble of voices carried to Will while he waited. Eventually a thin line of flickering light appeared as the door opened a crack. "Come in, then, if you dare."

Will sensed that the rough tone was forced, an awkward addition that did not belong to the voice. He quickly tied the horse and stepped toward the door.

"Not the sword. That stays outside!"

Will opened his mouth to protest, then shrugged. Sometimes you simply had to trust your instincts. He sheathed his sword, unstrapped the scabbard, and leaned it against the outside wall of the cabin. Then he stepped up to the door.

The crack widened, revealing a small room dimly illuminated by firelight and a couple of sputtering candles. He stepped in and looked around curiously. A few rough items of furniture barely relieved the starkness of the cabin's single room.

But his immediate attention was drawn to the occupants. A middle-aged man stood warily by the fireplace. His narrow gaze followed Will's every movement while his hand fidgeted beside the handle of a long-bladed knife. Huddled on the far side of the cabin sat an old woman. A cloak covered her stunted and misshapen body and a shawl held close about her head hid her face entirely. Her posture suggested she was a hunchback.

Will's travels had brought him into contact with many strange people. He could readily imagine what the idle ignorance of superstitious villagers might make of a hunchbacked old crone. It wasn't hard to guess why they had hidden away in the heart of a 'haunted' wood.

Finding himself in a home, even a rude one, made him acutely aware of his fatigue. "May I sit?"

A wooden chair lay unused beside the old woman, but the man nodded toward a low stool at the opposite end of the room. Will slumped onto it gratefully.

"Do you have any hot food? I will gladly pay for it."

The man bent to a metal pot suspended over the fire. His eyes scarcely leaving his guest, he scooped a generous portion into a wooden bowl. He handed it to the weary soldier along with a lump of bread.

Will took it eagerly and ate, scooping it out with his fingers. The stew seemed to contain lumps of fish, and he couldn't remember when he last enjoyed a meal so much. He cleaned out the bowl with the bread, not looking up until it was all gone.

"I must be gone well before dawn. I am a member of the King's Guard and I have urgent business in Stantony." He paused. "And I must avoid the local villagers." Neither of his hosts responded, but he could tell he had captured their interest.

"Can you guide me to the edge of the forest and direct me toward Stantony?"

The man spoke at last. "It is not possible. I have a game leg, and my...sister is unable to guide you." His face was unyielding.

"But you must! I will never find my way in the dark. And my errand is pressing."

There was no further comment. Will could see the man's curiosity had given way to stubborn determination.

"Can you at least wake me, then, three hours before the dawn?"

"We will wake you." This clearly presented no problem; most likely they would be glad to see the last of him.

The man apparently wanted to say more. Choosing his words carefully, he said, "It cannot benefit you to speak of your visit here. If you have any...gratitude for our hospitality, any respect for our solitude, you will leave us in peace." His face was stern, but he could not wholly suppress a tone of pleading from his voice.

"I'm sure I can be well away from here without needing to talk to anyone," Will replied. "If you guide me," he added significantly.

Will could see that the man was torn between the desire to be rid of him as expeditiously as possible and the need to remain secure in their haven, far from prying eyes. He decided to help them with their decision.

"I was pursued deep into the forest by a woodcutter and his friends. I think they mistook me for a nomad raider."

The man frowned in annoyance; the woman appeared shaken by the news.

"If I spend tomorrow wandering around the forest, they may find me. And you, too."

The man looked at Will darkly, then shot a glance at the woman who had become restless and distracted.

"All right," he growled. "You have your way. We will guide you as you ask."

Will could no longer ignore his exhaustion. Whether or not his hosts would play false, he needed to sleep. He mumbled his thanks and cast himself down on the floor.

HE WOKE to someone shaking him roughly. He squinted up into a face outlined by the flickering light of a single candle. Then he realized where he was. Surely he had only just laid down.

"It is time. You must go."

Will sat up reluctantly and rubbed his eyes. A warm skin had been placed over him while he slept, and he found to his surprise that his sword lay beside him. He stood up and strapped it on.

Will's horse snorted a welcome as they emerged from the cabin. The man hobbled around the side of the house for a moment and reappeared with the saddle. Will recalled with shame that he had gone to sleep without first taking care of his mount. It appeared that his hosts had made good his omission. He moved guiltily to the horse's side and tightened the girth straps.

Whatever the reputation of these people, they had treated him with kindness and respect, even though he was a complete stranger.

The man thrust a loaf of bread into his hand. "My sister will guide you."

Surprised, Will looked around for the woman. He glimpsed her dimly through the morning mist standing nearby. Fumbling in his pouch, he removed several coins and pressed them insistently into the hand of his host. After mumbling a brief protest, the man accepted them willingly enough.

As they prepared to leave, the man approached his sister and spoke quietly in her ear. She nodded impatiently and headed for the path, glancing back to be sure Will was following. She led him further upstream, then turned away across a clearing onto another fainter path.

The woman proved nimble enough in spite of her deformity. With a horse in tow, Will was hard pressed to keep up with her. It quickly became apparent to Will that he would never have found his way without her help.

She led on without pause until the first faint lightening of the sky heralded the coming of the dawn. The trees had thinned noticeably.

Soon they passed through a final patch of very dense woodland and arrived at the edge of the forest. Rolling hills dominated what could be seen of the distant skyline. The woman would go no further.

"Which way is Stantony?"

She did not speak, but pointed to a road, barely visible off in the distance.

He mounted his horse and looked down at her earnestly. "Thank you. You have done more than you can know by helping me. When my task is complete, if it is in my power, I will help you and your brother."

As he walked his horse clear of the forest, a voice called softly after him, "Fare well, king's man!"

He turned back, utterly astonished. For the voice was not that of an old crone, but the sweet tones of a girl who would soon be a woman.

But she was gone. He caught a last glimpse of her gliding off into the trees, and remembered the flash of white disappearing past him in the forest.

He set off without delay, his thoughts distracted by his guide. What lay behind that closely drawn cloak? Was she a witch, able to change her age and shape at will? Or simply a youth playing at an old crone? And if so, why? Intrigued and dissatisfied, he rode reluctantly away from the answers.

He had almost reached the road when he noticed three horsemen riding down from a ridge that overlooked the entire area. They chose a route which would soon intersect with his own. As they drew closer he saw that two of them were youths and the other scarcely more than a boy.

After a hurried consultation, the boy separated from the others and galloped back along the road in the opposite direction. The lad leaned forward over his horse, urging it to greater speed, but could not resist glancing frequently back over his shoulder.

Hoping to avoid them, Will kicked his heels into his horse's flanks. In response they spurred on their mounts and soon cut him off.

The youths—one slight and fair haired, the other taller and riding a skittish bay stallion—were armed, and as they approached they drew their swords importantly. Will had no intention of allowing them to delay him for long. He slowed his horse to a stop, drew his own sword and lay it across his knees. The eyes of the fair haired youth widened, and he glanced nervously at his bigger companion.

"Throw down your sword, stranger, or we will not answer for the consequences," the dark haired youth commanded.

"Is it always your custom to greet travelers in this way?" Will asked evenly.

"We know who you are," the youth sneered in response.

"Yes, you can't fool us," blurted the fair haired one. "We know you've been with *her*." He shook his sword indignantly. "We saw you. You're a nomad, no matter how *she's* made you look."

"I have no time for superstitious foolishness," Will replied scornfully. "I have an urgent errand for the king that cannot be delayed. Move aside!"

The fair youth glanced anxiously after his departed friend. Guessing they had sent for help, Will spurred his horse at them, determined to break through and trusting in the speed of his horse to outdistance them.

But the dark haired youth swung his horse into Will's path and swiped at him with his sword. Will barely ducked in time. He was immediately forced to raise his own sword to deflect another blow.

Warming to the task, his opponent soon rained blows on him. The youth had clearly been trained to use a sword, and Will was forced to parry vigorously. He was too eager to be dangerous, but the tall youth would be a competent swordsman one day.

Will thrust half-heartedly, unwilling to hurt him. But it was becoming evident he would not break free without taking the initiative.

Encouraged by his friend's boldness, the fair haired youth pressed in on Will from behind. Seeing his enemy momentarily distracted as a result, the larger youth aimed an energetic blow at Will's head. Will reacted too late to parry the stroke effectively. Glancing off his own sword, the blade gouged a deep tear down the length of his cheek.

Will's free hand flew to his face in disbelief. In a few moments, this credulous young fool had done him more injury than a stronghold full of Rogandan soldiers in a whole night. Blood flowed freely from the stinging wound.

His assailant paused, almost as surprised as him. Then, a new light in his eye, he returned to the attack. His friend advanced confidently from the other side.

Riled now, Will charged his attacker. He wanted to hurt him, to return pain for searing pain. He lunged for his sword arm, intending to take him out of the fight. But the youth's bay lurched forward, carrying its rider full onto the point of Will's sword. He reeled back, crashed to the ground, and lay still.

The fair haired youth gaped at his friend, wide-eyed with horror. Then he wheeled his horse and galloped off as though pursued by an army of demons from hell. His sword quivered point down in the ground, discarded in his haste.

A quick examination with his hand convinced Will he had suffered nothing worse than a flesh wound. He turned back to the fallen youth. Seeing him lying in his blood brought Will a deep pang of remorse. The youth had done nothing worse than trying to defend his home against a supposed invader. Such needless waste.

Why did it have to end like this? He shook his head, frustrated and angry at the senseless stupidity of it.

The youth had brought it on himself. Yet that knowledge failed to satisfy Will's need for self-justification. It was two nights—could it truly have been so recent?—since he had killed the two Rogandans. Anyone would excuse him for that, and his countrymen would unanimously praise him. But this?

If only he could have those few minutes over again. He wrestled unhappily with his thoughts. Never in his life had he found himself so bound in the grip of shame.

Harsh cries aroused him. A group of horsemen, riding hard, was almost upon him. Their armored leader rode a powerful charger and wielded a battle-ax. He was tall and dark haired. When he saw the fallen youth he bellowed out a roar of fury. Will hastily sheathed his sword still bloodied and urged his horse to a gallop.

Hurried glances over his shoulder showed the dark haired leader pursuing him closely. The others had fallen behind. Spurring his horse unmercifully, the ax man was gaining ground steadily.

Will kicked his mount hard in the ribs, and it sprang away with renewed energy. Another glance a few moments later showed his pursuer slipping behind. Carrying a heavy man in armor, the charger could no longer maintain its burst of speed.

The man bellowed and wept in frustrated rage. Finally abandoning the pursuit, he sent a despairing curse racing after his fleeing quarry.

Long after every sign of the chase lay far behind, the words still haunted the troubled young soldier: "His blood is on your head! Forever! For EVER!"

RUFE WOKE TO BRILLIANT SUNSHINE. He sat up and groaned. His stomach wanted to violently escape his body. He'd clearly overslept, yet no one had roused him, and there was no sign of other soldiers. The large barn in which he slept, normally a hive of activity in the morning, was strangely silent and empty.

Where was everyone? Lord Gramm always inspected the soldiers early each morning. Something must be going on. Had the soldiers been summoned to a village? If so, how could they have gone without disturbing him?

Or worse still, had Edgar finally made his move? A nasty suspicion crept in on him—Edgar's wine last night must have been drugged. Thoroughly alarmed and furious at being so easily duped, Rufe pulled on his boots, strapped on his sword and hurried outside. He squinted in the sudden light. His shadow clung closely to his body —he had almost slept the morning away.

Almost immediately he met two of Edgar's henchmen. They greeted him casually, but their manner said they had been waiting for him.

"Are you with us?" The tone was deliberately matter-of-fact even though the question was blunt.

Rufe sensed that a great deal hung upon his reply.

"Yes, I'm with you." Rufe could not remember a time when he had so consciously and deliberately set out to deceive someone. But he had built a reputation as a man of his word, and he could see that the soldiers accepted his answer at face value.

The men visibly relaxed. Rufe wondered what had been planned for him had he responded differently. He glanced at them with contempt. It would take more than this pair to dispose of him.

"Come with us. Things are moving along very nicely. Gramm is out of the way, and Edgar is whipping up the rabble right now in the town square. The nomads will soon be in for a big surprise."

Rufe set off after them, racked with indecision. What could he do? He looked at the men walking hastily ahead of him and decided there might be a simple way of buying more time.

He quickened his pace and caught up with them. Positioning himself between them, he placed his arms loosely around their necks. He responded to their startled looks with a genial smile. Then he abruptly squared his shoulders, stepped back and drew their heads together with a single fluid movement of his powerful arms. With a sickening thud the two men slumped senseless to the ground.

Rufe bent down and put his ear to their mouths. Yes, they were still breathing steadily. One at a time, he picked them up in his great arms as a father might carry a child, and shifted them back to the barn, carefully laying each of them on a palliasse. After stopping for a moment to admire his handiwork, he once again headed for the town square.

Rufe cautiously circled the soldiers on the edge of the square, bending low to remain inconspicuous. Hands on his hips, Edgar stood on top of an old wooden cart in front of the soldiers. He was working them gradually and persistently, like a man breaking a horse.

But a few stubborn dissenters were not yet convinced.

"What about Lord Gramm and his knights?"

"How many times do I have to tell you?" The hard edge in Edgar's voice suggested his patience was wearing thin. "They're ill. All of them. I can't help it if their food doesn't agree with them.

"Mind you, it serves them right if you ask me," he added, dropping his tone sarcastically. "They wine and dine like kings every day while we survive on scraps."

Rufe knew it wasn't true, but a spontaneous growl of agreement from the crowd indicated Edgar had struck a chord. He pressed home his advantage. "But I'm not interested in feasting. I want to strike a blow for my king!

"The nomads have had it all their own way. It's time we took the fight to them. We're the king's soldiers. But are we cowards?"

Edgar's challenge evoked a loud chorus of denials. He almost had the crowd where he wanted it, and Rufe could think of nothing to do or say to stop him. Soon it would be too late.

Rufe concluded reluctantly that it was too late for him to intervene effectively. No one could stop Edgar now except Lord Gramm.

The lord must be somewhere nearby, probably drugged and under guard. Rufe hurried off, on the lookout for another soldier who was not at the meeting. As he ran he mumbled a fervent prayer that Lord Gramm would be conscious when he found him.

. . .

A BUZZ of voices rose on the far side of the square. A lone horseman appeared, picking his way through the crowd toward the center of the square. The voices fell silent as he passed through their midst, and all heads turned to follow his progress. Steam rose in clouds from his horse. Judging by its step it was almost spent, although it still tossed its head proudly.

The rider's face bore a gaping wound, and his eyes probed the crowd with restless intensity. Many soldiers stepped back involuntarily when they saw his appearance.

The man drew his horse to a halt just before the wagon where Edgar glared darkly down at him, annoyed at the interruption. He looked up, and even Edgar flinched when confronted with his ruined visage.

"Where is the commander?"

"What business is it of yours?" Edgar replied.

The rider eyed Edgar coolly before answering. "Raiders have attacked the village I kept watch over. My task is to alert the commander."

Someone called out. "It's Will Prentis. From the King's Guard."

A hubbub arose. There were loud cries of "To horse!" Men began arguing and milling around in confusion.

"Be silent, you idiots!" Edgar roared over the din. "Do you want another fool's errand to a burned-out village?"

"Wait!" The rider's clear voice rang out. "He is right. The village is destroyed. It is already too late."

Edgar seized his opportunity. "Listen to this man. There is nothing more to argue about. We must ride for the nomad encampments at once. We will plunder them as they have plundered us."

"No! Listen to me." The rider rose in his stirrups, and his voice carried commandingly. He turned to Edgar. "Who placed you in authority here?" he challenged loudly.

Edgar scanned the crowd and nodded to several men who immediately pushed their way toward the front. The other soldiers backed away. The rider swung his horse around and drew his sword. It was caked with dried blood. Edgar's men surrounded him, though they hung back warily.

"Your task," Edgar called out, "was to raise the alarm as soon as your village was attacked. And yet you say it is too late to save it." He pointed accusingly at the rider and addressed the crowd. "This man's village was destroyed while he escaped with a flesh wound. I say the raiders chased him, and he hid until they had gone. He is a coward and a traitor who deserves to die."

Edgar's men closed in, probing for a weakness.

11

Silent as a cat, Thomas padded through the dark and drafty corridors of the castle. During the winter months, every fireplace hissed and cracked, pitting blazing fire against the creeping chill. At this time of the year many of the fireplaces were deemed unnecessary, though, and the cold seeped slowly from the enclosing walls, setting Thomas shivering and longing for sunshine and the open air.

Whatever the season, the castle bustled with life and energy, even with the king away; Hilda the Grim, who oversaw the kitchen hands, pageboys, and chambermaids, saw to that. Sudden woe befell any idle hand coming into range of her ever-restless eye. But the castle was so vast and its corridors so labyrinthine that not even Hilda could oversee it all at once. That morning Thomas had seen no sign of her, not even the scurrying of her minions at the rumor of her approach.

He had been sent by his father with a message for the Hunt master. Ferreting the man out proved a challenge worthy of Hilda herself. Thanks to the cleaning girl who pointed out the old hunter's refuge, though, Thomas had finally tracked him to his lair. He startled the master out of a peaceful midmorning nap.

His message delivered, Thomas set off to find the castle entrance and the relative warmth of the stables. His journey took him through unfamiliar and lightly trafficked sections of the castle. At one point, he paused beside a narrow window that offered a distant glimpse of the river and the forest beyond it.

He fell to thinking about the carefree afternoon, seemingly years ago, when he had found the stone. The Thomas of those days was long gone, largely as a result of that discovery. And what did he have to show for it? He was confused and often unhappy, he had made a bitter enemy, and the power of the stone was lost to him.

Thomas had seen very little of Simon since their fight in the stables. For some inexplicable reason Simon had not told his father about his attack with the pitchfork, or even about the fight. Whether he was saving it until he could extract the maximum revenge, or whether he had some other motive, Thomas couldn't tell. Simon had not forgiven him—of that much he was certain—although that didn't help him suppress the shame of his own behavior.

His musing was interrupted by the welcoming crackle of a huge fire, issuing from the open doors of a large room. Although he had only seen the room on a few occasions, Thomas recognized it at once—the king's personal audience chamber. After a furtive glance into the chamber, he stepped inside and pushed the doors partly closed. The fire roared encouragingly just inside the doors, and he positioned himself before it, gazing about him in admiration.

A large table stood in the center of the room, surrounded by many elegantly carved chairs. The largest chair, almost a small throne, faced him at the far end, commanding the table.

Full suits of ancient ceremonial armor stood tirelessly at attention along both main walls. His father had brought him here once as a small child, and Thomas had taken some convincing that the suits did not conceal real knights. Even now he couldn't help shooting sudden glances at them, half expecting to surprise them in some tiny movement.

Imposing as they were, though, the suits of armor were not the main feature of the room—the chamber was dominated by huge wall hangings. Twelve tapestries adorned the walls, each featuring the deeds of a different king. The history of Arvenon appeared to be woven into the giant hangings, but Thomas could not name even one of the kings. He was disappointed to find no tapestry depicting Steffan II, the current ruler.

The largest and most lavish showed a young man astride a restless charger, the light of battle in his eye. A desperate struggle raged below him. His hand was raised high and behind him an eager troop of horsemen restrained their steeds with difficulty, waiting for his hand to fall.

It was his face that captured Thomas. The weaver had portrayed a young man with the air of one born to rule. His face showed a determination that reminded Thomas of Will. And with the imminent prospect of battle and perhaps death, the youthful warrior exuded a calmness that Thomas envied.

"Impressive, isn't it?"

Thomas leaped in alarm at the sudden voice. He whirled, wide-eyed. An old man stood behind him, gazing upward at the hanging. The man seemed vaguely familiar, but Thomas couldn't place him. He wore simple attire—not as lavish as might be expected of a noble, although certainly not the attire of a serving man, either. Thomas had been so absorbed he hadn't heard the man enter the room.

"Do you know who he is?" The old man smiled inquiringly at Thomas, inclining his head upward to indicate the youth in the giant tapestry. Thomas shook his head.

"It's Steffan the First. Our current king was named for him."

The man seemed unconcerned at Thomas's intrusion. Emboldened, Thomas decided to try to satisfy his curiosity. "What's going on?" he asked, pointing up at the hanging.

"The tapestry shows the Battle of Samoth, fought almost one hundred and fifty years ago. Arvenon was a smaller and weaker kingdom then, struggling to survive against the larger and more aggressive Kingdom of Rogand.

"The king, Rufus II, fought two inconclusive battles against the invading Rogandans, before he was finally brought to bay near the village of Samoth."

The old man's reply raised more questions than it answered. But he appeared to be in a talkative mood, so Thomas decided to wait and see what else he had to say.

"The Arvenian forces were outnumbered five to one, and the battle went badly for them. The king's only son was mortally wounded almost at once.

"The battle wore on into a second day. By midmorning, the king's son finally died, and the Arvenian army was on the brink of collapse. Just when it seemed the battle would be irretrievably lost, Steffan arrived. That moment is depicted on the tapestry before you.

"Steffan was the newly crowned king of Erestor, a small neighboring kingdom allied to Arvenon. He realized that if Arvenon fell, Erestor would be next, and he didn't hesitate to throw his full support behind Rufus. Erestor's army was small, but it included some of the finest cavalry ever seen up to that time."

The old historian had warmed to his task, and Thomas listened, fascinated and totally engrossed.

"Steffan's arrival was unlooked for by either side, and his horsemen swept through the right wing of the Rogandan army like a scythe. Rufus somehow rallied his surviving troops and attacked the enemy's left wing. It, too, quickly folded. Then the Rogandan center found itself under attack from two sides on narrow fronts. Most of the Rogandan soldiers milled around in confusion, unable to get at their enemies.

"The issue was decided just before sunset. A detachment of Erestorian archers arrived at the battlefield, and immediately began raining a deadly hail of arrows into the Rogandan ranks. The invaders held for a while, then turned and ran. Steffan's cavalry cut them down as they fled, all the way to the River Ange. Only the darkness saved them from total destruction. As it was, only one in three returned to Rog to face the wrath of their king.

"Rogand's power was broken, and Arvenon knew peace for many years."

"But didn't you say that Steffan was king of a different country?"

"Yes, I did. Rufus was gravely wounded in the final stages of the battle. The king had fought so well, only to see his son killed and his line ended on the day of his greatest victory.

"But he had a daughter. He offered her hand to Steffan there and then. Steffan accepted it, and Rufus proclaimed him the new king almost with his dying breath.

"Once it became known, there was dissent within the kingdom, of course. But the marriage brought legitimacy to the new rule, and Steffan combined the kingdoms and quickly strengthened and extended them. Most important of all, he proved to be a wise and just king, much loved by all. Just like our own king."

Thomas decided that while his luck held, he would keep the man talking. "Who are the other tapestries about?"

"The greatest kings of Arvenon, before and after Steffan. The tapestry to the left of Steffan's depicts Rufus II. Steffan himself commissioned it, in honor of the deeds of his late father-in-law."

"Who is that one to the right?"

The old man didn't answer. He held up his hand for silence. Voices could be heard in the corridor outside, rapidly becoming louder.

"You'd best be off." He pointed to a small door at the far end of the room. Thomas scurried through it, pulling it shut behind him just as the approaching voices reached the main doors of the chamber.

As the door closed, he heard a respectful greeting, "My Lord Duke, I see you have arrived already..."

And then it hit him. The old historian was the Duke of Erestor, the king's uncle, and, in the absence of the king, the regent of the kingdom! No wonder he knew so much about the Arvenian kings—it was his own family history. Thomas was mortified.

He had seen the duke many times, but mostly from a distance, and always before today dressed in a manner befitting royalty. He felt the blood rush to his face as he realized that he had not bowed to the duke. Worse, he had dared to speak to him, and hadn't done so in an appropriate manner. He hadn't even thanked him, a courtesy due to any commoner, much less a duke. He shivered at the thought of his father learning of the conversation.

He set off along the corridor before him toward a door at the far end. It was closed, but he opened it slowly and peered through it into a small antechamber. Two more doors lay to the left and the right, and another stood open opposite. Through the far door he could see what appeared to be a major corridor of the castle.

Thomas headed quickly through the antechamber toward the corridor, anxious to be gone. Before he reached it, though, he again heard voices in the corridor outside. One, loud and strident, he knew at once, and realized to his alarm that he was on a collision course with Hilda the Grim.

Hilda would want to know why he was sneaking around the castle, where he had been, where he was going, and who he had been bothering. He glanced at the doors on either side, chose quickly, and went through the one on the left, praying as he did that the room would be empty.

His prayer was answered, not only in the affirmative, but far beyond his expectations. In a day of marvels, he had stumbled on the most marvelous thing of all: a mirror. He had heard of its existence and knew what it was called, but had never seen it till now.

It stood almost as tall as him, mounted on a frame of exquisitely carved mahogany. It was truly a gift befitting a queen. Thomas knew without needing to be told that he did not belong in this room.

Nevertheless, he was drawn to it like a moth to a flame. He gazed in wonder into the mirror, clearer by far than any still pond on a calm day, and saw a tousle haired, gangly youth staring back at him. Although his mother had asserted it a hundred times, it nevertheless surprised him to see strong traces of his father in his own face.

As he stared, his curiosity was aroused: what would he look like when he was a man? Perhaps things would improve for him. Maybe he would be happier then.

He recalled his first glimpse of Will. The stone had transformed the young soldier from an ordinary man-at-arms into a knight, a vision that surely revealed Will's destiny. Could the stone show him something of the future of the pale youth before him in the mirror?

He reached down into his pouch and fumbled around, finally grasping the stone in his right hand.

Nothing happened. It wasn't surprising—the stone was now useless, after all—but he was still disappointed. He continued to stare absently into the mirror. Then the image seemed to shimmer, and a subtle change became apparent. It took him a few moments to identify it; the image before him had scarcely altered.

It had something to do with the eyes. He peered intently into the eyes and staggered backward in disbelief. The madness in the eyes. His eyes. His wolf's eyes. How could he bear it?

He instantly released the stone, and his eyes were as before. But it was too late. He could not undo what he had witnessed.

These eyes did not presage rabies. They spoke to him of the ruin of hope, the death of normality, the triumph of insanity in his life.

He fled the room and the castle in utter dismay.

12

Rufe's search had finally paid off. A solitary soldier stood outside a small barn on the outskirts of the town. He appeared alert and nervous. The barn doors were shut and barred. Rufe debated with himself for a moment before deciding to risk a bluff. He walked purposefully toward the soldier.

The man tensed instantly, his hand flying to his sword hilt. "What do you want?"

"Edgar sent me. You're watching Gramm, aren't you?"

"So you're with us?" The soldier's hand relaxed again. "Why did he send you?"

"He thought you might need to be reinforced."

The man looked worried. "Is there trouble?"

"No. Everything's going according to plan."

As he said it he sent his huge fist crashing into the soldier's jaw. The man slumped to the ground and lay still. Rufe hastily unbarred the doors and threw them open.

Once his eyes adjusted to the dim light inside the barn he saw prostrate forms laid out everywhere. After a quick search he found Lord Gramm and went straight to his side. The noble lay senseless, but breathing steadily. Rufe shook him firmly, but to no avail. His knights lay strewn around like wheat stalks scythed by a reaper. Edgar must have drugged them heavily.

His heart skipped a beat at the sheer audacity of it. But Lord Gramm could not punish those responsible if he didn't know who they were. And Edgar was shrewd enough to keep even his own accomplices in the dark. Knowing Edgar, someone had already been set up to take the blame.

Rufe quickly despaired of arousing even one of them. Then he heard a low moan coming from a corner of the barn. He headed toward it hopefully.

The sight that awaited him stopped him in his tracks. Several young men lay together, many of them severely wounded. Appalled, Rufe approached more closely. He recognized a squire of one of the knights. The squires must have put up a fight.

He discovered the source of the moans. A young man, ghostly white from shock and loss of blood, stirred weakly. He seemed to be drifting in and out of consciousness.

Drugging Lord Gramm and his knights was treasonous folly. But the brutality before him was beyond everything. Confronted by the pale, motionless young forms, Rufe's feelings of powerlessness vanished like an early mist before the sun. The urge to make Edgar pay became so compelling it felt almost like physical pain.

The insistent needs in the barn tugged at his heart. But every other fiber of his being drew him irresistibly into the eye of the storm brewing outside. He rushed out of the barn and sprinted toward the square.

His first glimpse of Edgar revealed him talking to a stranger on a horse. His spirits leaped when he recognized the man as Will Prentis. But what were they saying? He pushed to the front at the same moment Edgar pronounced judgment. Rufe caught a brief glimpse of Will's ruined face as his friend swung his horse around, surrounded by his attackers. Then he reached the cart.

Edgar finally spotted the giant guardsman. Fear showed on his face, and he called loudly for help. But he was too late.

Rufe vaulted into the cart before Edgar's sword had cleared its scabbard. Edgar had time for one hasty swing. Rufe blocked it with a lump of wood from the cart and kicked him hard in the midriff. He doubled over, and Rufe brought both fists crashing down onto his head.

He turned to the astonished crowd and indicated Edgar's prostrate body. "This...this *fool* drugged Lord Gramm and locked him in a barn."

They stared back uncomprehendingly. Most had drawn well away from the ring that closed around Will. Perhaps they hadn't heard him over the confused buzz of voices.

But Will's attackers heard. Several of them wavered, their faces betraying first shock and then horror. Fully half of the group slunk away and melted into the crowd. That left five. Two of them rushed at Rufe. The rest redoubled their attack on Will.

Still the crowd wavered. Rufe glared at them in disgust. He bent down to Edgar's limp body, heaved it up and hurled it at the two men clambering onto the cart. One of them was knocked to the ground. The other dodged it and pulled his friend to his feet.

Rufe drew his sword and leaped off the cart. He was dimly aware of one of Will's attackers going down. Then he charged howling at his enemies.

Furious, he flailed about with great slashing strokes, taking fierce delight in the frantic dodging of his opponents. His superior strength and reach forced them onto the defensive.

But he soon tired. And his opponents fought with the savage desperation of doomed men.

One of them got behind him. Suddenly he was fighting for his life. The sword became slippery as a cold sweat loosened his grip. Then he steadied himself, feinted toward one of the men, and dodged free. Sobered, he placed his back to the cart and struck out with renewed energy.

Other guardsmen joined the fray at last, and his attackers once again lost the initiative. Small knots of men struggled back and forth around the cart.

Within minutes it was over. Two of Edgar's remaining cronies had thrown down their swords. The other three lay dead. A soldier of the King's Guard lay beside them.

Rufe turned his back on the carnage and looked around for Will. He soon spotted him striding purposefully in his direction.

Will Prentis had always been his friend. Now they had fought together, alone and against the odds, and prevailed. Resolutely ignoring Will's damaged cheek, Rufe smiled a welcome. Will sprang past him onto the cart without even acknowledging him. Open-mouthed, Rufe stared after him.

Will stood to his full height. "You men. Gather round. Now!" The soldiers obeyed slowly, avoiding the bodies. Bewilderment showed on their faces.

"Listen to Rufe Sarjant. You need to hear what he has to say." Will turned to him at last and beckoned him up.

Rufe smiled up at him warmly. "I'm glad you're back, Will."

Will merely nodded. "Make it brief," he said bluntly.

Rufe scurried up onto the cart. This was a day of surprises. He pushed aside his questions and faced the men. "I found Lord Gramm and his knights. They're in a barn near here. Unconscious, all of them. They should recover after Edgar's drugged wine wears off. Some of their squires may not be so fortunate.

"It seems Edgar had plans for us. He talked about revenge against the nomads. But I think he was more interested in looting them."

Rufe began to warm to his task. "I suspect..."

Will cut him off cold. "I need five volunteers. Men who can't ride fast or fight hard."

No one stepped forward. Will turned swiftly to Rufe. "Choose them when I'm finished. And make sure they're reliable. They must tend the wounded, guard the traitors, and explain everything to Lord Gramm when he recovers."

He inspected the crowd, frowning. He seemed to be assessing them. "Thanks to Edgar's treachery our numbers are reduced and we are without our leaders. We must do the best we can."

He drew himself to his full height. "I have come from the nomad stronghold." Exclamations of amazement and disbelief greeted his words. Rufe gaped at Will, utterly astonished. He felt as though he was seeing him for the first time.

Will raised his hand for silence. Such was the force of his presence that the soldiers obeyed without hesitation. He swung around to Rufe. "My saddlebags. Get out the nomad clothes."

Rufe jumped down and retrieved them, tossing them up to Will.

He held them high. "The men who wear these are not nomads. They are Rogandan soldiers, led by a Rogandan lord. I speak their language and passed myself off as one of them.

"They want to provoke our king to fight the nomads. Even now they ride for Danford. They plan to sack the city. If they succeed, the king will be forced to turn on the nomads. You can imagine the rest." He pointed down at Edgar's still form. "This greedy fool would have played right into their hands."

"Why should we believe you?" someone in the crowd called out. "Maybe you're lying like Edgar."

Rufe reacted without thinking. "You're the ones beyond belief," he shouted, jumping up beside Will. "You listen to a self-serving liar. But you can't recognize the truth when it's shoved under your noses. Well, anyone who says Will Prentis is lying can argue it out with me." He thrust out his chest and glared at them belligerently.

This earned him a brief smile from Will. For a moment his friend seemed less aloof. Then he turned back to the soldiers, and his voice rang with authority.

"Choose quickly. The fate of our kingdom hangs in the balance. I will ride to Danford, even if I must face the Rogandans alone. Who will dare to ride with me?"

Rufe stared first at the crowd then back at Will. The soldiers stirred restlessly. Will's challenge hung in the air, his marred face confronting the soldiers like a rebuke. Yet he seemed completely calm. Rufe could not suppress an irrational notion that even if no one joined him, Will would somehow beat the Rogandans single-handed.

Will had changed. He may have become distant and unreachable, but he wouldn't have to ride alone.

Rufe stepped forward. "I will ride with you," he said quietly.

Will nodded an acknowledgment. Still he waited, arms folded across his chest. There was complete silence.

Then one soldier stepped out from the crowd. "I will, too."

Another followed. "And I."

"Me too."

Just as a falling rock dislodges others, the momentum gathered. The lone voices became a chorus and the chorus an avalanche of cheering.

Will tolerated their enthusiasm for no more than a minute. He held up his hand one last time. "Get your horses and weapons and return here at once. We must ride as we've never ridden before."

As they dispersed Rufe heard him add under his breath, "And pray that we arrive in time."

THE SOLDIERS at first made good time. They rode north swiftly through the open country surrounding Stantony, before swinging west to ford the broad river that wound lazily across the plain.

Will and Rufe led the way to the other side and turned to wait for the others. The water, just three feet deep, flowed gently, but the ford was narrow. There was barely enough room for two wagons to pass in the middle. The soldiers pressed toward the crossing, which soon degenerated into a confusion of splashing horses and shouting men.

Will jumped his horse back into the river and swam it across, scrambling up the opposite bank. Rufe heard Will's voice through the din, calling the men to a halt. The chaotic surge toward the river ceased abruptly, and the ford cleared. Will's voice rang out again, shouting instructions. As if by magic, a disciplined column of soldiers began crossing four abreast.

Will followed and led them west again without pause or comment. They climbed for almost an hour into rising foothills and crossed a pass, descending again into undulating terrain that stretched as far as the eye could see.

Every now and then the column of soldiers stretched out too far, and Will dropped back and urged on the laggards. Increasingly he glanced up at the sun, sinking slowly over their left shoulders, before frowning ahead across the hills.

Finally, returning from one of his trips down the line, he drew his horse alongside Rufe's.

"We're moving too slowly," he announced. "I'm going to ride ahead. I've already selected twenty men with fast horses."

Rufe's jaw dropped. As if to emphasize Will's words, several riders moved forward resolutely. Rufe recognized among them some of the best fighters in the troop.

He looked back at Will, dismayed. The soldiers had regained their sense of purpose since Will arrived. What would happen now?

"Who'll lead the troop if you leave?"

"You."

At first Rufe thought he was joking. But Will's face showed otherwise. Rufe was so flabbergasted he was unable to respond. All his life kings or lords or knights had been there to give the orders. Nothing had prepared him for this.

"I can't lead them!" he finally blurted out.

"Why not?"

"Because...because I don't know what to do."

"All you have to do is get the men to Danford as quickly as possible," Will replied. "If you find the Rogandans there, attack them without delay. If not, get inside the gates and defend them."

"The men won't follow me."

"Of course they will. If they'll follow me, they'll follow you."

Rufe shook his head, frowning. "It isn't the same." Will made it sound so straightforward, and he felt like a stubborn child trying to complicate a simple chore. For Will, leading seemed as natural as breathing. But it wasn't that way for him. "I don't have your qualities."

Will had been listening patiently, as though Rufe's objections would vanish once he was allowed to express them. But now he spoke pointedly. "There isn't time to consider personal feelings. Our mission is too important. The whole kingdom might be on the brink of disaster."

Rufe wanted to protest, to point out the obvious shortcomings that disqualified him. But when he opened his mouth, nothing came out.

"You needn't worry. I'll let the men know." With that, Will trotted back down the line again, calling out to the men as he went.

Rufe was stunned. The matter had been settled before he could even consider it as a serious option.

Will returned after a few minutes. "I've spoken to the men," he said. "You're in charge now. I'll see you in Danford!"

He raced away, followed by his select group of soldiers. His final instructions reached Rufe faintly over the drumming of hooves: "Keep the men moving!"

Will's hand-picked soldiers rode hard. They soon dipped out of sight behind the hills ahead. Each time they reappeared they had dwindled in size until Rufe could no longer see them at all.

Once Will had gone Rufe realized how much he had been depending on him for purpose and direction. Now he felt utterly alone.

With Rufe at their head, the main body of troops rode on in silence. Cresting a ridge, Rufe looked back and noticed that the line had stretched out too far again. He headed back to urge the stragglers to quicken their pace, fully expecting to be ridiculed. To his surprise, they responded obediently.

Will had taken complete command of the troops before leaving Stantony and no one had raised as much as a murmur. That was amazing enough. But the soldiers' meek acceptance of his sudden delegation to Rufe was nothing short of astonishing.

Rufe still wasn't quite sure how it had all happened. But one thing stood out very clearly: Will Prentis had become difficult to refuse.

"There, beyond those hills."

Rufe's gaze followed the soldier's pointing finger across the seemingly endless prospect of rolling hills. Yes, he could just make it out: a tiny strip of silver reflecting the late-afternoon sun. The River Dan. Beside it lay the town of Danford. Their goal was at last within reach.

Rufe strained ahead for a glimpse of Will and his troop. But he knew it was irrational. They were long since out of sight.

After hours in the saddle, both men and horses showed their weariness. But Rufe could not shake off a mental picture of a sea of nomad-clad horsemen sweeping away Will and his tiny force. The time had come to pick up the pace.

WILL'S troop charged through the last village before the walled city of Danford. Only the barking of a dog marked their passage. They swept onto the final stretch of road past an abandoned cottage, sending some hens squawking under an old wagon overgrown with weeds. Then all was quiet except for the drumming of hooves.

Will halted his men under the cover of the last stand of trees before the walls of Danford and peered out into the dusk. The gates had already been closed for the day. All appeared peaceful.

"Wait here. I'm going to see who holds the gates."

Will removed his helmet and drew his cloak around him to hide his sword. Head down and slouching forward in the saddle, he headed toward the gates. To all appearances he was just another weary traveler, his horse plodding with fatigue.

The night-watchman challenged him well before he reached the wall. "The gates are closed. Be off with you!" The words were carefully articulated, but the speaker could not disguise a heavy accent.

"But I need shelter for the night." Will glanced back over his shoulder. "You can't turn me away! It isn't safe out in the open."

Coarse laughter greeted his statement. Apparently he had said something amusing.

He wondered if their sense of humor had a limit. "It's rumored there are nomad barbarians abroad tonight."

The laughter ceased abruptly.

A spear whistled through the air and quivered in the ground beside him. "Begone!" His horse laid back its ears and tossed its head wildly. Will swung the animal around and galloped away from the gate. Echoes of renewed laughter chased him out of earshot.

He pulled his horse up inside the safety of the trees. "They've taken over the gates already. We don't have much time."

"Are the gates closed?" one of the men asked.

"Yes, although they've left the portcullis up." Will looked around him and cursed. "They probably aren't strong enough to hold off a determined assault, even by twenty men. But we have no ladders, no ropes, nothing. Not even a horn to alert the people inside."

A soldier spoke up. "Could we get the portcullis down? Cut the ropes that hold it up, maybe? That would keep the Rogandans out."

Another answered. "Not a chance. One of the guards showed it to me when we were stationed here. It's raised and lowered by heavy chains. Neither the winder nor the chains are even visible from outside the walls."

Will's mind churned as the darkness deepened. He glanced away toward the distant hills, little more than an outline against the sky. Rufe and his men were out there somewhere. He prayed they would arrive in time.

Someone broke the silence. "If the portcullis is up, we can get inside it."

"How does that help us?" Will demanded.

"We won't last long outside the walls once the Rogandans arrive. But maybe we can defend the tunnel between the gates and the portcullis."

"Yes, and spend our time dodging boiling oil from the gate-house," another voice chipped in sarcastically.

"No, wait. It's worth thinking about." Will had no better ideas. And a desperate situation called for desperate measures. "Don't forget their task is to open the gates, not defend them. They won't be boiling up a vat of oil. Anyway, supplies like oil and rocks aren't stored at the gate-house. They're only taken there during a siege." Will sincerely hoped he was telling the truth.

"But we can't just ride in. The minute they see us coming they'll drop the portcullis. After their friends get here and finish us off, they'll wind it up again and let them in."

Will pondered for a minute. "Then we'll have to make sure they don't realize twenty men are at the gates until it's too late."

"How do we do that?"

"A while back we passed an abandoned wagon. We'll hide inside it. Once we get it past the portcullis we can use it to barricade the entrance." He jabbed his finger at several of the men. "You four, go back and get it. And be quick about it!"

THE DAN WOUND its way like a glittering serpent through the plain before them. The troop had broken free of the hills at last.

Without slowing, Rufe twisted around in the saddle and reviewed the column stretched out behind him. After weeks of frustration and idleness Will had promised them a real opportunity to do at last what they came for. There had been so many false alarms, though. Would the Rogandans be there?

He felt certain they would. And the soldiers thought so, too. Glancing back at them he could sense the expectancy in their ranks, the suppressed nervous excitement. The setting sun caught their spear tips and set them flickering like dancing fireflies. It was an impressive sight. The king's soldiers were riding to war.

Once they reached level ground, still a league or more from the town walls, Rufe drew them up to speak to them. The deepening dusk masked their faces, but tension charged the silence. For some of them this would be their first real fight. It was no practice drill with blunt swords—the Rogandans were hardened killers. But the men would find what they needed. They were the king's soldiers.

Rufe was not afraid. Whenever fear came visiting he simply called to mind the image of a witless boy, alone in a razed village. Even the heavy burden of leadership had begun to melt away beside the imminent prospect of vengeance.

"If Will Prentis is holding the gates against the Rogandans," he called out, "stay together until we reach them. Press the Rogandans toward the walls. Don't let any of them escape!

"And stay silent until they spot us. We have the advantage of surprise—let's make the most of it. We may never get a better chance to destroy them.

"The King's Guard should stay close to me." He drew his sword and held it aloft. "For the king and for Arvenon!"

The men roared it back. "For the king and for Arvenon!"

Rufe Sarjant spurred his horse toward the distant walls. The ground trembled as eight score horsemen galloped after him into the gloom.

RUFE HEARD the fighting before he saw it. The ringing clash of metal on metal and the cries of battle revealed a struggle immediately before the gates. He urged his weary horse to a final effort and charged toward the press, his men close behind.

A burning wagon blocked the entrance, its flames dimly illuminating the struggle. On the far side, a perilously small number of dark forms held at bay the raging nomad-clad soldiers of Rogand. Dozens of hand-held torches weaved a frantic rhythm through the air as the frustrated raiders crowded into the entrance trying to reach the defenders. But the flames kept them back, and the entrance had been blocked so effectively that only two or three men could attack at once.

At the sight of his enemy an involuntary roar exploded from Rufe's lips. Behind him the roar grew in volume, swelled by scores of other voices.

For a moment the fighting stopped as startled heads turned away from the walls. A ragged cheer went up from before the gate, then died as the Rogandans renewed their assault with reckless ferocity.

A line of horned horsemen swung around to face the new threat. They barely had time to turn before Rufe's soldiers crashed upon them like a tidal wave, shattering the line. Rufe plunged through into the heart of the Rogandan troops with the guardsmen surging into the gap behind him. His weariness forgotten, he pressed urgently toward the gates.

Horn-helmed heads beckoned on every side. Rufe's sword danced among them. A fierce joy flooded through him, energizing his wildly swinging arm.

The Rogandans gave ground reluctantly. But the king's soldiers would not be denied. Cheering wildly, they swept aside the last raiders and broke through to the defenders.

First to reach the wagon, Rufe leaped from his horse and ran to find Will. The fighting had been heaviest here, and he picked his way appalled among the ghastly debris of battle.

Then he stopped cold. Before him lay Will Prentis, his lower body crushed beneath a fallen horse. The flickering light revealed his final agony, preserved in his contorted face. Rufe trembled violently and uncontrollably. His mind became numb.

Somehow his feet returned him to his horse, and he found himself back in the saddle. He stared unseeing, first toward Will and then to the battle still raging around him. The trembling slowly faded, replaced by an icy calm.

He looked out upon his enemies, and a deadly wrath mounted within him. Then, as violently and indiscriminately as a volcano spewing fire, he erupted.

Rufe spurred his horse savagely. Ears flattened and nostrils wide, it propelled its giant rider into the thick of the battle.

None could hold their ground before him. He soon formed the vortex of a whirling turmoil of destruction. Friends and foes alike fell back in terrified confusion before his berserker fury.

How long it continued he could not tell. But there came a time when his enemies had all fled or perished. Dimly he became aware of a nagging sense of pain and loss. Then he remembered where he was, and grief flooded over him.

People with torches emerged from the town and began searching out the wounded. Rufe heard his name spoken in awed tones by other soldiers, although none approached him.

He had no desire for company. His terrible passion was spent, and a confused sense of shame began to nag at him. Tired and downcast, he slipped away into the darkness alone to wrestle with his feelings.

13

The days had shortened, and the air held a new chill when the king finally returned to Arnost with his army. A huge crowd cheered their arrival, and this time Thomas was a part of it. Olaf led in the King's Guard, and Thomas searched everywhere for the distinctive red hair of Will. To his bewilderment, he saw no sign of him.

The king followed his Guard, waving to the crowd. But he seemed grim faced to Thomas. Others noted it too, and many expressed surprise. Hadn't the king's soldiers won a great victory at Danford? Some began whispering darkly of an end to peace and a beginning of troubles.

To his growing disquiet, Thomas had discovered nothing of Will. He had plenty to distract him, though—he was fully occupied in the stables attending to the horses that returned with the king the previous day. Many were in poor condition. His father had been absent for much of the afternoon and finally returned just after sunset.

"Have you heard about your friend?" his father asked gruffly.

"Which friend?" Thomas replied warily, uncertain about what might be coming next.

"The guardsman, Will Prentis. The one who left you his chain."

"No. Have you seen him?" Thomas couldn't conceal his eagerness.

His father shook his head. "He came back in one of those covered wagons. Seems he was badly wounded in the battle at Danford. He's quite a hero, I'm told."

"Wounded?" echoed Thomas, torn between alarm and pride at the news. "Where is he?"

"In the barracks, I imagine."

THOMAS SET off for the barracks, surprisingly reluctant to meet with Will now that the time had come. He had been stalling for a couple of days, not because he wasn't eager to see his friend, but because he was unsure of his welcome. A lot had changed in the short months since the king left for the border region. Thomas's life had changed irrevocably in that time, thanks to the stone. By all accounts Will's had, too.

Will Prentis's name was on everyone's lips since the soldiers returned to their families. Of course, Thomas knew better than to believe without question the reports spreading like wildfire through the town. His own experience had taught him that wagging tongues love to exaggerate. There was always a kernel of truth underneath, though, and it seemed that Will had somehow been responsible for saving the town of Danford. His serious wounds added further weight to his reputation.

The victory at Danford had left its mark on all of the soldiers. It was obvious even to Thomas that they had returned from their campaigning with a new confidence. It wasn't exactly a swagger—more an air of robust self-belief. And Will wasn't the only subject of idle conversation. People also spoke in awed tones of another guardsman, a one-man army called Rufe Sarjant.

As he approached the low stone building that housed the King's Guard, Thomas fingered Will's chain anxiously. If Will didn't want to see him, returning the memento at least gave him an excuse for being there.

When Thomas asked for directions to Will Prentis, the soldier on duty dismissed his request peremptorily. "He's not available."

"I need to return something to him."

"Then give it to me."

Something in Thomas rose up at the soldier's imperious tone. He shook his head stubbornly. "No. He entrusted it to me."

The soldier looked down at Thomas skeptically. When it became obvious that the youth was not going to leave, he shrugged. "What's your name?"

"Thomas. Thomas Stablehand."

The man called across to another soldier. "Hey, Red. Go see if the chief wants to speak to a Thomas Stablehand."

Confronted with this evidence of Will's new status, Thomas's stubborn bravado evaporated. He shrank back, trying to be inconspicuous. The soldier, meanwhile, totally ignored him.

The inevitable rejection felt like an age in coming, and Thomas fidgeted uncomfortably, debating with himself about slinking away unnoticed. He had been a fool to think Will would be willing to see him.

Eventually, the soldier called Red reappeared. To Thomas's surprise, the man addressed him directly. "He'll see you. Come with me."

The soldier on duty scowled at him. "Make it quick," he commanded. Thomas scurried after Red, leaving the sentry muttering loudly about the chief never getting well with people pestering him all the time.

Red left him without introduction at the door of a small but cheerful room. A fire crackled importantly opposite the doorway, and sunlight streamed through a small window. A man lay on a low bed talking quietly to a giant guardsman.

Thomas hung back just outside the doorway. The man looked up and beamed a welcoming smile. Thomas started as he realized that the scarred visage belonged to his friend Will.

"Thomas! Come in. It's good to see you again at last." He eyed Thomas approvingly. "You've grown up since I last saw you." He winked at the other soldier. "We'll have to find a place for him in the King's Guard before too long." Thomas, still wounded from their last conversation, was too astonished to reply. Now he felt even more discomfited.

The other soldier excused himself. "I'll see you tonight, Will."

"Thanks, Rufe. I'll look forward to it."

At the sound of the name, Thomas again started. The burly guardsman caught his expression, and Thomas saw a shadow pass across his face, a fleeting look of pain. Then he was gone, striding off down the passageway.

Thomas stepped into the room awkwardly. "I brought your chain, Will."

Will accepted it gravely. "Thank you for keeping it safe." He slipped it around his neck. "But now I want to hear all about your doings. What have you been up to with the horses? What's been happening in Arnost all these months?"

The unexpected warmth of Will's welcome and interest soon thawed Thomas. Their conversation rambled on, and he quickly rediscovered his old pleasure in the company of his friend. They skirted the recent past, it was true, but that seemed to suit Will as well as it suited Thomas.

As he was leaving, Will insisted that he visit again, frequently. Thomas felt sure he meant it.

"But I don't want to tire you out. The guard outside said that too many people were pestering you."

Will laughed out loud. "The men seem to have taken it upon themselves to protect me. The truth is that I've hardly seen anyone except Rufe since we arrived back in Arnost.

"Pestering me?" He laughed again, heartily, almost as if rediscovering laughter. Thomas didn't need the stone to tell him that Will hadn't done much laughing in recent days.

"You're good for me, Thomas. I need a lot more than just armies and battles in my world. Come again, and make it soon."

Thomas left the barracks with a new smile on his own lips. He couldn't remember when he last felt so content. Even the scowl of the sentry didn't shake him.

"WHAT HAPPENED when you reached the gates of Danford, Will?"

Thomas had seen a great deal of his friend in recent days, but he had rarely found him in much of a mood to talk about the battle. Today Will had been more forthcoming, and he was determined to make the most of the opportunity.

"We approached the gates in an old wagon. Most of the men were hidden in it. The Rogandans controlling the gates tried to scare us away, then when that failed, they threw spears at us. One of the men was wounded in the leg. But we made it into the passageway between the portcullis and the gates, and upended the wagon to block the entrance.

"They tried everything to dislodge us. Their options were limited, though. They couldn't make too much noise, in case they roused the people inside Danford."

"Why didn't you make noise yourselves?"

"We tried, believe me. But no one heard us, and the Rogandans kept us busy dodging arrows and spears from above.

"Eventually Drettroth and the main body of raiders arrived, and things really livened up. The Rogandans inside the gatehouse tried dropping fire on us, but it only set the wagon alight. That made it even harder for Drettroth's men to get at us. They tried opening the gates to attack us from behind, but one of our men almost made it into the city to rouse the guard. They didn't try that again. I guess they decided to just wait for Drettroth to finish us off.

"Our situation was desperate. We were being picked off one by one. Around that time I was trapped under a horse and lost consciousness. I remember nothing more about the fight.

"I woke up the next day with my legs crushed, and the king's personal physician fussing over me. But I'm told that Rufe arrived just in time."

"What about our soldiers inside Danford?"

"Once the main battle started, I suppose the people in the city were finally roused. They say that the Rogandans held out for hours in the gatehouse. But they were all killed eventually.

"Drettroth lost half his force killed or wounded in the battle. But the important thing was that his plan was completely exposed."

"Are we at war with Rogand, then?" To Thomas, the prospect was more thrilling than frightening. He didn't doubt for a minute that the Rogandans stood no chance against Will Prentis and Rufe Sarjant and all of King Steffan's soldiers.

"Not yet. King Agon sent emissaries claiming that Drettroth had acted alone, without his authority. The king knows that isn't true, though. It's probably only a matter of time. Don't spread that around, by the way. There are enough rumors already."

"I won't!" Thomas vowed eagerly, flattered to be holding an important confidence.

There was one other question on Thomas's mind. He hesitated for a while, then curiosity won out. "Is it true that Rufe Sarjant is a berserker?"

Will frowned. "That's a harsh title for a man like Rufe."

"I think so, too," the youth added hastily, seeing Will's reaction. "Rufe seems so gentle." Thomas had, indeed, seen plentiful evidence of Rufe's thoughtful concern for Will during his recovery.

"He's the kind of person who'd rather help people than harm them," said Will.

Thomas nodded wisely. "I guess people just made it up."

Will shook his head emphatically. "No. I didn't witness it myself, but if half the reports are to be believed, Rufe accounted for almost as many of Drettroth's raiders as the other soldiers together."

So it was true. Rufe was a man of contradictions. "I wonder why he became a soldier."

Will shrugged. "I don't know. The choice might have been made for him; he's descended from a long line of soldiers." Will stretched an absent finger up to his face and smoothed the scar on his cheek. "Either way, sometimes life takes unexpected turns." He gazed off into the distance, as if deep in thought. "Everyone's good at something," he finally concluded. "Unfortunately for Rufe, he happens to be very good at killing."

In the weeks that followed, Thomas became directly involved in Will's convalescence, and the soldiers gradually came to accept his presence in the barracks. Mostly, though, the two of them went riding together.

"Walking causes me considerable pain," Will told him. "It's easier when I'm riding, because the horse takes my weight instead.

"The problem is that I need to completely relearn my riding technique. I always relied on my legs to guide the horse, especially when both hands were occupied. But I don't have much strength in my legs now. I need you to help me develop a new way of riding."

"I'm happy to try," Thomas promised him. "I'll need my father's permission to spend time away from the stables, of course."

With the king himself frequently checking on Will's progress, the request was readily granted by Thomas's father. It seemed that Will could have pretty much anything he wanted, within reason.

By the time a month had passed, Will's confidence in the saddle had been fully restored.

"I'm ready to fight on horseback again," he said. "When it comes to horses, Thomas, you're a master."

Rufe Sarjant was also impressed. "I wasn't sure I'd ever see Will assured in the saddle again," he admitted.

Other soldiers had witnessed Will's improvement, too, and Thomas began to develop a reputation for his horse skills. Thomas was more than delighted with the affirmation, although he was careful not to show it.

Soon after, it was announced that Will Prentis had been appointed second in command to Olaf, captain of the King's Guard.

The appointment was wildly popular among the soldiers. The Danford veterans—the soldiers who had followed Will on the epic ride to the Battle of Danford—felt they had a special claim on his leadership. These men were the envy of every other soldier. Everyone wanted to serve under him.

To the king, busy locating and training soldiers as fast as he was able, Will provided an ideal rallying point.

THEIR HORSES GRAZED NEARBY as Thomas sat with Will beside the river. "How did you get the scar, Will?"

The question was casual, but the reply was terse. "When you fight, you expect to get wounds."

Presuming that his friend was sensitive about the effect of the scar on his appearance, Thomas promised himself he wouldn't mention it again. He said no more, contenting himself with tossing pebbles into the river.

It was Will who broke the silence. "Being a soldier is not what you think, Thomas. People get killed, people who shouldn't."

"You mean the villagers? That wasn't your fault. Besides, if it wasn't for you, more of them would have died."

"Not just the villagers. Sometimes..." Will hesitated, seeming to choose his words carefully. "A soldier does things...things he doesn't intend." He shrugged helplessly, as though it was too hard to explain.

"I know just what you mean." Thomas desperately wanted to prove his maturity, to show that he understood, too. "It doesn't just happen to soldiers. I've done things I didn't intend as well." The words were out before he realized what he was saying.

Will, his interest aroused, turned to him curiously. "What's happened, Thomas? Tell me about it."

Thomas, flustered, didn't know how to respond. Will continued to stare at him, saying nothing, but clearly expecting an answer. What was he going to say? He had to say something, or Will would think he was boasting to impress him. The silence was becoming uncomfortable.

"I...Well, it was a few months ago. You see, there was this thing. I found it. A stone, I mean. A little stone..."

He hadn't planned it—the idea of telling Will would never have occurred to him—but once he started, there was no turning back. Hesitantly at first, then with growing abandon, Thomas spoke, and the story of the stone poured out. As he spoke, he took to his feet and began pacing around, unable to suppress his agitation. The story burst out, like a river swollen by the spring thaw bursting its banks. Apart from the fight with Simon, he held nothing back. Will did not interrupt him.

The relief of getting it out was more than he could ever have imagined. It was only when the pressure had been released that he became consciously aware of it.

Finally, the flow stopped. He sat down abruptly, exhausted and panting a little.

Will, his face inscrutable, still said nothing. Thomas began to worry, his relief giving way to fear that his friend would think him mad.

Finally, Will spoke. "You're not lying, Thomas. That much is obvious to me. But even so, it's a difficult story to believe!"

He stared at Thomas thoughtfully for a time. "Let me see your stone," he finally commanded.

After a moment's hesitation, Thomas reached into his pouch and retrieved the stone. He handed it to Will, who took it and examined it closely.

"I remember it," he announced. "A family heirloom, eh?" He aimed an ironic grin at Thomas, who felt his cheeks flush in embarrassment at the reminder of his old lie.

Will held the stone and gazed fixedly at Thomas, frowning. "I can read your thoughts," he exclaimed in surprise.

Seeing the alarm on Thomas's face, he chuckled, and tossed the stone back to Thomas. "I was only jesting," he reassured him. "But the look on your face, Thomas!"

Then slowly he became grave. "I'm sorry. I can't begin to imagine what it must be like to have lost such a power after having it. So you really see nothing at all with it now?"

Thomas shook his head mutely. He cradled the stone in his hand, and looked at Will. The scar again caught his eye, and without intending to, he found himself staring at it. At once, as if in a dream, he saw through the scar to a distant scene. A young man lay on the ground. He frowned in concentration.

"What is it, Thomas? Do you see something?" Will's voice sounded far away.

"Yes. It's a young soldier. With dark hair. He's lying face down. I think he's dead; there's blood everywhere. There's a tall man with a battle-ax."

A stinging slap across his cheek jerked him back to the riverbank. A second slap knocked the stone from his hand to the ground. The furious face of Will hovered inches from his own, the scar livid. Will's eyes were wild with rage, and an accusing finger jabbed emphatically and painfully into his shoulder. "Don't...you...EVER..." Will spat, "do that again."

Then he turned on his heel and hobbled away to his horse. He mounted and rode away without a backward glance.

Thomas stood, shaking uncontrollably, and watched him until he had disappeared. Then he numbly retrieved the stone and secured it. He paced aimlessly up and down the river, distressed and restless.

When he had finally recovered himself enough to ride away, he left with a tight knot in his stomach and a feeling of utter hopelessness.

To Thomas's total astonishment, Will appeared as usual for their next ride. He behaved as if nothing had happened.

Only once did he refer to the previous incident.

"I believe your story about the stone, Thomas, if it's any comfort to you. But don't ever try it out on me. Understood?" The words were spoken mildly enough, but danger lurked behind them.

Elated, Thomas agreed eagerly. It seemed to him a very small price to pay for the restoration of their friendship. He felt like he had just been released unexpectedly from a deep, dark dungeon.

The vision of the young man left him bemused. Whether it was real or imagined, present, past, or future, he had no inkling. Could it signal the reawakening of the stone, or had it simply been imagination? Why had Will reacted so sharply?

The stone continued to show him nothing whenever he tried it. Unable to find any way of unraveling the mystery, he eventually abandoned the attempt.

Neither of Thomas's parents had much to say as they ate their evening meal. Thomas, more interested in eating than in talking, didn't care at all.

One thing had been nagging at him, though. Spoon halfway to his mouth, he paused long enough to ask, "Do you know where Ben is? I haven't seen him today for a while."

There was no response. Ignoring the question, Thomas's father said, "A child was savaged by a dog in the town today."

"Did the hounds get out again?" Concerned, Thomas again paused briefly in his assault on the food. "I'll bet it was Toby. That animal's savage; something needs to be done about him."

"It was Ben." His father's tone was so casual that at first Thomas wasn't sure he had heard properly.

"What?"

"Ben mauled a young child."

Thomas's spoon dropped to the table with a clatter. "You can't be serious. It couldn't have been Ben."

"It was Ben. The child's mother described the dog exactly. Simon told me himself."

Thomas's heart skipped a beat. "He's lying," he blurted. He couldn't control the shrillness in his voice.

His father frowned. "Why would he lie about it?"

Thomas's mouth clamped shut; what could he possibly say? A chill of dread crept over him.

"It wasn't the first time, either." His father's tone allowed no contradiction. "Ben attacked Simon during the Feast of St. Stephen. I saw the wounds myself."

So that was Simon's game. Thomas felt the blood drain from his face. He could scarcely breathe. "I promise I'll keep a closer eye on him from now on," he managed.

His father shook his head with finality. "You can't have an animal attacking people. I overlooked it the first time, Thomas, against my better judgment, because I knew how much you cared about the dog. But no more. I put him down this afternoon."

Thomas propelled himself from the table, knocking over his stool. He ran from the house, into the deepening gloom, sobbing his rage and grief. The uncaring stars stared down at him.

Simon's revenge was complete.

14

Life changed dramatically for Thomas in the weeks that followed. The changes had been in turn astonishing, exciting, frightening, and utterly disheartening. After the initial disasters were in the past, though, he dared to hope that his new life might even prove rewarding.

It was Will who was responsible for his change of direction. He had appeared one afternoon as Thomas exercised some horses, waiting patiently until he had finished.

"You have a lot of skill with horses, Thomas. You seem to understand how they think. I know very few others who can handle them so naturally."

Thomas had felt himself blushing deeply at the compliment.

"I need your help," Will had continued, his face becoming serious. "We're training soldiers as fast as we can, and they need to learn to ride and handle horses."

Thomas was astonished. "Why should you need help with that? Surely all of your recruits can ride already."

Will shook his head firmly. "No, they can't. Many of them are sons of poor farm laborers who don't own horses. A lot of them have no idea how to get into the saddle, much less ride. And if they were responsible for the care of their own horses, the animals wouldn't last for long.

"It's becoming a major problem, and it's slowing down our training. I've spoken to your father, and he understands the urgency. He's willing to release you, so you can help us out."

"But they'll never listen to me! I'm not even a soldier."

"No, but you're a horseman. And one of the best I've seen. You'll be fine."

"But..."

Will waved his hand dismissively. "It's important, Thomas. The king needs this army."

And that was that. Thomas started the next morning.

It didn't take more than a single day of training before Thomas's worst fears began to be realized. He had no experience of command, and his students were quick to take advantage of his lack of confidence. Grumbling at his instructions soon turned to loud complaints. His voice became more and more shrill as he tried to get them to listen. By noon on the second day, most of them were openly ignoring him and even mocking him. Worst of all, almost no progress had been made in teaching them the horse skills they needed. Thomas had not been able to hold their attention for long enough to teach them anything. He was discovering the hard way that teaching is not possible when a student is unwilling to learn.

He had never been more unhappy. He was a total failure, and he knew it. At that moment his father's lowliest job as an unskilled stable hand felt out of the reach of his capabilities.

Then, at his lowest ebb, the situation miraculously changed.

It was late on the second day of training. One of the students had been hopping around, wild eyed, squawking like a chicken in a mocking impression of Thomas yelling. He finally came to a halt, panting from his efforts, but rewarded with riotous applause from the others.

Thomas stood speechless, fighting back tears of anger and frustration. Then he looked up and saw Will standing nearby, silently watching. He had almost certainly seen the entire performance.

Will hobbled purposefully toward the youths. He was soon spotted, and a buzz of excitement swept through their ranks. They instantly fell silent, standing aside respectfully to make way for him. The contrast could not have been more marked. Thomas's heart sank even lower.

Will addressed them calmly, without raising his voice. "All of you want to become soldiers." Heads everywhere nodded eagerly. "I'm told that some of you hope to join the King's Guard." Will paused and surveyed the throng of enthusiastic faces. Dismayed, Thomas felt certain they would instantly stand on their heads if their captain asked it of them.

Will lowered his voice slightly, and the recruits leaned forward. "I'm sure you're all aware that soldiers of the King's Guard are skilled horsemen. Do any of you fit that description?" he asked mildly.

He turned toward Thomas, acknowledging him with a nod. "You're fortunate to have Thomas to teach you. He's the best chance you have.

"And in case you didn't know, I'll be asking him for recommendations for the Guard. He won't be suggesting your name unless you have excellent horse skills, unwavering discipline, and a positive attitude." He paused to let his words sink in. Thomas could see some of the recruits beginning to color.

"Oh, and one other thing. Thomas happens to be a friend of mine. When you treat him with respect, you're treating me with respect." Then Will's voice took on an iron edge. "If I should find any of you showing him disrespect, I'm going to take it *personally*."

He wheeled, and left them gaping after him in stunned silence.

Thomas realized that his next move was crucial. Stung by the way his students had belittled him, and remembering Will's reaction on first seeing him mount a moving horse bareback, Thomas made a quick decision. Walking briskly to the nearby enclosure, he selected a horse without a saddle or bridle and slapped it on the rump, guiding it into the open. He clicked his tongue, and the horse moved off at a brisk walk.

Thomas ran along beside the horse, took a firm grasp on its mane and, after a quick skip, vaulted up onto its back. Then he steered it with his legs, heading back toward his students. A couple of them watched open-mouthed. The rest were uncharacteristically silent.

He brought the horse to a halt, and remained on its back, towering over them. "It's your turn. Who's ready to try that themselves?" Every one of them remained silent.

Thomas turned to the ringleader among his students. "Well?"

His former tormentor had nothing to say. He looked down, shuffling his feet, unable to meet Thomas's glare.

Thomas slid down from the horse's back and moved to one side. "If you want to learn to ride as well as I can, then join me over here. Right now. I won't be wasting any more time on the rest of you."

Most of them joined him immediately. None of the others were far behind, although swallowing their pride was clearly a struggle for some of them.

Thomas didn't give them time to think. He sent them off immediately to find a horse of their own, and he kept them working hard without a break until well after the normal time for their evening meal.

He had no further trouble after that.

Even before he had finished with the first group, he began training a new set of recruits. No repetition of Will's speech was ever necessary. Thomas didn't need it.

THANKS TO HIS STUDENTS, Thomas soon became aware that idle tongues around the town had found a juicy new topic for gossip: the royal succession. Almost a year had passed since the attack on Danford and the border towns. But the new army that had been steadily building before their eyes offered a constant reminder to the townsfolk of the uncertain times that lay ahead. The king was greatly loved, and his loyal subjects expected to see his line continue. Where, then, was his heir?

According to rumor, the king would soon depart on a mission to bring home a bride. The king's uncle, the Duke of Erestor, would act as regent until he returned.

THE SWEAT TRICKLED FREELY down Thomas's brow as he plunged the pitchfork into another bale of hay and hefted it into the air. He was definitely getting stronger, he decided, but the thought offered little comfort at the end of another long day with still more work ahead. He glanced briefly at the ruddy glow of the sunset and then returned to the haystack.

"WHY DO YOU DO IT, THOMAS?" his mother fussed. "You have a job, an important one. It isn't necessary to work in the stables as well. You'll get sick if you keep this up." His father ignored the glance she shot in his direction. She was hopeful indeed if she expected help from that quarter.

Thomas ignored the question, too, and sank onto a stool. He picked up a spoon and began poking at the steaming gruel she placed in front of him.

Why did he do it? He wasn't sure himself. It certainly wasn't to prove something to his father; that would be a futile waste of time. His father acted as though his exertions were only to be expected. He'd certainly never encouraged Thomas to slow down, much less stop.

Was he trying to prove something to himself? Or was he simply clinging on to the old, the familiar? Too weary to be long bothered with trying to figure himself out, he plodded his way through the bowl of food before him.

. . .

"You've done wonders with them, Thomas." Will stood beside him, openly admiring Thomas's second group of recruits as they wheeled and trotted in formation. "What have you taught them?"

"The simple skills, mostly. Caring for their horses and learning to understand their needs. Controlling them, and learning to ride without using their hands."

"And there've been no major injuries. That's an achievement."

"Well, I've taught them how to fall without breaking a limb, of course. But you've forgotten the miller from the first group. That break was a bad one—I'm not sure he'll ever walk properly again." Thomas hung his head at the memory.

"Don't blame yourself for that, Thomas. I saw what he was like myself. A lot of these youths are terrified of their horses at first. But those who can't master that fear will never learn to ride safely. We can be grateful he survived the fall."

Will turned to Thomas, a thoughtful expression on his face. "Don't be afraid to ask, even demand, more from these lads, Thomas. Not all of them will be capable of it, but some will rise to a challenge."

Will left Thomas basking in the warm glow of his praise. Somehow, Thomas reflected, Will knew how to get the best out of his men. He never interfered or told Thomas how to do his job, just offered a timely word of encouragement or a well-placed suggestion.

How had Will guessed that he would be so well suited to this kind of work? It was now clear, even to Thomas, that he had a gift, not only of handling horses, but of passing on the skill to others. As his confidence increased, so did his effectiveness and his enjoyment in the role.

The next day Thomas initiated extra training for the more capable recruits. Before he had finished with them they could ride bareback confidently, control a horse without a bridle, and mount and dismount from a moving horse. No one from the first group was selected for this honor. If Will ever noticed, he never mentioned it.

Thomas's charges were now more than ready to learn to fight on horseback, a skill that he could not teach them. Nevertheless, he had won their respect. Beginning with past students from the second group, his former trainees sometimes found time to visit him, both to laugh behind their hands at the newest recruits, and to ask for advice on the finer points of horsemanship.

WITH THE ADDITIONAL demands of his advanced class, Thomas no longer found time to help his father. His father never commented on it. But he noticed. More than once in Thomas's presence, he observed pointedly how helpful Simon had become around the stables, and how he could no longer manage without him.

With difficulty, Thomas held his peace. Simon belonged in the past, and he was determined to keep it that way. He didn't want to think about Simon. Doing so led to memories, painful memories. Memories of loss. Memories of a blinding red passion and a strange and frightening desire to wound and kill.

And he could not think about Simon without thinking about the stone. Since the incident with Will the stone had lain undisturbed in his pouch. For the first time in many months Thomas was truly contented, and he had little desire to risk that for any reason. The stone was as unpredictable and mysterious as it was powerful. Even apparently closed to him, it had somehow managed to threaten his friendship with Will, the friendship he valued more than any other. So he left it alone and untouched.

The stone was not absent from his mind, though. Far from it. He imagined it brooding in his pouch, like a snake, coiled but still deadly. At best he and the stone were observing a truce. He didn't question its potential to visit trouble upon him still. Nevertheless, he doubted that he could bring himself to part with it.

STEFFAN the Second of Arvenon frowned, unable to hide his displeasure. He stood at the window of his apartments in Castel

Citadel and glared out in frustrated anger toward the mountains in the distance, beyond the fields where banners fluttered above the tents of his army.

From the moment of his arrival here in Castel, everything had proceeded favorably, very favorably indeed. The marriage negotiations had been quickly concluded, and only the nuptials remained to be celebrated. A treaty between Arvenon and Castel had met with approval on both sides and was in the process of being drawn up.

Now there were unexpected delays. King Istel, at first eager to conclude the arrangements, suddenly could not see his way clear to give up his daughter Essanda until after her nineteenth birthday, another three weeks away.

Steffan did not want to be so long away from his kingdom in these uncertain times. And if, as promised, he remained after the wedding for a further two weeks before escorting his bride to her new home, the risk of bad weather interfering with the journey would steadily increase. Snow sometimes came quite early to the mountains, and the journey south might become unnecessarily hazardous.

He exchanged glances with Lord Bottren, a high-ranking nobleman and close friend who had journeyed with him from Arnost. Then he turned his attention to Count Gordan, a cousin and confidant of the King of Castel. The count was about his own age and seemed to share his outlook on life and also many of his views on issues of strategic policy. He had seen much of Gordan throughout the negotiations, and found himself liking the count and hoping he would become both a good friend and a useful link between the courts of Castel and Arvenon.

"I just don't understand the delay, Gordan," he said frankly.

The count sighed. "There is no hidden agenda, Your Majesty. The reason is simple, and personal. Now that the day approaches, the king finds it more difficult than he expected to say goodbye to his daughter. She reminds him so much of his beloved wife. I'm sure it would not be an issue had he not lost the queen to the fever five years ago."

"And why has my request been refused to spend time with the princess?"

Gordan winced. "Our customs are, perhaps, different from yours, Majesty. The king expects that you will have the rest of your life to enjoy the company of the princess. Who will, of course, soon become your queen."

There it was again—this time the king was certain of it. A brief look he couldn't identify had flashed across Gordan's face. The count would deny it, but the topic of the princess clearly made him uncomfortable for some reason.

What had he been missing about the girl? She was certainly young, almost eleven years his junior, but by all accounts she was intelligent and accomplished beyond her years. Her looks were much less important than her lineage and her childbearing potential, but there had even been hints that she was very attractive. Those hints were becoming increasingly difficult to believe.

It was all beginning to seem too good to be true. So far he had seen the princess only briefly and at a distance, so heavily appareled in finery that he was not confident he would even recognize her in different circumstances. If only he had been allowed to spend some time in her company, surely his questions would have been answered.

"She's not mad, is she, Gordan?" The question had been plaguing him, and it just slipped out.

The count looked genuinely astonished and alarmed. "Mad? Of course not! How could you suggest such a thing, Your Majesty?"

The king decided to let it drop for now. Another issue had been weighing on his mind, and he might as well get that out in the open as well. "I know of the Rogandan threats, Count Gordan. Do they have any bearing on the sudden hesitation of King Istel?"

Gordan's face hardened. "Our policy in Castel is not dictated by the threats of Agon, Sire." When the king did not reply, he steadied himself and went on. "You clearly have unprecedented access to the state secrets of Castel. My compliments to your agents," he offered ironically, bowing low.

"I can assure you that my agents are working only on behalf of

Castel, not against it. Our kingdoms are soon to be allied by marriage and by treaty, Count. You can always count on us for support."

The count bowed once again. "Thank you for your kindness, Your Majesty. I will convey your words to My Lord the King."

He excused himself and left.

"What do you make of it, Bottren? Did I go too far?"

The nobleman paused thoughtfully for a moment before answering. "No, Your Majesty. I don't think there's any harm in letting them know that King Istel's hesitation troubles you deeply. Or in hinting that we know more about their affairs than they might have guessed."

"Keep our agents looking into this business of the princess. I want to understand what's behind it."

"Certainly, Your Majesty."

The king cast his gaze once more to the distant mountains. "Agon appears to be spreading his tentacles far and wide. But he's hopeful indeed if he thinks he can bully kingdoms this far from Rogand."

"Let us not underestimate Agon, Sire. He is a ruthless and ambitious man. And he has demonstrated a talent for the unexpected. I fear he might have surprises in store for us all yet."

"Thank you for the reminder, Bottren. You're right, of course. I will be giving a great deal of attention to the problem of Rogand just as soon as the issues with Castel have been resolved and my marriage is behind me. Indeed it cannot be denied that this marriage has itself been partly prompted by the ambitions of Agon."

He dismissed the nobleman and stretched out on his bed, allowing his mind to wander. Affairs of state paraded restlessly through his mind. Of late such thoughts had increasingly been displaced by hopeful brooding around affairs of the heart. The two streams swirled about in his head, competing for his attention.

"I KNOW the wedding delay has tested your patience, Steffan." King Istel's voice had taken on a soothing tone.

Steffan bowed. "I'm sure Your Majesty has had his reasons."

Istel sighed. “Please do not suspect me of fomenting intrigues. There are none. My daughter celebrates her nineteenth birthday in one week. The following day she will become your bride.

“Forgive the sentimental foolishness of an old man. It is hard for me to give up my beloved daughter, even though this marriage has my full blessing.

“Perhaps, too, it is difficult for me to embrace change. As you know, I married a woman twenty years my junior, and even now my son is only twelve years old. I have been surrounded by the young, and I try to keep pace with them, but every year it becomes harder.”

Steffan bowed again. “One week will pass quickly.”

“I thank you. But there is another matter I wanted to discuss with you.”

Steffan could not help noticing that as usual King Istel did not dwell for long on the topic of the princess.

Every attempt to ferret out the mystery surrounding his future bride had been frustrated. Men who had much to say on other subjects found little of substance to contribute when the princess was mentioned. It almost seemed as though the nobility of Castel had formed a conspiracy of silence around the subject. He was committed to the marriage, because he needed the alliance. But it was becoming increasingly apparent that his bride-to-be was not exactly what he had been hoping for.

“Every trader coming from Rogand reports that Agon’s soldiers are on the move,” Istel continued, a grim look on his face.

Steffan nodded. “We have received the same reports.”

“And my agents tell me they appear to be heading west. You have been building an army, Steffan. I fear you will soon find yourself in need of it.”

Steffan decided to be blunt. “Will Castel stand with us?”

Istel did not hesitate. “We will. Our army does not compare in size with your own, much less with the hordes of Agon. But we will fight with you if you are attacked.”

Steffan scanned the face of his future father-in-law. He seemed sincere and in earnest.

"I will be frank," Istel continued. "Castel needs this alliance. If Arvenon is overwhelmed, Castel cannot expect to stand for long." The king could not hide the concern in his voice.

Throughout the negotiations, the strategic needs of both kingdoms, in addition to the Arvenian succession, had always formed the basis for the alliance. But now Istel had stated his vulnerability openly and more directly than ever before. Steffan wondered at the reason for this further frankness.

"And there is one final thing. We have recently received disturbing news from one of our agents." Istel seemed to be choosing his words carefully. "He has stumbled upon evidence that one of your nobles—unfortunately he has not been able to identify which one—has held discussions with Agon."

Steffan's immediate response was disbelief. What kind of game was Istel playing?

The Castelan king was watching his face carefully. "This agent has proven very reliable. Always. He has never failed us." He seemed genuinely concerned. "I am truly sorry to be giving you this information."

Could it be true? Steffan frowned deeply. His court was so far away, and he had been held up here, unnecessarily, for so long.

"You have been planning to remain here for two weeks after the wedding before returning home. At my insistence." Istel looked worried. "Perhaps you should return sooner. If you leave one week after the wedding, the journey through the mountains might be easier, too."

Istel clearly took this alleged threat seriously. Steffan decided he would send a message to the duke. Just in case. His uncle would know what to do.

Steffan left Istel's audience chamber more confused than ever. Why delay the wedding? Why insist he remain in Castel after the nuptials? What was Istel hiding about his daughter?

And how could he benefit from telling Steffan about the claims of treachery? It would only reinforce Steffan's eagerness to return to his own kingdom earlier.

There was much to think about. Commoners saw the king as all powerful. But there were so many situations over which even a king had little control.

King Steffan, plagued with questions, surrounded by unknowns, and far from home, faced the truth and admitted it to himself. King though he was, he felt uncertain and vulnerable.

15

Thomas and Rufe sat side by side in a small tower room, soaking up the rays of the midmorning sun that streamed in through a high window. The castle was a cold place at the best of times, and the weather was gradually becoming cooler. The sunlight offered a pleasing addition to the warmth from the fire in the grate. They sat in silence. Rufe was comfortable with silence, and Thomas liked him for it.

The tower room had long been a favored hideaway for Will and Rufe, an occasional refuge from the many pressing demands on their time. The room was sufficiently remote to be private, but it took some steady climbing to get there. At first Rufe had pressed Will to choose a more accessible location, but Will insisted on hobbling up the long flight of steps, almost in defiance of his injury.

From the time Thomas first learned about the retreat, both men made it clear that he was always welcome there. Nevertheless, many weeks had passed before he found the courage to join them regularly.

The fact that they thus honored him astonished Thomas. Of late even the soldiers, not known for showing deference to anyone but their own, had been treating Thomas with respect. He put it down to his friendship with Will. But if he could have known it, the reason had much more to do with his own growing reputation as horse master. He was developing into an effective leader, and it was obvious to everyone except himself. Once again he attributed his success to Will, and in particular to Will's early intervention on his behalf.

But whatever the reason for it, he derived much simple delight from the fact that his opinion, his counsel, and even his company were actively sought by the two people in the world he most admired.

Thomas leaned back in his chair and allowed his mind to wander. He tried to imagine the king and his embassy far away in Castel. Had the marriage negotiations been successful? A messenger had arrived from Castel early this morning if rumors could be believed. Perhaps there would be news. If so, Will would be certain to know the details.

At some point Thomas knew he would be expected to marry, too. How was he supposed to make that happen? If you were a king, you sought a suitable alliance, and sealed the agreement with a marriage. A wife was included in the deal. But it didn't work that way for commoners. The castle boasted some attractive young women, to be sure. One or two happened to be very attractive indeed. But Thomas couldn't think of a single reason why any of them would be interested in him. In the presence of girls he somehow lost the ability to speak. If a girl was particularly attractive he sometimes couldn't even think straight.

These woeful thoughts were banished by the arrival of Will, accompanied by Tolin, the dour quartermaster general of the king's army. Tolin, slightly flushed from the climb, entered the room with voice raised and gesturing emphatically. Tolin was one of the few soldiers willing to disagree with Will, who didn't seem to mind at all —in fact he seemed to appreciate it.

"You should be out there with them, Will. Rufe, too. Sending a thousand men into the countryside without their leaders is like asking a child to ride a horse without a bridle."

"They're hardly leaderless, Tolin," replied Will patiently, pausing at the door to catch his breath. "Count Ranauld is an outstanding leader, and doesn't need any help from us. Several others are developing nicely, too. They just need a chance to establish themselves, and they'll do that better without other people yapping at their heels all the time."

Seeing Tolin's mouth open for a rejoinder, Will quickly steered the conversation elsewhere. "When can we expect more horses?"

Thomas suppressed a chuckle as Rufe aimed a wink in his direction. Will certainly knew how to handle the old veteran. When it came to stores, supplies, weapons, and all the necessities of provisioning an army, Tolin's knowledge was nothing short of awe-inspiring. And it didn't take much to get him talking about the subject.

"We've got ten more due in later today. Someone will need to meet them at the city gates. Someone competent this time. That last groom was a disaster—we don't need spooked horses stampeding through the market again."

Tolin jerked a thumb pointedly in Thomas's direction. "Why can't you send Thomas?"

Will raised an eyebrow inquiringly at Thomas.

"I don't mind. I'll go meet them," he replied, trying to sound matter-of-fact even as he felt himself coloring at the compliment. He had no teaching today—most of his competent students had joined Count Ranauld's training exercise, and since it was market day the rest had been given the day off.

Thomas stood up to go. "Any news of the king?" he asked, pausing at the door.

"A messenger came today from Castel," Will told him. "The negotiations went well. Wedding preparations have been proceeding, and the marriage should take place within days. The king will probably stay on for a while afterward, and return with his bride before winter sets in."

"And what of Olaf and the soldiers?"

"Olaf has been received with great honor, and the King's Guard are quartered with him in the castle. The rest of the men are camped outside the city walls."

"Ridiculous." Tolin never seemed reluctant to offer his opinion. "It made no sense taking a force that size to Castel. What was Olaf thinking?"

Will shook his head. "It wasn't ridiculous at all. The king certainly didn't need two thousand of his best men to protect him from bandits on the road. But there's no harm in showing a potential father-in-law that his daughter will be well protected. Or in reminding him of the benefits of a strong ally. Rulers of small kingdoms never sit easily on their thrones in troubled times."

The conversation rambled on. After a while Thomas, his curiosity sated, took his leave and headed for the city gates. The horses would be welcome; it seemed like the growing army could never get enough of them. Will had convinced the king he needed a mobile force, so the king sent agents ranging far and wide looking for suitable mounts. A steady stream of horses had been arriving ever since, creating ongoing challenges in feeding and stabling them.

No one knew when this army might be needed. But Will did not expect the day to be long delayed, and he did not intend to be caught entirely unprepared. The level of activity around the castle had increased dramatically, placing extra demands on everyone who worked there. With the constant arrival of new horses, Thomas knew his father must be pushed to the limit as well. The worry in his mother's face confirmed it. But the young horse master's own role consumed all his attention, and that was entirely to his liking. He no longer had any desire to help his father.

THOMAS MADE his way to the main gates of Arnost. He passed through them, beyond the pair of guards who stood idly on each side of the main entrance. They ignored him, just as they ignored almost everyone who came and went. Their role was to maintain order, not to grant or deny access to the city, and they hindered no one who went peacefully about their own business.

He took up his position just outside the walls, beside the main road that led through the gates. From here the road was visible far off into the distance, but he could see no sign yet of the horses.

Thomas had chosen a good location to wait. He stood there fascinated by the endless tide of humanity that ebbed and flowed through the city gates. Men and women, merchants, commoners, and the occasional minor noble mingled together, some loud and energetic, others heads down and with no interest in any affairs but their own.

Observing people never ceased to fascinate him. Careful observation could reveal a great deal to a practiced eye. As he well knew, a treasure trove of insights and secrets lay concealed inside every person, buried too deep for even the keenest observer to glimpse. Nevertheless he harbored no lingering desire to return to the days when he used the power of the stone to peep into the souls of the unsuspecting. Nor had he forgotten the mirror and the awful madness in his own eyes. He was willing to go to great lengths to avoid any fulfillment of the stone's prophetic vision.

He could now acknowledge that he had abused that power. Perhaps, from the security of at last having something worthwhile and significant to do with his life, it was easier to be honest with himself. Or perhaps it was because the stone was closed to him. Either way, he was not proud of the way he had acted, and he liked to think that he would do it all very differently if he had his time over again. But there was no point wasting regrets on the past. He had more than enough responsibility to occupy him in the present.

He glanced across the plain that stretched south and west beyond the city walls. A wide variety of stalls always spilled out into the fields on market day; on this particular occasion a cattle market seemed to be the main focus. Small clusters of the animals could be seen everywhere, surrounded by curious onlookers, and the sound of lowing drifted toward him across the fields.

In the far distance on the road he thought he could see a small group of horses. But it could just as easily be cows. He returned his attention to the people around him.

Thomas soon discovered that he was not the only person standing around at the gate. A tall grim-looking man occupied a position across the road from him. He had been there for some time with no apparent purpose. Thomas studied the stranger closely. He had become adept at doing so surreptitiously, facing elsewhere and looking sidelong at his subject, then rapidly shifting his gaze forward if the person under scrutiny happened to glance in his direction.

Something about the man seemed not quite natural, but at first he couldn't put his finger on it. People didn't usually stand around in a public place for no reason. Some, like the guards, found themselves there because of their work. Others, like him, were waiting for someone or for something to happen. And a few idlers could always be seen hanging around a crowd. None of the usual reasons seemed to fit, though.

Eventually he figured it out. He felt sure that this man was working hard at looking inconspicuous. His curiosity now thoroughly aroused, Thomas studied him even more closely.

The man wore a long greatcoat that fell to his ankles. The weather, while cool, definitely did not warrant such a thick garment. A quick scan of the crowd revealed a few others similarly attired and similarly engaged. As he watched, a driver momentarily lost control of his cart. It swung off the road and knocked into one of the men. The man reacted instinctively, reaching up to grab the startled driver and yanking him off his cart. Then the man subsided as quickly as he had erupted, and released the driver with a rough apology, "Sorry, friend. No ill intended." He spoke with a strange accent.

Thomas tore his eyes away from the scene and stole a glance at the first man, who stood watching the incident with a look of fury plain on his face. Then the anger vanished, and his face again revealed only careless passivity. So complete and rapid was the change that Thomas had to tell himself that he had not imagined it. Then the man turned and looked directly at him, and this time Thomas was not sure he had diverted his gaze quickly enough.

Fully alert, but anxious not to be discovered, Thomas shifted his attention back to the road. He could now clearly see a group of horses being led by a few men on horseback, not far off and making their way toward the city gates. He sighed and shifted his feet, feigning boredom and impatience. But the strange men occupied his attention entirely. He felt sure that during the scuffle he had caught a brief glimpse of a sword under the foreigner's coat. What could it mean? His thoughts swirled frantically around the possibilities.

After what seemed like an eternity, he risked another sidelong glance at the first man. His attention was elsewhere. Without consciously planning it, Thomas reached down for the drawstring of his pouch and groped in for the stone. Its power flared instantly, and he stared open-mouthed. The intruders were Rogandan. They might disguise their garb and their speech, but no secret could be hidden from the stone. Their true purpose was laid bare, and what he saw chilled him to the bone.

Then he discovered that the man had become aware of him, fully aware, and he read his death in those eyes. He realized with a start that he had been staring openly, his guard lowered and his pretense at indifference exposed.

At this crucial moment the long-awaited horses arrived. He took in the situation in a moment. A young man, not much older than himself but richly dressed, appeared to be in charge of the party. Three other older men each led three horses with halters behind their own mounts.

The young nobleman led a single horse—a bay mare. The mare was not saddled, but it had reins rather than a halter, suggesting that the young man had recently been riding it bareback.

Thomas seized the opportunity. "You've arrived at last!" he exclaimed loudly. "Come with me, and I'll show you to the stables."

He quickly took the reins of the bay mare from the surprised young nobleman and swung up onto its back. The mare shied away, pulling against the restraint of the reins. The noise and bustle of the crowd was clearly spooking it. Thomas spoke quietly to the animal, and it settled again.

Taking the lead, Thomas rode quickly through the city gates looking neither to the right nor to the left. No one tried to prevent him. It was slow going trying to force a way through the densely packed throng that crowded the road to the castle.

Once well clear of the gates, Thomas dismounted and returned the reins to their owner. "You'll find the stables just below the castle.

Ask for Axel, the stable master. I'm sorry, but I must leave you—I have an errand of pressing urgency." Without waiting for a reply he pushed his way into the crowd.

After several minutes of frustrating struggle Thomas had made very little forward progress. The milling throngs were clogging the road hopelessly. He peered behind him and saw that the group with the horses had advanced almost as much as he had.

Then an idea came to him. Pushing through the crowd in the opposite direction, he made his way back to the horses. The young nobleman was working hard to keep the mare under control, and doing admirably given the circumstances. Eyes bulging and ears laid back, the horse pulled this way and that struggling to free itself.

Taking the reins of the mare once more, Thomas leaped onto its bare back and pulled back savagely on the reins. The mare reared, almost throwing him, and screamed in protest. All eyes turned in his direction. He urged the horse forward, leaning down and slapping it hard across the ribs. The crowd scattered as horse and rider plunged forward, barely missing a cart and almost trampling several people. He shouted a warning at the top of his voice as the horse careered wildly up the road, the crowd parting magically before it. The mare charged on, completely out of control, and it took all of his skill to keep his seat.

The horse slowed only when the road drew to an end at the castle. Then, panting and quivering, it came to a complete halt. He slid off its back and, handing the reins to a surprised guard, ran into the castle courtyard yelling frantically for Will.

Half the castle was in an uproar by the time Thomas finally managed to locate Will. He found him at the stables, talking to the stable master.

Breathless and agitated, Thomas came to a stop and stood doubled over panting stupidly, unable to speak. His father eyed him for a moment as a man might gaze at a carnival curiosity, then turned his back on him and resumed his conversation with Will.

"I must speak with you, Will!" Thomas blurted, finally recovering himself enough to interrupt them.

His father faced him. "As you can see, Thomas," he said, speaking with exaggerated patience, "Will is busy right now." He again turned his back on his son.

"But this is urgent!"

"And so is my conversation," snapped Axel, spinning around, visibly annoyed now. "Your rudeness is intolerable! If you must behave like a child, do it elsewhere so we can finish talking in peace."

Thomas bristled. Of all people, why did Will have to be with his father at that moment? But nothing mattered except for the urgency of the situation. Calming himself, he spoke again, forcefully, and directly to the young deputy captain. "Will, I must speak with you. Right now. It cannot wait."

Will turned to him, then glanced back at the storm brewing on the face of the stable master. "What is it, Thomas?"

"I must speak with you alone."

Thunder appeared briefly on his father's face, then he abruptly turned on his heel. The storm receded into the distance.

Will cocked an eyebrow quizzically at Thomas. "It seems you have my full attention," he observed.

Thomas did not hesitate. Like water from a burst dam, his story poured from him, beginning with his suspicions of the strangers and ending with the alarming revelations of the stone. He spoke rapidly and concisely, skipping over unnecessary details but omitting nothing of importance.

Will did not interrupt him. As he listened, a deepening frown furrowed his brow.

Thomas at last finished his account and paused, breathless.

"You've done well, Thomas. Very well indeed! But there is much to do." Will punched his hand in frustration. "I've been blind! Stupid!"

He set his face to the castle and hobbled toward it as fast as he could manage. Spotting a soldier, he shouted to him, "Get me Rufe Sarjant. Hurry, man!" Wide-eyed, the fellow took to his heels, disappearing into the castle courtyard.

Rufe's huge frame soon appeared, and he quickly joined them, curiosity evident on his face. Will drew him aside, beckoning to Thomas to join them. A small cluster of soldiers gathered nearby, peering uneasily in their direction.

"Rufe, listen carefully. I need you to go with Thomas to the city gates. Take as many soldiers as you can mount quickly, but do not delay. When you get there, Thomas will point out a number of men. Kill them all. Don't let any escape."

Rufe threw a surprised glance at Thomas. "Can Thomas really be certain who deserves to be put to death?" he asked doubtfully.

"He can," Will replied flatly. Seeing continuing hesitation in his friend's eyes, he added, "There's no time to explain now. Don't fail me in this, Rufe!"

That was enough for the giant guardsman. He sprinted toward the gathered men, calling loudly for horses.

Thomas stirred, the anticipation of the impending action affecting him strangely. For the first time he felt like a man, and yet also newly aware of his own mortality.

"I'm going to need a sword."

Will shook his head emphatically. "You won't be doing any fighting. You're no soldier—you wouldn't last two minutes."

An old wound, buried deep, stirred uncomfortably.

"We cannot afford to lose you," Will continued, real alarm in his voice. "You're much too important!"

The old scar vanished from his consciousness, forgotten.

Rufe reappeared astride a horse and leading another. Thomas took the offered reins and swung into the saddle. Only seven soldiers had quickly found mounts; others would have to follow as quickly as they could.

Rufe set off immediately, heading away from the castle. Taking a deep breath, Thomas dug his heels into his horse's flanks and followed.

THOMAS SHRANK INTO A DOORWAY, not wanting to watch but unable to tear his eyes from the terrible ritual of death before him. It was not going well for Rufe and his men. Four of them lay dead along with all four guards from the gate, and between them they had accounted for only one of the Rogandans. Another had died at the hand of Rufe.

Rufe, positioned behind a small cart, battled grimly against two men. All three of his remaining soldiers stood desperately at bay, outmatched in skill and visibly nearing the end of their strength. Even as Thomas watched, one of them went down, and his victorious opponent moved to join the fight against one of the others. At this critical moment three new soldiers arrived from the castle and plunged into the battle, restoring the balance at least for a while.

The Rogandans had been ready for them when Rufe's little group rode up to the gate. Thomas had barely pointed out the first of the foreigners before they found themselves under attack from all sides. The attackers showed a callous disregard for commoners—several bystanders lay unmoving on the ground, unable to flee quickly enough to get out of the way.

The Rogandans were few in number—Thomas had counted eight —but they were battle hardened and well armed. Their long cloaks hid more than swords; Rufe's men found their thrusts turned aside by chain mail, and they had only small shields for their own protection.

Rufe had at once been set upon by three attackers who quickly realized he was the leader. Only his longer reach kept him alive in those first frantic moments. He had backed up to a wall to avoid being surrounded, bellowing loudly, "To me!" The gate guards, standing stupidly at their posts and watching open-mouthed, sprang into life and headed for Rufe. The distraction gave him the chance to catch one of his attackers off guard. He ran him through the throat.

A guard from the gate pinned a Rogandan against a wall with his spear. The man's mail coat protected him as he twisted this way and that trying to get free. A second guard came at him from the side, dancing back and forth as the frustrated Rogandan aimed blows at him. The whole pantomime would have been comical but for its deadly intent. Eventually they succeeded in bringing him down.

That was the high point of the battle—everything had gone horribly wrong since. The Rogandans were simply too ruthless, too well trained, and too strong. Where were Will and the other soldiers?

Thomas watched tensely as Rufe rained blows on his two opponents. He felt sure his friend would prevail. But the other soldiers?

Then he noticed a movement out of the corner of his eye. One of the Rogandans had brought down his opponent and was heading in his direction! He knew the man—it was the one he observed at the gate—and the man had clearly recognized him, too. He began backing away fearfully and discovered to his horror that he had no safe path of retreat. Battle raged on both sides, and a dead end alley lay behind him. He desperately tried to open the nearest door, but it was shut fast and barred.

The Rogandan closed in. Thomas edged away, heart pumping wildly. He blundered into a discarded basket, stumbled, and fell heavily, hitting his head. For a moment the whole world spun before his eyes, but as his vision cleared enough he saw his attacker almost within reach, a mocking smile on his lips. Thomas shrank back in helpless terror as the man raised his sword to strike. But the blow never came. The Rogandan stopped short, a look of surprise flashing across his face. A red-tinged spearhead protruded through his neck. He went down hard, twitching violently, then lay unmoving.

Thomas, his head pounding, looked up dazedly. An image of Will on horseback swam into view, concern on his face. Seeing Thomas unhurt, he paused only for a minute.

"Get yourself to safety, Thomas. Now!" he commanded, pointing to a horse wandering nearby. Then he turned away, shouting instructions. A large group of soldiers plunged into the battle. Thomas saw two more Rogandans go down, then the remainder fled into the back streets with soldiers in hot pursuit. Will didn't wait for the outcome but spurred his horse through the gates. Two noblemen and a sizable group of soldiers followed him.

Thomas picked himself up and staggered toward the horse. Mounting it, he turned his back on the destruction and headed for the castle.

16

To Rufe it felt like an age had passed since the fight at the gates of Arnost. In fact it was no more than a few hours. He peered uneasily across the river, trying in vain to detect movement on the far shore in the moonlight. How many more times could his men deny the Rogandans the passage of the ford? He knew another attempt would not be long delayed. He passed the back of his hand across his eyes. How good it would be to rest, to sleep. When would this night of blood and death come to an end?

His thoughts returned again to Will. The young deputy captain had returned to the city soon after the Arvenian soldiers had finally dispatched the last Rogandan at the gates. Rufe, exhausted from the struggle, felt only relief that the threat had been dealt with. But Will had seen that this incursion was merely the beginning. Rufe found himself quickly summoned to a conference with Will and the duke.

Will addressed himself to the regent. "This is not Danford over again, My Lord. The Rogandans have not come here to raid. I believe they intend to occupy Arnost. I'm confident we will soon discover that an army is hidden somewhere nearby."

The duke appeared doubtful. "Where could anyone hide an army near here without us knowing?"

"Surely not in the woods across the river," Rufe had said.

Will had been far ahead of them both. "I've given it some thought," he said. "The only likely place is the Dark Forest, just across the Arn River. It's vast and unpopulated—you could easily hide an entire army in there. But it's only two hours hard riding from Arnost."

"What do you propose?"

"The only place an army could easily cross the Arn River is a small ford on the main road east. I'm confident that two or three hundred soldiers with enough archers could prevent a crossing. With Count Ranauld away from the city we do not have enough men available. But we should round up as many as can be found, and send them to the ford. They can act as though they're involved in a training exercise.

"The Rogandans won't realize yet that their men at the city gates have been discovered. Hopefully they won't do anything more than observe our soldiers. In the meantime, we must send men to find the count. Without some of his thousand, we will have no hope of holding the ford for long."

"Will you lead the men to the ford?"

"I will go with them, but Rufe should lead the defense. If the Rogandans are there, I will return immediately. There will be much to do if Arnost is to remain safe."

Rufe did not feel equipped to take charge of the defense, but he knew Will well enough not to waste his breath protesting. The regent moved quickly to put the plan into action.

Will had been vindicated. Once they arrived at the ford, watchmen soon spotted observers in the woods across the river carefully monitoring their movements.

The pretense at a training exercise had worked, too—almost. Everything had gone smoothly until some of Rufe's men became a little too enthusiastic, stopping and searching every wagon that happened to cross the ford. The true situation must have gradually become apparent to any interested observer.

The Rogandans attempted a crossing before reinforcements arrived, and it had been a near thing. Small groups of mounted men with concealed weapons had ridden into the ford and quickly discovered it openly held against them. A determined assault in force at that moment would certainly have carried the day. But the cautious approach of the Rogandans cost them crucial moments, and reinforcements sent by Ranauld galloped up even as they were massing for their first serious attack.

In the long hours that followed, Will had joined Rufe and his men twice. Each time Will brought a few more soldiers to join the defense along with wagons full of spears, fresh clusters of arrows, and spare bowstrings.

His presence alone was worth hundreds of fighters. While he was there the men's spirits lifted visibly and weary hands gripped their weapons more tightly.

Once Rufe asked him what he had been doing, but Will deflected the question, simply saying that he was needed elsewhere and reminding Rufe that holding the ford was enough for him to be thinking about. Will was right, of course. He always was.

The sound of axes carried into the night. During the current lull in the fighting Rufe's men were hard at work strengthening a long wooden palisade he'd ordered built. He needed it to protect his men, and particularly his archers, from enemy arrows.

Although his archers were few in number, they had played a critical role in preventing the Rogandans from forcing the ford. A deadly hail of arrows rained down on the attackers each time they entered the ford, felling men and horses and staining the water red.

The crossing soon degenerated into a bloody chaos. The Rogandans could make no use of their superior numbers. Sending in more men would have been pointless.

The river was broad and the water thigh deep at the crossing. The shallow section was little wider than a single wagon, and it doglegged twice before reaching the near side. The river flowed across it swiftly. Smooth stones large and small lay underfoot, slippery with moss, making it impossible to cross quickly. The ford could safely be navigated with ample time and due care. Forcing a passage against a determined enemy was another matter entirely.

Soldiers who lost their footing were quickly swept away downstream. Those who couldn't swim drowned, and many who could swim were dragged under by the weight of their gear. The wounded had no chance at all.

Any who made it through the confusion were ridden down on the far bank by horsemen with lances or met by a determined line of soldiers charging with spears lowered. Enough had made it across, though, to steadily reduce the ranks of the Arvenian defenders. Arrows from across the river found their mark, too, resulting in a constant stream of casualties even when no assault was underway. The palisade had offered some respite between Rogandan sallies.

Rufe's defensive strategy might have been simple, but he applied it with firm resolve. So far it had worked. Rufe himself was first into battle and last to retire. He wasn't Will, but the men followed him willingly enough. Too many had followed to their deaths. There were so many Rogandans. Before the daylight failed he had seen the opposite shore and the woods beyond it crawling with them.

On his last visit Will left him with the words, "I need you to hold until daylight, Rufe." He meant to do it. But unless the Rogandans withdrew or the king's men abandoned their defense of the ford, before long few of his soldiers would be left to defend Arnost.

The enemy soldiers attacked heedlessly, like cattle driven to the butcher. Will had warned him about it. "Don't expect them to give up," he said. "They're led by Drettroth."

"How do you know?" Rufe had asked.

"I can sense it," Will replied. "And the signs are there. Have you wondered why the Rogandans at the gates didn't just slip away when they had been discovered? That's Drettroth. He's not interested in explanations or excuses. His soldiers succeed, or die in the attempt."

"RUFE! COME QUICKLY!" A scout beckoned urgently.

He hurried toward the man. "What's happening?"

"They've been building rafts below the ford. Dozens of them!"

Rufe groaned inwardly. It had been too much to hope that the

Rogandans would be satisfied with an endless series of failed attempts on the ford. He peered across the river. The moon offered light enough to faintly see the activity on the far bank.

A river crossing by raft would be extremely difficult and unpredictable. The river was too wide and the current flowed too swiftly to offer any certainty about where the rafts would land. But the Rogandans could rely upon an overwhelming superiority in numbers. Rufe could not ignore the threat posed by the rafts. He would be forced to divide his force or risk being outflanked.

"How long do you think we have before they launch?"

"It's difficult to be sure. Maybe an hour. But no more."

Before Rufe had time to take any action, though, another soldier alerted him to a large body of horsemen riding in from the direction of Arnost. Moments later Will himself arrived at their head. The news spread quickly and loud cheering erupted from Rufe's men. Best of all, Will had brought with him as many soldiers as Rufe already had. He seemed to have developed a habit of showing up just at the crucial moment. How did he do it?

Will located Rufe, and the two leaders stood together for a long moment without speaking. The moonlight revealed a Will weary to the point of exhaustion. Clearly he had not slept this night. But that was equally true for them all.

Rufe felt great satisfaction at the prospect of facing battle with his friend rather than alone. He was relieved, too, at the thought that his captain would now take charge of the defense.

"They've built rafts," Rufe told him.

Will nodded in the dark. "I expected that."

Somehow his friend always managed to stay one step ahead. "How did you guess?"

Will shrugged. "It's what I would have done," he said simply.

"What do we do?"

"I've made some preparations."

Several wagons arrived as they watched, and men quickly began unloading them. Count Ranauld also arrived and joined the two men.

Will drew them both aside. "Rufe, I need to call on you for one more effort. When the Rogandans launch the rafts they will make an all out attempt to secure the ford. The rafts are little more than a diversion, and I will deal with them. But I need you to hold the ford. They'll throw everything they've got at you.

"I also need you to demonstrate your tactics to the count. He will relieve you, and he needs to understand exactly how you've managed so effectively to beat back a vastly superior force for all these hours.

"Once the immediate attacks have been dealt with, Rufe, I want you to take all your men back to Arnost. Make sure they get food and especially sleep as soon as you get there. Check that the defenses of the city are sound, then get some rest yourself. Don't keep pushing yourself. I'll be depending on you when I get back, and I need you alert and refreshed."

"What about you? You're exhausted, too!"

"Don't worry about me. I'm no longer needed elsewhere, so I can finally help out here. I'm determined to make sure that Drettroth is denied passage of the river until noon tomorrow. After that I'll get out fast, and everyone with me. When you return, make sure that the duke is clear that all of his preparations must be completed by noon."

"I understand." Pushing down his weariness, Rufe set off immediately to explain the defenses to Ranauld.

RUFE'S MEN waited patiently for the attack. They had forgotten their weariness in the excitement of the arrival of Will and his reinforcements. Ranauld's new reinforcements waited with them, tense and nervous in anticipation of their first action.

Much distant shouting accompanied the launch of the rafts across the river. The eyes of the Arvenians were drawn to the broad sweep of river below the ford. Many shapes moved slowly in the dim light, out over the surface of the water. There must have been almost two hundred rafts, each bristling with a small thicket of spears that glinted in the moonlight. So many! Flights of arrows flew through the sky from the defenders to meet them, but the watchers saw dark shapes raised against the missiles. The Rogandans had prepared a huge wooden shield to protect each raft.

Then came a surprise. A small point of light arced slowly through the air toward the rafts. It came down directly onto a wooden shield raised above a raft, and burst as it landed. A splash of light flared out as it spewed liquid fire. The fire ran across the shield, setting it ablaze, and down onto the raft and its occupants. The shield was quickly thrown overboard. Small figures could be seen writhing on the raft, covered with flames. Some cast themselves into the river. Screams of pain carried across the water.

The defenders watched in amazement as more and more tiny lights sailed through the air toward their targets. Some landed on the water, sputtering before disappearing beneath the surface. Others fell onto the rafts, spreading fire and terror among the attackers.

Rufe's men did not cheer. The scene was too terrible for any response but silent horror. But new hope rose in them. They already trusted Will completely and depended on his leadership. They had heard the stories from the Danford veterans, and knew their leader somehow had the knack of arriving at the critical moment and turning disaster into victory. Now they were witnessing it for themselves. The battle for the ford would become a new story of legend. And they were part of it.

When the Rogandans released their expected attack on the ford, a deafening roar rose up from the defenders. They had hurled back attack after attack at great loss and almost to the limit of human endurance. But now they determined they would never be overcome, whatever the cost and no matter what the enemy threw at them.

The battle raged on, and slowly a night of blood and horror passed and gave way to a dawn of unspeakable weariness.

RUFE and his men reached the city walls soon after dawn. They rode through the gates slowly, utterly spent but proud and erect. The wounded followed close behind in wagons.

The countryside around the city was no longer recognizable. No farmhouses or buildings of any kind remained, and smoke still rose from burned fields and dwellings. They had ridden through a wasteland.

Before they could pass in through the gates they had to make way for a few wagons leaving the city laden with women, children, and the elderly. They soon discovered that a long line of such wagons had already departed, heading west or south, away from the fighting. These were the last.

Rufe discovered that the city had been emptied of everyone except soldiers and those few able-bodied men and women who had stayed to provide for their needs. All the cattle from the market had been rounded up and herded into the city. Any usable supplies had quickly been gathered from every farm within miles. Anything that remained had been put to the torch.

An enormous amount of crucial preparation had been carried out, and in a remarkably short period of time. Rufe began to understand what Will had been doing in the hours before he returned to the ford. He also realized why it hadn't been possible to immediately send all of Ranauld's men to reinforce the defenders.

Drettroth must have hoped to take the city by surprise. Now he would find it held in strength against him. He must have expected to supply his army from the rich farmlands surrounding Arnost. Instead he would find a barren wilderness. If he expected to starve the city into submission, he would eventually discover that it had been well stocked and its hungry dependents sent elsewhere.

Rufe suddenly thought of Thomas. Without his alertness they would certainly have been overtaken by a terrible disaster. He decided to seek him out as soon as he had an opportunity.

He located the Duke of Erestor and delivered Will's message. The regent had not been idle. The last wagons had departed. Adequate supplies had been gathered. Final repairs to the city walls were almost complete. The duke may have weathered a few too many winters, but he was capable and had the situation well in hand.

Having seen to the welfare of his men, Rufe took the opportunity to snatch a few hours sleep.

The sun was high in the sky when he woke. There was no news of Will. Noon came and went with still no sign of the captain or his men. Rufe was bent on gathering some men and heading back to the ford, but the duke overruled him. “Will knows what he’s about,” he said calmly. “He’ll be back when he judges the time is right.”

Two more hours passed before a line of wagons rolled slowly into view. The duke sent out mounted soldiers to escort them in. Rufe met them at the gate, eager for news.

“We left the captain several hours ago,” one of the wagon drivers reported. The man carried a leg wound, bound with bloodied bandages. He spoke through clenched teeth, struggling with pain and pale from loss of blood. It was obvious that every man capable of fighting had remained at the ford.

“The Rogandans managed to get a few rafts across the river, a long way downstream, out of our sight. Our scouts discovered them before they reached us, and we managed to drive them off. But they attacked the ford again at the same time. We held on, but lost a lot of men. The captain sent us off as soon as it was safe to leave. That was midmorning. He was determined to hold until noon.”

THOMAS JOINED RUFE, and they waited together with growing anxiety as the afternoon drew on. Rufe paced restlessly along the city wall, muttering to himself. More than once he was determined to mount a horse and head off alone to find out what was happening. Thomas talked him out of it with difficulty.

Late in the afternoon more wagons appeared in the distance, moving slowly. Before they reached the city a group of horsemen came into view, far behind but heading for the city.

Rufe ran from the wall, calling loudly for men to join him. A mounted party quickly formed and galloped away from the walls. When they reached the wagons, a few men detached themselves from the group and climbed onto the wagons. The wagons picked up speed, and before long the gates opened to receive them.

Rufe and the other horsemen dwindled slowly into the distance.

Who would they encounter? Would it be Will, with whatever remained of his force? Or the first contingent of the victorious Rogandans? Now it was the turn of Thomas to pace anxiously along the wall. The horsemen met and merged in the distance. Thomas could not tell if they met as friends or foes.

After what seemed like an age, Thomas could make out a large body of horsemen. They were hundreds strong, surely too many for Will's party. Had Rufe now been lost as well, undone by his rash impatience to rejoin his captain?

But now behind this group an even larger body of men could be seen, spreading out across the plain. As the first group drew closer, riders could be seen looking back over their shoulders, and urging weary mounts to greater efforts. It was Will and his men! Rufe must have joined them.

They arrived in good order and passed proudly through the gates. Will and Ranauld rode with them, both apparently unscathed. Ranauld led them in.

Will waited at the rear, not entering the city until all his men were safely inside. His arrival was greeted with noisy jubilation by the men on the walls, and the sound of cheering rose on the afternoon air.

BEFORE THE SUN set an immense army had spread out across the plains before the city and could be seen setting up camp. The city was invested. The siege had begun.

Men gazed in awe at the vast extent of the enemy encampment. Then they looked around them anxiously, trying to assess the strength of the city walls.

The Rogandan losses at the ford, great as they were, appeared to be about as significant as a few broken ears in a cornfield. But however strong the enemy army might be, the watching soldiers took great heart from the return of Will Prentis. Where Will led, men would follow. And no matter the odds, they were certain he would lead them to victory.

VOLUME 2—THE SHAKING

17

The Duke of Erestor banged his fist down hard on the table and glared angrily at the Council members seated before him. The hubbub gradually died down, and all eyes turned in his direction.

"May I remind you, My Lords, that our situation is difficult enough already without us bickering with each other? Any sane person," and with this he locked eyes with the pompous Lord Sinnett, who colored and quickly lowered his gaze, "can see that all available manpower is needed for the defense of the city. Each of us has servants to see to our basic needs. Beyond that we must all make sacrifices for the sake of our mutual security. Do I make myself clear?"

He paused for a long moment. The nobles had gone quiet.

Will, standing behind and to the left of the duke, glanced at the assembled lords. They were a reduced group in more than numbers. Several of the more astute nobles, like Bottren, Dongan, and Owein, had accompanied the king on his delegation to Castel. Others, such as Gorein, Storr, Burtelen, and Leile, had hurriedly departed for their holdings in the south and west to strengthen defenses and raise armies. Many of those who remained were essential neither to the king nor to the kingdom. Yet even as their relevance diminished, by some mysterious logic they had apparently deduced that their importance had increased.

Good men still occupied seats at the table, but sadly they were now outnumbered by lesser brethren. Count Ranauld briefly caught his eye, disgust evident on his face. Will kept his face impassive.

The duke rose to his feet and cleared his throat. "As you are aware, we have been very fortunate indeed to have at our service Will Prentis, the deputy captain of the King's Guard." He nodded to Will. "I am today confirming him as commander of the army. As of now, all soldiers in Arnost will come under his direct authority. I am appointing Count Ranauld," and the duke paused and bowed in his direction, "to act as his deputy."

Loud murmuring greeted his announcement. A nobleman answering to a commoner? It was unprecedented. The duke raised his voice and talked them down. "Our king holds Will Prentis in very high esteem, and before he departed he advised me to strongly consider such an appointment should the need arise." He paused to let that sink in.

"Any of our soldiers will readily confirm," he continued, "that he has long been commander in all but name. He commands the complete loyalty of every one of our soldiers, and I expect no less from each of you.

"I need hardly remind you," he concluded, "that without the commander's extraordinary efforts over the last two days, every one of us would be dead or enslaved."

Will could not help noticing the subtle emphasis the regent placed on his new title, reinforcing his status.

The duke paused again, and directed his gaze pointedly around the table, offering a challenge to anyone who dared take it. No one said a word.

Then the silence was shattered as Count Ranauld surged to his feet, his chair skidding noisily back across the stone floor behind him. His voice rang out as he raised his goblet high. "To the commander!" One by one the others stood with him, a few without hesitation, others more slowly.

At last only the Earl of Pisander retained his seat. The earl, who ran the king's foreign spy network, lived for intrigue. He also had a high view of his own importance. Leaning casually back in his chair, he studied each nobleman's face in turn. Will's eyes he ignored. Then slowly he rose to his feet, raised his goblet and aimed his gaze in the direction of Will. "To the commander," he averred firmly.

THOMAS TOOK A DEEP BREATH, steadied his nerves, and strode through the door. He had not been alone with his father since before the incident with Will, and he was not looking forward to it.

A few hours ago his mother Marya had left the city in a wagon, heading for safety with most of the other women. She hoped to join her brother and his wife, living far away south on a farm with three children that Marya had never seen.

His mother had not gone willingly, though. She desperately wanted to remain with her husband and her son. Axel, reinforced by a decree from the duke, overruled her protests. Thomas felt sure that his father did not want to be separated from his wife, either. But he was a practical man, and her safety was his highest priority.

Thomas found his father seated at the table preparing food. He glanced up briefly when Thomas entered then returned to his work.

The youth was determined to make an attempt at peace. "I'm sorry I interrupted your conversation with Will."

His father did not respond for a while. Then he said, "When you were a little boy you were bitten by a horse."

Thomas, who had heard this story many times, was curious that his father chose to mention it now.

"The wound wasn't dangerous, but it took a long time to heal. You were very upset. Your mother believed you would never want to go near horses again. She thought the incident shocked you most because you loved the horses and couldn't understand why one of them would want to hurt you.

"I believed there was a chance your interest could be recaptured. I spent many hours with you, helping you to overcome your fear. At first you were resistant, but gradually you regained your confidence, and you began to rediscover your love for them."

Thomas hadn't heard this before. He listened intently, his interest stirred.

"I taught you first how to recognize their moods, and later how to manage them whatever mood they were in. You were a fast learner. I taught you to ride, too. You were the youngest rider I ever saw."

"I know you taught me to ride," Thomas acknowledged. Nevertheless his father's comments were a revelation to him. He hadn't been aware that his father had a role in the development of his unusual ability to read and respond to horses. It gave him a lot to think about.

"You were good with horses and a hard worker. I always hoped you would succeed me one day," the stable master continued. "I remember the day I presented you to the king. I was proud of you.

"You used to be happy back then." He sounded wistful. "I don't understand what happened. Everything changed."

His father was right—it had all changed. Because of the stone. But how could he explain it to his father? He wouldn't be able to make him understand.

"Back then you wanted to be with me—with your mother and me. Now you only seem to care about Will Prentis and Rufe Sarjant and their friends."

Shamed by his father's words, Thomas didn't know what to say. It was all true. They had grown apart, and it was his fault. And to think that his father might be sad about it—he hadn't expected that.

"You've become a different person, Thomas. You fought with Simon, didn't you?"

Thomas looked down, then finally nodded uncomfortably. "Yes." He wanted to tell his father it was Simon's fault, but he couldn't honestly say that.

"Why would you do that?" His father seemed baffled. Then he glanced at his son sharply. "He told me you attacked him with a pitchfork. Is that true?"

Thomas felt himself coloring. How could he possibly explain? *Simon had my stone!* His father would not understand, and he couldn't blame him.

He saw his father's eyes narrow in anger and disappointment. For a while neither of them said anything.

"There was a time when you used to treat me with respect." His father started up again, and his voice had taken on a harder edge. "I don't like what you've become, Thomas. Yesterday I finally understood that you care nothing for me."

"I said I was sorry." Thomas finally found his voice again. "But I needed to interrupt you—it was urgent!"

"It was obvious to me that your message was urgent—when I finally found out what it was. It wasn't the interruption that showed your lack of respect. It was your refusal to deliver the message in my hearing. What possible reason could you have for doing that?"

He had paid such a heavy price for the stone. Now, as he felt the full impact of his father's words, he began finally to grasp just how much it had affected their relationship. For the first time Thomas actually considered sharing his secret with him.

"There was a reason. A good reason."

"Well?" His father spread his hands inquiringly. "What was it?"

Now he came to it, Thomas could not imagine how to begin to explain the whole complicated, messy story of the stone. Nor could he imagine how his father would receive it. He stood there wrestling with his thoughts and feelings. Should he make the attempt? He couldn't decide, so in the end he managed only an evasive non-answer. "It's difficult to explain."

His father aimed a look of disgust at him. "It doesn't seem difficult to me. It's very simple: you care nothing at all for me, or for your mother."

This accusation was so untrue. He cared deeply about his parents. And it was so unfair. From the way his father behaved at times, Thomas could just as easily claim that he cared nothing for his son.

"You're a very important person now. Too important to have anything to do with the likes of us."

He looked at his father in disbelief. Could he really have misunderstood him this much?

Thomas had found himself, entirely to his own surprise, doing a job that counted for something, and he wanted to do the job well. He also wanted his efforts to be noticed and appreciated, and he couldn't pretend otherwise. But it had never entered his head that he was more important than his parents. He simply didn't think like that.

His father's barbs drove from his mind any thought of telling him about the stone. He felt only anger and hurt.

Then came the final injury. Simon appeared in the doorway of Thomas's bedroom, a mocking smile on his lips. It was obvious that he had been listening to the conversation. Worse, his father was not surprised to see Simon—he had known that he was there. And Thomas had actually considered revealing the secret of the stone.

How *could* his father say all this to him in the presence of Simon? Now it was his turn to wonder what possible reason could excuse such behavior.

"Oh, Simon will be sharing your room from now on," his father informed him casually. "His uncle has gone south for safety, and Simon has no one else to stay with."

Thomas stood there speechless. Seeing the look on his face, his father said curtly, "If you don't like it, you can always go stay with your friends in the castle."

Thomas said nothing. He pushed past Simon into his room, gathered his few possessions, and left.

Bells rang loudly, and the gathered throngs cheered deliriously as King Steffan of Arvenon strode purposefully and majestically into the cathedral, between two long lines of armed men standing importantly at attention. The men, selected from his own guard, stood resplendent in their dress uniforms.

Doubts still ravaged his mind. To add to the uncertainties about his new bride, there was now the disturbing fact that he had received no word from Arnost for several days. New messengers had been sent, but they had not yet returned.

All these distractions the king pushed from his thoughts. He reminded himself of the reasons why he had sought this alliance. Each of them remained pressing. He was committed now, and he was determined to go through with it. Today was his wedding day, long considered and long anticipated, and it deserved his complete and undistracted attention. If there were problems to address in Arvenon they could wait until the following day. If Istel had been playing him false in some way, he would deal with it later. And deal with it firmly.

He made his way to the front of the cathedral, with Lords Bottren and Owein following close behind. A bishop in a flowing gown and tall miter greeted them and showed them to their positions.

A trumpet fanfare heralded the arrival of the princess and her retinue. After a stately entrance accompanied by rapturous applause, she made her way slowly to the front of the church. Steffan watched closely, trying without success to get a clear glimpse of the young woman behind the thick veil that covered her face. Her gown was a stunning white waterfall of lace, glittering with diamantés. His eye was drawn from the exquisite veil, topped with a diamond tiara, down to the long string of pearls around her neck supporting a large sapphire pendant. The overall effect was dazzling. Steffan pulled himself to his full height, gazing admiringly upon his regal bride.

Trumpets sounded, monks chanted, and choirs sang. The bishop solemnly intoned the rites. The bride and the groom exchanged vows promising love, honor and fidelity until death parted them. He spoke boldly; she so faintly he could barely hear her. Then he placed a ring on her delicate finger.

The bishop spoke of the joys and trials and the rights and responsibilities of marriage and parenthood. Steffan, half-listening through the distractions of the day, was struck by the simplicity of the message. The prelate painted a picture of the basic hopes and needs of human life. His homily would have been equally at place in the wedding of the poorest and most humble couple in the kingdom.

Amidst the pomp and splendor of the royal wedding, the bishop was choosing to remind the groom that the basic benefits of life did not exist merely for the pleasure of kings. Steffan heard the entreaty and silently promised himself that he would not forget it.

The bishop offered words of blessing, and it was done. A triumphant fanfare rang out as he led the bridal couple to a balcony and presented them to the enthusiastic crowd, who waved banners and cheered wildly. King Steffan found himself caught up in the joy of the throng, and smiled back in unfeigned delight.

Finally the wedding party, invited guests, and a large contingent from among the nobility of Castel, proceeded to a massive hall in the castle where a sumptuous banquet had been laid out. The tables groaned under the weight of an overwhelming assortment of food both local and exotic, beautifully presented. Round loaves of bread made from fine-ground flour stood piled high on wooden platters, still steaming, fresh from the oven. Every kind of meat had been prepared, from fish, fowl, and whole pig carcasses to the finest cuts of venison and beef. An unparalleled selection of fresh and dried fruit competed with sweetmeats, honey cakes, and delicious desserts for the approval of the revelers. The best wine from Lestanor flowed freely as well as copious quantities of the excellent local ale.

Harps and lyres offered a soothing background to the feast, and pipers waited at the ready for later in the evening when guests might wish to dance.

Steffan had been warned in advance that Castelan custom prohibited the bride from removing her veil until after all the celebrations were complete. Further, since for that day she was exalted above all others in honor as she was in beauty, she was not expected to speak but simply to bask in the attention and admiration of all. So she remained demure and silent throughout the feast that followed the ceremony.

This was no intimate family occasion. Ambassadors from all the neighboring kingdoms had attended the wedding and were present at the feast. Each of them came in turn to the bride and groom throughout the meal and presented fine gifts and fine words.

The Rogandan ambassador managed to be particularly insufferable, delivering a speech full of empty sentiment in words dripping with honey and a tone dripping with sarcasm. The man returned to his seat and sat smugly surrounded by toadying ambassadors of lesser status who hung on his every word. Whenever Steffan glanced in his direction, he raised his chalice and proffered an exaggerated bow.

As the afternoon and evening wore on, the celebrations became increasingly tiresome to Steffan. The desire grew in him to dispense with partying and to escape the nobles and ambassadors who vied for his attention. More and more he wanted to be alone with his bride, to converse with her at last and to see her face.

He took every opportunity, though, to study his father-in-law. King Istel imbibed freely and celebrated more and more loudly as the wedding supper proceeded. Occasionally, however, Steffan caught him staring at his daughter with a look akin to anguish.

The night was well advanced before Steffan's frustration finally came to an end. He left the revelers and the banqueting hall and was ushered to his wedding chamber. Servants respectfully helped him out of his ceremonial garments and into comfortable attire of smooth silk before bowing deeply and leaving him. His bride was, he knew, somewhere nearby being likewise prepared. He waited, eager and impatient, for her arrival.

SOLDIERS on the wall ducked involuntarily as a large rock sailed over their heads, crashing into a house behind them in the city. Will stood on a battlement beside the gates, watching. The Rogandans probably did not know that the houses close to the wall were unoccupied. He was more than happy for them to waste their shots demolishing houses instead of focusing on the wall.

More challenging were the fireballs the attackers had launched, starting fires and keeping his soldiers busy trying to put them out. At least one large blaze was still burning out of control, and a pall of smoke hung low over the city.

In the first couple of days of the siege Will had set the defenders to work building their own catapults. They built especially large ones with the result that their engines had greater range than those of the Rogandans. For now. The defenders also had an unlimited supply of ammunition to quarry from the rocky outcrop on which the castle was built.

The Arvenian soldiers had quickly put the catapults to good use, forcing the Rogandans to hastily remove their new encampment and re-site it further back out of range. A few even larger catapults were now under construction in Arnost. Will didn't want the besiegers to become too comfortable.

For the Rogandan catapults to reach the city, they were forced to operate well within the range of the defenders. One lucky shot from Will's men had already destroyed a Rogandan engine, and most of the enemy soldiers had been hastily pulled back for their own protection.

From his position atop the wall, Will raised his hand, then lowered it. The gates swung ponderously open, and a large group of mounted soldiers issued out and galloped toward the Rogandan catapults. Most of them engaged enemy soldiers, but a few rode up to the catapults and quickly poured oil over them. Other soldiers then threw torches onto the catapults. Within moments all of them were ablaze.

The Arvenians wheeled and galloped back to the city even as groups of Rogandan cavalry formed behind them. They raced through the gate, and it swung shut in the faces of the pursuing Rogandans, who were met with a hail of arrows from the wall and quickly retreated.

The defenders jeered and shook their fists at the fleeing Rogandans. They shouted with delight at the sight of the burning catapults.

The sally had bought the city some time, and it was good for morale. But Will was under no illusions. Before long there would be other larger engines to take their place. And they would be well defended next time.

Will's thoughts went to the king far away in Castel. Was he aware that his capital was under siege? Messengers had been sent, but it was difficult to know if they had been able to get through.

But what exercised Will most was the inaction of the Rogandans. Their catapults kept the pressure on the defenders, to be sure. But Drettroth had more than enough men for a direct assault on the city. Why was he not attacking? And in the unlikely event that the Rogandan lord was content to simply starve the city into submission, he certainly did not need an army this size to maintain a siege. What was he planning to do with the rest of his soldiers? There were far too many unknowns, and it made Will uncomfortable.

The duke joined him on the wall, interrupting his musing. "I see your sally was successful, Will."

"Yes, My Lord. It has given us some breathing space, at least for a while."

"How are the men?"

"In good heart. A lengthy siege will test their resolve, though."

"Some of the lords are pressing for a Council of War. They want to know what we're planning."

Will raised an eyebrow quizzically. "What do they expect, My Lord? It will take a very large army to lift this siege. We do not have anywhere near enough men to do it."

"I know. We will meet with them and try to help them see reality. Unfortunately, few of them have any comprehension of the ways of war."

The duke sighed. "Most of them are more of a hindrance than a help. A rock from a catapult damaged a small part of the servants' quarters of the Earl of Pisander earlier today, and he has taken the opportunity to demand a new and more luxurious dwelling.

"I fail to understand why he didn't leave when he had the chance. His holdings are within my own Duchy of Erestor, west of here. He would have been safe there, and he is of little use in Arnost. His spies cannot reach him while he's locked up in here."

Will shrugged sympathetically. "I do have a proposal I could present to the Council, My Lord. People are usually easier to manage when there is some kind of a plan."

The duke looked at him doubtfully. "We must preserve the king's army if we are to preserve his city."

"My plan does not put the army at risk."

The regent frowned at him. "Don't expect me to approve any plan that puts you at risk. The men believe in you, and I depend on you. I cannot afford to have anything happen to you."

"I understand, My Lord."

The duke offered no further comment.

This particular issue was far from settled, though, and Will had the feeling that the regent knew it as well as he did. Perhaps, like his commander, the duke was simply planning to choose his timing carefully before picking a fight.

18

The afternoon dragged on interminably. Thomas hefted another heavy stone and lugged it to the wall, puffing and blowing as he went. He loathed this work, but he could think of nothing better to do.

He could hardly have felt more miserable. Only a few days ago he had been on top of the world. As horse master he had an important role, a job he loved and excelled at. Now his students patrolled the wall or put out fires; the army had little use for horsemen during a siege. Back then his free time had been spent relaxing with Will and Rufe. Now both men were so busy that he rarely caught a glimpse of them.

The pinnacle for Thomas had been his discovery of the Rogandans lurking at the city gates. His quick reaction had played an important part in saving the city. And the stone, inert for so long, had responded in his moment of need and exposed the designs of the invaders. Now his intervention seemed small and insignificant, overshadowed by the heroic defense of the ford and the drama of the siege. And he had since found the stone closed to him once more.

On one of the few occasions he had seen Will, his friend had noticed that he was bored and inactive.

"Perhaps your father could use some help at the stables," he had suggested.

But Thomas would not go back to the stables. He had wasted no time finding something else to do. Builders were hard at work strengthening the wall, and he soon found himself helping them.

The work was difficult and dangerous, the more so when the Rogandans began lobbing rocks the size of ponies over the wall. The stone mason in charge of the section of wall where Thomas was working became increasingly upset and irritable as time wore on. Thomas soon became a target. "Can't you work faster?" "Are you deaf? I told you to put it over there!"

When Thomas made a mistake mixing mortar, the mason lashed out unmercifully. "Don't you know anything? You're worse than useless! You create more work than you're doing."

Shoveling manure at the stables would have been preferable to this. But Thomas knew that he could face neither his father's accusing silences nor Simon's smugness. He decided he had little choice other than to persist.

Life had an uncomfortable way of turning on you just when everything seemed to be going well. And given the circumstances of the siege, it seemed highly unlikely that any further changes would be for the better.

"WHAT ARE we doing to break this siege, My Lord?"

"Why are we just sitting here while the Rogandans pillage our land?"

"When will the king return from Castel with his army to relieve us?"

The duke endured the carping of the nobles with increasing annoyance. Finally he held up his hand. The clamor continued unabated.

"Silence!" he bellowed, a look of fury on his face. "I shall dismiss you from this chamber and this Council if you continue to behave in this way."

Some of the nobles appeared affronted, but the noise subsided.

After a few moments of silence, the Earl of Pisander spoke up. "I think my fellow nobles are simply wondering if our excellent commander has prepared a plan for dealing with the Rogandans."

"The city walls are solid, and we have enough men to defend them, My Lord," Will replied calmly. "My plan is to ensure that the Rogandans stay out, while we remain safe inside."

"A safe plan indeed, Commander. No one could accuse you of being unduly adventurous." A couple of the nobles snickered. "Do you have no thought of taking the fight to the Rogandans?"

"Our estimate is that the Rogandans have twenty thousand men in their army. We have almost twenty five hundred—barely enough to protect the city. I would be a poor commander indeed if I committed our soldiers to battle against such odds without a very compelling reason, My Lord."

"Are you afraid to fight unless the odds are in your favor, Commander?" Pisander asked quietly.

Will, who had thus far never managed to engage in any fight where the odds were in his favor, did not bother to reply.

"If you think he's afraid, why don't you issue him a formal challenge, Pisander?" Count Ranauld broke in, his voice icy calm.

"Don't be ridiculous, Ranauld. You know that a nobleman cannot duel with a commoner."

"That problem is not insurmountable. I am his Second In Command. Issue the challenge to me. I would be delighted to defend his honor."

Pisander went pale. "Come, My Lord. You entirely mistake me. I meant no slight on our gallant commander. Everyone knows he has no cowardly bone in his body. I was merely hoping to learn if he might have some plan of action."

"As a matter of fact I do." All eyes turned immediately to Will. He looked to the duke for permission to speak. The duke frowned, but inclined his head.

"We need to find out what Drettroth, who leads the Rogandans, is planning to do. His army is very large, much larger than he needs for a siege. And he was never planning a siege, anyway—he expected to take Arnost by surprise. I suspect that Arnost was only ever intended to be a stepping stone, and that he has other plans for this army."

"How do you propose to uncover Drettroth's plans," retorted Pisander, "given that our best agents have uncovered nothing? Are you planning to write to him and ask for the details?"

Will ignored Pisander's sarcasm. "I'm proposing to visit the Rogandan camp myself and learn what I can."

The duke was on his feet in an instant. "Certainly not! It would be suicide."

"My Lord Duke," said Pisander reasonably, "surely we should at least hear the commander out."

"How could you possibly get in there undetected?" Ranauld protested.

"There are twenty thousand men milling around out there. No one can keep track of them all. I speak Rogandan, which means I should be able to bluff my way out of any difficult situation."

"But even Rogandan soldiers have duties to perform," protested the duke. "A soldier doesn't just wander around wherever he wants."

"I'm not planning to go as a soldier, My Lord. I'll go as a priest. Their armies never go anywhere without them. And no Rogandan soldier would dare to ask questions of a priest."

"But what if you meet other priests?"

"I know something of how they behave. When I was young, my friends and I used to imitate the priests. I was thought to be pretty good at it."

"When do you propose to do this?" asked Pisander.

"I'll go tomorrow night as soon as it's dark. There's a place where I can easily be lowered over the wall. I'll find my way to Drettroth's tent, discover whatever I can, then I'll be out of there before dawn."

"It's a bold plan," Pisander admitted. Others around the room murmured their agreement.

"It's far too risky," asserted Ranauld.

The duke had the last word. "I'll never allow it," he said flatly.

Nevertheless Will was determined to go. He fully understood the risks, and the thought of being caught was too awful to entertain. But an attempt had to be made. And he was confident that the duke would be brought to see the sense in it.

Of late Will had discovered, to his wonder, that in the end people mostly acceded to his requests and embraced his proposals. Perhaps it was because he had developed a reputation of making suggestions that were more than usually useful. Perhaps people believed in his luck.

CONFIDENT THAT HE would be proceeding with his plan, Will began serious preparations for his foray into the Rogandan camp even before receiving agreement from the duke.

His confidence was soon tested. The duke sought him out not long after the conference. The regent appeared harried and frustrated.

"Pisander has been bleating in my ear since the minute the meeting ended," the duke complained. "He insists that we must find a way to get information. He says that his agents are either missing or outside the city and unable to report. Frankly, even if they all suddenly appeared tomorrow, I wouldn't set much store by anything they had to say. They somehow managed to completely miss the arrival of twenty thousand Rogandan soldiers in the Dark Forest."

The duke sighed deeply. "He's right, though—we do need information. But not at the cost of your life, Will. This plan is madness! I will not let you walk alone right into the middle of the entire Rogandan army."

"I understand your concern, My Lord. Believe me, I have no desire whatsoever to fall into the hands of Drettroth either. We have met once before, and I doubt that he remembers the meeting warmly," said Will, a grim smile on his face.

"But what is he planning to do with all those men?" he continued. "I can't imagine he'll leave them sitting here for long. Nor can I see him waiting out a siege. If we don't get some idea of his intentions soon, My Lord, we might not have another opportunity. He'll leave enough men here to keep us quiet, and disappear off with the rest to who knows where."

"But even if we discover his plans, what can we do to prevent them?"

"We can find a way to get messengers through the Rogandan lines to warn other cities that he's on the way. Given enough time to prepare, they might be able to avoid capture. Drettroth will be forced to tie down more of his forces laying siege, or waste men storming heavily defended walls."

The duke did not want to be convinced. "Even if you're right, why does it need to be you?"

Will shrugged. "Who else speaks Rogandan fluently, My Lord? Who else even knows what Drettroth looks like?"

Hearing no response from the regent, he added, "And who else would be willing to make the attempt?"

The duke could not deny the need to discover Drettroth's plans, and he had no answers to Will's questions. He left with his face betraying his frustration.

Before twenty-four hours had passed, the regent had acquiesced. Will did not ask for or expect his enthusiastic blessing; he knew that would be too much to hope for.

A SOFT TAP at the door of his apartments stirred Steffan into life. "Enter!" he commanded.

A servant woman appeared at the door and bowed low. "Her Majesty, Essanda, Queen of Arvenon, and Princess of Castel, awaits your pleasure."

"You may send her in," he replied, trying not to sound eager. He leaped to his feet, ready to greet his bride.

The woman bowed low again and backed out of the door.

A few moments later Queen Essanda entered the room. The

contrast between her earlier impregnability and her current appearance could not have been more marked. They had dressed her in a flimsy gown of transparent material, and every line and curve was fully revealed in the candlelight.

Steffan stood with mouth agape and stared. Everything instantly became clear—the reason behind the secrecy, the hesitation of the king, the awkwardness of the Castelan nobles. He had been preparing himself for the unexpected, but he hadn't been anticipating this. How had they managed to keep it hidden? A mixture of emotions assaulted him: disappointment, anger, shame, pity, but most of all astonishment.

"Do I displease My Lord?"

Her trembling voice startled him out of his reverie. He looked at her face and saw a small tear starting on one cheek. Compassion rose within him. He remembered that the princess, too, had feelings. She surely deserved his consideration.

He moved to the four-poster bed and sat down. Patting the bed beside him, he said to her gently, "Come and sit here."

She obeyed at once, and placed her dainty hand into the larger hand he offered her.

"How old are you, child?" He put the question as delicately as he knew how.

"I am fourteen," she said importantly. "It was my birthday yesterday."

Steffan could think of nothing to say. At almost thirty years of age, it had taken time to reconcile himself to a bride of nineteen. Nothing had prepared him for marriage to a child, barely pubescent.

"I know what is expected of a wife," she offered calmly, blushing faintly. "My nurse explained it to me."

He winced, then hurried to disguise it. He knew men who would not hesitate to bed such a wife. But he would never do it.

"In my kingdom we do not usually marry a girl until she is a little older," he began tentatively.

"That is usual in my father's kingdom, too," she returned. "But Pappa explained that it was important for me to marry now."

She looked up at him with her big round eyes. "I have always known that my father would choose me a husband to help his kingdom," she said gravely. "I am willing to do my duty to my father. And to my husband."

Unable to think of anything to say, he remained silent. What should he do? He needed a mature bride who could deliver and mother an heir. He could arrange to have the marriage annulled, and return her to her father. But how could he return home empty handed?

It had not been easy to find a suitable bride. Essanda seemed a perfect choice: from royal stock, shaped by similar customs and even speaking the same language. Where would he begin looking again? How eager would the next king be to hand over a daughter if he backed out this time? And what would the idle tongues of the gathered ambassadors do with the scandal?

And these difficulties, great as they were, were far from the only considerations. In such uncertain times, Arvenon needed dependable allies as much as Castel did. How could the new alliance possibly survive an annulment?

Steffan began to see that Istel had cleverly steered him into a position from which it would be difficult to escape.

Essanda had waited patiently through his long silence, but now she looked up at him uncertainly. "I overheard Gordy—I mean My Lord Gordan—talking to my father. He said you would be angry at first. But he said you are a good man, and that you will treat me kindly." Her big eyes peered at him entreatingly. "Will you be kind to me?"

As he gazed back into her calm and hopeful face, admiration stirred within him. He could not begin to imagine what this situation must mean for her—a carefree child one day, wife to a strange husband from a foreign land the next. Her childhood had been ruthlessly stripped away, replaced by the stern prospect of a life of duty as queen and mother.

Heavy expectations had been placed on her young shoulders. Far too heavy. Yet somehow, in spite of her frailness and vulnerability, she managed to radiate courage and determination.

"Yes, I will be kind to you."

He realized as he said it that he had made his decision. She would remain his wife in name, and one day become his wife in practice. Arvenon would have to wait a while longer for an heir.

"Count Gordan is a wise man," he noted. To himself he added bitterly, *But he has betrayed my trust and squandered the respect I held for him.*

He turned toward her and took both of her hands. "You are my queen now, Essanda. But I will not yet ask you to take on the full responsibilities of a wife. That must wait until you are older. Do you understand?"

She nodded.

"But it will remain our secret. You must tell no one. Can you remember that?"

Again she nodded, a serious look on her face.

Galling as this situation was, it wasn't difficult for Steffan to see how it had come about. In spite of a long history of friendly relations, Arvenon and Castel had engaged in very little direct communication in recent decades. During the reign in Arvenon of Steffan's grandfather, King Leonid III, the Castelan succession had been contested. In an attempt to strengthen their case, both of the claimants had sought to secure Leonid's endorsement. He had steadfastly refused to interfere in the affairs of another kingdom. The eventual winner had resented his lack of support, and the two kingdoms had grown apart as a result.

These quarrels had seemed little more than ancient history to Steffan when he found himself searching for a bride, and apparently King Istel had seen it the same way. Nevertheless, Steffan was now paying a heavy price for the long isolation.

"I don't understand it," he mused. "Why did Actan never mention your age?"

Lord Actan's lands bordered Castel, and he had informally acted as Arvenon's ambassador since before the reign of Steffan's father. Actan died only weeks before Steffan's first approach to King Istel, leaving no heir. Had he remained alive, he would certainly have briefed Steffan fully. But why had he never mentioned details of the royal family earlier?

Her soft voice broke in on his thoughts. "Perhaps he did not think it was important." Then abruptly she smiled, and dimples appeared in her cheeks. "He was nice. He used to give me sweetmeats."

Essanda's reply startled him. Steffan, thinking aloud, had not been looking for an answer. He especially would not have expected a child to offer such a response. She was almost certainly right, though.

Still speaking largely to himself, he added, "I wonder that none of the other ambassadors ever mentioned it."

"Perhaps they thought you knew already."

It was indeed the logical conclusion, but still surprising from a fourteen-year old. Steffan began to look at the girl with new eyes. He had heard she possessed wisdom beyond her years—maybe some of what they told him was true.

Then her little mouth formed a pout. "I don't like some of the ambassadors," she asserted.

"Why not?"

"Some of them are bad men."

"Which ones?"

"The Rogandan lord is *horrible*." Her face wrinkled in disgust. "Do you know he said terrible things about you and your kingdom?"

"He said terrible things to you about me?"

"Oh, no. He was talking to someone else. I was nearby, but he didn't think I was paying attention. He thinks I'm a half-wit.

"I'm not, though," she said seriously. "I just sit quietly and look somewhere else, and people seem to think I'm not there. I learned that from my Pappa. He says that peacocks strut to attract attention, and eagles soar to avoid attention."

The girl was full of surprises.

"What did the Rogandan say?"

"He said, 'Let the Arvenian fool marry the half-wit child. Very soon we will deal with him and his upstart kingdom. Then Castel will not last long, either.'"

"Are you sure that's what he said?"

She looked offended. "Of course I'm sure. My Pappa says I have a very good memory."

"Did you tell your Pappa what he said?"

"Yes. I tell him everything I hear the ambassadors say. And what the nobles say, too."

Steffan immediately found himself very interested indeed in what the girl might be able to tell him.

Long into the night they sat side by side on the bed talking, her delicate form dwarfed by his sturdy frame. When her yawns outnumbered her words, he picked her up tenderly and placed her into the large bed, tucking her in and bending down to kiss her on the forehead. Then, taking a feather pillow and a quilt, he stretched out on the floor at the foot of the bed.

There was a great deal to think about, and it was almost dawn before he finally surrendered to sleep.

THE SKY gradually darkened until only a faint outline of the distant hills remained. In Erestor, far to the west beyond those hills, the sun would have just disappeared into the ocean. The duke stood on the wall and gazed off into the night, pierced by a pang of homesickness. When would he stand again on the battlements of his castle in Maranelle and smell the fresh salt air and watch the fishing boats glide home on the evening tide?

He sighed and turned his attention once more to the Rogandan encampment. The lights of countless campfires twinkled across the plain. He knew how deceptive the peaceful scene below really was. Reality yielded a grim and very different picture. Whenever armies faced each other the angel of death hovered patiently somewhere nearby.

A torch appeared on the steps leading up to the wall. The giant frame of Rufe followed close behind it and with him a strange figure the duke did not recognize. The stranger was clad in a dark hooded cloak of homespun wool. A wide black leather belt loosely encircled his waist, and black leather shoes covered his feet. The face beneath the cowl was painted with long streaks of deep blue. The effect was singular and disturbing.

The stranger was Will Prentis. The transformation in his appearance was nothing short of astonishing.

"I would never have recognized you," the duke acknowledged, assessing him closely in the torchlight.

"It took some time to get it right," Will said casually. "My red hair would have given me away, so I dyed it black. Provided I can remember the right greetings and chants, I can't imagine any way I could be detected."

"I hope you're right," said Rufe worriedly.

"You're like an old mother hen," Will laughed. "Don't worry, Rufe, I'll be back at the gates well before dawn. Just make sure someone is there to let me in!"

Rufe personally lowered him over the wall. Will disappeared slowly from sight as Rufe steadily played out the rope. Eventually the rope went slack, and a couple of quick tugs from below signaled that Will had made it safely to the ground. Rufe retrieved the rope, coiling it as he drew it back in.

The duke went off to his bed to get some sleep. Rufe settled down on the wall to wait.

Cocks crowed in the city, heralding the dawn. The sun rose slowly, ushering in a new day of life and toil, and dispensing its rays impartially to Arvenians and Rogandans alike. But Will had not appeared, and the steadily growing light revealed no sign of him anywhere near the gates.

The duke reappeared on the wall as dawn was breaking. He placed his hand comfortingly on the shoulder of the giant guardsman. "Don't worry, Rufe. He's simply been delayed. He always comes through in the end."

But the morning drew on, and still they waited. Afternoon came and went and yielded to a new evening. A whole day had passed without a single attack upon the city. The entire countryside seemed to be holding its breath.

The missing commander did not appear, and their hope began to fade slowly with the light.

Something had gone wrong. Badly wrong.

19

Steffan ambled happily hand-in-hand with his mother along a beach in Erestor, the fresh sea breeze playing with her long dark hair. Then, for no apparent reason, a fisherman standing beside his boat picked up a mallet, and began rapidly laying into the side of his vessel. A staccato hammering sound punctuated each stroke. The odd behavior was accompanied by an urgent voice, "Your Majesty! Are you awake, Your Majesty?"

The king emerged groggily from his dream and opened his eyes to the half light just before dawn. The voice and the hammering continued, more insistent than before.

He groaned and sat up, his back aching from lying on the floor. He struggled sleepily to his feet and made his way to the door.

When he opened it he was greeted by an apologetic Lord Bottren. "I am very sorry to disturb you, Sire. But there is important news. King Istel has learned that Rogandan soldiers now occupy the mountain pass that leads south into Arvenon."

Steffan exclaimed loudly in anger.

"There is more, Your Majesty. Before the pass was closed a messenger came through from the duke in Arnost. A large Rogandan army has now besieged the city."

Steffan looked at his friend in disbelief. “It has come so soon.” He bowed his head for a moment, covering his face with his hands. Then he straightened again. “Agon chose his timing well,” he observed bitterly.

“King Istel has convened a Council of War. It will commence as soon as you arrive.”

Steffan returned to his room and dressed quickly. Essanda still slept, and he moved about quietly so as not to disturb her. He slipped away to join Bottren as dawn lit up a sky heavy with rain clouds.

Led by a Castelan retainer, they made their way to a modestly sized audience room in the castle. The room was dimly lit by small windows high on one wall and warmed by huge logs crackling loudly in a large fireplace. Steffan could make out King Istel and a small number of Castelan knights and nobles. Count Gordan sat beside the king. The light was too poor to easily read their faces, though, and he wondered if that suited his new father-in-law on the morning after the wedding.

The other Arvenian lords, Owein and Dongan, had already arrived and were seated at one end of the table.

“Welcome. Your Majesty, My Lord,” King Istel greeted them, nodding to each in turn. “It gives me regret to rouse you in this way so soon after our joyous celebrations, but a common enemy threatens both of our kingdoms.”

Steffan held his peace. He knew he was going to need to choose his words carefully. Having suddenly found himself at war, he could not afford the luxury of fully indulging his anger over Istel’s deception.

“I assume you have been briefed, Steffan?”

“I have,” he affirmed.

“Please be seated.” The king indicated two unoccupied chairs beside Dongan.

Steffan did not move.

“Is there a problem?” Istel’s voice was even.

“I will be frank, Your Majesty and My Lords. We find ourselves in dark days, in greater need than ever before of true friends and trustworthy allies. We have made a treaty and pledged ourselves to each other for good or ill. Yet all parties have not approached this alliance with equal candor, and the conduct surrounding the birth of our accord has threatened its very existence. You have conspired together to take advantage of our trust and deceive us." He made no attempt to disguise the anger in his voice.

A number of the Castelan nobles shifted uncomfortably. Bottren looked startled, and Owein and Dongan rose from their seats. Gordan's face was unreadable.

"Please, please," said King Istel placatingly. "Let us not be hasty, Your Majesty." He stood slowly to his feet. "I presume you are referring to my daughter's age. That is a minor matter which time will soon mend. Let me assure you that I myself..."

Steffan cut him off cold. "I know what you intend to say, King Istel. I don't doubt that your speech has long been prepared. You will, from your own experience, sound the praises of marriage to a woman many years your junior. You will extol the virtues of your daughter and remind me of her lineage, her qualities and her great potential. You will assert that the deception is of no consequence. And you will remind me that our kingdoms have the best chance of weathering the coming storm if we do it together. Spare me your words! I do not need them to help me choose a course of action. I have already decided."

"What do you intend to do?" Istel asked directly, his voice betraying his uncertainty.

"Essanda will remain my queen." Several of the Castelan nobles exhaled audibly. "And she will stay here in Castel until she is older." King Istel sank heavily into his chair, unable to hide his relief.

"But it will be on my terms. She will have her own apartments, as befits a queen of Arvenon. Lord Owein will remain here to oversee her continuing education and preparation. I request that Count Gordan be placed in charge of her security." The count looked to his king, who readily bowed his head in acquiescence.

"There remains the question of access to her family." Steffan could see Istel stiffen. "She will have unrestricted access to her brother. Access to her father will be subject to the condition that neither our marriage nor issues of state will ever be discussed between them." Istel slumped back into his chair. Once again his relief could not be concealed.

"Do not think, though, that I will forget your deception, My Lords. Your conduct in the days to come will have considerable bearing on the decisions I take once this immediate crisis has passed."

Istel was clearly unable to speak. Gordan rose to his feet on behalf of his king. "Your response is very gracious, Your Majesty, and we thank you sincerely for it. I know I speak for His Majesty and all his nobles when I say that Castel will stand firm with Arvenon, whatever troubles may lie ahead." He bowed deeply to Steffan.

Steffan acknowledged his statement with a curt bow of his head. "With your permission, I would like to request a brief conference with the Lords Gordan and Owein before we begin the Council, Your Majesty."

"Of course." Istel rose slowly to his feet and stood bent before the table, leaning on his hands. He appeared old and tired. "I, too, thank you, King Steffan. We have both been put to the test, and you have shown yourself to be the better man." Then he straightened and faced Steffan squarely. "I swear to you, though, that I will prove a truer kinsman than I have a friend."

Steffan bowed and withdrew with the two lords. When they were alone he turned first to Owein. "When I am absent from here, as I surely will be soon, I charge you with the responsibility of caring for the queen. She is barely fourteen years of age, and has much to learn to prepare her for her role.

"She is an intelligent girl, though," he observed. He fixed Gordan with an ironic gaze. "She has also provided me with as much useful information in a few hours as the best agents of Castel and Arvenon could uncover in several weeks."

Gordan colored slightly, and bowed low to cover it. "We will work hard to ensure that information flows much more freely from Castel in the future, Your Majesty."

"I will look forward to it," he replied tartly.

Then Steffan addressed the count with a gentler tone. "Gordan, I believe you have a special relationship with Essanda."

"She is as dear to me as my own life, Sire," Gordan acknowledged.

"Then while she remains in Castel I place her security in your hands. If you wish to undo some of the damage you have done yourself in my eyes, you will not fail me in this."

"She will not suffer harm while breath remains in my body," Gordan vowed.

"Then let us return to King Istel's conference. We have a war to win, and Agon has the initiative."

Will moved away from the wall and took stock of his surroundings. The moon rode high obscured entirely by clouds, leaving the night comfortingly dark. He did not expect Rogandan soldiers to be located anywhere nearby, but he could not rule out the possibility of night patrols.

He closed his eyes and focused his thoughts inward, immersing himself in the imagined world of the Rogandan priests. It didn't hurt to be well prepared.

He expected it would take a while to locate Drettroth's headquarters. Once he had done so, he needed to quickly find a suitable place to hide within earshot. How he would accomplish all this was far from certain, but he felt sure that opportunities would present themselves at the right moment.

Above all, he knew that he needed to appear confident and inconspicuous, just another priest going about his business. With his heart pounding in his chest, he set off boldly toward the nearest line of campfires.

He had gone only a few paces when dark figures erupted all around him. Before he could react at all, a gag had been stuffed in his mouth, his arms pinned, and his hands trussed. It was over in barely two heartbeats.

"Exactly as the traitor promised!" A harsh voice laughed with satisfaction.

His captors bustled him through the outer line of Rogandan campfires, barking a rough password when challenged. Will's mind whirled as he was hurried on deeper into the encampment, struggling to adjust to the disastrous change in his circumstances. Most galling of all was the knowledge that he had allowed himself to be betrayed.

They drove him forward unmercifully, pushing and shoving roughly if he fell behind, until they had almost traversed the full extent of the Rogandan camp. Finally they reached what appeared to be their destination.

He was pulled to a halt outside a strongly guarded tent. The tent stood at the top of a low hill with a commanding view of the surrounding encampment. After stating his business to a guard, one of his captors briefly disappeared inside. He soon re-emerged, beckoning for Will to be taken in.

Will found himself thrust into a spacious tent, well lit by many clusters of candles. Lord Drettroth sat in a large and comfortable chair, his teeth bared in a self-satisfied smile. Beside him stood a thickset brute with bulging muscles and a demeanor of arrogant self-confidence. He radiated pure evil, and the casual malice in his face made Will's blood run cold.

The guard forced Will to his knees, and on a signal from Drettroth his hood was thrown back and his gag removed.

"Ah, Commander," Drettroth said mockingly. "It is so good of you to pay me another visit. I have often wanted to renew our acquaintance since our last all-too-brief meeting.

"Yes, do not fear," he added. "I know who you are, in spite of your vain attempt to disguise your appearance.

"Search him thoroughly," he commanded the guards. Many hands probed him roughly, covering every inch and seeking out anything he might have secreted in a hidden pocket. They found nothing. Drettroth nodded at the door, and the guards left.

"Forgive me, I have not introduced you to my own commander."

He turned to the other man. “Luzik, this is the recently appointed commander of the rabble of Arvenon. He goes by the name of Will Prentis, I am told. A commoner, like you.

“I see he has acquired a scar since I last saw him,” Drettroth mused. “That is certainly in keeping with a priest of our Dark Gods. The scar seems lonely, though, don’t you think, Luzik?”

Luzik came forward and grabbed Will’s chin roughly in one fist. Will averted his eyes as the evil face drew close to his own. Luzik’s rank breath almost made him gag.

“I see what you mean, My Lord. But that can soon be mended.”

Luzik whipped out a knife and slashed it viciously across Will’s other cheek, then wiped it clean on Will’s robe before putting it away. Blood ran down Will’s chin and dripped onto the floor of the tent.

The man stepped back to peruse his handiwork.

“Untidy lout!” he shouted. “You’ve befouled Lord Drettroth’s clean floor.” He slapped Will so hard on the side of the head that he fell over sideways.

Luzik dragged him back onto his knees again, and he knelt there, dazed and wretched. Warm blood trickled out of his ear, and a loud ringing dulled his hearing. His face stung from the open wound on his cheek.

“Twice you have interfered with my plans,” Drettroth spat. “You will not receive a third opportunity.”

Then he relaxed, and his voice took on a genial tone. “But I forget my manners. You must have many questions. I understand that you came here hoping to learn something of my plans.

“Before we examine what I have in mind, though, I regret that we will need to excuse Luzik. He has business to attend to. But I can promise you a much closer acquaintance with him tomorrow evening.”

Will did not like the look of the smile the two men exchanged.

Drettroth turned and nodded to his commander, who got up to go. As he walked out of the tent he backhanded Will across the head again, knocking him to the ground once more. He leaned down closer to Will’s still-ringing ear.

"That's just a small taste, scum!" he growled, his voice dripping with venom. Then with a parting leer he left.

"Guard!" Drettroth called peremptorily. One of the sentries came into the tent and bowed.

"Untie the hands of our guest. And give him water. We don't want him wilting before tomorrow's entertainment."

The guard untied him and left the tent, returning with a skin of water that he threw across to Will.

Drettroth stood, and with exaggerated courtesy waved Will to a chair beside a large table covered with maps. After a moment's hesitation, Will pulled himself off the floor and went to the chair, taking the skin with him.

Drettroth leaned across the table and selected a large map. It covered Arvenon, Castel, and the other kingdoms that flanked them. The map stretched south as far as the border of Lestanor.

He waved his hand over the seaward region of Arvenon, to the west. "Once I have annexed Arvenon, the Duchy of Erestor will become a separate country again. Historically it never belonged to Arvenon anyway. It will be ruled by one of your own nobles—after he has delivered Arnost to me as promised.

"He will not be popular, I fear." Drettroth chuckled. "He will be expected to recruit for me a large detachment of the fabled Erestorian cavalry. And you do have some excellent archers—I felt as though they were making a special effort to impress me at the ford. I'll be needing a company of archers from Erestor as well."

Drettroth again bared his teeth in a grimace he no doubt intended as a smile. Will wondered how he could speak so lightly of an event that resulted in the loss of so many of his own men.

"All of these recruits are going to see a great deal of heavy fighting," the Rogandan continued regretfully. "I wouldn't wonder if few ever return to honor their new ruler.

"And then there is also the annual tribute to consider. The new ruler will have to squeeze very hard indeed to extract that much gold from his subjects.

"He will find a way, though. Or I will replace him with someone more energetic."

Will was appalled to think of the price that his countrymen would pay for this treachery. And the traitor was an utter fool if he truly thought he could negotiate to his own advantage with the Rogandans.

Who could it be? Will rapidly ran through the possibilities. Pisander came at once to mind, with his connection to Erestor and his arrogance. But it could be anyone.

Then an awful thought occurred to him—could it be the duke? Surely not. The notion was absurd. He refused to even consider it.

"We are here." Drettroth stabbed a finger at a point on the map that boasted a tiny illustration of a city and the label 'Arnost'.

"If you had my men at your disposal, where would you take them next?"

Drettroth's smug inquiry sounded more rhetorical than genuinely curious. Will didn't bother to answer.

"West to Erestor? North to Castel? Both at once?" Drettroth sighed deeply. "It is difficult to choose between so many delightful alternatives," he lamented. "But I have made my decision. I will be sending some of my men west to Erestor. Others will stay here. In the morning, though, I, along with a large contingent of my army, will depart southward for Ranwood.

"Once we reach Ranwood some of my men will go on to Stonehold. I'm told it's a solid little fortress. Very poorly defended, though. My scouts have advised me that people are coming and going as if there was no war going on at all. These townspeople will soon discover otherwise.

"Ranwood and Stonehold will become important bases for securing Arvenon. Along with Arnost, of course."

Drettroth's self congratulation made Will squirm. To the Rogandan lord, this appeared to be a game. It wasn't just boasting—Drettroth was taunting him. He was playing with Will as a cat plays with a mouse. And there was no reason to hold back. He was freely handing out vital information, but there was nothing Will could do with any of it.

"Once Arnost has been yielded to Luzik on my behalf, he will remain for a time to carry out a very special task that I have given him. I intend to make an example of Arnost. Even you will have a role.

"I have been told how much your soldiers depend on you. Imagine how disheartened they will be when your lifeless body is discovered outside the gates of the city, horribly disfigured. The story will spread quickly, I'm sure."

Will worked hard to keep his face impassive. The truth was that he felt sick to his stomach.

"As for the soldiers in Arnost, they have opposed me, so all of them must die. None will be offered the privilege of serving in my army.

"Sadly, the citizens of Arnost will suffer a similar fate. The streets will run with their blood, except for a lucky few who will be allowed to flee in every direction to proclaim the fate of those who dare to oppose me."

So Drettroth did not yet realize that few people remained in Arnost except soldiers. He did not know everything, and the reminder gave Will new heart.

"Are you a religious person, Drettroth?" Will asked on impulse.

His question brought Drettroth up short. The brow of the Rogandan lord began to darken in anger at his captive's insolent familiarity. Then abruptly he threw back his head and laughed.

"You are a remarkable young man. Perhaps you have decided that I can do nothing worse to you than I am already planning. You are quite right, of course.

"But still it is a curious question. Why would a fly caught in a web ponder the metaphysical standing of the spider?

"I could almost wish you were leading an army for me. I am far too accustomed to being told what men think I want to hear—not one of my men is bold enough to say what he really thinks.

"But I could never trust you." He rounded on Will. "You must be Rogandan by birth—how else could you speak our language so well? Why then are you leading an Arvenian army? What made you turn on your countrymen?"

Seeing he could expect no answer from Will, Drettroth shrugged. "No matter. I know of an effective way to deal with traitors."

Will wished his betrayer in Arnost could hear this conversation.

"But I have not answered your question. Perhaps you have heard the rumors." Drettroth raised an eyebrow questioningly.

Will knew of no rumors and must have looked blank because Drettroth quickly continued.

"Apparently not. Some of my men have suggested that I was once a priest," he explained. "Such talk has no foundation in fact, although it is true that I have made a careful study of the Dark Gods.

"I have little time for the priests and their arcane rituals," he said with disdain. "They bore me.

"But I do believe in the Dark Ones," he averred fervently. "I have seen far too much to doubt their existence."

A haunted look came into Drettroth's eyes. "Do you believe in Malzakh the Destroyer?" he asked.

Will hesitated for a moment, then shook his head.

Drettroth's teeth showed in a grim rictus. "You will!" he promised. "Oh, you will. And very soon now."

Will averted his face in denial. He sincerely hoped that the Dark Gods were nothing more than an evil figment of Rogandan imagination. He flatly rejected them on the basis that such a horrible travesty of the purpose of life and death could not possibly be true.

Will could not help thinking that the nature of the Dark Gods went a long way toward explaining the character of the Rogandans. They believed that Nehrvina the Awful gave them life. When they were full of years she also took it back. Nehrvina satisfied her ravenous hunger by devouring the spirits of her children when they had thus been released.

Malzakh the Destroyer neither gave life nor took it away. He simply preyed on those who died an untimely death. Nothing but eternal terror awaited his victims. He did not devour their spirits entirely, but instead endlessly feasted on them in turn, allowing the passage of time to restore what he had taken before rending them again.

The only release came for those whose untimely deaths were especially undeserved. In time Nehrvina claimed back their souls, stealing them away when Malzakh was distracted, and consuming them herself.

The priests promised some relief, however, for the faithful who were lucky enough to be taken by Nehrvina. As a reward for a lifetime of worship, the Awful One placed their spirits for a time in Paradise, a place of unlimited pleasure, without pain or suffering. It was no eternity of bliss, though; eventually all must succumb to her insatiable appetite.

With such uncertain alternatives awaiting them, it was little wonder that the fear of death cast a constant pall over the lives of the Rogandans. Much of the energy they brought to life was spent in an effort to avoid dying.

And there was little incentive to behave well, apart from the fear of retribution from rulers or revenge from the wronged. They believed that the same fate would overtake the most depraved and the most decent, provided they lived to the same age. An early death was therefore the only real evil.

Not surprisingly, these beliefs made them indifferent soldiers. Rogandan rulers had responded by encouraging a popular sect which taught that death in battle was entirely undeserved, and that soldiers would therefore escape eternal torment in the clutches of Malzakh. Further, they would immediately be admitted to Paradise if their service was sufficiently wholehearted.

Nevertheless the shirking of Rogandan soldiers was proverbial. That was probably why Agon appointed leaders like Drettroth and why he in turn cultivated a thug like Luzik. With nothing but terror awaiting them beyond the grave, a more immediate source of terror was needed to drive Agon's soldiers forward into battle.

No, Will did not believe in the Dark Gods. His aunt had believed, though. He remembered the fear in her eyes as her final fever grew. As the prospect of an untimely death became ever more apparent she had even belatedly tried to appease Will. Unwilling to forget the depth of her cruelty toward him, he had reacted to her deathbed overtures with disgust. She deserved the fate she anticipated.

Will glanced across at Drettroth. "I myself intend to cheat Malzakh," the Rogandan lord asserted determinedly. "May his dreadful hunger instead be satisfied by the enemies of Rogand!

"Every true Rogandan believes in the Dark Gods. Except perhaps for Luzik. He is no believer—power is the only god he worships. He, too, will learn to see things differently in time, perhaps before many more winters have passed." He bared his teeth in a nasty smile.

Drettroth yawned hugely, and Will had to suppress himself from imitating his captor. "It is becoming late, and I have a long day ahead of me tomorrow. And I fear that I am keeping you awake.

"I regret that this will be our final meeting. I leave for Ranwood in the morning, and you must wait here for the return of Luzik.

"I trust that you have enjoyed our time together. If not, I am sure when you meet the Destroyer you will find yourself wishing that my hospitality had been greatly extended."

He bowed mockingly to Will and left the tent.

The candles in the tent burned low. Will tried to sleep but sleep eluded him. His face throbbed from the wound on his cheek, and all night he lay restless and regretful, tortured by the consequences of his own stupidity. The duke and Rufe had been right. He had been a fool to make this attempt. Even if he had not been betrayed, there was little chance he could have found his way to Drettroth's tent and learned anything useful in the course of one night.

There was a fine line between bravery and bravado, and he had crossed the line. He had leaned on his luck once too often, and now it had run out.

. . .

THE SUN ROSE AGAIN, and almost an entire day passed. Will had many weary hours at his disposal, and he took the opportunity to berate himself at his leisure. His courage dwindled away completely as the day progressed. He knew he had no hope.

He thought of his friends. The duke and his soldiers would grieve for him, but Rufe would miss him the most.

He thought, too, of Thomas, and wondered what would become of him and his stone. He remembered the day by the riverbank when he had slapped the stone from his friend's hand. He hadn't fully believed the story about the stone until Thomas described the dark haired youth lying dead in a pool of blood, and the father with the battle-ax. Then he knew it must be true. He wondered if Thomas realized that Will himself had slain the youth.

Yes, he had regrets. But for the most part his life had been full and rich, even if it had been short. He had aspired to lead the King's Guard, and he had become commander of the king's army. For a couple of days, anyway.

Now it was all ending. The same foolhardiness that propelled him to such heights had now become the cause of his downfall.

FROM THE MOMENT that Drettroth departed Will could hear guards constantly all around the tent, but no one approached him or even spoke to him. Occasional furtive glances outside showed that the tent was surrounded by men dressed in the same garb as Luzik. Will guessed that they were members of Drettroth's personal guard, or possibly Luzik's. He had no doubt that they knew what to do should the 'priest' attempt to escape.

When he became hungry he searched the tent thoroughly for food but found nothing to eat. He rationed the skin of water carefully to make it last until evening, even though he knew there was no real point to it.

The sun had sunk low in the sky before Luzik returned. He could hear the Rogandan commander shouting orders and the sounds of heightened activity outside. Still no one came for him, so he went to the entrance of the tent to see for himself what was happening. Being careful to stay out of sight, he peered cautiously outside.

"Round up more men," he heard Luzik calling to other members of the guard. He could see a crowd of soldiers beginning to gather around the low hill where the tent was sited. No doubt they were being called together for the evening's entertainment. A regular dose of random violence would cultivate their fear of Drettroth and his cronies.

"And make sure no priests are among them." Luzik jerked a thumb meaningfully in the direction of the tent. No doubt Luzik didn't want awkward questions when Will's turn came and the onlookers got to see a priest being put to death. Perhaps Luzik thought he could avoid any confrontation with the priests even while showing his soldiers he wasn't afraid to lay hands on one of them.

Then Will noticed a couple of captives, bound and standing miserably off to one side of the hill. They appeared to be Arvenians—probably peasants who were unlucky enough to be in the wrong place at the wrong time.

Moments later the first of the peasants was brought to Luzik. He stood silently before the muscle-bound monster. Will could see the fear on his face, but he did not plead for his life. Luzik's sword flicked back and forth until blood was flowing freely. Still the man made no sound. Disappointed, Luzik drew back his arm and cut him down as casually as a man might swat a fly.

The second peasant was pushed forward. He fell to his knees, begging loudly for mercy with a tremulous voice and many tears. Luzik probably did not understand a single word of Arvenian, but he took the fellow's meaning well enough and seemed delighted by his behavior.

Luzik began dancing around the man, leaning in closer from time to time to inflict wounds that caused pain but not death. Will prayed that the man would cease his noise and shorten his misery. But the fellow did not understand, and his pleas redoubled, punctuated now by wails of pain and terror. Luzik intensified his dance, glee evident on his face.

Then out of the corner of his eye Will noticed one of Luzik's guards capering around in a mocking imitation of his leader. Although the fellow was careful to stay out of Luzik's line of sight, the guards nearest the tent had seen it, too.

"Look at Suveg!" one of them whispered. They watched his antics for a moment.

"Thinks he's so clever, Malzakh bite him!" said the other.

"Ridiculing Luzik openly? He's a half-wit!"

"He's always hated Luzik."

The gathered soldiers didn't seem to have noticed Suveg, but most of Luzik's guards were now watching him instead of their leader.

"Look! Luzik's spotted him. Now he'll get it!"

The guard was right. Suveg desisted from his dance, but a moment too late. Luzik stood rooted to the spot, staring at him.

Luzik plunged his sword into the captive without ever taking his eyes from his mocker. The frantic pleading gave way to a long rattling sigh, and the captive's voice finally ceased.

Suveg took his leader's meaning. He stood uncertainly for a moment, then he turned and fled.

"After him!" Luzik bellowed. "Do not lay a finger on him, though. He's mine."

Guards took off after the man, Luzik following close behind.

"I'm not going to miss this." One of the two tent guards disappeared in the same direction, closely followed by his companion.

Will poked his head outside the tent and looked around. The soldiers still remained in position around the hill, bored and restless, but not moving away. None of Luzik's guards were anywhere in sight.

They had left Will unattended. He'd been offered a chance. A fool's chance, maybe, but still a chance. His courage flickered back into life. He probably had no more than a minute to act on it.

He stepped outside the tent and faced the soldiers. Every eye turned in his direction. They stood silent, watching to see what he would do.

He filled his lungs and thrust his arms wide. Then he opened his mouth to the sky and an unearthly sound issued forth from deep in his throat. The eerie noise grew in strength, carrying clearly in the late afternoon air.

As one man the soldiers fell to their knees and bowed low to worship.

20

The soldiers grumbled under their breath as members of Luzik's personal guard rounded them up and herded them toward the commander's tent. They had long since tired of these messy exhibitions of Luzik's barbarism, but none dared to risk his wrath by openly showing it.

Haldek went with them, reluctantly as ever. Not for the first time he wondered what he was doing camped outside a foreign city, surrounded by thousands of others who didn't want to be there either. It didn't help that they were led by men they universally feared and despised.

They had fought one battle so far, and it had been brutal. Haldek lost friends at the ford. Good friends. He himself had been driven multiple times into the attack, and he knew beyond doubt that he was very lucky to still be alive. How many other such battles could he survive?

The Arvenians had fought like demons. Their reckless ferocity unnerved him. Didn't they fear Malzakh? Perhaps they served a different god who was more merciful than the Destroyer.

His mind wandered back to his years of sentry duty, first at Agon's castle in Rog, later at the stronghold in the wilderness, then back at

Agon's castle again. Patrolling a wall at all hours of the night was never comfortable, but he now realized that he'd had it easy. He would choose sentry duty every time over fighting in battle. Only partially disabled soldiers and old men patrolled Agon's walls now, though. Every able-bodied man had been pressed into service in Drettroth's invasion army.

The soldiers bunched together, their eyes on Luzik. Haldek found himself right at the front of the crowd, almost directly in front of the action. Two peasants had been found for Luzik to play with. How could the ugly brute think it made him look good to carve up defenseless farmers in front of a crowd?

The first man died calmly and with real grace. Perhaps Nehrvina would honor his courage and rescue him from the Destroyer.

The second man showed himself craven. As Luzik toyed with the fellow, Haldek tried to imagine what it would be like to be trapped in such circumstances. He wondered how bravely he himself would die.

In the middle of it all, Luzik's attention abruptly shifted elsewhere, and he and his men vanished over the other side of the hill, apparently chasing one of their fellow guards. Haldek did not entirely understand why they had left, but it appeared that Luzik was settling an old score. The show seemed to be over for the evening, though, and Haldek waited impatiently for the commander to return and dismiss them.

Then a priest stepped out from the tent. Haldek groaned inside. Priests were even more frightening than Luzik.

Everyone knew that you didn't mess with them. They interceded with Nehrvina on behalf of the faithful, and if you found yourself in Malzakh's clutches you were going to need all the help you could get. Equally important, as a reward for their service the priests were destined to become gatekeepers in Paradise. If you were ever lucky enough to arrive there, you'd better hope you could find one of them willing to let you in.

Haldek spotted dried blood on the priest's face and cloak. He had apparently cut himself on one cheek, and he had a scar to match it on the other cheek as well, long since healed. It was unnatural the way the priests did that to themselves.

The man spread his arms and uttered the Call to Fear. Along with every man present, Haldek fell to his knees to worship. He did it without a second thought.

After the multitude had made obeisance, the priest cried out, "Rise, faithful servants of the Dark Gods."

The soldiers rose to their feet.

"All Hail, Terrible Nehrvina, Giver of Life and Dread Receiver of the Spirits of the Dead," intoned the priest.

"All Hail!" echoed the soldiers faithfully.

"Grant your servants long years in the land, to worship Your Awful Majesty."

"Long years!" they echoed fervently.

"Should our lives be cut short, deliver us from the feared hand of your Merciless Brother, we beseech you."

"Deliver us!"

"All Hail, Nehrvina!"

"All Hail!"

"All Hail, Nehrvina!"

"All Hail!"

The priest was warming to his work. He thrust his arms high to the heavens, and his voice rang out strong and true. The soldiers responded with increasing enthusiasm to his energetic delivery of the familiar ritual.

"All Hail, Fearsome Malzakh, Terror of the Living Spirits of the Dead."

"All Hail!"

"Satisfy your great hunger with the spirits of our enemies."

"Our enemies!" the soldiers cried.

"Do not imprison our spirits, but release us to your Gracious Sister, we humbly pray."

"Release us!"

Haldek bellowed heartily along with the rest of them, his spirits rising.

Then he noticed that Luzik had returned along with his guards. The commander at first seemed puzzled as he took in the scene, then angry. But after a moment he came and stood to one side of the priest, facing him with arms crossed and a smile of amusement on his face. He appeared to regard the holy ritual as a joke and the priest as nothing more than a clown.

Haldek stared at Luzik with a profound sense of violation. The sadistic leader was rightly feared by every soldier, but why should he be allowed to show disrespect to the gods?

He glanced around him. The priest continued to intone the ritual at the top of his voice, and the soldiers still responded wholeheartedly. But Haldek could see that others had noticed Luzik's behavior, too, and they were not pleased either.

The liturgy came to an end. Then, unusually, the priest threw back his head, and the strident Call to Fear rang out once more. The soldiers fell obediently to their knees and again bowed low.

Haldek raised his head and saw that everyone was not bowed as they should be. Luzik remained on his feet, his smile now more mocking than amused. Half of his guards had knelt with the soldiers. The others clustered nervously behind their leader.

The priest's arms began to shake violently. His eyes rolled back in his head until only the whites were visible. Haldek knew that the gods granted this kind of ecstatic trance only to the most devoted of their priests. He had seen it a couple of times before. In each case the priest had become the mouthpiece of the gods and pronounced some truly frightening judgments.

Those guards who were still on their feet fell trembling to their knees and bowed low to the ground. Luzik, though, appeared to be thoroughly entertained by the priest's behavior. He gave the impression that he couldn't wait to see what was going to happen next.

The priest slowly turned to Luzik and fixed him with his unseeing white eyes. Then a quivering finger moved slowly in the direction of the commander and singled him out.

A terrible voice issued from the throat of the priest. "Do...you... *believe*?"

Haldek waited breathlessly for Luzik to give an answer. The question seemed to take the commander by surprise. He opened his mouth, then glanced around at the expectant soldiers and shut it again.

What would he say? If he answered "Yes," then he must explain his insolence in standing during the Call to Fear. If he answered "No," his life was instantly forfeit.

Luzik gave no answer. He evidently sensed a dangerous mood in the men. Haldek felt it, too—a simmering anger was slowly bubbling its way to the surface.

"*Do*...you...believe?" the priest demanded.

Still there was no reply.

"Malzakh has been scorned. He is wrathful," the priest announced ominously.

The commander reached down for his sword, then snatched away his hand as a low growl escaped from hundreds of lips. Let him dare to lay a finger on the priest. Haldek licked his lips involuntarily at the prospect of witnessing—even participating, he thought recklessly—in the commander's demise.

The priest thrust out an arm imperiously toward the soldiers. "A mina!" he commanded.

He was going to invite the gods to pass judgment. Now it was certain that someone would die. A ripple of fear ran through the crowded mass of soldiery. Haldek looked at the face of the commander and thought he sensed a whiff of panic. Luzik had lost control of the situation. Malzakh hovered nearby, and the commander seemed to sense it.

A soldier pulled himself to his feet and placed a tiny halfpenny coin in the hand of the priest. The mina was the most common of coins, with a snake on one side, representing the gods, and a mouse on the other, representing the people. The priest was calling upon the gods to choose between himself, as their representative, and the rest. Surely the gods would vindicate the priest.

"Reveal the source of the blood guilt, Mighty Destroyer!" the priest cried, tossing the coin high into the air.

Every head came up to follow its progress. It fell to the ground and rolled a short distance before stopping. Several soldiers scrambled after it, and one raised it from the earth with trembling hands. “The mouse!” he cried.

Gasps escaped from the throats of hundreds of soldiers. The gods had pointed to the people.

“A peka!” demanded the priest.

A penny was thrust into his hand. One side held the head of the king, Agon, and the other a walled town. Haldek swallowed nervously as the priest invoked the name of Malzakh again and spun the coin high into the air. If it revealed the head of the king, then the guilt lay with the leaders of the army. If it revealed the town, then the masses were implicated.

Whole regiments had been put to the sword when such a coin toss went against them. Every man present held his breath as the penny fell to the earth.

Once again soldiers surrounded the fallen coin and bent over it, though none dared to pick it up. “The king,” a voice called at last, and the men erupted in relief at their escape.

The priest’s arm swept commandingly across Luzik and his men. Dozens of soldiers sprang up and encircled them at a distance, ready to prevent any escape.

“The coin,” the priest commanded. A soldier retrieved it and handed it to him.

One last time he invoked the name of the god. One last time he flung the coin high. This time it must choose between the leader and his men. If it revealed the walled town, every one of Luzik’s guards must die. If it revealed the king, the commander himself would become the victim.

The door of escape still remained ajar for Luzik. Haldek glanced across at the commander and saw him tense but rooted to the spot. He must have been a gambler—he was taking his chances. The priest had risked his own life on a toss of the coin, and Luzik appeared willing to do the same.

The coin spun lazily through the air, turning over and over. It landed, rolled, and came to a halt. Soldiers approached it reverently. Haldek's heart skipped a beat as one of the men raised his head to the eager throng. "The king!" he cried triumphantly.

"No!!! This man..." Luzik's cry of fury was drowned by a mighty roar as soldiers, and even his own guard, pressed forward to seize him. Fear lent him tremendous strength, and he burst free, only to be tackled to the ground by a writhing knot of enraged men. The soldiers would not be cheated.

Luzik's sword was removed and his arms pinned to his side. Haldek cheered with the rest of them as Luzik was dragged forward to face the priest. They stuffed a gag into his mouth, and men laughed in scorn at his frantic stifled attempts to speak.

Soldiers forced Luzik to the ground, and he lay struggling on his back with arms and legs pinned from every side. Although he twisted and turned he could not break free.

A curved blade was pressed into the priest's hand. His white eyes fluttered as he raised his hand to the sky.

"Receive your trophy, Dread Malzakh!" he cried, and the knife plunged down, once, twice, a third time.

Luzik's muffled screams of terror faded to a gurgle and ceased. Men cheered themselves hoarse. Hardened soldiers clung together, and some wept openly.

The sun sank abruptly below the hill, and Haldek became aware that he was cold. The soldiers began to disperse, their passion spent. Justice had been done, and they left satisfied.

A hand grasped Haldek's shoulder. He spun round and found himself looking into the eyes of the priest, now deceptively normal. He started as he saw a look of recognition flash across the priest's face. It made no sense, though. He didn't know the man—he had never seen him before.

"I need your help."

The priest, whose presence had been so commanding, now appeared weak and frail. He pointed, and they set off through the spreading dark in the direction he indicated, the priest leaning on Haldek's arm for support.

"You must take me to...to the gates of the pagan city."

"Surely not, holy one!" Haldek protested.

"Do not question the will of the Dark Ones," the priest returned weakly.

Haldek subsided and led him on meekly through the dark. The request of the priest baffled the soldier, but he knew better than to question one who had the very ear of the gods.

They moved ever more slowly as their journey progressed—the priest seemed spent after his ecstasy and his appeal to the gods. He leaned more heavily on the arm of Haldek. Occasionally soldiers looked at them curiously, but no one approached them.

After what seemed like hours they came at last to the final line of watch fires. A sentry challenged them rudely.

"You dare to question a priest?" Haldek retorted incredulously. The sentry mumbled an apology and waved them through.

They stumbled on until the gates of the city towered above them. The priest finally released his hold on Haldek's arm. "Leave me now," he commanded, his voice feeble with exhaustion. Haldek obediently stepped back away from him.

The priest took an uncertain step forward, then abruptly swooned and slumped senseless to the ground.

Haldek took one look at him, then turned tail and fled from the gates in terror.

21

Will woke to the cheerful sound of birds singing outside his room. Sunlight streamed in through a window over his bed. He had no idea where he was, and for a moment he could recall nothing of the immediate past. Then it all came rushing back: his capture, the conversation with Drettroth, his sleepless night and long day of waiting in the tent, the confrontation with Luzik, his invocation of the Dark Gods.

He realized he must now be in Arnost. He did not know how long he had slept, but his weariness had not left him entirely. His eyes still hurt, too, and he rubbed them gingerly.

He sat up and examined himself. The priestly robe had been removed, and he had been washed clean, but the scent of death seemed to linger in his nostrils. He had gone to the Rogandan camp an unbeliever, but he knew now beyond doubt that the Dark Gods were real. Had he simply brought down an evil man—well deserving of death—by his own bold cleverness and three lucky coin tosses, or had he been the unwitting tool of the Dark Gods, following a purpose and a plan beyond his comprehension?

He felt again the blade in his hand, rising and falling, rising and falling. He had called down the Dark Gods, and they had responded.

He knew that the ecstatic trance had somehow gone beyond his own skillful pantomime. He remembered the fierce joy that suffused him as he struck Luzik, and knew that it had not been natural. He remembered the commander writhing in terror beneath him, an unbeliever no longer. He had wielded the knife on Malzakh's behalf, and he felt sure that Luzik knew it.

When it was over, he had been close to collapse. Without the help of the Rogandan soldier he knew he would never have made it back to the city. How strange that he had turned to the very person who helped him at the Rogandan stronghold in the wilderness. The man did not recognize him, of course. The scars, the robe, and above all his masquerade as a priest ensured that.

He had been left utterly spent, sapped of all strength. His lack of sleep did not account for his weakness. The brush with the Dark Gods seemed to have drained away his life energy, leaving him exhausted and empty. And darkness had seeped in to fill the void.

Even now the horror of it all still filled his mind. In the fresh light of day, Will wondered how he could ever be clean and free from the darkness again. He covered his face with his hands.

A knock on the door broke across his grim thoughts.

"May I come in, Commander?" The duke stood in the entrance way, smiling down at him.

"My Lord Duke!" He bounded out of bed, and immediately sank back down again, unable to stay upright.

"Are you wounded?" the duke asked, concern on his face.

"No, My Lord, just a little lightheaded," Will replied, feeling foolish.

At that moment the cathedral bells began to peal loudly. Will looked out of the window, alarmed. "What's happened?" he asked.

"You've returned," said the duke with a smile. "Every person in the city is celebrating."

Will stared at him in disbelief. "They're ringing the bells for me?"

"They would have rung them earlier," the duke confirmed, "except I insisted they wait until you were awake."

"How long have I slept?"

"All night and half a day. It's early afternoon."

Will groaned. "We have so little time! We cannot afford to delay." He stood again, more slowly this time. "We need to convene a meeting of the Council, My Lord, so that I can share what I have learned. And I need to see Rufe Sarjant. And Thomas Stablehand. I fear I won't be able to stay here for long."

The duke frowned. "Don't expect me to approve any new forays into the Rogandan camp," he said decidedly. "Given the time you were gone and the condition you were in when you were found, I'm guessing we're lucky to have you back at all."

Will made no reply.

"What happened in there?" the regent demanded.

Will felt a shadow pass across his eyes. "I will not willingly talk about the details, My Lord. But you are right about being lucky. I am fortunate to be alive.

"I do know what Drettroth is planning now, though, and we must find a way to prevent him."

The duke nodded. "I will call together the lords as you request. We will meet before the day ends. I will also call for Rufe and Thomas. But first you must tell me what you have learned about Drettroth."

"Gladly, My Lord."

Will quickly told of his conversation with Lord Drettroth and the departure of the Rogandan lord with a large part of his army. He outlined Lord Drettroth's plans and made it clear that no town or city in Arvenon remained safe. The circumstances around his capture and subsequent escape he barely mentioned. He said nothing either of Luzik or of the traitor. But he asked the duke to double the guard on the city gates immediately.

When Will had finished, the duke studied him closely for a long moment without speaking. "I can see you have not told me everything, Will," he concluded. "Far from it. Nevertheless, I trust you, and I will allow you to choose your own time for speaking more freely.

"And in spite of my resistance to what seemed to me a fool's errand, I freely acknowledge that you once again proved to be right. You made it back, and with the information you went there for."

Will responded with a tight smile. "I do recognize that it was foolish of me to make the attempt, My Lord, and I promise you I will be more cautious in the future."

"I am gratified to hear you say it," the duke replied.

"You passed lightly over your escape," he continued. "Yet it is obvious to me that much more could be said. Rufe reported that he heard a disturbance in the Rogandan camp at sundown, not long before you appeared.

"He never gave up hope, you know. He watched all night, all day, and into the next evening. It was he who found you at the gates. He saw you arrive, and he thought he saw a Rogandan soldier helping you. The fellow bolted the minute you arrived at the gate."

Will's thoughts were drawn once more to the Rogandan. It had been so surprising to encounter him again.

"I imagine there is a tale here well worth the telling," said the regent. "It seems your legendary luck has brought you through again, no doubt with the help of your own considerable resourcefulness.

"I will arrange for food and refreshments to be brought to you. Give yourself time to recover before you attempt anything more. I will send for you when the Council has been convened. And I will arrange for Rufe and Thomas to come to you soon."

"I am grateful, My Lord."

The duke paused and studied Will again for a moment. "I don't know what lies behind your other request, but the guard on the city gates will be doubled at once, and they will be instructed to be especially alert."

Will thanked the duke again, and bowed deeply as he left the room. He did not believe for a minute that the regent could be the traitor. But he knew instinctively that it was never wise to assume anything.

Already he was planning his next moves. He must leave the city as soon as possible and find a way to get to Ranwood and Stonehold ahead of Drettroth's army. He would entrust the preparations to Rufe.

But first he needed to expose the traitor. The city would never be safe until he did. For that task he needed the help of Thomas and his stone.

"CHOOSE FOUR MEN, Rufe, and make sure they're ready to leave at a moment's notice," Will commanded. "I need hardy travelers and good fighters, equally proficient with the bow and the sword. And excellent horsemen, too." The rapid flow of instructions left Rufe looking dazed.

Thomas had rarely seen Will so grim. He wondered if his friend might be angry with him for some reason.

"Thomas will choose the mounts later, including a spare. I want seven horses, Thomas, built for endurance but capable of speed," Will continued sternly.

A man in the livery of the duke entered the room and bowed. "I bring a message for the commander from the regent," he announced importantly. Will stepped aside to receive the message.

Rufe leaned over to Thomas with a grin on his face. "Don't take it personally, Thomas. I've seen him like this before," he confided. "It seems to happen whenever he gets himself a new scar."

He again assumed a serious countenance as Will dismissed the duke's messenger and rejoined them, but still managed to fire off a wink. Thomas, grateful for Rufe's cheerful encouragement, couldn't suppress a smile.

Will caught him smiling and looked back and forth between the two of them for a moment, his expression unreadable.

"I've just been called to the Council of Lords," he finally told them. "I need you to accompany me, Thomas."

"Me?" Thomas asked incredulously, certain he must have misheard.

"Yes. I'll explain more on the way there."

They set off with Will leading, striding along with restless determination in spite of his limp. "When we get to the meeting, try to stay out of sight, Thomas. Don't say anything. If anyone asks what you're doing there, I'll handle it.

"I'm bringing you to the Council for a reason. One of the lords is a traitor." Before Thomas even had a chance to register his shock, Will plowed on. "I need you to find out who it is. Use your stone."

"But...the stone...it isn't reliable!" Thomas sputtered. "Usually it doesn't show me anything at all."

Will brushed aside the objection. "You found out about the Rogandans at the gate."

"Yes, but that was an accident. I mean, I didn't control it. It just happened."

"Well, I don't have any other options. I must find out who it is. And I'll need you to help me get some proof, too."

Thomas, already nervous at the thought of appearing at the Council uninvited, now became thoroughly alarmed. Will's expectations were completely unrealistic.

"Don't worry about it," Will said casually, apparently guessing at his thoughts. "It'll work out."

Thomas followed Will dejectedly, like a whipped cur trailing its master. Fortunately, when they arrived at the meeting no one even noticed Thomas—the attention of the lords was entirely upon Will. Such a hubbub greeted his arrival that the duke was forced to rise to call them to order.

"My Lords," he shouted. "Please! One at a time."

As the din subsided, the Earl of Pisander spoke up. "I am sure I speak on behalf of us all when I say that it is gratifying to see your safe return, Commander." The other lords echoed the sentiment, and Will acknowledged it with a bow.

"Commander," began the duke, "please tell us what you learned at the Rogandan camp."

"My Lord Duke, My Lords." Again Will bowed. "Almost the first thing I learned was that there is a traitor among us. I was betrayed."

His statement was greeted with an uproar. Once again the regent called them to order, but this time it took longer for calm to be restored.

"That is a serious charge, Commander. Do you have proof?" one of the nobles asked, frowning.

"Not yet, My Lord."

"Did you learn the name of this supposed traitor?" another asked.

"No. His name was not mentioned," Will admitted.

"I don't have time for this!" Pisander said disgustedly, rising from his chair with open contempt on his face.

"Do you have another more pressing engagement, Pisander?" asked the duke pointedly. Pisander glowered, but he sat back down.

"Perhaps you could tell us something of Drettroth's plans," suggested the duke.

Will accepted the duke's change of direction and began outlining what he had heard. As Will spoke, Thomas fiddled with the drawstring of his pouch, trying to remain inconspicuous. He finally got his hand into the pouch and grasped hold of the stone. He scanned the faces in the room, willing the stone to show him something, anything. It was useless.

Will continued, with frequent interruptions and interjections. Now that he had made his accusation, the goodwill shown him at the start of the meeting had greatly diminished.

In spite of the urgency of discovering the traitor, Thomas found his mind wandering. One of the nobles was regularly popping something into his mouth when he thought no one else was watching. Thomas watched more closely, trying to catch what it was. It looked like dried dates. Thomas had seen such delicacies at the market. They were rare and expensive—from Lestanor or somewhere like it. Where would a noble find dried dates during a siege? He must have hoarded a supply.

Another of the nobles constantly scratched his scalp. Thomas harbored a perverse satisfaction at the thought that even lords suffered from head lice.

A third noble, the man the duke had called Pisander, was hiding something in his cloak. Thomas started. How did he know that? He released the stone and saw nothing. He grasped it again, and once more the impression became clear. He was sure of it. He focused all his attention on the man.

Pisander continued to participate in the conversation, but Thomas perceived that one thing only dominated his mind—the parchment secreted in his cloak. It worried him, and it excited him, and his thoughts returned constantly to the urgent need to keep it safe and undetected. Above all he feared losing it.

And there was something more on the edges of his mind. Thomas could not establish the precise reason, but Pisander wanted the meeting to end, and to end quickly. There were pressing things he needed to do.

"I'm sure this is all valuable information if you're a soldier. But I can't see what relevance it has to us," Pisander was saying. "I propose that the commander and the duke—and Ranauld, of course—go away and discuss it together. Come up with a strategy, and call another meeting later for us to consider it." He rose once again from his chair as though the matter was now settled and the meeting at an end.

"Sit down, Pisander!" the duke ordered irritably. "The meeting will not finish until I say it's finished."

Thomas looked across at Will, trying desperately to catch his eye. Will's attention seemed to be fully engaged in the interaction with the nobles. He was looking everywhere except at Thomas.

Other nobles had become restless, too. It appeared that soon the duke would call the meeting to an end. Thomas became desperate. He coughed.

A couple of the lords looked in his direction, but still Will did not notice him. "Who's he?" one of them demanded, pointing at Thomas. "What's he doing here?"

All heads turned in his direction. Remembering the murderous scrutiny of the Rogandan intruder at the city gates, Thomas had the presence of mind to snatch his hand from his pouch before meeting anyone's eyes.

He looked up and found Pisander staring at him suspiciously, eyes narrowed. "Boy!" Pisander called. "What do you have in your pouch? Bring it here at once. Something of mine went missing recently. Something valuable. It's small, but it's an heirloom."

The mention of the word *heirloom* aroused Will's attention immediately. He looked across at Thomas sharply. Thomas stood still, nervous and shaking, his eyes fixed pleadingly on his friend.

"I'm speaking to you!" bellowed Pisander. He rose from his chair and began moving toward Thomas. Will got there first.

As he drew close he shot Thomas a questioning look. Thomas leaned in swiftly to his ear. "He's got something hidden in his cloak!" he whispered urgently. "A parchment."

"Who?" asked Will blankly.

"Him! Pisander!" hissed Thomas as the earl stormed up to them.

Will positioned himself in front of Thomas. Pisander glared at him, but Will refused to budge. He addressed the regent without ever taking his eyes off Pisander. "My Lord Duke," he said calmly. "May I suggest that everyone returns quietly to their seat?"

"Get out of my way, you upstart commoner!" spat Pisander.

"Return to your seat, Pisander!" commanded the duke. "Or if you prefer, my guards can arrange it for you," he added caustically.

Pisander stood staring venomously at Will for a moment, a look of pure hatred on his face. Then he turned to go. As he did, he stabbed a finger directly at Thomas. "Your turn will come!" he promised. Thomas could not keep himself from trembling.

Will walked across to the duke and spoke quietly into his ear for a long minute. The duke nodded, and Will returned to his position in front of Thomas.

"The commander has a request," the regent announced. "I expect every one of you to comply with it."

Will wasted no time. "My Lords, could each of you please remove your cloak and place it on the table in front of you? The cloaks will be briefly examined, then returned to you shortly."

His words caused a sensation. Several nobles were on their feet in an instant, complaining loudly about the insolence of the request. Pisander shoved back his chair and drew himself erect. "I will not tolerate this any longer," he announced and strode purposefully to the door.

Will nodded to the guards standing at either side of the door, and they crossed their spears, preventing the noble from leaving. "This is an outrage!" he fumed.

"Remove his cloak," Will commanded. A comical struggle ensued between the writhing earl and four guards as they attempted without success to remove the garment. Pisander protested vigorously at the top of his voice throughout the entire process.

After watching for a few moments, Will walked over to the guards. "Hold his arms," he commanded. They did so, holding the earl steady as Will poked his hand methodically around the folds of the cloak. Pisander became increasingly frantic as the search progressed, shouting threats at Will, the guards and even his fellow nobles, who observed the proceedings wide-eyed but did nothing.

Finally Will withdrew his hand triumphantly and held up a large parchment. Pisander went pale, but bellowed even more loudly, "How dare you! Return that to me this instant. That document is sensitive. It is to be seen only by the king!"

Will handed the parchment to the duke, who opened it and began reading to himself. His face grew hard, and he rounded on Pisander. "So is this how you demonstrate your allegiance to your king?" he asked quietly.

Then he addressed the assembled nobility. "My Lords, I will read this letter to you, and you can draw your own conclusions."

"No!" Hearing Pisander start up again, Will gathered up the earl's cloak and shoved the end of it into his mouth. An urgent mumbling continued, but the bellowing ceased.

"*To the Earl of Pisander,*" the duke began. "*Now that we have your commander in our custody, we are entirely satisfied as to your good will. He will be dealt with appropriately.*

"*This letter is your guarantee of safe conduct when our forces take over the city. Show it to my commander, Luzik, when you open the gates to him as promised. Your reward will be delivered only when Arvenon is entirely under our control.*"

"The reward in question," Will broke in bitterly, "was to rule Erestor as a Rogandan puppet. Drettroth plans to make it a separate kingdom again. Pisander was expected to raise armies for Drettroth and bleed the duchy dry to pay tribute to Agon."

The duke resumed reading from the letter. "*One final matter,*" he continued. "*I am searching for a small trinket that was stolen from me and taken to your country. It is a small stone, blue and purple in color—an old heirloom of no consequence to anyone but me. If you return it you will be richly rewarded with gold.*"

At the mention of the stone, Will again directed a sharp glance at Thomas. Thomas could see others staring at him, too, and one or two glanced curiously at his pouch.

"The letter is signed *Drettroth,*" concluded the duke, "and marked with his seal." He turned to Pisander with a look that spoke of death.

Pisander spat the cloak from his mouth and fell to his knees. "Have mercy, My Lord! I meant no harm—Drettroth misunderstood my intentions."

The duke looked down on him with disgust. "I am no longer surprised that we heard nothing of the Rogandan invasion. It must have taken a lot of effort on your part to keep it quiet. And I wonder about the fate of those agents who mysteriously went missing.

"You'll die for this, Pisander, I promise you. And soon, too. But we'll extract every last detail from you first." He turned to the guards. "Take him to the dungeons!" he ordered.

"I WONDER how Drettroth came to know of your stone?" Will looked at Thomas wonderingly. With the traitor unmasked, the commander had hurried him out of the meeting as quickly as he could.

Thomas shrugged. "I don't know," he said miserably.

"Unfortunately, some of the nobles probably suspect you have the stone that Drettroth is searching for. And after what just happened in there, a few may even guess what the stone is capable of. I regret to say I am not certain they can be trusted to keep it to themselves.

"I am truly sorry, Thomas. It is my fault that your secret has been put at risk."

Thomas could think of nothing to say.

"You are no longer safe here. You know that Rufe and I will be leaving the city soon. I can't command you—you're not a soldier—but I invite you to join us. Our path will be difficult and dangerous, but nowhere is safe in Arvenon anymore."

Thomas brightened at once. It was the best news he'd heard in a long time. "I'll come with you!" he said enthusiastically.

Will looked surprised, but seemed to accept the reply at face value. "Good, that's settled, then. I wanted to ask you anyway, but didn't think it was fair. I will admit that the stone could prove useful to us. And your skill with horses will be very welcome.

"Choose us some mounts, Thomas. There will be seven in our party now, and I need a spare mount, so we will want eight horses. I will join you again later. But first I must speak with the duke."

"It is necessary for me to leave again, My Lord." Will stood with the duke on a castle battlement overlooking the city.

The duke sighed. "I have been expecting this conversation."

"The fate of the kingdom will not be decided here. I must get to Ranwood and Stonehold ahead of Drettroth."

"We don't have enough men for you to fight your way through the Rogandan siege, Will. And their commander—Luzik wasn't it?—will be doubly on the lookout now that you've escaped."

"We don't need to worry about Luzik, My Lord. He is dead. I killed him myself."

The duke looked startled. "I suppose I shouldn't be surprised," he finally managed.

"They will not remain leaderless for long, but I am hoping they might be less vigilant than usual. And I think we can arrange a distraction for them at short notice. I am planning to slip past them in the confusion."

"Your departure would be a major loss for us. I imagine Ranauld can take charge of our defense, though. He is a capable man." The duke sounded resigned.

"He would be my choice, too."

"You're right, of course, Will. Your abilities are wasted here. I will quickly draw up letters of introduction. Your appointment as commander of the king's army will not be limited to command at Arnost."

"Thank you, My Lord."

"How many men will you take with you?"

"Just six others. A small group will travel faster and avoid detection more easily."

"Rufe?"

"Yes. And Thomas."

"A wise decision, for his own sake," the duke returned shrewdly.

"And four other soldiers hand picked by Rufe."

The regent nodded his acquiescence. "Be careful, Will," he warned. "No one has unlimited luck, not even you. And we cannot afford to lose you."

Will bowed deeply and took his leave.

THOMAS STOOD BESIDE HIS HORSE, stroking its neck and speaking to it quietly. The animal tossed its head and nickered softly in response. He had chosen a large bay stallion for himself, and he was looking forward to finding some even ground where he could give the stallion its head.

He wore a long waterproof riding cloak and a wide-brimmed leather hat found for him by Rufe. The guardsman told him that the outfit made him look older, and he was trying to effect a manner of casual indifference. He actually felt young and very self-conscious.

Rufe and his four new companions waited nearby. All of them had eaten and drunk their fill and loaded the saddlebags of their horses with supplies. The other soldiers wore swords at their waists and carried long bows slung across their shoulders. Quivers filled with arrows bristled on their backs.

"Who is the spare horse for, Rufe?" one of the soldiers asked.

"I don't know," he replied. "I asked Will the same question, but he wasn't in a talkative mood. I guess we'll find out soon enough."

While they waited, Thomas glanced up at the sky. Clouds covered it completely. Neither the moon nor any stars were visible. It was as good a night as any for sneaking away from the city.

Abruptly Will joined them. "Are you all ready?" he asked.

"Yes," Rufe replied on their behalf.

"Good. Introductions can wait until later. A diversion has been prepared for the benefit of the Rogandans. We will leave soon after it starts. Stay to the right when we pass through the gates, and keep me in sight. If we meet any Rogandans, leave the talking to me. Thomas, please lead the spare horse."

They made their way to the city gates and waited quietly beside them. Before long, fireballs began sailing overhead in the direction of the Rogandan camp. Will had called upon the new long range catapults, and the near side of the enemy encampment was under attack. Soon distant cries carried to them on the night.

The sounds of confusion spread, and still Will waited. Then finally he called softly to the gatekeepers, and the gates swung open. The small company rode swiftly through the gates and disappeared into the darkness.

THEIR DEPARTURE WAS REPORTED to the duke as he stood on the battlements. He dismissed the messenger and peered out into the gloom, trying irrationally to catch a glimpse of Will's party in the distance.

After a time he abandoned the attempt and stared off into the west. Would he ever see Erestor again?

The duke sighed and closed his eyes for a moment. War was for the young and the bold, a time for daring deeds and feats of renown. All he wanted was a warm fire and a quiet life in his home far away.

He sighed again, then climbed down the stairs and headed for his bed.

22

Thomas stood up in the saddle, flexing the muscles in his back and stretching his legs. After a few hours on horseback he was beginning to feel stiff. The going had been slow and frustrating, and he found himself longing to break out into the open for a canter.

Once clear of Arnost the riders had briefly swung north and soon found themselves climbing steadily. After about an hour they had swung west, and by the time a couple more hours had passed they were heading directly south. They encountered no one; the Rogandan besiegers seemed entirely unaware of their departure. The almost total darkness had aided their escape, but now it hampered their progress as they picked their way slowly across uneven ground.

Thomas had no idea where they were going, and didn't care. All the ties that bound him to Arnost had gradually been severed. Between the death of Ben, the departure of his mother, and the new coolness between him and his father, he had begun to feel like a stranger in his own city. The upheavals associated with the siege only made it worse. With Will and Rufe leaving as well, nothing remained for him there. The city had become a place of confinement, with growing danger to him both from without and from within. By some mysterious means Drettroth was aware of the stone, and even some of the Arvenian nobles may have seen enough to guess at its secret. No, he was delighted to be gone.

The night was well advanced before Will allowed them to rest. They came to a halt within a stand of pines, although the trees offered little protection from the biting wind. None of them suggested a fire—Rogandan soldiers might be patrolling anywhere, and they could ill afford to take chances.

Once the riders had seen to their horses, Rufe distributed some dried meat, and they huddled together chewing on it and sharing a skin of wine.

"You all know Rufe, and I'm sure you know Thomas, our horse master," Will began. Thomas felt himself coloring at the suggestion that he would be known by strangers. He seriously doubted that these men would ever have heard of him. Thankfully his embarrassment would go unnoticed in the dark.

"Rufe, please introduce our new companions," he continued.

Rufe pointed first to a big man with broad shoulders. "This is Ander. He's from Erestor originally." Thomas couldn't see his features in the dark, but he remembered dark hair and a round face from their time waiting for Will at Arnost.

"Glad to be with you," Ander offered, "and hoping I can be of some use. Once I find out what we're planning to do, that is." He apparently followed his comments with a grin, because Thomas could see teeth glimmering in the dark. Will didn't respond.

After a brief pause, Rufe pointed to a thin man with an angular face and drawn cheeks. "This is Nestor. Everyone calls him Nes. He's from Arnost." Nestor appeared to nod his head by way of acknowledgment, but remained silent.

"And finally, the twins: Rellan and Kuper." He pointed out their lithe forms. "They're also from Erestor."

Thomas peered at them curiously. They had the same lean figures, but from his observations earlier in the evening he would not have picked them as twins. They bowed slightly. Like Nestor, they didn't speak, although Rellan noticed Thomas staring and offered him a grin and a wink. Thomas quickly averted his gaze, embarrassed.

"We're going to rest a while." Will's matter-of-fact tone almost made it sound like a routine training exercise. "Tomorrow a guide will be joining us. He'll ride the spare horse."

Ander spoke up. "A guide? Do we need one? Many of us know our way around. I for one have traveled widely in Arvenon."

"I have also traveled extensively, both within Arvenon and beyond," Will replied. "But this guide is said to be without equal. There may be times when it could cost us our lives if we choose the wrong path. And wasting even a single day could cost the kingdom dearly, if it happens at the wrong time."

Ander said nothing further.

"Rellan and Kuper can take turns at watching. The rest of you get some sleep while you can. We will leave before dawn."

THOMAS WAS unused to sleeping out of doors on hard ground and could not find a comfortable position. The others apparently had no such difficulty; he soon found himself surrounded by the sound of snoring.

Eventually weariness overcame his discomfort, and he felt himself beginning to drift off. To his own great surprise, a single thought dominated his mind as sleep gradually overtook him: he hadn't said goodbye to his father.

THOMAS WAS STARTLED from sleep by vigorous shaking of his shoulder. A rough hand clamped down firmly across his mouth while a voice hissed urgently in his ear. "Sshhhh!"

Instantly alert and dimly recognizing the sharp features of Nestor, Thomas suppressed the urge to struggle against the hand that restrained him. Harsh voices sounded from beyond the tree line—not close, but not far away, either.

He lay still until Nestor released him, then rose quickly and silently and made his way to the horses. Some of them were restless, and he went among them speaking softly to them. The horses settled even as the voices became more distant and faded away. By now his eyes had adjusted to the darkness, but he could still see very little in the pre-dawn gloom.

Thomas headed toward a low mumble of voices nearby. His other companions huddled around Will as their leader fired off instructions.

The meeting apparently finished as he arrived. Seeing Thomas join them, Will turned to him. “Stay with the horses, Thomas—don’t let them wander. We will return soon.”

With that, Will, Rufe, and the other men vanished into the night. Thomas returned to the horses, and settled down to wait.

The hours dragged by. At one point, early in his vigil, Thomas thought he heard a distant shout, but couldn’t be sure. There was no other sign of his companions. Eventually the sky began to lighten as dawn approached, but still there was no sign of the men returning.

Thomas became increasingly anxious as time passed. What if they had all been killed? For the first time in his life, Thomas found himself confronted with the prospect of being totally alone. He had fled with barely a second thought from the only home he had ever known, but he knew he could never fend for himself out here. Without Will and Rufe he would be utterly helpless.

The stone had brought him here. Once again he asked the unanswerable question: why him? Why was he the one who found it? He thought of it as ‘his’ stone, but he knew it didn’t belong to him. It wasn’t even his secret anymore. The Rogandan commander at least was aware of it. And wanted it badly.

Did it actually belong to Drettroth? He doubted it. The Rogandan’s reference to his ‘heirloom’ had echoed his own old lie so closely. No, somehow he felt sure that the stone didn’t truly belong to anyone. He understood only too well, though, the desire to possess it, and what it could lead to.

He was struck by a sudden and disturbing thought—was it possible that this whole war was somehow connected to the stone?

. . .

THE SUN HAD CLEARED the top of the trees before his companions returned. Thomas was relieved beyond words to see them, but his discomfort did not leave him. The world had become frightening and unpredictable, and he no longer knew his place in it. Surrounded by wide open spaces, all he could see was how small he really was.

Somehow he had to find his way through. Friends counted for something. And Will Prentis and Rufe Sarjant were no ordinary friends.

"What happened?" he asked Will.

"We followed the Rogandans back to the main force. There were a lot of them, and we had to be careful to avoid being seen." Will appeared matter-of-fact about it. "I went in close to hear what they were saying," he added.

"Did you hear anything useful?"

"Not much. It was mostly the grumbling you hear from soldiers anywhere," Will replied, briefly tossing a glance in the direction of his own men. "I did get a rough idea of the direction they're headed in, though."

Thomas must have looked worried, because Will added, "I doubt we'll see anything more of them for a while.

"We need to pick up the pace," he concluded. "They're on foot, but they're moving more quickly than I expected."

THEY RODE HARD MOST of that day. Apparently Will now valued time more than he feared detection, at least for the moment. Their path at last took them across open ground where the horses could run, and Thomas gave the stallion its head. For a time he forgot his troubles as the countryside rolled away effortlessly beneath the hooves of his bay.

By the time the sun had set they were climbing steadily, up and up through a succession of foothills. It was completely dark by the time they ascended a steep and winding path that led to a monastery, set on the shoulder of a small mountain. Seeing what lay before them, Ander mumbled something fiercely under his breath and spat in the direction of the walls.

Will dismounted and approached the entrance. Calling loudly, he banged the pommel of his sword hard on the large wooden gate, barred and bolted against the night.

For a time there was no response. Then a voice called out faintly from within, "Who travels abroad, and why do you disturb the peace of this house of God?"

"Open in the king's name," Will called back. "I am here on the king's business, and it will not wait! The sooner you let us in, the sooner we will be on our way. Open up, I say!"

After a delay Thomas heard the sounds of bars removed and heavy bolts drawn back. Finally the gate swung open, and an old man in the habit of a monk stood before them. A frayed rope belt secured a well-worn robe to his wiry frame, and a long gray beard flowed freely down over his chin. His physical presence might not have been commanding, but a pair of bright and intelligent eyes peered out at them from behind the flaming torch he held before him.

"Welcome, travelers! My name is Brother Elias, and I welcome you to the Monastery of St. Rodrig the Martyr. Come in out of the cold. Enjoy some refreshment before a fire." He bowed and swept the torch inward, pointing toward a group of dark buildings. As they came inside the monastery walls, two monks greeted them and led away their horses to a stable that hugged the wall beside the gates.

They followed Brother Elias to a low structure topped by a large chimney from which smoke billowed forth invitingly. Once they were inside, two other monks appeared and, without instruction, silently set about preparing food and drink while their older companion saw to the comfort of Will's company. They soon found themselves seated on low benches facing a sturdy wooden table beside a roaring fire. They were served bread and cheese along with a thick vegetable gruel ladled from a steaming pot over the fire. The food was very good, and with a full stomach and surrounded by the warmth of the fire, Thomas found his head beginning to sag with weariness.

Brother Elias must have noticed, because he turned to Will and said to him, "Mattresses filled with fresh straw will be brought for you all, and warm blankets. You may spend the night in such comfort as we can offer, here before the great fire."

The monk's offer sounded very appealing indeed to Thomas. He was not alone, either—Kuper visibly relaxed, and Rellan permitted himself a long sigh of anticipation.

Will, though, had other ideas. "I thank you for your kindness, but our business cannot wait. I must speak with Brother Vangellis. I believe he is staying here?"

Brother Elias appeared troubled. "Why do you wish to speak with him?"

"My business is with him alone," Will replied, his face betraying no hint of his intentions.

The monk paused for a long minute, then nodded to one of the Brothers, who disappeared into the night.

They waited for what seemed like hours. Then the monk returned. He bowed to Brother Elias. "I was unable to rouse him."

"Perhaps your business can wait until the morning," Elias suggested, turning to Will.

Will shook his head emphatically. "It cannot. If you are unable to rouse him, I will do it gladly," he said bluntly.

Brother Elias looked alarmed. He turned back to the monk. "Perhaps you could try a little harder," he suggested. The man bowed once again and left the room.

Eventually he reappeared, accompanied by an overweight monk who staggered into the room—awake, but only just. The new arrival stood on his feet unsteadily for a moment and looked about him. He opened his mouth as if to say something, then clamped it shut again. Finally he slumped down onto a bench, glancing around uncomprehendingly. He was clearly very drunk.

"Allow me to introduce you to Brother Vangellis," said Elias gently. Thomas glanced at the old monk in surprise. He might have expected the man to be angry—surely Vangellis was bringing disrepute to his order. But instead Thomas sensed only compassion in his voice. Thomas shook his head. He had never understood the ways of the religious.

At the sound of his name, Vangellis stood again, attempting an exaggerated bow before flopping back down onto his bench with a self-mocking smile. The other travelers gazed at him, some with amusement and some with disinterest. Ander stood and stared, making no attempt to disguise his contempt.

Will got up and walked over to him. “My name is Will Prentis,” he said. “I command the armies of the king, and I need your help.”

“How...can...such as *I*...help...such as *you*?” Vangellis paused as though checking to make sure it had come out right, then, apparently pleased with his efforts, grinned expansively.

“You must come with us, as a guide,” Will said.

Vangellis smiled again, weakly this time. “A mish...TAKE. You have the wrong *man*,” he said, slowly and carefully articulating each word.

“There is no mistake, I assure you,” Will replied.

“With regret, then, I musht decline your mosht generous offer.” Vangellis slurred, then paused and nodded, apparently to himself.

Ander could hide his disgust no longer. “You cannot be serious, Will!” he burst out. “This drunkard? Guide *us*?!” Shocked at Ander’s disrespect toward his commander, Rufe got to his feet and glared at him. Ander saw it and quickly subsided.

Will ignored him. “We have brought a horse for you,” he said to Vangellis. He turned to the twins. “He may need some help. Get him outside and onto the horse.” Rellan and Kuper got up and moved swiftly toward the startled monk.

“Wait!” The ringing command from Brother Elias carried enough authority to halt the twins in the act of lifting Vangellis bodily from his seat. Elias turned to Will, genuine alarm on his face. “You cannot do this! Surely you can see that the man is not fit to travel.”

“He’ll soon sober up once he gets some fresh air,” Will replied mildly.

“So you thank us for our hospitality by forcibly kidnapping one of our order?” Elias protested.

"I mean no disrespect. But our need is very great." Will spoke with simple sincerity. "Is Vangellis a member of your order, then?" he asked.

"Well, no," the Brother admitted. "Not exactly. He is my guest. And under my care."

Will already knew that about Vangellis. And much else besides. Even without the stone, Thomas could see that. Will did not reserve his tactical skills entirely for the battlefield.

"It makes no difference," Will asserted. "We must all make sacrifices at times, and his skills are greatly needed." His tone was diplomatic, but his words took on an iron edge. "We will take him with us. By force if necessary."

Brother Elias looked from Will to Vangellis and back again. The anguish on the old monk's face made Thomas squirm. But Will was unmoved.

Elias gazed intently at Vangellis for a long moment. Then slowly the tension eased from his face. He seemed to have come to a decision. "God's purposes seem strange to us at times," he said. "But he knows what he is doing." He turned back to Will. "You must allow him a few minutes to pack some warmer clothing and a few possessions. The Brothers will use the time to prepare provisions to send with you in your saddlebags."

Vangellis looked up at Brother Elias as though the old monk had slapped him. Elias came to his side, and whispered in his ear before helping him up and ushering him from the room.

"Go with them," Will told the twins. "Stay out of their way, but don't let them out of your sight." They nodded, moving off swiftly.

They were gone for long enough that Will became restless and sent Nestor to hurry them along. Nestor returned a few minutes later, followed soon after by Brother Elias, Vangellis, and the twins. Vangellis was wrapped in a heavy cloak and dragged behind him two bulging saddlebags. His face was flushed and his eyes wide and moist. He looked pitiful. Thomas wondered what had passed between him and Brother Elias. Whatever it was, Vangellis had apparently accepted that he must go.

True to Elias's word, food had been prepared for the travelers. The monks with the provisions accompanied them to their horses. Thomas discovered, to his surprise and delight, that the animals had been rubbed down, fed, and watered. Clearly some of the monks, at least, understood horses. He quietly approached the monks who held the reins and thanked them for their efforts. They bowed silently in response.

The food was stowed, and the riders prepared to mount. All except Vangellis. He shuffled to the gates, clearly expecting to join the party on foot.

"You must ride," Will told him. "We have no time for further delay."

"I cannot...ride a horse," Vangellis asserted. "I will walk."

"What kind of guide is this?" Ander muttered sarcastically.

That earned him a rebuke from Will. "Enough!" the commander growled.

Will turned to Thomas. "He's going to need some help. Make it quick."

Thomas dismounted and went to Vangellis. "Riding is not difficult, with a bit of practice," he assured the monk, drawing the spare horse closer. The horse snorted and shook its head vigorously, pulling against the reins. Vangellis backed away in terror.

Based on his experience at teaching novices to ride, Thomas could see at once that Vangellis would make no progress tonight. Probably not anytime soon, either. He looked up at Will and shook his head.

"Thomas, you're the best rider, and the lightest. He's with you."

Thomas sighed inwardly. Riding double was not going to be pleasant, especially with an inexperienced rider scared of horses. "Rufe?" he called out hopefully to his friend.

Seeing Rufe approach him with a purposeful stride, Vangellis began to panic. A lot of struggling and yelling followed before Elias intervened. He took Vangellis to one side and spoke quietly to him for a time. Eventually the monk calmed down and submitted to the inevitable.

The saddle was removed and Vangellis hefted by main force onto Thomas's bay by Rufe and Nestor. Before he could fall off, Thomas vaulted up behind him and reached around him for the reins.

That night's ride was a deepening nightmare for both Thomas and the unhappy monk. Controlling the horse from behind Vangellis became more and more difficult as Thomas grew increasingly weary. Vangellis had no idea how to move with the horse and was bounced around unmercifully. Many times he would have fallen but for Thomas. Without a saddle it took a prodigious effort to keep the monk on the horse, heavy and uncoordinated as he was. His wine-induced stupor gradually wore off, or perhaps was relentlessly shaken out of him. He groaned more and more frequently and eventually began to cry out in pain after the worst of the jolts.

Will halted them well before dawn. By then everyone in the party was on edge. Ander was muttering under his breath, and some of the others were noticeably restless. Thomas felt so tired he didn't care. The monk was too miserable to do anything except position himself as far as possible from the others. He limped away clutching his saddlebags and moaning softly.

When dawn came none of them had managed to sleep much. But Will was impatient to be gone. He called the men together, and they huddled bleary eyed around him. "I don't want a repeat of last night's experience," he began. "Thomas, you're going to stay here and teach Brother Vangellis to ride.

"Nes, I need you to stay and protect them. The rest of us will try to get to Ranwood ahead of Drettroth. His main force has been traveling by foot, but they will be getting close now. We've had too many diversions, and now we don't have a lot of time." At the mention of diversions, Ander threw a scowl in the direction of Vangellis.

Will and his party mounted without pausing to eat. "Too bad you're going to miss out on the fun," Ander said to Nestor with a grin. "Enjoy the babysitting," he concluded with a wink at Thomas.

As they headed off Will called back to Thomas, "You have two, maybe three days. Make it count." Then they were gone.

23

Steffan trudged into his apartments and collapsed onto the bed. Once again he had returned completely exhausted after another day of wrestling. The daily struggle around a table with his father-in-law and his nobles did at least have one benefit—it was making the prospect of fighting on the battlefield seem positively appealing.

Istel's promise of support had been entirely sincere, and Steffan had to acknowledge that the Castelan king was showing real energy in raising armies and training soldiers for the defense of the allied kingdoms. The problem was that Istel thought only in terms of defense. Steffan, far from home and cut off from his kingdom, wanted action. He was all for setting off for Arvenon tomorrow with an army at his back.

Istel pointed out that they would be operating blind, with no idea of Agon's intentions. And if the reported size of the Rogandan army was accurate, any false move could prove fatal. Steffan countered that wars were not won by sitting safely inside a fortress while your enemy roamed freely, pillaging your land, burning your crops, and picking off your weaker cities at his leisure.

He had his own soldiers, of course—two thousand of his best. But he knew they were far too few to win a war on their own. He would need Istel's help even to keep his army intact if he wanted to break through the Rogandan soldiers holding the pass into Arvenon.

If only he had brought Will Prentis with him instead of old Olaf. Will would be crafting plans and coming up with ideas. And he had a way of inspiring confidence and hope. Steffan had come to depend on him so much. It was strange to think that he wasn't many summers past twenty years of age.

Will was probably stuck inside Arnost at that moment, unable to do anything useful. That was good news for the capital, of course. Somehow Steffan couldn't imagine it falling to the Rogandans with Will in charge of the defense. But he would have been much more useful here with the king. Now the war would have to be won—or lost, he thought grimly—without Will's help.

Essanda's young face appeared over him, a look of concern creasing her brow. "You are tired, My Lord."

"I told you not to call me that, Essanda!" he snapped irritably. The face abruptly disappeared, and he quickly repented. "I'm sorry. I didn't mean to yell at you."

"That's all right," she said generously. "A king has many worries, I know." She sailed back into view. "What should I call you?"

"You can call me Steffan. But no more of 'My Lord'!" He frowned at her in mock anger.

"I will call you Steffan when it's just us," she decided. Then her mouth formed a stubborn line. "But I will call you 'My Lord' when we are with company."

He smiled at her affectionately. "That sounds like a good compromise, Essanda," he agreed.

She vanished behind him. Then her hand appeared and began to gently stroke his hair and his neck. It felt very soothing.

He sighed in appreciation. "Where did you learn to do that?"

"My mother always stroked my hair when I was sad or upset. It made me feel better. I thought you might need to feel better, too."

"You're a remarkable girl, Essanda."

"'My Lady', if you please," she teased, adding "Steffan" with a self-conscious giggle.

He smiled again, then closed his eyes and allowed himself to drift off as she continued her stroking. It took only moments before he was asleep and dreaming. They were pleasant dreams, without hint of wars or conferences or turmoil.

SEEING that he had fallen asleep, Essanda climbed up onto the bed and lay down beside him. Soon the two of them floated far away, released for a time from the daily troubles of mortal kings and queens.

NESTOR DID NOT STAY with Thomas and the monk for long. No more than two minutes after the others had left, he mounted his horse and disappeared. He returned briefly after a short time. "There's a stream just over that rise," he told Thomas, pointing to a low ridge a short walk away. Then he disappeared again. Thomas headed in the direction he had indicated and found the stream. The water was cool and fresh, and he felt much better after splashing his face and taking a long draft.

When he returned he found Vangellis snoring loudly. He briefly debated with himself about waking the monk, but eventually decided that his new student would learn more effectively if he started the day with a bit of sleep. It also gave him the opportunity to carefully examine his horse. Thankfully the stallion did not seem to have suffered lasting ill effects from the long journey bearing two riders.

Vangellis woke a couple of hours later to find that Thomas had prepared a modest breakfast from bread and cheese he had discovered in his saddlebags. Thomas had also filled a couple of skins with fresh water from the stream.

"Please join me," Thomas said simply. "Nes seems to be off somewhere, so we will have to enjoy breakfast on our own. My name is Thomas. Thomas Stablehand."

"I am Brother Vangellis, as I'm sure you are well aware by now," replied the monk with a self-mocking smile. He sat down very delicately beside Thomas, wincing as he made contact with the ground. "So you're supposed to teach me to ride." He sounded very skeptical about the prospect.

"We won't get on a horse today," said Thomas. "I thought you might be a bit uncomfortable."

Vangellis looked both surprised and delighted. "I doubt that your leader will be pleased," he ventured.

"Will won't mind. He's happy to leave the teaching to me," Thomas replied confidently. The monk looked at him with obvious curiosity. Thomas ignored it and went on. "Getting on a horse isn't the first and most important thing. It's understanding how horses behave, what they like and dislike, what's good for them and what isn't," he explained. "For example, normally I would never ride double. My horse tolerated it last night—we have an understanding. But it isn't good for him, and I wouldn't do it without a reason.

"Last night I put your interests first. We need to get you to the point where a choice like that isn't necessary."

"But I don't like horses. I've been scared of them all my life."

"That's probably because you think they're unpredictable. Or because you had a bad experience when you were young. Either way, I've found that accurate understanding takes away the fear. Once you know why they behave as they do, you can predict their reactions, and avoid situations that upset them. Well, most of the time," he added with a grin.

Thomas began with simple explanations, and demonstrated each point with the help of one of the horses. Vangellis often asked for clarification, and Thomas was surprised by his perceptive questions. Warming to the obvious interest of his pupil, Thomas shared more freely and deeply the important lessons he'd learned about horses. With this new understanding, the monk was able to begin to move beyond his fears, and soon demonstrated a natural empathy for the animals. The horses seemed to respond to him, too. Before the end of the day, Thomas concluded that Vangellis had real aptitude as a horse handler. Possibly more so than any student he had taught at Arnost. It didn't guarantee that he would do well in the saddle. But it was a promising beginning.

From time to time during the day Vangellis had become restless and asked for a short break. He would head off out of sight for a while, taking his saddlebags with him. When he returned he was ready to begin again. The time alone seemed to calm him, so Thomas soon agreed to these breaks without hesitation.

Nestor returned as the sun was setting. He brought with him a pair of hares that he had shot with his bow. He quickly skinned and cleaned the rabbits, and as soon as it was dark he set about building a fire to cook them. Thomas wondered about the wisdom of a fire but did not question Nestor. The location where they had camped was well concealed, and he was sure that their protector would not take unnecessary risks.

"Where have you been, Nes?" Thomas asked him.

"Protecting you doesn't mean sitting here waiting for a fight," he replied calmly. "I've been scouting around for miles in all directions. No one dangerous is anywhere nearby. Once we've eaten I'll smother the fire. It's very unlikely we'll be troubled tonight."

The rabbits were delicious, especially when accompanied by a few drafts from a skin of wine that the Brothers had packed in their saddlebags. Vangellis didn't say much during the meal, but he shared the wine enthusiastically.

The next day Thomas began teaching the monk to ride. By then the monk could tolerate short periods in the saddle in spite of his soreness. Thomas could tell quite quickly if a person was going to be able to ride well; Vangellis would never be among the best, but he had the makings of a competent rider. His natural feel for horses helped him sense changes in the mood of his mount. Now he just needed to learn to respond quickly and appropriately. By the end of the day Thomas was satisfied with his progress, but he became increasingly aware that Will could return at any time.

Thomas woke early on the third day, impatient to resume their lessons. When Vangellis got up, he disappeared as usual with his saddlebags. This time Thomas followed him. Although he felt a twinge of guilt about spying, he was determined to see what the monk was doing. He carefully kept out of sight as he followed deeper into the trees.

Vangellis came to a stop and looked behind him. Thomas barely pulled back out of sight in time. After a pause he peered from behind a tree. Vangellis was pulling a wineskin from one of his saddlebags. His hands were shaking as he lifted it to his lips and drank a deep draft. Then he closed his eyes and sighed deeply. The trembling in his hands ceased.

Thomas remembered a conversation he had overheard between his parents. An old uncle of his mother's had injured his back and could no longer work. The doctors offered no relief, and to dull the pain he turned to wine. Thomas remembered the sadness in his mother's voice as she talked about how far he had fallen. The wine robbed him of so much, but he could not give it up. He was totally and helplessly dependent on it.

Thomas moved slightly, and a twig snapped loudly under his foot. Vangellis started. "Who's there?" he called sharply.

After a moment's indecision, Thomas stepped out from his hiding place. He felt ashamed, but it was the monk who reacted with guilt, trying to conceal the wineskin behind his robe.

"Do you have problems with your back?" Thomas blurted out, immediately feeling stupid for asking the question.

Vangellis sighed and brought the skin into the open again. "No, Thomas," he said sadly. "The wine helps me cope with a different pain." Another twisted smile played across his lips. Then he shrugged and took another short draft before returning the wineskin to his saddlebag.

Nothing further was said by either of them, and Thomas resumed the training as if nothing had happened.

. . .

In the end they saw no sign of Will's party for almost four days. Late that afternoon the twins appeared. They had been riding hard, their horses covered with sweat. Nestor was with them. Thomas felt sure their protector had spotted the twins well before they arrived.

"We need to be ready to leave the minute Will arrives," Kuper announced. He glanced over at Vangellis, sitting upright on his horse. "Can he ride?" he asked doubtfully. In response, the monk kicked his heels into the horse's flanks, and they moved away at a trot, the monk moving rhythmically up and down with the horse. "Not bad," Kuper admitted, surprise evident in his face. Then he ignored Vangellis and turned his attention to more pressing matters. "We're going to water our horses. Make sure you're ready."

While Kuper and his brother moved off to the stream, Thomas and Vangellis gathered their few possessions, packed them away and mounted their horses.

Will, Rufe, and Ander arrived only minutes later. "Is he ready?" Will asked Thomas, jerking his head toward the monk. Thomas nodded. "Then let's go. There are fifty Rogandan horsemen behind us."

They moved off immediately. Will did not even look at Vangellis to check his riding skills, and Thomas swelled with pride at the implied compliment to both his teaching skills and his judgment.

They didn't stop again until it was almost dark. Will would have ridden further if he thought the horses could manage it. But most of the animals had been ridden long and hard, and the riders could ill afford horses pulling up lame. There was no sign of a pursuit. For the moment they seemed to have either lost the Rogandans or left them far behind.

The journey had not been without incident. Vangellis fell twice, and was very fortunate to have avoided serious injury. Considering his lack of experience, Thomas thought he had done well. No one learned to ride well overnight, and they had passed over difficult terrain.

The second fall was especially bad, and Thomas had no doubt that the monk carried serious bruising. They had been riding through a narrow pass when Ander pressed in close to Vangellis, spooking his horse. An experienced horseman would have handled the situation with ease, but Vangellis quickly lost control and fell heavily. Ander cursed Vangellis loudly and repeatedly, blaming the incident on his incompetence. Will, clearly annoyed, had finally cut him off. Ander fell silent, but his antagonism toward the monk was now more obvious than ever. Vangellis said nothing, but, at the first opportunity after they stopped, Thomas was not surprised to see him slip away with his saddlebags.

Once the horses had been seen to, they huddled together around some food and wine packed by the monks.

"Did you get to Ranwood before Drettroth?" Thomas asked Will.

"Yes," he replied. "But less than a day before his army. We arrived early in the morning. I'm not sure the townspeople were happy to see us."

"You can't blame them," Rufe said. "One minute they're happily going about their business, and the next the commander of the king's army rides in and tells them to flee for their lives."

Kuper took up the story. "Will found the local lord and told him he needed to empty the town before nightfall. The lord wanted to call a meeting of the town elders, appoint some scouts to go check for immediate danger, and send out messengers to tell the farmers to sharpen their pitchforks just in case!"

"First time I've seen Will really angry," Ander enthused. "He went to the market square and yelled for silence. Told them the Rogandans were coming and that no one left in town by nightfall would be alive to see the dawn. Ordered them to forget their possessions and run. There was total panic!"

"It did the job," agreed Kuper. "Most of the people were gone within three or four hours. After that it was a few older people who needed help to leave."

"How did the lord take that?" asked Nestor.

"He wasn't happy at first," Rellan replied, with obvious understatement.

"The lord is a fool," Ander added derisively. "He knew that Arnost was under siege, but did nothing to prepare for war."

"He is not a bad man," said Rufe. "He did everything he could to help the townspeople leave quickly and safely."

"It wasn't his fault," Will agreed. "Good leaders in peacetime aren't always the best leaders in war.

"The town was indefensible," he continued. "No wall, no garrison of any size. It would have been a massacre. And given the location, the Rogandans would have settled in and used the town as a base."

"Not now," grinned Ander.

"What did you do?" Thomas asked. He was entirely captivated by the unfolding story, but tried hard to keep his tone matter-of-fact.

"As soon as people started to leave," Ander responded, "we went through the town and laid out flammables. Dry wood and straw, leaky barrels of oil. Placed them everywhere. The whole place was a bonfire just waiting to be lit."

"Then we found a good spot just outside the town and waited," said Kuper.

They all paused, clearly lost in their memories. Thomas couldn't bear the suspense. "What happened?"

"We waited until the Rogandans arrived," said Rufe. "It was almost dark. They came in, slow and stealthy, and spread out looking around. They couldn't find anyone. When night came on they posted guards, and settled into the houses to sleep."

"We lit fire arrows," Kuper continued, "dozens of them. We sent them sailing in, one after another. It was a beautiful sight! Beautiful and deadly. Once the fires started they spread incredibly quickly. You should have seen the town burn," he said, awe in his voice. "The flames lit up the night sky like it was day."

"The Rogandans knew where we were by then," Rufe said. "The arrows gave us away. We took off in a hurry, but we were close in to the town, so they were never far behind us."

"How many Rogandan soldiers died in the fires?" Thomas wondered aloud.

Vangellis didn't wait for an answer. He got up abruptly and left the group. The soldiers stared silently after his retreating form until well after he was gone.

"We don't know," Will finally replied.

"A lot," said Rufe simply.

Nothing further was said for a long time.

Nestor finally broke the silence. "Where to next?"

"We'll go on to Stonehold," Will replied. "We're part of the way there already."

"There's one road in and out," said Ander. "The Rogandans will use it—they're probably on it already. Even if we can get onto the road ahead of them, we won't be able to use it to get out."

"That's why we brought a guide," Will replied.

Ander grunted dismissively.

Will ignored it. "Ander and Nes, take the first watch. The rest of you get some sleep. We'll be moving out as soon as it's light."

It took Thomas a long time to get to sleep that night. When he slept his dreams were disturbed by images of a burning town and screaming men.

"THE ROGANDANS ARE on the road to Stonehold in strength," Kuper reported. "We won't be able to get past them. We need to find another way in. And we need to do it quickly."

Will turned to Vangellis. "Do you know of an alternative route?"

"Yes," the monk replied. "There's a mountain trail. I've walked it a couple of times. But it's rough. I don't know if horses will be able to manage it."

"We're about to find out," said Will. "We don't have a choice. How long will it take us?"

"About the same as using the road. It might save us a bit of time. The road winds around a lot because of the landscape. This path is slower going, but it's also shorter because it's more direct. It will depend a lot on the horses."

For the next few hours they alternated between slow, cautious riding and leading their horses on foot. The path was extremely rough, and even when the sun had cleared the horizon Thomas still had to pick his way carefully.

Occasionally the trail widened, and they were able to make better time. Eventually, they crested a ridge, and Stonehold lay below them. The drawbridge was down to provide access across the moat, the portcullis was raised, and people and carts were coming and going. No one at the stronghold seemed to have any awareness of their peril. Thankfully, the Rogandans were nowhere in sight, but Thomas knew that was likely to change very quickly.

Will brought them to a halt. "Rufe, you're with me. The rest of you stay here. Be prepared for a rapid departure," he warned them.

Will and Rufe picked their way down the trail. As they neared the road below, Rellan called down a warning. "Riders! Off in the distance. You don't have long!"

Will and Rufe waved back an acknowledgment as they reached the road below. Then they galloped to the town, crossing the drawbridge and coming to a halt before the gate.

Thomas was much too far away to hear anything, but it was clear that Will was remonstrating with the guards at the gate. He was pointing repeatedly down the road. The guards were not responding.

From their position high up on the trail, Thomas and his companions could now clearly see Rogandan riders in the distance, approaching at a gallop. If the portcullis wasn't lowered soon, it would be too late.

"Hurry!" groaned Kuper between clenched teeth, tension evident in his voice.

Rufe drew his sword and started waving it around. The guards leaped into action at last and lowered the portcullis to deny Will and Rufe access to the fortress. A few bowmen appeared on the wall, and the two men beat a hasty retreat across the moat with arrows beginning to fall around them.

Just as their horses began clambering back up the trail, the first Rogandan riders appeared. The horsemen quickly clattered across the drawbridge and spread out around the wall, but they soon scattered as the archers on the wall began targeting them instead.

Several of the invaders lingered near the portcullis. Then slowly, ponderously, the drawbridge over the moat began to rise into the air. The Rogandans had no way to prevent it. The last of them fled across the bridge before it could be raised high enough to block their escape.

The invaders spotted Will and Rufe fleeing up the trail, and a sizable group of riders began a vigorous pursuit. Kuper, Rellan, Ander, and Nestor quickly unslung their bows and fired off a couple of volleys. Several pursuers fell to the deadly hail, and the others backed off. It was clear they did not intend to abandon the chase, though.

Vangellis took the lead, and the whole party began hastily retracing their steps. At times they caught glimpses of the Rogandans following them. It was a large group, but they stayed out of bowshot range.

After a couple of hours, the monk turned aside from the main trail and led them onto a hidden path that sloped steeply upward. They climbed for a while, until the path emptied onto a broad plateau. With open ground before them at last, they let their horses run, continuing at a rapid pace for the best part of an hour.

The monk eventually led them off the plateau, and they dipped down out of sight. The path up to the plateau must have been missed by their pursuers, because there had been no recent sightings of them.

Will called them to a halt to rest their horses.

“What happened down there?” Rellan asked.

“Will couldn’t convince the guards about the danger,” Rufe replied. “They refused to close the portcullis without an order from their local lord.”

“How did you change their minds?” Thomas asked.

"Will started yelling at them in Rogandan, and I drew my sword and began threatening them. They finally took the hint."

"Only just in time, as it happened," said Will.

Vangellis took the lead once again when they set off, and they continued until nightfall.

With the sun setting, Will decided they had done enough for one day. They dismounted and shared a simple meal.

"You've led us well," Will told Vangellis. "We couldn't have made it to Stonehold in time without your help. The Rogandans would have captured the town."

The monk dipped his head slightly, but otherwise didn't respond.

Will continued. "We seem to be a long way ahead of them now. We can afford to get some sleep tonight."

"What will we do tomorrow?" Kuper asked.

"I've been giving that some thought," Will replied. "Drettroth undoubtedly had plans once he had taken Ranwood and Stonehold. After the last couple of days, I have a feeling those plans will have changed. I can't even guess at his next movements. He still has his army, though, and there's very little we can do against so many."

"What do you mean?" Thomas asked in surprise. "Look what you achieved at Ranwood. With only five of you!"

"Right. We destroyed one of our own towns."

Thomas opened his mouth to argue, but quickly realized it was wiser to say nothing. He closed it again without speaking.

"Drettroth's had the initiative for too long," Will continued. "We need an army. It's time we joined the king. We ride north for Castel in the morning.

"Get some rest," he concluded. "We will leave at dawn. The Rogandans that followed us from Stonehold will be tracking us as soon as it's light. And if our pursuers from Ranwood ever manage to figure out which way we went, we'll have two groups chasing us."

"Don't you think the group from Ranwood will give up?" Thomas asked hopefully.

"Not a chance," Will replied. "It won't go well for them if they return to Drettroth without us."

24

"Have you been here before?" Will asked Vangellis.

The monk shook his head.

They had been riding for several hours with just two short breaks. They knew that the Rogandans had found their tracks and were following them. They also knew that their pursuers were not far behind.

For some time they had been following an animal trail, but now it branched. One way led down, the other led up.

"Which way should we go?" Will asked the monk.

The downward trail appeared to offer easier going—when Thomas looked ahead along the ascending path, it seemed as if the trees were closing in around it.

Vangellis glanced toward the lower path, then peered thoughtfully for a long time along the upper path. Finally he turned to Will. "The upper path," he said.

Ander grunted derisively, but said nothing.

"The upper path it is," Will ordered without hesitation, pointing along the ascending trail.

"The lower path is the obvious choice. Nes, I need you to make it look like that's the one we took. Rellan and Kuper, go with him."

A low outcrop of rock ran alongside the upper path for the distance of a couple of bowshots. While Nestor and the twins trampled the lower path to make it look as if a group of riders had passed that way, the others dismounted and led their horses onto the rocky outcrop. Ander followed behind to make sure they left no hint of their passing.

By the time Nestor and the twins rejoined them, the sun was well past its zenith. The three soldiers had followed the other trail until they could leave it without their change of direction becoming obvious.

The monk's instinct ultimately proved to be right. The ascending trail continued to climb until they had crisscrossed their way to the top of an escarpment. At the top they once again caught sight of the lower trail. It wound its way into what appeared to be an extensive boggy morass. At that point the trail disappeared. On the other side of the bog, the only way forward led eventually into a box canyon. Riders following the lower trail would eventually be forced to retrace their steps.

They set out to find a place to camp, leaving Nestor behind at the top of the escarpment to watch for any sign of the Rogandans. He caught up with them not long before the sun completely disappeared below the western horizon.

"Did you see them, Nes?" Will asked.

"Yes. They took the lower path."

"How many of them?"

"Almost fifty. It's a large group."

"Have they camped?"

"Yes. Right on the edge of the bog. They'll probably waste most of tomorrow finding a way through it."

"With a dead end waiting for them on the other side," grinned Rellan.

Kuper glanced across at the monk. "We would have been caught in a trap if we'd taken the other path."

"A lucky guess," muttered Ander.

Vangellis said nothing. In the group he never spoke at all unless asked a direct question. He seemed a totally different person from the curious student Thomas had taught to ride.

While Vangellis never obviously appeared to be drunk, it was clear to Thomas that the monk's closest companion was his wineskin. Whenever they stopped, Vangellis wasted no time disappearing off with his saddlebags. If others had their suspicions, nothing had been said. But at the previous stop Thomas had noticed Ander watching the monk closely with narrowed eyes.

THE NEXT DAY they broke camp again before dawn. Will wanted to open up a big lead over their pursuers. They headed west, trying to skirt some rugged terrain that lay directly in their path northward. By the time the sun passed noon, they had made their way down to a succession of low hills covered with tall grass. At last they began to make good time.

Riding in open country again Thomas felt his spirits lifting. He knew that danger could be lurking anywhere—a Rogandan army might be waiting over the next rise for all he knew—but he decided not to think about it. The day passed without incident, and, setting off before dawn once again after another night with too little sleep, they headed northwest.

Will sent Nestor ahead to scout for any sign of trouble. Not long after sunrise he appeared in the distance, riding hard toward them. Wary and alert, they reined in their horses and waited for him to join them.

"Rogandans!" he said urgently. "I almost stumbled into their camp."

"Did they see you?"

"I don't think so."

"How many?"

"It's a big camp. Hundreds of tents."

"They'll have patrols out," Will said. "We can't stay in the open. Vangellis, I need you."

They all dismounted while Will, Nestor, and Vangellis huddled together for several long minutes. Finally Will called them together. "We're heading south. It's the wrong direction, but there's a forest only an hour's ride away, and we should be able to avoid detection there. We'll ride through its outskirts westward until we're clear of the Rogandans."

They set off immediately, riding fast. Time passed, with no sign of the forest, and Thomas became increasingly anxious. He couldn't help looking back repeatedly over his shoulder, half expecting to see an army chasing them.

Being chased by fifty Rogandan soldiers had been frightening. But he had a feeling that Will and Rufe would somehow find a way to outfight, outwit, or simply outrun them. But an entire army?

As he wrestled with his anxiety, memories—unwanted and unwelcome—forced their way back into his mind. He relived the fight at the gates of Arnost. He saw again the Rogandan soldier moving in to finish him off.

There was a time when he had imagined himself as a soldier in his daydreams. It had seemed so exciting. Now he knew better. War was no adventure—it was horrible beyond words.

Within the hour they reached the first outliers of a great forest that stretched east-west as far as the eye could see. Will called them to a halt between two huge trees. They peered back the way they had come, but there was no sign of pursuit. Thomas began to relax a little.

"We'll rest for a few minutes," Will said.

As the words left his lips a faint crack sounded nearby. Every soldier reacted instinctively. Nestor's sword appeared in one fluid movement as he spurred his horse toward the noise. Rellan and Kuper's bows were taut almost before the sound faded away.

A figure detached itself from behind a nearby tree and sprinted deeper into the forest. Rufe got there first and gave chase. He was almost upon the fleeing form when the spy tripped and fell sprawling. Moving with a speed that belied his size Rufe slid from his horse, pinning the figure to the ground with the point of his sword.

A quavering voice said a few words in a language Thomas could not understand.

"It's a girl!" Rufe exclaimed in surprise.

"She's Rogandan," said Will. He rode up and spoke to her, apparently in the same language.

The girl returned a rapid reply, her tone becoming bolder and more insistent with every word. Will spoke again, but she cut him off, impassioned and increasingly shrill.

Rufe dragged her to her feet. She was possibly a couple of years older than Thomas. Between the fire in her eyes and the dark tangle of her long hair she looked quite wild.

"What's she saying?" Ander asked.

"She seems to be some kind of servant who's run away from the Rogandans. She says we must take her with us. Either that, or she insists we kill her right now."

"Those are our options," Ander agreed. "Now that she's seen us she can betray us."

"Safer just to kill her," Nestor said dispassionately.

Vangellis bristled. "Not if you expect to keep me as your guide," he said, his jaw set in a tight line.

Ander opened his mouth to reply, but Will got in first. "Enough!" he said firmly. "She's coming with us. For now, anyway."

TO THE RELIEF of Thomas they stopped to make camp well before the sun reached the horizon. Will had asked Thomas to ride double again, and the experience had been very unpleasant. The girl, whose name was apparently Elbruhe, had been hefted up behind him with instructions from Will to hang on to Thomas. She had clearly never ridden before and spent much of the first hour alternating between whimpers and squeals of terror. She eventually quietened down, but managed to poke him in the ribs almost continuously in her frantic attempts to hang on.

They attended to their horses and shared a simple meal. Afterward, Will drew Elbruhe aside, and the two talked for a very long time. Elbruhe seemed to do most of the talking. Thomas glanced over from time to time; more than once he spotted the girl sobbing.

Will eventually rejoined the others. They had positioned themselves in a circle as if warming themselves around an imaginary fire. Everyone was there except the girl, who was presumably preparing a place to sleep, and Vangellis, who was off on his own somewhere.

They sat without speaking for what seemed an age. Will appeared more than usually thoughtful.

Eventually Ander broke the silence. "What did you learn about the girl? Will the Rogandans come looking for her?"

Will shook his head. "I doubt it. The Rogandans care more about their animals than their slaves."

"How did she become a slave?"

"She said she's an orphan. That's shameful in their eyes. If the Dark Gods took your parents, they must be angry with you. People follow the example of their gods. I know something of it myself."

"So she ran away?"

"Yes. She decided it was better to starve to death alone in the forest than go on living as a slave. She's witnessed things no one should have to see. And terrible things have been done to her."

Will had nothing more to say, and the conversation ended there.

Later, Thomas lay gratefully beneath his warm blanket, shutting out the cold wind that roared through the tops of the trees above him. He tried to catch glimpses of the stars through the restless branches of the trees, and pondered his own misfortunes. Thanks to the stone he was caught up in events he could not comprehend, let alone control, swept away in a current he could not resist. Not long ago he had never known real danger. Now he flirted with danger every day.

But for all that, the good far outweighed the bad. He tried to imagine the life of the Rogandan girl, and could not. He had grown up with parents—parents who loved him. He knew that even his father cared about him. He had never gone hungry, never been beaten without cause. By the time sleep took him his troubles had given way to a heightened sense of gratitude.

In the morning Will approached him. "We leave within the hour, Thomas. Try to teach the girl what you can about riding. It might make your life easier," he added with a wry grin.

Thomas went over to her. A small stream ran nearby, and she had clearly bathed in it. Her hair was still an unruly tangle, but she seemed more presentable. He beckoned her to follow him, and after a long moment of indecision she did so.

As she followed him to his horse, he decided he couldn't blame her for hesitating. He pitied her for her sufferings, whatever they were, and it felt good to be able to help.

"This is a horse," he said. "Horse!" he repeated in a louder voice, feeling instantly stupid as he realized she couldn't understand a word. She ignored him, moving to the horse's neck and stroking it. The horse responded to her confident touch, allowing her to lean into it.

She couldn't ride, but she clearly knew horses. That should make his task easier. "I'm the horse master. I teach people to ride," he said, trying to sound important but managing only to feel foolish. She continued to ignore him.

His attempts to instruct her turned into nothing more than an exercise in frustration for Thomas. He realized for the first time how much his teaching relied on words. Normally he spoke first, then demonstrated, and followed up with more words to reinforce the lesson. Now he was reduced to the demonstration, and she clearly neither understood nor cared what he was trying to convey.

She soon became bored and wandered off. He coaxed her back, but not for long. Eventually he had almost been forced to drag her back to the horse, and she became very testy. The others stayed away, but he noticed them throwing sidelong glances in his direction, and more than once caught them smirking.

Finally he had abandoned any thought of teaching her to ride. In exasperation he placed himself in front of her and grabbed her hands, showing her how to hang on to him. This drew a mocking laugh from her, which stung and discouraged him.

They finally set off with Elbruhe seated behind him once again. She held on as instructed, but the outcome certainly hadn't flattered his skills as a teacher. The obvious amusement of some of the others didn't help, either.

As the day progressed, Thomas sensed that she was bouncing less and moving with the horse more. She no longer poked him in the ribs, either. She seemed to be learning from him indirectly, copying his movements and becoming better attuned to the animal. Her obvious progress made the journey easier for both of them, but Thomas felt frustrated.

When they camped for the evening, he lay awake trying to make sense of his own reaction. He realized he'd become accustomed to actively participating in the adventure as others learned to ride. On this occasion, they might have been riding the same horse, but the learning process hadn't been a shared experience in any way, and it left him feeling disconnected and dissatisfied. He recognized that it wasn't the fault of either one of them—the absence of a common language was an insurmountable barrier—and he drifted off to sleep having resolved to be less sensitive and more sympathetic to the girl in the future.

A couple of hours before dawn Thomas was awakened by a piercing scream. Every soldier was instantly alert and on his feet. Will appeared in the gloom and moved to Elbruhe, clamping one hand firmly over her mouth and bending low to whisper in her ear. She writhed under his grasp for a few moments, then became still. He released her, whispering again into her ear.

"It was a nightmare. Nothing more," he said to the curious onlookers. "Nes, make sure no one was nearby to hear that. The rest of you get some more sleep."

Thomas couldn't get back to sleep, though. And from Elbruhe's restless tossing and turning, he guessed that she couldn't, either.

The following morning Elbruhe discovered that the monk understood some Rogandan. After that she sought him out whenever they were not traveling. Vangellis, who had made it obvious that he preferred his own company, seemed to accept her presence with equanimity. She prattled away to him almost without pausing for breath. How much he understood Thomas did not know, but he rarely said much in return.

At one point Thomas found himself briefly alone with Vangellis. "How much do you understand of what Elbruhe says?" he asked.

"I understand Rogandan a lot better than I can speak it," the monk replied. "I don't understand everything she says, though. She talks so fast," he added with a smile.

"What does she talk about?" Thomas ventured.

"I don't think it's my place to say," the monk replied.

"Does she talk about...people?" he persisted.

The monk smiled and said nothing.

She fascinated Thomas, and he couldn't pretend otherwise. From the beginning, though, he decided not to try out the stone on her. It probably wouldn't have shown him anything. But even if it did, he knew that spying on her wouldn't have been right. That was a path he'd trodden before, and he wasn't going to do it again.

Clearly Elbruhe had experienced more than her share of pain and suffering in life. The monk had told Thomas that the wine helped him cope with pain. He didn't seem to have meant physical pain. Maybe the two of them understood each other.

THE NEXT DAY Thomas decided to let Elbruhe ride in front, so she could experience riding more normally. He held the reins around her, and found that she was now able to hold herself in position without needing his help.

Sitting behind her he couldn't help noticing the way her hair bounced to and fro in the wind. Her wild appearance was greatly diminished—she'd found a way of removing most of the tangles from her hair—and it felt like he was seeing her for the first time.

As the morning gradually wore away Thomas began to find it unsettling to be sitting behind her. Reaching around her waist with the reins meant his arms bumped against her continually. He couldn't help noticing the soft roundness of her body, skinny though she was. Had she found it distracting to ride behind him, holding him tightly? He hoped so, though he scarcely dared to admit it even to himself. If she did, she showed no sign of it.

At one point they slowed while traveling over uneven ground. His arms swung around more than usual, making constant contact with her. After a few minutes of this, she turned her head and glared at him. Then tossing the hair fiercely from her eyes, she spat a stern rebuke into his face. Finally she paused, before adding "Delou-ahn," sarcastically.

Will, riding nearby, laughed out loud.

"Well, tell us what she said," said Rufe mischievously.

"She said, 'Keep your hands to yourself!'" he replied with a grin. "Then she called him 'Sweetheart.'"

Every one of the soldiers burst out in uproarious laughter. Thomas felt himself coloring beet red.

The remainder of the ride was a nightmare that couldn't end soon enough for Thomas. He tried to hold his arms away from her body, but it wasn't possible to control the horse without touching her at all. Upset with her for humiliating him, he felt tempted to dream up a biting response. But he knew that the language chasm would defeat him even if he found something suitable to say.

It was so unfair. And why did Will have to tell everyone what she said?

The soldiers were still chortling over the incident when they finally stopped for the day. Elbruhe clearly enjoyed the attention, and she looked down her nose condescendingly at Thomas as she dismounted.

Turning her back on him, she went to his horse and hugged its neck, speaking baby talk to it. The horse seemed to enjoy her attentions. Then she walked away without a backward glance.

Thomas turned to the horse and glared at it. "Traitor!" he muttered accusingly. The horse whinnied and shook its head.

The monk unexpectedly sought him out. "Don't take it to heart, Thomas," he suggested gently. "She was cruel, I know. But she's used to being mocked, and I think she enjoyed serving it out for once. She doesn't mean it."

Thomas knew the monk meant well, but it didn't placate him. He decided to avoid Elbruhe entirely. If she noticed at all, it didn't bother

her. She soon sought out Vangellis and chattered away happily to him as usual. The monk listened patiently as always.

Thomas ended the day annoyed with Elbruhe for humiliating him, angry with the soldiers for laughing, and peeved with the monk for being kind to her. The brush down he gave his horse was less enthusiastic than usual, too.

Something happened the next morning that caused Thomas to forget his grievances. Not long after Thomas had woken, he was startled by a loud wailing. The haunting quality of the sound sent a chill up his spine. The whole camp was astir in moments. He looked around for Elbruhe, but the noise wasn't coming from her. It was coming from the monk.

To the surprise of Thomas, Will ignored Vangellis and his wailing and hobbled over to Ander. "What have you done?" he demanded, stiff with anger.

The burly soldier's face displayed a hardened wariness. "He's supposed to be our guide. I've had enough of following the advice of a drunk!"

Will approached Ander until their faces were inches apart, and stared him down. "Lay a finger on him or his possessions again, and you'll deal with me!"

Ander could not meet his eyes. He dropped his gaze sullenly to his feet.

"You're on double duty. For the rest of this week. You're getting off lightly, too—don't push me, or I'll come up with a real punishment." Will's tone was even and controlled, but the menace in his voice was unmistakable.

The wailing continued uninterrupted, adding a bizarre backdrop to the confrontation.

Thomas felt completely bemused. What had just happened?

Will headed to Vangellis and tried to talk to him. The monk ignored him.

It was the girl who finally managed to get through to him. She took his arm and led him aside, speaking in soothing tones. A few minutes later the wailing stopped. Thomas could hear the monk quietly sobbing for a while, then that, too, came to an end.

Rufe was standing apart, frowning. "What's going on?" Thomas asked bemusedly.

Rufe nodded in the direction of the monk. "It seems Ander slashed all his wineskins in the night."

"Oh. So you knew about the wineskins?"

"Everyone knew," Rufe replied. "Will didn't mind as long as he stayed alert. He never wanted to be here, and we all thought it would help him stay calm."

Rufe's comments were a revelation to Thomas. He had imagined the wineskins were his secret with Vangellis. He wondered what else might be obvious to everyone. What were they saying about him and Elbruhe? He felt a blush coming on, and quickly excused himself.

They eventually set out much later than usual. Outwardly, at least, the monk seemed calm. This time Elbruhe rode double with him instead of with Thomas. The young horse master felt nothing but relief. He couldn't think straight when she was around.

25

The party had barely departed when Elbruhe called to Will. After a brief exchange they resumed their journey. Just thirty minutes later the girl called out again, more urgently this time. The horse she shared with Vangellis had come to a stop, and she quickly dismounted. The monk all but fell from the horse. He lay on the ground where he landed while Elbruhe fussed around him.

Will rode over and bent low over his horse to examine Vangellis. Elbruhe spoke rapidly and vehemently, punctuating her words with animated gestures. Will replied, pointing firmly in the direction they had been traveling. She became very agitated, waving her hands dismissively toward Will and the rest of the party. She then turned her back on Will and knelt down beside the monk.

Will waved Rufe to his side, and the two of them carried on a conversation in low tones. Thomas could not hear what they were saying.

Finally Will ordered them all to dismount. "Vangellis is not well. We'll stay here for a while until he improves."

"He's faking it," Ander sneered, speaking under his breath so that those nearest him could hear but Will could not.

Rufe heard, though. He pushed himself in front of Ander, towering over him. “If you’ve got something to say, then say it to Will,” he challenged, his voice trembling with anger.

“There’s no problem,” Ander replied hastily in a tone that suggested Rufe was turning an acorn into an oak tree.

Rufe stared down at him without speaking, then turned on his heel and left. Thomas noticed Ander roll his eyes dismissively at Rufe’s back as the giant guardsman moved away. Thomas got up and left, too. He felt like he’d witnessed one skirmish too many in Ander’s tireless campaign against the monk.

THE SUN PASSED OVERHEAD and began its journey toward the western horizon, but Vangellis hadn’t improved. He was getting worse. When they stopped he had been shaking with fever. Now, several hours later, his fever raged unchecked and the trembling had become more violent. He vomited repeatedly, even though nothing remained to be purged from his stomach.

At one point Thomas spotted Ander stealing a furtive look at Vangellis as he passed by. Thomas wondered what he was thinking. Did he feel remorse for what he’d done? No reasonable person could think that Vangellis was faking his illness. But Ander couldn’t be relied upon to be reasonable where the monk was involved.

Elbruhe was tending Vangellis, and Will hovered nearby. Vangellis lay prone, although from time to time he seemed to be seized by some kind of fit. As Thomas contemplated the scene Nestor happened by. “What’s happening to him, Nes?” Thomas asked.

“He’s got the barrel fever,” the veteran replied.

“What’s that?”

“He doesn’t have his wine anymore. He’s come to rely on it,” said Nestor. “Now the craving’s got hold of him.”

“How do you know?”

“Seen it before,” he replied.

“What can we do?”

“We can wait.”

"Wait for what?"

"To see if he survives. This time tomorrow we should know."

"You can't mean he's going to die!" Thomas protested.

Nestor shrugged. "He might. Seen it before," he repeated.

Thomas couldn't bear the uncertainty. He joined the little huddle around Vangellis to see if there was anything he could do.

Seeing him arrive, Elbruhe addressed him sweetly, ending with a teasing "Delou-ahn."

"Elbruhe wonders if her sweetheart might fetch some fresh water," Will said, managing a tight smile.

Thomas stood there dumbly for a moment, then fled in search of a water skin. A small stream flowed about fifty paces away, and he filled the water skin there and hurried back. Elbruhe ran it over a damp piece of cloth until it was dripping wet, then placed it across the monk's forehead.

She spoke again to Will, a serious look on her face.

"She wants some 'feverwort'. We need to find a way of breaking his fever."

"What's feverwort?" Thomas asked.

"It's a herb used by the Rogandans to treat various ailments," Will replied. "Fever is only one of them. I've seen the plant before; my aunt used to grow it. It has a broad green leaf and a small pale white flower. If we're lucky we might find some near the stream."

The description didn't sound very detailed, but Thomas set off hopefully to look for the herb. Will followed close behind him.

After a long hunt Thomas found something that vaguely fit Will's description. The flower was pale lavender, though, not white. Nevertheless he headed hopefully to Elbruhe to show her what he'd found.

Seeing it set her off on a tirade.

"Well, I don't know what to look for," he said defensively. "I've never even seen it."

Will reappeared, just in time. "Apparently that's poisonous," he explained to Thomas. "The leaf of feverwort is broader, and darker in color. And the flower needs to be white."

Thomas plodded off to have another try. As he passed Elbruhe she poked out her tongue at him and gave him another earful. "Thanks so much for your helpful explanation," he retorted.

Walking past the twins he overheard Rellan saying to his brother, "Listen to them. Just like an old married couple," while Kuper chortled loudly. Thomas scowled at them and walked on, pursued by gales of laughter.

It took him almost an hour, but Thomas eventually found a plant that he felt certain was feverwort. Grabbing two large handfuls, he sprinted back to the camp, and held it out expectantly to Elbruhe. She leaped up excitedly, and, to his complete astonishment, planted a joyful kiss on his cheek. Then she turned away, calling loudly for Will.

Thomas stood there dumbfounded. When he recovered himself he decided to get more water. His cheek still tingling, he set off for the stream, fervently hoping that no one had noticed.

He returned to the camp at the same time as Will, who wasted no time calling for Rufe.

"We need to build a fire."

Rufe was clearly taken aback. "That's a big risk!"

"Nevertheless, we will do it. Avoid green branches. Try to keep the smoke to a minimum."

Elbruhe boiled water over the fire and used the leaf of the herb to make a steaming broth. Then she lifted the monk's head and carefully poured some into his mouth. He sputtered and coughed, spilling most of it. But she gently persisted, returning the broth to his lips again and again, making sure he swallowed a few drops at least each time.

By nightfall there were hopeful signs that the fever might be easing. If they thought he was through the worst of it, though, they were sadly mistaken. The monk's problems were just getting started. None of them got any sleep that night.

It began just after dark. The monk was lying quietly with Elbruhe close at hand to check on his condition. The twins were on watch, and the others had started to think about sleeping.

Then suddenly Vangellis had begun screaming in terror, slapping at himself and rolling on the ground. “Get them off me!” he shrieked.

The camp was instantly in an uproar. Will and Rufe rushed to him, ready to help. But they could not understand what his problem was.

“What is it? “ Will demanded. “What’s on you?”

He ignored Will and kept screaming, and scratching himself frantically. Great welts appeared wherever he made contact with bare skin.

Will grabbed his head with both hands and forced the monk to look at him. “What...is...the...problem!”

“Insects! Crawling over me!” Vangellis gasped. Then his eyes widened. “Biting, biting!” The screaming resumed, more panicked than ever.

At that point Nestor stepped in and took control of the situation. “Hold him down and cover his eyes! He’s seeing things that aren’t there. He’ll hurt himself if we don’t stop him.”

“Do what he says,” Will ordered.

Rufe, Will, and Nestor surrounded him and tackled him to the ground. His twisting and writhing became frenzied, but they held him down. Thomas tore a strip off his blanket and fashioned a simple blindfold. He fastened it around the monk’s face, trying to ignore the madness in his bulging eyeballs.

Will stuffed some cloth in his mouth, and the shouting was reduced to a wild mumbling.

Eventually Vangellis became calm.

Gradually they released him. They began with his mouth, then uncovered his eyes. After a few minutes without further struggling, they finally released him entirely.

Elbruhe spoke to him soothingly, and helped him drink some more broth.

He lay with his head in her lap, entirely spent. In his weakened state from the fever, Thomas could not imagine how he had found the energy to fight so hard.

That had only been the beginning. As the night progressed the monk had to endure further invasions of insects, then snakes, and later rats crawling all over his body. Each time he suffered the indignity of being forcibly restrained.

Thomas and his companions later realized that covering the monk's eyes did nothing to diminish his visions. And nothing could prevent him from feeling the intruders crawling over his flesh. The hours of darkness must have been a waking nightmare to him.

Thomas realized at one point that he hadn't seen Ander at all during the night. He had certainly never approached the monk, and seemed to have stayed well clear of the others. When dawn came Thomas looked around, and couldn't see him anywhere.

Ander reappeared only minutes later.

"Anything happening?" Will called out to him.

Ander simply shook his head. He looked tired, too.

Will must have sent him off scouting. Yet Will didn't seem to have left the side of Vangellis at all during the night. Then Thomas remembered Will talking to the twins. They had disappeared as well.

Thomas hadn't given a thought to security; the drama involving the monk had fully absorbed his attention. Apparently it hadn't distracted Will from his other responsibilities, though. How did he do it?

Elbruhe must have been tired, too. Thomas greatly admired the way she cared for Vangellis. She was tireless, tending to his every need with gentle compassion. He would have admired her even more if she hadn't taken to snapping at him all the time. Thankfully he didn't understand a word, and he was grateful that Will chose not to enlighten him.

Two full days dragged slowly by before the monk's crisis finally appeared to be over. Vangellis was left too weak to move, but both Elbruhe and Nestor now hoped that he would survive.

Thomas thought back to his conversation with Nestor two days previously. The idea that the monk might die had seemed so extreme to him at the time. But the soldier had been right. Life could be far more fragile than Thomas imagined.

In the end they remained at the campsite a further four days.

Even then the monk was barely capable of sitting on a horse. Thomas sat behind him once more, steadying him, and Elbruhe rode alone for the first time. No one questioned her right to join the party or to ride one of their horses. At some point she had crossed a mysterious threshold and become one of them.

KUPER AND RELLAN RODE IN, bringing their horses to a halt beside their commander.

"Any sign of Rogandans?" Will asked.

Kuper shook his head. "No sign at all. We seem to have lost our pursuers. Ander and Rellan and I have scouted far and wide, and no Rogandans are anywhere near us."

"What about the army we caught a glimpse of?"

"Long gone. Their tracks show that they headed west, toward Erestor."

Will nodded. "So there is no immediate danger," he said.

"Has our delay created a problem?" asked Kuper.

Thomas had been asking himself the same question. The commander had without hesitation put the needs of Vangellis ahead of everything else. Perhaps he felt responsible for the monk since he had compelled him to join them. They'd been held up for six days, though, and Will had seemed so determined to avoid wasting time. Thomas had the impression that the fate of the kingdom might be hanging in the balance.

Will shook his head. "I'm not concerned about the delay. My most pressing priority was to prevent Drettroth from carrying out his immediate plans at Ranwood and Stonehold—there was real urgency behind that. We need to find the king, but I never expected we'd be able to reach him quickly. Not with so many Rogandans roaming the countryside."

Kuper nodded.

"Let's keep moving," said Will. "We won't be traveling far today."

Thomas had no idea how Will juggled his various responsibilities. He was simply glad it wasn't his job.

They rode slowly but steadily along the fringes of the great forest for a couple of hours, until Nestor returned from forward scouting and reported that he'd found a village within the forest. A small trail intersected their path about thirty minutes ride away. He had followed it far enough to see it broaden into a well-used road. A goatherd had told him about the village. Nestor guessed it was a couple of hours further on, riding slowly.

Will called them together and announced they would divert to the village. After the unexpected delay they needed to restock their provisions, and it offered an opportunity to warn the local inhabitants about the Rogandan invasion and ask them to spread the word. The villagers might also have remedies to help speed the recovery of Vangellis.

By the time they reached the village Vangellis was close to collapse. They helped him from the horse and stretched him out on the ground while Will sought out the village headman.

The village might have been home to fifteen families, and it soon became apparent that it was poor indeed by any standard. Livestock, normally abundant in a reasonably prosperous village, were hard to find here; a couple of small pigs ran squealing from the horses, and a half dozen scrawny chickens pecked hopefully around a small cluster of rude huts. The children ran around naked, and the clothing of the adults was poor in both quality and condition. The villagers themselves looked thin and weathered, as if worn down by too many cares. Thomas had never seen poverty like it.

No young men at all could be seen. Thomas guessed that the young men would be pressed into the service of the local lord, either as soldiers or working in his fields.

The village lay in a large clearing, well within the boundaries of the great forest. Trees had been cleared on either side of the village and meager crops struggled for life in small strips of cultivated earth. The land had probably been cleared gradually over many generations.

Thomas discovered through Rufe that the village was on the northern boundary of the domain of a minor baron. Most of his holdings lay south of the forest, although a couple of other larger villages lay near at hand to the south and also within the forest.

Will appeared with the headman, who didn't appear to be any better clothed or fed than the rest of them. The fellow looked anxious. Thomas expected a headman to seem more confident and authoritative.

Will explained that the party had a sick man who needed care, and wanted to rest and restock supplies. The headman looked even more worried, but he nevertheless arranged billets for them all. Each of them would be placed in a different household, except for Thomas and Vangellis who were sent off together.

Elbruhe made it clear through Will that she was to be notified immediately of any change in the monk's condition. She had plenty to say, and Thomas nodded wisely and listened intently as if he was hanging on her every word. She was clearly annoyed by his behavior, a fact that brought him considerable satisfaction.

Before they dispersed Will called them together.

"I've warned the headman about the Rogandans. He's sent messages to the nearby villages. He's also sent word to his local lord. We can expect a visit.

"Ander and Nestor, you take first watch. I want to know the minute anyone comes near this village. Something doesn't feel right here. These people are harmless, but they're living in fear. Be ready to be roused at any moment.

"Rellan and Kuper, take over the watch at dusk."

VANGELLIS AND THOMAS had been assigned to an elderly couple, and their hosts ushered them into a small hut. A small fire burned inside on a simple hearth with a rough stone chimney to catch the smoke. The chimney was surprisingly effective, but smoke still filled the hut, and Thomas soon found his eyes watering. Vangellis was too tired to pay any attention to their surroundings. The man pointed him to a small space that had been cleared on the floor, covered by a rough blanket. Thomas helped him to lie down before sitting on a three-legged stool proudly produced by the woman.

Small strings of onions, leeks, and other dried vegetables hung from the roof. The woman slowly retrieved a few and began to prepare a meal. Her husband watched her mournfully. Neither of them said a word, and Thomas found himself unable to think what to say, either.

Not long after dusk the woman indicated that the food was ready to eat. Vangellis was in no condition to join them, so Thomas found himself eating with his hosts, sitting on his stool while they sat on the floor. The meal consisted of a vegetable stew served in wooden bowls and a large slab of dark bread.

The bread had arrived just before they sat down to eat. A young girl brought it to the woman, stretching up on tiptoes to whisper in her ear before hurrying off. The hosts set aside no bread for themselves, but their eyes followed closely every piece on its journey to Thomas's mouth to be chewed. He guessed that the bread had been sent by the headman, intended for the guests only.

The stew was thin and the vegetables scrawny. The bread was tough and strongly flavored, but it was bread. He softened it by dipping it into the stew before attempting to chew it.

The portion served to Thomas didn't go close to filling him, but he didn't ask for more. From the condition of the man and the woman, they weren't used to eating any better themselves.

A portion of bread and stew had been set aside for Vangellis, so after Thomas had finished eating he thanked his hosts and carried the monk's food to him. Tearing off small pieces of the bread and dipping them into the stew, he placed them into the mouth of the prone man. Vangellis moved his jaws half-heartedly a few times before swallowing the pieces whole.

A blanket for Thomas had been placed near Vangellis. He lay down, peering across at the man and woman in the dim light provided by the fire. They had also lain down, but he could see no sign of blankets. He realized that they must have given up their blankets for their guests.

Uncomfortable at the thought of the cold night that lay ahead of them, but unsure about what to do, Thomas lay for a long time unable to sleep. After thirty minutes of restless indecision he could stand it no longer. He stumbled out of the hut in the darkness and made his way to his horse to retrieve some blankets.

Back in the hut again he returned the borrowed blankets to their original owners. They peered at him with wide eyes, saying nothing. But they accepted the blankets without hesitation.

Thomas tucked a blanket around the monk and settled down for the night. He was more tired than he realized, and soon drifted off to the sound of the monk's rhythmic snoring.

Once asleep, he dreamed. He found himself walking alone across a courtyard in the castle at Arnost. Water bubbled merrily from the spout of a fountain and sparkled in the late afternoon sunlight.

Walking beside the fountain, something on the ground caught his eye. Bending down to examine it, he was astonished to discover that it was his stone. He fumbled for the pouch at his belt, anxious to discover how it had fallen out. But his stone was still in its place.

Completely baffled, he opened the drawstring and took out the familiar object. Then he picked up the stone from the ground and compared them. They appeared to be identical.

Abruptly something struck him hard from behind, on the back of his head. He pitched forward, both stones flying from his hand into the fountain. Down, down, he fell. The last thing he saw before blacking out was the base of the fountain. It was covered with stones, every one identical to his own.

CONFUSED AND DISORIENTED, Thomas struggled to return to wakefulness. Someone was bending over him, shaking him gently.

Vangellis swam into view. "Sorry if I startled you," he said. "You were calling out in your sleep."

Thomas frowned. His surroundings mingled strangely with lingering elements of his dream, and it was difficult to re-establish reality.

After clearing his head he peered up into the concerned face of Vangellis and realized that the monk looked different.

"Are you feeling better?" he asked. Vangellis looked very pale, but otherwise more normal than he had appeared for many days.

"Yes," he replied. "I think I am."

They were alone in the hut. Vangellis pointed to two small wooden bowls. "Fresh milk," he said. "I suspect this is our breakfast." He drank the contents of one of the bowls and gave out a sigh of satisfaction. A white mustache briefly appeared above his lips before he wiped it away with his sleeve.

The monk studied the hut and its contents carefully. As he did so, a frown gradually furrowed his brow. "I need to speak with Will," he said, and marched determinedly from the hut.

Thomas jumped up from the floor. Gulping down his milk, he hurried out after Vangellis. Elbruhe would have his hide for letting the monk dash around so soon after his illness. He had to run to keep up—the monk was in a hurry.

Vangellis quickly found Will, who stood in the village square talking to the other soldiers. Everyone was there except the girl.

The monk walked up to them and nodded in greeting.

"How was your meal last night?" Vangellis asked. His voice sounded casual, but Thomas detected an edge to his tone.

"I've eaten better," Kuper replied with energy.

"Smallest meal I've been served since I was a boy," Nestor added. "I had to send the woman back to prepare more. Twice."

Others grunted in assent. "A soldier can't fight if he doesn't eat," Ander asserted.

Vangellis nodded his head calmly, but his voice was tight. "We're condemning these people to death."

"What are you talking about?" Nestor demanded.

"We ate as much food in one night as the entire village would have eaten in a week. Maybe more. Food was already in very short supply for them. Another couple of days with us staying here, and they won't make it through the winter."

Rufe waved his hand in denial. "We'll pay them. There's no need for them to starve."

"Pay them with what?" Vangellis demanded.

"With money, of course," Rufe replied, baffled by the question.

Vangellis shook his head, trying to remain patient. "People like this have no use for money."

He looked Will in the eye. "Pay them, and you guarantee their deaths. Their lord will never believe they were given money. He'll conclude they stole it from us."

There was a pause, then everyone started talking at once, but Will cut them off. "He's right," he said.

He faced the monk. "What do you suggest?"

"We need to give them food. Not money."

"We can give them a deer," Rellan suggested.

Vangellis shook his head stubbornly. "They won't be allowed to kill deer from the forest. Deer will be reserved for the lord. Ask them!"

Will held up a hand for silence. "There's no law prohibiting us from killing deer. We will hunt some ourselves," he said. "But we won't give them to the villagers. We'll tell them to invite people from the nearby villages to come to a feast. We'll hold a market. They'll need to bring some food to trade. We'll sell meat in exchange for vegetables, then invite them all to the feast.

"Some of the meat and most of the vegetables will stay here for the local villagers. The rest we'll take with us as provisions."

Vangellis paused for a moment, thinking. He nodded once, tentatively, then again decisively. "I think that might work," he said with a smile.

"That's settled, then," said Will. "It will mean another delay, but we're not leaving until we find out what's been going on in this village anyway. Safeguarding these people is no less our duty than fighting the Rogandans.

"Rellan and Kuper. Go find us two or three large deer. Nestor and Ander, you're on watch. I'll speak to the headman."

Before they could disperse, Elbruhe appeared. She took in the scene with a single glance. Making her way to the monk's side, she took him firmly by the elbow. Then, frowning fiercely across at Thomas, she rattled off a couple of choice phrases, clearly savoring each word as it left her mouth. The sarcasm in her tone required no translation. Finally, chin held high, she took charge of Vangellis and defiantly steered him back in the direction from which she had come.

Her performance was appreciated enormously by the men. They applauded noisily, accompanied by some hooting and hollering. The villagers, hard at work tending their strips, paused for a moment and stared at them all curiously. Rufe, grinning from ear to ear, gave Thomas a wink.

There was no point whatsoever in responding. With a sigh of resignation Thomas turned away and headed off to tend to the horses.

26

Steffan sat motionless on his destrier watching the columns march past. Captain Olaf no longer led Steffan's soldiers to war—advancing years and infirmity had finally caught up with the old veteran, and he was confined to his bed in Castel Citadel. Lord Bottren had taken command of the Arvenian army, at least for the moment. Once again Steffan found himself wishing he had Will Prentis at his side.

Essanda had risen early to see him off. He could still picture her, a thoughtful frown creasing her young face. Steffan had assured her that everything would be fine. He had the feeling she wasn't convinced, but she was trying hard not to show it.

The truth was that he was bursting to go. Careful planning was well and good, but Steffan had long since wearied of the endless round of debate and negotiation. He was longing to do something, to take the fight to the Rogandans at last.

Eventually he had reached the point where he could bear it no more. He sought out King Istel and vented his spleen—at length, and at considerable volume. His father-in-law had taken a long hard look at him, then finally conceded that the time for action had come. Things had moved remarkably quickly after that.

The soldiers were marching on Deadman's Pass, still blocked by the Rogandans who had occupied it on the day of Steffan's wedding. Clearing the pass would present the new joint force with their first real challenge.

Steffan's army was ready to fight, and he couldn't wait to see his men take the initiative. He found it inconceivable that a small band of Rogandans could hold them up for long.

THERE COULD BE no doubt that Will's market was turning out to be a big success. Over two hundred people had appeared from neighboring villages and farms, lured by the promise of trade and especially the report of a feast. It was obvious to Thomas that very little feasting happened around here, so it wasn't surprising that people became enthusiastic once they had overcome their initial reticence.

The twins had returned from the hunt with a large buck and three does. At that moment two of the does were roasting over a fire in preparation for the feast. The buck and the other doe had been carved up and traded for vegetables, cheese, bread and other items of food.

Nothing had been wasted. The hide, the antlers, the bladder, and even the entrails all had their uses and the local farmers had quickly taken up what seemed to be a rare opportunity to trade them. The raw meat had been cut into long strips and wrapped in vine leaves to keep them fresh. Business had been brisk as soon as the meat was offered for trade. The new owners would undoubtedly smoke the strips to preserve the meat. The families in the region would benefit greatly from the additional variety in their diets over the winter months to come.

Will had already turned over generous supplies of food to the headman for distribution to the other families in the village. The man had brightened considerably. In fact, he had almost smiled. And the feast hadn't even started yet.

The villagers were not the only ones looking happier. Thomas had never seen Vangellis so relaxed—he almost seemed normal. Even Elbruhe had flashed Thomas a smile. She also paid him a compliment. At least that's what she appeared to be doing, and Thomas was more than willing to take it at face value.

JUST BEFORE DUSK, with the feast well underway, Will gathered together the members of his party.

"Nestor just warned me that a group of riders is approaching from the south. He estimated there are at least twenty of them. He and Ander will watch them closely to make sure nothing surprising happens.

"Thomas and Vangellis—keep out of the way. I don't want anything to happen to either of you. Make sure Elbruhe stays with you.

"The rest of you know what to do. Don't start any trouble, but if I give the signal, don't hesitate."

Thomas and Vangellis, with Elbruhe following them, withdrew to a suitable spot beside one of the huts. From there they should be able to observe everything that happened without interfering or unnecessarily putting themselves at risk. Vangellis spoke quietly to Elbruhe, who listened intently with a deepening frown.

Will must have warned the headman, too, because the sounds of merriment quickly began to die down, and people scurried away. Soon only Will stood in the open. Flanked by a giant bonfire, he was biting off chunks of meat from a large piece of venison.

Before long a group of riders rode into the village. They were led by a rotund man in late middle age with a long scar across his face. He sent probing glances around every point of the village before approaching Will.

"Who authorized this debauchery?" he demanded.

"I did. Come and enjoy some of the venison—it's very good, and there's plenty here for all."

"Your life is forfeit for poaching the king's deer, fool."

"And who are you to decide matters of life and death on the king's behalf?" Will asked calmly.

"I am Baron Rudungen. I represent the king here."

"I also represent the king. I am commander of the king's armies. My name is Will Prentis."

"Where are your armies, then, Commander?" the baron asked, mockingly searching around him.

"The placement of the king's armies is not a subject for idle chatter in times of war."

"Hah! You talk big, but my men will soon bring you down to size." The baron nodded to the nearest of his soldiers, and they began to close in.

Will raised his right arm, and two arrows flew through the air and buried themselves into the shields of the two men nearest to Will. "Withdraw your men, or next time your head will be the target, Baron," Will called out.

The baron's men halted, peering around nervously trying to spot the archers.

"I see you have been expecting us. Well your bold talk doesn't deceive me," the baron sneered. "My spies report that you have only five soldiers with you. You're badly outnumbered."

"And my spies tell me you brought only twenty men. Some of them are looking a bit pale. I wonder how many have actually fought a battle before. They may discover that parade ground tussles with wooden swords do little to prepare you for the real thing. My men have fought the Rogandans many times, and always against much worse odds than this. I'm sorry, Baron, but if you were planning to pick a fight with the king's commander you should have brought an army."

Will's words had been skillfully chosen and were having their effect. Some of the baron's men appeared nervous and fidgety. Thomas could see that more than a few were indeed looking pale.

The baron said nothing. He was clearly calculating the odds and trying to think of a way to turn the situation in his favor. Finally he came to a decision.

"I see no reason for bloodshed," the baron offered reasonably. "Let's settle this in a more civilized fashion: my champion against yours, hand-to-hand combat with no weapons. If your man wins, I will allow you to leave here without interference. If my man wins, all of you will return with me to my castle in chains.

"Either way, the vermin here who call themselves villagers will learn to regret their little party today."

Will's face became stern. "I guessed that you might have been responsible for the poverty in these parts. It seems I was right.

"I accept your challenge," he continued, "but with one alteration. If my man wins, you will come with us to the king. Bound and as our prisoner. If we make it past the Rogandan army waiting for us, you will get an opportunity to explain your actions today directly to the king. And you will be held accountable for the brutal oppression of your subjects."

The baron laughed, a cruel and mocking sound. "We will see," he said. "Choose your champion." He called to his men, and one of them dismounted and stepped forward. Thomas gasped. He was a big brute of a fellow with a thick neck and a cruel face. The baron rode to his side and bent down to him, whispering in his ear. The man nodded once and began stripping off his weapons.

"Rufe," Will called. Rufe appeared, very close to the position where Thomas and the others were hiding. Will came over to him. "This baron intends treachery," he said, speaking quietly. "Be careful. Whatever happens, this is going to end in a fight, and we're going to need you."

Rufe nodded. He stepped forward, handing his weapons to Will. Ander, Nestor, and the twins were nowhere to be seen.

When Rufe moved into the open the baron's soldiers gasped. Their man might have been big, but Rufe was bigger.

"Let me warn you against treachery, Baron," Will called. "Many of your men will die unnecessary deaths here today if you play me false."

The baron did not bother to reply. He waved his man forward impatiently.

The two men circled warily, looking for an opportunity. Then the baron's man charged and wrapped his arms around Rufe, pinning one of Rufe's arms to his side. He began to squeeze. The baron's soldiers cheered excitedly.

A lesser man could not have withstood the crushing pressure, but Rufe tightened his own great muscles and began pounding his opponent's head with his free fist. After a few moments the man released his hold and stepped back, shaking his head to clear it.

While he was still dazed, Rufe charged him, fists raised, and rained heavy blows to his upper body. The man chopped downward onto Rufe's left arm, forcing him to step back wincing with the pain.

The fight wore on, with both men landing punishing blows but neither able to knock the other from the contest. The baron's champion was not able to deliver an easy victory, and Thomas could sense the tension rising. The baron's men were becoming restless.

Then Rufe's opponent reached behind his back, and knives appeared in both hands. Rufe reacted instinctively, running at him then dropping into a slide that carried him right up to the waiting man. At the last moment Rufe spread his legs enough to encompass the right leg of the other. Even as the man reached down to stab him, Rufe snapped his legs together in a scissor movement. Thomas heard the sickening crack of a leg breaking, and the knife-wielder crashed to the ground with a cry of agony.

After that chaos ensued. The baron loudly called his men to arms, and Rufe and Will were soon fighting for their lives. First two, then three, then four of the baron's men fell from their horses, arrows protruding from their chests or necks. But the remaining soldiers soon located the archers and moved to engage them. The stream of arrows ceased, but not before three more men lay unmoving in the dust.

Small knots of men writhed to and fro across the village square, the dying rays of the sun adding a faint red tinge to the scene. The twins fought back to back, their blades dancing among the many targets around them. Ander and Nestor fought nearby. A couple of soldiers brave enough to test their strength and swordsmanship quickly paid with their lives; others soon learned to stay out of reach. Will and Rufe had likewise fought their way to each other's side. They each accounted for an enemy before the others drew back warily.

So far the baron's extra numbers had made no impact. Half of his men milled around uselessly, the skillful tactics of Will's fighters keeping most of them out of the fight. They got their chance only when one of their own went down.

The baron stayed on the sidelines, shouting instructions in a fury. Thomas could see that some of his men would have turned and run, but they feared their leader even more than their enemies.

The fight had reached a dangerous point for Will and his men. They were visibly tiring. Thomas felt sick to the stomach as he recalled the struggle at the gates of Arnost. Even as he watched, Rellan sustained a heavy blow to his left arm. He was now unable to do more than defend himself. Worse, Ander, who had been fighting ferociously, tripped and went down. Enemies immediately swarmed over him, stabbing downward, until Nestor's desperate swordsmanship forced them back.

The baron's remaining soldiers cheered and joined the struggle with renewed hope and energy.

At this crucial moment, with the balance tilting in favor of the baron, it abruptly shifted again. A ragtag group of men unexpectedly appeared on the fringes of the battlefield, moving steadily toward the struggle. They were farmers, armed with picks, axes, and even rakes.

The baron greeted their arrival with unconcealed rage. In response to his furious instructions, several of his men peeled off immediately to confront the new challengers.

The farmers had no skill at arms; they brought little more than raw courage to the battle. The baron's men, however, knew exactly how to deal with peasants. The soldiers fell on them savagely, threatening an imminent bloodbath. First one, then a second farmer was struck down, and the others showed signs of wavering.

But the looming slaughter never happened. In the first moments of confusion, Rufe glimpsed an opportunity and seized it. Pushing through the distracted opponents that remained before him, he ran to the baron and dragged him from his horse. He threw the noble roughly to the ground, planted a foot firmly on his chest and pinned his neck with the point of his sword.

"Throw down your weapons. Now! Or the baron dies," he bellowed.

The baron squirmed under his foot. But the sharp weapon at his throat left him no choice. "Do as he says," he hissed.

"Speak...LOUDER...Baron," Rufe suggested, poking down with his sword to emphasize each word. "I don't think they can hear you."

"Do as he says!" the baron shrieked.

His soldiers complied immediately.

Few in the village slept at all that night. The baron spent an uncomfortable night trussed up and gagged, guarded by Nestor, who was not gentle with him. The gag had been applied after an incessant stream of threats and curses from the noble.

The villagers gathered the dead and laid them out while the able-bodied among the baron's surviving soldiers, supervised by Rufe and Kuper, labored digging graves in the cemetery beside the village.

Fortunately, Vangellis seemed to have largely recovered from his brush with the barrel fever. During the night he worked tirelessly among the wounded, ably assisted by Elbruhe. Thomas ran errands for them, fetching water and stoking fires. He also searched in the woods around the village for feverwort. The search was difficult and frustrating. He hunted in the dark aided only by the flickering light of a torch, and it took him almost three hours. But he continued until his persistence was rewarded. He handed over the leaves without expecting or receiving any praise for his efforts; all of them were too weary to care about such niceties.

In the morning the headman humbly approached Vangellis and asked him to conduct funerals on behalf of the villagers, who counted two of their own among the dead. Vangellis seemed strangely reluctant, but after some hesitation he agreed, to the obvious relief of the headman. Thomas was surprised by his reticence—he was, after all, a monk. But there was much that Thomas found difficult to understand about Vangellis.

Will gathered the villagers. The local families and those from neighboring villages huddled together. Many of them sobbed and wailed piteously. The deaths had added further grief to their already difficult lives. Not all among the visitors were personally affected, but every one of them appeared downcast. Thomas was not surprised. They had come for a feast, not a funeral.

Will also gathered the soldiers, both his own and the baron's. The baron arrived, too, led in by Rufe. The noble glowered darkly but said nothing. Indeed it was not possible for him to speak. Will had decided he could not trust the baron to remain silent, and did not want him disrupting the proceedings. So the man whose pride and arrogance had led to the deaths stood there with a gag in his mouth, hands tied behind his back, and a face like thunder.

All of them gathered in the tiny cemetery at one end of the village, between two deep trenches close by and a larger group of newly dug graves positioned off to the side. Carefully constructed wooden crosses adorned the graves of the two villagers. The other graves, dug for the fallen soldiers, boasted nothing better than rude crosses fashioned by their comrades from sticks.

Will nodded to Vangellis, and he stepped forward slowly. The monk seemed ill at ease. He stood with head bowed for so long that Thomas began to feel uncomfortable. But everyone else seemed to be waiting respectfully, so Thomas tried to mimic their calm demeanor.

At last Vangellis lifted his head. "All of us must one day face God to give account. And when we come before him, we do so without the benefit of earthly rank or status."

Thomas threw a glance across at the baron, who frowned and mumbled angrily behind his gag.

"All of us have done wrong. We deserve the condemnation of a just and righteous God," Vangellis continued, coloring as he said it.

"But God offers pardon and hope. Forgiveness, undeserved, and unearned."

Thomas glanced across at the graves, wondering if every one of the men lying within them was worthy of a free pardon after what they'd done.

The monk walked slowly to the grave of one of the soldiers and lifted the simple cross from the mound, raising it high. "God's gift of life comes through one who was punished in our place. He offers pardon to all who will humble themselves to receive it."

Thomas felt sure he could see tears glistening in the eyes of the monk, but Vangellis again lowered his head, and Thomas could not be certain.

"The promise of resurrection and life forever with God," the monk continued in a low voice.

He uttered some words of ritual, and the mourners filed past the open graves. Then the baron's men were set to work filling them in.

After the last grave had been covered with earth, Will called the baron's surviving soldiers together. Along with the local headman, the headmen of two neighboring villages had been invited to witness Will's conversation. The soldiers stood restless and anxious, uncertain of their fate and bone weary from a night of hard work immediately after a deadly battle. More than half their number now lay under the earth keeping company with generations of departed villagers.

"You have done great wrong here," Will told them. "Not just by attacking the king's commander without reason or provocation, but by actively aiding in the oppression of these villagers. Your duty as soldiers is to protect the defenseless, not to steal from them the necessities of life and rob them of hope. You will carry your shame with you to your graves.

"No such behavior would be tolerated in any soldier of mine. Nevertheless, I recognize that you were doing the bidding of the baron, and it is he who will be primarily held to account.

"All of you have worked hard during the night without shirking or complaint. That counts for something. You have been fortunate to survive. Some of you are wounded, but all of you can ride if you travel slowly. I'm sending you back."

Faces lifted in surprise and relief.

"But you will carry a message to whoever rules in the baron's absence. We will stay here for a time to attend to our wounded. During that period, if any soldier comes within a day's ride of this village, the baron will die immediately.

"When we leave, the baron will go with us. If he survives the journey he will face the king. Our sovereign is a just ruler, and I do not expect him to be pleased with the baron's treatment of those under his protection, nor with the attack on his commander.

"As soon as I have opportunity I will send men to visit this region. If I discover that the abuse of these villagers has continued, I will return. With an army next time.

"Make sure this message is delivered. In full. Do you understand?"

One of the soldiers, an older man, stepped forward. "The message will be delivered, Commander," he said. "I give you my word. We are grateful to you for your mercy."

"Then go in peace," said Will. "Be aware, though, that I will not be so generous next time, if I meet you in similar circumstances.

"May you find yourselves serving a better master in the days to come," he concluded.

With that he sent them off. They left with their horses but not their weapons.

Once they had gone, Will turned to Thomas.

"I have a task for you, Thomas. The baron's former soldiers," he said, jerking his head in the direction of the newly filled graves, "won't be needing their mounts anymore. I'm giving them to the villagers. I want you to show them how to care for horses. There should be time for you to teach a few of the basics of riding, too."

He turned to Nestor. "Have you spent time behind a plow?"

"Almost from the time I could walk," the veteran confirmed.

"Then show the villagers how to harness their new horses to their plows. Maybe we can still bring some good out of this...this nightmare," he concluded, waving his hand vaguely around the village.

Following his gaze Thomas could still see remnants of the recent battle. A few trees bristled with stray arrows, the dirt was stained with dark blood in many places, and discarded shields and weapons lay in piles where the villagers had stacked them. Even a few signs of the feast remained, incongruous amidst the detritus of war and the fresh mounds of earth.

Nestor pointed over to the pile of weapons. "Are you going to give them to the villagers as well? We could show them how to defend themselves."

Will shook his head. "There won't be a future for these villagers if they try to fight their local lord. If they put all of their energy into farming they'll survive. With the help of the horses they might even thrive if the new lord gives them half a chance.

"No," Will continued, "it will be up to us to make sure they're treated properly and well defended."

Elbruhe had not attended the funerals; she remained with the wounded. Vangellis joined her as soon as the ceremony was over.

"Let's go check on Ander and Rellan," said Will, setting off for the hut that had been turned over to the monk to care for the wounded.

Following the example of their commander, Thomas and the others turned their backs on the dead and set their faces toward those who might still benefit from their help.

27

The battle for the village was over, won decisively by Will and his men. The battle for Ander's life had just begun. The outcome of this latest struggle was far from certain.

The monk had been kept busy throughout the night. Rellan's left forearm had been broken in the dying stages of the fight, and Vangellis quickly set it and applied a splint. A few villagers and a number of the baron's soldiers had also required treatment for various wounds.

The best of his attention, though, had been devoted to Ander, who lay unconscious and weak, barely clinging to life. Ander had been stabbed repeatedly before Nestor was able to drive off his attackers, and he had lost a lot of blood.

Vangellis bound up his wounds and staunched the flow of blood. Most of all the monk now feared fever and the wounds turning septic. He brewed a fragrant potion consisting of feverwort and a number of other herbs, and with the help of Elbruhe delivered it persistently into the mouth of the stricken soldier. At least some of the broth went down each time Ander swallowed.

The monk had also prepared a noxious-smelling paste. He

applied it liberally to long strips of cloth which he used as poultices when dressing the wounds.

Thomas, who had come to the hut with the others and contrived to stay on when they left, watched the process as closely as he dared. Knowing he would be instantly dismissed if he got in the way, he sat quietly in a corner and tried to remain as unobtrusive as possible.

He had never had an opportunity like it to study Elbruhe unobserved, and he watched her delicate movements with wide-eyed fascination as she attended her patient. She was so completely absorbed in the task before her that she never noticed her audience, nor the rapt attentiveness that accompanied her every gesture and sigh.

The young woman in turn, while never neglecting the soldier, seemed to be focusing almost her entire attention on the monk. Neither of them said more than an occasional word, but she seemed to anticipate his needs, handing him dressings or instruments almost before he reached for them.

How had the monk managed to capture her interest so entirely? Thomas felt a pang of jealousy as he pondered this important and seemingly unanswerable question.

His new train of thought caused him to study Vangellis himself. Thomas's own attentions were now divided between Elbruhe and the monk, just as the girl's were divided between the monk and Ander.

Vangellis, though, allowed himself no distractions. His attentions were concentrated exclusively on his patient.

It occurred to Thomas that the tireless efforts of Vangellis were bent entirely on the recovery of his onetime persecutor, the man who had so callously plunged him into his own near-fatal crisis. If the monk felt even the slightest animosity toward Ander, he showed no sign of it.

The others occasionally appeared in the room. Most often it was Will and Nestor, and early in the evening Thomas decided to leave with them after one of their visits. He was beginning to feel hungry and tired.

"What do you think, Nes?" Will asked, once they were clear of the hut. "Will they be able to save him?"

Nestor paused for a moment, then simply shook his head.

At that moment animated noises came from another hut where the baron was being held. Will frowned darkly, and made as if to go in there. But with an effort he restrained himself.

“Perhaps our noble guest is less than satisfied with his accommodations,” he said tightly. “Could you please take a turn at watching him, Thomas?”

“Yes, of course.”

Thomas went to the hut, ducked his head and entered. The interior was illuminated by the red glow from a small fire which provided warmth as well as light. The baron was chained to the central pole of the hut, secured by an ankle iron.

The baron had not been at all pleased about being chained. Thomas witnessed the whole incident. An old woman had produced the chain. She put it into Will’s hands and left without a word.

Will sought out the headman, showing him the chain and asking about the woman. “Baron put this on ’er husband as punishment,” the headman had explained. “’er man was old and frail, but Baron ’ad ’im chained to a post out in the open. Middle o’ winter. When Baron left we built a small shelter round ’im. But Baron’s men came back later. Tore it down. Tried to shelter ’im ’erself, she did. But ’e didn’t survive for long. The cold nearly got ’er, too.

“No blacksmith ’ere. So we ’ad to cut off ’is foot. To get ’im free, y’ see, so we could bury ’im. We never told ’er. Terr’ble sick, she was. Almost died.”

Will had clearly been sickened by the cruelty of the punishment. “What crime had the man committed?” he asked.

“’e didn’t bow when Baron rode past. Couldn’t do it, y’ see. Twas ’is back. Gave out years ago. Too long workin’ in the fields.”

Will said nothing in response. But he gave the chain to Nestor, who was able to release the ankle lock. Then Will took the chain and clapped the iron onto the baron’s ankle himself, securing his hands firmly in front of him with a length of rope.

The baron had plenty to say about it. The commander had little patience for his ranting or for his threats. When he showed no signs of subsiding, Will delivered a couple of stinging slaps to his face and stuffed the gag back into his mouth.

Now, many hours later, the baron did not look quite so lordly. His rich clothes were filthy, and his eyes were wild and staring. The gag was still in place. It must have been very uncomfortable.

Rellan sat in one corner of the hut, pale and clearly in pain. If the baron had been hoping for sympathy from him, he would have been sorely disappointed. Rellan had offered to watch the baron for a few hours, since only Rufe, Nestor, and Kuper were now available for patrol. The injured soldier was clearly reaching the end of his endurance.

"Will asked me to relieve you, Rellan. You need to get some rest."

"Thank you, Thomas," he replied wearily, climbing awkwardly to his feet and leaving the hut without a backward glance.

Thomas sat down, and immediately became aware that the baron was urgently trying to catch his eye. He looked everywhere except at the baron, who began jigging around in an almost maniacal fashion to draw his attention. After a few minutes of this, the situation became ridiculous. Eventually it became maddening.

Finally the inevitable could be denied no longer. Thomas looked at him. The look on the baron's face was so ludicrous that a mad laugh burst from Thomas before he could prevent it. The baron's face instantly turned to fury, which caused Thomas to blush and look away again.

For a few minutes nothing happened. Then the baron apparently mastered himself, and the whole pantomime began again.

When Thomas finally made eye contact with his prisoner again, the baron was desperately trying to communicate something.

"Mmm...mmm. Ummh-mmhh!"

Thomas didn't know what to do. The baron started up again, even more urgent this time. "Mmh! HMM!"

Eventually Thomas realized he was trying to communicate that he wanted the gag removed. That seemed like a bad idea. Thomas decided he should ignore it. But then what if the baron really needed to say something—something important? Would Will be angry when he found out?

After agonies of indecision, Thomas concluded that no real harm could come from letting the baron say what was on his mind. He was in charge—he could take whatever action seemed appropriate. Moving to the baron's side, he removed the gag.

"Untie my hands this instant," demanded the baron in a commanding voice.

The baron was so accustomed to giving orders, and Thomas so accustomed to doing as he was told, that he almost obeyed. Then he checked himself. What would the baron order him to do next? And the man was a prisoner—he wasn't supposed to be giving orders at all.

Thomas sat and did nothing. He watched as the nobleman wrestled with his anger before eventually mastering himself.

"I need to relieve myself," the baron said in a reasonable voice. "I can't do that unless you free me. Please release my arms."

The appeal took Thomas completely by surprise. How could he deny such a request? But what if the baron had trickery in mind? A ruse of some kind would be entirely in character for a man like him.

Not knowing what to say he said nothing. The baron waited for a couple of minutes then repeated his request, this time through gritted teeth, slowly emphasizing each word as if talking to the village idiot. Thomas, thoughts churning with indecision, still remained silent.

Abruptly he thought of a way of being certain about the baron's intentions. He reached down to his pouch and fumbled for the drawstring. Then he noticed his prisoner watching him curiously, and memories of the Earl of Pisander flooded into his mind: '*Boy! What do you have in your pouch? Bring it here at once.*'

He released the pouch hastily and resumed his confused silence.

Stealing occasional glances at the baron from the corner of his eye, Thomas could sense a storm brewing. Having seen him in action during the battle, it wasn't hard to imagine that the lord was accustomed to instant obedience whenever he uttered a demand. He had now issued a peremptory command and followed it with a polite request. Thomas had not responded to either of them. Predictably, the baron erupted.

Assaulted by a barrage of expletive-laden threats, and alarmed that the yelling would arouse the entire village, Thomas rapidly came to a decision and acted immediately on it. He attempted to stuff the gag back into the baron's mouth. The nobleman clamped his mouth shut uncooperatively. Thomas drew back the gag. The stream of curses resumed immediately.

But not for long. Guessing what would happen and moving like lightning, Thomas jammed the gag into the newly open mouth.

"MMMHHM! UHMMMM! MMWAHHHMM!"

Apoplectic with rage, the baron's eyes opened so wide they looked like they would pop. Thomas tried his best to settle back down and ignore the wild man before him. Many tense minutes passed before the storm appeared to subside.

Then Thomas noticed a dark stain appear on the baron's clothing and slowly spread downward. Startled, he looked at the man's face. The baron had turned beet red and tears of frustrated fury welled in his eyes. Seeing the state of this previously commanding figure unnerved Thomas completely.

It hadn't been trickery. The baron had made the most basic and reasonable of human requests and he had denied it. He knew about the cruelty of the man, and his head told him he deserved this and much, much more. But he was a nobleman. Nobody treated nobles like this and got away with it. What would the king say when the baron told him how he'd been humiliated? What would the consequences be for Thomas? But it was too late to repair the situation now.

The baron finally subsided completely. It was a good thing, too, because Thomas could no longer meet his eye. He didn't dare even to glance at the man. Time continued to pass, slowly and agonizingly.

Will had not forgotten Thomas, though. Eventually an old woman arrived in the hut. She came to Thomas, not speaking, but patting him on the shoulder and waving him to the door. He recognized her as the one who had given Will the chain. Her weathered face crinkled into a sad and toothless smile as he wearily dragged himself to his feet.

As he left he saw her settle herself down. She didn't avoid the baron's eye. She fixed him with a stony glare, and he averted his gaze.

For Thomas, this guard duty proved to be one of the most miserable experiences of his life. It was dark when he finally emerged from the hut, and he looked expectantly to see the first signs of dawn in the sky. He was surprised to learn he had only been in there for three or four hours. The sun would not be rising for many hours yet.

He hadn't eaten, but he didn't feel hungry. He dragged himself off to bed and after tossing and turning for a couple more hours eventually fell into a deep and troubled sleep.

When Thomas rose in the morning he realized that he'd seen no sign of Vangellis, and the monk's blanket did not appear to have been disturbed. No one was in the hut, but once again fresh milk had been left along with a small lump of bread. He gulped down the milk and hungrily bit into the bread as he pushed outside. A dull morning awaited him, with dark clouds rolling across the sky from the west. Ants swarmed on the ground near the hut, anticipating rain.

Curious about Vangellis, and eager to see Elbruhe, he headed for the hut where he expected to find them, carefully avoiding the place where the baron was being held. He hoped fervently that Will would not ask him to guard the prisoner again, and wondered if he could find a way to say no if he was asked.

Nestor was leaving as he arrived. Belatedly, and somewhat guiltily, it occurred to him to wonder if Ander had made it through the night.

"How's Ander, Nes?" he asked.

Nestor screwed up his face and peered up at the sky before turning to him to answer.

"He's alive. Barely. The monk's been up all night with him. Not sure what he's trying to prove. Doesn't owe him any favors."

The soldier spat and glanced at the sky once more before disappearing behind one of the huts.

Before Thomas could step inside he noticed Elbruhe striding purposefully in his direction. He smiled and opened his mouth to greet her, but she ignored him completely, pushing past him into the hut with neither a word nor a backward glance. He frowned, trying to think what he'd done to deserve her reaction. Completely at a loss, he shrugged helplessly, ducked his head and followed her into the hut.

He arrived inside into the middle of an argument. Elbruhe was expostulating fiercely in Rogandan. Her arms were jerking about as she emphatically drove home every point, and her tone was brimming over with emotion. But her voice was lowered so as not to disturb the patient. The scene was almost comical.

Thomas didn't need to understand Rogandan to get the drift of it. Vangellis had been up all night tending to his patient, while Elbruhe finally got some sleep. Now she wanted to reverse the roles. He was politely but firmly refusing to do it. The monk clearly had a stubborn streak, and the girl's best efforts made no difference at all. He wouldn't budge.

Finally, she threw up her hands in exasperation and turned to the patient. Thomas at last remembered Ander, and looked across at the soldier.

What he saw shocked him. If the man had seemed pale and weak before, he now appeared almost spectral. Thomas had seen corpses before, and Ander's sallow complexion reminded him of a corpse.

Vangellis knelt at his head gently mopping his brow. Elbruhe was right—the monk looked close to exhaustion himself. His mouth was moving, but Thomas couldn't catch what he was saying. Was he whispering to his patient? Thomas felt a little stupid when he finally figured it out. The monk was praying.

A life and death struggle was being fought in the hut. Ander's life was a small lamp with its oil almost spent and its wick flickering weakly. Vangellis was protecting the tiny flame, shielding it from the elements. The fact that his task seemed utterly hopeless did not appear to dismay him at all.

The monk's face was lit by a number of candles as well as the fire in the hut. But his face almost appeared to have a light of its own.

How was that possible? Puzzled, Thomas stared at him intently. He watched closely for many minutes, and with increasing astonishment. It was true—he hadn't imagined it. The monk was, quite literally, glowing. Thomas gazed at him in wonder, feeling like he had never seen him before.

Something strange and beyond his comprehension was taking place in that room. Thomas was superstitious of course. He had a robust fear of God, sometimes remembered to pray to the saints—especially when he was in trouble—and had enough sense to be terrified of ghosts. What was happening in the hut felt different, though. He was glimpsing something far beyond his grasp, but it made him feel stronger, more hopeful about life.

Although he didn't feel in any way frightened or alarmed, he knew for certain that he did not belong there. His legs carried him from the hut almost involuntarily.

Once outside, the sense of awe quickly began to dissipate. But Thomas had emerged with an unshakable conviction that Ander would recover. He couldn't say why he believed that, and it certainly made no sense. But he didn't doubt it even for a minute.

Humming brightly to himself and with a spring in his step, he set off to check the horses. The sun was setting low in the sky before he realized that Elbruhe had been absent from his thoughts all afternoon, and he hadn't even noticed.

AFTER A DAY and a half of heavy rain the weather cleared. There had been no sign of the baron's soldiers; it seemed that the new steward was taking Will's message seriously. The baron himself was now allowed to spend the daylight hours out of doors. But he was still chained, and anchored to a pole. His gag had been removed on the understanding that he would not speak. He kept his end of the bargain, but his dark looks and threatening demeanor still said plenty to anyone willing to pay attention. As long as he didn't speak, though, Will chose to ignore his behavior.

Many of the villagers avoided him entirely. Even chained he still terrified them. A few paused whenever they passed by and glared at him, though, crossing themselves to ward off evil as they left.

The village was a scene of continuous bustle. Thomas had been teaching the villagers to care for the horses. A few of them could not overcome their fear of the animals, but many others now approached them confidently and were quickly learning how to handle them. In another day or two, Thomas hoped to have three or four of them in the saddle.

Nestor had also begun to show them how to plow their fields behind a horse. The farmers were clearly startled at how much more could be achieved with the help of their new animals. The village was changing before their eyes. The grim faces and the quiet despair that greeted them when they first arrived already seemed a distant memory.

Thomas had not visited Ander again, but he remained eager to know how he was progressing. His companions uniformly predicted a gloomy outcome; Thomas believed otherwise but kept his opinions to himself. Will seemed willing to tolerate a further delay in reaching the king until the situation was resolved. One way or the other it would surely be settled before long.

Late in the second day after Thomas had last seen Ander and the monk, Elbruhe came running out of the hut calling excitedly. No one could understand a word she was saying until Will arrived and relayed her unexpected news. Ander was awake.

All of them ran immediately to the little hut and crammed inside it. Nestor was already there. Elbruhe tolerated the presence of the new arrivals for no longer than a minute before shooing them out again.

They all returned the next day, this time by invitation. Thomas unabashedly pushed his way to the front to get a better look. Ander was not only awake, but sitting up, supported by Elbruhe who had rushed back to his side as soon as her invitation had been delivered. As they arrived she was helping him sip from a bowl filled with steaming broth.

Ander offered them a barely audible greeting and managed a

weak smile. The soldiers returned hearty, if muted, congratulations, then lapsed into silence. Thomas could sense their surprise, though. Their companion may have looked frail, but he was very much alive. He even had some color in his cheeks.

Thomas took the opportunity to study the monk closely. He appeared entirely normal. There was nothing unusual about his appearance. Thomas could no longer detect any visible glow from him, but there was a calm composure about his presence that seemed different from before. After a brief smile of greeting he ignored the visitors and quietly went about his business.

The most remarkable change was in Ander. His eyes barely left the monk. Looking at the convalescent soldier, Thomas found himself remembering Ben, his faithful mastiff, lying quietly at his feet attentive to his every movement.

ANDER LEFT the hut for the first time a couple of days later. He was too weak to go far, but everyone was heartened by his obvious progress. Within a week he was able to move about more freely, and Will asked Thomas to assess his ability to ride.

Thomas led Ander to his horse. The animal whinnied in pleasure as its master greeted it and stroked its neck.

"Do you think you'll be able to ride again soon, Ander?"

"My wounds are healing well, but they may open up again if I ride too soon," he replied. "It shouldn't be too far off, though. Maybe three or four days. I'm sure Will is eager to be on the move again."

"Will won't leave until you're ready."

They stood there without speaking for a time. Thomas finally broke the silence.

"It didn't look good for you in there, Ander. But somehow I knew you were going to make it." He wanted to say more, but he couldn't find the words.

"It wasn't good. I was in a very dark place." A faraway look came into Ander's eyes. "I couldn't find my way out. There was a bright light, way off in the distance, but I couldn't get to it. I was lost." Ander paused, remembering. "Then he called me."

"Who?" asked Thomas.

Ander looked at him, uncomprehending.

"Who called you?" Thomas repeated.

"The monk, of course. Brother Vangellis."

Ander turned back to his horse, patting its neck.

Thomas was too shocked to reply. He had never heard Ander even refer to the monk by name, much less use his title.

Before long all the soldiers were calling the monk 'Brother Vangellis'. None of them even seemed aware of the change.

Thomas couldn't bring himself to do it, though. It wasn't any lack of respect. It wasn't actually anything to do with the monk. He'd come face to face with something outside his comprehension, and he couldn't figure out how to respond to it.

If he adopted the monk's title, deep down inside himself he sensed that he would be crossing a threshold. His world would change, and he would change with it.

'Brother Vangellis.' Such simple words. But he couldn't say them.

That left him with a dilemma. He had nothing against the monk, and didn't want anyone to think he was making a point by staying away from his title. He soon discovered, though, that with a little creativity it was possible to avoid referring to a person by name at all.

LATER THAT AFTERNOON they gathered to say goodbye to Rellan and Kuper. Rellan held his arm loosely in a sling. He wouldn't have full use of it any time soon, but he looked a lot brighter even than a couple of days ago.

"Are you sure you want us to leave, Will?" Kuper looked concerned.

"Don't worry about us," Will replied. "With or without you, we can't fight our way through a Rogandan army. And I need you to get to Erestor and find Lord Burtelen. He should have raised an army by now, and we're going to need it.

"Make sure he personally receives the messages I've given you. Hand them over yourself—don't give them to anyone other than him."

"Understood."

Will turned to Rellan and jabbed a finger at him. "I don't want to see you again until you're fully recovered."

Rellan managed a smile. "You'll see me sooner than you think. I won't stay away a minute longer than I need to," he vowed.

The twins eased their mounts forward as everyone called out farewells. As they passed Thomas, Rellan winked at him.

"Stay out of trouble," he grinned, jerking his head toward Elbruhe.

Kuper laughed out loud. Thomas felt a blush coming and hoped no one was watching him too closely.

As the twins spurred their horses and rode out of the village, the baron smirked to himself. This upstart 'commander' didn't have too many soldiers left to command.

Soon they would leave to find the king, and this Will would undoubtedly take him with them. Many long leagues lay between this village and the king, though, and they couldn't expect him to ride while he was chained. An opportunity to escape would present itself, and now there were two enemies fewer to worry about.

He scowled as he thought about his own soldiers. The cowards had made no attempt to rescue him. When he got back to his castle there would be scores to settle.

His eyes narrowed as he surveyed the village and its inhabitants. They dared to plow their fields with his horses, and stand in judgment over him as they passed by. Their turn would come.

He moved uncomfortably, causing his chains to rattle, which further fueled his anger. So his captors thought they could chain him up like a dog, did they? Commoners and rabble, every one of them. He would find a way to make them pay.

28

Almost another week passed before they finally left the village. Ander's recovery had progressed remarkably well, and he almost looked his normal self. For his sake, Will refused to consider leaving sooner, but by the end of that time the commander was becoming noticeably restive. He had made certain that all of them were thoroughly prepared in advance so that nothing further would delay their departure.

Although all members of the party now had their own horse to ride, they were still able to leave a dozen animals for the villagers. The locals had selflessly given up some of the horses to neighboring villages. As a result, three villages now had four horses each as well as people trained in the care and use of them. Thomas made sure that each village had more than one mare; in time, small herds could be established.

Adequate supplies of feed would need to be set aside for the winter months, but plenty of suitable fodder grew nearby, and the children could help to gather it. The villagers had already completed the construction of crude stables to shelter their precious new assistants.

Every person in the village turned out to bid them goodbye. By prior agreement, each member of the party had prepared a small gift for their hosts. Thomas gave his favorite horse brush to his hosts. They knew that he was the army's horse master, and understood the value to him of this gift. They thanked him many times.

The old man had a new sparkle in his eyes of late. He came close and pinched the cheek of Thomas affectionately. The old woman embraced him with tears in her eyes. She had spoken several times of her own son, taken from her many years previously to serve the baron. The monk had once asked her if Thomas reminded her of her son, and she readily confirmed his suspicion. Thomas had no difficulty imagining how his own mother might feel in similar circumstances, and he made sure his farewell was warm and unhurried.

All of the villagers approached the monk, bowing and touching his cloak reverently. Some brought children for him to bless. He appeared uncomfortable and embarrassed by the attention. They either didn't notice or didn't care.

As they mounted, the headman approached Will.

"Thank y'. All o' y'," he said, bowing low respectfully. "Don't know 'ow to pay y'. For all y' kindness, y' un'erstand."

"No need for payment," Will replied with a smile. "We're pleased we could do something to help get the village back onto its feet."

The headman bowed low once again.

Then he lowered his voice. "B'ware o' Baron," he confided. "'im'll 'urt y' if 'e can."

"We understand. Thank you for the warning."

Thomas glanced over at the baron, who sat atop his horse with hands tied firmly in front of him and the rope secured to the horn of his saddle. He glared at the villagers and his captors alike with creased brows and open anger on his face. The headman was clearly right. They would need to guard the nobleman like an enemy soldier.

They waved a final farewell, and rode out of the village.

Nestor and Rufe had scouted for many leagues to the north, west and east and discovered no sign of the Rogandans. Based on this information, and after a lengthy consultation with the monk, Will decided to head directly north for Castel to seek out the king. He knew they were very unlikely to be able to avoid the Rogandans entirely. They would need to find a way through Deadman's Pass, and Will fully expected to find it held against them.

The weather remained fine once they cleared the great forest and rode north through open grasslands. For three days they made excellent progress, stopping only briefly to rest their horses and to sleep. They ate and drank during the brief rest breaks, and slept for no more than four or five hours before setting off again before dawn.

By the evening of the third day, both the monk and Elbruhe had become well accustomed to the saddle. Observing them, Thomas felt they looked as though they had been riding most of their lives.

Very little passed between any of them, even when they stopped for the night. Weeks of intensity and high drama had given way to a single focus on reaching the king. Thomas was glad of the respite; he needed time to ponder everything that had happened. His old life in Arnost now seemed like a distant memory. A few weeks ago he hadn't even met some of the people who had now assumed significance in his life—people like the monk, and, well, Elbruhe. He felt himself blushing again, grateful that no one was nearby to notice it.

The baron had scarcely spoken since they left the village. Thomas thought he could see the nobleman's scowl deepening as the leagues rolled away beneath the pounding hooves of their horses. Thomas wasn't the only one aware of it, either—he noticed both Will and Rufe watching their prisoner more closely than ever.

With the forest now far behind them, the riders began to notice a range of mountains off in the distance. The mountains drew ever nearer as they journeyed north. After a few days the terrain was noticeably changing, and there were signs that the grasslands were coming to an end. Before long they found themselves climbing steadily, and encountering isolated stands of trees.

A tree line became visible ahead in the foothills of the mountains and gradually gained definition as they approached. Tall pines stretched east and west as far as the eye could see. Will consulted with Vangellis before deciding that it was time to turn west to find the break in the tree line that signaled the entrance to the pass into Castel.

It was well past noon, with the sun moving steadily across the sky on its way toward the western horizon, when Nestor appeared ahead in the distance, riding hard toward them. It could only mean one thing.

"Head for the tree line!" Will ordered urgently. They turned their mounts north again and dashed for the safety of the trees.

Nestor did not reach them until they had almost made it to the trees. Riders were now clearly visible behind him.

"How many?" Will called as soon as he came into earshot.

"No more than a dozen," he called back. "Others on foot, but far away."

"Follow me!" Will called as they plunged at last into the trees. He led them in deeper until they came to a natural dell, sheltered from sight until they were right upon it.

He called them to a halt, and immediately dismounted. All of them quickly followed his example.

"Thomas, take the horses to the far side of the dell, and try to keep them quiet. Ander, take care of Brother Vangellis and the girl. Take the baron with you. You won't be fighting—I need you to keep them out of harm's way.

"Rufe and Nes, come with me. If they find us, they'll get a warm welcome."

"Commander!" called the baron. "You could use an extra fighter. It's time to put aside our differences for a while. Untie my hands and let me have a sword."

Will turned to the nobleman, and Thomas felt his heart skip a beat. Surely Will would never agree to such an idea.

"When this is over I'll return the sword, and we will continue as before. You have my word. I will put my case before the king."

Thomas glanced from Will to the baron and back again. It was true that they were badly outnumbered, with only three uninjured fighters to defend them all. But surely the baron's promise couldn't be taken seriously.

Will's face set hard. "I don't trust you, Baron. You demonstrated clearly at the village that your word means nothing." He turned to Ander. "Keep him out of sight," he told him.

Ander nodded. "Don't try anything, Baron," he growled.

The nobleman ignored him.

Ander took up a position on the far side of Rufe, directly in front of Thomas and the horses. The baron stood behind Thomas, and Brother Vangellis and Elbruhe positioned themselves at the rear.

Thomas glanced around behind him, eyeing the baron doubtfully. He couldn't help remembering his guard duty in the hut.

Seeing the look on his face, the baron addressed him quietly. "Don't worry, boy. I wouldn't want to see anything happen to you." Then, more quietly, he added "Yet," with a nasty smile.

Thomas faced forward again, sweating uncomfortably and trying hard to convince himself that he could simply ignore the nobleman's words.

They all settled down to wait. Time passed, and Thomas began to hope that they would remain undetected.

Then they heard the voices of their pursuers, calling out to each other as they searched among the trees. Thomas wondered if they would be making so much noise if they had been aware of the reputations of their outnumbered quarry.

The Rogandans drew closer, and one of them soon passed by very close to their hiding place. He didn't enter the dell, though, and Thomas dared to hope the soldier would leave without discovering them.

He stole another glance back at the baron, and was horrified to see the prisoner with a knife, having almost severed the bonds on his hands.

With the Rogandan so nearby, Thomas couldn't call out. Instead, he urgently reached forward to alert Ander.

At that crucial moment, though, Thomas was struck on the head and fell heavily to the ground. Dazed, he picked himself up in time to see the baron mounted, and spurring his horse out of the dell. Clearing their cover the nobleman let forth a shout of challenge that echoed through the trees. The Rogandan immediately turned toward the sound, calling loudly for his companions.

Other soldiers soon appeared. Two of them set off after the baron, whose fleeing form was already lost to sight. The others swarmed into the dell.

One soldier was met by an arrow and tumbled from his horse, dead before he hit the ground. An arrow intended for a second soldier instead took his mount in the neck. The horse screamed and went down, throwing its rider almost at the feet of Will. The commander dispatched him with a single stroke and immediately looked around for new targets.

Another soldier came at Thomas, sword raised to strike. The youth released the horses and threw himself to one side. He escaped the attack, but could only watch helpless as the Rogandan scattered the horses.

The dell soon descended into a chaos of shouting soldiers, flying arrows, and the clash of swords. Thomas remained kneeling where he was, trying to remain inconspicuous.

Nestor got off several more arrows before three soldiers attacked him at once. He was soon fighting for his life.

Another soldier came at Rufe. The giant guardsman ducked under the attacker's wild sword swipe, picked up a branch, and used it to knock the man from his horse. Rufe was on him before he had a chance to get up. He'd barely dealt with this opponent before two more were on him.

Ander also quickly came under attack. He had been assigned the task of protecting the monk and Elbruhe, and he did so with energy that belied his recent injuries. He called anxiously to the monk and the girl, urging them to hide among the trees.

Will much preferred to fight on horseback, and grabbed the reins of a riderless horse and swung himself into the saddle. Rufe soon followed his example, and the two of them rode to the aid of Nestor, who took advantage of the distraction to find a mount himself. Although still heavily outnumbered, they coordinated their efforts to draw the attackers away from Ander and the others. The main conflict soon shifted westward out of sight of Thomas.

The sounds of battle gradually diminished, and Thomas dared to hope that those sheltering in the dell had seen the last of the fighting. He looked around, trying to locate each of his companions. The monk was nowhere to be seen, but he spotted Elbruhe not far away, peering cautiously from behind a tree. Ander leaned on his sword, breathing hard. He had fought bravely and effectively, but it had clearly taken a big toll on his reduced resources.

One riderless horse wandered nearby, and Thomas quickly secured it. He could see no sign of the other horses, but he decided not to go searching for them until the outcome of the battle was decided. They probably weren't too far off. He peered off into the trees to the west, looking for any sign of returning soldiers.

Ander shouted a sudden warning and moved to engage a Rogandan soldier who rode in from the opposite direction. Thomas, still holding the reins of the horse, drew back and watched the conflict from a safe distance. Ander soon showed himself to be the more experienced fighter, but his reactions had slowed, and the other soldier made up for his lack of skills with a seemingly endless supply of energy. Thomas felt confident about the ultimate outcome, but nothing could be taken for granted.

Totally absorbed in the scene before him, Thomas was startled into sudden alertness by a high-pitched cry, "TO-MMAAASSS!" He spun around in time to see a second Rogandan spurring his horse toward him, a spear pointed at his heart. He threw himself frantically out of the way, barely avoiding the spear thrust. Without Elbruhe's warning he could not have escaped.

He scrambled quickly to his feet, ready for a second attack, but the rider had already turned aside to pursue a new target. Thomas watched with helpless horror as the soldier overtook the fleeing form of Elbruhe and ran her through.

Heart pounding and screaming her name, he ran to her side, utterly heedless of his own safety. He reached her in a moment and knelt beside her.

Ander, having dealt with his previous opponent, appeared on horseback and chased the attacker out of the dell. Thomas did not even notice.

Elbruhe lay face down, with blood soaking the clothing on her back around a gaping wound. He gently turned her toward him onto her side. She gazed uncomprehending up into his face for a moment, then life flickered briefly in her eyes. A crooked smile passed across her lips. "Delou-ahn," she murmured.

His anguished tears blinded him as he sat down and drew her to himself. Hopelessly he racked his brains, trying to imagine some way to staunch the bright red flow from her back. But no answers came, and he simply clung to her.

Then he felt her body relax. She sighed, a long and weary sigh, and breathed no more.

A tight knot came into his throat, and bitter tears flowed freely, dripping down onto her face. He sat unmoving, cradling her head in his lap. Entirely unconscious of his surroundings, he saw only her face, peaceful at last, and her empty staring eyes.

HE WAS STILL THERE when Vangellis found him. The flow of tears had ceased, and he sat numb and unmoving, unaware of the world around him, as if frozen in time.

Vangellis drew close, and, reaching down, gently closed her eyes. Thomas started as if slapped, and looked up at the monk. Their eyes met, and, finding compassion and grief in the eyes of another who had truly cared about the girl, he was completely undone. He began to weep loudly.

The monk bent low once more and carefully removed the burden from his lap. Then, drawing Thomas to his feet, he enfolded him in a giant bear hug.

Thomas abandoned himself to his grief then and wept without constraint, his entire body wracked with heaving sobs. Vangellis held him tightly.

In time the torrent ceased, and Thomas, once more calm, stepped back from the monk. He didn't understand how, but it felt like he had been washed clean inside. His grief had not left him, but he was surprised to discover that he felt some measure of peace.

They stood without speaking for a time.

Finally the monk spoke up. "We can't stay here, Thomas," he said. Then almost to himself he continued, "But I won't leave her like that."

He turned to Thomas and asked him, "Will you help me prepare a grave?"

Thomas simply nodded in response.

They set out together to find a suitable resting place. Before long they came upon a grassy sod beside a small stream where wildflowers covered the ground, pale and delicate. Neither of them spoke—they didn't need to. This was the spot.

Thomas returned to the dell and retrieved a fallen spear. He marked out a section of ground and used the spear to begin carefully removing the turves. He put the grass and the flowers to one side and began digging into the moist soil underneath. The monk got down on hands and knees to help him.

After thirty minutes they had laid bare a shallow grave. They went together to the dell and retrieved her body, carrying it to the open grave and lovingly positioning it within. Then Vangellis led Thomas to the stream, and they rinsed their clothes as best they could, staining the clear water bright red. Thomas did it absently, his thoughts far away.

The monk fashioned a small cross from wood, securing the pieces with tough twine torn from a creeper. He placed it into the ground above her head.

"I will not leave Elbruhe to the harsh mercies of her Dark Gods," he said quietly, as if speaking to himself aloud. "She questioned me many times about our own God—he had captured her imagination, and, I believe, her heart, and it is into his gracious hands that I commend her spirit."

He said much more, speaking of hope and of a final resurrection. But Thomas heard little of it. His mind wandered down pathways of the past, remembering an independent spirit, a face framed by wild hair, the lash of a sharp tongue, and the weary attentiveness of a nurse laboring through the night. Most of all he thought about everything she had come to mean to him, and the magnitude of what he had so suddenly and irrevocably lost.

Then they slowly covered her body with the moist earth, repositioning the turves on top of the mound. Thomas could not bring himself to cover her head. He turned aside while Vangellis completed the task.

Thomas lingered by the graveside, unable to will himself to embrace the future. Vangellis disappeared, perhaps wanting to allow him some solitude.

The monk returned after about an hour, holding the reins of a horse.

"I found him wandering nearby," he explained. "Do you think you could find us another one?"

Thomas did not respond immediately, but finally he nodded and accepted the reins offered by Vangellis. He mounted the horse and set off.

He did not want to stop thinking about Elbruhe and his loss, and he felt almost guilty about focusing on anything else. But at the same time it was a relief to have something to do.

He began his search at the dell, carefully avoiding the place where Elbruhe had fallen. A number of bodies lay there, and he belatedly and guiltily wondered what had become of his other companions. All of the slain wore Rogandan garb, which came as a relief to him. Seeing them lying there evoked no response at all in him. That in itself felt strange given the intensity of the grief he had just experienced. He clicked his tongue and guided his horse away from the dell. He didn't look back.

Another horse was grazing quietly not far away, and he took its reins and led it back to the stream. Vangellis knelt beside the grave with his head bowed, apparently praying. Thomas was not willing to disturb him, but one of the horses whinnied and shook its head, causing the monk to look up.

The monk joined him and accepted the reins, swinging himself into the saddle. They both sat silently on their horses for many minutes. Then Vangellis turned his horse's head and slowly headed off through the trees.

After pausing a moment longer, Thomas followed him. *I won't ever forget you*, he promised silently, brushing at the new flow of tears that welled up in his eyes and trickled down over his cheeks.

"THOMAS! LOOK, A RIDERLESS HORSE," Vangellis called. Thomas peered in the direction he was pointing and saw the animal through the trees off to their left.

"We'd better remove its saddle and bridle," the youth replied. "If the reins get caught in some branches the horse will starve."

They picked their way through the trees and emerged into a small clearing.

"We seem to have found its rider," said the monk, pointing to a figure lying face down on the ground.

Even from a distance Thomas could see that it was the baron. At the sight of their betrayer Thomas felt intense anger rising up within him. He wanted to hurt the man, to make him pay.

He dismounted and marched over to the baron, bending down and flipping him onto his back. He stepped back at once, retching involuntarily.

The baron was dead. His killers had not treated him kindly. He lay with his intestines hanging out and the ground soaked with his blood. The look on his face made it obvious that he had died a particularly painful death.

Vangellis came to his side and winced. "They certainly made a mess of him," he exclaimed. "A terrible way to die, poor fellow," he concluded.

Thomas glared at him. "Poor fellow?" he said indignantly. "He deserved everything he got and more! Elbruhe would be alive right now if it wasn't for him!"

To his annoyance, he felt his lower lip tremble uncontrollably as he spoke her name. His own weakness made him angrier than ever. "I hate him! I hate the sight of him," he spat. He turned away and paced up and down restlessly, trying to master his feelings.

After a few minutes he looked back and saw the monk gathering rocks into a pile at the baron's head.

Seeing him looking on, Vangellis paused for a moment. "The ground is very hard here," he said. "We can't dig a grave without tools. I'm planning to cover him with branches. Would you like to help me?"

"No! I won't do anything for him. The vultures can have him if they want. They'll probably choke on him!"

Thomas turned angrily on the monk. "Why are you doing this for him? I know you cared about her." His lip betrayed him again and forced him to silence, tears of frustration welling in his eyes.

"Yes, I cared about her," Vangellis acknowledged. He paused, a thoughtful look on his face. "You're going to have to forgive him, Thomas."

"Forgive him?! Never!" Thomas vowed fiercely. "I'll hate him until the day I die."

"He's beyond your hatred now."

"I don't care. After what he did, he doesn't deserve to be forgiven. Ever!"

The monk did not respond for a full minute. Then he said softly, "Do all of *your* actions deserve forgiveness, Thomas? Have you never given anyone reason to hate you for what you did to them?"

Thomas looked at him sharply, expecting accusation but finding no sign of it in the monk's eyes. If anything, Vangellis looked ashamed.

Thomas opened his mouth to absolve himself, but an image came flooding into his mind. He saw a pitchfork, saw himself lunging with unbridled rage, to hurt, to wound. He remembered the terror in Simon's eyes.

He clamped shut his mouth and turned away.

Somehow his fierce anger toward the baron had ebbed away, but a stubbornness rose up in its place. He would not forgive. He would *never* forgive.

The monk resumed his labors without assistance from Thomas. The youth instead busied himself with the stray horse.

As Thomas waited for Vangellis to finish, the reality of their situation gradually sank in. They had no idea what had become of Will and Rufe and the others. If any Rogandans appeared they would find themselves undefended. Even the baron had been armed with a knife and trained to defend himself; their prospects would be worse than his.

Thomas started to become restless. Vangellis was taking too long.

Finally he could wait no longer. "We need to go!" he said, unable to keep a tone of irritability out of his voice. "It isn't safe here."

The monk must have decided he'd done enough, because almost immediately he ceased his efforts. He stood by the graveside with head bowed for a few moments then turned away and mounted his horse. They picked their way out of the small clearing and resumed their journey. They were heading away from their friends, but Thomas felt confident that Nestor could track them wherever they went. Assuming he was still in a position to do so.

They traveled for about an hour, with Vangellis taking the lead. As much as possible they stayed among the trees, and saw no one. By then the light was fading fast.

The monk brought his horse to a stop and turned to Thomas.

"We have no way of knowing what's happened to Will and the others," he said. "I don't doubt for a minute that they're still alive. And they will come looking for us.

"They will follow us because they feel responsible for our safety. But the truth is that I have become a burden to them. They no longer need my services as a guide. The pass to Castel is somewhere nearby, and they know which direction to take to find it. And once Will rejoins the king he will have his choice of local guides.

"What about you, though, Thomas? I know you have a long-standing friendship with both Will and Rufe, and you are the army's horse master. But why did they bring you on such a perilous journey? Do you have some key role to play that I am not aware of? Or did they bring you away from Arnost to protect you from something or someone?"

The monk's questions shocked Thomas. His guesses were close to the mark—uncomfortably so. Was the reality of his situation this obvious to everyone? Or was the monk simply an exceptionally shrewd observer?

Vangellis had also raised an uncomfortable question. Was he himself also a burden to Will? He knew that Will and Rufe, and the others, too, would defend him without hesitation. Even if it put their own lives at risk. Surely that made him a liability, because he could offer little in return. They had no need of his particular skills with horses. And the stone was of little use out here, even if he could be confident it would work reliably for him.

Then he found himself wondering if he should have tried the stone on the baron. Perhaps he could have anticipated his treachery and saved Elbruhe's life. But even in his grief Thomas could see that playing guessing games with the past was pointless. The past could not be changed. What was done was done.

Vangellis still waited patiently for a response. And Thomas discovered that his perspective had undergone a major shift.

"It isn't just you," he acknowledged. "I'm a burden to them as well."

"Then I have a suggestion," Vangellis told him. "The others will catch up with us tomorrow if we rest tonight, and we will rejoin them and continue to slow them down.

"But there is another way. I know of a remote monastery up in the mountains—we can reach it in three or four days. We'll be safe from the Rogandans there. Our friends will no longer need to worry about us."

"But will they know we've gone somewhere safe?"

"They won't know for certain. I think they will guess, though."

"I hope you're right. Will needs to join the king. He needs an army."

"The monastery, then?" Vangellis asked.

"The monastery," Thomas agreed.

29

"It happened over here." Ander led them to the place where Elbruhe had lain.

"She's been moved," said Will.

"You're right," Nestor affirmed, and immediately set off, head down, following the trail of blood.

They followed the trail for several minutes. "Thomas couldn't have carried her this far on his own," Rufe asserted.

"No," Will agreed. "Brother Vangellis must have been here, too."

They soon found themselves in a small clearing beside a stream, looking at a new mound with a small cross at its head. They dismounted and stood in silence, taking in the scene.

"It was a brutal end to a harsh life."

The others looked at Will in wonder, astonished at the tremulous tone of his voice, and even more surprised to see the tears that trickled down his cheeks.

Finally Rufe spoke up. "They chose a peaceful place to lay her to rest, though," he offered.

"They did," Will agreed firmly, his voice steady again.

They stood without speaking for many minutes.

"Brother Vangellis would have seen her off properly," Ander said finally.

The others nodded their agreement.

Will turned away from the grave. "We can't delay longer. Let's find out what's become of our Thomas and Brother Vangellis," he said.

They mounted and headed off after Nestor who had already found the trail and was following it swiftly on foot, leading his horse.

They followed only for a short time before Nestor halted.

"They turned aside here," he announced, "before continuing on their original path."

They followed him into a small clearing. A small pile of rocks had been fashioned into a simple cairn, and a small mound lay beneath it. A horse grazed beside the mound.

The mound proved to be mostly fallen tree branches and leaves. They removed a few of the branches and found a body freshly laid out beneath the pile. It was the baron.

"Looks like the Rogandans have saved our king some trouble," Nestor suggested dryly.

"This fool has cost us far too much time and loss already. Let's be on our way," said Will, throwing a branch or two back onto the mound.

"The horse?" asked Rufe.

"It can go wherever it wants to," he replied. "Looks like Thomas already removed the saddle and bridle," he concluded, pointing to some items lying on the other side of the cairn.

The afternoon light failed and quickly gave way to dusk, forcing them to abandon the search until daylight. They ate slowly and lay down to sleep as soon as Will had assigned each of them a turn at sentry duty through the night. After the riding and the fighting that lay behind them they were soon asleep.

In the morning Nestor led them on. The trail was going cold, and he consulted with the others more than once before leading them forward. He always found the right path.

The afternoon was wearing on when they finally halted before a rocky incline.

"They're a long way ahead of us," Nestor said. "They must have traveled on during the night."

"The monk knows his way around," Will replied.

"I suspect we'll find that they abandoned their horses here," Nestor suggested. "The trail goes on and up, and they were traveling by foot."

"I think I know where they're going," said Will. "There's a remote monastery somewhere up there in the mountains. Brother Vangellis will certainly know where to find it."

He paused for a moment, then continued. "We're not going to follow them any further. We no longer need a guide, and Thomas will be safer there than anywhere we might take him."

Rufe nodded. "Young Thomas'll be all right. He's in good hands."

"None better," Ander agreed.

"Then let's not delay any longer," Will concluded. "It's time we found the king."

THOMAS and the monk had been climbing steadily throughout the afternoon. Their progress was slower now, since they were traveling on foot.

They had set the horses free as soon as the going became difficult for the animals. Vangellis explained that the monastery did not maintain food or shelter for horses, so there was little point in keeping them any longer than they were useful.

When they paused for a meal late in the day, Thomas discovered to his dismay that they were eating the last of their provisions.

"How are we going to survive without food?" he demanded.

Vangellis, who appeared entirely unconcerned about their predicament, paused in his eating and gazed across at Thomas.

"Three or four days without food would do us no real harm. It might do us some good. Perhaps it would help us remember the lot of those who never have enough to eat."

Thomas colored, remembering the way his hosts in the village watched him eat the bread.

"But you need not worry," the monk continued with a smile. "I have spent many years wandering alone in many different places, and I have learned where to find things to eat. We will not go hungry.

"I also know how to keep us safe from any predators that might be roaming these mountains. Apart from predators of the human variety, that is," he added seriously.

They lit a small fire that night. Vangellis chose dry wood that gave off little smoke, but they had spent the entire day climbing ever upward through difficult terrain, and the likelihood of anyone coming upon them seemed very remote indeed.

Once he lay down, Thomas fell quickly into a deep sleep. He dreamed that he was riding alone across open grasslands. He was going somewhere on an important errand, but he couldn't quite remember what it was. Soon he came to a wide and swiftly flowing river. He could see no place to safely cross it, but for some reason it seemed important to do so.

He dismounted and led his horse down to the water's edge to take a drink. Then he heard a voice calling his name.

"TO-MMAAASSS!"

He looked up, startled, and saw Elbruhe standing on the opposite bank of the river. She was calling to him, urgently trying to tell him something. But he could barely hear her over the noise of the water, and he couldn't understand a word she was saying, anyway.

Impulsively, he mounted his horse and rode it into the river. There was no other way to cross. The horse struck out strongly for the other bank, but they were quickly caught in the current, and swept downstream.

Thomas turned his head to keep his eyes on Elbruhe, but her form dwindled rapidly in size and soon disappeared from sight. He faintly heard her call his name one last time, "Toooomm-maaasss...!"

He woke with a start and sat up, panting for air. The night was cold, but he found himself covered with sweat.

Everything around him was still pitch black. Stars twinkled high overhead, but as yet no glow had appeared in the eastern sky.

Then he heard a strange wailing sound. Could it be Elbruhe calling him? Then he remembered that she was dead. The hairs tingled on the back of his neck.

The fire had burned down, and only coals remained. In the dim light he could see no sign of Vangellis. The monk was not there.

He heard the sound again. This time it seemed more clearly human, more anguished. Had Vangellis gone to identify the source of the noise? He had a feeling that the monk would not be frightened by strange cries in the night.

He got up and crept carefully in the direction he had heard it coming from. Once he was away from the glow of the embers his eyes gradually adjusted to the darkness. He picked his way among the trees until he came to a clearing.

An indistinct form was faintly visible across the clearing from him. Sobs shook the dark frame, punctuated occasionally by a low wailing. He had found the monk.

Thomas stood there for a few minutes, uncertain how to respond. Did the monk need his help in some way? Or would he feel that Thomas was spying on him?

Eventually he took the easiest solution and quietly slipped away. He returned to the campsite and lay down again beside the coals. But he could not get back to sleep. He lay awake, picturing the monk sobbing alone in the clearing, and wondering what could have reduced him to such a state of distress.

The first hint of dawn finally began to glow in the eastern sky. A dark mass of clouds overhead had hidden the stars; the clouds slowly became visible, their outlines tinged with orange and yellow. As the light grew in strength the colors became richer and more varied. Captivated by the display, Thomas for a moment forgot all else in the extravagant dawning of a new day.

The light grew brighter, and the vivid colors slowly yielded to bold whites and grays. With the performance coming to an end, Thomas began to find it increasingly difficult to understand how such beauty could coexist so casually with the pain and loss in the world. How could God send a sunrise like that after the brutality of Elbruhe's death?

The sun had cleared the treetops before the monk returned to the campsite. He showed no signs of his pre-dawn distress. In fact he appeared more peaceful and composed than Thomas had ever remembered him.

"I've brought some berries," the monk announced with a smile, revealing a dark blue treasure trove secreted in a fold of his cloak. "They're delicious," he promised. The blue-stained teeth exposed by his grin amply reinforced his assertion.

Thomas tried one, and they were indeed delicious. The two of them quickly disposed of the pile, and both sat back sighing contentedly.

Vangellis was different—that much was obvious—and Thomas was very curious to know the reason. But he didn't quite know how to approach the subject. After a moment's reflection he decided to ask about something that had baffled him for quite some time.

"Why did Ander hate you so much?" he asked.

The monk didn't answer immediately. He sat gazing up into the sky for so long that Thomas began to wonder if he'd heard the question.

"I'm not sure," Vangellis finally offered. "Perhaps someone he cared about had been treated badly by a member of the clergy. When that happens, it's easy to just lump all of us in together. You find a worm in your apple, and you lose your taste for apples."

He paused again.

"And when he first met me I would have given him no reason at all to question his assessment," he acknowledged with a sad smile.

"He doesn't think that way now, though."

"No," the monk agreed. "He doesn't hate me anymore."

He fell silent again, and his eyes narrowed, apparently remembering the events in the village.

"He couldn't hate you after you healed him."

The monk shook his head. "I didn't heal him. God did that."

Vangellis must have been in a talkative mood, because almost without pause he continued.

"When Ander first woke up, Nestor was in the room. He never says much, as you know. But he had a few things to say to Ander. He told him that everyone else had long since given him up for dead. Said he'd asked me what I was trying to prove, staying up day and night caring for him. Told Ander he owed me a debt he could never repay. Then he got up and left the hut.

"It was nonsense, of course. Ander owed me nothing. And I told him as much after Nestor had gone.

"Ander didn't seem surprised by any of it. He never said a word; he just took it all in. But he followed me everywhere with his eyes. He looked like he was...well, I can't quite describe it."

"I know what you mean," Thomas said. "He was in awe of you."

The monk clearly found that thought uncomfortable. "He came to trust me," he countered. "I think that was the main thing that changed."

The conversation lapsed for a while, and they sat in silence.

After some time, Vangellis turned to Thomas.

"Did I disturb you last night?" he asked directly.

Thomas felt himself flushing a bit, and didn't immediately answer.

"I'm sorry I interrupted your sleep," the monk continued, not offering Thomas an opportunity to deny it.

"Something happened last night," he said tentatively. He paused for a while, then apparently decided to speak more freely.

"A lot has happened to me since Will dragged me from my bolt hole at the monastery. I was very unhappy about it at the time, but I'm grateful to him now.

"To begin with, Ander showed me a great kindness by depriving me of my wineskins. Perhaps kindness wasn't his intention at the time, but the truth is that anything I've done for him since was merely a partial repayment for the greater good he'd already done for me.

"Then we went to the village. I have visited many such villages, and seen similar oppression, although thankfully not often quite that bad. But those people needed help, help that I could offer. Help that I had *vowed* to offer. I managed to escape reality in the monastery, but I couldn't escape it there in the village.

"Then came the opportunity to care for Ander." He paused and gazed heavenward again. "Showing love in practical ways to people who hate you changes you as well as them," he said quietly.

"Then there was the fight. And the loss of Elbruhe. She had suffered so much during her life and received so little. But she gave whatever she could so unstintingly. It was a slap in the face to me. I had tried to escape from the world—to escape something I'd done. I ran away like a coward."

He turned to Thomas, a look of determination on his face.

"I'm through with running. I won't do it anymore."

Thomas didn't know what to say, so he said nothing.

"I need you to understand that, Thomas. Because I'll need to leave you at some point."

At this last statement, Thomas's reaction changed instantly from curiosity to alarm. Will and Rufe were now far away. He had left them out of a selfless desire to release them. But he had done so knowing he wasn't alone. He had lost Elbruhe, lost his friends, and now the monk was planning to abandon him, too.

"So you're going to leave me alone in this wilderness?" he blurted out.

"No, no! Of course not. I won't suddenly desert you," the monk assured him hastily.

Then he sighed. "I suppose I will have to tell you the whole story," he said. "I think after all this time I need to get it out of me, anyway. Are you willing to hear it?" he asked.

Thomas nodded, his curiosity aroused.

"I knew from my youth that I had a calling on my life," the monk began. "My father was a farmer, and he was a good man. But I had no desire to follow him, even though my family had farmed for generations.

"I took my vows on my twentieth birthday, and became apprenticed to an older man who had been serving as a monk all of his life. He was a kind and humble man, and I traveled with him for almost ten years, observing him and learning from him as he cared for the poor and spent his life in service. God was not an idea to him—he was a master like no other and his truest friend.

"I remained with him until he died, full of years and mourned by all who had known him. He had run the race and finished well, and I was filled with the desire to emulate him and his life of service.

"I believe I began well, too. For many years I traveled far and wide, doing whatever I could to care for those in need. There has never been a shortage of such people. I tried to bring God's hope to those who had no hope and to anyone who would receive it.

"I even traveled into foreign lands, learning something of their language and customs. Whenever I was welcomed by a man or woman of peace, I stayed for a time, then moved on."

"Is that how you got your reputation as a guide?" Thomas asked.

"I suppose so," Vangellis replied. "I certainly had opportunity to visit many different places over the years.

"At one time I found myself back in a particular region of Arvenon. People were surrounded by plenty, but suffering greatly. The local lord was not a good man; our own Baron Rudungen was an uncomfortable reminder of him.

"One day I came upon him by accident. A young woman in a nearby town had caught his eye and aroused his lust, and he had waited until she was alone and unprotected. She was little more than a girl. He was intent on taking from her by force what she clearly was unwilling to offer him freely.

"I knew this girl, and I could not bear to see her brutalized. I remonstrated with the nobleman, and he slapped me to the ground, vowing that he would have his way with her. He gloated that he had done the same many times and would do so many more. He boasted loudly that no one dared prevent him, even if they had the means.

"The girl had taken the opportunity to run off, and was nowhere to be seen. He turned his back on me, cursing, ready to set off after her.

"Something rose up in me. I decided that I had to save her, so I picked up a rock and struck him on the back of the head. He went down hard, and didn't get up.

"When I examined him I saw immediately that he was dead. Having cared for many sick people, I knew the signs. So I hid his body and left.

"It was a great mystery to everyone when he didn't appear. The girl was not suspected, since no one apart from me even knew that he had seen her. She wasn't aware of what I'd done. I wasn't suspected, either—none of the people, great or small, imagined even for a minute that I was capable of murder."

He paused and looked across at his companion. "Yes, Thomas," he said sadly, "I'm sorry to say that you're wandering the wilderness with a murderer."

Thomas sat there for a moment, not sure what to say. He simply couldn't see the monk as a bad man. "We've seen a lot of people die," he finally said. "Even a nobleman. Some deserved it, and some didn't. Was it so terrible that this man died? It sounds like he truly did deserve it."

A wry smile appeared on the face of Vangellis. "Are you saying that monks should be allowed to go around killing people, as long as the people are bad enough?"

"No, of course not! But it seems like...well, one mistake destroyed your whole life. Was there no way you could be forgiven? Is murder unforgivable?"

"No, that wasn't it. God can forgive murder. The problem is that I wasn't sorry I'd done it."

He paused for a moment.

"I knew that I should turn myself in," he continued, "but I kept putting it off. I tried to carry on with my work, but my heart wasn't in it anymore. You can't break your vows like that and then carry on like nothing has changed.

"I soon discovered that I'd lost all sense of purpose and calling. My life became a pretense, and my own hypocrisy became more than I could stomach. So I moved on, never able to settle, always restless."

He paused again, for longer this time.

"Then I discovered that alcohol can numb the pain and make you forget for a while. After that my downward slide continued faster than ever. Pretty soon I wasn't recognizable as the same person anymore.

"I'd fallen so far there didn't seem to be any way back. Eventually I ended up at the monastery where you found me. I probably would have ended my days there in a drunken stupor if Will hadn't dragged me away.

"Then came the withdrawals, a severe mercy I have Ander to thank for. It was soon followed by the pressing need to care for the helpless, and for a time I forgot myself as I became immersed in exercising my calling once again. Then there was the shock of Elbruhe's death. It confirmed to me that I had truly begun to care again.

"The death of the baron also showed me that I had been changing. He richly deserved punishment, but this time I had no desire to take it into my own hands. I didn't hate him, so he had no hold over me. And his death reminded me that God does not forget to dispense justice, even if it sometimes seems long delayed.

"Last night came the crisis. All this time I have thought myself incapable of repentance, and therefore lost to forgiveness. But I have changed. I'm sorry now that I took justice into my own hands. I repented of murdering the noble, abandoning my vows, and selfishly escaping into oblivion.

"My innocence is gone forever—I can't undo the past. But I can see now that living without integrity was always a choice. I can have my integrity back. Not for free, certainly, but I'm more than willing to pay the price.

"The amazing thing is that I truly know that I am forgiven. And last night I renewed my vows. I shed some tears, but I also had my first taste of real contentment for a very long time."

Thomas could see that Vangellis was, indeed, a different person. He had never seen him so peaceful, so happy.

"So I hope you understand now why I have to go back," he continued. "I must face justice for the murder that I committed."

Thomas found himself unable to respond for some time. Too many thoughts and feelings churned around inside him, and he had no idea what to say. He didn't want to see the monk go back. And he didn't feel at all like he was sitting down with a murderer. He felt like he was in the presence of the safest person he had ever known. He felt like arguing, but it was obvious to him that sooner or later the monk would leave, no matter what he said.

Ander had seen something unique in the monk. Thomas couldn't quite define what it was, but he could see it, too. And Thomas trusted him no less than Ander did.

Eventually he found his voice. "When will you go back?" he asked.

"There's no point in going now," the monk replied calmly. "The Rogandans almost certainly control that part of Arvenon. I'll need to wait until Will finds a way to remove them."

"He will find a way," Thomas asserted.

"I believe he will, too," the monk agreed.

Thomas harbored no doubts at all on that subject. For the first time, though, he found himself with mixed feelings about it.

"I know all this is a lot for you to take in," the monk acknowledged. "But I want you to know that I won't simply abandon you. I will do anything in my power to help you, Thomas."

Thomas replied without hesitation. "And I will do anything I can to help you, too, Brother Vangellis."

30

The going became easier as Thomas and the monk found their way onto an animal trail that was heading in roughly the right direction. After climbing for much of the morning, they were now following the line of a long ridge, and Thomas appreciated the easier going.

He had a lot to think about. The revelations of the previous day offered a new perspective on the monk's actions and behavior, and Thomas felt better able to understand everything that had happened since Brother Vangellis had joined them. At the same time he was still coming to terms with the death of Elbruhe, and struggling to control the ferocity of his own emotions whenever he thought about the baron. Underneath it all lay a nagging uncertainty about his own future. What would become of him?

Wandering along with his mind in another place, he suddenly noticed that the monk had halted abruptly.

"Move backward, Thomas. VERRRYY slowly."

Baffled, Thomas did not instantly obey. He shot a glance at the monk and saw him standing with his posture relaxed but his gaze fixed intensely. He followed the monk's stare. A huge brown bear faced them, less than a stone's throw off the path to his left. The bear stood tall on its hind legs, towering above them. Its mouth hung wide in a menacing snarl. Then, a growl issuing from deep in its throat, it began moving threateningly toward them.

Unreasoning terror gripped Thomas. Heart pounding, he broke into a cold sweat. His first instinct was to turn and run for his life. He would have done so, too, had not the monk opened wide his mouth and begun to sing. The bear halted in its tracks, head bent slightly to one side. Thomas, in amazement, looked first at the bear, then at the monk, then back at the bear again.

Warming to his task, the monk lifted up his voice and sang with complete abandon. He sang of the mountains and the skies, the forest and the plains, the birds of the air and the creatures of the sea. It was a joyous song, a psalm of praise to the Creator. As he sang he waved his arms above his head and swayed slowly from side to side, entering in wholeheartedly with his entire body. The bear stood perfectly still.

The song seemed to go on for hours, although it must surely have been only minutes. Eventually the joyful strains came to an end. The monk closed his mouth and lowered his arms.

The bear lingered until the last notes had died away. Then it dropped onto all fours, turned its back and disappeared off into the trees. For all the world it seemed as if the creature had waited politely for the song to finish before leaving.

"I think we should move off, Thomas. Mr. Bruin might have liked the performance so much he went to gather some friends for another one," the monk said with a smile.

Thomas needed no urging. They set off at a rapid clip, the youth unable to prevent himself from looking back continually over his shoulder.

"I DON'T UNDERSTAND what happened back there," Thomas began.

They sat huddled before a fire as the daylight dimmed around them. Thanks to prodigious efforts on the part of Thomas, it was a very large fire. He had gathered many loads of dead wood into a huge pile, each time forcing himself to go back for more. Whenever he reached down to pick up a branch, he fully expected a bear to appear from behind a tree and rise up to threaten him. He wondered if singing would work for him as well, and racked his brains for suitable songs just in case.

"This isn't the first time I've encountered a bear," the monk replied. "After I first took my vows I was walking in a forest on one occasion. I thought I was alone, and I was singing heartily. Then I looked up and saw a mother bear and her two cubs. My heart almost stopped beating. My singing stopped, too, and the bears didn't seem at all pleased. So I started up again, and they calmed down. I sang every song I could think of, and they gave me a very fair hearing. When I eventually ran out of ideas, they just left."

"So you were never frightened by bears?"

"Actually, the very opposite was true—I'd always been terrified of bears. From a young age I heard stories of the bear that attacked and killed my uncle. And I knew you can't outrun them. So my first bear encounter frightened and encouraged me at the same time."

"Have you met any bears since?"

"Yes. On two occasions. I serenaded my second bear, and we both left satisfied. The third bear wasn't interested in songs. He was hungry, and apparently I looked like food. As he moved in I lectured him sternly, but he wouldn't listen."

"What did you do?"

"I picked up a lump of wood in each hand and laid into him. For his benefit, I also quoted scripture from the book of Proverbs."

"Are you serious?! What did the quote say?"

"The passage says '*My son, do not despise the Lord's discipline and do not resent his rebuke, because the Lord disciplines those he loves*'," the monk replied with a grin. "I swatted him once for every word. We didn't make it to the end of the passage, though."

"Why? What happened?"

"He had a sudden change of heart, and he repented."

The image of Brother Vangellis sternly disciplining an aggressive bear was too much for Thomas. He couldn't help himself. He burst out laughing. The hilarity was too contagious to long resist—in short order the monk had joined him. Soon the two of them were laughing so hard that tears ran down their cheeks.

"My sides hurt," Thomas complained when they finally stopped.

"Mine do, too," Brother Vangellis replied, wiping his eyes with the sleeves of his gown. After a pause he added, "But I think we both needed that."

The sun had now set completely, and it was getting colder. Thomas threw more wood onto the fire, realizing as he did so that he was no longer anxious about the bears. He felt confident that the monk would keep both of them safe.

They sat for a while watching the flames reach out to embrace the new fuel. A large beetle emerged onto one of the fresh branches and scurried along it to safety. Thomas felt a little like the beetle. He'd barely remained one step ahead of disaster for weeks now.

The monk was studying him closely. "I can see you've been carrying a burden, Thomas," he offered gently.

How does he know? Thomas wondered.

"Yes, it's true," he finally admitted.

"Would you like to talk about it?"

Did he want to talk about it? Thomas stared into the fire, trying to make sense of his own thoughts on the subject. The monk waited patiently, his face outlined by the flickering flames.

"Why do things happen the way they do?" he finally asked. "Why me?"

The monk didn't reply.

Then Thomas realized that he'd made his decision. His long-standing questions about the stone still remained. They were questions that Will couldn't answer—maybe the monk could.

Haltingly at first, he began to tell the story of the stone, starting from the very beginning. This time he left nothing out, not even the incident with the pitchfork.

The monk asked questions from time to time, but mostly just let him speak.

The fire had diminished to glowing ashes before he finally came to an end.

"So no one knows about the stone except you and Will?"

"No one."

The monk reached across to the wood pile and began rebuilding the fire. With no immediate response coming from Brother Vangellis, Thomas began to feel worried.

"Do you think I'm damned?" he asked anxiously.

The monk looked startled. "Why would you think that?" he asked.

"Maybe the stone is evil."

The monk shook his head. "See this fire," he said, waving a branch that had just caught alight. "We use it to keep us warm, to cook our food, and to protect ourselves from wild animals. Our enemies also use it to destroy our crops and to burn down entire towns and villages."

He threw more wood on the fire. "Fire is not evil. It's people who are evil."

Thomas wasn't satisfied. "Well, I've used the stone in ways that are evil. Doesn't that make me evil?"

"All of us do evil things, Thomas."

He stared into the fire a moment before responding further.

"From what I've heard, you did begin badly with the stone. You paid a price for it, too. But I think you have learned from your mistakes. It's been a long time since you abused the gift of the stone."

"Is it a gift? It seems more like a curse!"

"It's a gift," the monk asserted firmly.

"Where did it come from?"

"I don't know. The monastery we are heading for has a library. Perhaps we might learn something there.

"But I have never heard of anything at all like your stone, Thomas. I don't want to build your hopes up."

Thomas sighed. He trusted the monk, and it felt good to have unburdened himself. He now realized, though, that he had irrationally hoped that Brother Vangellis would be able to help him. His wishful thinking simply wasn't realistic. How could anyone understand the stone? No one even knew it existed.

Then he remembered that Lord Drettroth knew. Thankfully the Rogandan lord was far away and had no idea where to find either him or the stone.

By noon of the next day they had reached the monastery. Built of solid stone, it had been established on a small but fertile plateau, high up in the mountains. Walking toward it they found themselves on a broad path that led first through a grove of apple and pear trees then skirted extensive fields. Brother Vangellis pointed out the carefully cultivated strips of land and explained that the monks grew corn and other grain crops as well as many types of vegetables. Goats and chickens fled from their approach as they made their way up to the thick stone wall that surrounded the monastery buildings.

The gates of the compound hung wide open. As they passed inside they saw a dozen monks sitting in the sunshine around a wooden table, enjoying a simple meal of bread, cheese, and wine.

Several of them leaped to their feet when they saw Brother Vangellis, greeting him excitedly. They crowded around him, all talking at once. The others hung back, looking uncertain and uncomfortable.

"What is the reason for all this excitement?" asked an old monk, frowning at them with mock severity. He stepped forward, and the little crowd parted before him. Approaching Brother Vangellis, he reached up and slowly placed a hand on each of his shoulders. Holding him there, he quietly studied his face for a long moment. Then he enveloped the younger man in a warm embrace. Thomas could see tears glistening in his eyes. Drawing back, he studied him once more with a happy smile.

"My friend, it does my old heart good to see you!" he exclaimed. "And it brings me great joy to see the sun once again shining upon your brow."

He turned to the other monks, who still sat silent and awkward at the table. “Why do you hesitate?” he asked, a tone of gentle chiding in his voice. “The return of a prodigal is always a cause for great rejoicing.”

They rose and faced Brother Vangellis, who greeted them with a self-conscious bow. They greeted him politely, if not warmly, although a couple of them muttered apologies for their half-hearted welcome.

“And who is this young man that you have brought with you?” the older monk asked. He turned to Thomas, presenting a round and cheerful face surmounted with wisps of snowy white hair.

“This is Thomas Stablehand,” Brother Vangellis replied. “He has seen a lot in his young life, and comes to you through great danger. He is horse master to the army of our king. Thomas, this is Brother Beneface, the abbot of this monastery.”

“Thomas, you are welcome here,” the abbot assured him. “May you find peace and rest in our community and refreshment for your spirit.”

“Thank you, Brother Beneface,” Thomas managed.

The abbot introduced Thomas to a young monk around his own age.

“Brother Hann will show you around, Thomas. I must borrow your friend for a while—I can see we have a great deal of catching up to do. He will join you later.”

With that he took Brother Vangellis by the arm, and steered him away toward one of the monastery buildings.

“Come with me, Thomas,” said the young monk. “Are you hungry? I will show you to the kitchen.” Then he added eagerly, “Do you really ride horses?”

“Yes,” Thomas replied, trying to sound matter-of-fact. “As it happens, I teach soldiers to ride horses.”

“Really? I’ve always wanted to ride a horse. Maybe you could teach me.”

“So you have horses here? Brother Vangellis didn’t think so.”

“No, unfortunately we don’t.”

"Then it won't be easy to teach you to ride," said Thomas with a grin.

"I suppose not," Brother Hann acknowledged sheepishly.

After a brief visit to the kitchen, from which they emerged laden with bread, cheese, and apples, the two of them wandered around the fields outside the monastery, enjoying the frequent bursts of sunshine through the clouds. They were soon chatting happily like old friends. The young monk's cheerful demeanor and infectious laughter soon put Thomas at his ease. He began to wonder when he had last felt so relaxed. The war with the Rogandans seemed a very long way away.

A bell rang from the monastery.

"I must go to prayers now, Thomas. I will show you to the guest rooms on my way there."

They headed toward a building along the inner wall of the monastery compound.

"You won't be alone, Thomas. We have another guest here already. It's very unusual for us to have guests at all—we're so far away from other people up here. And to have multiple guests at the same time is even more unusual."

He lowered his voice. "The other guest is a bit strange. I think he's suspicious. He's foreign, too."

At this news Thomas at once became alert. A cloud threatened to intrude upon his sunny afternoon.

"It's probably just me, though," Brother Hann added with a smile. "Brother Beneface would say I shouldn't be so quick to judge."

He led Thomas to a long building that hugged the inner wall of the compound. A single corridor stretched along the length of the building and provided access to half a dozen small guest rooms. Large windows along the corridor opened onto the monastery grounds and admitted light into the rooms, each of which had its own door and window.

The monk led Thomas to the first room along the corridor. "The other guest is staying in the room at the far end," he whispered.

Then, speaking more loudly, he said, "Make yourself at home,

Thomas. Come and go as you please. Two bells means that dinner is about to be served in the refectory."

Thomas had nothing to put in his room except the waterproof cloak and wide-brimmed hat he had brought with him from Arnost. He took off the cloak and hung it on a wooden hook in the wall opposite the bed. He placed the hat on a three-legged stool in the corner of the room. Then he left the room and emerged once again into the late afternoon sunshine.

The monks had apparently gathered in a small chapel; the sound of their chanting carried across the monastery grounds. Thomas headed out of the gates and wandered around the outer walls of the monastery, circumnavigating it entirely. The monastery faced north, and he discovered that it was perched almost on the edge of the plateau.

To the left of the main gates he found several large hen houses, a goat pen, and a number of small enclosures that turned out to be a piggery. Beyond them lay the fertile fields that provided crops for the monks.

To the right of the main gates a rocky outcrop separated the monastery buildings from a steep precipice. Far below, at the base of the plateau, Thomas glimpsed a wide river flowing eastward through rugged country.

A bell tolled twice, calling Thomas back to the monastery to join the monks for dinner. As he headed toward the gate he noticed a stranger leaning against a tree, studying him. Seeing that he had been noticed, the man immediately turned his attention elsewhere. Thomas decided to ignore him, and headed through the gates.

When he reached the refectory building he saw that the stranger had followed him in. Brother Beneface greeted Thomas at the door and ushered him inside. A smiling Brother Vangellis stood waiting for him.

The abbot welcomed the stranger at the door.

"Brother Vangellis, Thomas," he said, turning back to them, "I would like to introduce you to another visitor. His name is Harald. He speaks very little of our language."

He indicated a man who was bearded and dark in complexion, and medium in height. The man bowed slightly.

Brother Vangellis addressed him, speaking a few words in a language that Thomas did not recognize. The man's face remained blank, and he shrugged, indicating that he did not understand.

Brother Vangellis then smiled, and returned Harald's bow. Thomas copied him.

They took their places standing behind low benches in front of a long wooden table. As soon as the abbot gave thanks for the food everyone sat down, and a hubbub of cheerful conversation quickly broke out while a couple of monks served the food. The meal consisted of a thick vegetable gruel served hot, along with freshly baked bread. The food tasted very good indeed to Thomas after their limited diet in the wilderness.

Harald sat at one end of the table, speaking to no one. As soon as he had finished eating he stood up and faced the abbot, giving him a formal nod in acknowledgment of his hospitality. Then he left.

"He's Rogandan," Brother Vangellis whispered to Thomas.

"How do you know?"

"I spoke to him in Rogandan. I said, 'May no evil creature shadow your path'. It's a saying among Rogandans—they are very superstitious. The standard response is a special hand gesture to ward off evil. He pretended not to understand me, but his right hand instinctively began the gesture before he could stop it. I'm sure no one else noticed. But I did, and he saw that I did."

A wave of anxiety flooded over Thomas. He had felt sure they would be safe here.

His concern must have shown on his face, because the monk quickly added, "There's probably nothing to worry about. But we should watch this Harald, just in case. I will have a word to Brother Beneface.

"I was planning to share the monks' quarters with them, but I will sleep in the guest room next to yours instead."

Thomas thanked him more than once.

. . .

A SMALL SOUND startled Thomas into wakefulness. He lay unmoving in his bed, his eyes slowly adjusting to the thin strip of moonlight that shone through the heavy curtains across his window. Someone was in his room.

A vague shadow hovered near the opposite wall—the intruder seemed to be groping around inside his cloak. Moments later the figure slipped from the room. The door closed softly, and silence descended once again like a blanket.

Thomas lay without moving for a very long time. Then he got up and stole next door to the monk's room. Rhythmic snoring sounds issued from the prone form of Brother Vangellis.

Thomas shook him gently. The monk mumbled and turned over. Thomas shook him again. He woke with a start to see Thomas holding a finger warningly to his mouth.

"What's wrong, Thomas?" he whispered, becoming quickly alert.

"I just had a visitor," Thomas hissed. "He was poking around in my cloak. Maybe he was looking for the stone."

"You still have it?"

"Yes, I have it. I keep it with me. It wasn't in my cloak."

"There's no harm done, then. Don't assume the worst, Thomas. I doubt that your visitor knows anything about the stone. The man is probably just a common thief."

Thomas did not reply. He stood there feeling tense and unhappy and shivering uncontrollably.

"Go back to bed. I am awake now, and I will get up and watch the corridor here from my room until daylight. In the morning I will speak with Brother Beneface."

IN THE MORNING they set off together to search out the abbot. When they found him, he appeared a little flustered.

"Good morning, Brother Vangellis, Thomas," he said. "It seems that our visitor, Harald—if that truly was his name—is no longer our guest at the monastery.

"Certainly his possessions have been removed from the room he was occupying in the guest house. And I have just been informed that a quantity of supplies have disappeared from the kitchen. Our cook was most indignant."

At that moment another monk appeared, red faced. "The silver chalice we use for Holy Communion has gone missing, Brother Beneface. I can't find it anywhere in the chapel."

"Oh, well," sighed the abbot. "These are the risks you take when you welcome strangers into your midst."

Then, suddenly recalling his audience, he hastily added, "Please pardon me, Thomas. I meant no slight on you!"

Brother Vangellis chuckled. "As it happens, Thomas had a visitor himself last night, Brother Beneface. He woke to someone poking around his cloak in the dark. I suspect that your guest was little more than a thief."

"I fear you are right. We must pray for his soul, poor fellow."

The abbot turned to Thomas. "I am very sorry that your experience of our hospitality has not been entirely pleasant so far.

"I hope we can make amends, though. I will ask Brother Hann to free himself for a few days to keep you company."

Thomas thanked him sincerely, and tried to make it clear that the monks' hospitality had, in fact, been excellent.

They took their leave of the abbot and set off to join the other monks at breakfast.

"I think you can afford to relax again, Thomas," Brother Vangellis assured him as they headed into the refectory. "I suspect we've seen the last of 'Harald'."

31

For Thomas, the loss of Elbruhe lay constantly at the back of his mind, a dark shadow that brooded just beyond the reach of his normal awareness. It nagged incessantly at him until he turned his thoughts inward and dragged it into the open once again. But exposing it never seemed to offer him release.

Fortunately for him, he found the perfect tonic in Brother Hann. It was hard to feel gloomy for long around someone who was so unfailingly cheerful. And the young monk, being unaware of the situation, was entirely unaffected in his communication.

Thomas and Brother Hann were soon spending every available minute together. The two of them quickly became inseparable. Thomas had grown up without siblings and with no close friend his own age. In recent times almost all of his significant relationships had been with people much older than himself. The only exception was Elbruhe, but she was different in every imaginable way.

Brother Hann and Thomas were as unalike as anyone might reasonably expect a monk and an army horse master to be. But they made the simple discovery that they enjoyed each other's company. After the recent blows sustained by Thomas, he gradually came to appreciate Brother Hann's sunny disposition as a welcome breath of fresh air. For his part, Brother Hann listened with unfeigned amazement as Thomas told him about his years in Arnost, the Rogandan invasion, and everything that had happened to him since. Separated for a time from the turmoil of the recent past, Thomas found unexpected peace and solace in his days at the monastery, in spite of the grief that gnawed at him.

In the afternoon of their second day at the monastery, Brother Vangellis took Thomas to the library. It was a substantial building located at the southwest corner of the monastery grounds. Shafts of bright sunlight burst into the library through large windows facing directly west. The windows looked out over the edge of the plateau and commanded a magnificent view of mountains marching far off into the distance as well as vistas of the rugged terrain close at hand.

Many books lined a series of wooden shelves that ringed the room. A number of benches with stools stood in the middle of the room, and almost every available surface was covered with books, scrolls and manuscripts. Even some of the stools carried precariously balanced piles of books and papers.

Brother Vangellis introduced Thomas to the librarian, Brother Erastus, a thin man in late middle age with a long nose and sharp eyes. After welcoming Thomas the librarian fixed him with a penetrating gaze for a few moments before turning his attention to Brother Vangellis.

"So you've finally decided to visit an old scholar in his library, eh? If you took more time to study instead of forever scurrying around frantically, you might be better off," he suggested, wagging a long finger at Brother Vangellis. He sounded stern, but the smile creasing his face betrayed his true feelings.

Brother Vangellis ignored the bait. "You are privileged," he assured Thomas, "to stand in one of the largest libraries in the kingdom."

"*The* largest library in the kingdom," Brother Erastus corrected him, "apart from the king's own library in Arnost. *And* we have the biggest collection of old scrolls in Arvenon. We have books on almost every imaginable topic: history, philosophy, science, and, of course, theology, to name a few."

"Brother Erastus is rather proud of his collection," Brother Vangellis told Thomas.

"Rightly so!" the librarian replied with energy.

"Has no one told you that pride is a sin?" Brother Vangellis teased.

The librarian sighed deeply. "I am afraid your friend never was much of a scholar," he told Thomas. "But it doesn't prevent him knocking on my door whenever he needs me for something."

He turned back to Brother Vangellis. "I presume you do have a reason for interrupting my labors."

"Yes. I have an unusual challenge to offer you. I was wondering if you have ever come across any reference to a stone that confers special powers," the monk replied, coming immediately to the point.

"What kind of special powers?" the librarian returned.

"The ability to discern the thoughts of other people."

"Sounds like superstition to me," Brother Erastus asserted.

"Yes, it does," agreed Brother Vangellis.

The librarian turned to Thomas. "May I see the stone, please?"

Thomas was too shocked to reply. He turned to Brother Vangellis with dismay, wondering how much he had told the librarian.

"I've told him nothing, Thomas!" his friend protested.

"You didn't need to," Brother Erastus said calmly. "Some things are as obvious to me as the very large nose on my face.

"You give me far too little credit, Brother Vangellis," he continued. "Just because I spend so much time reading books doesn't mean I can't read people."

Brother Vangellis shook his head and shrugged helplessly. "He's an old rogue, Thomas," he said. "But I would trust him with my life. It's safe to show him the stone."

Still alarmed at the ease with which his secret had been laid bare, Thomas drew the stone slowly from his pouch and, after a moment's reluctance, handed it to the librarian. Brother Vangellis, who had never seen it himself, peered inquisitively over the librarian's shoulder.

"It's unusual," the scholar observed. "I've never seen anything quite like it. I collect rocks as a hobby, and I can tell you that this stone is made of different material from any rock in my collection."

He handed it back to Thomas. "It might be a sky rock," he suggested.

"What's a sky rock?" Thomas asked, quickly putting it away again.

"It's a rock that's fallen to earth from the heavens," the librarian replied. "Sometimes we see a streak of light across the sky at night. We're seeing tiny stars falling to the earth. Occasionally people find the location where one has landed.

"But a sky rock that gives you the power to see into other people's minds? I don't recall ever reading about such a thing, and I have read almost everything in our library at one time or another. But I am willing to take a fresh look at some of the older scrolls."

"Thank you, Brother Erastus," said Brother Vangellis, making a small formal bow and frowning at Thomas, who belatedly managed to blurt out a mumbled thanks of his own.

"Well, this has been as much excitement as I can cope with in one afternoon," said the librarian decisively. "Off you go, then," he added, shooing them out. "The sooner you leave the sooner I can get started on my search."

As they were moving out he placed a hand briefly on Thomas's shoulder. "You needn't worry, young man," he said reassuringly. "I won't breathe a word of this to anyone."

As the days passed it seemed increasingly unlikely to Thomas that the librarian would be able to discover anything about the stone. He decided to put the search out of his mind and enjoy the unexpected benefits of the sanctuary offered by the monastery. He knew that the war with the Rogandans must surely be continuing and that his friends might well be in peril. He also knew that he could not hide here forever. But each new day brought sunshine, laughter, and contentment in the company of his new friend. For now it was enough.

It therefore came as a shock when, almost a week after their arrival at the monastery, Brother Vangellis sought him out one afternoon and told him that Brother Erastus had uncovered some information about the stone.

The two of them hurried to the library to find Brother Erastus waiting impatiently for them to arrive. With no more than a hurried greeting, he led them to the western wall of the library. Removing a cleverly concealed panel in one of the bookshelves, he revealed a hidden lever. He pulled down hard on the lever, and the bookshelf swung noiselessly to one side, exposing a narrow opening in the floor that led down to a winding staircase.

They followed him down the stairs into a large room lit by wall-mounted candles. He pulled another lever, and the bookshelf above swung silently back into place, sealing the chamber.

Thomas glanced around the room in the dim light. A large table at one end of the room held a small collection of scrolls with a couple of oil lamps for illumination. The walls were entirely covered with small wooden cubicles filled to overflowing with scrolls.

"We keep our oldest scrolls here," Brother Erastus told Thomas. "The even temperature, the dry air, and the absence of sunlight have allowed us to preserve them for very long periods. The only alternative is to copy them. We eventually do that when they deteriorate enough, but it is an immense task."

Thomas had never learned to read and write, and the usefulness of expending such effort on ancient documents was not at all clear to him. However, Thomas guessed that Will might have appreciated this place. Will had learned his letters from his uncle, who was a trader, and had said more than once in his hearing that the skill could be valuable at times. Thomas decided to see it through the eyes of his friend. He nodded wisely in appreciation.

"Not only scrolls have been preserved down here," Brother Vangellis added. "The monks have retreated here more than once when the monastery was attacked."

"Has the monastery ever been destroyed?" Thomas wondered aloud.

"Yes, once," the librarian replied. "During the Rogandan invasion in the days of King Rufus II. The monks remained hidden, and thankfully almost all of the library was saved."

"Buildings can always be rebuilt, of course. Scrolls are infinitely more precious," Brother Vangellis added with a grin. Brother Erastus ignored the remark.

"Over here, Thomas." The scholar led them to the table. "When I found this scroll I realized that I had seen it before. When I last read it, though, I dismissed it as a fable.

"Not all historians are careful to separate fact from rumor and hearsay," he explained. "It can be difficult to discern old histories from old stories."

"Does it mention the stone directly?" Brother Vangellis asked.

"It does much more than that," the librarian replied. "It offers an entire history for it."

Thomas felt his heart beginning to pound. He felt restless, nervous, and excited in equal measures. "Can you read it to me?" he asked, his voice quavering with emotion.

"Of course," the librarian replied. "I'd suggest you take a seat," he said, pointing them to a pair of stools beside the table. "This is going to take a while.

"This scroll is very old. It is hard to accurately date it, but some clues suggest that it dates back two hundred years at least. The author calls himself Randolf of Clerbon—he is not known to me. And in the early part of the scroll he quotes an even older manuscript by another unknown author.

"This is what it says.

'Three talismans of great potency are abroad in the world, uncelebrated, unrecognized, and hidden from any certain knowledge. Perhaps I alone know their true history, long forgotten with the passing of many scores of years. I once learned of an ancient parchment, lost and mayhap forgotten by all save only an aged hermit. The old man had glimpsed it in his youth, and he described it to me as well as his failing memory served him.

Long did I search for it, and bitter and fruitless my labor seemed. Dark and tiresome would be the full tale thereof. At last, hope having deserted me, I stumbled upon it, the greatest treasure in my possession. Even now I have it before me, a faded manuscript, crumbling with age and arcane in script. Many candles burned to naught ere I found a way to decipher it.

Hear, then, the testimony of a scribe whose witness has been silent for many an age:

Long years have passed away since Goodman Tomas walked upon the earth. A poor farmer and simple he was, yet greatly beloved by all who knew him. He lived in a rude hut in but a small village.

One day his fortunes turned. Though his back had been bowed down with much labor, yet was he seen to stand again straight and tall. Tales grew up around his wisdom, and people journeyed from afar to seek his counsel. His insights failed him not, and his sayings gave birth to a bountiful supply of proverbs.

It came to pass that his village became a town, and the town a city, and he the mayor. His family prospered likewise.

Late in life offered he a gift unto the king of his country. Rude in appearance was the gift but great in effect, and the king, who was a good ruler, handled it wisely. His fortunes likewise changed, and he became powerful even as his kingdom prospered.

The story sprang up and spread abroad that Tomas had received a star from heaven that fell from the sky and landed in the form of a rock beside his hut. Great and manifold were the gifts bestowed by this rock upon its owner—gifts of insight, good health and influence among men. And behold, having received it freely from Tomas, the king rejoiced also in the selfsame gifts. Nor were the benefits denied to Tomas when he yielded up the rock. He continued as before until he had attained a great age.

So Tomas died, full of years, and in time the king also slept with his fathers. The son of the king prospered, too, and increased yet more in power. A subtle, but alas, not a wise king was he, and many enemies gathered themselves against him. The neighboring kingdoms rose up, bound together in hatred for the king and desire for the rock. Nevertheless, try as they might, they could not overcome him, such was his might in arms and his shrewdness in council. Finally, by treachery alone was he brought low, slain by the hand of one he trusted.

Thus lost the son of the wise king his kingdom and his life, all through foolishness and pride. The ruler who wrested control of his kingdom laid hands upon the rock, lusting to command every virtue of which he had heard so much. It benefited him nothing. Years of bitter fortune and failing prosperity passed, until in anger he caused the rock to be smashed into a thousand fragments and cast outside his palace.

And lo, it came to pass that certain peasants, chancing upon the pieces, found them pleasing to the eye. Taking them up, they bore them unto their dwellings. Anon it was seen that some of the virtue of the rock had passed into three of the pieces. One brought health and vitality, a second, great authority, and a third, insight into the hearts and minds of men.

Long and illuminating would be the history that chronicled the fortunes attending those who found the stones. Time revealed that the stones, as likewise the rock vouchsafed to Tomas, lost their virtue entirely when taken by force, at times remaining dormant for a generation. Only when a stone was gifted freely, or found by chance, was the virtue bestowed. The stones together were like the original rock in every respect but one—once a gift had been made of a stone, its virtue was thereafter withheld from the giver.

Some stones passed as heirlooms from father to son or mother to daughter. In time the gift was always squandered through pride or folly, or lost through violence or misadventure.

None can say where the stones are today. Long years have passed since last I heard aught of them. Many say they are lost forever, and some rejoice in their vanishment. Some say they are a gift from God to the wise. Others say they are a tool of the Devil to curse and ensnare all who receive them.

There was a time when one of the stones lay in my hand for a moment. Young and foolish I was, and greatly desirous of possessing it, though every opportunity was denied me. Now I am old, and wiser, and content with my lot in life. Who could envy those who bear the burden of such a gift?

The witness ended thus. My account concerning the ancient manuscript is accurate in every particular and my translation faithful and true. I, Randolf of Clerbon, swear it on my life.'

"This 'Randolf of Clerbon' appears to have written the last sentence in blood—most probably his own," said Brother Erastus, distaste plainly evident on his face. "But he continues, once again using ink."

'In the unrelenting passage of years since the scribe lived and breathed, many things have changed, and some remain the same. The role of the rock in shaping kingdoms, revealed in the manuscript, has never ceased. The true history of Arvenon and the surrounding kingdoms is incomplete without reference to the stones of power.

Such fateful talismans—how they haunt my dreams! Ever have I sought them, but alas, thus far to no avail. Much lore have I gathered concerning the three—the Stone of Vitality, that grants well-being and life beyond the span of other men, the Stone of Authority, that bestows power and influence for good or for ill, and the Stone of Knowing, that lays bare the hearts and motivations of others. I record here but a small part of this lore, in order that my labor shall not prove entirely vain, that my research shall not crumble to dust with my mortal body.

What, then, can be said of these stones? They respect neither rank nor status. They surrender their power impartially to saint and sinner alike. Certain boundaries do, however, encompass those who bear them. The potency of a stone is diminished by afflictions of the body or the spirit, especially when a stone is new to the bearer. Familiarity increases their virtue, though bearers assume fearful risks with overuse.

Such is the witness of those who lay greatest claim to discernment about the stones.

Nevertheless, overuse has never been chief among the perils confronting those who bear a stone. The principal danger has ever been the lust of others who desired the stones for themselves.

A stone fails of its purpose if a bearer has been killed to acquire it, no matter who carried out the murder. The same failure ensues if a stone is taken without consent.

Such limitations have never deterred the unscrupulous, though. The most cunning among them have ever recognized the futility of force, and sought instead to obtain the stones using fear and intimidation. That history must needs be told.

First, though, it is necessary to faithfully chronicle the properties of the stones. I will describe each in turn, for though their lineage is common, their likeness and behavior vary considerably.

The Stone of Knowing is said to be little bigger than a man's fingernail, smooth to the touch, and colored brightly with azure and magenta tones. The stone grants admittance—full and unfettered—to thought, intent, and motivation of every person upon whom the eye of the bearer falls. Certain parchment fragments, perplexing in nature, hint that even animals and birds lie within its reach, at least in small measure.

No memory from the past is safe—every secret buried deep must be surrendered to its power. The stone may offer glimpses of what is to come, but with no certain assuredness, since many a fork in the road awaits the traveler who journeys to the future.

An extraordinary weight bears down upon the hand that cradles this stone. It is said that, of the three, the Stone of Knowing holds the greatest potentiality for good or evil, depending only on the character of the one who bears it.

The Stone of...'

"AND THERE THE ACCOUNT ENDS," the librarian said. "The scroll is torn, and the latter part of it is missing."

He took in a deep breath and exhaled slowly as though marking the successful completion of a long and arduous journey. They all sat hushed and still for many minutes.

The scholar eventually broke the silence.

"The writer tells us he is Randolf of Clerbon. I have searched widely, and learned that Clerbon was once located in the region we now call Erestor. I have discovered no reference to this place in the last two hundred years. I therefore believe we can safely conclude that this scroll is at least as old as that."

Brother Vangellis shook his head in wonder. "Astonishing as this tale seems," he said, "it has about it the smell of truth, or something very near the truth. You have done well indeed to find it." He acknowledged the librarian with a respectful nod.

Thomas did not know what to say. Surely he should feel only relief to know where the stone came from. But the history of the stone was alarming, and it was difficult to grasp what it all meant.

Brother Vangellis got up. "I think it's time we went outside for some fresh air, Thomas," he said, looking at his young friend with concern in his eyes.

Brother Erastus put away the scroll and unsealed the entrance to the cellar, and they all emerged into the library. The late afternoon sun flooded the room with golden light; before long it would sink behind the distant mountains. Thomas realized they had been down there for longer than he had imagined.

As they emerged from the building, an agitated Brother Hann ran up to them.

"We've been looking for you everywhere!" He thrust Thomas's cloak and hat into his hands. He turned to Brother Vangellis. "Brother Dannel has your things. There he is now!" He waved frantically, and Brother Dannel ran over and handed over the meager possessions Brother Vangellis had left in the guest house.

"What's going on?" Brother Vangellis asked.

"A Rogandan force has surrounded the monastery," Brother Dannel replied. "One of the Brothers saw them coming and ran to raise the alarm. We shut the gates before they arrived, but feared we had locked you out."

"They're demanding we hand you over, Thomas, and you, too, Brother Vangellis!" Brother Hann exclaimed, unable to hide his dismay. "We have done all we can to remove every trace of you. It's something about Thomas stealing an heirloom belonging to their commander. The commander of their entire army is right here at the gates. His name is Lord Dead Wrath or something."

"He is lying about this supposed heirloom," said Brother Vangellis calmly. "Where is the abbot?"

"He is at the gate," Brother Hann told him. "He instructed us all to hide under the library. But what will happen to him?"

"That is in God's hands," replied Brother Dannel. "We must do as he has said."

THE MONKS and Thomas huddled together fearfully in the hidden room underground, listening to the Rogandan soldiers rampaging through the library above. Brother Erastus sat there with tears in his eyes. He had taken many armfuls of books down into the cellar, and would have gone back for more had they not restrained him. As it was they scarcely closed the opening in time.

The murmur of barely audible prayers filled the room, interrupted from time to time by crashes above as another bookshelf was pulled from the wall.

In the absence of the abbot, Brother Dannel was the most senior monk. He had been praying quietly for some time, but now he lifted his head and turned to Brother Vangellis.

"It is clear to me that you must make good your escape while you still can, Brother Vangellis," he said decisively. "You must take Thomas with you.

"The Rogandans will quickly realize that the river below us offers the only effective escape route from this region. They will send soldiers to watch the river."

"How can we escape from here?" Brother Vangellis asked.

"There is a tunnel down to the bottom of the plateau. It was built by the Brothers who came before us, for just such an emergency as we face now."

From the surprise on the faces of some of the monks, Thomas could see that not all of them were aware of this information.

"We will follow you later, if it proves to be God's purpose," Brother Dannel promised.

"There is a small coracle on the bank of the river below," he continued. "It will carry you to safety. Go quickly now!"

An older monk lifted a flagstone to reveal a large metal ring set into the floor. He tugged unsuccessfully at it. A couple of the younger monks joined in, and soon a piece of the floor pulled free, causing those tugging to fall backward. A draft of stale air rushed into the room, almost extinguishing the candles.

Brother Dannel handed a burning torch to each of them. "May the peace of Christ go with you!" he said fervently. His lips continued to move noiselessly as he breathed a silent prayer over them.

They stepped down onto the first steps of a long and winding staircase that stretched far below them into the dark. Treading carefully they began their descent, Brother Vangellis first, then Thomas.

After a few moments they heard the entrance to the tunnel close above them.

"What are they doing?" Thomas called anxiously. "Why don't they escape, too? How can Brother Dannel say they'll follow if it's God's purpose? Does God want them to die?"

Brother Vangellis did not answer. The monk trod purposefully down, down, not looking back. Thomas hurried after him as quickly as he dared, anxious to catch up.

Once Thomas glanced above him. He could see nothing. As they moved on, the dark closed in behind them, even as it stretched down before them beyond their sight.

Thomas thought about the scroll and the history of the stone. He turned it over and over in his mind, examining it from every angle. Lord Drettroth had surely discovered the truth, too. There must be another copy of the scroll at large in the world.

What if he catches me? But the stone won't work for him if he takes it from me by force! What did the scroll mean by fear and intimidation? Will Drettroth try to frighten me into giving it to him? I must never let him catch me! How did he find me here?

His mind flew from thought to thought while his feet kept moving, down, down, down, ever deeper. In time his mind became numb, and nothing remained except the endless staircase and the unyielding dark.

The End

The saga continues in
The Cost of Knowing

PART II

THE COST OF KNOWING

THE STONE CYCLE BOOK TWO

VOLUME 1—THE FORMING

1

King Steffan the Second of Arvenon stood at the entrance to the royal tent, staring moodily out across a sea of smaller tents. A new frown creased his brow as the view was obscured by the latest downpour. The rain, apparently untroubled by royal displeasure, had been sheeting down fitfully since midmorning.

He closed the flap and stepped inside, banishing the showers. If only his frustrations could be dealt with so easily.

"What can we do, Bottren?" he asked irritably. "We're in the field with an army—finally—and going nowhere."

Bottren didn't respond, and Steffan didn't expect him to. Their central problem had not changed in the last three weeks. They could not find a way south through Deadman's Pass into Arvenon.

The pass was proving to be aptly named. A group of Rogandan soldiers had occupied the pass immediately after Steffan's wedding, and completely blocked a narrow section of it with large rocks. Access between Castel and Arvenon was no longer possible. The nature of the terrain and the determination of the defenders meant that every effort to dislodge them had failed.

Steffan's army, with the help of Castelan forces under King Istel and his commander, Lord Eisgold, had tried everything. A frontal assault had been disastrous—Steffan lost so many men that three weeks later he was still berating himself for ever agreeing to it. Steffan's and Istel's best archers had rained arrows on the position; they stopped when they realized the Rogandans were retrieving the fallen arrows and shooting them back. Agile mountain men volunteered to scale the walls of the pass, but the rain had made the rocks slippery, and every one of the climbers eventually plunged to their deaths.

Without this pass, they would have to head northwest all the way to the sea and take ship to Erestor. Then they would be forced to march east across much of Arvenon before they could reach the same point. Even if the ships were available, they simply didn't have time. If only there was a way to break through.

The Rogandans had chosen to defend a section of the pass where the walls narrowed to a thin neck. It was located almost all the way to the Arvenian side. From the summit of the pass the rolling hills of Arvenon could be glimpsed over the heads of the defenders. Having the goal so close only increased Steffan's frustration..

No doubt Rogandans were roaming freely throughout Arvenon. The longer Steffan's army delayed breaking through, the sooner winter would creep upon them. Then it would be too late to do anything. The Arvenian capital, Arnost, might even fall if he was unable to break the Rogandan siege.

Steffan wondered what had become of Will Prentis. No doubt the defenders at Arnost were benefiting from his leadership, but once again Steffan wished he had brought Will to Castel with him instead of old Olaf. The deputy captain of the King's Guard might have been young, but he was energetic and effective. He would have forced his way through the pass somehow.

As Steffan's mind wandered, his thoughts found their way back to Essanda. He pictured her as he had seen her in their apartments in Castel Citadel, a smile playing across her young lips as she gazed intently at her new husband. She seemed to think highly of him for some reason he couldn't fathom. Lately he had taken to writing to her regularly. Young though she was, he could safely vent his frustrations with her, and having an outlet brought him some consolation. The letters she wrote back were thoughtful and sympathetic, and—he struggled for a moment trying to put his finger on it—artless. Yes, that was it. It wasn't that she was childish, or simplistic. She was actually very intelligent, and clearly trying to put herself into the role of a responsible queen. But somehow her carefree girlishness always managed to leak out. Steffan found it endearing.

The strangeness of his own thinking suddenly struck him. He was already forgetting he had been maneuvered into this marriage. And somehow it had apparently become settled in his mind that years must pass before his bride could become his wife in full measure.

Sighing deeply, he dragged his mind back to the problem before him. He decided to try to think like Will. To find a solution no one else had thought of, yet one that seemed so obvious after the event.

STEFFAN'S SOLDIERS moved into position just below the summit of Deadman's Pass, lining up behind a newly constructed siege engine. The engine resembled a tall tower on wheels. Thin metal shielding covered the front and sides of the monstrous wooden structure, and the platform at the top was broad enough to carry a dozen men and tall enough to overshadow the mound of rocks that blocked the pass.

At a signal from their commander, the soldiers began to push with all their might, even as horses at the front took up the strain and pulled. Slowly, reluctantly, the wheels began to turn, and the huge structure groaned as it inched forward up the pass. As it slowly crested the summit the horses were moved aside. The soldiers continued to push, and the siege engine gradually gained momentum as the road sloped downward. Soldiers inside the structure soon began to apply massive brakes to ensure it did not move too fast.

The best engineers of Castel had spent the previous week building the engine on the Castelan side of the summit, just out of sight of the Rogandans. Thankfully the rains had eased off, and construction had gone according to plan. But it had cost them another week.

Down the pass lumbered the engine, slowly and inexorably. Soldiers massed behind it, protected by its vast bulk. Harsh cries could now be heard from the Rogandans at the end of the pass. Arrows soon appeared, but the engine was barely in range, and most fell short. The remaining arrows bounced harmlessly off its protective shielding. Soldiers atop the structure now began firing back, their arrows easily reaching the defenders.

As the engine rolled closer, arrows from behind the barrier occasionally found their mark, and figures could be seen falling from the top of the engine.

Rogandan soldiers appeared, bearing large rocks which they attempted to place in front of their defenses. As soon as they left their protection they were met by a deadly hail of arrows. None made it back alive. A few achieved their purpose, though—some of the rocks would now prevent the engine from rolling all the way to the barrier.

As the siege engine approached the defenses Arvenian soldiers ran in front of it to remove the rocks, protected by a stream of arrows from the tower of the engine. Rogandan archers recklessly exposed themselves to prevent the attackers from reaching the rocks. One Arvenian went down, another, and then another. The rocks were removed, but not before seven of Steffan's soldiers lay unmoving before the barrier.

Now the attackers threw down jars of boiling oil from the tower. Cries of alarm could be heard as the jars shattered, spewing bubbling liquid over the defenders. Burning torches followed the jars and flames sprang up everywhere. The whole scene quickly descended into chaos. Few arrows now reached the top of the engine. Another signal was given and Arvenian and Castelan troops rushed from behind the engine and scrambled over the barrier. Within minutes loud cheering could be heard from the top of the siege tower. The defenses had been overwhelmed.

The battle for Deadman's Pass was over. The entire operation had taken less than an hour.

. . .

Steffan sat in his tent, eager with anticipation. He had just received word that the last rocks from the barrier had been cleared from the pass. Dusk was upon them now, and his soldiers were resting. Tomorrow he would re-enter his kingdom, an army at his back.

The king had just sent off a note to his young queen, informing her of the good news and warning her that before long he rode to war and to an uncertain future.

Some would undoubtedly think him foolish for investing time and emotional energy communicating with someone barely older than a child. But it was important to him, and he didn't care if others thought it strange.

It brought to mind something his father had told him soon after the death of Steffan's mother. He had just turned eighteen. While he greatly missed his mother, the world lay before him bright with hope and promise. His father, though, had borne the burdens of kingship for too many years, and he never recovered from the loss of his wisest counselor and most loyal supporter. He didn't openly show his grief, but it was barely four years before they buried him beside his wife, reuniting him in death with the one who had been his truest friend in life.

One day he had told Steffan that it was her companionship he missed the most. Recalling it, Steffan began to understand why his relationship with his young wife had already assumed such importance to him. He had no siblings, and he had essentially been alone since his parents died. Now he, too, had a companion.

There was nothing sexual in his response to Essanda—he had assigned that part of himself to a long hibernation. But he cared about her, and he was certain that she, too, had come to care about him. There was someone apart from himself in the world to whom his thoughts and feelings and concerns really mattered. He understood for the first time the significance of his father's words. A king, no less than any other man, needed to walk through life with a companion.

His thoughts were interrupted by the arrival of a messenger. "Our watchmen have seen riders approaching the pass, Sire. From Arvenon. Four of them."

"Friend or foe, bring them to me as soon as they arrive," the king instructed. "I need to know what's been going on in my kingdom."

The man bowed and left.

It was dark before the messenger returned. Four men entered the tent behind him, and the king's mouth opened wide with astonishment when he saw them.

"Will! Rufe! I thought you were shut up in Arnost. Has the city fallen, then?" he asked in dismay.

"No, Your Majesty," Will assured him. "Not as far as we know, anyway. The city was secure in the hands of the duke when we left it several weeks ago. They were well provisioned and well defended. I am confident they have been able to keep the Rogandans out."

His immediate concerns allayed, the king paused long enough to call for refreshments. He also sent to King Istel, asking him to join them at his convenience.

"King Istel will join us shortly. Who are your companions, Will?"

"This is Ander, and this is Nestor, Sire. They have traveled with us since we left Arnost."

"You are welcome," the king returned, as the men bowed.

King Istel arrived and was introduced to the men.

After satisfying himself that his father-in-law was comfortable, King Steffan addressed his attention to the new arrivals. "I am very glad to see you, Will! And you, too, Rufe. I will have great need of your skills in the days ahead."

Will bowed in response. "We are at your service, Your Majesty."

"So you left Arnost with only these companions?"

"No, Sire. Our party was larger at first."

"So where have you been and what have you been doing in the weeks since you left Arnost?"

"That is a long story," Will replied calmly.

"We can spare a little time," the king replied with a smile. "And I enjoy stories," he added, waving them to some empty seats.

2

The royal city of Varacellan, the many towered capital of the Kingdom of Varas, lay glittering like an elegant jewel in the afternoon sunlight. A stiff breeze whipped the flags on the lofty battlements of the royal castle, dispersing the fresh smell of salty air throughout the city. Tall ships lay at anchor in the harbor, sheltering from the heavy seas that pounded the coast beyond the inlet.

Varas was a small but prosperous kingdom encircled by Castel, Rogand, Arvenon, and the sea. A rugged and inaccessible coastline formed the northern border of Varas, but Varacellan, with its fine harbor, offered a haven that attracted ships from every corner of the continent and beyond. The capital had become the hub of a prosperous trade network, and goods flowed in abundance between the harbor and the main trade route south to Arvenon.

The broad River Aron formed much of the southern boundary of Varas, marking its border with Arvenon. Varas also shared a short and mountainous border with Castel to the west; otherwise the sea formed the longest stretch of the western fringe of the kingdom. To the east lay Rogand, across an impenetrable section of the Blue Mountains that extended along the entire eastern border of Varas.

Small as it was, Varas had somehow managed to retain a precarious independence over the years. That independence now appeared threatened as rarely before.

Within the audience chamber of the royal palace, a group of men waited restlessly, illuminated by the bright sunlight that flooded in through the broad windows. The faces of the men were grim.

"The Rogandan Ambassador is here, Sire."

"Show him in."

King Delmar of Varas sat in state flanked by four of his most senior advisors. The ambassador stepped into the room and bowed low. Delmar found the gesture more mocking than deferential. Was it because the Rogandan held his bow for slightly too long, or was it the poorly concealed smirk that flashed across his face as he returned to a standing position? Whatever the reason, his manner reeked of insincerity.

"Why are Rogandan soldiers massing at our southern border, Lord Grunsetz?" Delmar demanded.

"A mere misunderstanding, Sire," the ambassador replied with an oily smile. "Lord Drettroth simply wishes to ensure that Varas is not disturbed by any armed troublemakers fleeing Arvenon."

"We can secure our borders without your help," Delmar replied curtly. "And we are well able to manage our own relationship with King Steffan, too."

"I understand, Your Majesty. I trust you appreciate that Rogand would not want to see Varas drawn into Arvenon's quarrel with Rogand."

"I presume the 'quarrel' to which you refer is Rogand's unprovoked invasion of Arvenon."

Grunsetz frowned. "Your concern for Arvenon surprises me, Sire. Is there an alliance that Rogand is unaware of?"

"I said nothing about an alliance. But I would be a fool indeed if I ignored what was going on around me."

"Of course, Your Majesty. Rogand's concern is very simple. Castel has allowed itself to be aligned with the Arvenians, a decision that I fear their king may come to regret before long. Rogand simply wishes to avoid any similar...ah...misunderstandings with Varas."

"If Rogand wishes to avoid misunderstandings with Varas, you will withdraw your forces from our border."

"I regret that I can make no commitments on behalf of King Agon, Sire. But I will certainly convey your wishes to His Majesty."

"I am counting on you to do so," Delmar replied.

Lord Grunsetz bowed once again. "There is another matter I wished to raise," he said. "With your permission, of course."

"You may speak," Delmar replied.

"King Agon wishes to establish a treaty with Varas," said the ambassador.

Delmar eyed the man warily. What game was Agon playing? "What kind of a treaty?" he asked.

"A security pact. King Agon has learned that Rogandan traders are being attacked in Varas. He is concerned about the security of his people, especially now that they are being targeted."

"Rogandan traders are not being targeted. One trader was robbed here in Varacellan, and I believe he was injured. Investigations are being pursued vigorously. There are reports, though, that he contributed to the incident by cheating local merchants."

"King Agon views it differently. He wishes to establish a treaty that would allow Rogand to place soldiers in Varas to protect Rogandan traders."

"What?! So you are proposing to invade Varas, too?"

"Please, Your Majesty! Rogand has no such intention. King Agon's desire is to resolve this issue by means of a treaty."

"Varas will regard any intrusion by Rogandan forces as an act of war!"

"I implore you, Sire! What is to be gained by making an enemy of Rogand?"

"Let me return the question to you. What does Rogand gain by making an enemy of Varas?"

"May I speak frankly, Your Majesty? Rogand has little to fear from Varas. But King Agon wishes to offer Varas an opportunity to avoid any possibility of unnecessary strife."

"This audience is at an end, Lord Grunsetz. Your proposal will be considered. I will offer no more than that."

The Rogandan bowed once again and was ushered from the room.

THE DOOR HAD BARELY CLOSED on the ambassador before a heated debate broke out among Delmar's advisors.

"It's an outrage!" stormed Lord Radesen. "Grunsetz should be thrown out of Varas without ceremony!"

"We cannot fight the Rogandans and expect to win," Lord Lunevag countered. "Their army is simply too large."

"Is it possible that the Rogandans will invade?"

"Surely not. Why would they ask for a treaty if they were planning to invade?"

"Why demand the right to place troops inside our borders, then?"

"That is nothing more than a bargaining ploy. They are beginning negotiations with an unreasonable demand that can be withdrawn later as a gesture of goodwill."

"We must ally ourselves with Arvenon."

"What use would that be? The Arvenians cannot even defend themselves effectively—how could they aid us?"

"Rogand has not yet subdued Arvenon, for all Grunsetz's posturing. Their armies have been unable to take Arnost, if the reports are to be believed."

A new voice cut across the argument. "Varas should accept this treaty." Lord Tarestel spoke quietly, but all eyes turned to him at his words. "There is no other way we can avoid war. If we fight Rogand, our armies will be quickly overwhelmed. If we enter into a treaty we will at least retain some ability to determine our own destiny."

King Delmar frowned. He wasn't at all sure he wanted to encourage this particular line of thinking. "Your counsel is valued as always, My Lords," he said. "You are dismissed for now; please make yourselves available to meet again tomorrow. Lord Radesen, remain here for a moment."

Lord Radesen inclined his head in acknowledgment. The other advisors bowed and departed.

The king turned to the head of his judiciary, not attempting to hide his displeasure. "This matter of the Rogandan trader needs to be resolved decisively, Radesen! See that justice is done, and be prompt about it. And make sure that Grunsetz—and anyone else with even the vaguest interest in the affair—hears about the outcome and understands it fully. We don't need to give Agon a pretext for picking a quarrel with us."

Lord Radesen bowed deeply and hurried away.

Delmar watched him go with a heavy heart. Tarestel was right about one thing—Varas simply was not strong enough militarily to defeat Rogand. Should he have allied himself with Steffan? He had hoped that a neutral stance might allow him to avoid conflict with Rogand. But such hopes might be proving illusory.

Arvenon was a natural ally. The two countries shared a great deal in common, in language, culture, and religion. By contrast, the very thought of a treaty with Rogand stuck in his throat. And he was not at all convinced by Tarestel's argument that signing a treaty with Rogand gave Varas more influence over its own destiny. How could it be safer to invite a poisonous reptile into your home, when you could try to deal with it while it was still outside?

He had so little experience to draw upon. Why couldn't this crisis have waited a few more years? Throughout his brief adult years his course had never seemed smooth. For as long as he had been king, he had been forced to navigate a road filled with ruts and pitfalls. And it was abundantly clear that the path before him was about to become very bumpy indeed.

"You didn't share your own views after Grunsetz left the Council, Karevis," said King Delmar, "and I'd like to know what you think. I still cannot bring myself to believe that Agon wants to pick a fight with Varas. He's already fighting two kingdoms as it is. Maybe I'm just deluding myself, though. What do you think I should do?"

The two of them stood together on a palace balcony that overlooked one of the broad tree-lined streets of Varacellan. The breeze might have been fresh, but the weather was unseasonably mild. Locals and foreigners mingled freely, enjoying the late afternoon sunshine as they strolled happily along the street and browsed among the hawkers' stalls that offered tasty portions of food, bolts of colored cloth, cut flowers, and much else besides. Delmar wondered how many more such afternoons they would enjoy together in peace.

Lord Karevis had been leaning on the balcony gazing down at the sights below. He turned his attention away from the tranquil scene and faced Delmar.

"My heart says to fight," he replied. He paused for a long moment before adding, "I'm not sure that we can win, though."

Delmar sighed. "We have an army, but we're not sure we can take the risk of using it."

"Our soldiers are better trained and better disciplined than the Rogandans," Karevis asserted. "I have complete confidence in them. They will give a good account of themselves whenever it comes to a battle. My only uncertainty is how we can contrive to outmaneuver an adversary with such a significant advantage in numbers."

Delmar fell silent. Karevis had been born the same year as him and had remained his closest friend since childhood. They had played together, studied together, and trained together. They'd also quarreled and fought at times, but they'd never fallen out for long. Karevis was the brother Delmar never had.

Yet Karevis had never traded on this special relationship. Delmar routinely sought out his friend, sometimes to consult with him and sometimes just to enjoy his company. If other nobles ever found out, though, it wasn't because Karevis told them. Delmar had learned to trust his friend's discretion implicitly.

Though still a young man, Karevis now commanded the Varasan army, a role he had earned by dint of hard work combined with his very considerable abilities.

Delmar had always been impressed by his friend's strategic sense. And the commander had honed the skills of his soldiers to exacting standards. There was little doubt in Delmar's mind that the Varasan army could achieve more than any other army of equivalent size. He had no desire to throw away any of the lives of his soldiers to put his belief to the test, though.

In spite of the looming crisis with Rogand, Delmar still held out hopes that a settlement could be negotiated. He feared that his hopes may be nothing more than wishful thinking, though. Either way, he wouldn't need to wait long to find out.

King Delmar of Varas stood to receive his advisors as they filed into the room. Lord Karevis had already arrived.

He waited until they were all seated. "I've just received some very grave news, My Lords," he said. "The Rogandans have crossed the border. They have forded the River Aron and occupied the main pass into the lowlands."

This report was greeted with loud expressions of dismay.

"Are we at war with them, then?" asked Lord Lunevag.

"There hasn't been any real fighting," Karevis replied. "Our border guards were taken by surprise and overwhelmed. The army units stationed near the border have withdrawn and are awaiting orders."

"So much for Agon's interest in a treaty," said Lunevag.

Lord Radesen had thrust back his chair and was pacing around the room. "That means they've already overrun my estates!"

Delmar could smell the scent of fear among his advisors. It wouldn't take much for them to descend into panic.

"I intend to handle this situation personally, My Lords," he told them calmly, projecting a confidence he didn't feel.

"What do you plan to do, Sire?" asked Lord Tarestel.

"The difficulty of containing the Rogandan army has just increased significantly," he replied. "The Aron and the mountain pass have always been our strongest lines of defense. The loss of the pass in particular is a significant misfortune. I will contact Grunsetz and see if it is still possible to negotiate. I fear that our bargaining position is greatly diminished, though."

Some of the lords had a lot to say, and Delmar let them speak. Although many words were spoken, he heard little of any value. Lunevag and Radesen were still in denial, hoping irrationally that somehow life could return to normal. They were in for a rude shock. Privately, Delmar held out little hope that Varas would still exist as an independent kingdom by the end of another week. Whether they decided to fight or negotiate, the outcome would most likely be the same before long.

Tarestel largely kept his own counsel. The noble's wealth had always exceeded his power, and Delmar had long sensed that the discrepancy irked him greatly. The man had become craftier as he aged, if not wiser, and Delmar found himself wondering uneasily if Tarestel had his own agenda in this situation.

ONCE AGAIN KAREVIS had held his peace, and Delmar sought him out after dismissing the Council.

"Is the situation retrievable?" Delmar asked.

"While we held the pass we had a chance. It's hard to see how we can keep them out for long now, though." Karevis hung his head. "I strengthened the guard at the border, but I should have issued orders to expect an invasion, and to defend the river crossings and the pass at all costs."

"The fault does not lie with you," Delmar told him firmly. "I'm the one who failed to act decisively while I still had the chance. We've always had strong natural barriers on three sides, and our southern border has been secure thanks to good relations with Arvenon. It's become painfully clear to me that I've taken that far too much for granted." He shook his head, struggling to come to terms with his own blindness, and with the magnitude of the disaster that had been visited on his kingdom as a result.

"Until they invaded Arvenon, the Rogandans never had ready

access to our borders. Once they did, though, they didn't waste much time. Before long they'll control the entire continent."

Delmar placed his hands on his friend's shoulders and looked him in the eye. "Whatever happens now, do everything you can to protect our people. Don't fail me in this!"

Karevis looked downcast. But he nodded his agreement. "Should I join my men?" he asked.

"No. Send orders to resist further encroachments by the Rogandans, but not to actively initiate fighting before I've attempted negotiations."

Karevis bowed, and left to relay the orders.

Delmar knew he couldn't afford to delay. He had to act swiftly, not just because time was short, but because he needed to be actively doing something. He was frightened that if he allowed himself the luxury of thinking, he would quickly lose any hope of preserving his own self control.

There was so much he had planned to do. He wanted to enrich and strengthen the kingdom he had inherited, and broaden its alliances. He had expected to marry and have a family, and to one day grow old enjoying his grandchildren.

It was all too late now, though. The very best he could hope for was to fulfill his duty as king, and try to retrieve whatever he could from the wreckage.

King Delmar was bone weary by the time he arrived under a flag of truce with his aides at Rogandan army headquarters near the border with Arvenon. Having finally reached his destination, though, he found that his entire body was throbbing with nervous energy.

"Come in, Your Majesty." Grunsetz offered his usual oily smile as he ushered the king into his tent and pointed him to a seat. No refreshments or other courtesies were on offer. Delmar was not surprised.

"What brings you to my humble quarters?" the Rogandan asked.

"I'm here to negotiate," Delmar replied simply.

"Ah. Well advised, I'm sure. Perhaps I could have offered better terms at our earlier meeting. But no matter. Since your army has avoided bloodshed thus far, there is still an opportunity to reach a peaceful solution to the current disagreements. I know that Lord Drettroth is eager to meet with you."

Delmar did not like the implications of Grunsetz's comment. "Surely we can discuss details here, right now."

"That would also be my clear preference, Sire. Please understand that. But I am under strict instructions. Lord Drettroth is only willing to discuss details of an accord in person."

"What does he propose if I accept?"

"You will be escorted to his headquarters for the negotiations, protected by a special Guard of Honor in recognition of your rank. Your aides will be allowed to return to your capital to report on your behalf."

"You cannot be proposing that I go alone!"

"Those are my explicit instructions, Your Majesty. Lord Drettroth was most specific."

"And if I refuse?"

"You will be allowed to return to your army. Hostilities will commence immediately. Fighting has been delayed only out of respect for your stated desire to meet to discuss terms."

Delmar frowned. Discussing terms sounded a lot like surrender, and he had never made any such proposal. This situation was even worse than he had feared.

What choice did he have, though? He had been brought to Grunsetz by a roundabout route that gave him plenty of opportunity to review the size of the Rogandan army. He was sure that the detours had been entirely intentional. However good the Varasan soldiers might be, it was clear that the Rogandans had brought a large enough force to overwhelm Delmar's army, especially now that they controlled the pass and enjoyed ready access to the Varasan lowlands.

But going alone to meet Drettroth? Was it safe? Delmar glanced across at his aides. He hadn't brought them for protection—they were advisors, not soldiers. And even if they had been soldiers, he knew they wouldn't be able to safeguard him for long if Drettroth wanted him dead. By coming here, he had already placed his safety entirely in the hands of the Rogandans.

As for advice, he would just have to manage without his aides. He was more than capable of deciding for himself at the negotiating table anyway. The main implication of going alone would be the total lack of support. No doubt Drettroth would believe himself to be in a stronger bargaining position as a result. The Rogandan lord might be in for a surprise.

"I accept Lord Drettroth's conditions."

Another oily smile crossed the face of the Rogandan ambassador. "A wise decision, Sire," he said. "I am confident that you will be able to save your subjects much pain and suffering."

"Please excuse me while I instruct my aides," Delmar said.

The Rogandan bowed an acknowledgment, and Delmar turned to his chief aide and swiftly gave him messages for his noblemen back in the capital, and special instructions for Karevis and the army. He dismissed his aides and watched them ride away.

"If you please, Sire?"

Grunsetz ushered him toward a group of soldiers who were already mounted. Delmar's horse was led over to the group. He mounted it, and they rode away.

GRUNSETZ WATCHED them go with a self-satisfied smirk. Everything was proceeding exactly to plan.

He summoned another soldier and pointed away in the direction taken by Delmar's aides.

"Take a squad and follow that group of Varasans. They are heading for their capital, Varacellan. Stay out of sight until you find a suitable location, then kill them all! Not one of them must be allowed to reach the capital alive.

"Dispose of their bodies when you're finished. There must be no evidence left behind. And I want no mistakes! Do you understand?"

The soldier nodded.

"Report back to me when you have completed your mission."

Soon a large body of Rogandan soldiers set off after Delmar's aides.

Grunsetz was now free to carry out the next phase of his plans. With King Delmar out of the way, someone else must rule Varas. The ideal candidate would be a Varasan nobleman—someone very compliant. Grunsetz was confident he had found the perfect person.

He could barely contain his glee. Varas had as good as fallen, and with little more effort than plucking an apple from a tree.

Lord Drettroth would be pleased. Very pleased indeed.

3

The never-ending staircase finally came to an abrupt end. Brother Vangellis halted, having reached its lowest extremity. Thomas descended the few steps that separated them and found himself standing in a tiny room fashioned roughly from the surrounding rock. A small wooden door in the opposite wall provided the only way out.

The monk began tugging at a large iron ring set into the door, and Thomas quickly lent his weight to the task. Thomas strained until he thought the veins in his face would burst. At last, with a loud creak of protest from the iron hinges, the stout wooden door moved slowly inward. A steady stream of soil from outside poured into the widening crack.

As soon as the opening became wide enough, Thomas slid through the gap. He stood quietly for a moment and gazed around him. Nothing unusual caught his attention in the dim light provided by the moon, so he turned once again to the door.

The entrance was almost covered by bushes and soil, and Thomas began to pull energetically at the branches and roots that blocked it. Then he threw his weight against the door from the outside while the monk continued to pull on the iron ring from inside. Soon the opening had visibly increased in size. Brother Vangellis extinguished the torches and left them inside the small room. He joined Thomas outside, and the two of them shoveled away dirt with their hands until they were able to pull the door shut once more. Finally, they did their best to restore the vegetation that Thomas had removed.

Thomas moved away from the opening and paused to catch his breath. After the long journey in the confined atmosphere of the enclosed stairwell, followed by the exertion of his recent labors, the crispness of the evening air felt very refreshing. He glanced back toward the door, and to his surprise found himself peering about for a moment before he found it. Its location had been cleverly chosen. Even standing immediately before it, the lie of the land concealed it so effectively that it could not easily be recognized as a man-made opening.

Brother Vangellis had turned away toward the river. "Let's find this coracle," he whispered. Thomas could sense the urgency in his voice.

The ground sloped sharply downward, every inch of it covered with trees, bushes, and lush grass. They began crisscrossing their way methodically down the slope, fully alert for any sign of the hidden vessel.

Before long, Thomas heard a soft call through the gloom. "I've found it!"

Thomas followed the monk's voice down almost to the river bank. The coracle lay upside down beneath a large bush. They lifted it together and carried it to a clear patch of grass, flipping it over so that it sat on its base. It was small and light, but surprisingly capacious. It was most likely intended for one occupant, but the two of them would easily be able to squeeze into it. A single wooden board bisected the inside of the vessel, providing both stability for the frame and a crude seat for passengers to sit on. A couple of paddles had been secured under the wooden board.

Thomas looked at it doubtfully. The river was wide and fast flowing, and the vessel seemed small and frail. Brother Vangellis, however, was clearly delighted with it.

"This brings back happy memories, Thomas," he said.

The look of incredulity on Thomas's face must have been obvious even in the moonlight, because the monk hastened to add, "But I haven't forgotten that we'll be navigating in the dark. And fleeing from the Rogandans."

While speaking, he reached into the coracle for the paddles and placed them on the seat within easy reach. Thomas picked one up and examined it. A relatively short shaft led down to a pair of broad wooden blades. He practiced dipping it in and out of an imaginary river.

"You'd best leave the paddling to me, Thomas. For a while, at least. Can you help me carry the coracle to the water?"

As soon as they placed it in the river, the little craft threatened to spin away with the current. Brother Vangellis held onto it tightly, and motioned for Thomas to get in. The boat wobbled precariously as he climbed aboard, and he sat down in a hurry to avoid being pitched into the water. The monk wasted no time. In one fluid motion, he pushed off from the bank, stepped nimbly into the boat, and took a seat. Planting his paddle confidently into the water, he angled the blade into the current and steered the coracle out into the middle of the river.

The moon provided just enough light for Brother Vangellis to keep the coracle away from the banks and avoid protruding branches and rocks. He clearly knew what he was doing.

Thomas, nervous and uncomfortable, tried not to move more than he needed to. As time passed, though, and the water seemed to be mostly staying in the river where it belonged, his anxiety about Drettroth overwhelmed his uncertainties about the coracle.

"It was Harald, wasn't it?" he finally asked.

"I fear so, Thomas," the monk replied. "It seems he was more than just a wandering thief. I don't doubt that many other such 'travelers' were sent throughout Arvenon with instructions to watch out for you."

Thomas shook his head, totally overwhelmed as he grasped for the first time the scale of the manhunt mounted against him. So much deadly strife lay behind him. Apparently there was to be no end to it.

His thoughts churned restlessly as he struggled to absorb this new reality. The broader implications slowly began to dawn on him, too. He was not the only person affected by this development.

"The Rogandans seem to know I'm traveling with a monk," he said. "I'm sorry that you're involved as well now."

Thomas knew that the monk had already experienced more than enough trouble of his own. He was nevertheless relieved beyond words that he wasn't fleeing for his life alone. Brother Vangellis had confidently taken charge of the coracle, and Thomas was entirely willing to follow his lead whenever they decided to leave the river.

The trouble wasn't limited to them, either. He was painfully aware that many others had been drawn into his problems as well.

"What will become of the monks?" he asked.

"I don't know. They are in God's hands."

Thomas didn't find the monk's answer reassuring. But God would have to take care of his own in this case. No one else was in a position to do it.

The dark outline of the plateau slowly diminished as the current swept them further downriver. Brother Vangellis leaned forward, peering intently into the darkness ahead. After some time he broke the silence.

"We've put some distance between ourselves and the monastery now, Thomas, and it's difficult to navigate in the dark. I think we can afford to stop and rest for the rest of the night. We can continue our journey in the morning."

Thomas wasted no time in agreeing. The monk steered the coracle toward an inlet where the water flowed less swiftly, and with a few powerful strokes he guided them to the bank.

They had no food and no blankets to wrap themselves in, and they couldn't risk lighting a fire. So they simply lay down on the river bank and tried to sleep. Thomas failed miserably—he spent most of the night cold, hungry, and restless. Worst of all, anxiety about the future threatened to overwhelm him.

Just before dawn he fell into a restless sleep, filled with nightmares. When he woke, he couldn't remember any of the details. His dreams hovered just out of the reach of his conscious mind, although the feelings of dread lingered.

Brother Vangellis was nowhere to be seen. He had gone to sleep long before Thomas—gentle snores had begun to sound not long after they lay down—and he must have woken before Thomas, too. The figure of the monk soon reappeared in the pre-dawn half light, though.

"Follow this little stream for a short distance, Thomas. The water upstream tastes fresh, and you might benefit from splashing some of it on your face, too."

Thomas followed his advice. Filling his belly with water was better than leaving it entirely empty, but his stomach still grumbled, and he came back feeling wretched. He was starting the new day as he had ended the previous one—cold, hungry, and anxious.

As soon as it was light they set off again. Once the current had them in its grip, Brother Vangellis turned to Thomas. "I'm sure you're feeling as hollow as I am," he said. "Let's travel for a couple more hours, then we can pull in and find something to eat. In the meantime, let me give you a chance to control the boat yourself."

The monk demonstrated how to steer and handle the craft. At first, whenever Thomas tried to paddle, the coracle simply spun around in a circle. Brother Vangellis showed him how to angle the blade with his wrist while sweeping the paddle through the water to move the vessel forward.

After some practice, Thomas began to grow in confidence. He successfully directed the boat from one side of the river to the other and back again. Then he tried a bit too hard, and nearly pitched both of them into the water.

His teacher waved off his embarrassment with a laugh. "Don't worry, Thomas. The world isn't likely to end if we capsize. If it does happen, though, don't try to climb back in while we're in the water. It won't work. We'll need to swim for the bank, and tow the coracle along with us."

"Won't it sink?"

"No, it should float. Some air will get trapped underneath a coracle if it flips over cleanly."

The sun had risen above the trees before they landed the craft again. Thomas found his spirits rising with the sun. Having something to do had improved his state of mind considerably, and the anticipation of food helped even more.

"HOW DO you know if mushrooms are good to eat?" Thomas asked. They had been wandering inland for a couple of hours, and had already collected a small pile of mushrooms that promised to take the edge off their hunger.

"Experience, Thomas. Bitter experience at times," his companion replied, offering him a wry smile. "I have been very sick indeed after eating mushrooms that looked and tasted delicious. After a while you get to know what's safe and what isn't."

"That's good to know," said Thomas. "But I'm left with the same question."

The monk smiled. "You're right. Next time we find mushrooms, I'll try to point out what to look for. A tip for beginners, though—stay away from mushrooms with white gills."

In the end, they added a few berries to their collection, and, best of all, a young wild turkey. The turkey was unlucky. If they'd been less famished and the bird less plump and self-satisfied when they stumbled upon it, the outcome might have been different. But the turkey would now be joining them for dinner, notwithstanding its noisy objections. They finally headed back to the boat with arms laden and bellies rumbling loudly.

The turkey needed to be cooked, so lighting a fire had become a necessity. It was difficult to imagine that any Rogandan soldiers could be close enough to observe the smoke. Nevertheless the monk carefully chose a small natural clearing surrounded by tall trees, and sent Thomas off looking for dry timber to feed the fire. After what seemed an interminable delay waiting for the food to cook, they finally found themselves feasting heartily.

By the time they lay down to sleep, the fire had burned down to glowing coals. For Thomas, soaking up the warmth with a satisfyingly full belly, the trials and worries of the previous night seemed far away.

THOMAS WAS startled awake by a hand shaking him. "We need to go!" Brother Vangellis whispered urgently into his ear. Thomas sat up and squinted around him in the half light. Dawn was close. A thin line of smoke rose high into the air from the remains of the fire. Nothing else unusual could be seen, but he could faintly hear rough voices calling in the distance. They didn't sound near, but they couldn't have been too far off, either.

Clouds of dust rose as the monk hurriedly scooped dirt over the ashes of the fire, ending the telltale line of smoke. Observing that Thomas was fully awake, he motioned toward the river. They hurried to the coracle and launched it, praying that they would make it past the Rogandans before being discovered.

The monk steered them out into the current. In the semi-darkness they saw no one, and after a while they dared to hope that they had made a clean escape.

The light grew steadily brighter as they drifted silently downstream. Looking ahead, Thomas noticed a disturbance in the river off in the distance. He turned to Brother Vangellis. "What's that?" he asked, pointing ahead nervously.

"White water," the monk replied. "There are rapids ahead. Crouch down and hang on tight—I'll try to steer us through them."

The noise of the river grew ever louder as they approached the rapids. Thomas gripped the sides of the coracle and bent down as low as he could. He peered over the top of the boat, trying hard to convince himself that the monk knew what he was doing. The boat picked up speed as the current swept them into the roiling waters. The little craft bucked and swayed violently, and for a few anxious moments it seemed that they must surely capsize. But then the rapids spat them out the other side, and they were through the worst of it. The monk deftly swept his paddle in and out, guiding them to calmer water.

Thomas sat up again and stretched, trying to relieve the tension in his muscles.

“That was fun,” said Brother Vangellis with a grin.

Thomas didn’t respond, but his opinion must have been obvious, because the monk laughed when he saw the look on his face.

Ahead of them the river swung right in a broad sweeping curve. A wide beach covered with yellow sand lay on the inside of the bend. Brother Vangellis began guiding the boat into the slower current near the beach. Then Thomas noticed a man sitting on a log on the far side of the beach. Spotting the coracle, the man leaped to his feet and called out a single word of warning. Thomas didn’t need to be told that the man was Rogandan.

A number of other men appeared on the beach. One approached the water’s edge and called out to them, in their own language but with a heavy accent.

“BRING THE BOAT IN TO THE BEACH NOW, MONK!” he shouted. “WE WANT THE BOY.”

He spread his hands in a gesture of appeal. “Turn him over to us,” he called. “I guarantee that he will not be hurt, and you can go on your way. Disobey, and both of you will die!” The man fell silent and stood with arms folded, waiting to see what they would do.

Brother Vangellis did not hesitate even for a moment. He vigorously paddled the boat away from the beach and back into the swifter current.

Thomas looked fearfully toward the gradually diminishing figure of the Rogandan on the beach. The man had begun waving his arms and pointing emphatically toward them. Thomas watched with increasing alarm as four horsemen galloped across the beach and splashed their horses into the river. They surged out into the strongest part of the current and set their horses swimming after the coracle.

It could not be doubted that they would reach the boat before many minutes had passed.

IT WAS obvious to Thomas that the pursuit on the river had reached a critical stage. Two of the riders had quickly given up the chase when their horses struggled to keep up and fell behind. But the other two continued in hot pursuit, and one had now swum almost to within a stone's throw of the coracle.

Both riders had long since slipped off the backs of their horses into the water. They glided along beside them, firmly gripping the manes of their mounts in one hand.

Thomas was finding it difficult to breathe. A tight knot had been twisting inside his stomach, and his heart was racing. He forced out an agitated question. "Should we have done what the Rogandan said?"

The monk's face was set in a firm line. He was too busy paddling to do more than spit out words between strokes.

"His guarantees...mean nothing...Only Drettroth...can offer guarantees...And Drettroth cares...for no one...just his own...interests... You've seen that."

Thomas could only nod mutely.

"We're not...that desperate...It's not over...Not yet, Thomas."

Thomas knew that the horses could not keep swimming like this for much longer. And the water was cold. The soldiers must surely be suffering. The monk was visibly tiring, too, although he had refused an offer of help. The chase was coming to a head, and soon.

The nearest soldier had urged his mount to a final effort. With the prize seemingly almost within his grasp, he began to stretch out a hand to grab the side of the coracle.

"Thomas! The nostrils."

Thomas understood. He grabbed the spare paddle and began scooping sheets of water at the horse. The creature snorted and tossed its head. Seeing the rider straining harder to reach the boat, Thomas redoubled his efforts, directing an almost continuous stream of water at the face of the horse. Unable to breathe freely, the animal began to panic. It jerked away from the coracle, and the rider lost his grip on its mane. He quickly kicked out toward the boat on his own.

As the soldier approached, Thomas lifted the paddle free of the water, and began swinging it down hard at the swimmer's arms. The soldier dodged the paddle while still attempting to swim closer. As he strained forward to grasp the coracle, Thomas finally landed a heavy blow on his arm. The blade of the paddle split in two with a loud crack and broke away from the shaft. The soldier cried out in pain and pulled away. Nursing his injured arm, which was almost certainly broken, he struck out weakly for the shore.

During the confusion the other horse had drawn closer. His rider approached more cautiously.

Thomas tried to splash water toward the horse with his hands. Without a paddle he was forced to scoop much more vigorously, and the coracle began to rock dangerously. Then Brother Vangellis cried out a sudden warning. They had been swinging around another bend in the river, and Thomas looked up to see a new set of rapids foaming white almost immediately before them.

As they approached the turbulence an arrow fell into the water near the coracle. Startled, Thomas looked across the river and saw the right bank lined with soldiers. Even before they reached the white water, arrows began falling around them. Then they were into the rapids. The last rider and both horses were swept in after them, and Thomas caught a brief glimpse of heads dipping in and out of the foam.

Brother Vangellis suddenly leaned violently to one side. Thomas turned to him, thinking he had been hit by an arrow. But then the coracle capsized, and all was chaos. Somehow Thomas sucked in air before the waves covered his head. Then the current took him. The turbulent waters tossed him around unmercifully, and he barely managed to thrust his head above the surface for an occasional breath. Miraculously, he had not been smashed into any rocks, but the rapids still battered him relentlessly.

The turbulence ceased abruptly. Before he could clear the water for another breath, he was grabbed firmly from behind. Reacting instinctively he tried to fight against the arm that held him, but the grip was too strong. He was pulled under the coracle and thrust upward into a vacant space beside the seat plank. Gasping, he filled his lungs with air.

The arm had belonged to the monk. Both of them clung to the upended seat, craning their necks upward into the life-giving pocket of trapped air, and let the current carry them. Occasional arrows rattled off the hull of the boat, and others sliced into the water around them. But the coracle hid and protected them.

Once again it seemed that the Rogandans had no access to a boat. The rain of arrows soon ended but many more minutes passed before the monk dived under the boat and disappeared. Thomas heard a slow series of taps on the hull and guessed that the monk was letting him know that it was safe to emerge. He dived clear himself and surfaced to a river empty of enemies.

The monk began to tow the coracle to the riverbank. Thomas tried to help as best he could. The rapids had exhausted him, though, and he spent more time hanging onto the boat than towing it.

Brother Vangellis was almost spent, too, and it felt like an eternity before they finally reached the bank. They dragged the boat out of the river, then both collapsed onto the grass that grew almost down to the water's edge.

They lay there without moving for many minutes. Then the monk sat up, wincing as he stretched his limbs. "We need to keep moving, Thomas. Even if they think we're dead, they'll still look for us. They'll try to get you to Drettroth, whatever state you're in."

Thomas groaned, then slowly sat up himself.

"We've lost both of our paddles," said the monk. "I will see if I can find something we can use instead."

He headed for the trees near the river's edge and disappeared into them. Before long he returned with a couple of branches, and a bundle of thick reeds tucked firmly under one arm. The largest branch was a thick limb that would probably only be useful to push them off from the bank. The other branch was shorter with a sturdy fork splitting the main limb halfway down its length.

The monk sat down and began tightly winding the reeds across and around the fork to create a crude blade. "You'll find a stream over there, Thomas," he said, pointing downriver a short distance. "We have nothing to carry water in, so take a long drink while you have the chance."

Thomas took his advice and headed to the stream. He returned to find the monk examining his makeshift paddle critically. "This might work, at least for a while," he said, waving it through the air.

Brother Vangellis wasted no further time, heading straight for the coracle. He examined the hull briefly. "It doesn't look like the arrows have done any real damage," he said. With an effort he flipped the coracle over. "Are you ready, Thomas?"

The youth nodded and joined him. They lifted the boat into the water, and Thomas clambered in stiffly. The monk put the two branches into the boat and climbed in himself, more gingerly this time. He used the thick limb to push off from the bank and slowly they began to move forward as the current caught them.

Brother Vangellis used his new paddle sparingly, mostly angling it like a rudder to steer them into the faster-moving water.

Once they were underway he turned to Thomas. "I think we should just drift for as long as we can. We'll have to pray that there are no more Rogandans—and no more rapids—waiting for us."

Thomas felt too weary to offer more than a nod in response.

"There's something else I need to say, too." The monk paused, apparently choosing his words. "It was no accident when the coracle capsized in the rapids. I did it intentionally. I knew I was taking a big risk; we could have drowned. But I decided that the risk from the Rogandans was greater. I owe you an apology for putting your life in danger in that way, especially since I offered you no choice."

Thomas shrugged. "We're alive. And we're still free," he said. Finding nothing else worth saying, he fell into a brooding silence.

The immediate danger appeared to have passed, but Thomas could not relax. He had long since recognized just how much trouble the stone had brought him. But it was becoming clear that his real troubles were only beginning. The stone was unreliable, and largely closed to him. All it brought him now was deadly peril, and for so little return. And yet, although he could not clearly articulate the reasons, he was not willing to even consider giving it up.

Perhaps the stone had some kind of hold over him. If so, he had undoubtedly brought it on himself; he remembered the scroll saying something about fearful risks resulting from overuse. Even the writer of the scroll had been ensnared—he said that the stones haunted his dreams—and he had never as much as seen them.

"Have you been thinking about the scroll?" asked Thomas.

Brother Vangellis returned a tired smile before shaking his head. "I'm sorry, Thomas. After all the excitement I haven't had the energy to think about anything much at all."

Thomas was not deterred. "I've been wondering about the writer of the scroll. Randolf of Clerbon, wasn't it? How did he find out so much about the stones?"

"I don't know. It must have been frustrating for the poor fellow, though—always searching for the stones, but never finding them, and constantly acquiring knowledge that he couldn't use."

"Maybe he wasn't able to use the knowledge himself, but he answered some questions for me."

"Which questions?"

"I always wondered why the stone behaved so strangely with the two rabid animals; all it showed me each time was a wolf. But according to the scroll, the stone doesn't reveal as much about animals. And I never understood why the stone revealed nothing about Will's thoughts when I first met him. It changed his appearance, but that was all. But I'd broken my arm."

"And the scroll suggested that pain diminishes the power of the stone." The monk finished the thought for him.

"Yes. At the time I had very little experience with the stone, too, so maybe that was another reason. The scroll said that the power of the stone increases with familiarity. That certainly matched my experience."

Thomas fell silent again, and Brother Vangellis apparently had nothing further to say, either.

The scroll had explained so much, but there were questions it hadn't answered, too. Why was the stone largely ineffective now? He felt sure that Randolf of Clerbon could have given him a reason. If only Brother Erastus had found the entire scroll, and not just the first part of it.

He also didn't understand why he had seen wolf eyes in his own face when he looked in the mirror. After his fight with Simon, the stone hadn't been working at all, so why did it work then? And why wolf eyes? The scroll talked about afflictions of the spirit affecting the stone, and he had certainly been in turmoil since the fight. Did that have something to do with it?

Maybe it had been about his future. He had sensed at the time that the wolf eyes pointed to a possible destiny, one that he had been desperate to avoid. Thankfully, the scroll had indicated that the stone's glimpses into what lay ahead should not be taken as certain. And yet the stone's vision of Will's future had come so close to the mark. It was mystifying.

Thomas tried to recall everything the scroll had said, but his attention wandered. His fears about the future began to rise up again and press in on him. He couldn't think straight, and he soon found it impossible to concentrate. As the boat continued to drift peacefully along with the current, his thoughts churned and boiled like the rapids.

The afternoon wore on as they floated downstream, allowing the river to take them wherever it would. The coracle was too small to allow them to lie down or stretch out, and Thomas felt increasingly uncomfortable. It was also now many hours since he had eaten, and hunger began to gnaw away at him. After a time he began to feel thirsty, too, but he knew enough not to drink from the river. Eventually, his weariness overshadowed everything, and he found himself drifting in and out of sleep sitting up, in spite of the discomfort.

The countryside that slid by them was untamed and apparently unsettled. The sun set, and still they floated on.

Just after sunset they passed a scene that caused them to shrink down fearfully in their little craft. Many small fires burned brightly in a huge clearing, and armed Rogandan soldiers sat around the fires feasting noisily. The smell of cooked food wafted tantalizingly across the water. They drifted by undetected, but long after the fear had faded Thomas still struggled to rid his mind of images of warm fires and hot food.

By the time day was about to break, Thomas could bear it no longer. His aching muscles, empty stomach and growing thirst had reinforced the fear that dragged at his will and sapped his energy. "If we don't stop soon, I'll go mad!" he finally exclaimed.

"If you can wait just a little longer, Thomas, I think we will soon be able to leave the river for good." The monk's voice was calm, although Thomas could sense his concern.

Now that the silence had been broken, Thomas's anxieties burst forth. "Why did the Rogandans try to kill us? Doesn't Drettroth know what will happen if he tries to take the stone by force? I don't understand it."

"Even if Drettroth knows, his soldiers may not," Brother Vangellis replied. "His men clearly know that he is searching for you, and they may know you have something he wants. But I doubt that he has told anyone about the stone. I doubt that he could trust even his own commanders if they knew what it was capable of."

Thomas peered uncertainly at the monk in the gloom. "Do you want the stone?" He couldn't help blurting it out.

The monk laughed, but there was no mirth in it. "You need not fear me, Thomas," he replied. "I don't envy you the burden of this gift, if I can borrow from the words in the scroll."

Thomas shamefacedly recalled everything that the monk had done to help him, and the huge risks he had taken for his sake. He suddenly felt very contrite. "I'm sorry. I shouldn't have said that."

Brother Vangellis laughed again, more cheerfully this time. "Forget it," he said. "I've promised to help you in any way I can, and I mean to make good on that promise."

Thomas didn't know what to say. Perhaps sensing that, the monk quickly changed the subject. "As soon as there's enough light, we can find a suitable landing place. We have two options. We can hide the coracle so we can use it again. The risk is that the Rogandans might find it. They're certain to search the riverbank for any trace of us. The alternative is to let it drift on without us. They may eventually find it, but they won't know for certain where we abandoned it."

The choice was an easy one for Thomas. "I don't care if I never see a coracle again!" he said.

"It's decided, then," the monk replied. "We need to look for a large stream that empties into the river. That's where we'll land. A fast flowing stream will remove our footprints."

Thomas didn't respond. His mind drifted off, away from the coracle, the river, and even the Rogandans. For the first time in what seemed like an age, he found himself thinking of Arnost, and wondering if the siege still continued. Somewhat guiltily, he spared a thought for his father in the city, and his mother away at her brother's farm. Then he realized that in his preoccupation it hadn't occurred to him to wonder what had become of Will and Rufe and their other companions. He would have expected Will to have an army behind him now, and to be fighting the Rogandans. But Drettroth didn't seem interested in battles. He was too busy chasing the stone.

As his thoughts continued to wander, he reluctantly faced the fact that Elbruhe no longer constantly inhabited the back of his mind. Even in the extremity of his present circumstances, he still felt guilty about allowing her to be pushed so far from his conscious awareness.

Everything was changing. He tried to remember what his life had been like back in Arnost before the stone and before the Rogandans came. But he couldn't recapture it. Everything he had cared about was now beyond his reach. His old life, like the old Thomas, was gone.

Some measure of tranquility eventually came to him as the sky began to lighten in the east. He fixed his gaze into the heavens, watching the last of the stars disappear as the strengthening light swallowed them up.

After a while he turned his attention to the monk. "They'll never stop chasing me, will they?" It was a statement more than a question.

Brother Vangellis regarded him silently for a long moment. Then slowly he shook his head.

A COUPLE more hours passed before the monk spotted a suitable stream in the right terrain.

"This is it, Thomas. We might as well leave the coracle in the river and swim for the bank. Jump in quickly before we're carried beyond the stream."

Thomas launched himself into the river, struggling to reawaken cramped muscles. The monk followed him in, flipping the coracle over before swimming away from it. "If the Rogandans find it capsized, they might decide that we drowned in the rapids," he said. "If we're fortunate."

The little craft had disappeared from sight before they reached dry land.

Stepping ashore into the mouth of the stream, they allowed it to lead them away from the river. The monk did not halt until the stream had begun to narrow noticeably. After drinking deeply from its cool waters they clambered out onto some rocks.

They sat there for a while soaking up the sun. Then, putting the river and the stream behind them, the two fugitives disappeared into the wilderness.

4

"How many soldiers did you see?" Kuper asked.

"Hundreds, at least. We'll need to find a way around them." Rellan lifted his good arm and pointed vaguely toward the tree line off to the south.

"Hold the horses while I take a closer look."

Kuper clambered up almost to the top of the ridge, then bent low as he approached the summit. He knelt down and peered over the top. Dozens of tents stretched out before him on either side of a large stream. Groups of horses were tethered around the outer boundaries of the camp. A large number of small fires could be seen dotted around the site. A cluster of men had gathered around each of the fires. Kuper lay downwind of the camp, and the smells wafting toward him suggested that a good few of the soldiers were preparing food. It was the smoke that had first betrayed the location of the camp.

Between the camp and the ridge, flocks of sheep huddled together in fenced pens made of rough timbers. A few milking cows had been tied to posts nearby. Kuper wondered what had become of the shepherds and farmers and their families.

He climbed back down and rejoined his brother. "The Rogandans don't seem to be expecting trouble—they haven't posted sentries.

There are plenty of soldiers coming and going, though, so we can't stay here."

They remounted and set off hastily toward the distant forest.

Not for the first time, Kuper found himself battling with frustration. Will had entrusted them with the responsibility of reaching Lord Burtelen in Erestor and returning to Castel with the army that the nobleman had been raising. It had seemed like a straightforward assignment. But their journey had not been going smoothly. At first they made good time after leaving Will and the others in the village. But in the last few days they had spent far too much time avoiding Rogandans, with the result that they were much further south than they should have been. Steffan's Citadel, the gateway to the Duchy of Erestor, now lay to the northwest through dense forests, rather than due west across rolling hills.

Halfway to the forest they paused to rest their horses.

"Too many Rogandans for my liking," said Rellan with mild understatement.

Kuper nodded. "There must be thousands of them roaming around Arvenon."

"I wonder if Lord Burtelen is going to be happy about leaving the Duchy undefended."

"I've been wondering about that, too."

They sat in silence for a few more minutes before resuming their journey. The sun had dipped below the tree line by the time they reached the outskirts of the forest. As the trees closed in around them, they crossed a well-worn path that ran southwest into the forest. The path seemed to be running at least partly in the right direction, and after a moment's hesitation they turned onto it.

Almost immediately, faint cries of alarm reached them from further along the track. Both of them reacted instinctively, digging their heels into their horses' ribs. They galloped along the path, keeping their heads down to avoid low hanging branches.

Ahead of them the path broadened into a clearing that held a cluster of houses. One of them sprouted roaring red flames, and a torch had just been thrown onto the thatched roof of another. A small band of Rogandans scurried around among the houses, grabbing pigs and chickens, and hunting down panicked villagers.

Kuper had his bow in hand even before he brought his horse to a halt. Three arrows flew and three Rogandan soldiers fell before the raiders even realized they were under attack. A fourth soldier, a big brute of a man, had just stood up with a triumphant shout, lifting high a squirming pig. Rellan rode him down, his sword swinging from his good arm. Three raiders remained, and they decided to run for it. Only one made it to his horse, leaping onto its back and urging it toward the forest. He never made it out of the clearing. An arrow took him in the neck, and he crashed to the ground dead.

A strange calm settled over the scene, disturbed only by the roar and crackle of the fires. A few distraught women knelt weeping beside the still forms of their loved ones. Some of the men stood grim-faced and trembling as they beheld the ruin of their village.

One man, bowed with age, came to the twins.

"I am the headman," he said. "My heartfelt thanks to you on behalf of all my people. We are extremely grateful for your intervention."

"You need to leave quickly," Kuper told him. "These soldiers were just a foraging party. More Rogandans will come when they don't return. An entire army is camped in the fields north of here."

"Do we have time to bury our dead?" the man asked.

"You'll be taking a big risk," Kuper replied. "We can't defend you. We can't even stay to help you. Are any of you able to ride a horse?"

The man nodded. "Some of the men have ridden before."

"Then tell your women and children, and any men who can't ride, to leave at once with whatever they can carry. Send riders to watch all the entrances to the village. You can use the raiders' horses. The rest of the men can do what is necessary for your fallen. They can follow the others on horseback as soon as they have finished here. They can also flee if the need arises."

The man nodded once more. "I will do as you say." He called a number of men by name and gave them instructions. They left immediately to do his bidding.

When he was finished, Kuper took the opportunity to ask for directions. The headman was able to give them detailed instructions, kneeling down and drawing in the dirt as he talked.

Kuper thanked him in his turn. Then the twins mounted their horses and bade him farewell.

"Thank you again for your kindness," the headman said, bowing his head in gratitude.

"May better fortune smile on you in the days to come," said Rellan.

They turned their horses back onto the path and rode away. They soon passed a group of fugitives, mostly women with small children, who had already left the village and were heading deeper into the forest. Most of the women carried heavy burdens, but they set down their loads as the twins rode by and waved to them, calling out their thanks.

Rellan and Kuper stayed on the main path until it crossed a wide stream. Then, following the headman's instructions, they turned onto a smaller path that headed due west. The path was barely visible at first, but it soon became wider and better established. They pressed on until it was almost dark, then turned aside from the path to find a suitable place to sleep.

The next day they rose at first light and continued their journey westward within the boundaries of the forest. They saw no further sign of the Rogandans. And, even though they mostly traveled on established paths, they saw no signs of human habitation. At times they felt as though eyes were upon them, but they never caught as much as a glimpse of another person. Deer sometimes crossed the path off in the distance, but never close enough for Kuper to take a shot.

When they camped that night they took turns to watch. It was not necessary for them to discuss the arrangements—they simply came to an unspoken understanding, just as they had so often done from the time they were children.

In the half light before dawn Kuper found himself on duty. He sat with his back to a tree, his head drooping low. Even to a careful observer he would have appeared to be fast asleep. But he was awake, with senses fully alert.

The horses, standing off to the side of the twins, were unusually skittish. Kuper's bow lay within easy reach, and he was ready for trouble. But he did not move a muscle. As the minutes passed, the horses gradually settled. All appeared to be calm.

Then the stillness was shattered. The horses exploded into action with squeals of protest. A small figure sprang onto the back of one of the animals, urging it forward. He was hanging on to the halter of the other horse.

Kuper was on his feet in an instant, his bow stretched taut with an arrow ready to release. The diminutive thief looked back as he raced away, and Kuper hesitated. Then he lowered his bow, and the horses disappeared into the forest.

Rellan, now fully awake, looked at his brother questioningly.

"He was just a boy," Kuper told him. "I couldn't do it."

Rellan acknowledged this decision with a shrug. "I would have let him go, too," he said.

Without the horses, their task had become much more difficult. With no better options on offer, they shouldered their bows and began following the path on foot.

The fading light of late afternoon found them further west than most men could have traveled in a single day. But they were lithe and fit and on a mission. Apart from occasional brief stops to fill their water skins in a stream, they had walked or jogged almost continuously.

With dusk approaching they slowed their pace and began looking around for a place to spend the night. Then Rellan straightened, closing his eyes and lifting his nostrils to the breeze. "I smell smoke," he said, turning his gaze upwind into the spreading gloom. "It's faint, but it's unmistakable."

"I can't smell a thing," Kuper replied. "But then your sense of smell has always been uncanny."

"Shall we find out what's going on?" Rellan asked.

Kuper nodded. "Getting horses is our biggest priority. Where we find people we're likely to find horses. With any luck, they might be willing to help us once they find out what we're doing."

"We don't know who they are, of course."

"No, we don't. There's always a risk. But they're not likely to be Rogandans. And the fact that we're not, either, will probably be enough to earn us a welcome. Anyway, we don't have to reveal ourselves before we take a look at them."

"Agreed," said Rellan. "I'm willing to chance it. And where we find a fire, we're likely to find food," he added with a grin. "I'm hungry!"

Kuper set off after his brother as he began picking his way among the trees.

They had to walk for several minutes before Kuper also began to smell the smoke. Not for the first time, he marveled at the sensitivity of his brother's nose.

With the fire close nearby, they began to move more cautiously through the trees. Before long they could hear the crackle of the flames and catch glimpses of the glow. Not knowing if sentries were posted, they separated and approached independently.

Kuper moved forward until a single tree separated him from the small clearing that boasted the fire. A group of cloaked figures sat around it, feasting on the remains of a deer. There was nothing especially alarming about them. Kuper and Rellan had sat around many such fires themselves.

Bows and quivers of arrows lay beside some of the feasters. And the occasional glint of metal at their sides told him that all of them were armed. None of that was surprising, though—these were dangerous times.

As Kuper watched, his brother stepped out from the shadows into the firelight. "Greetings, friends, and well met," said Rellan, stretching out his good hand and allowing them to see his other arm in a sling.

All of them leaped to their feet, drawing swords or knives. "Who are you, and what are you doing here?" one of them demanded. They spread out to surround the intruder.

"I'm just a weary traveler, attracted by the warmth of your fire and the smell of your food," Rellan replied brightly. "My brother and I thought we might join you in the hope of sharing your hospitality."

At the mention of a brother, Kuper also stepped forward into the firelight, hands empty and palms outward. "My greetings to you, as well," he said cheerfully as they spun around to face him. He moved slowly and deliberately to the fire and sat himself down in front of it, sighing loudly and contentedly. Rellan joined him.

The others watched them warily for a while. One of their number, a tall bearded man with a prominent scar across one eye, finally nodded to the others, and they came and joined them at the fire. All of them remained watchful.

"May we share your deer?" Rellan asked.

The others looked to the man with the scar. "Help yourselves," he replied.

Kuper hadn't realized how famished he was until they started eating. Everything went quiet for a while as they hungrily devoured slice after juicy slice of venison.

Eventually Kuper wiped his mouth with his sleeve and sat back, smiling and contented. Rellan, limited by his one good arm, had been making slower progress. But he, too, eventually managed to satisfy his hunger.

Their hosts still hadn't relaxed, so Kuper decided to take the initiative. "Our sincere thanks to you all," he said, nodding politely in acknowledgment of their hospitality. "My name is Kuper, and this is my brother, Rellan. We are traveling to Erestor on the king's business, and lost our horses this morning to a thief."

At the mention of horses and a thief, a couple of the men started noticeably. Their leader, however, remained unmoved. "I am known as Scar," he said evenly. "Anyone who trespasses in this domain must give an account of themselves to our leader. We will treat you with respect if you come with us willingly. We would prefer to avoid trouble."

Kuper assessed them calmly. His instincts told him that Scar could be trusted. "We will come willingly," he promised.

Scar issued brief instructions to the other men, who immediately began clearing up the site. They sliced the remaining strips of meat from the deer, disposed of the carcass, and covered the fire.

Scar turned to the twins. “Please remove your weapons,” he said. “We will take good care of them, and they will be returned to you as soon as our leader permits it. Later in our journey it will be necessary to blindfold you briefly. But for now please walk with us.”

After the twins had handed over their bows, arrows, and swords, the group set off, heading east along the path. They traveled at a brisk pace for over two hours, and Kuper found it galling to be retracing so many of their steps from earlier in the day. Then Scar and one of the other men blindfolded them, spun them around a few times, and led them into the forest. Their guides proved to be skillful and effective; Kuper rarely stumbled. After traveling for what must have been another hour, they finally came to a stop, and Kuper’s blindfold was removed. Rellan stood close by, gazing around curiously.

Kuper was standing in a huge natural clearing. In the moonlight he could see a large number of rough dwellings around the outer edges of the clearing. A giant bonfire burned brightly in the center of it. Men and women came and went from the dwellings, going about their business. If children also lived there they must have been indoors, most likely asleep, because none were visible, and none appeared as he watched.

A hooded figure stood before the fire, facing away from the newly arrived party. Scar led the twins forward, other men flanking them watchfully. The figure turned as they approached, and they found themselves facing a woman, her long dark hair flowing forward over her right shoulder. She was dressed like a man, and the firelight revealed a face both proud and stern. Sharp and intelligent eyes studied them critically.

“These men found their way to our fire, Anneka,” said Scar after a respectful bow. “They call themselves Kuper and Rellan,” he said, nodding to each of them in turn as he spoke.

“Where were your sentries?” Anneka demanded curtly.

“I hadn’t posted sentries,” he replied. “It will not happen again.”

She glowered at him for a moment, then turned her attention to the twins. "Your arm," she said to Rellan, "is it broken?"

"It is," he confirmed.

"How did you break it?"

"In a fight."

"With the Rogandans?"

"No, with the retainers of a minor baron."

She considered that for a moment, frowning. "Why are you here?"

"We are on our way to Erestor," Kuper said, breaking into the conversation. "We would have been far away by now, but our horses were stolen this morning."

"Who stole them?"

"A boy."

"You couldn't prevent a boy from stealing your horses?" she asked, a mocking edge to her tone.

"I could have stopped him," Kuper replied calmly. "But putting an arrow into the back of a child is not my way."

"Perhaps a small moving target is beyond your skill level," she suggested.

Kuper did not reply.

She sighed. "I will decide about you in the morning." She turned to Scar. "Find them a hut to sleep in. And guard them well. No more surprises."

Scar bowed, then led them away.

"She's a cheerful one," Rellan ventured.

Scar frowned at him. "Don't presume to pass judgment on your betters," he said. "We owe our lives and our well-being to her."

"No insult intended," he replied with a smile.

Scar and a couple of other men led them to a small hut that held nothing apart from four straw mattresses covered with blankets. The other men positioned themselves outside the hut. The brothers went inside, and the door closed behind them. Kuper heard a bar drop into position across the door.

Rellan moved straight to a mattress and stretched himself out on it.

Kuper did likewise. He lay on his bed trying to relax. After the frustration of their roundabout journey toward Erestor, their forward progress had now come to a sudden and complete halt. Nothing could be done about it tonight, though. Tomorrow was a new day, and they would have to face its challenges then.

He closed his eyes and almost immediately fell into a deep slumber.

5

"Is it wise to give Will Prentis command of the entire army, Sire?" Lord Bottren's face was impassive, but his concern showed in his voice. "Most of Istel's nobles are strongly opposed, and even some of our own people are less than enthusiastic."

Not for the first time that week Steffan struggled to master his growing irritability with this topic. "The decision belongs to me and Istel, Bottren. We've made it, and it's final!"

The two of them sat astride their horses on a rise, surveying a plain before them bustling with purposeful activity. Importantly, the plain was on Arvenian soil, a few miles beyond Deadman's Pass. To one side lay the main army camp, situated between the plain and a river that flowed down from the mountains near the pass. The camp had borrowed its name—Hazelwood Ford—from the nearby river crossing.

Soldiers drilled in companies, mounted troops galloped back and forth, and off to one side bowmen fired volleys of arrows into the air. Everything Steffan could see told him the troops were ready for action. Thanks to effective initiatives on the part of Will in the days since his arrival, their skills had been honed and their morale greatly boosted. Further, Steffan saw evident signs that the soldiers were becoming increasingly enthusiastic about their new commander. That was no surprise to him.

The soldiers might be in good condition, but the leadership was another matter. A constant undercurrent of intrigue and infighting among the nobles had been annoying Steffan immensely for weeks. Since the appointment of Will, though, the discontent had found a new focus and risen to a crescendo.

Coordinating the forces of two independent kingdoms was always going to be a challenge, and Steffan had felt embattled from the beginning. Thankfully, Istel supported him—on most occasions, anyway. Nevertheless, the squabbling and backbiting never showed any signs of relenting. At times the nobles around him seemed to have forgotten entirely who the real enemy was.

More than ever, Steffan was convinced that the army needed to be on the move, confronting the Rogandans. It wouldn't take long for Will to silence his detractors once the fighting started.

He turned to Bottren. "Find Will," he commanded, "and send him to me."

Bottren bowed his head in acknowledgment. Turning his horse, he kicked it into a gallop and disappeared over the rise.

"We now have an army of seven thousand men encamped in Arvenon with more expected to join them. What is our commander planning to do with them?"

'Our commander' had become the label of choice for the Castelan nobles when referring to Will. It was invariably delivered with a condescending sneer. At first the sneer had been subtle, at least to his face. Never subtle enough to hide it completely, but enough to avoid the appearance of a direct challenge. Of late, any pretense at veiling the insult had been abandoned, occasionally even in the presence of one of the kings.

Will ignored it. He answered to King Steffan, not to any of these men. His king had given him a job to do, and he meant to carry it out to the best of his ability.

Usually both kings sat in the daily Council of War, but on this occasion neither one of them was present. Their absence gave the nobles full freedom to vent their feelings.

"Is it true that you deliberately destroyed one of your own towns? Don't imagine you can do the same here in Castel!"

"Some of your soldiers are asking why you abandoned your capital to its fate. What do you have to say about that?"

Will held his peace in the face of their hostility. Reasonable answers never satisfied people asking unreasonable questions.

He wasn't surprised by their opposition. He'd faced similar challenges from a number of the nobles at Arnost. Even saving their capital had not softened the attitude of some of them.

They had been born to rule over commoners like him. The two kings had flouted every convention the nobles held dear by placing Will in charge of the army. The kings themselves were not affected, of course, because Will was still subject to them. But the appointment was a slap in the face for every one of the noblemen. It said more clearly than words that neither King Steffan nor King Istel had any regard for the ability of their nobles. They preferred to place the fate of their kingdoms in the hands of a commoner.

Defeating the Rogandans wouldn't help Will—it would surely only deepen the insult. The nobles would always believe they could have done better.

Bottren quickly located Will and arrived to find him still in council with the other lords. The sun might have been shining brightly out in the wide world, but storm clouds gathered in the council room at Hazelwood Ford. In spite of his own reservations about Will's new role, Bottren had no desire to see him fed to the baying hounds around the table. When delivering the summons from King Steffan, he added a note of urgency to the message.

Will responded immediately. Standing, he bowed stiffly, and left with his rescuer.

Bottren knew that once he was gone, the other lords would vent their spleen without restraint. At least Will wouldn't have to listen to it, though.

The two of them rode for a time without speaking.

"The mood looked ugly in there, Will," Bottren finally ventured.

Will simply shrugged.

Bottren studied the man riding calmly beside him. For a commoner his poise was nothing short of remarkable. He didn't seem at all overawed by the nobility with whom he now spent so much of his time. Scarred and stern of face, he looked every inch a soldier. The permanent limp he carried from his battle wounds only reinforced the aura that surrounded him. Will Prentis was almost certainly a veteran of as many clashes as any other person in the king's army. It was easy to forget entirely how young he was.

In a moment of sudden honesty, Bottren owned that he, no less than Istel's nobles, had been blinded by his prejudices. Yet he had seen how the Arvenian soldiers stood taller in Will's presence, and witnessed the growing enthusiasm in their cheers whenever their commander rode by.

Will's usefulness was not limited to the battlefield, either. Every Council of War benefited from his insights, and no practical matter seemed to escape his attention. Bottren himself had not fully grasped the importance of logistics until Will's careful probing had exposed a number of serious inadequacies in the planning around equipping and feeding the soldiers.

Even the Castelan soldiers increasingly deferred to Will. That was appropriate, of course, given his role as commander of the combined armies. The Castelan nobles, though, were well aware of this growing respect and vigorously sought to undermine it.

Bottren glanced at Will again, allowing himself to see the young commander with new eyes. For the first time he acknowledged what he knew his king had long since recognized: this grave young man was a vastly more capable leader than any of the nobles, and offered the best hope—maybe the only hope—of defeating the Rogandans.

"Don't let them get to you, Will—you're a better man than any of them." The acknowledgment was long overdue, but Bottren knew there was never a wrong time to begin giving credit where it was due.

"Thank you, My Lord," the commander returned simply. "It would seem that your confidence is not shared universally, though," he added with masterful understatement.

"Perhaps not," the lord replied. "But the king sees it the same way, and his opinion is the one that matters."

They rode on in silence.

A single concern troubled Bottren. He succeeded in pushing it down for a time, but finally it would not be denied.

"Is the Rogandan army really as big as our scouts report, Will?" he finally asked.

"Yes, My Lord, it is immense. Almost beyond counting."

"How will we defeat them?"

"I don't know," Will replied candidly. "But somehow we must find a way."

WILL, currently in the final stages of preparing for conflict, had been fully absorbed for several days. The looming battle would be his first as commander of the allied forces.

Rogandan forces had increasingly been concentrating near the small village of Pinder's Flat. It was uncomfortably close to Steffan and Istel's main camp at Hazelwood Ford, and the constant presence of Rogandans in the area had become a growing irritant. The two kings were determined to drive them away. The encounter would not decide the outcome of the war, but it would be an important test for the new allied army.

Planning was proceeding smoothly, at least on the surface, but nevertheless Will was troubled. He turned away from the maps spread out before him and faced King Steffan.

"I would prefer to fight this next battle with your own soldiers, Your Majesty."

"I understand, Will," the king returned. The request clearly exasperated him, but he was visibly working hard at remaining calm and reasonable. "I must remind you, though, that defeating the Rogandans is not the only objective in this action. We need victories, but we also need to build an effective fighting force that includes both Arvenian and Castelan armies. Victories can help us establish that, but only if we win them together."

"May I speak frankly, Sire?"

"Of course, Will."

The king's words suggested he was open to hear whatever Will had to say. The firm line of his jaw said something entirely different. Will decided to voice his concerns anyway.

"Your goal of a unified force might be better achieved with someone other than me as commander, Your Majesty. Perhaps you would be better served if one of your noblemen took command."

King Steffan stiffened. "I never expected this from you, Will," he growled. "I don't need you going soft on me."

The king's response stung, but Will remained silent.

"I've appointed the person best equipped to lead this army, and that person is you," the king insisted, jabbing a finger at him emphatically. "I'm not entering into discussion on this. My very kingdom is at stake!" Brows bristling, he frowned across at Will, who maintained his silence.

"I know the cooperation from some of Istel's people might be a bit half-hearted at times," he conceded, "but you simply need to find a way to work with them."

It seemed clear that the king had little understanding of the extent of the hostility of the Castelan nobles toward the upstart commoner. But Will knew he could not expose the true situation without openly criticizing the lords, and that was simply out of the question. And besides, the king was right. It was his responsibility as commander to resolve any problems that affected the army, including this one.

“May I request, then, Your Majesty, that you appoint a liaison to coordinate the Arvenian and Castelan forces on my behalf?”

King Steffan frowned. “Who did you have in mind?” he asked.

“Lord Bottren,” Will suggested. It was a risk, but he had the feeling that Bottren would be willing to work with him. And it might help ease tensions if the Castelans could interact with another nobleman instead of him.

“Consider it done,” the king replied, reaching for parchment, his quill, and the royal seal.

A VAST CLOUD of dust drifted slowly into the sky ahead. The ring of metal on metal sounded above the cries of men and the scream of horses.

Will and Bottren skidded their horses to a halt at the top of a rise. The village of Pinder’s Flat lay behind them. Below them, the placement of the rival armies could be clearly seen, even though men were fighting and dying little more than an arrow’s flight away. The extreme vulnerability of the Arvenian left flank was immediately obvious.

Bottren stared in horror at the conflict raging below. “What are we going to do, Will?” The look on his face bordered on panic.

Will rapidly scrutinized the scene before him, witnessing the growing confusion spreading from the hard-pressed left wing of the Arvenian ranks. The battle hung on a knife edge. If he didn’t respond decisively the struggle below him could quickly degenerate into a rout.

“Archers, My Lord, NOW! Bring up the Castelan bowmen! We drive off the Rogandan reserves, or our left flank collapses.”

Even as the wide-eyed Bottren galloped away, Will spurred his horse frantically down toward the heaviest of the fighting.

“To me, men! For the king and for Arvenon!”

Will crashed into the seething mass of men, his sword weaving a skillful web of destruction. Others took up the cry, "For the king and for Arvenon!", and pushed through the press to reach him.

Seeing their commander fighting on the field of battle gave new heart to Steffan's harried soldiers. The cluster of men gathering around him gradually grew in size. Rufe appeared from the Arvenian center and charged into the fray at the head of a grim band of horsemen. For the first time the Rogandan momentum was halted. Outnumbered five to one, Will's soldiers nevertheless began to surge forward.

Then a Rogandan horseman, clumsily avoiding the stroke of an opponent's sword, crashed into Will and almost knocked him from his horse. Rufe, witnessing it close at hand, was powerless to help in the melee. His face registered alarm, then slowly the alarm was replaced with rage. His face glowed red, and his whole body shook. Raising himself high in the saddle and roaring ferociously, he broke upon his enemies like a wave.

The Rogandans fled in terror from the madman, some throwing away their weapons in their haste. A gap opened up in their front line, and it quickly widened as Will's men began to push vigorously into it.

At this critical moment Bottren arrived with the archers. A steady shower of arrows flew over the heads of the combatants and fell among the soldiers gathered in the Rogandan rear. Some turned and fled. Others pressed forward to escape the deadly rain, and collided with those fleeing Rufe's berserker fury. The chaos spread, and soon the entire Rogandan front line began to disintegrate.

The Arvenian army, so close to collapse only minutes before, instead began to visit ruin upon the Rogandan forces. Superior numbers did nothing to help the invaders as men became trapped and helpless in the middle of the Rogandan lines. Foot soldiers were crushed and trampled in the press without ever facing an Arvenian soldier.

The eager embrace of Malzakh awaited many Rogandans that day. But more than enough escaped to whisper abroad a rumor of the wrath of Arvenon and the terror that awaited its enemies.

. . .

At Pinder's Flat, Will became commander of the combined army in more than just name. Steffan's soldiers embraced him with the same enthusiasm as their countrymen at Arnost. They were willing to go anywhere with him, and said so openly.

The small detachment of Castelan archers were also quick to adopt him. Will had assigned them a crucial role in the battle, and when it was over he swiftly acknowledged that they had carried out their task flawlessly. He also openly accounted to them a generous portion of the credit for the victory. It soon became clear that the Castelan soldiers were glimpsing for the first time a leader they might follow without hesitation into the valley of the shadow of death.

The Castelan nobles were another matter entirely. The battle was not even over before the recriminations started. When the leaders finally met to review the battle the atmosphere in the room almost crackled with tension.

"What madness led us to Pinder's Flat?" one of Istel's nobles demanded with a sneer. "The terrain favored no one but the Rogandans!"

The speaker, Lord Eisgold, had bitterly opposed Will's leadership from the beginning. Will held his peace. He glanced across at Bottren and saw his second-in-command pale with anger.

"The conditions were so appalling it left me no choice, Sire," Eisgold spat, turning to King Istel. "Your soldiers would have been massacred if I'd left them exposed in the position *he* assigned them." His thumb jerked toward Will. "It was only thanks to my considerable experience that they were extracted without a catastrophe."

Will smiled grimly to himself. It was true that the extraction had been well executed. If the soldiers had been led into battle with the same enthusiasm, the outcome would never have been in doubt.

"This looming massacre you speak of, Eisgold," Bottren interjected. "How many men did you lose?" His voice trembled with suppressed rage. "What was your death toll before you decided to abandon your post? I heard it was as many as four or five!" he sneered.

Eisgold rose from his chair in a rage. "Are you accusing me of cowardice?" he bellowed.

Everyone began shouting at once. Many of the nobles leaped to their feet, gesticulating wildly.

"SILENCE!"

The word came almost simultaneously from the lips of both sovereigns. One by one the nobles fell silent, and resumed their seats. Istel's face glowed red with anger, but Steffan's revealed an icy calm. The two kings exchanged glances, and Istel nodded, deferring to his younger ally.

"None of you will speak until invited to do so," King Steffan commanded emphatically. He paused to allow them to recover themselves.

"In *my* assessment," he asserted, "Pinder's Flat was indeed a near calamity. Disaster was averted only by the quick action of our commander. At considerable risk to himself!"

Istel's noblemen glowered, but said nothing.

"Will, do you have anything you wish to say?" King Steffan offered.

Will paused, his mind racing. How should he respond? What could he possibly say that would make any difference?

It was obvious that Eisgold's action was intended to finish him. Some of his supposed allies were determined to see him fail, whatever the cost to their own cause.

Will's plan of battle had been simple. He had chosen a position to the south of Pinder's Flat. The site was protected by marshland on the left, preventing any flanking movement from that direction. The left wing he entrusted to King Istel's men under Lord Eisgold. The best of King Steffan's troops took the center with Rufe at their head. A lightly wooded slope climbed away to the right of the site. The wood prevented any rapid deployment of soldiers, but it was not impenetrable. Will accordingly assigned a sizable contingent of Arvenian troops to the right wing to guard against any attempt by the Rogandans to turn his right flank. Castelan archers stood close by in reserve to be quickly deployed wherever they might be needed.

The Rogandans vastly outnumbered his force. But that would probably always be the case in this war. And victory should have been readily within their grasp, if Eisgold had not removed his soldiers as soon as the fighting started. If the Rogandans had exploited the gaping hole on his left wing more quickly and effectively, the battle would have been over, and decisively so, in a couple of hours.

He knew that Eisgold's soldiers were not to blame. In fact he had heard that they were seething. They had been ready to fight, and were bewildered at being withdrawn so quickly from the battle. Now, with a victory won and praise and honors distributed freely elsewhere, they resented having being sidelined.

The perverse obstinacy behind Eisgold's behavior was maddening. Facing the Rogandans on the battlefield seemed straightforward compared to battling the Castelan nobles. Will could summon little enthusiasm for a campaign of this type. But he could not afford to retreat. The stakes had risen significantly, and Will wondered if the king fully realized the gravity of the situation. If he stumbled, the king would not long be able to continue to support him. And given the absence of an obvious successor, along with the disunity and lack of combat experience of the nobility, his removal had the potential to deal a fatal blow to the Arvenian cause.

He pushed down the sinking feeling in his gut. There was no room for weakness or self pity. He was now fighting for his life on two fronts, and he had to win both wars. There simply was no other option.

The king was still waiting patiently for his response.

"I have a question, Sire."

"Ask it," King Steffan replied.

"How would you respond if one of your soldiers withdrew from the heat of battle without orders?"

The sovereign did not hesitate. "I would have the man executed.

There is no room in my army for deserters or cowards." He glanced across at Istel, who nodded his acquiescence.

"And if one of your noblemen withdrew?" Will continued.

Eisgold bristled, but did not speak.

"I would have the man immediately relieved of command. *If* I was in a good mood," King Steffan growled.

Again Steffan glanced across at Istel. A deep frown creased the Castelan's face. After a moment's hesitation he nodded again, firmly.

"You asked if I wished to speak, Your Majesty," Will offered calmly. "I do have something to say," he continued, getting to his feet.

"There are times when decisive action on the part of a leader can mean the difference between victory and defeat in a battle. Occasionally the situation demands such a rapid response that there is no time to seek confirmation from the commander.

"Today's battle at Pinder's Flat was *not* such an occasion," he asserted bluntly. He paused to let his meaning fully sink in. "Nevertheless, I would suggest that we choose to view today's action as a learning experience."

Will bowed in deference to the two sovereigns and waited for them to respond. King Istel nodded his assent at once. King Steffan glared darkly at the nobles for a moment, then nodded as well.

"As long as I am commander, though," Will continued, a hard edge in his voice, "if any leader orders a troop withdrawal again without my authority I will not hesitate to request that Your Majesties take the strongest possible action against that leader."

He gazed slowly around the table, locking glances briefly with any of the nobles willing to meet his eye. Then he sat down.

Lord Eisgold was one who boldly met his stare. He glared back at Will with an undisguised look of pure hatred.

6

The fire sizzled and spat as fatty juices dripped down onto it. Thomas turned the makeshift spit one last time, confident that the hare was finally ready to eat. He examined the meat carefully, searching for the most evenly cooked portion. Having selected a leg, he tugged at it hopefully. To his delight it came away readily in his hand—surely the meat would be tender. Then he carefully handed the prize to Brother Vangellis.

The monk, his brow furrowed in concentration, took a bite and chewed it critically. Then he delicately pulled away pieces of meat with his teeth until only bone remained. Finally he licked his fingers clean.

Thomas, anxious and impatient, could restrain himself no longer. "Well?" he demanded.

The monk frowned a moment more, then beamed him a broad smile. "Wonderful, Thomas. Beautifully cooked! And a fine piece of meat."

Thomas exhaled in relief and grinned back at him proudly.

Life in the wilderness had been harsh. With the weather gradually becoming colder, he rarely felt warm enough during the long nights. And he nearly always ended the day hungry, even though they spent many of their waking hours searching for food. But he knew he had toughened up a lot. He might be lean, but his muscles had firmed up visibly and he'd developed physical strength he never had before. He was a different person from the awkward youth who had ridden away from Arnost.

For the first time in his life he was learning to fend for himself. He knew how to use available materials to start a fire, he knew which berries to pick, and he could now identify mushrooms that were safe to eat.

Today had been his crowning achievement. He had fashioned a trap, caught a hare, made a spit, lit the fire, and skinned, cleaned, and cooked his catch. Every action had been carried out by him entirely on his own.

The monk's approval was immensely gratifying. With the verdict behind him, though, there was no further reason to hold back himself, and Thomas attacked the hare without further ceremony. Brother Vangellis looked on with a smile for a moment before joining in the feast.

After the food was gone Thomas sat back with a sigh of satisfaction, gazing at the fire flickering at the entrance of the cave. The surrounding terrain hid the entrance very effectively, and they had not hesitated to select the cave as their dwelling place almost as soon as they discovered it. It was small, but dry and sheltered from the prevailing winds. And it was adjacent to a reliable spring, an important consideration since they had no containers suitable for storing water.

Their new home was serviceable, if somewhat primitive. They made whatever improvements they could. They built a fire pit just inside the mouth of the cave. They gathered quantities of firewood and stored them at the back of the cave. They searched out suitable vegetation to soften the ground they slept on. And they had almost finished constructing a large covering made of wood to shield the entrance of the cave from the elements during bad weather.

They had not seen a single person in the weeks since they left the river, nor any signs of habitation. If there were villages in the vicinity, they had not been able to discover them. Isolated as they were, Thomas was not exactly lonely. Brother Vangellis was an ideal companion; he was knowledgeable, even-tempered, and easy to get along with. But Thomas missed other company more than he was willing to say. He would have given a great deal to see Will and Rufe again, and another day or two with Brother Hann would have been worth twenty tasty hares.

He could hardly complain, though. Disappearing from sight was exactly what they had been trying to do. And he himself—or rather his stone—was the reason for their exile.

"I don't understand it," Thomas said. "Why does the stone only work occasionally now? The scroll said nothing about the stones behaving this way."

"A large portion of the scroll seems to have been lost," Brother Vangellis replied. "Perhaps your questions would have been answered in the missing sections. It's also possible that the scroll's author didn't know everything about the stones."

"But it's almost as if the stone wanted to save Arvenon."

"What do you mean?" the monk asked.

"Since I found it again, that's all it's done. It exposed the Rogandan soldiers at the gates of Arnost, and also revealed the man who had betrayed Will and planned to hand the city to the Rogandans."

"What about the time when it showed you something about Will?"

"I may have got that wrong. I don't really know."

"But Will only believed your story about the stone after that happened. I suspect you did see something that really took place."

"Perhaps you're right. Maybe that needed to happen for Will to believe in the stone. Otherwise, I may not have been able to convince him about the Rogandans at the gates."

"So you're saying that the stone doesn't want the Rogandans to take over Arvenon?"

"I don't really know," said Thomas. "If the scroll is right, that isn't at all how it works. It doesn't seem to have a will of its own. It would be nice to think that the stone doesn't want Lord Drettroth to get it, though."

"It's hard to believe he really has any claim on it."

"How could he have a claim on it?" Thomas asked, bewildered.

"You first found the stone near Arnost. But how did it get there? Was Drettroth aware of it then? Was he involved in some way? There's a lot we don't know."

Both of them had many more questions than answers. When Thomas lay down to sleep, he couldn't get the stone out of his mind. Was there a pattern they were missing? Why did it work the way it did? Would it only come to life in a crisis now? The scroll didn't give that impression. If Randolf of Clerbon was to be believed, the stones —like the rock before them—were simply there to be used. Wisely or foolishly. There was no hint of anything more than that.

And what about Lord Drettroth? If the scroll was right, he couldn't take the stone by force and expect to be able to use it. Was he aware of that?

Or did the Rogandan leader have some reason to believe that he could induce Thomas to give him the stone? Perhaps Drettroth had access to the entire scroll. Had it given him ideas about how he might make use of fear and intimidation? Thomas tried to imagine how far Drettroth might go and what he might do to persuade him to hand it over. He soon decided not to think about that anymore.

When Thomas did eventually get to sleep, his dreams were troubled.

THOMAS WOKE to the patter of rain outside the cave. He opened his eyes and glanced around. The dull light showed him the figure of Brother Vangellis, still sleeping soundly.

He looked up, squinting at the sky outside the cave, and cried out in alarm. A small figure stood framed in the gray morning light. It was a boy, scantily dressed, and dripping wet from the rain. He stood in the entrance, staring in at them.

The minute Thomas's cry rang out, the boy disappeared.

Brother Vangellis sat up, startled. "What's the matter?" he asked, peering around groggily.

Thomas was on his feet, just inside the cave, staring out into the rain. "Someone was here! Right here, at the entrance to the cave."

His companion got up and joined him. "Who was it?"

"It was a boy. He was looking at us!"

"So we're not alone after all," the monk said quietly.

Thomas found it difficult to hide his agitation. Even here, hidden in the wilderness, they had been discovered. "I thought we were safe here!" he said in dismay.

"I don't think there's much reason to worry, Thomas. It was just a boy. We don't seem to have any Rogandan soldiers here yet."

As they stood gazing out, the boy reappeared. He came from the direction of the stream, and stood in the rain, looking pitiful.

"Hello," said Brother Vangellis.

The boy did not respond.

"Do you live near here?" the monk asked. With still no reply, he tried again. "Do you need our help?"

The boy betrayed no sign of understanding him.

Brother Vangellis then spoke a few words in another language. Still no response. He tried again, apparently in a different tongue, and the boy came to life, speaking rapidly and urgently.

The monk turned to Thomas. "Well, that's a surprise. I wondered if he was a nomad. But not so. He speaks Rogandan."

"Rogandan?!" Thomas became more alarmed than ever.

"Please, Thomas—you'll frighten him away!"

The boy was indeed on the brink of running away and hiding again. Brother Vangellis spoke to him again, and he calmed down.

"I don't care if he runs away! I'd be happy if he left and never came back."

"That wouldn't help us. He knows we're here now. But he isn't a threat. His mother is sick, and he's scared."

"What are we going to do?"

"Go with him, and see if we can help his mother," the monk said calmly.

Thomas shook his head in disbelief. “You can’t be serious! We could be captured.”

“There’s a risk, it’s true.” Brother Vangellis paused for a moment, thinking. “Why don’t you stay here?” he finally asked. “I’ll go with him, and come back as soon as I can. If something goes wrong, you’ll still be safe.”

Thomas made no attempt to hide his dismay. “What if you’re taken? How will I be able to keep the stone safe on my own?”

“You are more capable than you realize, Thomas,” he replied, “and you’re stronger than you were as well. But if you should come to be alone, I don’t believe you will ever find yourself entirely abandoned. Help can come from unexpected quarters.”

His words failed utterly to comfort Thomas.

Brother Vangellis tried to reassure him. “You needn’t be concerned. I’m sure I will be back very soon. If these people meant to harm us, we would have had Rogandan soldiers in our cave this morning instead of the boy.”

It was obvious that Brother Vangellis would go, whatever Thomas said. So he said nothing. But he didn’t try to hide his anxiety. His obvious agitation clearly troubled the monk, but he left anyway.

In the end, Thomas had an entire day to wrestle with his discomfort. He wavered between feeling alarmed about the future and worried about the safety of his friend and protector. He felt too agitated to follow his normal routines, so he ate nothing all day apart from a few nuts that had been left in the cave.

By the time the sun set, with still no sign of the monk, his anxiety had become unbearable. He couldn’t decide whether to risk sleeping in the cave, or to hide nearby where he could watch the cave in safety. A part of him was tempted to assume the worst and conclude that his friend had been captured. But it would have meant fleeing on his own, and that notion was simply unthinkable. In the end he found a vantage point up a nearby tree, and sat down to watch.

His hunger kept him awake at first, along with the discomfort of his perch. But eventually weariness overtook him. At one point he snapped awake to find himself starting to fall. After it happened a second time, he climbed down from the tree and lay down at the base of the trunk.

He woke to the sound of someone calling his name. Bright daylight shone around him—he appeared to have slept through half the morning. Stiff and uncomfortable, he picked himself up and glanced around. Brother Vangellis was standing outside the cave, looking tired and worried. No one else was in sight.

Thomas headed for the monk, peering warily about him as he stepped out from the cover of the trees. As far as he could tell, they were entirely alone.

"I was concerned about you, Thomas. It's good to see you safe."

"Where were you? I thought something had happened to you!" Thomas couldn't keep the distress from his voice.

"I was caring for the boy's mother. She has a serious injury and she'd lost a lot of blood. I stayed with her all night, and I'm hopeful she will recover. I promised to visit her again tomorrow."

Thomas looked at him wide-eyed. "Surely we need to flee! We're not safe now that we've been discovered!"

"I can't do that, Thomas. Not until she's out of danger."

"But she's Rogandan. They're the ones trying to capture us—the ones who've invaded our country! Why is her health more important than anything else?"

"She's a person, just like us. And I imagine that her life is as precious to her—and to her family—as my life is to me," Brother Vangellis replied quietly.

"But you never even met her until yesterday."

The monk sighed. "No, but I have met her now. And her family."

He paused and looked Thomas in the eye. "I could stay away. But what if she died as a result, and Lord Drettroth's soldiers never appeared? She would have died for nothing."

"And what if Drettroth's soldiers appear when you're at her house? You might end up dying instead," Thomas exclaimed.

The monk smiled sadly. "Life doesn't always offer us sunny days and simple choices. Sometimes you have to do what needs to be done, and let the future worry about itself."

"But what if more than one thing needs to be done? How do we decide between them? Healing a sick person might be important, but it isn't the only thing that matters. Lord Drettroth and the whole Rogandan army are chasing us. We can't let him get the stone!"

Brother Vangellis didn't answer.

Thomas couldn't think straight. He didn't have the monk's certainty when it came to making hard choices and taking risks in the name of doing what needed to be done. He needed time to master his disordered thoughts, so he set off aimlessly, heading away from the cave. Brother Vangellis didn't follow him. His friend had apparently decided he needed time to himself.

As he wandered, Thomas found himself wrestling with competing thoughts and feelings. One part of him wanted to flee, and to do so immediately. He couldn't do it without Brother Vangellis, though. He was only beginning to realize how much he'd come to rely on his mentor.

Another part of him, though, could not begrudge his companion's unquestioning care for this nameless Rogandan family. Deep down he knew that the monk was right.

Will hadn't hesitated to help Baron Rudungen's villagers, even at risk to himself and his men. He had clearly decided that it would be callous to deny assistance to the vulnerable when in a position to offer it. This situation was no different. The fact that the woman was Rogandan didn't change anything.

His biggest struggle was in deciding what he should do himself. Visiting the woman seemed pointless—he couldn't speak her language, and he wasn't at all sure he could make any kind of useful contribution. And the responsibility for the stone weighed heavily on him.

His mind was still churning when evening fell. He joined Brother Vangellis in the cave as usual.

Thomas asked a question that had been nagging him all day. "What's a Rogandan family doing living in Arvenon?" he said.

"Apparently a few families fled Rogand some years ago. They've been hiding out in the wilderness ever since. They didn't tell me why they left."

They conversed a little more, but Thomas didn't offer to accompany the monk the next day.

HE WOKE ONCE AGAIN to full daylight. His companion was nowhere to be seen; he was clearly fulfilling his promise to visit the sick woman again.

For a time Thomas busied himself looking for food, trying to convince himself that he was where he needed to be. The truth was, though, that he was miserable and lonely. More than once, as the day wore on, he would gladly have gathered his courage and set off after his friend. But he had no idea where to go. In the end he gave up any pretense at being usefully occupied, and sat down in sight of the cave, waiting for the monk to return.

Life had changed beyond recognition since the arrival of the boy. Nothing felt straightforward anymore. And yet, although Thomas never openly acknowledged it, he had always known that hiding away in the wilderness couldn't last forever. He hadn't wanted to think about the future. Now the future had arrived.

Brother Vangellis hadn't returned by nightfall, and Thomas fell asleep at the base of the tree again.

HE WOKE around dawn with someone calling his name strangely.

"Toomaz!"

He peered out suspiciously into the half light. The boy was standing outside the cave. His shoulders were stooped, and he looked downcast.

"Toomaz!"

When there was no response, the boy turned and stared into the trees behind him. He appeared to be receiving instructions from someone hiding out of sight.

Fully alerted now, Thomas didn't move. After several minutes had passed, a Rogandan soldier stepped out from the trees, then another. Soon half a dozen men stood in the open, looking around them.

Last of all, another person was dragged into the open, his hands bound before him. It was Brother Vangellis.

The monk looked around him, then his voice rang out. "Flee, Thomas!"

He paid for his warning. A heavy blow from one of his captors felled him, and he went down hard. He didn't get up.

Thomas looked on in horror. His first instinct was to turn tail and bolt. Knowing he hadn't yet been spotted, though, he forced himself to pause and take stock so he could plan his next move sensibly.

The unthinkable had happened—his guide and companion had been captured. Will or Rufe would try to dream up a way of freeing the monk. But Thomas wasn't a soldier, and he didn't doubt that any attempt on his part at heroics would be sure to end in disaster. The monk was right; he had to flee.

The Rogandans almost certainly had trackers among them. If he ran blindly, they would hunt him down sooner or later, and probably sooner. It was abundantly clear to him what he needed to do.

The Rogandans were already spreading out, beginning their search. Thomas slipped away through the trees, heading for a nearby stream. After a few minutes he reached it. Stepping into the middle of the flow, he began to follow it downstream, heading away from the Rogandans.

He knew it was important to step out of the stream onto rocky ground to hide his footprints. After many minutes, though, he still hadn't found a suitable place. The stream was getting wider, and he guessed that the river could not be far away now.

He paused to take a long drink, then trudged on until the river came into view. Crouching down low, he moved stealthily forward. No other person was in sight. Very slowly and carefully he approached the mouth of the stream. Still seeing no one, he slipped into the river and surrendered himself to the current. He stayed close to the bank and swam slowly downriver, shivering in the cold water. He left the river when he came upon a suitable place to land.

Climbing out, he moved away from the water. He searched among the trees until he found a fallen limb that promised to be large enough to support his weight. He dragged it close to the water's edge and left it there.

Then he hid himself among the trees. As soon as night fell, he would once again take to the river.

He sat down on the ground and considered his situation. He had very few options. His first instinct had been to head deeper into the wilderness, although with no plan beyond avoiding capture. But the river had now become his only alternative. If he went with the current, he had no idea where it would take him.

He had to get away from the Rogandans—that much was clear. Lord Drettroth could not be allowed to take possession of the stone. But where would he be safe? Even in the wilderness the Rogandans had somehow managed to track him down. He could try to find a place that was not controlled by the invaders. But some of his own countrymen—men like Pisander—might betray him if they learned about the stone and gained the tiniest inkling of what it could do. Even Will might not be able to protect him.

He no longer had a guide to follow. But what use was a guide, anyway, when there was nowhere safe to go?

Utterly miserable, he buried his head in his hands and did battle with self pity.

When the daylight eventually failed, he made his way back to the river and dragged the tree limb into the water. He eased himself in and slowly guided it to the middle of the river. The water was cold, and he knew he wouldn't be able to stay there for long.

He drifted with the current, supported by the branch. The sounds of the river filled his ears, and he could see nothing except the stars above him peeking through thick clouds.

He fell to thinking of Brother Vangellis. What would his captors do to him? He remembered the blow that had felled the monk, and hoped he was not seriously injured.

It was clear that his own fears about visiting the sick woman had been well founded. The two of them almost certainly could have avoided capture by running away. But he knew that Brother Vangellis would never have been able to live with himself if they'd done that. And Thomas could not have retained his own self respect if he'd tried to force the issue.

He had been right about the risks. But in spite of the dire consequences, he knew that Brother Vangellis had been right, too, and in ways that mattered more.

The monk had done his best to respond to the needs of those around him, and ended up paying the price himself. Others might think that such behavior was stupid. Thomas, having personally benefited so much from the monk's assistance, could never see it that way. If he had the opportunity to say anything to Brother Vangellis at that moment, it wouldn't be words of reproach. He would instead apologize for failing to offer his unqualified support when the monk had simply set out to do what compassion told him needed to be done.

What would become of Brother Vangellis now? He didn't like to think about it.

What would become of him, for that matter? He might still be free, but his own future felt no less uncertain.

He would have given a great deal to have his friend with him again. Thomas never had more reason to appreciate the cheerful hopefulness and steady companionship of the monk.

But Brother Vangellis was gone, and he was truly alone.

7

Kuper woke at dawn, disoriented and not immediately sure where he was. Thin shafts of sunlight peeked through small cracks in the walls around him, revealing his brother on a straw mattress surrounded by blankets. It all came flooding back. He sat up and stretched. He had woken to a dawn that, like so many before it, promised many more risks than certainties. They would need to keep their wits about them.

Rellan was already awake and using his good hand to gingerly massage the muscles of his other arm in the sling. Seeing that Kuper had woken, Rellan turned to him with a crooked grin. "I can't wait to gaze once again upon the gracious countenance of our hostess," he said.

"Don't push her," Kuper replied firmly. "We're going to need her help."

Rellan winced with pain as he continued his massage.

Kuper looked at him in concern. "Is something wrong with your arm?"

"It's very sore this morning. I'm not sure if it's because of all the action yesterday, or the way I slept on it last night."

Kuper had him remove the sling and gently pull up his sleeve.

The flesh of his forearm was discolored and covered with angry-looking bruises.

"That looks bad! Maybe they have someone here who can help."

"It's nothing," Rellan protested.

Kuper shook his head stubbornly. "It isn't nothing. I need you back to full strength, Rellan. You'll be of no use to anyone until those bruises heal. You have to rest, and that's an end to it."

THE MORNING WAS WELL advanced before Anneka called for them again. As they left the hut, Kuper nodded toward his brother's arm, raising his eyebrows inquiringly.

"Don't worry about me," Rellan replied. "We can think about my arm later."

Scar took them to a corner of the clearing where Anneka sat flanked by several men. In the afternoon light she appeared less mysterious, but equally stern. Scar pointed to a pair of rude chairs that faced the others, and Kuper and Rellan seated themselves. The woman nodded Scar to a seat, then turned her attention to the twins.

"My name is Anneka, and I lead this community. These are troubled times, and we live a precarious existence here. If my welcome was lacking last night, it is because we are not always sure whom we can trust." She pointed toward the children running noisily around the clearing, and to a small group of elderly men and women sitting together in the sun. "We have many mouths to feed. Even more since the Rogandans came. And there are never enough strong arms and capable hands to provide for them."

She paused, studying them silently for a moment. "In our world we meet foes more often than friends. Which are you?"

"We are merely soldiers of the king who wish to be on their way," Kuper replied. "Removing the Rogandans from Arvenon will ease your burden. You can help bring that day closer by aiding us now."

As they spoke, the quiet clip-clop of hooves reached them as a small group of horses were escorted across the clearing. They were led by a diminutive figure who hummed cheerfully to himself as he walked. Seeing the horses, Rellan pursed his lips and issued a piercing whistle that rose and fell melodically. One of the horses whinnied in response and pulled away toward him. The lad restrained it with difficulty.

"I'm delighted to see that my horse has found its way to a good home," said Rellan, a cheeky grin spreading across his face.

"Mine, too, apparently," said Kuper, spotting his own horse in the group.

Anneka's face hardened. "Are you accusing us of stealing your horses?" she demanded.

"I can't speak for my brother," Rellan replied, "but such a thought certainly never crossed my mind! I am merely overwhelmed with joy that our lost mounts have been recovered and can now be restored to us."

Kuper's brow furrowed as he looked at his brother. Rellan had always been known for his impudent brashness, but choosing the right moment wasn't always his greatest strength.

Anneka was not amused. She frowned as she looked back and forth between the twins and the horses now disappearing from the clearing. "Perhaps there is a simple way of settling this," she said. She turned to Kuper. "You claim to be a bowman. How good a bowman?"

"I am not entirely without skill," he acknowledged modestly.

"Then let us put your skills to the test," she said. "Yours against those of our best archer. If you win, take two horses of your choice and go. If you lose, you will abandon any claim on our horses, and remain here to work for us until I release you. Do you agree?"

Kuper looked at Rellan, who winked at him. Kuper frowned back at his brother in frustration. Their horses had been stolen from them, and now he was expected to win them back. They should have been well on their way to Erestor right now. No one except the Rogandans would benefit from this foolishness.

The harsh truth, though, was that he couldn't see that he had another option. "I agree," he said reluctantly.

"It's a pity I can't use my arm," Rellan told her. "I'm the better archer."

She glared at him, not impressed.

"He isn't boasting," Kuper admitted. "It's the truth."

Anneka sent away one of her men, and he returned with a young man who carried a bow slung over his shoulder. The new arrival greeted the two strangers warmly. "I am Hender. I understand we will be competing for some horses," he said to Kuper with a grin.

"We're competing for much more than that," Kuper replied testily. His brother might find this situation amusing, but he saw very little to smile about.

At that moment two men rode slowly into the clearing. They approached the group, and the first man dismounted, offering a quiet greeting to the leader. Seeing his arrival, others wandered over to greet him. A small crowd of men, women, and children had soon gathered.

The other man looked harried. Riding was clearly uncomfortable for him, and he dismounted awkwardly. His companion led him to Anneka and introduced him.

"All of us are very grateful to you!" the newcomer exclaimed. "My people could not have managed without the food you sent us. We have been traveling much more slowly than we hoped; we have so many children with us. Even with your help, the first group will not arrive here much before sundown tomorrow."

Looking around him, he caught sight of Kuper and Rellan. "You are here, too!" he cried out joyfully. "Our rescuers!" He rushed to Kuper and took his hand, shaking it vigorously.

"These men were there when you were attacked?" Anneka asked. She looked skeptical.

"No," he replied, "but they arrived very soon after." He pointed to Kuper. "I've never seen such a bowman," he said enthusiastically. "Six arrows, and six Rogandans went down. And his friend here killed their leader. With his sword."

Anneka looked back and forth between them all. Finally she turned to Kuper. "Why did you help them?"

"We were passing by," he said, "and saw that they were defenseless. We couldn't just leave them to be slaughtered."

"The odds were against you," she said.

Kuper shrugged. "There wasn't time to consider the odds."

She nodded to herself. "You can have two horses," she said decisively. "We should be aiding you, not hindering you. Please pardon my doubts." She looked up toward the sun. "If you set off soon, you should be well on your way before night falls. I will send someone to guide you."

Kuper nodded his agreement. "Thank you for your offer of a guide. We will accept it gratefully." He pointed to his brother. "May I ask a favor, though? Do you have anyone with healing skills? My brother's arm needs some attention."

"I am the healer in this community," Anneka replied. "I will take a look."

She drew closer, and Rellan presented his arm. She probed his forearm thoroughly. She didn't appear to be making much of an effort to be gentle, and Kuper winced more than once on behalf of his twin as he looked on. One or two of the other onlookers seemed a bit surprised at her roughness as well. It seemed clear to Kuper that his brother had managed to get under her skin, even in the short time they had been with her.

Rellan bore it all without comment.

"Who set the arm?" she asked.

"A monk who was traveling with us," Rellan replied.

"He seems to have done the job properly," she conceded, somewhat grudgingly.

"He was a capable healer. And almost as gentle as you," Rellan replied, regarding her with a straight face.

The look she gave him made it perfectly clear what she thought, both about him and his comment. Nevertheless, she carefully pulled down his sleeve and reapplied his splint. "It's badly bruised, but you haven't broken it again," she said. "Don't move the arm any more than is necessary. I suggest you delay your departure. I will examine it again in the morning."

He bowed in gratitude and beamed at her innocently, a smile lighting up his face.

She scowled at him in response, turning on her heel and walking away briskly.

Kuper steered his brother away from the crowd. "What were you thinking?" he asked. "Riling her won't help anyone!"

Rellan flashed him a grin. "What a magnificent woman," he said happily.

Kuper groaned. He knew his brother well enough to see the signs of a looming disaster, and he had no idea how to head it off.

IT WAS clear that they were going to be stuck there for some time, so Kuper decided to make himself useful. He kept his eyes open for a while to learn where help was most needed. Eventually he ended up spending the afternoon assisting with the repair of a roof, in readiness for the coming winter.

There was little that Rellan could do to help with physical work, but he likewise wasted no time finding other ways of occupying his time. Soon after climbing onto the roof, Kuper looked down and saw his brother at the center of a noisy and enthusiastic group of children. Rellan was pretending to be a one-armed monster, lurching around slowly with an arm outstretched to grab them. Whenever he caught someone, they always quickly managed to escape. The children deliberately placed themselves almost within reach, then sprang away whenever he came too close, squealing with excitement. Later Kuper noticed the children sitting around his brother, hanging on his every word while he told them stories.

Most interesting of all, Kuper had spied Anneka shooting frequent glances toward his twin. From a distance he had the impression that more often than not she wore a frown. But there was no doubt that, for better or for worse, Rellan had managed to capture her attention.

The next morning Kuper rose early and set off into the forest with one of Scar's traveling companions to chop wood. Upon his return he found that Rellan had collected his bow and was giving some of the older boys tuition on archery.

When Anneka sent for Rellan late in the morning, his twin hurried along behind him. Kuper was unable to shake off the feeling that a disaster was imminent and that he was powerless to prevent it. He had tried to warn his brother the previous night, but at such times Rellan had a frustrating habit of giving every appearance of hearing him out, then doing exactly what he had been warned not to do.

When they arrived, Anneka avoided eye contact with Rellan, focusing her attention solely on his arm.

"Thank you very much for your thoughtful care for me," Rellan said brightly. "I didn't expect to find such gracious help hidden away in the wilderness."

Anneka pointedly ignored him. Kuper concluded that she probably thought he was mocking her.

She continued to examine Rellan's arm. She seemed a bit more careful this time, but Kuper still felt glad it wasn't his arm beneath her probing fingers.

"Your arm is improving. But you need to rest it properly if you want it to heal." As she spoke, she looked up into his eyes for the first time. What she saw there clearly disconcerted her. At first she colored, then she frowned in intense annoyance.

"I don't know what you think you've been doing with the children," she burst out angrily. "Many of them have been through a lot, and they don't need you talking nonsense to them."

His response was one of innocent bewilderment, which did not improve her mood.

"I was merely recounting some of my adventures," he said mildly, "and telling them how fortunate they are to live in such a place as this, with a wise and thoughtful leader who takes care of all their needs."

"It's true," one of the bystanders blurted out. "I overheard him."

Kuper noticed that a small crowd had quietly gathered, and that they were observing the interaction with keen interest.

"One of the young girls asked me what I do at bedtime when I'm feeling sad," Rellan continued. "I told her that I find a happy thought and think about that. She asked me, 'What kind of happy thought?'.

So I suggested she think about something nice that happened that day, and come up with ways of showing she was grateful the next morning."

"He did say that," another observer confirmed. Anneka frowned.

"She asked me what happy thought I was going to take to bed with me that night, and how I could show I'm grateful in the morning. I told her that I would go to sleep thinking about their kind leader who is mending my arm, and that I would specially thank her in the morning."

"I heard that, too," chipped in another person. Someone stifled a snort of laughter.

Anneka rounded on the bystanders crowding around them. "Don't you have anything else to do?" she snapped.

They scurried away. Kuper went with them, and Rellan followed after first thanking her gratefully once again.

The latest incident had clearly agitated Anneka. Later he heard her yelling at someone, which hadn't happened before in his hearing. He noticed others looking at each other with raised eyebrows.

Soon after that Rellan disappeared. Kuper kept an eye out for him. As the day wore on he had the impression that Anneka was doing the same.

Darkness fell without any sign of his brother. At one point Kuper was standing alone, leaning against a tree, when Anneka joined him.

"Thank you for all your help, Kuper," she said. "You've been working very hard, and all of us appreciate it."

"It's the least I can do," he replied.

They stood together in silence for a while. "Have you seen your brother?" she finally ventured.

"No, I have no idea where he has gone."

She sighed. "I wish he was more like you. I don't know what it is, but I find him extremely irritating. I've found myself wondering if he's setting out to vex me deliberately."

Kuper laughed. "It isn't just you," he said. "You're not the first person to find him annoying. There were times when he drove my mother crazy, much as she loved him."

Anneka smiled grimly. "Without having met her, I feel a strong sense of connection with the poor woman."

Kuper laughed again. "In his defense, though, I should say that not everyone finds him irritating—it's just a lucky few." He paused for a few moments. "I told you that he's my brother," he continued. "He's actually my twin, although we're not identical twins, as you can see, and we're very different in many ways. I know him well. He is strong willed, it's true, and can be provoking at times. But he's also loyal and courageous. And by nature he's kind and very generous."

"Perhaps I have been a bit too harsh with him," she said with another sigh. "I don't know what's come over me. I've been snapping at people all afternoon, and feeling very ashamed about it."

They talked about other matters for a few more minutes, then she excused herself and departed, leaving Kuper with much to think about.

Rellan finally appeared late that night. He slipped under his blankets without a word. Kuper looked at him questioningly, and he responded with nothing more than a wink. Then he rolled over and immediately went to sleep.

The next day Kuper noticed Rellan watching the comings and goings around Anneka closely. As soon as his brother saw her alone, he headed over to talk with her. Kuper watched anxiously. His brother pulled a large bunch of wildflowers from beneath his coat and handed it to her. She looked surprised. They exchanged words for a while, and she actually smiled. Then he said something else to her, and she stiffened. She threw the flowers on the ground, spun on her heel, and departed, white with anger. Rellan bent down and carefully picked up the flowers. He left them on a table and came over to Kuper.

"What just happened?" asked Kuper anxiously.

"Yesterday afternoon I went searching for flowers for Anneka," his brother told him. "When I gave them to her she thanked me and asked me what had prompted the gesture. I told her that I could see how hard she worked, and thought that she might enjoy something of beauty to take her mind off her many responsibilities.

She liked that. Then I also said that she'd seemed grumpy and unhappy yesterday, and that I hoped the flowers would cheer her up."

Kuper shook his head and covered his face.

"Well, she *was* grumpy!" Rellan retorted. "Everyone could see it. What good does it do to pretend to ignore something when it's so obvious?"

Kuper just groaned.

"Don't worry," Rellan said with a grin. "She'll get over it. She's too good a person to let such a small thing bother her for long. And they were very nice flowers."

Kuper shrugged. What else could he do?

Anneka reappeared after an absence of a couple of hours. She behaved normally, and even examined Rellan's arm again, managing to stay calm and detached while doing so. Before he left she apologized to him for her earlier outburst. Rellan apologized in his turn for having offended her. Having thus declared a truce they both went about their business.

Late in the day refugees began arriving from the destroyed village, and every adult in the community was soon very busy. That evening Kuper and Rellan found themselves sharing their small hut with several others.

On the afternoon of the next day Anneka called for Rellan once more and examined his arm. Kuper noticed that she was more gentle this time. She seemed relaxed, even with a crowd of people nearby.

"The swelling on your arm is finally going down," she said. She turned to Kuper. "You will be able to resume your journey again tomorrow."

"Then there's time for an archery contest this afternoon," said Rellan brightly.

People responded immediately, calling excitedly for Hender. He was close at hand and stepped forward with a smile. Loud cheers erupted around him.

Anneka tried to look severe. But then she shrugged. "Oh, very well," she said.

The people crowded around their champion, slapping him on the back and urging him on.

Kuper fetched his bow and moved to the center of the clearing with Hender. Rules were agreed upon, and the two men took their places. The onlookers stood back to give them space.

The first contest called for a single shot at a stationary target. Two pine cones were spotted high up in a tree across the clearing. They were so far away that Kuper could barely see them. He was given the first shot. He pulled the bowstring back to his ear and let fly. The arrow streaked away toward the target, and rattled the pine cone, dislodging it. Many people applauded politely, and some of the newly arrived refugees cheered.

Then Hender took aim. A hush came over the crowd. The onlookers exhaled as he released his arrow, and a collective sigh chased it on its way. The arrow flew straight to the pine cone, knocking it to the ground. Someone ran to the tree and held up the arrow. It had skewered the cone neatly. The entire crowd erupted in cheers.

Kuper applauded with them, a smile of appreciation on his face.

The second target was a pair of small rocks, one for each contestant. This time, Hender would shoot first. A volunteer threw the first rock high into the air, and Hender drew his bow and fired. The arrow flew to the rock and hit it squarely, sending it tumbling through the air. Once again the crowd erupted.

The second rock was thrown, and Kuper took his shot. As he released the arrow a bird flew past. The arrow barely missed the creature, and the crowd gasped. The arrowhead shaved the side of the rock, causing it to wobble a little on its way to the ground.

"Lucky bird!" shouted Rellan enthusiastically, prompting bursts of laughter from the crowd.

The final test required the contestants to land an arrow into the center of a round knot high up in the trunk of a large tree across the clearing.

Kuper took his time before releasing his arrow. It sailed across the clearing and embedded itself right in the middle of the knot.

"Hooray!" shouted Rellan, to more laughter.

Hender drew his bow and fired, then rapidly nocked another arrow and fired again. The first arrow landed right alongside Kuper's arrow, so close the two were touching. The second arrow split the two down the middle. Everyone in the crowd shouted themselves hoarse. Rellan shouted along with them.

Kuper congratulated Hender and shook his hand. "You bested me, fair and square," he said with a smile. The crowd cheered again, honoring both their champion and the gracious loser.

Anneka stepped forward and held up her hands for silence. She waited until the noise had subsided. "There's been little reason to celebrate in recent days," she called out. "But tonight we will hold a feast in honor of Hender, and in honor of a worthy contest. It will also be an opportunity to bid farewell to our new friends, who are leaving in the morning." Groans and sighs of disappointment greeted this latest news.

"Hunters will soon be off to bring us fresh meat," she called. "Prepare a bonfire!"

Another cheer went up at her words, and a buzz of excitement filled the air as the crowd dispersed. Dry wood was gathered in the center of the clearing and the fire built up once again. Spits were erected in anticipation of the spoils of the hunt.

The twins did not see Anneka again until later in the evening. The celebration was well underway, and they had been sitting with Hender enjoying fresh venison and quiet conversation. The bowman had just left them to join a group of revelers. Someone found a lute, and men and women jumped to their feet to dance. Hender was pulled into the circle by an attractive young woman who appeared to be on very friendly terms with him. The two of them were soon spinning and whirling with a sea of couples in time to a popular Erestorian folk dance.

The twins rose to their feet and nodded respectfully as the leader approached.

"It's a good thing our fate didn't depend on me defeating Hender," said Kuper.

"Your departure will be our loss. Your bow and your help would have been very welcome among us," she said. "And you, yourself, of course," she added with a smile.

"What about me?" Rellan asked, a wounded expression on his face.

She shot him a dark look, but didn't bother to answer.

"We haven't talked a great deal about what is going on in the rest of Arvenon," she said, changing the subject. "We hear so little news of the outside world."

"You know that the Rogandans are roaming freely throughout the countryside," Kuper replied. "I believe you're also aware that the king is in Castel with his new bride, and that Arnost is besieged. You may not have heard, though, that one of the lords was planning to betray the king. He has been imprisoned in Arnost. He came from Erestor," he added, "so you may know of him."

She reacted sharply. "Who was it?"

"The Earl of Pisander."

"Pisander?" She spat the name. "A dungeon is too good for him! I hope the rats gnaw his bones." She paused while she mastered her anger. "Please excuse me. Let us speak of something else," she said.

"Is the pass into Erestor open?" Kuper asked. "We need to get through as soon as possible."

"No, the Rogandans are besieging Steffan's Citadel, so the pass is closed. There is another way, though. It is difficult, and impractical for a large company. But a small party should be able to get through. I have promised to send a guide with you. He will help you find the way."

"We are grateful for your help," Kuper replied.

"It is the least I can do, if only to mend my sorry welcome when you first arrived."

Rellan had been listening quietly. But at this point he broke into the conversation, a serious expression on his face. "There is one other boon you could grant, if you were willing," he said.

She looked at him suspiciously. "What is it?" she asked.

"The honor of accompanying me in the dance," he said, bowing formally.

She was too shocked to respond. Without waiting for an answer he grabbed her hand and pulled her toward the dancers. Kuper could see the blood rising in her face and winced, waiting for an eruption. But the dancers raised a cheer as they saw their leader apparently joining their merriment, and she quickly mastered herself. Soon the whole company was hooting and hollering in delight as Rellan used his one good arm to deftly lead her through the dance in time with the music.

Kuper had no doubt that Anneka had yielded for the sake of her people, and he wasn't looking forward to her reaction once the dancing was over. His unease grew as the evening wore on.

Other men partnered her briefly on the dance floor, then Rellan claimed her once again for a lively jig.

As the dance ended it apparently became plain even to Rellan that she had reached her limit. He escorted her away from the dancers, to the cheers and applause of the crowd. She acknowledged them with a wave and a smile, but her smile seemed forced to Kuper.

She walked right past Kuper without pausing. Rellan trailed along in her wake. Soon they disappeared behind some trees, out of sight of everyone. Their raised voices ensured that Kuper was still able to hear them, though.

"How dare you humiliate me like that!"

"Where was the humiliation? You heartened your people enormously by joining in their fun."

"Don't throw that back in my face. You forced me to do it!"

"And you were going to force us to stay here to work for you. After stealing our horses!"

"Aargghh! You are the most insufferable, most arrogant, most presumptuous man I have EVER met!"

With that, she stormed off into the night.

Rellan joined him, kneading the muscles of his healing arm. "Well," he said with a tight smile, "this has been an evening I won't forget in a hurry."

. . .

THEY ROSE AT DAWN. As they readied themselves to leave they were joined by their promised guide, a wiry man who introduced himself as Yosef.

"Your leader has not come to bid us farewell," Rellan observed.

"Her movements are not always predictable," Yosef replied. "We may see her yet."

Other people were already about their business as they mounted up to ride out of the clearing. Seeing them leaving, a number of men, women, and children hurried over to speak with them.

"My children love you, Rellan! Thank you for spending time with them."

"Thank you for helping with my roof, Kuper."

"How will I learn to be a proper archer, Rellan? Please come back soon."

"Go get the Rogandans, Kuper!"

One little girl came up to Rellan, and said to him very seriously. "Our leader likes you."

He smiled back at her. "I like her, too."

Many of the recently arrived refugees also came to wish them well, and to offer again their heartfelt thanks.

Last of all, Hender came up to Rellan, looking a bit sheepish. "Where did you find the flowers?" he asked quietly. Rellan laughingly gave him directions.

Mostly for Rellan's sake, Kuper kept an eye out for Anneka. But she didn't come.

They finally managed to get away, with people calling farewells after them. They continued to wave back until the clearing was out of sight.

After they had been traveling for several minutes, their path took them past a giant fallen redwood. Once they were beyond it, Kuper looked back and saw a lone figure standing on the fallen trunk. It was Anneka.

Following his gaze, Rellan turned in his saddle. He raised his arm high in farewell.

She watched them silently, her face unreadable. She did not wave back.

Her figure slowly dwindled in size as they rode on, until the path turned, and they saw no more of her.

"That's curious," said Yosef, stealing a sideways glance at Rellan. "In all our years in the wilderness, that's the first time I've seen her with flowers in her hair."

Rellan visibly relaxed. His cheeky grin reappeared, and he winked at his brother. "Anneka and I will meet again," he said. "I feel it in my bones."

8

"You don't have to like it, Karevis. But if you're not willing to follow instructions you'll be replaced by someone who is."

Karevis glared at Lord Tarestel, making no attempt to conceal his contempt. He had never liked the man. Tarestel had always seemed a little too willing to sacrifice the greater good of the kingdom for the sake of his own advancement. He had never been too obvious about it, though. Karevis likened him to an eel—very slippery and with the potential for a nasty bite. Now he had far exceeded the worst expectations even of Karevis.

"So you're going to rule Varas as a puppet of the Rogandans?" Karevis asked him.

Tarestel answered slowly, with exaggerated patience. "I've explained it already. The Rogandans are holding the king, along with the aides who accompanied him. He has not been harmed, but that is certain to change if we choose not to cooperate. Grunsetz has given me an ultimatum—either I act as Lord Protector of the kingdom, or he will appoint a Rogandan to do it. Surely even you wouldn't want to see that happen!"

"What is being done to free the king?"

"You simply don't understand, do you? Your precious world is gone! Gone! And the king with it. Everything is changing around us. Soon Arvenon and Castel will be gone, too."

Tarestel was becoming excited. "The Arvenians and the Castelans resisted, so their *people* are going to pay." He began jabbing his finger at Karevis. "Their people will suffer because of the choices made by their leaders! We can't let that happen here. We have to work with the Rogandans. It's the only hope our people have!" Tarestel came to a halt, his passion abating.

Karevis frowned. He didn't like Tarestel, and he didn't trust his motives. But what he was saying seemed to make sense. Uncomfortable sense. Karevis remembered the words of the king, possibly the last words he would ever hear from his friend: *Do everything you can to protect our people. Don't fail me in this!*

The moment that Tarestel had echoed Delmar's directive, Karevis knew he had no choice. Much as he disliked it, he was going to have to work with the man.

He raised his hands in a gesture of surrender. "I understand. You will have my support." It was his turn to jab his finger at Tarestel. "But only for as long as it protects the people! Do you understand?"

Grunsetz handed Tarestel a parchment covered with numbers. "It has proven necessary to levy another tax," the Rogandan announced in a bored tone of voice.

Tarestel scanned the document, his alarm increasing every moment. "This is monstrous! You can't be serious!"

Grunsetz shrugged. "The cost of occupying and protecting Varas is proving to be significant."

"But there will be riots!"

"You need not fear for your safety. We now have our soldiers stationed in every city and throughout the countryside. Rioters will be dealt with ruthlessly."

"But this will beggar every family in the country!"

"Some of your countrymen are lazy. Perhaps you need to

encourage them to work harder," the Rogandan suggested. "Of course there are other ways of raising the money. Our previous levies don't seem to have troubled your coffers at all. If you are so concerned for your countrymen, perhaps you could help them out this time and pay your fair share." Grunsetz treated Tarestel to one of his nasty smiles.

Tarestel felt himself beginning to sweat. "I won't be able to govern effectively once this becomes known."

"That's your problem, Lord Protector. If I recall correctly, you volunteered for this position. You seemed to believe that your king had done an extremely poor job of ruling Varas, and that you could do so much better. If the task is no longer to your liking, I'm sure another of your countrymen can be found to take your place. Perhaps someone a little more pliable next time."

"But how could I—or anyone else for that matter—possibly come up with this much money?" Tarestel asked in despair.

"You must squeeze, my dear Lord Protector," Grunsetz replied. He raised his fists by way of illustration and tightened them slowly. "Squeeze! And if that doesn't do it," he added, "then squeeze some more!"

LORD KAREVIS HEADED to the tent of Zornath, the Rogandan liaison, in response to his latest summons. Karevis might be commander of the army in name, but the Rogandan held all the real power. Zornath allowed Karevis to continue to issue directives to the Varasan officers, but not before every word had been carefully vetted.

The Rogandan was like a terrier yapping at his heels, never leaving him alone for an instant. And Karevis wasn't alone in his suffering, either. A host of lesser Rogandan 'liaisons' had been sprinkled liberally throughout his army, and every one of his officers now shared his pain. Zornath had placed his men well—the Rogandan seemed to catch the faintest whisper from the Varasan ranks, often before Karevis himself became aware of it.

A few of the Varasans had even become informants, reporting on their fellow soldiers. Karevis could hardly bear the shame of it. He knew that most of his men shared his disgust, but there was little that any of them could do about it.

Many times Karevis had found himself thinking that his situation could not possibly get any worse. But he had been wrong, so very wrong. Every single day he seriously considered resigning his position. So far he had refrained from doing so. He stayed for one reason only—he knew that his men would suffer in a multitude of ways if he left. He still retained some ability to shield his subordinates from the most painful decisions of his new masters, and he would remain for as long as that continued to be true.

The guards stopped him when he arrived at Zornath's tent. He stood outside, like a fox at bay, waiting for the hounds.

"Ah. Come on in, Commander," called the Rogandan, finally noticing him. He stepped inside the tent, and Zornath pointed him to a stool. The liaison was himself seated in a large armchair. Karevis sat down, pretending he didn't notice the discrepancy.

"I have some wonderful news," Zornath said, flashing one of his toothy smiles.

Karevis braced himself. Thus far, the Rogandan's notion of good news had never matched his own. Not even vaguely.

"Lord Drettroth has ordered the Varasan army into the field," Zornath told him, beaming with delight. "Is that not splendid? There is nothing soldiers love more than being on campaign!"

Clearly it was wonderful news as far as Zornath was concerned. Karevis had rarely seen him so cheerful.

"What does Lord Drettroth have in mind?" Karevis asked, not expecting an answer.

Normally, Zornath loved to keep him in the dark. On this particular occasion, though, the liaison appeared to be in an expansive mood. "Our destination is Arvenon. Your soldiers have many fine qualities, Commander, I am sure. But in Arvenon they will have one particular advantage over our own men—they speak the same language as the Arvenians. This skill will undoubtedly prove very useful when dealing with the local people."

Karevis pondered the news. Using a common language to communicate with the Arvenians was all very well. But Drettroth didn't need an army for that. Going on campaign sounded much more to the point. More trouble was brewing, because nothing would ever induce him to fight alongside the Rogandans against the Arvenians. He was certain the vast majority of his men would feel the same way.

Sooner or later he was going to reach a breaking point. If things had been bad before, they were about to get a lot worse.

He wondered if Tarestel was aware of Drettroth's plans. "How does the Lord Protector view this development?" he asked the liaison.

Zornath flicked his fingers dismissively. "It is no concern of his. There are more than enough Rogandan soldiers stationed in Varas to ensure the security of his rule. He has no need for the Varasan army."

Karevis wondered how Tarestel was liking his role as Lord Protector. He wouldn't be surprised to learn that the ambitious nobleman was finding life as a Rogandan vassal every bit as distasteful as he was himself.

His musings were interrupted by the liaison.

"Efficiency will become of paramount importance once our army is on the march," Zornath told him. "Some of your men are not communicating effectively with their liaisons. Get me a list of names of all of your men who speak Rogandan. They will be assigned secondary roles as translators."

The Rogandan appeared to lose interest in the conversation. "Deliver the list by noon tomorrow, Commander. And do not be late!" he commanded. "You are dismissed," he added in an imperious tone, dropping his gaze to a document lying in front of him.

As the commander left Zornath's tent, he wracked his brains for the thousandth time, trying to conjure up a way of extracting his army from the clutches of the Rogandans. But as always, his mind was blank.

Why hadn't they fought while they still could? If the Rogandans had defeated them, as would have been likely, the outcome for the people of Varas could scarcely have been worse than it was now. And his men would have fought like tigers. The Rogandan army would have been left considerably weakened.

Instead, the Rogandans had been able to send their most feeble soldiers to Varas as occupiers, and use the Varasan army to swell their ranks in Arvenon.

He didn't doubt that King Delmar would have chosen differently if he'd had his time over again. But it was too late. And there was no point in blaming his friend; the king must surely have paid a heavy price of his own. Karevis had no way of knowing exactly what had become of Delmar, but by now he knew enough about the Rogandans to make some intelligent guesses.

He returned to his quarters in a gloomy mood, troubled by dark forebodings.

ESSANDA FROWNED UP at Count Gordan. "Why is everyone so unhappy these days, Gordy?" she asked.

The noble was sculpting a tiny image of a horse from a piece of wood. He glanced up from the carving and gave her an affectionate look. "People are frightened, Your Majesty. They're worried that the Rogandans might defeat us," he replied. He bent his head again, returning to his labors.

He was refreshingly direct with her, as always. It was something she especially appreciated about him. Other people usually told her what they thought she needed to hear.

To most adults she was invisible. She had always been shown appropriate deference, of course, first as Princess of Castel, and now as Queen of Arvenon. But she was just a child to most of them. Sometimes they even said so out loud. And in her presence, too. To them she was a delicate doll—a bit fragile, and needing to be handled gently. She wasn't seen as an independent person in her own right.

Count Gordan treated her as if she was intelligent. She liked that.

"But Steffan—His Majesty, I mean—isn't going to let them win. I know he has great faith in his soldiers."

Count Gordan contented himself with a grunt of acknowledgment. She didn't quite know how to read it.

"Why don't people like Will?" she asked.

"Will Prentis?" He put down his knife. "You seem to know quite a lot about what people think," he said, raising an eyebrow.

She smiled innocently at him, but didn't reply. He was right, of course—she did know a lot. She heard things. She could probably thank her invisibility for that, at least in part. She could also thank her new husband. He had apparently decided that she was intelligent, too, and she suspected he told her much more than he should have.

"People don't like Will because he isn't a nobleman," Count Gordan said. He glanced around the room, apparently satisfying himself that they were alone. "And also because he's smarter than any of us nobles," he added with a grin.

"He can't be smarter than you!" she protested.

"Thank you, Your Majesty," he said, bowing his head low. "You honor me greatly."

He looked at her seriously. "I believe that I am a useful diplomat, Your Majesty. Your father seems to think so, anyway. But the truth is that when it comes to war, Will *is* more clever than me—more clever than any of us. Much more so. He seems able to out-think his opponents. And, just as important, men are willing—even eager—to follow him into battle. None of the nobles can make the same claims. And many of them can't forgive him for it."

"How do you know all this, Gordy?"

"I have my ways of finding out what people think, too," he said.

She looked at him questioningly. "Is there anything we can do to make it easier for the nobles?"

He shook his head, admiration in his eyes. "You never cease to amaze me, young Essie," he said, calling her by the affectionate name he had used since she was a small child. "You give the appearance of being so naive and unaware, but you quickly see to the heart of it, as always."

She looked at him quizzically. "What do you mean?" His familiarity did not offend her in the least—he had been almost like a second father to her, and she felt secure in the knowledge that he loved and admired her.

"I meant, Your Majesty, that most people sympathetic to Will would be thinking about ways of strengthening him at the expense of his critics. You turn your attention instead to the source of the problem."

He paused for a moment. "I have given the matter a great deal of thought," he admitted. "I'm sorry to say that I don't have any good answers, though." He sighed. "Everyone is proud and stubborn at times. For some strange reason, though, people with few accomplishments and abilities can be the proudest and most stubborn of all. The only real achievement some can claim is to have brought down people better than themselves. If you can call that an achievement."

A gong sounded, announcing dinner. He rose and took her hand, leading her from the room.

THAT NIGHT as she lay in bed, Essanda remembered a tale she had heard from one of her father's oldest advisors.

"A fool set a fire at the home of his rival," the advisor had said. "He looked on gleefully while the fire took hold, and he actively discouraged his neighbors from fighting the blaze. Soon the fire could not be contained. To the arsonist's delight, his rival lost everything.

"Meanwhile, though, the fire spread out of control and engulfed the whole town. Before long it consumed the home of the fool, too, along with all of his possessions.

"What did the fool learn from this disaster? He convinced himself that the fault lay with his rival, since the fire had spread from his house. He abused his victim publicly, demanding compensation. His victim had no compensation to offer, of course. Both men were ruined, along with the entire town.

"The fool lost everything except his folly. The greater fools, though, were the townsfolk, who stood by and did nothing when they could have saved their neighbor's home and prevented the destruction of their town."

Essanda didn't know what she could do to help against the Rogandans. But she drifted off to sleep determined not to stand by and watch her kingdom fall because she'd done nothing to save it.

9

Thomas had only been in the water a short time before he began to feel the cold acutely. He tucked his arms in to his body and began kicking his legs, but it didn't help. Soon he was shivering uncontrollably.

It was clear that he couldn't stay in the river. Releasing the branch that had supported him, he swam to the bank opposite from where he had started. He hoped there was at least a small chance that the Rogandans were only occupying one side of the river.

Locating a place to land, he dragged himself out onto the bank. Then he got up and began squeezing water from his clothes. The night air was cool, and he knew he needed to dry himself and find somewhere out of the wind as quickly as possible. Teeth chattering and arms hugged to his chest, he headed inland.

After picking his way through the foliage for a few minutes, he found a small animal track heading away from the river. He turned onto it instinctively, following it until it widened into a small clearing. An animal had been digging near the base of a tree, leaving loose soil scattered around. The soil had been exposed for long enough to have dried out thoroughly. After a moment's consideration, he stripped off most of his clothes—everything except his trousers and the pouch holding the stone—and put them to one side. Then he picked up handfuls of the dirt and began spreading it over his body. He kept at it until a thin coating of mud covered him. Finally he wrung out his clothing as best he could. Then he set off again, following the animal trail where it continued across the clearing.

It didn't take long before the mud began to dry on his body, leaving behind a clinging layer of dirt. He brushed at the dirt as he walked, managing to remove most of it. His clothes were still too wet to put back on, but his body was nearly dry, and he was no longer shivering quite so violently.

When the trail led him into an area of denser undergrowth, he turned off the path. Having found a piece of ground covered with soft grasses, he gathered together several fallen branches still covered with leaves and made a low shelter. He hung his clothes on the outside to dry, and crawled in. The grass was cold on his bare skin, but he was so tired he drifted off to sleep anyway.

He woke in the night to the haunting cry of an owl. Crawling out from beneath his shelter he hunted for his clothes. They had blown away in the breeze, and it took him a few minutes to find them. They were almost dry, so he put them on and climbed back under the branches.

He lay there thinking about his urgent need for food and better shelter, especially with the weather becoming cooler. Above all he knew he must remain truly hidden. The harsh reality of his isolation pressed in on him. Once again he wondered where Brother Vangellis was, hoping fervently that he was not badly hurt.

The loss of the monk's companionship was a heavy blow, and he wished they could have remained together. The monk was beyond his reach, though. He was alone in the wilderness with no hope of rescue.

It would have been easier than ever to lose control of his emotions, but he knew the time had come to toughen up. He simply could no longer afford to indulge in self pity. His mental toughness needed to match his newly developed physical strength. He had to survive on his own.

. . .

The morning was half spent when Thomas first heard the horse. He had been checking his snares, and finding them empty had followed the animal trail back to the river. Arriving at the water's edge, he peered out cautiously, looking for boats or any other sign of the Rogandans. He had seen people on the river more than once, and had even spotted a soldier on the opposite bank on one occasion. But up to now there had been no sign of pursuers on his side of the river. No one had come anywhere near where he had been hiding for the past few days.

He left the river when he heard loud whinnies from further along the path. His heart beat a frantic rhythm as he hurried off the path and hid himself. Was he about to be discovered at last?

After a few minutes a horse and rider came into view, heading along the path. He guessed that the horse must have propelled its rider into some of the low hanging tree branches that overhung the path, because the man had both blood and bruises on his face. The rider was cursing the animal roundly. Thomas could not understand a word he was saying, but his meaning was very clear.

As he drew nearer to the river, the rider dismounted. He roughly wrapped the reins around a branch, then picked up a stick from the ground and laid into his horse with it. The terrified animal drew back and reared up, screaming in fright.

Muttering loudly, the man set off on foot toward the river.

As he disappeared from sight, Thomas peered back along the way he had come. No other riders were in sight—this soldier was apparently traveling alone. Thomas looked first at the animal and then ahead to where the rider had disappeared.

Could he dare to steal the horse?

He looked on anxiously—the soldier could return at any minute. If he was going to do it, he needed to move quickly, but still he hesitated. What if the man reappeared at the very instant he stepped into the open?

He stood rooted to the ground in an agony of indecision, breaking out into a cold sweat as the moments fled away. Finally, his heart pounding in his chest, he acted. Full of apprehension, he approached the horse. It watched his approach with eyes bulging, and began to pull away. He spoke to it quietly, drawing upon all his experience with the animals. The horse calmed down, and he loosened the reins and led it away. Incredibly, the soldier still did not appear.

The moment he was out of sight of the place where he had found the horse, Thomas climbed into the saddle and rode away, bending low to speak soothingly into the animal's ear.

Once well clear of the area, he drew in a deep breath and exhaled loudly. He couldn't believe it. By now the Rogandan would have returned to find his horse gone. With luck, the soldier would assume that it had broken free and wandered off. The way he had treated the animal could only make that outcome seem more likely.

Thomas twisted around in the saddle and checked the saddlebags. The soldier had thoughtfully bequeathed him dried meat, a large chunk of cheese, and some stale bread, along with a water skin. Thomas even found a warm coat crammed into one of the saddlebags.

His situation had improved dramatically, beyond his wildest imagining. Having started with nothing, he all of a sudden found himself with a horse, a water skin, food, and warm clothing. He still had one problem, though. He had no idea where he was, and even less idea which way to go. After pondering the situation for a while, he decided to head east, away from the river. He would keep away from roads and travel mainly at night. Most of all, he would stay as far as possible from any Rogandans.

THE HORSE PICKED its way through the undergrowth between towering trees. Paths were almost non-existent here in the deep forest, suggesting that it might be an excellent place to remain hidden. Assuming Thomas could cope with the loneliness. He decided not to think about that.

The ground sloped steadily downward, and the sounds of a

stream somewhere ahead penetrated through the trees. The horse made for the water, and Thomas let it have its head. The trees parted to reveal a narrow path, with a small stream bubbling away merrily beside it.

The horse stepped into the stream and lowered its head to drink. As it did so, Thomas gulped down the last mouthfuls from his water skin. When the animal had finished he dismounted and refilled the skin from the stream.

Thomas felt like stretching his legs, so he set off down the path, leading the horse. He walked on for about half an hour. Then, around a bend in the path, he spotted something that stopped him dead in his tracks. Further down the stream sat an old and misshapen crone, dressed in black, facing away from him. She was rocking backward and forward, making a peculiar keening noise.

Thomas had never seen a witch before, but he had heard people talk about them, and she seemed to match the description perfectly. Everything about her suggested menace and extreme danger. He stood there transfixed, his skin crawling and his eyes almost popping out of his head. His horse, unconcerned, began grazing on some grass beside the stream.

In the improbable hope of exposing her character, Thomas reached down and untied the pouch at his waist. He thrust his fingers in for the stone, and clutched it in his hand. To his surprise the crone suddenly appeared harmless. She seemed more frightened than frightening. He released the stone, and the impression went away. He grasped it again and caught a glimpse of grief and pain. The stone did not permit him to read her fully, but it was evident that there was nothing evil about her. In spite of her appearance, he sensed an air of quiet dignity and decency about her. The overwhelming impression, though, was one of great distress.

More curious than alarmed now, he put away the stone, and approached her cautiously. As he drew near it became obvious that the strange sound he had heard was a dismal combination of sobbing and wailing. Sensing the depth of her anguish, his heart went out to her, unappealing though she was.

He tried to imagine what Brother Vangellis might do if he was here. He stopped a little distance from her. "Hello," he called. "Is there anything I can do to help you?"

At the sound of his voice she leaped into the air with a startled cry and spun around toward him. Her face was hidden within a large hood, but her reaction plainly revealed her terror.

He showed her his empty hands. "I won't hurt you."

Her body shook as she faced him. She seemed completely dismayed to have been discovered. Having spent so long hiding himself, Thomas felt considerable sympathy for her reaction.

"Can I help you?" he repeated.

She faced him without speaking, no doubt entirely unwilling to trust him.

He sat down on the path, wanting to demonstrate that he had no intention of harming her. He tried to study her without seeming to stare. Why was she hiding away in this remote place? And who was she? She might have been ugly, but an old crone she was not. The nimbleness of her movements made it plain that she was anything but old.

He tried again. "Are you in pain?"

She remained silent, so he decided to wait.

Eventually she must have decided to take a risk. "My...my father. He is very sick." Her voice sounded strange—unnaturally husky.

Once more Thomas found himself wishing that the monk was with him. He himself was no healer, and he guessed there was little he could do to help. "What's wrong with him?" he asked.

"He has a high fever."

Thomas looked at her with surprise. "A high fever?"

"Yes. I am afraid...that he will die." Her head was bowed and her face hidden, but a teardrop appeared from within her cowl and fell to the ground.

"Do you have any feverwort?"

"What is that?" she asked tremulously. Her hand disappeared into her hood, and she appeared to be busy brushing at the tears that now flowed freely.

"It's a herb that can be used to bring down fever."

"What does it look like?" The dullness of her tone conveyed no expectation that any herb could make a difference.

He described it to her briefly, then began searching around the banks of the stream. She also looked, but only half heartedly.

Thomas found it first. He called her over and showed her the plant's broad green leaf and pale flower.

She bent her head to look at it. "We can try," she said, sounding resigned. She seemed thoroughly dispirited. "I will take you to him."

He followed her shuffling steps away from the stream and into the trees. He studied her from behind as they walked. Her back was disfigured with a prominent hump at the top of it, and her right shoulder stood higher than her left. She looked hideous, and he quickly found himself looking anywhere but toward her back. Had it not been for the reassurance provided by the stone that she was harmless, he would never have dreamed of approaching her, much less going anywhere with her. But he'd also heard the monk say that beauty or ugliness on the outside of a person was not a reliable guide to what they were like on the inside. He promised himself he would try to remember that.

They soon came to a small cabin, and she disappeared inside, holding the door ajar for him. He followed her in. The light inside the single room of the cabin was dim, but he was able to make out the figure of an older man on a bed. The man was tossing and turning and moaning. Thomas approached him and felt his forehead. It was burning up.

"Do you have any warm water?" he asked.

She shook her head, but went to a fire that had burned low and stirred it up. Then she threw on a piece of wood. A metal pot hung over the fire, and she added water to it.

Thomas tried hard to remember what Brother Vangellis had done in such cases. He knew that the monk had used the feverwort to make a broth. But did he use the stem, the leaf, the flower, or all of them? How much water should he use? He simply didn't know.

Then a vague memory stirred in his mind. He recalled the monk talking about berries and mushrooms and what was safe to eat. He had pointed out some flowers that were good to eat and others that were poisonous. Then he had used feverwort as an example of a plant with an edible flower. At least that's what Thomas thought he had said.

The woman came to him with a bowl filled with warm water. Thomas hesitated until he began to sense her uneasiness. He took a snap decision and threw in the entire plant—stem, flowers and all. He sincerely hoped he was doing the right thing. Something needed to be attempted, though—it appeared that the man would be in serious trouble if he didn't receive help of some kind soon.

Thomas stirred the water and quickly noticed a pleasant aroma filling the little room. The man continued to toss and turn, calling out in his delirium. He said something incoherent, then began groaning. Twice he mumbled, "Elena," before resuming his groaning. Thomas guessed that the woman's name was Elena, because more tears emerged from within her hood as soon as she heard the name.

The color of the water had now changed with the addition of the feverwort. Thomas knew he was taking a risk feeding it to the man, but the soothing aroma gave him hope, and the man's condition added a sense of urgency. He asked for a spoon and used it to begin feeding drops of liquid into the man's mouth. He remembered that the monk usually prayed while he was doing this. Just in case it made any difference, he mumbled something under his breath that he hoped was suitable. He had no confidence that God had even heard him, but he'd done the best he knew how.

After continuing to spoon in the broth for a while, he handed the task to the woman. She was eager to help, and it was better than having her standing anxiously beside him wringing her hands as she had been doing.

"I'm going to attend to my horse," he told her, and slipped out of the cabin, heading for the stream.

The horse nickered a greeting as he approached. The two of them had quickly come to an understanding—Thomas was delighted with the freedom of being on horseback once more, and the horse seemed very contented with its change of master. He led the animal to the hut and removed its bridle, saddle bags, and saddle. The man's condition was uppermost in his mind, and he couldn't face the idea of entering the cabin and finding him worse. So he put off his return and gave his horse a thorough rub down instead.

Eventually the inevitable could be delayed no longer. He opened the door and went inside. To his surprise the woman looked almost relaxed. He bent low to examine the patient. The man was still unconscious, but he no longer appeared quite so restless. He had stopped moaning, too.

The bowl was almost empty of water, so the woman went to the fire and refilled it.

"Would you like me to feed him again?" Thomas asked.

She nodded and handed him the bowl. Thomas wasn't at all sure that he warranted the confidence she was apparently placing in him. If his treatment proved effective, the credit rightly belonged to the monk. Nevertheless, she seemed content to trust her father to his care. He resumed the task of patiently feeding drops of fluid to the man.

It soon became apparent that the woman had another reason for allowing him to take over from her. She was busying herself preparing food. The smells that began to fill the room reminded Thomas just how long it had been since he last enjoyed a good meal.

When the food was ready she pointed him to a stool and handed him a bowl. The food was simple—a stew with vegetables and some kind of meat—but it tasted very good. As he ate he glanced across at the cook. He could not see her face, but from the movement of her head she seemed to be alternating her gaze between her father and him. She appeared to be observing him particularly closely. He was enjoying the food far too much to be distracted by her scrutiny, though.

When he finished he closed his eyes and let out a long sigh of contentment. The woman had returned to her father and had resumed feeding him the fluid. She glanced at him briefly, then ignored him in favor of her patient.

Thomas began to feel restless. He wasn't needed at the moment, and he didn't know what to do with himself. "I think I will look for more feverwort," he told her.

She nodded, but said nothing.

He left the cabin and headed off into the forest on foot.

Several hours passed before he finally returned. He had been busy. As well as searching for feverwort, he had made and set a couple of rabbit snares. It wasn't clear even to him why he had decided to set snares. He told himself that he wanted to repay the woman for the meal. Setting snares was an odd way of thanking her, though, considering he was nothing more than a visitor. He was behaving as though he had settled there.

By now the light was fading. He checked on his horse, then approached the cabin. In the act of opening the door, he hesitated, and eventually knocked softly instead. The woman came to the door and opened it. Although he couldn't see her face, he had the impression that she was surprised at his timidity. She waved him in.

"I've found more feverwort," he said, handing her a large bundle of plants.

She nodded her thanks and laid them out to dry near the fire.

He headed over to her father. The man had not woken, but he did seem more settled.

With the light in the cabin almost gone, the woman lit a couple of candles, placing one of them near the head of her father. Then she laid some blankets on the floor beside him.

"Please," she said to Thomas, indicating a simple mattress across the room. Then she lay down on the blankets. Thomas had the feeling that she had given him her own bed, but he didn't like to argue. He lay down himself.

DAYLIGHT GREETED him when he woke. Two small windows were set into opposite walls of the cabin, and the shutters had been opened. Dim light was shining through them determinedly. He sat up and looked around. The woman was awake and tending to her father. He was still lying down but had clearly regained consciousness. The man spoke to her softly, and Thomas could not hear what he was saying. Noticing that his visitor was awake, the man turned to him and regarded him silently.

After a couple of minutes of this scrutiny, Thomas began to feel uncomfortable. Apparently sensing his unease, the woman turned to her father and spoke quietly to him. The older man gazed at her thoughtfully for a moment, then turned back to Thomas.

"I understand it is you I have to thank for my recovery," he said.

"Please don't mention it," Thomas replied awkwardly. "I may not have done anything much at all—it's possible you would have recovered on your own."

The man seemed to soften a little. "From what my daughter, Elena, has told me, I very much doubt it," he replied. "I am Rubin," he continued. "What is your name? And how do you come to be here?"

"My name is Thomas Stablehand. I have been traveling with a friend—a monk. He taught me about feverwort. He was taken by the Rogandans a few days ago." To his own embarrassment, he was unable to keep a quaver out of his voice. He steadied himself. "I am trying to hide from them."

"You will be safe here," the woman said. She sounded eager.

Rubin frowned for a moment. Then he seemed to relent. "You are welcome to stay with us," he said, "at least for a while. Other people do not seem to find us here." He looked significantly at his daughter. "Not often, anyway."

She looked back at her father without speaking.

"Thank you for your kindness," Thomas replied. "I do not wish to impose on you."

Rubin nodded his acknowledgment but did not speak.

Thomas again began to feel uncomfortable. "Please excuse me," he said. "I must see to my horse." He got up and left the cabin.

As he led the horse to the stream, he thought about both the woman's eagerness and the man's apparent reluctance to host him. The daughter's motives were easy to understand—she credited him with her father's recovery. As for her father, he didn't blame him for his hesitation. The simple truth was that the man knew nothing about him.

And there was indeed one thing of great consequence they did not know about him. He knew that the Rogandans would never stop searching for him. His hosts had no idea that by allowing him to stay with them, they would sooner or later be putting themselves at great risk. But could he bring himself to abandon human companionship once again, and set off alone into the unknown? Where would he go? How could he bear it?

As he wrestled with his conscience it occurred to him to wonder why they were hiding away, so far from the rest of the world. What secrets did they have of their own? The more Thomas thought about it, the more uneasy he began to feel. Would he be safe if he remained with them?

Then a memory came to him of the woman wailing at the stream. The stone had shown him that she was no threat. It was hard to imagine her encouraging him to stay if she knew it would put him in danger.

Even without the stone, he suspected that in time he would have come to recognize the gentle spirit hidden behind the woman's deformity. She was an object of pity rather than fear. He had never seen her face, concealed as it was beneath her expansive hood, but once or twice he had caught fleeting glimpses of her chin or her cheek. She appeared to have unsightly red splotches across her skin. He had the clear impression that she was surpassingly ugly, and he was grateful that she thoughtfully hid her face from sight.

He came to a decision. He would stay, at least for now. But he would be truthful with his hosts, and tell them that he was being hunted relentlessly by the Rogandans. Then they could decide for themselves whether they wanted to ask him to leave.

The challenge would be to explain why the Rogandans wanted him so badly. How could he do that without exposing the secret of the stone?

10

Kuper stared absently at the flickering flames as his brother threw another branch onto the fire. After several days away from the saddle, a long day of riding had left him feeling weary. They had finally stopped as the sun was setting.

Given their remote location they had no qualms about building a fire to banish the evening chill. He glanced across at his brother once again. Rellan seemed uncharacteristically withdrawn since leaving the community in the clearing. At that moment he sat gazing into the fire, apparently lost in his thoughts.

The afternoon had seen them climbing the slopes of a mountain after emerging from the forest in late morning. With daylight fading, they had reached the shores of a vast natural lake that stretched out before them like a small inland sea. The highest mountain peaks still towered above them, but they had reached their immediate destination.

"Tomorrow we will find a way around the lake and into Erestor," Yosef said. "Fortunately, we've had no rain in the past week. The path is dangerous at the best of times, but it can be extremely treacherous when it's wet."

"I had no idea there was any way across the mountains except through the main pass," said Kuper.

"The pass is certainly the simplest and most obvious way. It runs right through Steffan's Citadel. But the citadel gates are shut and barred right now. You can thank the Rogandans for that—they're camped in the fields below it. I've heard they're packed in so tight down there that a mouse couldn't sneeze without them knowing about it. There's no way past them to the citadel."

"A pity. I was looking forward to seeing the citadel again."

"You know it?"

"Yes. We grew up in a small village on the Erestorian side of the pass, and the citadel could be seen from our village. It was quite a sight."

"It's an impressive fortress," Yosef acknowledged.

Yosef unpacked and passed around some food from his saddle-bags, and talking ceased for a while as they ate.

Rellan finally broke the silence. "When did you join the community in the forest?"

"I went there with Her Ladyship—Anneka, as she now insists on being called—six or seven years ago. Her husband owned large estates in northern Erestor, and she lived there with him and their two-year old son. He was a good man. A jealous nobleman falsely accused him of disloyalty to the king, and the lords were preparing to try him for treason. But fighting broke out when soldiers were sent to bring him in. He was killed along with his son."

Rellan's eyes narrowed. "The nobleman who brought down her husband—was he called Pisander?"

"Yes, it was the Earl of Pisander. He didn't get that title until later, though. He was known as Lord Dunnridge at the time."

Rellan got to his feet and began pacing around restlessly.

"Pisander has been brought down himself," said Kuper. "And because of disloyalty to the king, too."

Yosef shook his head.

Rellan paused, his arms spread wide in exasperation. "Punishing other people for his own weakness? Other *innocent* people?"

Unable to think of a useful response, Kuper held his peace.

Several minutes passed before Rellan was able to master his agitation. Finally he returned to the fire and sat down again. “What did Anneka do?” he asked.

“She fled with his surviving retainers. I was one of them. She led us into the wilderness.

“A lot of people would have been crushed by what happened, but not her. She’s unusually capable—she’d never been content just to live in her husband’s shadow. And she’s caring and compassionate as well, which is why her people are so loyal.

“The crisis brought out her strengths more than ever. They were dark days, though, especially during the first couple of years. It was only the force of her will that kept us going.”

“The community seems to be well established now,” Kuper observed.

“Yes, although it’s never been easy. The hunting is good, but the soil there is not well suited to farming, and we’ve never been able to grow enough crops. Anyone who’s dispossessed—or even discontented—seeks us out, and we seem to have a never-ending number of mouths to feed. The Rogandans have made it much worse.”

The conversation lapsed, and they decided to build up the fire and prepare for sleep. They lay down, wrapped in their blankets, but sleep proved elusive. Rellan tossed and turned restlessly, and Kuper also struggled to get to sleep on the hard ground. As he lay there, Kuper thought about Pisander and the perversity of human nature. He was grateful that his captain and his king lived according to much higher standards. Both of them were consistently honest and direct in their dealings with other people. He recognized, too, that he had always taken that entirely for granted. He drifted off wondering where Will was, and what he was doing.

The next day found them navigating around the southern edge of the huge lake. There were no paths, so they picked their way carefully across steep slopes that supported little vegetation. A sheer rock face just above them capped the top of the slope; there was no way across it. Yosef warned them that the lower slopes were unstable, so they traveled as near to the top as possible. Even so, the soil was loose and slid away freely under the hooves of their horses. Kuper had no difficulty understanding how the slopes could become treacherous after a soaking rain.

At about the halfway point they crossed a steep hillside strewn with large boulders. As they moved forward in single file with Yosef in front, the ground crumbled away beneath their guide's horse. The animal stumbled, throwing Yosef from its back. In a moment he was sliding helplessly down the slope. The others watched in horror, powerless to stop him. Yosef's horse, ears back and nervous, stamped its hooves restlessly, threatening to destabilize the slope even more.

Halfway down the slope Yosef landed hard against a boulder. It held firm.

At the same time, Kuper dismounted and gave his reins to his brother. He carefully moved to Yosef's horse and calmed it. The flow of soil down the slope gradually ceased.

Yosef lay still for so long that Kuper became alarmed. "Are you injured?" he called.

"I'm fine!" Yosef called back. "I'm just catching my breath."

After a few moments more, Yosef cautiously began climbing back up the steep bank, loose earth tumbling down around him as he went.

He was exhausted by the time he reached the others. He lay quietly for several minutes, trying to recover from his exertion. "This is the most difficult section," he told them. "The ground becomes firmer just beyond the next ridge."

"We can find our way from here," Rellan told him. "If you return now, you should be clear of the lake before nightfall."

Yosef didn't immediately reply, so Kuper decided that further encouragement was necessary. "Rellan's right, Yosef," he added. "Once we get past the lake and swing north, we'll be back in familiar territory. You need to head back before your horse becomes unmanageable."

Yosef considered the situation for a few moments. Then he slowly nodded. "You're right. You know where you need to go from here. I doubt that I can be of much use to you anymore."

After satisfying themselves that Yosef was able to make his way back safely on his own, they parted. Dismounting and leading their horses, they picked their way carefully across the hillside. Once they reached firmer ground, they looked back and saw that Yosef had also made it beyond the unstable section of the slope.

Several hours passed before they were finally clear of the lake. In open country at last, they gave the horses their heads. Many leagues still lay between them and Maranelle, the capital of the Duchy of Erestor.

As they rode, Rellan threw off his sling.

Kuper drew his horse closer to his brother's and slowed a little. "What are you doing?" he called.

"I've had enough of it," his brother called back. "I'm going to need both arms for what's coming next."

An image of his brother dancing, with Anneka in his arms, immediately came to Kuper's mind. He kept his face impassive, but inside he couldn't help grinning. Both of them kicked their heels into the flanks of their horses and sped away, heading for the sea.

After waiting with growing impatience for three hours, Kuper and Rellan finally found themselves confronted with a minor underling to Lord Burtelen.

"We need to see Lord Burtelen urgently. We have an important message to deliver to him."

"Who is the message from?" asked the official. His dismissive tone said more plainly than words how little importance he placed on them and their message.

"The commander of the king's armies."

"Captain Olaf?"

"No. The new commander. Will Prentis."

"Who is this Will Prentis? I've never heard of him."

Kuper forced himself to stay calm. "He is the person who saved Arnost from the Rogandans. He is the one who requested the duke to send Lord Burtelen back to Erestor."

"That fellow? He's just a commoner."

Not for the first time in his life, Kuper wondered why it was that the lower the ranking of a minor official, the more self-important he tended to become. This man was almost insufferable, which suggested he sat a long way down the pecking order.

"We're not here to discuss this with you," Rellan interjected. "We're here to see *your master*. If you continue to block us, you will answer to the king!" His pointed emphasis on 'your master' was not missed by the official, who simply became more obstructive.

"Give me the message, and I will pass it on to His Lordship," he sniffed.

"We were instructed to hand it to him personally," Kuper insisted, struggling to remain civil.

"Well, I will see what can be done. Perhaps he might be able to find time, sooner or later, in his busy schedule to attend to you. Come back next week, and I might have better news."

A nasty smile came over Rellan's face. "You're clearly a very busy man. You must have many important things to do. We're only soldiers. Life is very simple for us." He looked at his brother complacently. "How many people have we killed in the last two weeks, Kuper?"

"Probably more than I can count on the fingers of both hands," Kuper replied casually.

Rellan turned back to the underling. He slowly looked the man up and down, starting at his feet, and ending by staring insolently into his eyes.

The man began to sweat visibly. "I'll find someone else for you to talk to," he squeaked, and scurried away without looking back.

Before another hour had passed Kuper and Rellan found themselves ushered into a small but ornate reception room. The walls were covered with paintings, mostly depicting military actions. Kuper gazed at them admiringly until Lord Burtelen was announced. He entered the room almost immediately, looking harried and red in the face.

"What's this I hear about a message from Will Prentis?" he asked.

Kuper passed on the messages entrusted to him.

Lord Burtelen paused to absorb them. "Where is Will now? And where is the king?" he asked.

"We left Will some time ago, My Lord. We were forced to divert more than once because of the Rogandans, but he should have joined the king in Castel several days ago. We don't know any more than that."

"He asks me to bring an army to Castel at once. That's out of the question. I haven't been idle—I have a small army ready to march. Most of the men are camped this side of the Citadel. They're well led, and they've been training hard. But winter will be upon us before long. And—more significantly—the Rogandans have a much larger force waiting on the other side of the pass." He paused, narrowing his eyes. "How did you get through, for that matter?"

"A local guide showed us another way through the mountains."

The nobleman frowned. "It wouldn't be good at all for Erestor if word got out about an alternative route across the mountains."

"I don't think you need to be concerned, My Lord," Kuper replied. "The way we took was not an established path. Without detailed local knowledge I doubt that anyone would find it. And it's difficult to imagine a large party using it. The going was extremely challenging, and we attempted it only because our need was pressing. We almost lost our guide at one point."

Lord Burtelen nodded, apparently satisfied. "I can see that the two of you are unusually resourceful," he said. "For now, take some time to rest and refresh yourselves. I will meet with you again in the morning." He clapped his hands, and a retainer hurried in to do his bidding. He instructed the man to arrange food and accommodation for Kuper and Rellan, then dismissed them all.

. . .

THE TWO MEN found themselves ushered to a table laden with food—freshly roasted venison with a wide range of cooked vegetables, along with seafood accompanied by leafy salads. A pile of tasty-looking pastries lay ready to hand, and goblets filled to the brim with rich red wine sat beside the plates.

Both of them stared wide-eyed at the lavish spread for several minutes before daring to eat. Once they made a start, though, they attacked the food with energy. The servings were generous, but the plates were nevertheless carried away empty.

After the rich meal they were led to a room containing a bath filled with steaming water. After taking turns soaking in it, they dressed themselves in fresh clothes that had been laid out for them. They were finally shown to a bedroom that boasted a pair of comfortable beds.

The room also contained a pair of embroidered couches. They weren't yet ready to sleep, so each of them selected a couch of their own and stretched themselves out. Neither of the twins had ever experienced such luxury.

"I don't know how we're going to get Lord Burtelen's army past the Rogandans," Kuper said.

"We need to do a lot better than getting an army past them," Rellan replied. "We can't leave the Rogandans behind to attack us from the rear, and we can't leave Erestor undefended for them to pillage, either."

They talked into the night without resolving anything. Eventually they retired to their beds.

Kuper went to sleep surrounded by unaccustomed opulence, but he didn't sleep well. He lay on the bed restless and frustrated, unable to find a solution to their dilemma.

THEY DISCOVERED the next morning that Lord Burtelen was both a shrewd interrogator and a man of action. He questioned them closely for almost two hours. As his questions finally came to an end, Kuper realized that the nobleman had picked them clean of information.

"Well, I can see that your Will is an energetic and effective leader as well as a gifted strategist," said the lord. "We're going to need those qualities in the days to come. And I'm gratified to learn that the Lady Neave—Anneka as she's known to you—is still alive, albeit in greatly reduced circumstances. The so-called justice carried out against her husband was a mockery. When all of this is over we must see what can be done about her situation."

Kuper stole a glance at Rellan. His brother looked pale and uneasy.

"On a happier note," the nobleman continued, "Erestor and Arvenon—and indeed the entire civilized world—will be a better place without Pisander playing his poisonous games."

He sighed. "But we still need to deal with the Rogandans. It hasn't escaped me that you are more than usually capable, both of you. So I'm going to put you to work. You understand the Rogandans as well as anyone in Erestor. You know the terrain around the Citadel. And you're willing to take risks when necessary to get the job done. I need you to come up with a plan to deal with the Rogandan army camped outside Steffan's Citadel. Go there and assess the situation. To assist you, I will grant you limited authority over my soldiers at the Citadel. You will command twenty men.

"Take your time. Come back to me with a plan in two weeks."

As he spoke he wrote on a parchment, dripped hot wax onto it and stamped it with his seal. Handing them the document, he dismissed them.

Kuper walked from the audience chamber in a state of bewilderment. "How did that just happen?" he asked, holding up the document. Rellan simply shrugged, lost in his thoughts.

They rode out of Maranelle before another hour had passed. As their horses climbed the low hills surrounding the city, Kuper looked back, admiring the colorful pennants waving from the fair towers of the city. Dark clouds were gathering on the horizon, providing a striking contrast to the varied blues of the sea. Tiny fishing boats with white sails dotted the broad bay, sailing home on the tide ahead of the coming storm.

The refined tranquility of the many-hued scene presented a striking contrast to the deep greens and browns of the rugged forested mountains of his childhood. Something stirred inside him as he gazed upon it. For the first time in his life he wondered what it would be like to leave war and soldiering behind, and to settle down and raise a family. He glanced across at his brother. Was Rellan also harboring such thoughts? Had he truly been foolish enough to surrender his heart to a woman of noble birth?

They crested the ridge above the bay, and Maranelle disappeared from sight. He shook his head, as if to clear it. Lord Burtelen had just set them an impossible task, and granted them two short weeks to achieve it. He turned his face away from peaceful daydreams and set his mind instead to the harsh realities of the road that lay ahead.

"The Rogandans are still sending soldiers into the forest," said Scar. "We kill their scouts, and they send more."

Anneka frowned. "How close to our settlement have they come?" she asked.

"Not very close. Not yet. But it's looking like they will. We need to decide what to do."

She glanced around the clearing, her gaze resting on children and on groups of the old and frail huddling together against the rain and the cold. So even this sanctuary was going to be denied her. She hardened herself and presented them with a face empty of emotion. They needed her to be strong. "How long do we have before they show up in force?"

"Maybe a few days. Maybe less." Scar didn't meet her eyes. "Perhaps we can begin preparations, just in case we need to leave in a hurry."

She shook her head decisively. Delaying the inevitable was pointless. All of them knew what they needed to do. "The very old and the very young won't be able to hurry," she said. "They need to leave now. Today. We can't wait until an army of Rogandans is yapping at their heels. It will take them days to reach the refuge, especially in this weather." She glanced up at the sky, scowling at the dark clouds that blotted out the sun. The rain had been unrelenting over the last few days, and it was going to make their task much more difficult.

"The refuge isn't big enough to accommodate everyone," Scar said. "We never imagined we'd have so many to care for."

She detected a hint of desperation in his voice, and willed herself to remain calm. "The most needy will take the huts. The rest of us will just have to manage as best we can."

She glanced at the men sitting around her, all watching her intently. Every one of them trusted her. The weight of that burden had not crushed her, though, because she in turn had learned to rely on them. The community had survived only thanks to their resourcefulness and sacrifice.

She looked them in the eye, allowing them to see that she was not afraid. "Most of us won't be going to the refuge yet," she told them. "Not while the Rogandans are roaming freely in the forest. Only the weak and helpless will go. They will need a few people to guide and protect them, of course, but no more than absolutely necessary. The rest of us will somehow have to make sure the Rogandans don't go anywhere near the refuge."

She paused, assessing their mood.

"We also need to make sure they don't find a way into Erestor," she added.

Her final statement met with a mixed reaction, as she expected.

"Why should we risk our lives for Erestor?" Scar asked bluntly. "No one there has ever done us any favors."

"We're not doing it for the nobles," she replied, shaking her head. "We'll be doing it for the common people. We already know what the Rogandans will do to them if given the chance." She added some iron to her tone. "You can think whatever you like, but this topic is not up for discussion."

Some of them weren't happy about it, but she could see that they accepted it.

"I have a suggestion," said Yosef.

She didn't hesitate. "Let's hear it." Yosef rarely had much to say, but when he did speak he was always worth listening to.

"Give me half a dozen of our better archers," he said, "and I'll make sure the Rogandans don't find their way to the lake. Scar can take Hender and the rest and keep them away from the refuge. Between us we'll steer them into the valley. They could spend weeks wandering around down there without injuring anyone except themselves."

She glanced around the group. Several others were nodding, including Scar. "That's settled, then. Scar, you'll have most of the men. I'll go with Yosef. All of us can join the others at the refuge whenever it's safe to do so. There will be plenty to do when we get there."

She nodded to another of her veterans. "Wilton, I'm placing you in charge of the women and children. Choose four men to go with you. Take whatever's essential, and leave the rest behind. If we're lucky the Rogandans won't find this place and we can come back later. Don't build your hopes up, though."

ANNEKA STAYED BEHIND to see the women and children off. Scar and Hender and a dozen others followed soon after them. Yosef gathered his small group and left, too, promising to wait for her on the trail beside the fallen redwood.

Her people had followed her, believing for better times. Now she stood in the middle of an empty clearing, surrounded only by silence and abandoned dwellings. So much effort had been spent in establishing this place, in making it a home. Now the Rogandans would find it and put it to the torch. All that they had built together over years would be gone in minutes, consumed in angry red flames.

It was hard, so hard, to lay down everything she had lived for, and to walk away. And not for the first time in her life, either.

She stood unmoving in the stillness and closed her eyes. Only memories remained here now. She remembered the joy of the dispossessed when they saw they had come at last to a place of safety. She thought of the babies born, the loved ones laid to rest beneath the greensward in the little graveyard through the trees.

She remembered, too, dancing in the firelight, intense eyes upon her, burning into her soul. She had been so angry with him. *Don't you torment me with hope. Don't you dare!* She recalled the sleepless night that had followed. And her foolishness the next morning in putting his flowers in her hair and for a fleeting moment allowing herself to feel like a woman again.

She opened her eyes once more. He had left, and it was a good thing. She would never see him again, and that was a good thing, too. Foolish sentiment was a weakness she simply could not afford.

She turned her back on the clearing, mounted her horse, and rode away.

11

King Steffan sat outside the Castelan royal tent, enjoying the warmth of the late afternoon sun in the company of his father-in-law.

"There's a matter I've been wanting to discuss with you," said Steffan.

"Eisgold?"

"Yes. I don't understand why you persevere with him."

His father-in-law looked pained. "These situations are never simple, Steffan. No throne is entirely secure without the support of the nobles—you know that as well as I do. And Eisgold is very well connected. If it proves necessary to push him aside, I'll do it without hesitation. But it's not something I can afford to do lightly. It would unsettle the other nobles, and I need their unqualified support more than ever right now."

"I fully understand your difficulty. Nevertheless, I'm not comfortable leaving Eisgold in charge of so many of your men," Steffan said frankly. "After the debacle at Pinder's Flat, it isn't clear to me that he can be trusted."

"The man is certainly stubborn at times," Istel acknowledged.

"But there can be no question about his loyalty. And I have no doubt that he will follow orders from now on."

"Even if the orders come from Will?"

"Even then."

Steffan frowned. "What makes you so sure?"

Istel sighed. "I was ready to relieve him of command myself after Pinder's Flat, in spite of the complications. But when I went to speak with him, he was most apologetic. Profusely so. He assured me that he now viewed his own actions as unacceptable, and that in future I would see a complete change in his attitude toward Will."

"Why the change?"

"He told me he realized that defeating the Rogandans was more important than any differences between him and Will. He said he understands that only one person can command, and that my choice of commander will have his full support, no matter who it is."

"Do you think he's sincere?"

"I do. Humble is not a word that I would normally associate with Eisgold, but he certainly came across that way."

"I wouldn't call him humble, either. He was singing the praises of his own military prowess when we first attempted to break through the Rogandans blocking Deadman's Pass. We both know how that turned out. We only succeeded thanks to the siege engine, and he opposed that idea vigorously when it was first suggested."

"Yes, he's no military strategist, whatever he might think. But it is possible to lead soldiers well without being a military strategist—Rufe Sarjant has proven that. Eisgold is both capable and effective as a leader. Men are willing to follow him. And there's no suggestion of giving him broader authority. Will is the one with overall command. Eisgold will stand or fall purely on whether he's willing to follow Will's orders."

"Are you completely sure he won't try a repeat of his little game at Pinder's Flat?"

"Yes, I am," Istel replied.

"Very well. You know the man better than I do. Let me make it clear that I still have strong misgivings. Nevertheless, I'm willing to give him an opportunity to prove his sincerity. But I'll be watching him. At the first hint of dissension, we need to replace him. I fully understand the challenges you will face if you remove him, but we cannot go into battle uncertain about how one of our key leaders will behave. There's far too much at stake!"

"I agree completely. I'll be watching him, too. Very closely. He's insisted that his attitude to Will has changed. If he gives the slightest indication that he isn't following through on that, he'll have to go. I won't give him another chance. The other nobles will just have to live with it."

THE LATEST COUNCIL MEETING, hosted for senior leaders of the joint army, had just broken up, and King Steffan and Will found themselves leaving the tent together.

The session had been called to monitor preparation for the next stage of the conflict with the Rogandans. To all outward appearances the meeting had been remarkably smooth. Lord Eisgold certainly seemed to have undergone a complete change of attitude. He still had many differences of opinion with the other leaders, and especially with Will, but he now readily deferred to the commander. He used Will's title sparingly, but said it without any hint of sarcasm.

King Steffan turned to Will. "It would seem that your detractors have finally decided to see reason," he said.

"I trust that it is so, Sire," Will replied noncommittally.

The king directed a thoughtful glance toward him. "People do change, Will. Lord Eisgold says that he has, and I need you to give him an opportunity to demonstrate it. You can be assured that I will not stand idly by if he fails to deliver."

Will nodded his acknowledgment. He didn't know the reason behind the king's request, but he guessed that it probably had as much to do with politics as with second chances. It was obvious to Will that Lord Eisgold had strong support among the Castelan nobility, and it was unlikely that King Istel would find it easy to move the nobleman aside, quietly or otherwise.

For his own part, he wasn't quite sure what to make of Eisgold's sudden transformation. He hadn't forgotten the hatred on Eisgold's face at the meeting after the battle at Pinder's Flat. And yet the nobleman was betraying no hint of animosity now.

Will had seen enough to recognize Eisgold's leadership abilities as well as his broad influence. If he truly had undergone a change of heart, there was no doubt that he would be a useful asset to the allied army.

Had he truly changed, or had he simply decided to mask his hostility?

Time would tell. In the meantime, given King Steffan's direct request, Will had no option but to give Eisgold the chance to prove his sincerity.

Bottren spotted Will alone on a ridge not far from Hazelwood Ford. The commander sat astride his horse, reviewing soldiers on exercise. It was too good an opportunity to miss, and the Arvenian nobleman wasted no time in spurring his horse in Will's direction.

"Commander," he said, greeting Will with a nod.

"My Lord," Will replied, bobbing his head respectfully.

The ghost of a welcoming smile crossed Will's lips, causing Bottren's eyes to widen momentarily in surprise. Such a display was rare indeed for the grave young commander, and Bottren took it as a high compliment.

Bottren knew that Will trusted him. Of late he had even wondered if Will might also count him as a friend, in some sense at least. He had no idea how that could possibly work in practice, of course. Friendship simply wasn't possible between nobles and commoners.

He thrust such fancies from his mind to focus on more pressing problems. "What do you make of Eisgold's new mood of cooperation?" he asked.

Will shrugged. "By all appearances he has changed completely. I'm still not entirely sure about it, though," he said candidly. "Perhaps I'm overly skeptical."

"My response is similar," Bottren told him. "I would like to believe in the sincerity of his sudden turnaround. But I'm not fully convinced. Not yet."

He paused for a moment, studying Will carefully. "Let me be direct with you, Will," he said. "I know you have little stomach for intrigue. Internal dissension may well be dying down, and it's obvious that our main attention must be on our real enemy. But when it comes to the motivations and intentions of the Castelan nobles, you can't afford to leave it to guesswork. Not when our last battle so nearly ended in disaster."

Will nodded. "You are right, My Lord. I have come to realize that I need to prepare for internal battles as thoroughly as I prepare to fight the Rogandans. I admit I've been slow to recognize that, but it is very clear to me now."

Bottren raised his eyebrows in surprise. He hadn't expected Will to be so easily convinced. "So what are you planning to do about it?" he asked.

"I've already taken steps," Will replied.

This announcement surprised Bottren even more.

"I asked Nestor to keep his ears open," said Will, "and he's responded energetically. To say the least." A wry smile appeared on his face. "I had no idea how well suited he was to this kind of work."

"Nestor? He came with you from Arnost, didn't he?" asked Bottren. "What has he been doing? Has he learned anything useful?"

"He's woven an extensive spiderweb that's already trapping an impressive amount of information. He seems to have no difficulty finding informants who are sympathetic and willing to help—he has soldiers and even minor Castelan nobles working for him. You are welcome to examine what he's discovered if you're interested. You'd probably make much more sense of it than I can."

"I'll be most interested to look at whatever he's discovered. Has he learned anything that sheds light on the intentions of Eisgold or the other senior Castelan commanders?"

"No. Nothing definite. Perhaps there's nothing worth uncovering about Lord Eisgold anymore. If there is, he's been wise enough to keep his own counsel. Either way, the king has asked me to give Lord Eisgold an opportunity to demonstrate that he now supports my leadership. I'm sure I don't need to tell you that I intend to honor his request."

"I see," said Bottren. "The king's request does not require you to close your eyes, though. And there can be no harm in continuing to keep a watchful eye on King Istel's nobles.

"I must say I'm greatly encouraged to hear about Nestor's initiatives on your behalf. They're a wise precaution, even if they prove unnecessary. And I hope you realize that your information gathering won't be limited to Nestor—you can count on me as well. I will be your eyes and ears among the nobility. My position there gives me opportunity to hear and see things that Nestor's contacts could never be a party to."

"I am grateful to you, My Lord," said Will with a bow.

"You don't need to thank me," Bottren replied. "Both of us are only trying to save the two kingdoms."

"Our resources are extremely limited," said King Steffan. "We can only afford to undertake one campaign at a time. The focus of that campaign needs to be the relief of Arnost." The Arvenian king sat beside his father-in-law in a hastily erected building in the camp at Hazelwood Ford, accompanied by the leaders of the combined army.

"I sympathize with your desire to see your capital freed," said King Istel. "I'm sure I would feel the same way. But should we make that our first priority?"

"I believe we must. For practical reasons—if we don't relieve Arnost now, we run the risk of seeing it fall to the Rogandans. And there are symbolic reasons as well. Taking control of our capital will demonstrate that the Rogandans have lost the initiative."

King Istel nodded an acknowledgment. "I propose we hear all of the alternatives before we decide," he said, glancing across at his fellow sovereign. King Steffan paused before inclining his head reluctantly.

"What was the strategy you were advocating, Eisgold?" King Istel asked.

"Some of us have wondered, Your Majesties, if our goal should be to prevent the Rogandans from making further gains. Rather than taking new risks, we could strengthen what we have. That would give us a base we can use later, to take back what we have lost."

"What do you think, Will?" asked King Steffan.

"I believe, Your Majesty, that there is only one way to end this war, and that is to defeat our enemy. We cannot do that by capturing or holding locations," he replied. "We must draw the Rogandans into battle, on terms favorable only to us. It must be a decisive battle. We must inflict on them a defeat from which they cannot recover."

"But how can we do that?" King Istel asked. "They have so many more men."

"We must choose a battlefield that denies our enemies the benefit of their superior numbers."

"Does such a site exist?" asked Lord Bottren.

"We must search until we find one," Will replied. "If we fail to destroy the Rogandans, sooner or later they will wear us down."

King Istel turned to the nobles. "My Lords?"

"Our combined forces are nowhere near big enough to fight a pitched battle against the Rogandans," said Bottren. "Nevertheless, I believe that Will is right, provided we can somehow lure the Rogandans into a battle that is not of their own choosing."

"To have any hope of winning, conditions would need to favor our forces massively," said Eisgold. "And yet I can't help feeling that our commander is right," he conceded. "We must act decisively. Time is on their side, not ours."

King Istel turned to his ally. "Steffan?"

"Reluctant as I am to delay the relief of Arnost, I can appreciate the good sense of Will's reasoning. I am therefore willing to put my preference aside and agree to pursue Will's strategy," King Steffan replied. "But I would like to know when our anticipated reinforcements will arrive. Has there been any word from Erestor?"

"Not yet," Will replied. "I sent two of my men, Kuper and Rellan, to fetch the army being raised in Erestor. They are good men, but they have been gone longer than I expected and nothing has been heard from them. Lord Bottren has since sent others, but as yet there has not been time for them to reach Erestor and return."

"I will not give up hope of Erestor arriving in time," said King Steffan. "But in the meantime we must make our plans based on the forces we have available to us."

The conference eventually broke up having achieved general agreement on strategy, at least in principle. Detailed planning had not yet begun.

Will's point of view had prevailed, and the man who had previously been his most bitter opponent had openly agreed to put aside his own ideas and support him. Common sense suggested that he ought to have been elated, but he nevertheless left the meeting with a vague sense of unease. Lord Eisgold's new mood of cooperation troubled him for reasons he couldn't readily identify. He told himself that he was probably being unreasonable. Nevertheless, he intended to keep a close eye on the nobleman. Meanwhile, he comforted himself with the awareness that if there was anything sinister to uncover, Nestor would be working hard to expose it.

"I've just received a communication from Count Gordan," Steffan told his father-in-law. The two kings sat alone together in Istel's tent in the late afternoon. They were sipping wine, and enjoying a few moments of respite from the seemingly endless burden of their responsibilities.

"Anything of significance?" Istel asked.

"He relays a request from Essanda. She wishes to visit our encampment at Hazelwood Ford."

"What?" Istel exclaimed, rising from his chair. "This is no place for a girl! What is Gordan thinking?"

"So she's just a girl now, is she?" said Steffan, tilting his head and gazing up at Istel from under a raised eyebrow.

Istel looked at him testily. "You know what I mean! Seriously, Steffan. We have enough battles on our hands—let's not fight that one again."

"You needn't worry," Steffan replied, an ironic smile on his face. "Joining battle with you is not any kind of priority for me."

Istel gradually calmed down and resumed his seat. "Why would she want to come here?" he asked. "I don't understand it."

"She says she is missing her husband. And her father."

Istel looked at him and frowned. "I'm not going to ask you what you think of this foolishness. The look on your face makes it all too obvious."

Steffan made no attempt to hide his grin. "I can't deny that a visit from our 'girl' would make a welcome change for me. I don't doubt that it would lift your spirits, too," he said, raising his eyebrow again.

"But the roads are not safe!" Istel protested. "Do you want to lose your wife before she's even become your wife in more than just name?"

A flush of anger flared on Steffan's face.

"Wait!" Istel cried. "Don't be angry. She's told me nothing! Following your instructions, no doubt," he added with a grumble. "But I know Essanda—don't forget that I'm her father. And I'm not stupid."

He sighed. "You're a good man, Steffan, and I'm grateful that you choose to treat my daughter so well. I dare say I don't deserve you as my son-in-law."

Istel's comments raised issues that were best left for another occasion. Steffan decided to stay with the main point. "There's nothing unsafe about the roads provided she is accompanied by a proper escort," he observed calmly. "It isn't an especially long ride from Castel Citadel, and there are no Rogandans between your capital and Hazelwood Ford."

Istel sighed again. "Very well, then. Have it your own way. She is your wife, after all. But make sure that Gordan leaves nothing to chance."

Steffan set off for his own tent with a new spring in his step, already composing a suitable reply in his mind. A visit wasn't going to be practical for a while. Dealing with the Rogandans was his highest priority, and he could not afford any kind of distraction in the immediate future. He would request Gordan to arrange for her to arrive in one week's time.

"How is your mother, Commander?" Zornath asked, accosting Karevis with one of his irritating smiles.

Karevis frowned. The question caught him completely by surprise, and he was at a loss to know how to even begin to respond. "My mother?" he asked blankly.

"I am told that one of our soldiers met her. In Varacellan. The capital, you understand."

Karevis frowned again, more bemused than ever. Surely Zornath didn't think it was necessary to explain to him that Varacellan was the capital of Varas!

"I have been assured that she is a charming old woman. Very proud of her son, too. As she should be." Zornath flashed another smile at him.

Karevis said nothing, but a chill began to run down his spine as he pondered the possible implications of Rogandan soldiers tracking down his mother.

Zornath eyed him silently for a moment. "I have some very good news," he announced. "Even you will think it is good news. Even you!"

His teeth appeared once again in a grimace that was probably intended as a smile. "Oh, I know what you think, my dear Commander. The opinion of your dear liaison is not enough to sway you. Oh, no!" He wagged a finger at Karevis and smiled conspiratorially.

"King Agon is planning to shower the people of Varas with his special favor. He desires to show the world the great wisdom of cooperating with Rogand instead of resisting. Your people must pay their taxes without complaint, of course. But they will be treated well. Very well, indeed. This truly is good news, is it not?"

Karevis frowned once more. He had no doubt there would be a sting in the tail of this sudden excess of Rogandan bounty. He just wasn't clear about the specific direction it might take.

"You and your soldiers also have a special part to play, of course," Zornath continued mildly.

Here it comes, thought Karevis.

"Lord Drettroth requires very little from the army of Varas. Very little, indeed. He asks only that you take your stand beside your Rogandan allies, defying the enemies of Agon, our mutual king."

Zornath rose to his feet and drew himself to his full height. "You will fight at our side, and together we will crush the Arvenians!" he cried, his face alight and his fists pounding energetically down onto the table before him. Then he sat down once more, his eyes glowing.

"Never!" said Karevis fiercely, his face set hard like granite.

The mood of the Rogandan changed in an instant. Springing from his chair and planting both hands on the table, he thrust his face threateningly toward Karevis, a look of thunder on his brow.

"Do not imagine—even for an instant—my *dear* Commander, that you, or your pitiful little army, can hope to defy me in this."

Karevis drew back in disgust from the stream of spittle that punctuated Zornath's every word. The Rogandan simply leaned forward even further.

"Every one of your soldiers has left behind a sweetheart...a wife...a child. Perhaps even a *mother*." He fixed Karevis with a nasty smile. "I care nothing for them!" He snapped his fingers dismissively. "Nothing! Their safety depends *solely* on your cooperation. Your *enthusiastic* cooperation. Think carefully, Commander. Think very carefully, indeed."

The Rogandan again stood erect, looking down upon Karevis in disdain. "You are DISMISSED!" he roared.

Karevis remained in his seat and glared back at the Rogandan for as long as he dared. Then he rose to his feet and marched defiantly from the tent.

He was beaten, though, and he knew it. He thought of his frail and defenseless mother and began to tremble with suppressed rage. His stomach twisted mercilessly into knots inside of him.

It had always been obvious that foreign occupation would leave the ordinary citizens of Varas vulnerable, but he had stubbornly refused to dwell on that, telling himself he had enough troubles of his own to worry about. He could remain in denial no longer.

He knew that Zornath had about as much human feeling as a viper. He and his kind would not hesitate to trample the helpless women and children of Varas. They would do it eagerly, too, if offered half an opportunity.

Karevis and his entire army were caught in a trap, and the iron jaws were beginning to close tight.

What could he do? How could he find a way to halt this relentless slide into horror and despair?

Such questions had become all too familiar—they plagued him constantly throughout his waking hours. He'd found no answers before, and he could not see any way of escaping now.

12

"Why do you need to hide from the Rogandans, Thomas?"

Rubin's question caught Thomas off guard. He had promised himself he would tell Rubin and Elena the truth about his situation, and he intended to do so. But he hadn't been able to figure out how to broach the subject without bringing the stone into it.

"I was staying at a monastery in the mountains, and the Rogandans invaded it. I escaped in a boat, and they apparently decided they wouldn't simply let me go."

It was obvious to Thomas that Rubin was not entirely satisfied with his answer.

"Leave him alone, Father," Elena chided. "We all have our secrets."

Not for the first time, he wished he could see the expression on her face. But in the days he had stayed with them he'd never caught so much as a glimpse of it.

Later that afternoon Thomas squatted by the stream dressing a rabbit he had snared. Elena sat beside him scraping the skin from some vegetables she had picked from the small garden beside the cabin. She chatted away happily, telling him about a brightly colored bird she had seen recently.

Listening to her talk, he remembered her taciturn manner and strange tone of voice when he first met her.

"I like the sound of your voice," he said.

She must have been taken aback by his compliment, because the flow of words dried up immediately.

"Thank you," she eventually managed.

"When we first met, you sounded so gruff. And you hardly said a thing."

She didn't respond.

He hadn't been with them long before he began to suspect that her manner of speaking was forced. Then one day he had surprised her talking to her father without any trace of the rough tones he was used to hearing. She had dropped the pretense after that.

None of them ever talked about it. He knew that Elena and her father had intentionally hidden themselves from the world. So he simply assumed she'd tried to make her voice as unattractive as her appearance to frighten off strangers.

Her father's earlier question emboldened him to pose a question of his own. "Why are you and your father hiding in the forest?" he asked.

She lifted her head and seemed to study him for a while.

She finally responded. "People in our village misunderstood us—misunderstood me, that is. Some of them were very superstitious. I was accused of being a witch."

Thomas remembered his own reaction when he first caught sight of her. It wasn't difficult to imagine why the villagers had feared her. But her appearance truly was misleading. She might be unattractive, but there was nothing evil, or even frightening, about her.

"I'm sorry," he said, and meant it.

"Father decided that I would never be safe until we went somewhere far from other people."

"How did you come to be like...like you are?" he asked. His question was awkward and indelicate, and he instantly regretted asking it.

She didn't seem to mind at all. "I was born the way I am," she said without hesitation. "It didn't become a problem until I started to grow up, though."

"How old are you?"

She paused before answering. "Females dislike being asked that question. Has no one ever told you that?"

Her tone carried a hint of rebuke. He had no idea what to make of it. An obviously insensitive question hadn't bothered her, but what seemed to him a straightforward query had gotten a reaction. How could anyone understand women?

She answered him anyway. "I'm probably a year or two older than you."

That was a surprise. He had already guessed that she wasn't as old as he'd first thought. But he'd still imagined her to be quite a bit older than he was himself.

That night as he lay in bed, he found himself thinking about her deformities. Her hunched back could not be hidden, but why was it necessary to conceal her face? Did she have a hook nose with warts on it? Did she have a mustache? On multiple occasions now he'd caught brief glimpses of her chin and the lower part of her cheek. Angry red splotches were always visible on her skin. Could it be leprosy? He shuddered. There was no sign of the disease on her hands, though. And the splotches did not always seem to be in the same location—they moved around. He didn't think leprosy did that. Did she have some other kind of skin disease?

The more his imagination worked away at it, the more hideous the possibilities became. In the end he called a halt to his creativity. He knew that the reality couldn't possibly match the runaway imaginings of his overactive mind.

Why was it so fascinating to dwell on the gruesome? He enjoyed a good ghost story around the campfire as much as anyone. Maybe it was only truly frightening if the horror was real. In this case he concluded that however monstrous Elena's face might be, as a person she was quite agreeable. He felt very sorry for her.

A part of him still wanted to catch a glimpse of her face, dreadful though the sight might be. The fact that it was out of reach only made it all the more tantalizing.

He sighed. At least he had the decency to feel ashamed of himself for thinking about her in this way. He rolled over and tried to get to sleep.

ELENA'S FATHER gradually warmed up to Thomas, and it didn't take long before Rubin seemed to very much appreciate having a male companion on hand. Thomas showed him how to make more effective snares, and he quickly became good at it.

Rubin already had a basic ability to ride, so Thomas attempted to teach him more about horses. He soon discovered, though, that mastery of that kind didn't come naturally to the older man. With only a single horse between them, Thomas decided there was no pressing need to pass on such skills anyway.

Rubin in turn began to expand Thomas's skills in building and maintaining dwellings. Thomas was already capable of carrying out small projects, as he had demonstrated following his contentious decision to rebuild the damaged barn for his father. But he still had much to learn. He could not readily account for the discrepancy between his incompetence as a laborer when rebuilding the wall of Arnost and his growing abilities in helping Rubin. He eventually decided that the difference mostly had to do with the overseer. Rubin showed considerable patience when Thomas made mistakes and openly expressed appreciation for his persistence as well as his growing aptitude. Thomas tried hard not to dwell for too long on the contrast between Rubin and his own father.

On a couple of occasions when roof repairs were required, Rubin was very glad to hand the task over to someone younger and more nimble than himself. Spending an hour or two working with Rubin became a regular feature of most days for Thomas.

Elena increasingly became part of his daily routine, too. As the days passed they often found themselves spending time together. She proved to be surprisingly good company.

"You've never told me about your mother," he said on one occasion.

"She died when I was little—not even five years old. She died during childbirth, and the baby died, too. I barely remember her."

"That must have been hard," he said.

"It wasn't so bad," she replied. "My childhood was still a happy one. My father was kind, and he found ways of spending time with me, as well as working hard to provide for us. But what about your childhood?"

He told her about his parents, and his life in Arnost. He didn't think there was a great deal to tell, but her gentle questioning gradually uncovered all manner of detail he wouldn't otherwise have thought to offer. She expressed particular interest in his role as horse master for the king's army, and more than once he had to remind himself not to bask unduly in her obvious admiration.

Over time they developed a pattern of spending time together each afternoon, wandering along the stream or sitting in a meadow talking. He learned a great deal about her life, first growing up in a town and later in the forest. She told him about the gradual process of alienation that caused them to flee to their hideaway. Whispers and little slights had gradually turned into open insults, accusations and finally threats. Thomas became angry on her behalf when he began to understand the full extent of everything she had been forced to endure so unfairly.

He in his turn told her about their flight from Arnost. He never referred to Brother Vangellis by name—the capture of his friend still felt too raw.

He shared nothing at all about Elbruhe. It seemed to him that it would be insensitive to describe his experiences with a normal girl, even one who spoke a different language and was therefore difficult to communicate with. He felt sorry for Elena and had no desire to make her uncomfortable.

"Are you happy here, Thomas?" she asked him one afternoon.

He had no need to consider his answer. "Yes," he said without hesitation, "very happy."

"Do you miss being around other people?"

He thought for a moment. "No," he replied. "I need to hide, too, if I want to avoid the Rogandans. And it isn't as if I'm entirely alone here."

"No," she agreed. "You're not alone."

The more he thought about it, the more it became clear to him that there was nowhere else he would rather be. Arnost had felt like home when his mother had been there. But it had changed for him in so many ways. No other place he had visited in his travels felt even vaguely like home. The monastery was the closest, but he was only ever there as a visitor, and as far as he knew the monastery had been completely destroyed by the Rogandans.

The truth was that as the days went by he felt increasingly detached from the outside world and from his previous life. Elbruhe had gradually slipped away from his conscious mind. He still thought of Brother Vangellis many times every day, but he knew there was no point in worrying about the monk when there was nothing useful to be achieved by it.

Elena became his constant companion, and it gradually became difficult for Thomas to remember what life had been like without her.

In spite of the many challenges she faced, she was calm, considerate, and unfailingly cheerful. He could not imagine why people had ever thought she was a witch. It was true that she was having an effect on him, but not because of any kind of spell she'd cast. Her impact was in no way evil. The monk had taught Thomas to fend for himself, and had begun to instill in him a new appreciation for the value of human life. Elena was helping him to recognize the beauty in a harsh and uncertain world, and to cheerfully embrace the simple joys that life had to offer.

Elena had not been crushed by the burdens of her life; somehow she had managed to rise above them. Bitterness had not taken root in her, and he often marveled at that.

. . .

Thomas had now been staying at the cabin for several weeks. On a number of occasions he found himself on the brink of telling Elena about the stone. But each time, for reasons he didn't understand, he had decided against it.

When he slept he often dreamed of her. In his dreams she never wore a hood, but even so he never managed to see her features. They talked together, but never face to face. Whenever he looked directly at her, her face was turned away from him.

On one occasion he dreamed they were walking hand in hand by the stream. She chatted away merrily, and his heart felt light. After he woke, though, he felt uncomfortable in her presence for almost an entire day.

Finally, one night he dreamed that they were talking as usual, but this time he turned to her and found that she was facing him. The voice he heard was Elena's, but the face he saw belonged to Elbruhe. He woke with a start to find himself drenched with sweat.

She rarely appeared in his dreams after that, and even then only for brief moments.

"Thomas, could you help me, please?" Elena called.

He joined her at the garden beside the little cabin where she was extending the borders of the cultivated patch.

"What's the problem?"

"This rock is in the way. I'm not strong enough to move it."

"Let me do it," Thomas replied. He bent down and lifted it easily. "Where do you want it?"

"Anywhere out of the way," she replied. "You're so much stronger than me!" she added with a little laugh.

"It's nothing," said Thomas modestly. He dropped the rock beside a tree and shook the dirt from his hands. "Bye," he said with a smile, and headed off into the trees.

"Where are you going?" she called after him.

"To the stream. I want to do some fishing."

"May I join you?"

"Of course," he replied.

Thomas had made himself a couple of thin spears with very sharp points and serrated edges, and hardened the points in the fire. Spearing fish in a river was not straightforward, but he had become quite adept at it. He had acquired these skills, along with so many others, from Brother Vangellis. He collected the spears from a hollow log where he kept them, and they made their way to the stream.

He selected a shallow spot where he had caught trout on previous occasions. Spear in hand, he squatted down at the edge of the stream and began watching for any sign of fish. Elena sat down beside him and dangled her feet in the water.

After a while with no sign of action, she began humming quietly, swishing her feet back and forth in time to the tune.

"Hey, stop it—you'll scare the fish away!" said Thomas.

"What fish?" she asked in a dreamy voice. "I can't see any."

He leaned forward and scooped a handful of cold water over her.

She jumped to her feet with a little shriek. Quickly positioning herself behind him, she gave him a small shove. Squatting as he was on the balls of his feet, he tumbled forward into the stream with a loud splash. He lurched to his feet with water pouring off him, and sprang forward to grab her by the arm. She danced back out of reach, squealing with delighted terror. Once safe, she stood well back from the stream with her hands on her hips, and regarded his sodden state with a merry laugh.

"You'll pay for this!" he promised, prompting a fresh burst of laughter in response.

She tried to keep her distance from him as they headed back to the cabin. As they approached it, though, he sidled up beside her and flung his arm around her waist, managing to drench her in the process. She squealed again, trying to pull away, but he had too tight a grip. They arrived with him growling like a wild animal and her giggling uncontrollably.

Rubin stood waiting for them, and he watched their approach with a guarded look on his face. Seeing his expression, Thomas began to wonder whether he approved. Feeling suddenly awkward, he let her go, and went inside to dry off in front of the fire.

When he came outside again, neither one of them was anywhere to be seen. They didn't appear until the afternoon was spent. Rubin looked serious, and Elena was silent. Thomas didn't know what to say, so he remained mute, feeling very uncomfortable. Their meal together was uncharacteristically subdued. All of them settled down to sleep with scarcely a word being said.

The next day Thomas briefly found himself alone with Elena. "Is your father unhappy with us?" he asked casually.

"It isn't my father," she replied. He had become accustomed to the melodic tone of her voice. Today she sounded surprisingly brusque. "I would be glad if we could avoid being familiar in future."

Her reply shocked him speechless. Eventually he found his voice. "I thought you were having fun," he protested.

"I can see that I was unintentionally leading you in an unhelpful direction, and I apologize for that," she replied, her tone distant. And with that she departed, leaving him gaping after her.

It was obvious that her father had a great deal to do with her change of heart. Thomas still felt hurt by her sudden aloofness toward him, though. The old Thomas might have tried to think up a suitably cutting retort. But he had no desire to be angry with her. He just felt miserable.

He spent the rest of the day off by himself, trying to make sense of Elena's unexpected rebuff. Females could be so unpredictable. Elbruhe's mood could change like the wind, but Elena had never been like that. She had always come across as steady and dependable. And thoughtful and kind, too. What had he done? How had he succeeded in changing her so completely?

She must have decided, no doubt with plenty of help from her father, that he wasn't good for her. No other explanation made sense to him. He tried to see it from her point of view. She'd enjoyed a simple life here with her father before he intruded on them. His arrival had just been a complication.

He'd been a burden to plenty of other people, too. He wouldn't like to hear what his father might have to say on this topic. He'd done nothing useful for Will since they left Arnost—he'd just been a liability. Well, he had taught Brother Vangellis to ride. But that was about the extent of it. And he hadn't done any favors for the monk, either, especially considering what eventually happened to him.

Elena had accepted him at first because she thought he'd healed her father. But now she was finally seeing him as he was. What did he have to recommend him, after all? When he examined himself frankly, he couldn't come up with much that was worth boasting of. The more he thought about it, the more painfully obvious it seemed.

He hadn't even been direct with them. He'd known from the beginning that staying here exposed Elena and her father to major risks, but he had never told them. When he was honest with himself, he knew he'd only been able to enjoy the present so much because he'd pretended the future didn't exist. His life here wasn't sustainable. He couldn't keep going on like he had been.

When dusk came, he found himself very reluctant to return to the cabin. In the end the cold and hunger drove him back. Rubin looked up at him when he came in, but Thomas avoided eye contact. Rubin made a few comments, behaving as though everything was normal, but Thomas couldn't manage more than one word answers and grunts. Elena said not a word.

The next day was little different, and Thomas became increasingly uncomfortable. Now that he felt so ill at ease in Elena's presence, he began to realize how much he'd come to take her company for granted. Maybe she resented that as well.

By the time the afternoon was well advanced, his need to be alone had become pressing. He saddled his horse and stuffed a few things into his saddlebags. The horse nickered and pushed at him with its nose. It was pleased to see him; he knew he'd been neglecting it for far too long.

As he mounted, it occurred to him that he could simply go and not come back. He could see no sign of either Rubin or Elena, and he knew it would be very odd to leave without saying goodbye. But maybe it was better that way, for all of them. It was clear that he wasn't wanted here anymore.

He rode away slowly, a tight knot in his stomach. Several times he looked back over his shoulder, hoping against hope that one of the others would appear and stop him. But no one came.

He departed more downcast than he could ever remember feeling. His life had become a succession of partings, and for reasons he didn't entirely grasp this one felt like the most painful of all. He wasn't sure how he was going to face being alone again. But there didn't seem to be any other option.

He followed the path beside the stream. He had no plan and no idea where to go. Leaving was the last thing he wanted, but he knew he had to put distance between himself and Elena. He had stayed with Brother Vangellis because he needed him, and it had ended very badly for the monk. He told himself he couldn't afford to do the same to Elena and her father.

All of that was true. But there was another reason why he had to separate himself from them now. He had to leave because he had overstayed his welcome, and they wanted him gone. He couldn't dwell on that, though. It was too distressing. At that moment he felt numb, and he needed to stay that way.

He'd been gone for about an hour when he heard faint voices, not too far away. Immediately wary, he dismounted and tied up his horse. Then he crept forward until he noticed the flicker of a fire through the trees. The smells indicated that a meal was being prepared. At any other time it would have made him feel hungry, but he couldn't think of his stomach when it was obvious he was listening to the harsh voices of foreigners. He remained still, watching intently, until he was able to confirm beyond doubt that the men around the campfire were Rogandan soldiers. Even this remote corner of Arvenon was not safe from their endless probing and pillaging. Before long they would discover Elena! They only had to follow the stream. What would they do to her? They would surely kill her on sight if they thought she was a witch.

He slunk away in a panic, his heart racing as he hurried back to his horse. Casting caution aside, he urged the horse at breakneck pace back the way he had come, ignoring the branches that whipped across his face as he galloped along the path.

The minute he reached the cabin, he leaped from the horse's back and ran inside. It was empty. He left the cabin and looked around frantically. Elena was nowhere in sight. Her father wasn't anywhere to be seen either. He searched near the little garden, but he found no sign of them there, either. He tried to calm himself to think. Where could she be?

Then a memory came to his mind, and he thought he might know. Not far downstream was a quiet meadow, quite near to the water. She loved to lie there among the wildflowers, watching the branches of the trees waving overhead.

He rode there with his heart thumping in his chest. She had to be there.

When he reached the spot he launched himself from the saddle and ran into the meadow. There before him was Elena, sitting quietly among the flowers. She turned to him.

"The Rogandans are here! Only an hour away—down the stream." His words tumbled out. "It's me they're looking for. I can't explain now, but you need to go. At once! You don't have a moment to lose. Take your father and find somewhere safe to hide."

She just sat there, her face invisible as ever. "You've decided to leave us, haven't you?" she said calmly.

"Yes. You'll never be safe while I'm with you."

"That's not why you're leaving, though, is it?"

"What does it matter? You need to hide!"

"I have to know the reason."

He frowned. This wasn't going the way he needed it to. How could he make her see the urgency?

"I know I'm not wanted anymore. But that's not the point!"

"Why do you care if the Rogandans find us?" she asked.

He couldn't believe what she was saying. "Why do I care? What on earth are you talking about?"

"Why do you care?" she insisted.

"Why? Because you...because you're more important to me than... than anything!" There. He had said it.

"But I'm deformed."

"What?! What difference does that make?"

"Young men don't care about girls who are deformed."

"Who told you that?!"

"Father told me."

"Well, he's wrong! You can't help being deformed. And it's not the way I think about you, anyway. Your looks don't matter to me. That's just the outside of you. It isn't who you are." He realized as he said it that it was true. He truly didn't care that she was deformed. And she *was* more important to him than anything in the world.

"This is all completely crazy! I have to go. They mustn't capture you. I'd die if anything happened to you! I need to lead them away from here. And you need to hide." He glared at her in frustration. How could he make her understand?

"You really do care, don't you!" she said in wonder.

"Arghhh! What will it take to convince you that you need to go?"

"We'll go," she said with sudden decision. "But there's something you need to know first." She left him and ran to the stream. He looked on bewildered as she stood in the stream with her back to him and her head bowed, water splashing around her. Then she did a little jig and bounced up and down once or twice, shrugging her shoulders.

Finally she faced him. He looked at her stupidly, blinking in bafflement. Her hunched back had disappeared, and her deformed shoulder was completely normal. An oddly shaped bundle lay beside her on the ground, and he realized he was looking at what had been her hump.

As he stared at her, perplexed, she threw back her hood, and for the first time he saw her face. His jaw dropped. He had always imagined that her face was monstrous, but nothing had prepared him for the truth. He stood gaping at her in astonishment.

She wasn't ugly. She was beautiful—beautiful beyond words. Her loveliness took his breath away. Completely confounded, he could find nothing to say.

Blushing faintly, she gazed at him, her face shining. Small drops of faint red trickled down her chin, and he belatedly realized that the splotches on her skin had been stains, probably from some kind of berry. It was all part of the disguise, no doubt intended to make her appear diseased. She had washed the berry stains off in the stream.

He stood there dumbfounded, rooted to the ground.

She came to him shyly, and looked up at him. After a moment's hesitation she took his hands in hers. "I'm sorry I couldn't tell you the truth, Thomas. I've been in disguise for so long it's hard to imagine myself any other way. It was Father's idea. Some people couldn't cope with how I looked—not like you see me now, anyway. He wanted to frighten everyone away so I would be safe. But I don't want to conceal myself anymore. Not from you. I want you to see me as I really am."

Thomas didn't answer. He was still struggling to breathe.

"I did hear what you were saying," she told him seriously. "And we will hide from the Rogandans." She looked at him plaintively. "Do you really need to go?"

He nodded. Reluctantly, but firmly. It had to be done. The Rogandans would find her otherwise.

"I couldn't let you leave without knowing the truth," she continued. "Once I knew for sure that you really do care for me, that is." She gazed up into his eyes. "I've come to care for you, too, Thomas. Very much." Another blush appeared, a delicate shade of pink that spread delightfully across her perfect cheeks. It made her even more beautiful, if that was possible.

"Will you come back for me?" she asked.

The anxious look on her face melted his heart, and helped him recover his voice at last. "I will return—I promise!" he stammered. "As soon as it's safe. Nothing will keep me away."

She walked him to his horse. He turned to her, unable to resist gazing upon her one more time. He wished he could stand there forever, drinking in the sight of her.

She surprised him by stretching up on tiptoes and leaving a soft kiss tingling on his cheek. He felt himself blush a furious red, which made her grin. He finally mounted his horse, but then sat there without moving.

"Weren't you in a big hurry?" she teased.

Another blush flooded his face as the reality of their peril broke through his daze. He'd been acting like a half-wit. He urged his horse forward. "Hide quickly!" he called to Elena. "I'll come back. As soon as I can."

The path beside the stream bent around, and he caught a final glimpse of her waving to him. Then she was gone.

Completely stunned by Elena's revelations, he followed the path without a conscious thought about where he was going. The image of her face after she had thrown back her hood was fixed in his mind, and he wanted to keep it there forever.

What an incredible transformation! He tried to recall his crazy imaginings about how monstrously ugly she must be. All along, her true appearance had been breathtaking, beyond anything he could possibly have dreamed up.

He had supposed that people called her a witch because she was ugly. But he saw now that they had been reacting to her astonishing beauty. *How can she look like that? It can't be natural.* It must have been nothing more than envy for many of them. And yet she had emerged unspoiled. He had never heard her speak a word of hatred or even anger toward the people who persecuted her.

Most amazing of all, though, she cared about him. She hadn't been impatient for him to go—she wanted him to stay.

It wrenched his heart to leave. But he knew he had to do it. It was up to him to draw the Rogandans away. He knew, too, that he had every reason to be afraid. He nevertheless rode away feeling stronger and more self-assured than he had ever felt in his life.

13

Driving rain chased the twins most of the way to Steffan's Citadel. They were long since soaked to the skin by the time they arrived. With too many of their fourteen days already behind them, they presented their credentials to the commander of the citadel and made their way immediately to the battlements, accompanied by one of his men. They gazed out over the plain that lay below the pass. A river ran through the meadows, and the ground on either side of it was covered with tents, campfires, clusters of horses and even a couple of small buildings. The river had begun to rise in the rain, and the Rogandans were busy moving tents further away from its banks.

"What have the Rogandans been doing?" Rellan asked.

"Very little," the soldier replied.

Kuper frowned. "Why are they here, then?"

The man shrugged. "They're not strong enough to take the Citadel. And we're not strong enough to drive them off. Maybe they just want to fence us in. Make sure we don't go anywhere."

"Until enough of them arrive to tilt the balance?" Rellan suggested.

The soldier shrugged again. "Their numbers have certainly

grown," he said. "I heard the commander say that every Rogandan soldier in western Arvenon is down there now." He waved his hand across the sea of tents.

"There is one thing they do," he added. "Every day, before dusk. They drag a few villagers up the slope toward the Citadel. Over there." He pointed to a level piece of ground beside the road that wound its way up to the gates of the fortress. "They slaughter them in front of anyone who's willing to watch."

"Can't you do anything to stop them?"

He shook his head. "They stay just out of bow shot range. We could go out and fight them, I suppose. They'd love to drag us away from the protection of these walls," he said, patting the thick stone of the battlements.

He spat, disgust evident on his face. "They're rabid animals that need to be put down. We just don't have an effective way of doing it."

Kuper left the walls none the wiser about a way of dealing with the Rogandans. The commander arranged dry clothes for them and directed them to a mess where they were served a simple meal.

As they ate, Kuper voiced something that had been on his mind for the last couple of days. "I don't understand why Lord Burtelen is so different from the other nobles," he said. "To start with, he's very impressed with Will. Then he gives us twenty men. Why? Apparently it's just because we're resourceful."

Rellan shrugged. "Lord Burtelen is like the king. If you're good at something, it doesn't seem to bother him if you're a commoner."

"You're right," Kuper replied. "He might not care about us being commoners, but I wish he'd given us a task we could succeed at. He's expecting us to remove an entire army of Rogandans. How are we going to do that? I don't have any clever ideas."

Rellan shrugged again.

With no solution in plain view, they decided to sleep on it.

As they prepared to rest, Kuper turned to his brother. "What's eating you, Rellan? You've barely said a word since we left Maranelle."

With no reply forthcoming, Kuper decided it was time to be more direct. "It's Anneka, isn't it? Or Lady Neave, or whatever her name is."

Rellan just looked back at him with haunted eyes. Knowing his brother well, Kuper waited patiently, saying nothing.

Eventually Rellan found his voice. "When we were in the forest I began to think something might be possible between us," he said. "Even when Yosef told us where she'd come from, I didn't think it needed to make a difference."

He paused for a long time, and Kuper waited him out.

"I was only fooling myself. Lord Burtelen made that clear. She's a noblewoman, and she belongs with her own kind. Once this war is over, the king will put her situation to rights, and that will be an end to it." He fell silent.

Kuper sighed. "I thought it might work out for you at first, too," he said. "I don't think I've ever seen you so alive. But I didn't know about her background then. It changes everything. What you're saying is right—people like that don't end up with the likes of us."

THE NEW DAY brought them no insights into an effective way of dealing with the Rogandans. The commander of the citadel arranged for them to meet with the twenty soldiers assigned to them, then they joined him in conference. They were still together when another soldier brought in a report.

"A large band of Rogandans has moved into the forest, Commander," he said.

"What do you think they're doing?" the commander asked.

"Some of the men think they're probably trying to find a way around the Citadel," he replied.

Kuper shot a glance at Rellan. The look on his face reflected the alarm he felt himself.

The brothers excused themselves as soon as they could reasonably do so, and found a quiet place to talk.

"Do you think there's any way they could discover the path around the lake?" Kuper asked.

“It doesn’t seem likely,” Rellan replied. “If they captured Yosef, though, or someone else who knows the way, they could force it out of them.”

“We have to stop that happening,” Kuper said. “I wonder if Anneka and her people can prevent them from getting to the lake.”

Rellan shook his head. “She doesn’t have enough people to pick a fight with a large band of Rogandans.”

“We need to find out what’s happening.”

“I agree. We could take some soldiers with us. Enough to deal with the band of Rogandans.”

“No.” Kuper shook his head. “The alternative route wouldn’t stay a secret for more than a day if we did that. It needs to be one of us.” He looked his brother in the eye. “It needs to be you.”

“If you think I want to see Anneka again, you’re wrong.”

Kuper could clearly see the conflict on his brother’s face. Rellan wanted to stay away, and he wanted to see her, probably in equal measure. Kuper decided to let his brother come to his own conclusion.

After a long pause, Rellan looked up, his face showing no emotion. “I’ll go,” he said. “This isn’t about Anneka. It’s about preventing the Rogandans from getting into Erestor.”

Kuper nodded. “In that case,” he said, “you might as well leave immediately. I’ll brief the commander.”

Rellan left to gather his things. “Be careful,” Kuper called after him.

RELLAN HAD the lake in sight when the light failed. As the sun set, the rain started again in earnest, and he spent a miserable night huddled under some trees. He tried lighting a fire, but the wood was too wet, and he eventually gave up.

Dawn came without any let up in the downpour. He set off early and soon arrived at the lake. Water was pouring into it from a number of swollen rivers and streams, and the level had risen noticeably in the few days since they left. He set off around the lake, riding as long as it was safe to do so. Once the ground became less firm he dismounted and led his horse on foot.

Yosef's prediction was right. With several days of heavy rain, the slope had become unstable, and forward movement was extremely treacherous. It was very slow going, and he lost his footing more than once. On one occasion the ground broke away beneath him, and he avoided tumbling down the slope to the lake only by hanging on grimly to the reins of his horse. The animal somehow managed to hold its ground and support him as he slipped and slithered his way back up the slope. By the time he finally reached the horse, he was completely covered with mud.

The afternoon was almost spent by the time he reached more solid ground. He found a stream and cleaned off the mud as best he could, then searched out a vaguely sheltered location to spend the night. The rain continued fitfully, and he spent the night soaking wet and shivering. When a stiff breeze sprang up, it chilled him to the bone.

When the new day came, he set off once again, sodden and miserable.

ANNEKA STOOD with Yosef under a large overhanging tree. The tree provided some shelter from the rain, but it made little difference since they were wet already. The other men had taken up positions nearby, and everyone had settled down to wait. For all they knew their waiting had no purpose. The Rogandans might never come there.

Since he had the larger group, Scar had agreed to send out a couple of scouts. They would keep him informed about the movements of the Rogandans. The scouts would also seek out Yosef's party from time to time. There should be some warning at least before any of the enemy came their way.

By the time a couple of hours had passed, Anneka was already bored. She suspected that this task would become very tiresome very quickly. Then Yosef drew her attention to one of the other men. He was vigorously waving his arms. They waved back, and he pointed behind them toward the lake. They turned to see a horse and rider heading toward them, coming from the direction of Erestor.

Yosef put an arrow to the string of his bow and waited. As the rider drew near he turned to Anneka. "The rider reminds me of someone. But he doesn't look quite right." After a couple more minutes he laughed. "Of course," he said. "It's Rellan! But he's missing his sling."

Anneka's heart skipped a beat. What was he doing here? Then she took a firm grip on her emotions and let her mind take over. She was very good at it. She'd had years of practice.

When Rellan drew close, Yosef stepped out from under the tree and hailed him. Rellan's immediate response was to reach for his bow, then he recognized Yosef, and called back cheerfully. He dismounted and approached Yosef, greeting him warmly.

Then he noticed Anneka. Glancing into her eyes for a moment, he nodded and said, "Hello," before snatching away his gaze and turning his attention back to Yosef.

"You look like you've been bathing in mud," Yosef told him.

As the two of them exchanged banter, Anneka stared at him in surprise. She'd been bracing herself for a barrage of cheeky flirtations. Instead, he seemed strangely reserved.

She waited for a pause in the conversation. "What brings you back, Rellan?" she asked, keeping her tone level.

Some kind of emotion flashed across his face as he turned to her, then he seemed impassive again. "My brother and I were at the Citadel," he said. "Lord Burtelen sent us there. We learned that the Rogandans had sent a force into the forest, and we were concerned that they might be trying to find a back door into Erestor. I've come to assess the situation." He hesitated. "We also thought your community might be affected." His voice trailed off.

"Nice of you to think of us," she said, a touch of sarcasm in her tone.

Once again an emotion flickered briefly across his face, followed by a faint flush.

Why did I do that?! He hadn't even been trying to annoy her. Well, not this time, anyway. She didn't understand her own reactions at times.

Yosef broke in, clearly trying to steer the conversation somewhere safe. "We're aware of the Rogandans, Rellan. Anneka wanted to prevent them finding the other route into Erestor. That's why we're here."

"Just the two of you?"

"No," Yosef replied with a laugh. Anneka remained silent, not trusting herself to avoid another sarcastic retort.

At that moment Yosef's other men began appearing, apparently unwilling to miss out on whatever might be happening. They greeted Rellan warmly. Seeing him with Anneka, a couple of them gave him a wink.

Anneka broke in on their chatter. "Rellan is just here to find out what the Rogandans are up to. He'll be leaving shortly." She turned to him. "Scar has a couple of scouts out there. Keep an eye open for them, and give them our greetings if you see them."

Her intention had been to bring the conversation to an end, but she hadn't reckoned on her men.

"Do you know what the Rogandans are planning?"

"Have you heard what the king is going to do?"

"Has this rain flooded the Rogandans out yet? I hear they're camped in the meadow below the Citadel."

"Is anyone in Erestor gathering an army to fight them?"

"Wait! Be quiet, all of you!" It was Yosef who cut them off.

They fell silent, looking at him.

"You've just reminded me of something," he said. "Something that might be important. My great uncle—he died in his nineties—told me about a disaster that happened when he was a boy. There was an unusual amount of rain that year, and it triggered a landslide into the lake. A huge amount of water overflowed into the river and swept away everything along both banks of the river. The guards on the

Citadel walls saw the whole thing happen before their eyes. Apparently people talked about it for years."

He turned to Rellan. "You've just been there. Could we trigger a landslide?"

"The slopes are very unstable," Rellan replied. "I nearly didn't make it here. But I'm not sure how we could cause a landslide. Especially without ending up in the lake ourselves."

One of the other men spoke up. "It should just be a matter of rolling something down the hill. We used to do it as children where I grew up. One time we managed to create a landslide big enough to block the entire river for hours. Enough water built up that it caused flooding downstream when our little dam burst. We were in big trouble when the adults found out that we caused it."

Rellan raised his eyebrows. "Sounds like it's worth an attempt."

"Let's go do it, then!"

The men would have rushed off to the lake in a group if Anneka hadn't broken in. "Stop! We're not all going to try it. Apart from the fact that it's too risky, it's unnecessary." She pointed to the last speaker. "Jon, you can come with Yosef and me. And him." She jerked her thumb at Rellan. "The rest of you get back to your places."

They grumbled but followed her orders. It was quite clear to Anneka that if they could arrange it, every one of them would choose vantage points that allowed them to witness the action.

"We'll split into pairs," she instructed. "Yosef, you're with me. Get your horses. We'll meet back here."

She fetched her horse and made her way back to the meeting point. The others hadn't arrived yet, and she found herself alone with Rellan. She busied herself with her saddle.

"Are you angry with me?" he asked.

"Angry with you?" she said. "Why would I be angry with you?"

He shrugged. "You're right. There's no reason for Lady Neave to even notice someone like me."

His reply took her aback. So that's why he was so withdrawn. Well, she could soon set him straight on that.

"There is no Lady Neave. She ceased to exist seven years ago. I'm Anneka. That's all."

She could see he wasn't convinced.

"The king will make it right," he said. "Lord Burtelen is planning to speak to him about it."

"It isn't up to them," she insisted. "That life is over. I don't want it back!"

He said nothing. He just gazed at her. He continued for long enough that she ceased feeling embarrassed and began to feel irritated. What did he think he was doing? And where were the others? Why were they taking so long?

"What are you expecting from me?" she asked him testily.

"I want to dance with you again in the moonlight," he said with a sudden grin, briefly exposing his former self. Then he subsided, his new restraint replacing the old brashness. She decided reluctantly that she preferred the brashness.

"I'm not expecting anything from you," he said. He looked into her eyes. "What about you? What are you expecting from life?"

She didn't bother to respond. The truth was that she expected nothing from life. Not for herself. Nothing at all.

"What about joy?" he persisted. "Do you have room for that?"

His question unsettled her. She thought she saw compassion in his eyes, and she wasn't sure she could cope with that. She set her face. "Don't talk to me about joy," she said stiffly. "I buried it along with my two-year old son."

He looked at her strangely. "Can anyone be truly alive without joy?" he asked. He paused, studying her silently. He spoke again, slowly, apparently trying to find the right words. "You don't have hope, either, do you?"

Hope? she thought dully. *I buried that, too.* Maybe her world lacked color, but she'd trained herself not to think about it. Until he came along, brim full of life and constantly poking and prodding at her.

He smiled sadly. "I wanted to help you find it again. I believed I could do it—that we could do it together. But I was wrong. I'm sorry." He bowed his head, as though he couldn't look at her.

She opened her mouth to speak, then closed it again. She wasn't sure whether to yell at him or to burst into tears. How did he manage to unsettle her so?

She did the only thing she knew how, and pushed her feelings down, deep, where they couldn't distress her.

The arrival of Yosef and Jon saved her further awkwardness. She wondered darkly if they had deliberately delayed their return to give Rellan time with her. They all mounted, and set off for the lake without further comment.

When they arrived and dismounted, Rellan produced a very long coil of rope that he had brought with him, and threw it over his shoulder. Then they left their horses and walked beside the lake, trying to locate a suitable spot.

"A steep slope might work the best," said Jon. "Somewhere with a lot of loose rocks."

"There's a section like that further along the shore," Yosef said, and set off walking carefully.

They reached the location without incident. Yosef pointed. "That's where I slid halfway down the slope," he said.

"And over there is where I slid down yesterday," Rellan added, also pointing.

"It's extremely dangerous," said Yosef. "We'll need to be careful."

Jon found a rock that was a suitable size for him to handle. He hefted it and threw it as far down the slope as he could manage. It didn't roll at all, immediately sinking into the soft earth instead. The soil around it slid down a short distance, but then stopped.

Jon was clearly disappointed. "This isn't going to be easy," he said.

Yosef headed down the slope toward another rock, larger than the one Jon had thrown. "Give me a hand, Jon," he called. Jon joined him, and together they lifted the rock. As they did so, the ground beneath them slowly began to move.

"Get out of there!" Anneka shouted.

They began scrambling up again, but the soil fell away faster than they could climb.

The soil was moving downhill slowly enough that they didn't

seem far out of reach. Anneka ran toward them, hoping to grab one of their hands. Then the ground began to slide beneath her as well. She screamed involuntarily.

She looked up to see Rellan running away from them, up the slope. Even at this moment of crisis, a detached part of her mind registered surprise and disappointment at his cowardice. Then he reappeared, trailing rope behind him. He must have found something to secure the rope to. He quickly tied a loop with the other end and slipped it over his shoulders and under his arms. Then he leaped down the slope in her direction.

She began sliding more quickly and screamed again. She looked up to see Rellan skidding down rapidly toward her.

"Grab my legs!" he cried.

She reached out and grasped hold of his legs. The rope pulled tight, and he stopped sliding abruptly, almost shaking loose her grip. She slipped down further until her muddy hands were barely clasping his ankles.

Slowly he began to bend his knees, pulling her up with him. Then he reached down with one hand and grabbed her arm. He clenched her so tightly that she cried out in pain. But he did not loosen his grip. He continued to pull her toward him until she was close enough to wrap her arms around him. He released her arm then, and pulled her in close.

The two of them looked down. The entire slope was flowing away beneath them. Yosef and Jon were nowhere to be seen. A wave created by the landslide traveled slowly across the lake. Eventually it reached the other side and swept up the opposite bank. The ground on the other side in turn fell away into the lake, creating an even bigger wave that slowly but purposefully moved back in their direction. When it hit, it rushed up the slope toward them. She watched in silent horror as it reached their feet, threatening to suck them down into the lake. She clung to Rellan more tightly than ever. His arms enfolded her unwaveringly.

Then the wave was gone. The water in the lake slowly began to ebb away. The top section of the natural dam must have collapsed, because the water level continued to fall until the lake had been half emptied.

As the water receded, Rellan began climbing slowly upward, supported by the rope. Anneka was dragged along with him. Realizing that he must be limited to the full use of only one arm, she began trying to cooperate, scrabbling at the slope with her legs while still clinging fiercely to him with her arms.

Eventually they reached the top, both of them falling down prostrate in utter exhaustion. She clung to him still, and he drew her head gently in to his shoulder.

The enormity of what had happened gradually overwhelmed her, and she began to shake uncontrollably. For so long she had kept her feelings firmly in check. Now the barrier that held them at bay was more fragile than ever, and her emotions welled up overpoweringly. Wrapped securely in Rellan's strong arms, her face buried in his chest, she finally yielded.

She began to weep, quietly at first, then with increasing abandon. She wept for Yosef and Jon. She wept for the loss of their home in the forest. She wept for the pain and suffering in the world, and for the evil and injustice that had made her sanctuary necessary. Finally, a reservoir of tears was released that had never been breached, and she wept long and bitterly for her lost husband and her infant son. She did not weep because she chose to; she wept because her grief could no longer be contained.

In time she became silent. Pain and loss still surrounded her, but somehow a tiny deposit of peace, unexpected and unlooked for, had lodged itself deep within her being.

Eventually they got to their feet. She placed her hand in his, and their fingers intertwined. Then they carefully began to retrace their steps back across the ruined slope.

KUPER LEANED on the battlements and looked down over the meadow. The scene was deceptively tranquil. The Rogandan soldiers were responding to a brief break in the incessant rain and had emerged from their tents. They appeared to be enjoying a midday meal.

Kuper wondered where his brother was at that moment. He tried to imagine his reunion with Anneka.

A voice cut across his thoughts. "What's that noise?" One of the soldiers was leaning forward over the battlements, his head cocked to listen.

Kuper heard it, too. A distant rumbling sound was slowly growing in volume.

Activity in the meadow abruptly ceased. All the Rogandans were staring upstream. Suddenly they scattered, frantically trying to get away from the river. Shouts of alarm sounded faintly on the wind, quickly blotted out by a deafening roar. A massive wall of water swept into view. Nothing could stand before it. Huge trees were uprooted and swept away like straws in the wind. The mighty wave surged across the meadow, engulfing it in an irresistible flood.

Men ran to the battlements and gaped in awe, rendered speechless by the stupendous scale of the destruction. The peaceful meadow below them had been transformed into a raging sea. Kuper stared down at the maelstrom, completely dumbfounded. The water continued to pour in, unabated and roaring its fury.

Many minutes passed before the torrent began at last to show signs of subsiding. The soldiers crowding the battlements still did not move. Dazed and speechless, they stood rooted to the spot.

Kuper was the first to tear himself away. It was clear to him what he needed to do. Spotting the commander standing on the wall with the rest of his soldiers, he sought him out and drew him aside. "With your permission, I'm going to gather my men," he said. "As soon as it's safe to ride down there, I will lead them into the forest to hunt down that Rogandan band we heard about."

The commander nodded his approval. "There will be other strays as well. I will see to it that they are dealt with."

"One other request," Kuper added. "Can you send a message to Lord Burtelen? Please inform His Lordship that the way to Castel is now open!"

VOLUME 2—THE KNOWING

14

"Our scouts appear to have identified a suitable location for the battle, My Lords." At Will's announcement the persistent murmur of background conversation ceased abruptly. A great deal depended on this choice. Everyone present knew that the fate of two kingdoms would be determined by the looming encounter.

"There are unmistakable signs that the Rogandans have been massing their forces." Will told them. "They clearly want to draw us into a decisive battle. As you all know, the Rogandans outnumber us significantly, and they will be looking to inflict a heavy defeat upon us. They will set out to end our resistance once and for all."

"With the additional levies we have been able to raise from Arvenon and Castel, we have ten thousand men," King Istel said frankly. "How big is their army?"

"Based on the reports of our scouts, Your Majesty, our best estimate is that the Rogandans have nearly three times that number."

An undercurrent of murmuring broke out at Will's words.

He waited until the noise had died down. "Neither side has a substantial contingent of archers," he continued, "so archers are not likely to prove decisive. Cavalry, however, is a different matter. Only four thousand of their men are mounted. Our mounted strength is close to three thousand men, which means we have a cavalry force almost as large as theirs. That fact will have an important bearing on our plans."

"What about the reinforcements from Erestor?" one of the nobles asked.

"We still haven't heard from any of the messengers we sent west," King Steffan replied.

"We do know that a large Rogandan force was sent to Erestor," Will added. "They were almost certainly not strong enough to breach the defenses of Steffan's Citadel, but that may not have been their purpose. Their intent may have simply been to prevent Lord Burtelen from reinforcing us. And even if Erestor somehow found a way of sending us additional men now, it's unlikely they would reach us in time."

King Steffan nodded his agreement, although with obvious reluctance. "Will is right. We have no choice except to work with what we have," he concluded grimly.

"We must never lose heart, though," King Istel said. "Numbers alone do not decide battles."

Will bowed to the Castelan king, acknowledging the wisdom of his comment.

The commander turned to Lord Bottren, who retrieved a large map and approached the table. As Bottren began to spread it out, one of the nobles spoke up. "You say we've found a suitable location," he said. "How do we know the Rogandans will be willing to fight on a battleground they didn't choose?"

"They will come to us wherever we are, My Lord," Will replied. "They want to meet us in battle. And they will like this site. They want us to face them in the open, because they don't believe we have any hope of winning a pitched battle. They won't imagine there is any chance they can lose, given their vast superiority in numbers. So we will be offering them a lure they cannot resist.

"The challenge we face is a simple one," he said. "We need to find a way of ensuring that most of the Rogandan soldiers are not actually able to join the fighting. If we can do that, their advantage in numbers will not help them. This battleground does not guarantee us success. It does allow us to choose a strategy that suits us, though. If our strategy is good, and we execute it well, we have a chance. Once the battle begins, our primary goal will be to maneuver them into a position where most of their forces cannot participate."

He pointed to the map, and the men gathered around the table leaned forward to get a closer look.

"This site features a broad plain, bounded by a tall escarpment on the eastern side known as Torbury Scarp, and a group of low hills on the western side. Both the northern and southern ends of the plain are open. We propose to occupy the northern end.

"The cliff face of Torbury Scarp is steep and inaccessible both to horses and to men—climbing it is not an option. We will place it on our left. The hills across from it on the other side of the plain form a natural boundary for the field of battle on our right flank. The area between these two natural boundaries is broad enough to allow plenty of freedom for battlefield maneuvering. It's also broad enough to encourage the Rogandans to think they can deploy their entire army to full advantage. They will expect to be able to outflank us."

He paused to make sure everyone understood.

"Let me explain the strategy. I am proposing to form up our men three lines deep, facing south, with the escarpment rising above us on our left and the hills away to our right. The Rogandans will enter the battlefield from the south. The obvious place for them to outflank us will be on our right where there is more open space. When the two armies engage, though, we will instead allow them to drive a wedge into our line beside the cliff face of Torbury Scarp. It will appear to them that they have broken through on our left. The left side of our line will fall back rapidly, drawing the Rogandan forces into a stretched out line along the cliff face.

"While this is taking place, half of our cavalry—positioned on our right flank—will engage the Rogandan cavalry. We will be outnumbered more than two to one, but we must nevertheless find a way to drive the Rogandan horsemen from the field. I believe we can do it. I have seen our men, and I have fought the Rogandans. Our mounted soldiers are better trained, better led, and they are better fighters. Our riders must get behind the Rogandan army and drive them further into their new position along the escarpment.

"The rest of our foot soldiers will swing left and stretch out to form a new line opposite them. The Rogandans will now be positioned with the cliff face at their backs, and our men stretched out in front of them. They will be blocked on their left—the southern side—by our cavalry.

"The remainder of our cavalry will be waiting to the north on a ridge that commands an outlook over the whole site. Initially this will be at the rear of our position but as the battle progresses it will become our left flank. As the Rogandans continue to drive their wedge further forward along the cliff face, hoping to spill out around our new position and attack us from the rear, our cavalry will advance down from the ridge and engage them. The result will be that the Rogandans are blocked on the northern side as well. This movement will complete the containment of the Rogandan army.

"By then their soldiers will be spread, many men deep, across the whole length of the escarpment. Most of them will be unable to reach our soldiers, so they won't be able to fight. But they'll get in the way of those who are fighting. The more vigorously we can push their line back toward the cliff face, the more the Rogandans will trip over each other. Their numbers will be of no use to them—the press of men will eventually prevent any of them from fighting effectively."

The minute Will finished speaking, others jumped in energetically with their own comments and questions. Everyone had an opinion, and the debate became heated at times. Many of the lords were very impressed, though, and didn't try to hide it.

The meeting came to an end with a lot of questions still to be answered. There were always risks, of course, but the two kings approved both the site and the battle plan, and they did so enthusiastically.

While King Steffan was bringing the meeting to a conclusion, Will glanced around the table, assessing the expressions on the faces of the nobles. Nothing that he could see revealed open hostility, but he knew that most of the lords were well able to mask their true feelings and intentions.

Thanks to the vigorous efforts of Nestor, though, Will was no longer reduced entirely to guesswork to understand what the nobles around the table were thinking. Apart from his own liaison, Lord Bottren, Will knew that two of the lords had come to this meeting strongly supportive of his leadership while a couple more were largely positive. The remaining four—Lord Eisgold among them—were saying very little, either in public or behind closed doors. They were certainly not speaking negatively, which was something.

Neither Will nor Nestor had been able to discover clear signs that intrigue was still alive and well among the nobles. If it still existed at all, it had gone deep underground.

The only thing that mattered was how the nobles would behave when they found themselves fighting together for their lives and their futures. On that front at least, Will had not been able to detect any obvious cause for alarm.

"TODAY IS the day that Essanda is coming to visit." King Steffan groaned and buried his head in his hands. With a site chosen for the battle and active planning underway, the timing couldn't have been worse. "What was I thinking when I agreed to that?"

King Istel smiled grimly. "You might remember that I thought the idea was absurd from the beginning," he said, shaking his head. "In any event, it's much too late to do anything about it now. And I imagine she'll be as safe here at Hazelwood Ford as she would be in the capital."

When Queen Essanda did arrive at the main camp, Steffan was far too busy to meet her. The best he could manage was to send a warm greeting along with his apology. The message was delivered through Count Gordan, who had accompanied her from the citadel.

It was the early hours of the morning before Steffan was able to return to his tent. He opened the flap and stepped inside to find the tent dimly illuminated by the light of a couple of candles. He had arranged for a separate section of the tent to be set aside for his young wife, behind a canvas partition. Expecting her to be asleep, he moved through the large tent as quietly as he could.

As he headed for his own sleeping quarters at the opposite end of the shelter, he heard a voice softly call his name. He turned to see Essanda's head appear briefly around the flap that partitioned off her room. Her head disappeared again, then a few moments later she emerged with a cloak thrown over her nightgown and a blanket draped loosely around the cloak. Even so, she was shivering slightly in the cold.

"Hello, Steffan," she said, with a sleepy smile. "I am so happy to see you again at last."

"I'm sorry to have woken you, Essanda. But I am delighted to see you, too," he said affectionately.

She gazed across at him with bleary eyes, studying him critically. "You haven't been getting enough sleep."

"You're right. There's been a lot of demand on my time."

She gave him a little frown, shaking her head. Then she yawned hugely.

"It seems that both of us need some sleep," he told her, stifling a yawn of his own.

She nodded. "I will not distract you," she said determinedly. "We can talk tomorrow." She gave him another drowsy smile before heading back to her room.

"Sleep well," he called softly after her.

He waited until she had disappeared, then he made his way to his own sleeping quarters. Too tired to properly undress, he shed his cloak, pulled off his shoes, and climbed onto his bed as he was, covering himself with a mixed assortment of blankets and coats. He lay there for a moment thinking about Essanda. She had managed to show care and concern for him, young as she was. He resolved sleepily that he would not allow her to outdo him.

Rolling onto his side, he closed his eyes. He was so tired that he drifted off to sleep at once.

STEFFAN WOKE TO FULL DAYLIGHT. He jumped up from the bed in alarm—there were things he should have been doing instead of sleeping the morning away. Hurrying outside the tent, he found a table laden with food and drink waiting for him. He stood there squinting at it in the bright daylight.

A servant was on hand ready to offer assistance.

"Where did the food come from?" Steffan asked.

"Her Majesty arranged for it, Sire. She also insisted that you not be disturbed before you woke up."

He groaned. He glanced down at the meal spread out before him. It did look appealing, and he was hungry. He shrugged and sat down. Before long he was attacking the food energetically.

"Where is my wife?" he asked.

"I do not know, Sire. She left quite early."

He raised an eyebrow curiously—he couldn't help wondering what she was doing. He turned his attention once more to eating.

He left when he had arranged for dinner to be served for the two of them in his tent.

AS HE RETURNED at the end of the day, Steffan found himself uncertain about what to say to Essanda. He spent his days preparing for war. But she wouldn't be interested in that. He realized how much he still had to learn about her—they'd had so little opportunity to spend relaxed time together. What did she do with her days back at the capital? He arrived feeling uncharacteristically apprehensive and unsure of himself.

He need not have worried.

When he entered the tent, she rose and greeted him warmly, giving him an affectionate kiss on the cheek.

"Did you have a good day?" she asked, appraising him with her searching look.

"All things considered, it was good enough," he said. "Thank you for asking. How was your day?"

She smiled, pausing to pour him a drink before replying. "It was very enlightening."

He looked at her quizzically. What did that mean?

She giggled when she saw his face. "You look so serious," she said.

"I'm sorry," he said. "Preparing for war is serious business. But tell me how your day was enlightening."

"Some of my father's nobles are not excited about having a commoner as their commander," she began.

He looked at her sharply. "Who have you been talking to?" he asked, more brusquely than he intended.

She looked a little offended, and he quickly apologized for his tone of voice.

"I haven't been *talking* to many people at all," she told him. "I've been doing a great deal of listening."

He was not surprised. He already had a high regard for her ability to ferret things out. "What have you discovered?" he asked.

"That the nobles will follow the agreed plan of battle. But Lord Eisgold might have a plan of his own in store."

He waved his hand dismissively. "That rumor has been around for a while. But your father knows him better than anyone, and he doesn't believe it. I've been keeping a close eye on Eisgold myself, and he gives every indication that's he very supportive of Will."

"Has he always been supportive?" she asked.

"No, not at first. But he's changed."

"What was the reason for the change?"

"Your father wasn't willing to put up with his previous obstructiveness, and he clearly realized that. The man isn't stupid. And it's not impossible that he simply decided that Will's ideas were worthy of his support."

She offered him an innocent smile but said nothing.

Then she changed the subject. “Where will you be during the battle?” she asked, a frown of concern creasing her young brow.

“You needn’t worry,” he told her. “Istel and I have promised Will that we will stay well away from the fighting.”

She sighed with relief.

“Will was concerned that the need to ensure our safety could prove to be a distraction at critical moments. This battle will be challenging enough—none of our fighters can afford distractions. It’s galling, but I know he’s right.”

He adopted a look of reluctant resignation, winning him a pleased grin from Essanda.

They ended up speaking of many things. Later, when he reflected on the conversation, he realized that they hadn’t talked at all about the kind of things most noblewomen seemed fixated upon. He’d done most of the talking, and she had listened. In fact, almost all of her contributions had been gentle questions that teased out a considerable amount of information from him.

THE ARMY OF ERESTOR, finally on its way east, now stretched out for miles. It had taken far too long to get the soldiers through the pass at Steffan’s Citadel and over the soggy mire that had once been the road below it. Huge sections of the countryside below the citadel had been swept away by the torrent, leaving behind a swamp that now made travel of any kind extremely difficult. Getting a few thousand men and horses through this quagmire had proven to be a logistical nightmare. The last of the men were finally traveling on solid ground, but it had taken far longer than Kuper could ever have imagined.

Kuper and Rellan had been busy, not least because they had acquired new responsibilities. In view of their service to the Duchy, a grateful Lord Burtelen had extended to them a considerable degree of authority over the army that was now on the march. Neither of them were required to command men directly, but they had been granted unfettered access to the senior commanders and given a voice into both the tactics and the overall strategy of the force.

"We need to find a way to pick up the pace," Kuper said to his twin as they rode together near the front of the column.

"Yes," Rellan agreed. "The sooner we go, the sooner we can get back."

Kuper laughed. "The forest life seems to have acquired a new appeal for you," he said with a grin.

Rellan looked pained. "Anneka wasn't at all happy with me when I left."

"So the two of you had another of your raging arguments, did you?"

A resigned look flashed across Rellan's face. "We have had one or two. Life certainly hasn't been boring since I met Anneka."

"No. And I can't imagine that's likely to change any time soon," Kuper said.

"I hope not," Rellan replied with energy. "She certainly is a lively one," he added, a wry grin appearing on his face.

"You have yourself to thank for that. By all accounts you're the one who's brought her back to life," Kuper told him.

Rellan replied with a wink.

Both of them fell silent for a time. When Kuper next glanced across at his brother he saw a faraway look in his eyes. "What are you thinking about?" he asked.

"Anneka, of course. She was furious with me when I was about to leave. She wouldn't speak to me. Then when I mounted my horse she burst into tears and stormed off. I couldn't figure out what was going on."

Kuper looked at him in disbelief. "Are you serious? You really don't know? It's perfectly obvious to everyone else."

"What do you mean?"

"She's worried about losing you! She took years to get over the loss of her husband and son. She eventually managed to do it, but only after you arrived on the scene. Finally she's started to think she might have a future worth living for. Now you're going, too. Off to war! There's nothing at all complicated about it."

Rellan was frowning. "I thought it must have been something I said."

Kuper shook his head. "You're hopeless."

"Sounds like it should be easy to resolve, then," said Rellan, his face brightening. "I'll send her a message."

"There's only one way you can resolve it," Kuper told him. "And that's by returning alive and in one piece."

"Let's get on with it, then," Rellan replied. "Time to get them moving." He kicked in his heels and headed back down the column.

Kuper rolled his eyes. Rellan's intentions were wonderful, but impossibly unrealistic. You couldn't simply decide to ride off, win a war, and come back again. There was never any certainty about anything when you were a soldier.

Kuper looked back at the line of men and horses stretching away into the distance and sighed. The coming days promised to be more than usually challenging.

15

Brother Vangellis groaned. He opened his eyes and strained once again to see around him in the dark. It was futile, and he quickly gave it up. The cold seemed to penetrate through to his bones, and his hunger gnawed at him constantly. *O God, Father of all, whose Son commanded us to love our enemies...*

The incessant drip-drip-dripping of water frayed at his nerves, but it was better than the cries of pain and wails of despair that otherwise punctuated the stillness from time to time. He decided to close his eyes again and wait for the morning. *Deliver them, and deliver us, from hatred, cruelty, and revenge...*

He'd lost count of the days since they had brought him here and thrown him into the dungeon. Cold and alone in the dark, his sole comfort was the liturgy, fixed in his memory, that he used to mark his passage through each day. He greeted the new day with morning prayers, marked the arrival of noon with matins, and ended the day with vespers. The familiar ritual remained impervious to circumstances, in stark contrast to his emotions. The litany remained fixed and unchanging, unlike any hopes he might have entertained for a future that now seemed doubtful in the extreme.

With no window to the outside world, he didn't exactly know

when the sun rose and set, much less the actual moment of noon. But a tiny amount of dim light did penetrate his cell during daylight hours, and he was given a little bread and water at what seemed to be the start of each day. He marked this meal with special thankfulness.

Only once had he been called before the master of this stronghold. He had been quite literally dragged into the presence of Lord Drettroth and dumped on the stone floor.

He remained where he had been deposited, staring up at the Rogandan commander with considerable curiosity. His captor was tall, and simply clad in a black cloak. He might have been fifty years old—his black hair showed tinges of gray at the temples—but he was lean and muscular.

Many long minutes had passed before the Rogandan leader even bothered to notice his presence. He finally glanced down at his prisoner, fixing him in a piercing gaze. The monk saw intelligence in his face, and also sensed that a cold animal cunning lurked behind his calm demeanor. If the eyes offered any indication, the dark-clad nobleman had no acquaintance whatsoever with compassion. Brother Vangellis shivered involuntarily.

"Ah. The monk," the Rogandan had said, speaking smoothly in the language of Arvenon. "Are you missing your young friend? You will be reunited soon, I promise. Do you think he will enjoy the accommodations?" Drettroth had smiled broadly, apparently pleased with his own sense of humor.

And that was it. After those few words the Rogandan had dismissed him summarily. Brother Vangellis was bemused, unable to fathom the purpose of the visit, if indeed there had been a purpose.

As the guards dragged him away, Drettroth had spoken to the guards in their own language. "We might be able to find a use for him. Make sure you keep him alive."

Did Drettroth assume that his captive could not speak Rogandan? Or had he intended Brother Vangellis to understand his comment? The monk couldn't decide.

Nor could he guess how Drettroth might be planning to use him.

Perhaps his jailer thought he could induce him to put pressure on Thomas to hand over the stone.

Brother Vangellis didn't find it difficult to imagine the kind of inducements that Drettroth had in mind—he could threaten torture if the monk refused to cooperate, or hold out the offer of freedom if he did. He smiled grimly to himself. The Rogandan would discover that he was wasting his time.

Still, it was nice to know that they weren't planning to dispose of him. Not yet, anyway. And Drettroth's plans were entirely dependent on his men catching Thomas first. It was gratifying to know that they still hadn't managed to do so. That was another thing well worth being thankful for.

Brother Vangellis kept his eyes open as they dragged him back to his cell, and he made a couple of discoveries as a result. He noted first that prisoners were being held on other levels above the dungeon. They passed a large and surprisingly well-furnished cell occupied by what appeared to be a young nobleman. The prisoner peered out curiously at the monk as he was towed along behind the guards.

He also spotted a youth wandering around freely, if furtively. He looked a little younger than Thomas, and he appeared to be Arvenian, if his clothing and demeanor offered any indication. On impulse, the monk called out a friendly "Hello," but either the youth didn't understand him, or he chose not to respond. He slipped away instead into the shadows, leaving Brother Vangellis to wonder who he was and what he was doing there.

The guards didn't return the monk to the lower dungeon. They dumped him instead in a cell on the level below the nobleman. Perhaps the change was a response to Lord Drettroth's instruction to keep him alive. The cell with its stone floor and stone walls felt almost as cold as the dungeon, but a single torch flickered somewhere down the passageway, so it wasn't entirely dark. After bolting the iron door, they abandoned him once more to the loneliness of total isolation.

He wondered briefly what was going on outside in the wide world. That made him think of Thomas again, and prompted him to offer up a prayer of gratitude that his friend was apparently still enjoying his freedom.

His stomach rumbled, causing him to smile wistfully to himself. Going without food might not have been voluntary, but it nevertheless brought his observances to mind—it was almost time for his prayers. They could deprive him of food and warmth and companionship, but at least they couldn't take away the dependable familiarity of his disciplines or separate him from God.

THOMAS PEERED out warily from his vantage point behind a tree. The horses of the Rogandans stood close at hand, stamping restlessly.

He had resolved to release and scatter the horses before revealing himself. That would force the Rogandans to chase him on foot. His own horse was tied near the stream, hidden from plain sight but still within easy reach of the path. He should be able to flee quickly when the moment arrived.

He crept forward until the Rogandan soldiers were in sight. Wisps of mist were beginning to swirl slowly through the trees, but he was still able to see well enough. The soldiers had finished their meal and were sitting around drinking. If their boisterous talk and loud laughter offered any indication, they were not expecting trouble. Sentries were nowhere to be seen—to all appearances they had not bothered to post any.

Thomas took a deep breath to steady himself. He knew it was necessary to place himself at great risk if he was going to draw the Rogandans away from Elena and her father. But that didn't mean he had to let them capture him. He fully intended to make a clean escape.

Acts of daring seemed to come easily to Will, but Thomas was not like his friend. Will had embarked upon a surprising number of audacious exploits, even in the time Thomas had known him. But no one thought for a moment that Will was foolhardy. Thomas knew that if he had attempted the same things, he would rightly be seen as crazy.

And yet he was about to do something extremely reckless. And, strangely enough, although he knew he ought to be terrified, he found himself filled with unexpected resolve. Even the risk to the stone did not deter him.

He eyed the horses more closely. They appeared to be unguarded. He watched quietly for a few minutes more, looking nervously this way and that. Then he made his move.

Crouching low, he hurried to the horses. The animals became even more restless when he suddenly appeared among them. He did his best to calm them, but without a lot of success—there were simply too many of them, and he was too nervous to be able to give his full attention to the task.

He was about to begin untying the horses when he heard a sound. A soldier was heading in his direction! If it was a sentry come to check on the horses, he was lost. He was certain to be discovered. He shrank down fearfully among the horses, hoping the soldier would pass by without stopping.

The man seemed to be mumbling to himself. Thomas risked a glance in his direction and saw the soldier swaying unsteadily as he walked. He was clearly drunk. It soon became apparent that he had left the campfire to relieve himself. Everything depended on whether he would decide to check on the horses while he was there.

Thomas stayed low. His heart was racing, and he had begun to sweat. The horses became more restless than ever. Surely the soldier would come to investigate.

The Rogandan wasn't leaving. He stood there mumbling out loud. Thomas would have given a lot to be able to understand what he was saying. What should be do? He could run for it, but the soldier would be certain to see him. Drunk as he was, he would surely raise the alarm. Anything might happen after that.

Everything went quiet. Thomas hadn't heard the soldier leave, so he must still be there. The youth continued to wait, his anxiety increasing by the minute. What was the Rogandan doing? Had something alerted him? Was he creeping toward the horses right at that moment to investigate?

The pressure built until Thomas could stand it no longer. Anything would be better than just crouching there. He slowly began to stand, peering out anxiously to catch a glimpse of the Rogandan. He couldn't see him anywhere. Then a wave of horror washed over him as he realized that the man might be standing behind him, right this minute! Thomas broke out into a cold sweat. Overcome with dread, he spun slowly around.

No one was there. He gazed around in bewilderment. Finally he spotted the soldier. The man lay on the ground, right beside the horses. He appeared to have collapsed in a drunken stupor.

Thomas stood silently, watching for any sign of movement. The soldier didn't stir.

What should he do? Releasing the horses could not be done quietly. There was every chance it would wake the man up.

The Rogandan began to snore loudly. That decided it for Thomas. He would do what he came here to do, and if the man woke up, he would decide how to deal with it then.

The animals wore halters, and their ropes had been tied to the branches of trees. It was slow and tedious work for one person to release them all. He couldn't afford to let them wander, either. Before long someone would notice if horses began wandering around freely.

As he untied a horse, he looped its rope over his left arm. There must have been twenty of the animals, though, and it simply wasn't possible to manage that many at once. After freeing half of the horses, he tied their halters loosely to a branch. As soon as he was ready, he would do something to startle them—they should easily be able to pull free.

He began untying the remaining horses. After a while he moved almost without thinking from horse to horse, calming the animal, untying it, securing its rope to his arm, then on to the next one. He had two horses to go when he realized that something felt different. He paused, trying to make sense of his unease. Then it hit him—the soldier wasn't snoring.

He looked across to where the soldier was lying and discovered he wasn't there. He looked around and found himself looking into the startled eyes of the Rogandan. The man stared uncomprehendingly for a moment. Then his eyes went wide, and he opened his mouth and bellowed.

Everything happened at once after that. The first group of horses whinnied in fright and began pulling at their ropes. In a moment they were free and galloping away. His left shoulder was wrenched violently as the horses still tethered to his arm pulled in different directions. Wincing with pain, he somehow managed to slide the ropes from his arm.

The horses he had been holding were gone in a moment. One of them, wide-eyed and screaming, turned blindly and crashed into the Rogandan soldier, knocking him to the ground. He didn't get up.

Thomas ran for it, clutching his injured shoulder. He dashed back to his horse and untied it. The horse was spooked and difficult to manage. Somehow he clambered into the saddle. He was about to gallop away when he remembered that he needed to reveal himself so that his pursuers would set off in the right direction.

By the time he headed along the path the Rogandan camp was in an uproar. Men were running around, trying to catch horses. A couple of voices appeared to be shouting orders. Two men were already in the saddle, no doubt riding the horses he had been unable to release.

Someone spotted him, and a cry went up. He kicked his heels into his horse and set off along the path, bending down to avoid low hanging branches. He glanced back over his shoulder and saw through the thickening fog that both mounted soldiers were already in close pursuit. Other men were faintly visible running after them along the path.

His plan was not at all working out as he had expected. The pain in his shoulder had become excruciating now that he was bouncing along on horseback. He began to feel faint. He gritted his teeth and willed himself to stay in the saddle. He was determined to lead the Rogandans far away from Elena. Nothing else mattered.

The path wound its way into a denser region of the forest. The trees seemed to be closing in around him. The fog had also thickened considerably, and he could barely see further ahead than a couple of horse lengths. The chase became a confused blur, galloping blindly through the haze and somehow clinging to consciousness, in stubborn denial of his suffering.

Then abruptly a large branch appeared from out of the gloom. Rigid and unyielding, it knocked him from his horse. He fell heavily and rolled onto his injured shoulder. Everything went black, and he knew no more.

16

"Ah, Mr. Nestor! Please, take a seat."

Nestor bowed deeply. "Your Majesty." He joined Queen Essanda at the table, and they sat quietly for a few minutes gazing across the grassland that stretched out before them. Soldiers on exercise moved endlessly back and forth, conveying a sense of restless energy.

The battle scarred veteran stole a glance at the young queen. One of his contacts had arranged for them to meet on her first day at Hazelwood Ford, and he had quickly taken a liking to her.

Queen Essanda was remarkable for her age. He himself was a man of few words, but his taciturn nature hid his real strength—he was an unusually shrewd listener. He had a sharp memory, unending patience, and he knew how to ask the right question at the right time. He had rarely met his equal at this game. This little queen showed considerable promise, though. He had quickly discovered that her pretty young face masked a keen ear and an unusually perceptive mind.

"Are you well, Mr. Nestor?"

"I am, Your Majesty. Thank you for asking. But please, call me Nes. All my friends do."

That earned him a smile. “Mr. Nes, then,” she said cheerfully.

He smiled back. He had the feeling that she liked him, too.

At their first meeting she had shown considerable curiosity about the attitude of the nobles, especially toward Will. Nestor had been reluctant at first to say anything that might be seen as disparaging toward the nobility. But he had soon realized that her real concern was for the good of the two kingdoms. She didn’t seem invested in showing respect for people who didn’t deserve it, whether or not they were highborn. Like her new husband, she apparently valued people more for their integrity than for their social status.

“Have you been enjoying your visit to Hazelwood Ford, Your Majesty?” he asked.

She smiled briefly. “It’s been interesting.” Then she looked at him seriously. “I’ve heard something, and I’m hoping you can help me to understand it,” she said.

“I would be glad to, if I can.”

“It was something Lord Eisgold said,” she continued.

He raised his eyebrows in surprise. “He said it to you?”

“No,” she said, shaking her head. “He said it to some of our other nobles. But I was there as well.”

“They talk openly, with you there listening?” He didn’t try to hide his surprise.

She shrugged. “They talk in riddles. And they think I’m simple. That’s probably why they don’t mind talking when I’m around.”

He shook his head at the magnitude of their miscalculation. Anyone who thought she was a simpleton was making a big mistake. “Where did this happen, Your Majesty?”

“In a large barn. They go there to drink together. I went with some of their younger sons.”

“If you were there with others your own age, I’m surprised you got any chance to hear what the nobles were saying.”

“The sons don’t have much to say. I think they’re scared of me.” She giggled bashfully.

“So what was it you heard, Your Majesty?”

“Lord Eisgold said something strange. He said, ‘Even when every move of a game is played strictly by the rules, an apprentice might struggle to master the timing.' Some of the other nobles wanted him to say more, but he wouldn't. He didn't say anything else. They all left soon after that."

"You're sure that's what he said? Exactly that?"

"Yes, I'm certain. I have a very good memory," she told him proudly.

He sat there quietly, thinking. After a while he turned to her. "I've learned that the nobles refer to Will as the 'apprentice'. But what does he mean by the 'game'? I'm not sure," he said.

"I've been wondering about that, too. Do you think it might be the battle plan?" she asked.

He paused for a few minutes, deep in thought. "I believe you may be right," he said finally.

He leaned forward and lowered his voice. "You know from our last conversation that there have been vague rumors about the Castelan nobles, and about Lord Eisgold in particular. The rumors suggest that he might be planning a surprise for Will.

"The worst possible interpretation of what you've just told me is that Lord Eisgold intends to deploy his soldiers when it suits him, not when Will needs them. When the commander orders the Castelan soldiers into action at a crucial point in the battle, Lord Eisgold might decide to hold them back. The commander would be forced to join the battle personally in an attempt to save the day, just like he did last time. This time, though, he might not be so lucky. Once Will is out of the way, Lord Eisgold could throw the full weight of the Castelan army into the battle, and take the credit for the resulting victory."

He sat back in his chair. "That may not be what he meant at all, though. There are other less sinister ways of interpreting it. Lord Eisgold might simply mean that even if a battle plan is followed carefully, success will depend on how well the commander executes the timing of each move. That is undeniably true."

She didn't comment.

"I'm not at all sure that either King Steffan or your father would find this information incriminating," he continued. "I suspect that any alarming interpretation would be seen by them as far fetched. If I understand them rightly, they're convinced that Lord Eisgold had a change of heart, and now fully supports Will."

She nodded, confirming his view. "Would Lord Eisgold take the risk of doing something that might cause us to lose the battle?" she asked.

"Not intentionally. But it's possible he thinks he's smarter than he really is. He might believe he can get away with making a few changes to the battle plan without affecting the final outcome."

"Could someone try to talk him out of it?"

"I could ask Lord Bottren to speak to him. But if Lord Eisgold does have plans of his own, he'd simply deny it. And once he knew we were aware of his intentions, he'd make adjustments. Then none of us would be any the wiser."

She nodded slowly.

"And even if the worst reading of this is correct," Nestor pointed out, "Lord Eisgold may not actually deviate from the battle plan once the fighting starts. As it happens, I've recently learned something that supports that view."

She looked at him inquiringly.

"A servant overheard two of the Castelan nobles talking—two of the nobles most closely aligned with Lord Eisgold. One of them claimed that he's just talk. He said Lord Eisgold might like to give the impression that he's an independent thinker, but that he'll follow orders when it comes to the battle. The other nobleman agreed with him.

"That makes sense to me. It isn't just Arvenon's future that's at stake—Castel has just as much to lose. Lord Eisgold understands that as well as we do."

A thoughtful look came over her face. "Are you planning to tell Will any of this?" she asked.

He shook his head slowly. "We have nothing solid to tell him, Your Majesty. I'm not sure it would be responsible to distract him with vague uncertainties. How can a commander lead effectively if he doubts his own allies? Would it be responsible of us to suggest that in the heat of battle he might need to outmaneuver his friends as well as his foes? Will's task is difficult enough already." He raised his hands helplessly.

The two of them sat there for some time without speaking.

Finally the queen turned to him. "What are you going to do, Mr. Nes?" she asked quietly.

He shrugged. "Nothing, Your Majesty. It's hard for me to believe that Lord Eisgold really is planning to repeat exactly the same tactic he used at Pinder's Flat. He might be proud and stubborn, but I don't think of him as a fool."

She didn't look entirely satisfied. She sat staring off into the distance, a thoughtful look on her face.

There was nothing more he could say. He asked for permission to withdraw, and she granted it with a nod and a word of thanks. He left wishing that he had solid evidence, one way or the other. The signs were confusing, and he'd rarely felt so uncertain about how to read them clearly.

"What are you up to, Essanda?" Steffan had stepped into his tent to find his young wife parading herself in front of a mirror. She'd never shown any inclination to do that before. And she was wearing armor.

She didn't answer, but her deep blush confirmed that he'd surprised her at something.

"Where did you get the cuirass?" She was wearing a breastplate and backplate fastened together by leather straps. It fitted her surprisingly well. And it actually looked quite fetching.

"Do you like it?" she asked shyly.

"It makes you look much older," he said admiringly.

She fixed him with a mock frown. "I'm still just a girl, however old I might look. I hope you won't forget that."

He laughed. Coming closer, he took her by the shoulders and pulled her to him. But he contented himself with a kiss on her forehead.

"So why the armor?" he asked.

"We're at war, and I think that royals should dress appropriately. Do you like it?"

"I do. Although I'm not sure about the purple gown. I think white might suit the look better."

She looked down at her dress with a little frown of concentration.

"Putting on armor is well and good," he told her. "But don't imagine you'll be coming any closer to the fighting than this mirror."

She responded with a deep curtsy and a humble bow of her pretty head. Then she straightened and stood there silently, a delicate blush on her cheeks, basking in his obvious admiration.

She would make a queen worth waiting for. Assuming he still had a kingdom when the coming encounter was over.

THE ROGANDAN SOLDIERS huddled together in the early morning light as a biting wind blew through the camp. Haldek stood among them, chilled to the bone, wondering once again what he had done to deserve this particular fate. How did he come to be here in this strange land battling foreigners who fought like demons? He simply didn't understand the reasons behind it all.

The soldiers had been rounded up once again so the leader of their army could harangue them. The recently appointed Kulzeike had already earned himself a terrifying reputation. The previous commander, Luzik, now seemed positively genial by comparison. Where did Lord Drettroth find these monsters?

Haldek looked around him. Only Rogandan soldiers were present. Once again no Varasan soldiers had been rounded up. He was not sorry. The Varasans were savages who could not be trusted. They were supposed to be allies, but they had nasty tempers and seemed all too ready to pick fights with his countrymen. They had quickly built reputations as fierce fighters, too. Haldek made sure he stayed far away from them.

When Kulzeike arrived he mounted a platform erected for the

occasion. He surveyed the crowd before him, then spat contemptuously onto the ground. Apparently he did not like what he saw. "Are you soldiers, or are you WORMS?" the new commander roared.

Haldek kept his head down fearfully, anxious to remain as inconspicuous as possible. He wondered who would be singled out this time so that Kulzeike could make his point. But the commander showed no immediate inclination to satisfy his seemingly endless blood lust. For once it appeared that he had come here just to talk.

"Soon you will fight. Soon we will WIN!" Kulzeike looked out over them with a horrible grimace on his face that might have been intended as a grin.

The gathered throng gradually realized that something was expected of them, and a belated and very half-hearted cheer greeted their commander's pronouncement. His face grew ever more wrathful, and soon the men were cheering wildly. Haldek screamed with them, howling at the top of his lungs. Kulzeike seemed satisfied, and the din gradually abated.

"The fight—the real fight—will begin soon," Kulzeike told them. "Just this once, puny mice, you must fight like tigers. Then your job will be done. No more fighting. Just the spoils of VICTORY!"

He paused again. The necessary shrieking arose without any prompting this time. He waited for it to die down.

"These Arvenian fools believe they have our measure. But they are in for a surprise. A BIG surprise. Already we have a mighty army. But another army is on the march and will join us in the battle. Our enemies will be caught like fish in a net! We will squeeze the life from them."

The men delivered another obligatory roar, and then Kulzeike abruptly dismissed them. Haldek had never seen the commander in such a good mood.

He pondered the coming battle as they all shuffled away. Perhaps Kulzeike was telling the truth. Perhaps if they could just defeat the Arvenians this time, the fighting would finally come to an end. Then maybe he would be free at last.

That would finally be something worth fighting for.

THE SCOUT PULLED his horse to a halt beside Lord Burtelen and his aides. "A large body of soldiers is approaching from the south, My Lord," he said. "If they hold to their current path, they will intersect with us in two or three hours."

"Are they Rogandans?" the nobleman asked.

"They don't appear to be," the scout replied.

Lord Burtelen turned to his commander. "Alert the men just in case," he ordered. "I don't want us taken by surprise." The commander acknowledged the order and rode back down the column.

The nobleman directed his attention to Kuper and Rellan. "Go with the scout, and find out what we're dealing with," he told them.

They left immediately.

As they rode away Kuper drew his mount alongside the scout. "How many men are we talking about?" he asked.

"Hundreds, at least," the scout replied. "Probably fewer than a thousand."

Kuper raised an eyebrow. "Enough to make it worth avoiding a fight, then," he observed. "Can you take us someplace where we can observe their approach?"

"Certainly," the scout replied.

They rode for some time before the scout signaled to them that they needed to proceed more cautiously.

After a few minutes Rellan called softly to the others. "We're being watched," he said, nodding toward a lone rider off to one side.

"Let's just keep going," Kuper replied. "There are only three of us —we're not likely to cause them too much concern. We'll need to keep our wits about us, though, just in case we have to leave in a hurry."

They rode on, wary and alert, until they caught sight of the column of soldiers in the distance. They reined in their horses and observed the soldiers silently. After a time several men detached themselves from the column and rode purposefully toward them. Long before they arrived it was clear that they were not Rogandans.

The three of them decided to stay where they were.

"That's Ranauld!" exclaimed Rellan as they drew closer.

Kuper frowned. "I wonder what he's doing here." He didn't say it, but his first thought was that Arnost must have fallen.

The riders challenged them as soon as they came within hailing distance. "Who are you, and what is your business?"

"Greetings, Count Ranauld. We were sent by Lord Burtelen to ask you the same questions."

"I don't know you," the count replied. "Have we met before?"

"No, My Lord. My name is Kuper. My brother, Rellan, and I were part of the small group that accompanied Will when he left Arnost. Our other companion here is one of Lord Burtelen's scouts."

"Are you still traveling with Will?"

"No, My Lord. He sent us to Erestor for reinforcements. We are marching to join him, although we don't know exactly where he is."

"Is Lord Burtelen nearby?"

"Yes, your column will join his if you continue in the same direction for another hour or two."

Count Ranauld nodded. He gave a rapid series of instructions to his second-in-command, and then addressed Kuper. "Take me to Lord Burtelen."

They retraced their steps, riding fast, accompanied by the count and a couple of his senior men.

When they reached Lord Burtelen they found him in conference with another rider. The newcomer's horse was covered with lather from hard riding, and everything about him conveyed a sense of urgency.

"Ranauld!" Lord Burtelen called. "Well met. I hope you bring good tidings from the capital."

"Arnost still stands, I am glad to say," Ranauld replied.

"Turn aside with me, Ranauld," the lord said. "I've instructed my column to continue—it's time they picked up their pace significantly.

But we need to carefully consider our next steps. Kuper, Rellan, I want you with us."

The select group rode a short distance from the column and dismounted.

"I'm bringing three and a half thousand men from Erestor," Lord Burtelen began. "About one thousand of them are mounted. We've been planning to join Will Prentis to strengthen his army. What's your situation?"

"I have about a thousand men with me, two hundred of them mounted," Count Ranauld replied. "As you know, we have been besieged in Arnost from the beginning of this war. A few days ago we became aware that the Rogandans had lifted the siege. Their army simply melted away. At first we wondered if that meant that the war was over, but it seemed more likely that they'd just been ordered elsewhere.

"I saw no value in leaving twenty-five hundred good fighting men locked up in Arnost if a decisive battle was about to be fought. The regent agreed with me. We left fifteen hundred men behind to defend the capital, and I set off after the Rogandans with the rest. We've been trailing them ever since."

"How many men do the Rogandans have, and how far ahead of you are they?"

"They were more than a day ahead of us, but we've gained on them. They're still a good few hours away, though. Most of them are on foot, but they've been moving fast.

"It's hard to be certain about their numbers. They were joined by another army after they set out—we passed the place where the tracks merged a couple of days ago. I suspect that Drettroth is drawing all of his forces together for one big push. There may be as many as ten thousand of them."

Kuper gave out a low whistle.

The newcomer could restrain himself no longer. "May I speak, My Lord?" he asked Lord Burtelen. The nobleman nodded. "Will sent out a number of us in different directions in case reinforcements were in the area. A major battle is about to be fought. I expect it to begin tomorrow. As far as I'm aware, though, the commander has no knowledge of this new Rogandan army. It's very likely they will take him entirely by surprise."

"Do you know the planned site of the battle?" Lord Burtelen asked him.

"Yes, My Lord. The location is Torbury Scarp. I can lead you there. It is many hours away, though."

"Clearly there is considerable urgency about this," Lord Burtelen said. "Ranauld, I propose that you take control of the cavalry. I will place the mounted men from my column under your command, and you can send for your mounted soldiers as well. I suggest you set out immediately. Ride for as long as you have light, then continue as soon as the sun rises. If the battle is already in progress, you'll have to do as you see fit. If not, you can receive instructions from Will when you join him. I will follow as soon as is practicable with the remainder of our combined force."

Ranauld readily agreed to this proposal.

Lord Burtelen turned to Will's messenger. "You can accompany Count Ranauld to the battle site. But you'll need to give us clear directions first. Whenever possible, of course, we'll simply follow your trail." The messenger nodded his acknowledgment.

The messenger gave detailed directions to Kuper, Rellan, and some of Lord Burtelen's scouts while Ranauld was assembling the mounted soldiers. The cavalry departed without further delay. They were soon out of sight.

While the column continued to file past, Lord Burtelen gathered his commanders, along with Kuper and Rellan. "If we continue at this rate, we won't get there in time," he said. "The men can march until sunset. We'll feed them as soon as they stop. Then we'll empty the supply wagons. All of them. Each of the men can carry enough food for tomorrow morning. The rest of the supplies can stay where we dump them.

"In the meantime, send men into the countryside, one hour's ride in every direction. Requisition any wagons you find and bring them back.

"Once the men have been fed, we'll load as many of them as we can fit into the wagons. The ground ahead is supposed to be even, so the wagons can be driven slowly all night. It will be uncomfortable for the men, but it will have to do. They can sleep sitting up if necessary. We'll resume marching at first light."

"I have a suggestion, My Lord," Kuper said.

"Speak freely," the lord replied.

"The horses pulling the wagons will be working hard through the night. But we have a good few packhorses as well," Kuper said. "When we unload the men from the wagons, we could give the packhorses to any soldiers who can ride. Most of them won't want to fight on horseback, but the horses will get them there much faster and in better condition than if they march."

"Make it happen," Lord Burtelen said. "You and your brother can lead the group on the packhorses. Get the burdens off those horses now. You'll need them as fresh as possible in the morning.

"The rest of my men and Ranauld's men will follow on foot. It will be a forced march, but it has to be done."

Kuper spent the next couple of hours counting packhorses and finding soldiers capable of riding them. Rellan rode to Ranauld's column and did the same there. Very few of the packhorses had saddles, so the search was restricted to men who could ride bareback. In the end, they located three hundred packhorses. They stopped their search as soon as they identified the same number of competent riders.

Ranauld's men joined the main column, and Lord Burtelen urged them forward as fast as they could go. Together they marched into the east, destiny before them, and the sun setting at their backs.

17

Unknown faces swam fuzzily into view as Thomas struggled to return to consciousness. Intense pain assaulted him. The universe shrank to his shoulder and the agony radiating from it.

Strange voices sounded in his ear, speaking words he couldn't comprehend. Someone pressed a flask to his lips, and a bitter liquid spilled into his mouth. He coughed and sputtered. The liquid went down, mocking his feeble attempts to avoid swallowing it.

Someone stood over him and pressed down hard on his shoulder. A new wave of suffering crashed over him, pulling him down into blackness.

THE TORCH in the passageway sputtered on as Brother Vangellis sat in the semi-dark, uncomfortable on the cold stone floor. He closed his eyes, trying to remember the sights and sounds and smells of the outside world. It was too difficult.

Instead he began to sing. Apart from the guard who brought his daily ration of food and water, he had neither seen nor heard any sign of another person since being placed in his new cell, so he sang without restraint or self-consciousness.

After a while he realized he had strayed into the song he used to serenade the bear on his way to the monastery with Thomas. Momentarily transported in his memory back to that moment, he flicked open his eyes, half expecting to find a bear listening patiently nearby.

Instead he was startled to discover a person staring at him through the metal bars of his cell door. It was the youth he had seen wandering the passageways previously. The monk stopped his singing abruptly, halfway through a line.

"Hello," he said warmly.

The youth stared at him, a faint look of distaste on his face. "Are you insane?" he asked.

"That's a curious question," the monk exclaimed. "What makes you ask it?"

"Prisoners don't sing," the youth told him frankly. "Not unless they've gone soft in the head."

"I see," he replied with a smile. "I like to sing. So perhaps I am insane."

He gazed at the youth. The eyes that stared back at him revealed no appetite for life—it was almost as if their owner had aged prematurely. It disturbed him to see one so young in such a state.

"I am Brother Vangellis," he said. "What are you doing here, in a place like this?"

The youth paused, as if deciding whether or not to answer. "I am the food taster for Lord Drettroth," he finally replied.

The monk raised his eyebrows. "An important role. He must regard you as a trusted friend," he said.

"I hate him," the youth replied with sudden passion. "I hate everything about him!"

His response took Brother Vangellis by surprise. The monk's brows furrowed thoughtfully. "I suppose that makes sense," he finally concluded. "It wouldn't be fitting to ask a real friend to take that kind of a risk on your behalf."

"He is not my friend! He has no friends."

"How did you come to be here?" Brother Vangellis asked.

A look of pain—or perhaps shame—passed over the face of the youth. "I made a mistake. Now my life is over."

The monk shook his head in denial. "Your life doesn't have to be over because of your mistakes," he asserted.

"You're a monk. You wouldn't understand."

"I understand much better than you could imagine. I once thought like you do."

The youth looked at him skeptically. Then he shrugged. "It makes no difference," he said. "There is nothing I can do about my situation."

The monk shook his head again. "There is always something you can do. The choices before us may not seem obvious at times. But we always have choices."

They talked on, the imprisoned man calm and earnest, the one at liberty restless and unhappy. Eventually the youth left.

He came again, though, repeatedly, over the next couple of days. Slowly he began to thaw, and the monk's astonishment grew as the history laid out by the youth slowly took shape in his mind. The most important thing to Brother Vangellis, though, was the spark of life that gradually began to appear in the youth's eyes. Seeing it, he was content.

Hope did not naturally thrive in the stronghold of despair that was Drettroth's fortress. But, like a glimmer of light in a dark place, its presence was unmistakable once it appeared. Hope is as unpredictable as it is potent, and the effects of even a tiny dose of it can be far reaching, just as the fall of a single drop of water spreads ripples well beyond its point of entry.

THOMAS AWOKE SLOWLY to flashes of light playing across his face and a constant jarring and bumping. He dimly became aware that he was in a moving carriage. He squinted, trying to adjust his eyes to the light so he could see where he was. His shoulder ached—a dull throb intensified by each new jolt of the carriage.

He moved his head to look around him. Two men sat opposite him, one a soldier and the other in a blue cloak. Seeing that he was awake, the man in the blue cloak immediately reached into a bag. A small flask appeared in his hand.

Thomas's eyes grew wide as the man approached and firmly placed a restraining hand on his chest. Thomas twisted his head away, but the man forced the flask between his lips. Once again he tasted the remembered bitterness of fluid on his tongue. Once again he was pulled down into blackness.

HOPE CAME VISITING the young nobleman one morning as he sat in his comfortable but cheerless cell. It called so unexpectedly and came so well disguised that the nobleman was unable to recognize it for what it was.

It appeared in the form of a youth creeping furtively to his door.

"What would you do if you were set free?" the youth asked him quietly.

The nobleman had glimpsed the youth from time to time without ever having spoken to him, and he saw no reason to take either the question or the inquirer seriously. His reply was therefore terse and dismissive.

"Set free? From this prison? That hardly seems likely."

The visitor ignored his disregard. "I've heard you in the night," he told him. "Muttering. About your regrets."

Taken aback, the prisoner offered no response.

"What would you do if you were set free?" the youth repeated.

"Look, I don't know who you are, or why you've been spying on me," the nobleman replied testily, "but it's none of your business what I would do."

"If you had another chance, you'd act differently. I've heard you say so. Is it true?"

"Why are you asking me these questions!?"

The youth's mouth snapped shut. It was apparent he could see he was getting nowhere, and it clearly frustrated him.

And then he was gone.

The nobleman spent the rest of the morning trying to decide if he should have responded differently. He prided himself on his ability to read people, and in the end he concluded reluctantly that the youth, in spite of his blunt questions and his unusual manner, was probably genuine. He also acknowledged to himself that he had been unnecessarily discourteous.

As the hours passed, the youth's question began to haunt him. What *would* he do if he was set free? He was still pondering the matter when he finally drifted off to sleep.

The hours dragged by without any further sign of his visitor. Then, a full twenty-four hours after his first appearance, the youth abruptly emerged again.

The nobleman decided to aim for a new start on a different footing. "I apologize for my rudeness yesterday," he said.

The youth ignored his attempt at civility, instead going straight to the point. "Would you try to repair your mistakes if you were freed?" he asked.

The nobleman frowned.

"Would you make the attempt?" his inquisitor insisted.

"Of course!" he hissed.

The youth nodded to himself, apparently satisfied. "Do you have anything of value?" he asked.

The nobleman hesitated, then removed an armlet of silver from his upper arm and held it up.

"It will do." The youth reached out a hand for it.

The nobleman hesitated again. Then, deciding on impulse to trust his instincts, he shrugged and handed it over.

The youth slipped away without a further word, leaving as silently as he had come.

The day passed slowly, and the nobleman saw and heard nothing more of his strange visitor. He reluctantly began to conclude that he had been taken for a fool. His only consolation was the knowledge that here, imprisoned in this cell, he had no possible use for the armlet.

Each day in the late afternoon he was served a light meal. It was never enough to fully satisfy his hunger, but he didn't doubt that other prisoners fared much worse. Today his food was brought by a guard he had never seen before. The guard put down the food and departed without locking the cell door behind him. As he walked away down the passage, his hooded cloak fell from his shoulders. He left it lying where it had fallen.

The nobleman looked on, wide-eyed. Freedom beckoned. Could it really be that easy, though? Were guards lurking out of sight down the passageway, eagerly anticipating an excuse to begin mistreating him? He sat unmoving, paralyzed in an agony of indecision.

Finally the face of the youth appeared around his door, his brows furrowed in exasperation. "What are you waiting for?" he whispered fiercely.

His challenge stung the nobleman into action. He pushed at the door, wincing as it squeaked and groaned in protest. Then he slipped out of the cell, forcing the door shut behind him. Finally, he scooped up the cloak discarded by the guard and swung it across his shoulders, pulling the hood down low over his head to hide his face.

The youth beckoned, and he set off after him into the dark.

THE NOBLEMAN STOOD at a small postern door, staring out into the slowly fading light of dusk. The sun had only just set. The youth had led him on a winding route through an endless succession of dark passages until finally he felt the cool evening air on his face. Impossibly, he stood on the brink of freedom.

He turned to the youth. "Why are you doing this?"

In the dim light the expression on the face of his rescuer could not be discerned. "I can't mend my mistake," the youth replied. "Perhaps I can give you a chance to mend yours. That would be worth something to me."

For a moment setting aside his rank, the nobleman bowed low in honor of the youth.

"You need to go!" the youth insisted.

"You haven't told me your name."

"My name is Simon," he whispered back. Then he stepped inside without further comment, pulling the postern door closed behind him.

The nobleman stepped away from the walls, bending low as he ran toward the drawbridge that crossed the moat. He was relieved to see that the drawbridge was down.

His legs responded stiffly to the unaccustomed exercise, but he pushed on, not willing to lose even a minute. He needed to get across the bridge undetected, and he needed to do it quickly. He had no idea how long it might be before his absence was discovered. Perhaps not until the morning. But he couldn't take any chances. He thought about his mysterious rescuer, and hoped fervently that Simon's role in his escape would not be exposed.

As soon as he reached the bridge he stopped. Torches were positioned at various points across the bridge, but fortunately for him they had not yet been lit. Peering around him in the semi-darkness, he could see no one in sight. Taking a deep breath, he set out walking briskly across the bridge, his back straight and his head held high.

He passed the halfway mark without incident. Then he heard the sound of approaching hoof beats. Someone was riding toward the fortress. He looked quickly about him—there was nowhere to hide. The hoof beats grew closer, then he heard voices behind him, men shouting words he didn't understand.

He did the only thing he could do—he kept walking.

Two horsemen rode into view. He hugged the side of the bridge as he went and kept his head down. They rode past him without a second glance. He quickly looked behind him and saw men striding out onto the bridge, lighting the torches. He hastened forward, increasing his stride until he was all but running.

Finally reaching the end of the bridge, he followed the road a short distance until he came to a thick stand of trees. Then he moved off the road and peered out, watching for any signs of a pursuit.

None came.

The men finished lighting the torches and returned to the fortress. It was becoming clear that they hadn't even seen him.

What would you do if you were set free? Prompted by Simon's searching question, he knew exactly what he wanted to do. All he needed was a horse.

He poked around in the dark among the trees until he found a suitable fallen branch. Then he selected a place where the branches of a great tree overhung the road. Taking the lump of wood with him, he climbed onto a low hanging limb and settled down to wait. It didn't take long before a lone rider approached, coming from the fortress. As the horse passed below, he swung the piece of wood with all the force he could muster, aiming to knock the rider from his horse. The branch struck the horseman on the helmet, and he went down hard. Still armed with his tree branch, the nobleman scrambled down from the tree ready to do battle. But it was not necessary. The rider lay dead on the ground, his neck apparently broken by the fall.

The nobleman stripped the soldier of his weapons then dragged his body from the road and hid it among the trees. The horse had been spooked by his actions, and it took him a while to catch it. Once he did, he drew it aside under the trees and settled down once again to wait.

He needed to find the Rogandan army. Lord Drettroth was certain to be in constant communication with his army, which meant that he would be sending and receiving dispatches frequently. The nobleman's plan was to wait for the next outgoing dispatch rider, and simply follow him at a safe distance. The prospect of traveling through the night didn't trouble him at all; he was eager to get there as soon as he possibly could.

In the end almost an hour went by before another rider emerged from the fortress. The nobleman waited until he had passed, then swung in behind him. The challenge was to stay far enough away that he wasn't seen, but close enough that he didn't lose him.

The rider followed the road for some time before heading cross country over even ground. By then the moon had appeared low over the horizon, providing enough light for him to keep the silhouette of the rider comfortably in sight. The night wore on, each hour bringing him closer to his goal.

"THOMAS...THOMAS!...CAN YOU HEAR ME?"

The insistent voice that nagged at him was somehow vaguely familiar, but he couldn't place it. His head was swimming, rolling around groggily, not readily cooperating with his attempts to clear it. As self-awareness slowly returned he discovered that his left shoulder ached, and his head was thumping from somewhere behind his eyes.

Very reluctantly, he opened his eyes.

A dimly lit room lay before him. He was sitting almost in a corner of the room with a wall at his back. Along the adjoining wall sat the owner of the voice he had heard. It was Brother Vangellis. At the sight of the monk his eyes bulged, and his jaw sagged with surprise. His friend was chained to the wall by his ankles, although his hands were free. He had fallen silent, but he was looking at Thomas intently.

Thomas looked down and discovered that his own ankles had been chained and secured to the wall behind him. His left arm was strapped across his body in a sling, and his right arm was also chained to the wall.

Then he remembered the stone, and his heart skipped a beat. A hurried glance showed his leather pouch still secured to the belt around his waist. He strained his right hand toward it. But the chain was not long enough to allow him to reach it, and he gave up in frustration.

"Are you injured, Thomas?"

It all came back to him in a rush—releasing the Rogandans'

horses and injuring his shoulder, fleeing on horseback, a tree limb knocking him to the ground. Then he thought of Elena. He groaned.

"Thomas?!" The monk sounded thoroughly alarmed.

He looked up at his friend and shook his head. "I injured my shoulder. But I don't think I'm badly hurt." He peered around him and frowned. "Where are we?"

"We are guests of Lord Drettroth; this is his fortress. I don't exactly know where it is, though."

"How long have we been here?"

"I have been in this fortress since I was captured a few weeks ago. I was only brought to this room today, though. They brought you in here soon after."

Thomas took a closer look at the monk. "You look very thin."

His friend gave him a wry smile. "Perhaps you thought our fare was meager in the wilderness. Compared to the food here, we were feasting like kings."

Thomas closed his eyes and leaned back. It was impossible to get comfortable.

"I want to hear what's happened to you since we parted, Thomas. But there's something you should know first. Something I need to prepare you for."

The monk never had a chance to say what was on his mind. Both of them turned their heads at the sound of voices, doors opening, and footsteps approaching. Thomas felt his stomach begin to churn. He had no idea what was about to happen, but it surely couldn't be good.

18

Will stood alone on a hillside near Torbury Scarp, staring up at the blaze of stars in the cloudless sky. He knew that any further attempt at sleep was pointless.

So much would be decided on the day that was about to dawn. His men were in place, and everything had been done that needed to be done. Everything he knew to do, anyway.

His mind wandered back over the journey that had led him to this place at this time, with the armies of two kingdoms awaiting his word. Was it destiny that brought him here? Did something other than fate determine the rise and fall of kingdoms? He shook his head as if to clear it. Such matters were beyond his comprehension.

Will was a practical person, and he knew that even before the sun rose there was much that would require his attention. Taking a deep breath and pausing to settle his thoughts, he left the hillside and set off to find Lord Bottren.

THE SENTRY SAT BROODING by the fire, staring mindlessly out into the dark. His vigil seemed pointless. The Varasan camp was surrounded on both sides by the countless hordes of Rogand—it hardly needed him to be guarding it.

Try as he might, he couldn't manage to prevent himself from thinking about the pending battle. He was no different from most of his comrades—the very notion of fighting for the Rogandans left him cold. But they had no choice. He knew it as well as they all did.

He spat into the fire. A satisfying image came to his mind of Zornath roasting over the flames on a slow spit. Such a fate would be too good for that snake! He spat again.

All of a sudden a dark and hooded figure appeared at the edge of the firelight, almost startling the sentry out of his wits. The apparition became a man in a dark cloak, and the sentry leaped to his feet, reaching clumsily for his sword.

The man showed him a pair of empty hands before slowly squatting down beside the fire. The stranger greeted him quietly in the sentry's own language, then put a finger significantly to his lips. The sentry remained standing, sword in hand, staring wide-eyed at the cloaked figure and trying to decide whether to call out or not.

"I need to speak with Lord Karevis urgently," the man said quietly. The sentry still didn't move, so he added, "I have a message for him."

"A message?"

"For Lord Karevis," the stranger said patiently.

The sentry remained rooted to the ground, apparently too bemused to speak.

The newcomer sighed. "I've traveled all night to get here, and I'm very weary," he said testily. "I need to see Lord Karevis. Now!"

The stranger was clearly a nobleman accustomed to being obeyed, and the sentry responded involuntarily to his air of authority. "Come with me," he said apologetically.

Still watching the newcomer warily, the sentry led him past a seemingly endless succession of campfires, weaving his way among the huddled forms of sleeping men. Finally he came to a small tent.

A pair of soldiers stood guard outside.

"This man has a message for Lord Karevis—it's urgent!" the sentry told them.

The guards looked doubtful, but after a moment's pause one of them slipped into the tent. He soon emerged with the Varasan commander.

Karevis looked tired and drawn, but he clearly hadn't been asleep. He approached the stranger and peered into his hood. His eyes grew wide.

Once again the stranger put a finger to his lips. Karevis nodded, and immediately ushered him into the tent.

Then he gave an order to the sentry. "Find my second-in-command and bring him here right now. If he's asleep, then wake him up!"

Before he disappeared into the tent himself, the commander turned to the guards. "Do not allow us to be disturbed before dawn. Not under any circumstances!"

As the sun rose above the hills on the day of the battle, Essanda turned her horse off the road. She guided it southward onto a grassy plain that stretched away toward the horizon on one side, and ended in a series of low foothills on the other. Her destination was a distant ridge where she knew a major part of the cavalry of Castel waited to join battle. She glanced up at the sun, and urged her horse forward. She knew far more than she should have known about Will's battle plan, and she was keenly aware that timing was crucial—she couldn't afford to waste a minute.

She was supposed to be leaving Hazelwood Ford with Count Gordan that very day to return to Castel Citadel, and before long her escort was going to discover that she was missing. He would be horrified when he found out what she was actually doing. As for her husband...she decided not to think about that. Neither consideration swayed her, though, not even for a moment.

She called to her page boy, ordering him to pick up his pace. He looked hesitant and pale, and she experienced a brief pang of remorse for badgering him into joining her in this mad scheme. Not wanting to travel alone, and knowing she could expect no support from those she knew and trusted, Essanda had pressed him into her service. She had insisted that she needed him to protect her. But the terrified look on his face made it obvious that he felt the need for protection much more than she did.

If she was honest with herself, she was terrified, too. She was stepping into the inferno without any clear idea about how she might find her way out again. But given what she knew—or thought she knew—she had to do something. She would never be able to live with herself if she sat back and waited for the battle to end in disaster.

She put her head down and concentrated on the plain before her. She had allowed herself two hours to reach the ridge. A lot of hard riding lay ahead of them.

In the half light before dawn, away to the west, throngs of bleary eyed men tumbled down out of Lord Burtelen's wagons. The men were allowed to stretch their cramped legs while they broke their fast. Then they were loaded back into the wagons.

Lord Burtelen had realized that the men could be transported faster than they could march, and he therefore decided to abandon the wagons only when the terrain made it necessary. With the light growing steadily stronger, they were driven forward again, and at a much faster pace than had been possible during the night.

Meanwhile, Kuper and Rellan hastily gathered their riders. They mounted the packhorses and set off, following the trail of Ranauld's cavalry. Kuper kept the riders together. He had no more idea than any of them what awaited them on the battlefield. He knew only that they needed to travel fast.

As the sun cleared the horizon, he glanced across at his brother. Whatever was going through Rellan's mind in that moment, Kuper knew that his heart was far away, in a forest refuge on the border of Erestor.

There was never any point thinking about the future when you were heading into battle. Nevertheless, Kuper sent a silent prayer into the heavens. He asked nothing for himself. All he wanted was for his brother to be safely returned to Anneka.

He turned his full attention back to the task ahead. The sun was up, and they still had a long ride ahead of them. Unable to shake off the feeling that every minute counted, he urged his horse forward. Three hundred horsemen followed hard behind him.

THE SUN HAD BARELY RISEN over the battlefield when the distant beating of drums sounded faintly in the still morning air. The army of Rogand was on the march. Every head turned to the south, squinting into the distance, watching for the first sign of the enemy. The drum beat grew steadily louder as a formless lump wriggled into view. The blot on the horizon slowly took shape and became a solid line, then a wall of moving figures crowned by the tips of thousands of glistening spears. A dense cluster of horsemen covered the Rogandan left flank, but otherwise an endless wave of men had begun to flood the even ground between Torbury Scarp on the east and the low hills to the west.

"Hold steady, men," Rufe called. He managed to keep his voice level, even though his insides were roiling. He reminded himself that he only needed to deal with the enemy soldiers within reach of his sword. He didn't have to worry about how to stem this mighty tide—Will would be working on that.

He knew that the commander stood with Lord Bottren on a low hill behind Rufe's position to the right, almost in the northwest corner of the battlefield. He would be calmly assessing the enemy, deciding where best to move his pieces on the board spread out before him.

The wall of enemy soldiers drew closer. Rufe could guess what was going on in the minds of his men. Plenty of knees would be starting to feel weak. In the brief calm before the clash of weapons, he bellowed out a challenge to his men. "These men have come to burn our homes and butcher our women and children. WHEN are we going to let them do that?"

The men roared back their answer. "NEVER!"

The Rogandans were shouting now, and his men were shouting as well. Then the two lines met, and his world narrowed to thrust, block, twist, turn, thrust again. He heard a voice roaring above the din and realized it was his own. Faces came and went before him—sculptures of fear, anger, bewilderment. It soon became little more than a confused blur.

WILL PEERED through the dust at the battle raging before him. Rufe was holding the center as he knew he would. The left flank was beginning to yield, exactly as planned. On the right wing, his horsemen had already pushed back the Rogandan cavalry. The lines shifted back and forward, as men fought and men died.

Then he spotted movement on the right flank. The Rogandans had so many soldiers milling around, there was nowhere for most of them to go. The removal of the horsemen had opened up a gap and already Rogandan soldiers were spilling into it.

Will had anticipated this outcome, and a small cavalry unit had been held in reserve to deal with it. The reserve needed to be deployed immediately. If it wasn't done quickly, his entire right flank would be surrounded. The only possible outcome would be disaster.

He turned urgently to Lord Bottren. "Our right flank, My Lord—we've got to reinforce it. Now!"

His second-in-command peered intently down into the chaos below. "I see it," he said. He moved swiftly, barking orders as he went, with no trace of panic. Within minutes the cavalry reserve unit—the only reserve unit—had closed the gap, and the line had stabilized.

Bottren reappeared, and Will dipped his head in silent acknowledgment of his quick action. The nobleman quickly turned away, apparently to hide the smile of satisfaction that had flashed across his face. Will returned his attention to the conflict.

The Rogandans were beginning to pour into the breach on the

allied left flank, spreading out along the cliff face. Will's men were pivoting left to accommodate them. The enemy had so many soldiers that the new allied front line was forced backward, reforming further away from the escarpment.

Will's men made space as the Rogandans surged forward across the base of the escarpment. The Rogandan force was beginning to resemble a long stretched out wineskin. Will was planning to cork it at each end with his horsemen—the riders already in the field would seal off the far end, and Lord Eisgold's cavalry, waiting on a ridge to the rear, would seal off the near end.

The Rogandan cavalry must have been driven away, because some of Will's mounted soldiers had begun to reappear on the battlefield. They were attempting to plug the far end of the wineskin, away to the south.

The first Rogandan soldiers had reached the near end, to the north, and were already pushing hard at the thin line that held them in. There were so many of them that if they ever succeeded in escaping the containment they would quickly begin to swarm around the allied position. There was no time to lose—Lord Eisgold's horsemen must charge down to seal the northern end of the line, and they must do it immediately.

Will sent a dispatch rider hurrying to Eisgold with the directive. He did so with an acute awareness that the moment of truth had arrived. Would Eisgold follow orders, or would he withhold his forces at the crucial moment as he had done at Pinder's Flat? The pressure was growing by the minute—the position was deteriorating much more rapidly than Will could ever have anticipated. A wave of anxiety overwhelmed him for the first time on this momentous day, as the fate of kingdoms hung in the balance.

THE RIDGE WAS at last within reach, and the ground began to slope upward noticeably. For some time Essanda had been able to see Castelan horsemen massed at its summit. None of the soldiers had noticed her or her companion, though. The two of them had almost reached the steeper slopes of the hill before they were finally spotted. The moment they were seen, a rider detached himself from the ridge and rode swiftly to intercept them.

Essanda understood the distraction of the soldiers. The distant sounds of battle—the cries of men and horses and the clash of metal on metal—were penetrating faintly even to her current position.

"Your Majesty! What are you doing here?" She didn't know the soldier, but he had clearly recognized her.

"Take me to Lord Eisgold!" she commanded, feigning a confidence she didn't feel. The soldier bowed his head respectfully and swung his horse in beside her. She turned to her page boy. "Wait for me here," she instructed him.

The soldier guided her to the crest of the ridge, and they soon found themselves among the men. He took her to the middle of the line, and led her forward.

She steered her horse between the last of the riders into an open space before the waiting ranks. After taking a deep breath to steady herself, she turned to face them. Every head turned in her direction. She reached up and removed her helm, then she tossed her head to free her long unbound tresses. Her hair streamed out behind her as the wind caught it. The rays of the sun lit up her burnished breastplate, and the crisp white gown beneath it billowed softly about her in the breeze. A collective gasp escaped from the lips of the soldiers as they gazed upon her and realized who she was.

She exerted every ounce of her self control, presenting them with a stern and determined face. Inwardly, though, she glowed with satisfaction. She knew she was dazzling—she could see it in their faces. The men were giving her exactly the reception she had been hoping for.

Lord Eisgold rode up, his face red and his brows furrowed. "Essanda, Your Majesty! What on earth are you doing?" he demanded. "Who brought you here? This is no place for a girl!"

"I have come to salute my men," she replied, loudly enough that all could hear. They raised a cheer in response.

She was Princess of Castel, and Queen of Arvenon, and in that moment she knew that she had been born and raised for such a time as this. Young as she was, she understood what she needed to say and how to say it. She turned calmly toward the gathered ranks.

"Today you face great danger for king and country," she called, her young voice ringing out strong and clear. "Some of you may not return. You fight to defend those you hold dear, and we love you for it! I have come here now, on the eve of battle, to honor your courage and your sacrifice."

She fell silent, raising an arm high in salute. The men rose in their stirrups and cheered, banging their spears against their shields. The noise was deafening. She dipped her head low in acknowledgment.

Lord Eisgold stared at her in astonishment. His eyes flicked from her, to his men, then back to her again. The enraptured response of his soldiers was not lost on him. She smiled to herself, knowing that she had placed him in a difficult position. Her presence was good for the morale of his men. Even a fool could see that. But Eisgold did not want her there.

"My Lord, I know I must leave soon," she said, preempting him. "I do not wish to interfere with you carrying out your duty. I trust you will indulge me for a few minutes longer, though."

"Your Majesty," he acknowledged with a dip of his head. He cast an eye once again toward his men, then back to her. "Perhaps a moment more," he conceded. "Then one of my men will escort you to safety."

For the first time she allowed her attention to be drawn down to the battle raging below her. From this vantage point it was plainly evident that Will and his men were impossibly outnumbered. Surely the commander must call upon his Castelan allies soon!

As if in response to her thoughts, a dispatch rider galloped up, his horse in a lather. "The commander sends his respects," he said, addressing himself to Lord Eisgold. "His orders are for you to proceed with your attack as planned."

A ripple of nervous expectancy went through the waiting ranks.

“Was that the commander’s message? Did you convey it exactly?” Lord Eisgold asked haughtily.

“Yes, My Lord,” the rider confirmed.

“When is our attack expected, then?” Eisgold asked.

“Now, of course!” replied the messenger, a baffled look on his face.

“The message said *nothing* about timing,” Eisgold insisted.

The rider stared back at him in bewilderment. A few of the Castelan soldiers murmured openly.

“Well, don’t just sit there!” Eisgold shouted at him. “Return to your commander and clarify the order!”

Wide-eyed, the dispatch rider spurred his horse and galloped back toward the beleaguered captain of Arvenon.

So her instincts had been right—all of it was true. She hadn’t come all this way for no reason.

Essanda turned to Eisgold, holding her anger in check with difficulty. “By the time he returns, My Lord, it may be too late,” she said pointedly, once again speaking loudly.

Eisgold rounded on her. “With respect, Your Majesty,” he said curtly, “military strategy is not the province of girls.” He turned to one of his aides. “Escort Her Majesty to the rear,” he ordered.

“Not before I honor our flag,” she replied sharply, raising herself up in her stirrups and lifting a hand commandingly. The aide faltered. Eisgold frowned, and she moved swiftly before he could speak again.

Riding to the young man bearing the standard, she stretched out her hand and beckoned for the flag. The standard bearer lowered it to her, and she grasped it in both hands, kissing it reverently. Her action drew another cheer from the watching throngs. Once more she had their full attention.

Moving suddenly, she snatched the flag from the hand of the startled standard bearer. She separated herself from him and raised the standard high. “You have been called to battle,” she cried in her clear high voice. “Now is the time for deeds of renown! For the king! For Castel! For your commander!”

Spinning her horse around, she raced away down the hill toward the fighting. A mighty roar rose from fifteen hundred throats as a sea of mounted warriors surged down behind her from the ridge. Essanda saw the young standard bearer riding beside her, and thrust the flag back into his hands. He raised it high, adding his voice to the din.

Slowing her pace, she allowed the tide of men and horses to sweep by her. Once she found herself alone, she turned her horse and headed back up the hill. Lord Eisgold remained on the ridge astride his stallion, alone apart from a handful of his aides. Moments later, though, he galloped down the hill in pursuit of his men, his aides close behind him. He turned toward her as he rode past, and she plainly saw the fury on his face.

Lord Eisgold had followed through with his plan. And she had followed through with hers. She permitted herself a grim little smile of satisfaction.

Essanda rode alone up onto the empty ridge.

THE SUN HAD PASSED its zenith, and the battle was moving into a new and dangerous phase. Will's soldiers had been pressing hard on the Rogandans all along the line, forcing them back inch by inch toward Torbury Scarp, attempting to pack them in so densely they would be unable to fight effectively. But the enemy had shown plenty of spirit, and Will's men had been gaining ground more slowly than he had hoped. His battle plan was intact, but unless the allies could force the Rogandans back more decisively, they risked losing the initiative. Before long Will's soldiers must surely be worn down by sheer weight of numbers. The allied armies had already sustained fearful losses.

Will himself had become increasingly testy, and on occasion Lord Bottren had only restrained him with difficulty from charging down and lending his own weight to the fighting. In spite of his reckless impulses, though, the commander did not fail to recognize that he was needed where he was.

Then, slowly and inexorably, the tides of war began to turn, and

Will found himself struggling to find a way to prevent the complete collapse of the armies he commanded.

A throbbing boom-boom-boom pounded ominously in the distance, growing slowly in volume. Marching steadily to the drumbeat, an entire Rogandan army appeared at the southern extremity of the battlefield, unexpected and unwelcome, promising a bitter end to the hopes of Arvenon and Castel. The horde was so vast that Will did not even attempt to guess at their numbers.

Responding swiftly, he sent dispatch riders scurrying down to the right flank of the allies, at the far end of the battlefield. He watched on in nervous tension as the riders arrived, and the men sealing off the southern end of the Rogandan containment abandoned their previous strategy and swung around awkwardly to face the new threat. The enemy soldiers approaching from the south were so numerous that Will knew that his fighters would quickly be swept away before the coming onslaught.

Then the Rogandan commander struck his final blow. Behind the new Rogandan horde, Will and the watchers at his position could dimly glimpse the banners of the Varasan army. Together, the two new armies far exceeded the size of Will's entire force. Introducing the Varasans to the battle seemed to be little more than an idle boast, because the Rogandan advantage was overwhelming even without them.

The armies of four kingdoms had now crowded onto the field. Will stood and watched, and waited for the onslaught. He had no further reserves to commit, and no possible rearrangement of his armies offered any hope of defeating the forces now arrayed against him.

19

The door to the prison room swung open. Two guards marched in and positioned themselves near Brother Vangellis and Thomas. Nothing about their appearance or manner offered the faintest whiff of encouragement to Thomas. His stomach twisted tighter.

Another man walked in, tall and dark haired. Something indefinable about his bearing said he was a man accustomed to power. Thomas didn't need to be told that he wielded power ruthlessly and without mercy.

Nor did the man need any introduction. Without any possibility of doubt, Thomas was now face to face with the one man he had tried for so long to avoid.

Lord Drettroth glanced across at them and nodded, a smile of casual satisfaction on his face.

One last person walked into the room, and Thomas gasped in shock and disbelief. It was Simon. The youth's brows were furrowed, and his face wore a defiant frown.

A number of mysteries instantly resolved themselves for Thomas. He no longer had to guess how the Rogandan lord knew he had the stone—Simon must have betrayed him. Thomas had told Brother

Vangellis that no one else other than Will knew about the stone. But he realized belatedly that he had been mistaken. Simon had, of course, briefly held the stone as well. At the time Simon almost certainly had no awareness of what the stone was capable of. But he must have heard whispers from the Council meeting where Pisander was exposed, and put the pieces together. And so he had somehow slipped away from Arnost and found Drettroth.

The spitefulness behind Simon's actions was beyond comprehension. Thomas had witnessed so much suffering. The sacking of the monastery, the capture and mistreatment of Brother Vangellis, and now his own capture—all of it had come about simply because Simon hated him and wanted to see him suffer. Thomas wondered if he was satisfied. He certainly didn't look happy.

Drettroth broke in on his dark wanderings. "What a merry reunion this is!" he said, a humorless smile twisting his face. He turned to Brother Vangellis. "I did promise that you would soon be reunited with your companion, did I not? And here he is."

Drettroth turned to Simon. "I understand you've become acquainted with the monk as well, my Simon. You seem to have been spending a lot of time with him lately," he said. He watched their faces closely, before tipping back his head and laughing harshly. "Surely you're not surprised. I make sure I know what's going on in my own fortress."

He addressed Simon again. "You've been playing some little games with another of my guests, too. Don't imagine there will not be consequences. I take it personally when people decide to cross me."

The Rogandan licked his lips, and Thomas shuddered. He had no sympathy at all for Simon after his betrayal, but the Rogandan lord filled him with horror.

Drettroth turned his attention to Thomas. "It must have been quite some time since you last saw Simon," he said with an ironic smile. "You must be delighted to find yourself reunited with him once again."

It was clear that no response was expected of Thomas, and he offered none. The angry scowl on his face said all he wanted to say.

"I'm sure that's more than enough of pleasantries, though," said Drettroth. He turned to the guards and spoke to them rapidly in Rogandan. They left the room, closing the door behind them.

The Rogandan lord turned back to his prisoners. "We're all here for one reason. Simon, fetch the stone from Thomas."

Simon walked over to Thomas and knelt down, reaching out to his pouch. Thomas reacted violently, thrashing around in a vain attempt to deny him access to it. All he succeeded in doing was to make his shoulder hurt even more. In final frustration he used the only weapon available to him—he leaned swiftly forward and head butted Simon.

The younger boy cried out in pain and reeled back, rubbing his head vigorously and wincing. He approached again, more carefully this time, staying out of range as he opened the pouch and reached in for the stone.

Thomas yelled his frustration out loud, but he was unable to prevent Simon from emerging with the stone in his hand. Simon stood gazing at him for a moment, his face revealing more regret than triumph, then spun on his heel and headed over to Drettroth.

Drettroth watched the progress of the stone with an expression revealing both longing and gratification. When Simon reached him he stretched out a hand. "Give it to me!" he commanded.

Simon hesitated for a lingering moment, then handed it over. Drettroth twirled it slowly around and around in his hand, consuming it hungrily with his eyes. Then he permitted himself a smug nod. "There can be no doubt about it," he said with satisfaction. "It is the Stone of Knowing, as I expected. It has come to me at last!"

He turned to Thomas. "Perhaps you will be surprised," he said, "but I have no intention of keeping the stone. I will not be taking the slightest risk with this prize. I will not take it by force. It will remain with you. It will be yours until you freely decide to give it to me."

He gave Thomas an indulgent smirk. "You may find it difficult to imagine yourself giving me the stone, young man. The truth is that you will not just be willing to hand it over—you will be frenzied in your eagerness. After the proper encouragement, of course."

He returned it to Simon, then jabbed a finger in the direction of Thomas. The youth retraced his steps and restored the stone to Thomas's pouch, much more warily this time. Drettroth approached Thomas himself, and after a warning glare to discourage any repeat of the prisoner's earlier aggressive behavior, satisfied himself that the stone was indeed safely back in the pouch.

"You should understand how generous I have been in my treatment of you, young Thomas," Drettroth told him, "especially considering the amount of trouble you have put me to. It seems you had a dislocated shoulder. My men have reset it, and it will heal in time, provided you are careful," he promised. "And also assuming you live long enough," he added with another mirthless smile.

"You need to understand—all of you—that your future is entirely in my hands," he continued. "Perhaps you have hopes that your friends will somehow prevail against my armies, but that is no more than an idle fancy.

"Arvenon and Castel have capable soldiers—I am the first to acknowledge it. But between them they have proven incapable of assembling an army with any hope of defeating my forces. Even if reinforcements from Erestor had been able to reach them in time, and even if they had persuaded the troublesome Varasans to join them as allies, they still would not have enough men." He paused to let his words sink in.

Thomas wasn't convinced. Will and Rufe had defeated much larger forces before, and he was certain they would somehow find a way to do so again.

Drettroth saw his reaction and offered him a condescending smile. "You have no way of knowing it, Thomas, but a battle is being fought today. Right now, in fact. And I'm sorry to be the bearer of bad tidings, but by now your friends will have discovered the little surprise I have prepared for them. They know they are facing a much bigger army today, and they know it is not the entire Rogandan force. But they think the rest of my men are spread far and wide throughout every corner of Arvenon and Varas. They are so very wrong.

"I have long planned this battle, and I have secretly gathered together every one of my soldiers stationed throughout the whole of Arvenon—from everywhere except Erestor.

"I have even withdrawn the bulk of my occupying force from Varas. I will send them back as soon as their job here is done." He paused, sighing with contentment. It was becoming obvious to Thomas that the Rogandan liked the sound of his own voice.

"The end result is that I have assembled a second Rogandan army, one that is bigger in its own right than the combined forces of Arvenon and Castel." Drettroth's face glowed with pride, and he swelled with self-satisfaction. "That army has just arrived at the battlefield and is even now joining the fight.

"Your friends will have been very busy making plans. But all of it is for naught. There are simply too few of them. They will be overwhelmed. Even their much vaunted commander will not be able to rescue the situation this time.

"No, by the time the sun sets, the armies of Arvenon and Castel will be finished. The two kingdoms will be finished as well—they will be ripe for the plucking."

Thomas tried desperately to believe that it wasn't true, that Drettroth was lying, or at least exaggerating in his conceit. But he was not able to convince himself.

"None of this makes any difference to you, though, Thomas," the Rogandan continued. "I intend to get the stone, and the only question that matters is whether you are going to make it easy or difficult.

"The hard way will not be pleasant. Not for any of us. Look at our monk here, for example. I have a feeling that a man like him might take a very long time to die. The screams can go on and on. It's all very distasteful.

"And what about you? If, at the very last, you refuse to save yourself, I cannot in all conscience simply allow you to expire—I'm sorry to say I will need to make life unbearable for you. You will long for death, but it will be denied you. I must actively encourage you to rid yourself of the burdensome encumbrance of the stone. Prolonging your suffering will be the only way I can extend your opportunity to do that.

"By the time you do eventually yield—and I promise that you will!—you will beg and plead with me to end your life. By then, your death will be inevitable, of course. It will only be a matter of timing. As a reward, I may decide to be merciful and grant you a quick release from your suffering. Once I have used the stone to pick your mind clean of information, that is."

He shrugged, and spread his hands wide. "None of this is necessary, though. The easy way is for you to simply give it to me. If you do that, the monk doesn't have to die. And, more importantly as far as you're concerned, you don't need to die, either.

"I'm sure I can find a use for you both should you choose the path of common sense." He nodded in the direction of Simon and sighed eloquently. "Simon here has been doing a fine job as my food taster. I suspect that sooner or later I will need a replacement, though. I seem to have acquired so many enemies. I simply cannot understand the reason why." He raised his arms in a gesture of helplessness.

Thomas was already learning to loathe Drettroth as much as he feared him—he had no difficulty at all understanding why the man had enemies.

"A man like myself needs the protection offered by this stone. I can trust Simon to devote himself to ensuring that my food and drink are safe, because I know he is a coward at heart—he has already demonstrated that he will go to extreme lengths to preserve his miserable life. But not everyone is so reliable, and the stone will remove any possible doubt about the motives of every person I am forced to rely upon."

The idea of Drettroth having the power to read minds was the stuff of nightmares. Thomas refused to even imagine the implications.

Drettroth's eyes were alight, his face creased in a triumphant grin. "I have it at last!" He laughed, an evil cackle that inspired nothing but horror.

The Rogandan returned his attention to Thomas. "I have told you that a great battle is being fought, at this very moment. Perhaps you are wondering why I am not with my army. I care nothing for battles!" he said, waving an arm dismissively. "Battles are a means to an end, nothing more. And I have mustered such an overwhelming force that my soldiers cannot fail to win. Even without me there to drive them forward.

"No, I care for one thing only—I must have this stone!

"It should have been mine long ago. I once entrusted one of my servants with the task of retrieving it and bringing it to me. Instead, the fool kept it for himself and fled. I hunted him for years, and learned eventually that he had made his way to Arvenon. Since that time I have taken a very special interest in your kingdom."

So it was true—the stone *was* the reason for the war. That possibility had occurred to Thomas, but he had never believed it could actually be true.

"Perhaps the timing has proven fortuitous—my understanding of the stone was incomplete at that time. Now I am fully prepared, and more in need of it than ever.

"How the stone came to be in your possession, Thomas, I do not know and don't care. But it was only thanks to Simon that I learned you were the one who had it, and even then not until after you had fled your capital. You have led me a merry chase since that time. Your paltry efforts to hide from me were always doomed to futility, though." He gave Thomas a contemptuous smile. "You were a fool if you thought you could escape me. Once I put my hand to a task, I never give up. Never!"

Thomas turned his head away, unable to endure the gloating look on the Rogandan's face.

Drettroth continued. "You may not be aware, Thomas, but there are other stones, too, offering virtues of their own. I have certain knowledge of them, and I will not rest until all of them are in my possession! I will bring these virtues together to ensure the security and longevity of my rule. I intend to create an empire that will last beyond your wildest imaginings.

"I have worked unstintingly to arrive in this place at this time. Perhaps you will begin to see that your hopes and dreams are insignificant in comparison with the great tasks that I am undertaking. You cannot stand in the way of destiny. I will not allow it!"

A look of unshakable resolve commanded Drettroth's face. The Rogandan lord stood silent for a moment, his feet firmly planted and his arms folded.

"I will leave you now. Consider your options carefully, Thomas. If you are planning to refuse me, you need to take this one opportunity to explain to the monk why his life means nothing to you.

"I will return in one hour for your answer. Don't imagine that you can stall me—I am not a patient man."

Drettroth directed a penetrating look at Thomas. Then he left, pushing Simon out ahead of him. The door closed behind them.

Thomas turned to Brother Vangellis. "What am I going to do? Drettroth is evil, pure evil! If he gets the stone, there'll be no hope for anyone."

"You can't give him the stone, Thomas. Don't be fooled, even for a moment, into doing what he wants. And certainly don't give it to him because you think it will save me. He's the kind of man who would kill me anyway, just for the pleasure of it."

Thomas squeezed his eyes shut and shook his head in denial. It was beyond understanding. Why did the balance have to be tilted so strongly against people who simply wanted to live quietly and in peace—people who were just trying to do what was right?

He opened his eyes again, and narrowed them in anger. "This is Simon's fault! All of it. The miserable toad doesn't deserve to live."

"Don't be too harsh on him, Thomas. He is sorry for what he did. I believe he would take it back if he could."

"How can you excuse him? You've suffered as much as anyone, and it's all thanks to him!"

The monk held his peace.

Thomas shook his head hopelessly. "We did everything we could to hide from Drettroth," he said, "but it was useless—he caught us anyway. Pretty soon there won't be anyone left who's free.

"King Steffan doesn't want to control every other kingdom! And Will might be a great commander, but he isn't fighting just for the sake of it. Now that our kingdom has been invaded, he has no other choice.

"I don't understand it. Why do people like Drettroth have to win all the time?"

The monk did not reply.

"We can't even trust our own people," said Thomas. "Elbruhe died because Baron Rudungen betrayed us. Now Simon's betrayed us. Meanwhile, Drettroth has huge armies just waiting to do whatever he says. How can anyone possibly stand against him?

"Why can't good people have the power for once?" Thomas fell silent, hanging his head in misery.

After a long delay, Brother Vangellis finally spoke. "These are big questions, Thomas. I don't have simple answers for you. All I know is that we always have choices, whatever situation we're facing. We can choose to do what's right, or we can try to find excuses to justify doing what we know deep down is wrong. We can decide to act with integrity, even if we know it won't change the outcome. Even if it seems completely pointless, and everyone else around us has chosen the easy way."

"Does that mean the two of us have to decide to be tortured and to die?" Thomas asked, unable to keep the dismay from his voice.

"Perhaps it does," the monk replied. "But at least we won't be dying for nothing. Drettroth can't control the stone unless you give it to him."

"I know what the right choice is," Thomas said. "But how can I just sit here and watch them torture you? And what if I'm not strong enough when my turn comes?"

"God will give you the strength you need, if you ask him," was all the monk offered.

They both fell silent.

Thomas, distressed and restless, squirmed uncomfortably in his chains. He wasn't at all ready to die. He wanted to live.

In spite of his own convictions about what was right, he began to cast about in his mind, searching for any possible rationale that might permit him to simply hand over the stone and be done with it.

He began to question all of his assumptions. What made him think it was his responsibility to decide who should possess the Stone of Knowing? Surely that was arrogance on his part. The stone had only come to him in the first place because of pure chance. It was obvious that Drettroth had known about it for years.

And why was it his place to deal with Drettroth? There were plenty of people in the world much more important—and more capable—than a lowly stable hand. Surely it was up to them to decide what to do about Drettroth, whether or not the Rogandan had the stone.

His mind churned on and on. In the end, though, he knew that the monk was right, and that he was only looking for excuses. He was unable to shake off one simple fact—however it had come about, he was the one with the stone. That made it his responsibility.

Two things finally helped to settle him. One was Brother Vangellis. The monk had no say at all in what was about to happen, and it was almost certainly going to end very badly for him. Yet he was facing it with remarkable grace. Thomas had known for a long time how much he had to learn from Brother Vangellis. He was seeing it more clearly than ever in this desperate situation.

The other thing that helped him was the memory of Elena. She might be far away, but he had not forgotten her and all that she meant to him, and he was in no doubt about what she would encourage him to do, much as she wouldn't want to lose him.

His decision was made. He was not going to cooperate with Drettroth. Whatever the consequences.

Anxious and afraid, he watched the door, hoping against hope that Drettroth's return would for some reason be long delayed.

20

From her vantage point, Essanda could see the horsemen of Castel locked in a furious struggle for survival. Until now she had failed utterly to grasp the immensity of the task that lay before Steffan and his allies. The army of her enemies was vast beyond comprehending.

Nor had she understood at all the horror of war. She herself had called her soldiers to battle. She wondered now if any of them would live to see another dawn. She had no misgivings about her actions. She had done what needed to be done—of that she was certain. But in that moment the stark reality of the conflict below was too awful for her to bear, and she was left feeling ill and weak. A single tear escaped her eye and rolled down her cheek.

Alone on the ridge with a battle raging below her, she recognized that Lord Eisgold had been right about one thing—this was no place for a girl. Dizzy and anxious, and oppressed by the weight of the burden of responsibility she had taken upon herself, she crested the rise and headed her horse down toward the page boy who still waited below.

As soon as she rejoined him, they set off quickly, returning along the way they had come. No more than a few minutes had passed before a small group of riders appeared in the distance, racing toward them at full gallop from the direction of Hazelwood Ford. Long before she recognized the leading horseman, she knew who it must be.

The rider pulled his steaming horse to a halt before her. He said nothing, but his wide, reproachful eyes conveyed far more than words could ever have done.

A new teardrop emerged, quickly followed by another. Her tears threatened to become a torrent. The bold young queen had vanished, leaving behind a pale and frightened girl.

"I'm tired, and I'm worried, Gordy," she said, her voice trembling. "Please take me away from here."

THE ROGANDAN CAMP had long since emptied and the sun had passed its highest point in the heavens before Zornath sent for Karevis. "Our commander has reserved a little role for the army of Varas," the Rogandan told him condescendingly. "You will be privileged to witness the annihilation that must be visited upon the enemies of Rogand. And, as favored vassals and allies, you will be allowed to twist the knife into the Arvenians before they meet their final end. As a reward you will be granted a small share in the spoils of victory. The greatest reward will, of course, come from doing your duty." He flashed his teeth.

Karevis offered no response.

The Varasan army soon marched out in full battle array. They followed a much larger contingent of Rogandan soldiers—at least twice their number—onto the battlefield.

Zornath rode at their head, with Karevis close behind. If Zornath noticed a new aide riding beside the Varasan commander, he chose not to comment on it.

Soon the fighting could be seen and heard ahead. It was immediately obvious that the Arvenians and Castelans were already massively outnumbered.

Zornath turned to Karevis. "Now your men will join the fight. On to victory!"

Karevis drew his sword. He turned to his men. "You've heard what the Rogandans want from us. Now hear from your KING!"

The new aide accompanying Karevis spun around to face the men. Throwing off his helm, he raised himself in his stirrups. "I am Delmar, your king!" he shouted. "DEATH to the Rogandans!"

An astonished silence greeted him. Time seemed to stand still for a long moment as the soldiers of Varas stood frozen in a state of shock. For so long they had been threatened and manipulated. For so long they had endured humiliation and frustration. Now, as if by magic, their sovereign had reappeared, commanding them to turn on their oppressors. He was suddenly and unexpectedly offering them the fitting outlet for their pent up rage. Recovering abruptly from their surprise, they found their voices. A deafening roar erupted from their throats.

Everything happened very quickly after that. The first to die were the small number of informants in the Varasan ranks. The Rogandan liaisons followed swiftly after them.

Zornath, howling with fury, raised his sword and charged at Delmar. Karevis thrust his horse into the Rogandan's path, his own weapon lifted high. The horses screamed as they collided, and Zornath turned his wrath upon the commander. Raw hatred covered the face of the Rogandan as he aimed a vicious blow at his former subordinate. Steel rang on steel as Karevis blocked the thrust.

Shouting their battle cry, the army of Varas surged forward, their king at their head. Impatient to engage the enemy, the ranks parted and flowed around the two combatants. The men knew how much their commander despised Zornath, and were more than content to leave it to him to deal with the hated Rogandan serpent. None of them doubted the outcome for a moment, and none felt any need to remain behind to witness the contest apart from two of Karevis's senior aides. The aides waited patiently to one side, keeping well clear to allow their commander plenty of room.

Having lorded it over the Varasan soldiers for so long, Zornath found himself utterly ignored by them. This loss of face was the final indignity for the Rogandan. Incandescent with fury, he began raining blows upon Karevis until the air rang with the sound of their clashes.

The Varasan commander was not dismayed at all. How could he be, when this very contest had been the unwavering theme of his favorite daydreams? He had never dared to hope that it could actually happen. As the two of them traded blows, he felt an idiot grin of pure delight spreading slowly across his face.

Zornath's energetic sallies proved entirely ineffective, and he soon began to visibly tire. As his fury cooled, a look first of alarm, then of panic, began to distort his face. The smile on Karevis grew broader, and he began in his turn to press in relentlessly on his enemy.

The former tyrant began to glance frantically around him, no doubt seeking a way to break free. He could ill afford the lapse in concentration, though, because it led swiftly to his downfall. Karevis saw an opening and lunged forward, his sweeping stroke slipping through the guard of his hated enemy. Bearing a jagged wound to his neck, Zornath slid from the saddle and slumped to the ground.

Karevis only paused long enough to satisfy himself that Zornath would trouble his countrymen no more. Then, followed closely by his aides, he turned his horse toward the battle and set off after his king and his army.

The Rogandans had been taken by surprise when Delmar and his army smashed into them from the rear. The Varasans quickly thrust deeply into the Rogandan lines, and the battle had moved away from Karevis. As he rode forward he was forced to pick his way around piles of Rogandan dead. He was not at all surprised by the ferocity with which his countrymen had attacked their overlords, and he noted with satisfaction that few of his own soldiers lay among the slain.

Karevis knew he should be thinking about the strategic situation, but at that moment he did not care. There was just one thing he wanted, and so badly it almost felt like physical pain. He wanted to make the Rogandans pay.

THE TIDE HAD TURNED AGAIN with the defection of Varas. Nevertheless, victory was far from Will's grasp.

The Rogandan position now resembled a bent arm, with the forearm stretched along the escarpment, and a thick upper arm at right angles to it across the southern end of the battlefield. The upper arm was bordered by the Varasans to the south, and a thin line of Arvenians and Castelans to the north.

Bottren stood beside his commander, looking dispirited. "This battle is not turning out at all as we expected," he said. "The Varasans are doing a lot of damage to the Rogandans, though," he added, awe in his voice.

"They're doing their job a bit too well," Will replied. "Our men opposite them are struggling to hold their positions. They've been fighting since early this morning, and the Varasans are starting to force too many Rogandans onto them." He scanned the flanks once again. "Our biggest risk is over there," he said, pointing to the western side of the position.

"You're worried about the Rogandans breaking out?" Bottren replied.

Will nodded. "Their sheer numbers pose a huge problem for us. If they manage to burst out, they'll spill into the area behind our lines. Our men right along the escarpment will be surrounded."

"That would mean a complete collapse!" Bottren said.

Will nodded grimly. "We have a difficult choice to make, and almost no time to decide," he said. "We can hold our current positions. If the Rogandans break out, though, it will lead to disaster. The battle will be over." He peered across the battlefield. "There's another option that will buy us some time. But we'll have to reform our line completely. It's extremely risky. And we'll be saying goodbye to any hope of forcing a victory."

As they watched, the Rogandans broke through the defenders at the very top of the arm. The lines slowly bent and twisted to seal the breach. The breach was repaired, but even from this distance it was clearly achieved with considerable difficulty. Will didn't want to think about the cost.

"The decision has just been made for us," Will said. "It isn't a question of whether the Rogandans will break out. It's just a matter of time."

Will turned aside and rapidly issued orders. Dispatch riders were soon racing to every section of the allied lines.

"What are you doing?" Bottren asked him anxiously.

"I'm pulling our men back. We need to form a new line. Down here." He swept his arm left to right below their position. "The Varasans are already holding a similar line, across the southern end. I'm instructing our men nearest to their line to join the Varasans." He pointed away to the far end of the battlefield where the Varasans were fighting.

"We need to do it right now. We won't get another opportunity."

ANDER HAD QUICKLY EMERGED as a key leader in the thin Arvenian line that had swung around to face the second Rogandan army. He and his men had survived only because of the vicious Varasan assault on the rear of the new Rogandan force. Having now received Will's orders to push through the Rogandans and join the Varasans, Ander was eager to carry out these instructions as soon as possible. His men, vastly outnumbered and in continuous action for far too long, were perilously close to collapse. And the relative safety of the Varasan line lay near at hand—tantalizingly so.

"One more push, men. After me!" Ander bellowed. Willing himself to summon up a new burst of energy, he threw himself at the enemy soldiers before him. The men facing him saw what was coming and fell back to avoid him. They were keeping an anxious eye on the Varasans fighting behind them, though, and their caution quickly dissolved into confusion. A fighting wedge formed behind Ander, and together they carved their way deeply through the Rogandan line.

The men opposing them thinned considerably, then disappeared entirely as the Varasans stepped forward and attacked them vigorously from the rear. They were through!

Ander turned, determined to keep the gap in the Rogandan line open. He soon realized that he was not alone—a solid wedge of Varasans had quickly formed on either side of him. Seeing them, the Rogandans melted away, and the last of his men stumbled wearily forward to safety.

The Varasans stepped around him, and he found himself behind the front line. He leaned wearily on his sword, sucking in great gulps of air.

A Varasan leader appeared before him. The dust, sweat, and blood that covered the man could not mask the unmistakable air of authority about him.

"Well met!" he said with a grim smile. "I am Karevis. I command these men."

"I am Ander. My thanks to you, Commander!" Ander replied. "Your help was timely indeed. We were ordered to push through to your lines. Some others might need your help, too."

"Your line bunched into four groups," Karevis replied, speaking rapidly. "Yours was the first through, thanks to your own efforts. Two other groups have also made it through with our help. The fourth is in trouble. Can you come with me?"

Ander readily agreed. The commander led him swiftly to the left flank of the Varasan position where a large pocket of Ander's comrades fought desperately behind enemy lines. They stood back to back, surrounded entirely by Rogandan soldiers. The Varasan line was driving forward toward them, but the pocket was slowly being pushed further away.

Karevis wasted no time. Barking orders rapidly, he drew together a sizable group of his soldiers. With a newly energized Ander at his side, Karevis led a vicious attack on the Rogandan line to the right of the stranded men. Such was their ferocity that they drove clean through the enemy line. The rescued soldiers raised a ragged cheer as the two forces merged.

Now the tables were turned. Their swift action had left a cluster of Rogandans cut off from their main force. About one hundred men on the extreme end of the flank were now stranded, and the Varasans surrounded them and pressed in hard against them. Fighting side by side, Karevis and Ander drew the combined line tight. They forced their way back toward the main Varasan force, driving the trapped men before them. The rate of their forward movement kept the Rogandans constantly off balance. None of them escaped.

"Take your men out of the battle line and let them rest briefly," Karevis told him. "My men are fresher. And you've been having all the excitement."

"We're in your debt, Commander!" Ander told him gratefully, at once moving to follow his suggestion.

"Never fear," said Karevis. "There will still be plenty of them left once your men are ready for another round." Then he was gone, no doubt searching out the place where he was needed the most.

RUFE SARJANT COMMANDED the main body of men facing the Rogandans along the face of Torbury Scarp. Will had ordered a pivot backward to form a new line—at right angles to their current position—that would seal off the northern end of the battlefield immediately below Will's command post. The entire battle line, currently stretched out in front of the cliff face, would need to swing back in a sweeping arc. The men fighting at the leftmost, northern, end of the line would scarcely need to move at all. Those at the far southern end would have to retreat diagonally across almost the entire battlefield, fighting every step of the way.

Rufe knew he was in trouble as soon as Will's order had been relayed to him. He trusted his commander implicitly, and he didn't doubt that Will was fully aware of the risks attending this new maneuver. Will must have a compelling reason to issue such an order. He also knew that no help would be forthcoming to assist his men as they pulled away from the escarpment. They could not protect their right flank, either—Will would need to worry about that.

Rufe ran along the line, splitting his men into two parallel groups running the length of the battle line. The first group would need to stand and fight while the second group swung back a short distance. Then the second group would turn to cover the first group while they did the same. The pattern would need to be repeated until they reached their new position.

Such a maneuver would challenge the most disciplined of soldiers when they were fresh. Rufe's men had already been fighting for hours, as well as being heavily outnumbered. If some of the men moved too fast or too slow, holes would open up in the line. There was nothing he could do to prevent that, though. Will would notice the problem if it began to develop. He would have to deal with it.

Rufe issued orders for the movement to begin. Then without delay he set out toward the right of the line, where his men came nearest to the Varasans. These men would need the most support, because they had the furthest distance to travel.

The maneuver began. His men immediately came under intense pressure as the Rogandans spilled out from their containment and moved to the attack. As the previously solid battle line began to dissolve, Rufe was forced to call upon all of his skill as well as his indomitable spirit to keep his men alive and moving. At first, every minute that passed saw his men inch closer to their goal. But before long the rate of progress slowed dramatically. The men were soon reduced to fighting for their lives.

Rufe fought on with all of his considerable might. Strong as he was, though, he knew he could not keep the entire Rogandan army at bay.

WILL WAS KEENLY aware of the need to protect his right flank. Both ends of the original position had been sealed with cavalry, but now Torbury Scarp was becoming the left flank of the new position. That meant that the bulk of the men originally positioned on that flank—led by Lord Eisgold—could be redeployed. Many of the mounted soldiers had long since reverted to fighting on foot. Will therefore sent immediate orders to Lord Eisgold to remount as many of his men as possible, and lead them in support of the protruding right flank. The outer extremities of the right flank were already hanging dangerously out into blank space.

The efforts of the Varasans in support of his men to the south was not lost on Will. Witnessing the effective way they had been absorbed into the Varasan line was a source of immense gratification to him. As the day wore on, the debt owed by the allies to the Varasans only continued to increase.

However, it was immediately apparent to Will that Rufe's men were facing very serious problems. He could see that they would not be able to reach the new position assigned to them. Dangerous rents were already developing in the front line as different groups of men moved at different rates. If Will could not find an answer, and find it soon, his men would be engulfed.

21

As the door opened once again, Thomas began to tremble uncontrollably, completely incapable of mastering his anxiety. He glanced across at Brother Vangellis. How did he manage to stay so calm?

Lord Drettroth walked in, Simon trailing along behind him.

The Rogandan stood facing them, hands on his hips. "The moment of truth has arrived for you, Thomas." He held up a bunch of keys. "You can both be free in a matter of minutes. Or I can call in my team of assistants." He gave them another of his nasty smiles.

"Before we begin, though, the stone needs to be secured. Simon, bring it to me."

Simon approached Thomas and retrieved the stone. This time Thomas did not attempt to resist him. Simon brought the stone to the Rogandan and handed it over.

Drettroth grasped it with a gloating smile. "What is your decision, Thomas?" he asked. "Have you chosen common sense, or would you prefer for me to arrange painful and lingering deaths for the two of you?"

Thomas shook his head, unable to trust himself to speak.

"I will make it easy for you," Drettroth told him. "Just nod your head if you have decided to relieve yourself of this burden."

His face set stubbornly, Thomas shook his head firmly once again.

"I told you I am not a patient man," the Rogandan said, an angry scowl appearing on his face. "I will offer you one last chance. Take it while you can, or things will become very unpleasant. When your turn comes, you will beg for death, Thomas, but it will be denied you."

Thomas finally managed to bring his shaking under control. "I will NEVER give you the stone!" he replied defiantly.

Drettroth glowered at him. "We shall see, young man. We shall see. Simon, call for my assistants!"

Simon did not leave the room. Instead, he leaned closer to the Rogandan and whispered something into his ear. Then he drew back swiftly, putting distance between the two of them.

A look of utter astonishment came over Drettroth's face. Then he went purple with fury. "What have you done?" he screamed. He drew his sword, and strode menacingly toward Simon. The youth closed his eyes, but held his ground without flinching.

The Rogandan raised his sword high, ready to strike. Then abruptly he began to convulse, his body bending and twisting repeatedly, until his backbone began to arch, snapping backward and forward. He fell writhing to the floor, wracked with continuous spasms.

Simon stepped up to Drettroth and placed a foot firmly on his wildly twitching sword arm. Then he reached down for the sword. Prizing it from the Rogandan's fingers, he took a deep breath in an attempt to steady himself, then raised the sword and ran him through. Drettroth gasped a few choking breaths, then released a final rattling sigh. His body slumped, then lay still.

Thomas watched it all with mouth agape, too agitated to make a sound.

Simon flung the sword away as if it had stung him. It skidded across the room, coming to a halt not far from the monk. Then, apparently remembering his audience, Simon turned toward them. "He was going to have both of you killed," he told them passionately. "Whatever you decided. You do realize that, don't you?"

He stared down at the body of the late tyrant. "It's only fifteen minutes since he had his goblet of wine," he said, his voice beginning to tremble. "He swallowed a large dose of poison with it. It was his own poison—I took it from his collection. He told me that it came from the seeds of a tree with some weird name." He tore his eyes from Drettroth and looked at them once again. "His death would have been extremely painful if I hadn't finished him. I showed him more mercy than he ever showed to anyone else."

Neither Thomas nor the monk could find a word to say.

Simon passed an unsteady hand across his brow. "As his wine taster, I prepared his wine. He trusted me not to tamper with it because he always made me drink it first. I had to drink it this time, too, of course." He smiled weakly. "So I don't have long myself. Once the spasms start I need to make sure I go quickly as well."

The fingers of Drettroth's left hand were still clasped around the stone, and the youth unbent them until the stone tumbled out. He retrieved it, then hunted for the keys, which Drettroth had dropped when he unsheathed his sword.

Simon went to Brother Vangellis and bent over him, speaking quietly into his ear as he fumbled with the locks. The monk looked across at Thomas, and his eyes grew wide with surprise. What was Simon telling him? Thomas couldn't think of any secrets he'd kept from his friend.

Finally Simon managed to release the chains. Freed at last, the monk stood up and stretched his limbs, wincing as he moved back and forth. Thomas felt cramped and uncomfortable; no doubt the monk's muscles were in even worse condition given his long imprisonment.

Simon stood up and turned toward Thomas. The effort seemed to trigger a reaction, and he began to convulse. As the spasms intensified he urgently wrestled a small wineskin from his belt. He unstopped it and began to swallow noisily, fluid spilling around him as he hastened to get it down. A bitter almond smell tainted the air.

The effect was immediate. All at once his breathing became very rapid. He convulsed one more time, then he collapsed.

The monk hurried to him and bent low over his prostrate form. Then he straightened and turned to Thomas with a tear in his eye. "He's gone," he said.

Brother Vangellis stood respectfully before Simon's body for a few moments more, then he brought the keys to Thomas and worked at his manacled right hand until he managed to unchain it.

Then the monk stretched out his own left hand. On his open palm sat the stone. "Take it, Thomas. It's yours. I give it to you gladly and freely."

Thomas frowned, puzzled by his words and surprised by the look on his face. He slowly reached out his freed right hand and took the stone.

The impact was staggering. He was entirely unprepared for the unrelenting onslaught that assailed his senses as the stone blazed into life in his hand. The intensity of it rivaled anything he remembered from his early experiences with the stone.

His mind reeled as he struggled to bring order to the chaos of thoughts, impressions, and memories that flooded to him from the monk. Even so, many things at last became clear—baffling oddities that for so long had completely bewildered him. He closed his eyes, desperate for a pause in the flow, at least for a moment.

Chains rattled as the monk unsuccessfully tried one key after another in his attempt to remove the ankle irons from Thomas. Then a knock sounded at the door of the room, tentative at first, then with more force. Thomas snapped his eyes open in alarm. The monk froze.

With no response forthcoming to the knocks, the door opened a crack, and a head appeared. With the stone in his hand, Thomas immediately saw that it was a dispatch rider with information from the battlefield. He sensed that the overall report wasn't bad, but something had nevertheless gone wrong, and the messenger was presenting himself in mortal fear of the possible reaction of his master.

The door opened wider, and a cloaked figure came in. The messenger was immediately confronted with the body of the Rogandan lord sprawled on the floor before him. He stood there paralyzed with shock, a jumble of emotions washing over him as he stared down at his former lord. Wavering between relief and indignation, he looked up and saw first the body of Simon, then the discarded sword. Finally, he looked across at the monk, still kneeling over Thomas.

Thomas watched with mounting anxiety as the messenger drew the obvious conclusion that the monk had killed both Drettroth and his food taster, and was now attempting to free the prisoner. Thanks to the stone, Thomas knew the messenger's intent as soon as the man knew it himself—he would satisfy his growing outrage by taking revenge on his lord's murderer. He would first kill the monk, then forever frustrate his attempts to liberate the prisoner by killing him as well. The dispatch rider drew his sword and stepped toward them.

Thomas whispered an urgent warning to Brother Vangellis, who dropped the keys and stood to face the Rogandan. Thomas saw his friend glance across at the sword lying nearby beside Simon. Then a memory flashed into the mind of the monk: a memory of a young girl fleeing, glancing back over her shoulder as she ran. Of a lecherous nobleman turning his back on the younger Brother Vangellis, who immediately reached down for a rock.

His friend turned his face away from the sword, rejecting it emphatically. Instead he began speaking to the Rogandan in his own language.

Thomas could not focus on what was happening, though. The face of the young girl had filled his mind and was haunting his thoughts. Her beauty stamped her unmistakably. The monk's long, slow slide into despair had been triggered by his act of violence in defense of a young Elena. Thomas knew beyond doubt that it was her, that he had not somehow managed to substitute a younger version of her face into the story.

"Thomas, free yourself!"

Brother Vangellis's hissed warning snapped him out of his reverie. His friend's attempt to talk the Rogandan out of his intention was apparently proving futile. Thomas put down the stone and grabbed the key. Fumbling in his haste, he began trying keys in the lock on his left ankle iron. He found the correct key on his third attempt and released the lock.

"Run, Thomas." The words came to him as a whispered sigh.

Thomas looked up in alarm as the monk's knees began to buckle. Blood was seeping through the back of his robe, and he saw him grasp hold of the Rogandan as he fell. Frantically returning his attention to the final ankle iron, Thomas tried the same key. It didn't work! In a panic he began poking keys randomly into the lock. Would he never find the correct one? At last, after innumerable attempts, the lock clicked open.

Pushing aside the chain, he threw down the keys and grabbed the stone. He launched himself upward even as the Rogandan tossed the monk aside and thrust forward his sword for a killing blow on his final victim. Thomas scrambled aside with barely a moment to spare as the sword struck the wall where he had been sitting.

Before the Rogandan could attempt a second blow, Thomas darted past him and out the door. Energized by his terror, the escapee flew blindly down a passageway, darting down side passages whenever they presented themselves. He encountered no one, and eventually hid himself in a dark room filled with large barrels. If the dust around him offered any indication, this room rarely saw a visitor.

He was still alive. But at what a cost. Brother Vangellis was dead.

The rush of energy that propelled him from the room had dissipated, and his pent up emotions were finally granted release. His whole body quivered with shock. Overwhelmed by the devastating impact of the death of his friend, along with his own close encounter with death, he silently began to sob.

He struggled to comprehend what had just happened. By some kind of a miracle the monk had escaped torture and death at the hands of Drettroth, only to be struck down by a nameless dispatch rider. Why did it have to end this way?

Brother Vangellis was a man who had touched the lives of so many. Now he was gone, his passing unmarked and unheralded. The onus of mourning his loss had fallen entirely to a solitary fugitive huddling fearfully in the dark in an enemy fortress.

The stone had at least allowed him a glimpse of the monk's final moments. The last lingering impression as he slipped away was one of peace. In his journey through life Brother Vangellis had clambered toward the light, had slipped and fallen hard, but had found his way forward once again. He had run the race, and finished it at last without lingering regret.

It was true that Thomas had only known him for a relatively short time. But the significance of everything that had happened in that brief period, along with the key role that the monk had played in so much of it, gave the friendship an importance far beyond any reckoning based on the length of time.

Thomas allowed his memory to wander freely over the pathways he had traveled with Brother Vangellis since they had met on a dark night at the Monastery of St. Rodrig the Martyr. He recalled teaching him to ride, the monk's brush with death as a result of withdrawals, his intercession on behalf of the villagers, his healing of Ander. He remembered the encounter with the bear and their visit to the monastery, the flight down the river, and the monk's easy companionship and careful instruction in the wilderness. Most of all he remembered the patient smile and quiet wisdom of a selfless and trustworthy friend.

His bitter tears flowed unchecked as he grieved without restraint for Brother Vangellis, giving honor to his friend and mentor in the only way that remained to him.

In time his mind began to wander in different directions. The stone had revealed a great deal in the short period of time after the monk returned it to him. He began now to try to piece it together.

Brother Vangellis had been granted a great many insights by the stone as soon as Simon handed it to him. The monk had gained brief but unfettered access to Simon's mind. The same information became available to Thomas through Brother Vangellis once the monk had given him the stone.

The first thing Thomas recognized was that the stone had never truly belonged to him since the day he lost it so long ago. For all the intense pressure applied by Drettroth to coerce him into handing over the stone, it hadn't even been his to give. Back in the capital, once he had forcibly regained possession of the stone, it had allowed him to use it on rare occasions. But it was obvious now that its full virtue had passed to its finder: Simon. The youth had possessed it only for a few short minutes in the stables at Arnost before Thomas violently wrenched it away from him. It had granted Simon brief revelation about Thomas—the only person he had seen while it was in his possession—but the younger youth had not understood at the time that these insights were connected with the stone.

Simon had finally experienced its unrestrained power when he took the stone from Thomas at Drettroth's command. For the first time the secret ambitions of the Rogandan had been laid bare, and in plumbing the depths of his evil, Simon had understood at last the true nature of Drettroth's purpose. The Rogandan had freely acknowledged that he was actively seeking to bring together the three stones, and had claimed to have definite knowledge of them. Simon now saw that Drettroth intended to unite in his own person the power of good health and long life, authority over men and unlimited insight into the thoughts and intents of others.

But to his horror Simon had also glimpsed a darker purpose. Drettroth lusted to extend his own life indefinitely and was willing to go to any lengths to achieve that goal. He had secretly invested much of his energy pursuing a special understanding with his Dark Gods. Whether such a covenant had any meaning, and whether it could have delivered on his expectations, no one would ever know. But Drettroth had believed in its power, and he had been actively working to secure an unending supply of human sacrifice to establish and maintain the pact. His insatiable appetite for conquest could only be properly understood in light of this information.

For Arvenon, Castel, and Varas, a final Rogandan victory would have resulted in far more than a change of masters. The extent of the terror awaiting the ordinary people of the three kingdoms was more than Simon could take in. He knew enough about Drettroth, though, to be certain that the self-serving Rogandan lord would follow through on his plans without hesitation and entirely without consideration for his victims.

What the old Simon would have done with this knowledge was hard to guess. But everything had changed for the youth when he met Brother Vangellis. The unlikely friendship had stirred in him a desire for a new beginning, while at the same time bringing him unexpected hope. The first stirrings of change had caused him to arrange the escape of the young nobleman, who proved to be King Delmar of Varas. Once in brief possession of the stone, though, its disturbing revelations had brought Simon a new clarity of purpose. He immediately concluded that ending Drettroth's life must assume far greater importance than continuing to preserve his own.

Instead of calling for the torturers as instructed, Simon had gifted the stone to Drettroth, who at that moment had it in his hand. In a moment of supreme irony, the Rogandan lord had at last achieved his greatest desire only to discover that he had been betrayed. His life was about to end, and in excruciating agony. Far from cheating Malzakh, he realized he was imminently about to fall into the ravenous clutches of his insatiable god.

Having killed Drettroth, Simon could not reclaim the stone. But he handed it to Brother Vangellis who was able to learn a great deal from Simon, even though the opportunity was frustratingly brief.

The monk's surprise when looking at Thomas was not due to anything Simon was whispering to him. With sudden access to the mind and memories of Thomas, the monk had been startled to recognize Elena in the forefront of his consciousness. Although the monk never had an opportunity to express it in words, Thomas had been able to discern that Brother Vangellis took great delight in knowing they had found each other.

Thinking of his friend in this way triggered a fresh round of anguish in Thomas. He was aware that the monk could so easily have run for his life, as Thomas himself had later done. Brother Vangellis probably would have survived if he had fled. Instead he willingly chose to buy time for Thomas, and paid for that choice with his life.

Eventually Thomas was able to think calmly again. He pondered the monk's gift of the stone. His friend had told the truth when he assured Thomas that he had no desire for the burden of the stone's gifts. In turning it over to Thomas, though, he was ensuring that crucial knowledge and insights passed along from multiple people would not be lost.

Provided that Thomas, alone and defenseless in an enemy fortress, could somehow find a way to survive.

22

The men in Rufe's battle line had little time to think of anything beyond survival. A soldier beside Rufe took a blow to his helmet and went down hard, stunned. Two Rogandans rushed in eagerly to finish him off.

Rufe was not willing to give him up, though. Yelling a challenge, the giant leader thrust himself sideways into the gap, attacking both of them at once. Seeing his size and his determination, they hastily backed away. Rufe brought one of them down, causing the other to trip. Another Arvenian came to his support and dealt with the second man.

Rufe stretched an arm down to the fallen Arvenian soldier. He grasped it, and Rufe pulled him to his feet. The soldier shook his head a couple of times, but didn't hesitate before resuming his place in the line.

As the battle wore on, it became obvious that neither Rufe's role as leader nor his effectiveness in battle were lost on his enemies. The fight immediately became very dangerous for Rufe as the Rogandans began to specifically target him. Two men came at him at once. They went down, but three others quickly replaced them. Rufe knew he could not continue at this pace for long.

His men saw what was happening and moved vigorously to his aid. Soon Rufe stood at the center of a knot of men weaving back and forth, fighting frenetically. Rogandan soldiers crowded in, trying to bring him down. His own men threw themselves into the fight in his defense.

In the heat of battle Rufe stepped backward, stumbled over a body, and fell flat on his back. Sensing an opportunity, the Rogandans roared at the top of their voices and pressed in recklessly to the attack. One of them, a huge brute wearing a manic grimace on his face, stood over him and raised his sword high for the kill. Two of Rufe's men crashed into him from the side, knocking him from his feet. Scrambling up, one of Rufe's comrades thrust the Rogandan through. His companion, though, was cut down before he could find his feet.

Another Arvenian helped Rufe up. The big man immediately repaid him by blocking an enemy soldier who rushed in while he was distracted. More soldiers came at them both, and the fighting resumed its frantic rhythm. Rufe rushed to the defense of two more of his men and in turn was defended by two others.

In the melee the soldier immediately to Rufe's left went down. Rufe, already fending off another determined attack, could do nothing to help. The Rogandan attacker, instead of finishing off the soldier at Rufe's side, joined the assault on Rufe, drawing back his sword for a killing thrust. Exposed and distracted as Rufe was, the blow should have finished him. But another Arvenian, unable to impede the Rogandan in any other way, leaped forward and took the sword thrust himself.

Several frenzied minutes passed before Rufe could even turn to his rescuer. When he finally did, he found the man lying dead on the ground. Rufe didn't even know his name. Not for the first time that day, he owed another man his life. But there was no way for him ever to repay the debt. No chance even to thank him.

More attackers moved in against Rufe. He would not even be granted a moment to grieve.

Rufe plunged back into the battle with fresh determination,

though. There was a purpose behind the unselfish sacrifice of these nameless soldiers. All of them fought to end a pitiless invasion, a ruthless violation that left their land ravaged and their people murdered. They fought for the defenseless, for those who could not fight for themselves.

And beyond that deeper purpose lay a more elemental impulse. Rufe and the men beside him fought that day for their brothers, for men who had forged a kinship with their own blood. More than once today other men had laid down their lives for Rufe. More than once today he had very nearly done the same in return. He would not shrink from doing so again for the sake of those who remained.

Pain and suffering and bitter loss surrounded him on all sides. But it was a soldier's duty to fight, and, if necessary, to die. Rufe took his place in the battle line once more, shoulder to shoulder with his brothers in arms, ready to face whatever might come. In that moment, standing erect with them at his side, he was content.

FEW ARMIES COULD HOPE to retain cohesion under such conditions, and a lump came to Will's throat as he looked out over his men and witnessed again their quality, their fighting spirit and their sacrifice. It had become apparent that they were about to be overwhelmed in spite of everything they had worked so hard to achieve. He resolved that he would not stand by and allow them to face it alone.

"I'm going down there," he told Bottren decisively.

"But you can't!" Bottren retorted in dismay.

"I'm needed there. Much more than I'm needed here," Will told him. "You're in charge. If it comes to the worst, try to extract as many of the men as you can. I don't doubt that the Varasans will retreat in good order, and a good few of our men are with them now."

Bottren was opening his mouth to argue when a warning shout rang out behind them.

Will swung around to see a body of men riding in swiftly, skirting the low hills to the west.

Then another voice called, "They're ours!"

Unforeseen and unlooked for, and at the very threshold of disaster, a seemingly endless stream of riders poured onto the plain. Ranauld had arrived. Many of his horsemen carried hunting horns from Erestor, and with the battlefield before them at last, they raised the horns to their lips and blew. Wild and discordant, the sound swelled as it echoed back insistently from the escarpment.

Every head turned, across the entire battlefield. Rufe's men, embattled and almost overwhelmed, stood taller and gripped their weapons more tightly.

New hope awoke in Will. "Get their leaders up here urgently!" he called.

His dispatch riders raced like the wind to the column. They spurred their horses back up the hill with two men following close behind.

The leader dismounted and strode up the hill to Will and Bottren.

"Ranauld! It is good to see you," cried Bottren. Then his face fell. "Has Arnost fallen, then?"

"No! Arnost still stands!" Ranauld replied. "I've brought only a part of our strength. I'm sorry we couldn't get here sooner."

"Your help is timely beyond words!" Will told him. "You must have a thousand men down there. How did you find mounts for so many?"

"I have twelve hundred. These are mainly Burtelen's riders, though. Most of my men are on foot."

"Lord Burtelen is nearby? How many more men? When will they get here?"

"He has another three thousand, including my men. They are on foot, though. I cannot see how they could arrive today."

Will's brows bristled. He needed those three thousand, so badly. But he must work with what he had. "I need you to secure our right wing and stabilize our line," he told Ranauld. He quickly explained, and Ranauld set off without delay.

Will watched with awe as twelve hundred fresh soldiers poured onto the battlefield. Their impact was immediate. The right flank dangled no longer, and the Rogandans fell back rapidly as the horsemen swept across their line. Finding themselves free to disengage, Rufe's harassed soldiers turned their backs on the fighting and scurried back to their new assigned positions below Will. Their wounded, previously behind the line, now found themselves exposed. Rufe came last with a small group of soldiers, shepherding the wounded men.

The Rogandans now commanded most of the battlefield, and their weight of numbers soon began to be felt. Heavily outnumbered, Ranauld's men were driven back steadily toward the newly formed line behind them. The men in the battle line stepped aside and let the riders through, and most of the horsemen dismounted and rushed forward to strengthen the line.

The afternoon began to wear away. The Rogandans were far too numerous to be overcome. And Will's army was too stubborn to yield.

THE ROGANDAN COMMANDER, Kulzeike, was present on the battlefield. He himself had stayed out of the fighting, though. He harbored no doubts about the outcome, and he saw no reason to expose himself to the ever-willing clutches of Malzakh when he could leave it to his men to do the dying for him.

He had given his army everything it could possibly need to deliver a crushing defeat to the combined Arvenian and Castelan forces. Not least was their overwhelming superiority in numbers. And yet, in spite of everything, the fools had so far failed to bring their enemies to their knees.

The treachery of the Varasans at a critical moment was especially infuriating. It had plunged a knife into the back of his second army. Kulzeike was livid when he thought of their betrayal. The entire Varasan nation would pay in blood!

He still had more than enough men. But it was becoming clear to him that he was going to have to win the victory himself. Frustrating as that notion seemed at first, the more he thought about it, the more attractive it became. Being able to claim the glory personally offered considerable appeal to the commander. He was still new to this appointment. What better way to entrench himself as Drettroth's favorite?

The personal bodyguard of Kulzeike consisted of one hundred of the biggest, strongest, and most brutal men in the Rogandan army. None of them had seen any fighting today. He gathered them together and yelled at them for five solid minutes. Then he led them to what he deemed to be the weakest point in Will's northern battle line, near the western flank of the Rogandan position.

The men in Will's battle line had been in action all day. Kulzeike's attack smashed into them like a tidal wave. The defenders were unable to withstand the ferocity of the attack, and Kulzeike's assault quickly punched a gaping hole in the allied line. In those first frantic moments, the outcome of the entire battle hung in the balance.

In a day of surprises, though, another unexpected twist was developing. Even as Will prepared once more to hurry down to the fighting in an attempt to stem the tide by his own efforts, a new group of horsemen swung around the hills to the northwest and streamed unheralded onto the battlefield.

Will was not expecting their arrival. Even Ranauld had no knowledge of their movements.

The packhorses commandeered by Kuper and Rellan and their men were not sprinters, but they had more stamina than their swifter cousins, and they had plodded on steadily. The horsemen, riding bareback, were mostly hardy men from the mountains of Erestor. They were well accustomed to rough conditions and had been honed for war in Lord Burtelen's training camps. They were spoiling for a fight.

Kuper did not wait to find Will. He led his men directly into battle. His three hundred threw themselves into the struggle, right at the point where Kulzeike was rampaging unchecked with his bodyguard. Some of Kuper's men literally leaped from their horses straight onto their startled enemies.

In the heat of battle, Rellan spotted Kulzeike and recognized him as the key to the struggle. He plunged immediately into the attack. Kulzeike's bodyguards rallied around their commander, and Rellan was soon surrounded and in trouble.

The soldiers who had ridden to the battle with Rellan had no previous connection with him and no personal reason to specially look out for him. None of them stood ready to defend him with their lives. None except his twin.

Having dealt with an opponent of his own, Kuper looked up and recognized his brother's peril. Bellowing for support, he raced to Rellan's defense and threw himself at Kulzeike. He crashed into the Rogandan and bore him to the ground, his thrusting sword carving a brutal slice across Kulzeike's neck. Kulzeike did not get up.

The Rogandan commander's bodyguards reacted instinctively, several of them hacking mercilessly at Kuper while he was down and defenseless. For a moment Kuper struggled to rise. Then he slumped back down onto the ground, subsiding helplessly as his life ebbed away.

Rellan, his mouth agape, looked on with horror and disbelief. Then he exploded into action, attacking his brother's killers with deadly wrath. Unsettled by the sudden loss of their leader, none of the Rogandans were willing to abide his fury.

Having scattered his enemies, Rellan returned to his brother and stood trembling by his side. Numbed at the enormity of his loss, he struggled to accept what had occurred. All his life Kuper had been at his side. He was without doubt the best man that Rellan had ever known. And he had just saved Rellan's life, with never a moment's thought for his own safety. Why did he have to die?

Rellan's eyes brimmed with tears as he gazed down in anguish at his brother's body. He began to weep unashamedly, heedless of the battle raging nearby.

Finally, noticing the fighting drawing closer again, he recovered himself and called for help. Recognizing Rellan, another horseman came to his aid, and together they bore his brother from the field.

COSTLY AS IT proved to be, Kuper and Rellan's attack had restored the balance between the armies. It appeared that the day was set to end without either side able to force a decisive result. The Rogandans retained an overwhelming advantage in numbers, but the position of the battle lines, combined with the geography of the site, ensured that most of their soldiers were unable to reach their enemies. They were therefore reduced to milling around in the middle of the battlefield waiting their turn in the battle line.

Of the rival armies, Will's forces were in the most precarious position. The allies still had the Rogandans boxed in, which placed the initiative for any withdrawal with Will. He reluctantly began to consider the logistical challenges of pulling back from the battlefield. His difficulty was that any such action would immediately release the Rogandans. If they pursued his men with sufficient vigor, a retreat could easily turn into a rout. And if the Rogandans chose to surround Will's forces, they had the numbers to destroy them.

THE TIDE WAS ABOUT to turn one last time, though, with none of the combatants able to foresee what was about to happen.

Lord Burtelen's wagons had done their job. Having rolled his soldiers forward steadily through the night and then more rapidly throughout the whole of the following morning and into the afternoon, the nobleman formed the men up and marched them on at a relentless pace, permitting only brief and infrequent breaks. The forced march continued for the remainder of the afternoon. It brought them to the battlefield late in the day, but far sooner than Ranauld could ever have imagined.

A final barrier lay in their path: the series of low hills that formed Will's right flank. Instead of following the trail of the horsemen and marching around them, the men took the most direct route and tramped up and over the hills. The sun was less than an hour above the horizon when the first of them began to appear on the western fringes of the battlefield.

The earliest to arrive were the archers. They had traveled light, carrying nothing except their longbows and large clusters of arrows strapped to their backs. The hill face that fronted the plain was steep enough to discourage easy access from below, but the approach from the western side was more gentle, and the archers traversed it easily.

No horn or drum beat heralded their arrival. They moved silently into position, just over the crest of the final hill, and calmly began laying out their arrows. The entire Rogandan army lay spread out thickly before them across the battlefield, contained by the Varasans to the south and Will's men to the north. For the archers, the targets that blotted out the plain were abundant beyond their wildest imagining.

Thus far they had remained largely undetected. For most of the soldiers on the battlefield, the first hint of the archers' presence was the eerie whistle-whoosh of the arrows that soon poured, volley after volley, into the Rogandan ranks.

The effect was catastrophic. Men began to fall by the hundreds. The Rogandans immediately sent every available rider against them. Having no ready access up the slope of the hills, the horsemen milled around uselessly at the bottom of the hill face. The archers simply lowered their aim and sent the riders crashing from their saddles.

A sizable Rogandan force set out on foot, urgently sprinting toward the archers. There were far too many of them for the bowmen to deal with, but there was little need for concern. Before the Rogandans could begin clambering up the hill face, further elements of Lord Burtelen's thousands swarmed across the hills and took up defensive positions below the bowmen. These reinforcements were soon engaged in heavy fighting as they fended off the Rogandan attackers.

Some of the new arrivals had carried spare arrows, and they laid the bundles down beside the archers as they passed. With barely a break, the archers renewed their relentless destruction. The setting sun stained the clouds blood red in the west, and darts of death poured without pause out of the glowering horizon onto the battlefield. The human toll became staggering.

Will's men and the Varasans now fought with sudden hope and renewed energy.

All day the Rogandans had witnessed how thin the lines were that faced them, and they had never doubted that victory would eventually belong to them. Now, for the first time, doubt assailed them. A collective shudder ran through the thousands milling around on the plain. The fighting spirit of the army of Rogand began to crumble.

Men cast about desperately, searching for a haven from the deadly rain. The eastern end of the battlefield beside the cliff face of Torbury Scarp was out of range of the arrows, and Rogandan soldiers flooded into the area, pushing and shoving each other in an attempt to position themselves as close to the cliff face as possible.

Seeing this exodus, most of the archers gathered up their unspent shafts and scrambled down onto the plain, taking up positions behind the northern Arvenian battle line below Will, or behind the Varasan line to the south. The lethal hail resumed as the bowmen began firing over the heads of their fighting comrades.

Almost the entire battlefield was now within reach of the archers. The Rogandans, blocked by their enemies on three sides and by a sheer cliff on the fourth, had nowhere to go. No safe haven remained, apart from the established battle lines that ran across the northern and southern boundaries of the battlefield, and the new battle line to the west, below the original position of the bowmen. The archers avoided these areas for fear of hitting their own men, so Rogandan soldiers not in the battle line crowded together as near to the combat as they could. They achieved nothing except to hinder those of their countrymen doing the fighting.

. . .

WITH THE OTHER observers at his command post, Will watched stupefied as the archers methodically set about their demolition of the Rogandan army. Such an outcome was the sole purpose of his battle plan, but the nature and the scale of the carnage nevertheless numbed his senses.

It was obvious to Will that a decisive opportunity had finally arrived, and he immediately issued orders for an advance along the entire line. This time Bottren was unable to restrain him. No longer willing to remain an observer even for another minute, Will found his horse and set out to join Rufe. Cheers followed him as he rode along the line, and the men erupted the minute they realized that their commander would be joining them in the fighting.

As soon as he located Rufe, he dismounted. Seeing his friend still standing, Will greeted him with joy and relief. Rufe's face was grimed with sweat and dust and flecked with blood. His every movement betrayed his exhaustion.

"Were the archers another of your little surprises?" Rufe asked him with a weary smile.

"No. We will win today, and we have the archers to thank for it. But none of that credit belongs to me."

"We're still here and we're still fighting. You deserve credit for that," Rufe said.

Will shook his head. "The credit will go to all of you. But it's too early yet for anyone to claim credit. We need to finish this!"

FOR THE FIRST time that day, Will personally led his men to the attack, and in response they dug deep to dredge up a final reserve of strength. The entire line lurched forward. Slowly at first, then with growing momentum, they drove the Rogandans back.

The invaders had been told that overwhelming numbers would bring them an easy victory. Instead they had fought all day without prevailing. They had lost their leader, and with him much of their impetus to fight. Then they had endured death raining down mercilessly from the skies. Now, pressed back by an enemy that refused to yield, and jostled and crowded from behind by their own men, the Rogandan line began to totter.

Seeing the movement to the north, the Varasans began to force their way forward from the south with equal vigor. The last rays of sunlight illuminated the death throes of the army of Rogand, as the jaws of destruction slowly closed and ground it to pieces.

In the darkness and the confusion, a good few Rogandan soldiers managed to slip away from the battlefield. Nevertheless, as a fighting force the Rogandan army ceased to exist.

23

Thirst eventually drove Thomas from his hiding place. By then, several hours had passed during which he heard nothing, apart from a brief period of confused shouting two or three hours earlier.

He crept aimlessly through the empty passageways, having no idea at all where he was in the castle. At one time he passed a window that looked out onto a sky filled with stars, so he knew it was evening. Perhaps most of the inhabitants of the fortress were sleeping.

Eventually he decided to head downward whenever the opportunity arose. By this means he somehow found his way to the kitchens. Everything looked cold and abandoned, but he found water aplenty and drank until he was satisfied. After a brief hunt he found half a loaf of stale bread and an onion; he was so hungry that it seemed like a feast. He searched out a quiet corner and ate the food.

While foraging he was delighted to find an empty wineskin. After again slaking his thirst, he filled the wineskin with water and departed with it. He found himself a new hiding place and sat down to wait out the night.

With the coming of the dawn, he emerged once again, restless and weary after a night without sleep. He still saw no sign of any other person in the castle. The state of the kitchen finally convinced him that the fortress had been abandoned, and he eventually found the courage to explore the stronghold boldly from top to bottom as well as inside and out. No horses had been left in the stables. Even the dungeons had been emptied. The gates of the fortress stood wide open, and the drawbridge was down over the moat.

Behind the fortress stood a single tall tree in a broad meadow covered with green grass and dotted with white snowdrop anemones. Thomas hunted around until he found a metal spade, and he took it to the meadow. He began to dig two graves near the tree. The ground was soft, and he dug as well as he could with his single good arm. After what must have been hours, he felt confident the holes were deep enough to discourage wild animals.

He found a small cart behind the kitchens and wheeled it to the room where he had been imprisoned. Somehow he bundled Simon's body into the cart. Wincing with pain at every bump, he wheeled him awkwardly along the passageways, down the flights of steps, and over to the graveside. Then he carefully rolled him into the smaller of the two graves.

He anticipated more difficulty when he went back for Brother Vangellis, but the monk had become very thin during his imprisonment, and he was surprisingly light.

Drettroth he left lying where he had fallen.

By the time the light was fading, Thomas was bone weary, and his shoulder throbbed painfully. He had filled in both graves and gathered together a small pile of rocks to form a cairn between them. He managed to fashion a single crude cross, and he pushed it into the ground at the head of the mound where he had laid Brother Vangellis.

Perhaps no one in the world would truly miss Simon apart from Axel Stablehand, Thomas's father. But Thomas, at least, fully understood the magnitude of the debt owed by the people of Arvenon and Castel to Simon, and he spoke aloud a few halting words to honor him and to acknowledge his sacrifice. He also voiced his own remorse for the ways he had failed the youth. He said nothing of Simon's betrayal. In light of all the youth had done since, it seemed to Thomas that his earlier mistakes ought to be readily forgiven and quietly forgotten.

Finally he stood at the foot of the grave of Brother Vangellis. He paused, silent for a moment, eyes lightly shut and his thoughts drifting with the cool breeze that brushed at his hair. Then he opened his eyes and repeated aloud whatever words he could remember from the things Brother Vangellis had said at the funeral in the village and later by the graveside of Elbruhe. Finally, tears rolling freely down his cheeks, he spoke from the heart, honoring a man who had expressed his compassion unstintingly and without consideration for rank or status, one who had finally poured himself out in the most pragmatic way possible, by laying down his life for a friend.

WILL'S scouts found Thomas sitting alone at the gateway to the empty fortress. A horse was found for him, and he rode back with them to the camp at Hazelwood Ford.

He was greeted with genuine delight, especially by Will and Rufe, and they soon arranged for a reunion of the small party that had ridden away together from Arnost. Pleased as they were to find themselves together again after all that had happened, it was nevertheless a somber gathering. None of them had remained unchanged by the tide in which they had been swept along.

Thomas was grieved to learn that Kuper had not survived the battle. He was also disappointed to have missed seeing Rellan, who, after supervising the burial of his brother, had hurried back to Erestor at the earliest possible opportunity. Nevertheless, the review of the Battle of Torbury Scarp laid out solely for the benefit of Thomas scarcely had an equal anywhere, even among the kings and their nobles.

He listened with a mixture of awe and horror as Will, Rufe, Ander, and Nestor each took up the tale in their turn. None of them had any illusions about the reasons for the decisive victory. The battle had been won only thanks to a combination of circumstances entirely beyond their control. Yet it was also obvious to Thomas that no victory could have been won at all without their extraordinary efforts. He also rejoiced—and greatly marveled—that each of them had somehow survived when so many other brave men had fallen.

When the story was told, Thomas still had many questions.

"What was it like when the reinforcements from Erestor arrived on the battlefield?" Thomas asked.

"Watching Count Ranauld's riders pouring onto the battlefield—it seemed like an endless stream—was one of the most stirring sights I have ever seen," said Will. "Especially in light of what was happening at the time. And the arrival of Kuper and Rellan with their horsemen was no less significant. Neither group could have arrived at a more critical moment."

"For me it was the impact of the archers," said Rufe. "When the arrows first started coming in, fighting completely stopped for a few moments. Even the Rogandans paused to watch it. None of us could help ourselves.

"We were barely hanging on. And suddenly Rogandan soldiers behind the battle line started going down, far too many to count. Then it became chaos, with Rogandans running everywhere in a panic. The effect on their morale was ruinous. That's when I truly began to hope again."

"And none of it could have happened without Kuper and Rellan and their friends!" said Thomas. "What did you all say when Rellan first told you about the way they managed to remove the Rogandan army in Erestor?"

"We were completely dumbfounded," said Rufe.

Will was clearly still astonished by it. "The avalanche was a stroke of genius!" he said. "I've never heard of anything like it—an entire army destroyed in minutes, and with so little loss to ourselves."

They talked for some time in awed tones about the timely arrival of the soldiers from Erestor—entirely unexpected by either side—and how it had completely transformed the outcome of the battle.

"And what about Queen Essanda?" Thomas asked. "Is she safe? She seems to be a truly remarkable girl—or is she a woman?"

"She is remarkable. And thankfully she is safe as well," said Will. "She's little more than a girl, but without her intervention the battle would certainly have been lost not long after it started. Her efforts, assisted by some canny guidance from our Nes, completely unraveled the plans of Lord Eisgold."

"What's become of Lord Eisgold?" Thomas asked.

"He has been banished by King Istel," Will replied. "After the way he blatantly ignored orders at the critical moment early in the battle, he almost certainly would have forfeited his life if he hadn't fought so bravely later. After he actually committed himself to the fighting, he did all that was asked of him and more, and that is undoubtedly what saved him."

"And what about the Varasans?" asked Thomas.

"We couldn't have won without them, either," Ander told him. "They are ferocious fighters."

"They lost many men at Torbury Scarp," said Will. "So King Steffan lent King Delmar a large contingent from Erestor—over a thousand men—since they had seen very little of the fighting. The combined force has marched on Varas to retake it from the Rogandans."

"That shouldn't prove too difficult," said Thomas. "Drettroth withdrew most of the Rogandan army from Varas for the battle."

"So that's where the extra men came from!" Nestor exclaimed.

"From Varas, and from elsewhere throughout Arvenon," Thomas replied. "Drettroth secretly pulled together almost his entire occupying army. He intended to take you by surprise."

"He certainly succeeded in doing that," said Will. "But it's becoming clear you have a lot to tell us, Thomas. Start from the beginning, from the moment you and Brother Vangellis left us after the passing of Elbruhe."

The hours slipped away as Thomas related the full story of all that had happened, interrupted by a great many questions on the way through. His friends did not conceal their amazement as the tale unfolded. All of them were stirred when he told them of Simon's resolve in bringing down Drettroth. And, hardened soldiers though they were, none were unmoved when he related the willing sacrifice of Brother Vangellis on his behalf.

He omitted nothing from his account except Elena and the stone, and if it seemed remarkable that Drettroth should have pursued Thomas and the monk so tenaciously, none of them commented on it.

"So now I finally understand how King Delmar managed to appear on the battlefield at such a critical moment," Nestor remarked. "None of my sources could account for it at all."

"The thing I don't understand is why the Rogandans abandoned the fortress," said Thomas.

"Word must have reached them about the outcome of the battle," said Will. "It's surprising how quickly news travels, especially bad news. They probably all packed up and headed for Rogand. Our scouts have been reporting a constant stream of refugees heading east."

"I doubt they'll receive a warm welcome from King Agon," said Nestor.

"No," Will replied. "Drettroth is gone, but Agon remains. We now have an alliance with Varas as well as with Castel. All of us will need to strengthen our borders and rebuild our armies."

King Steffan paced back and forth impatiently, waiting to be informed of the arrival of Essanda.

Steffan had heard nothing about her exploits until after the battle. By then she had been escorted to Castel Citadel by Count Gordan as originally planned, even if her departure was somewhat belated. Steffan had been almost frantic with alarm when he first heard the story. He still felt agitated now, even though he knew she was safe and unharmed.

He had been entirely preoccupied with an endless round of official duties since the battle at Torbury Scarp, with no possibility whatsoever of traveling to the citadel to see her. Unable to speak with her, his frustration had grown until he felt like he was almost at breaking point.

In the end King Istel had decided he could bear it no longer. Taking matters into his own hands, he arranged for Gordan to bring her back to the camp at Hazelwood Ford. He held off telling his son-in-law until a few hours before she was due to arrive. Istel had been more than a little apprehensive about Steffan's reaction, but Steffan was delighted, to Istel's obvious relief.

Essanda was now due any minute.

"As far as I'm concerned she can't get here soon enough," said Istel. "You've been like a bear with a sore tooth from the moment I told you she was on her way!"

Steffan said nothing, but he managed a self-conscious smile.

A head finally appeared at the entrance of the tent where the two of them were waiting. "They've arrived, Sire."

Steffan burst out of the tent, almost colliding with Count Gordan. "I'll have words with you later!" he promised the nobleman fiercely. "Where is she?"

Essanda had just been helped from her horse, her face looking flushed after the ride. His protective instincts rose up at his first glimpse of her—to him she seemed both beautiful and fragile. And infinitely precious.

He ran to her and swept her into his arms. An overpowering jumble of emotions—brimming pride, intense relief, firm reproach—totally engulfed him, and tears flooded his eyes. He drew her away from his chest and pressed her forehead firmly to his lips.

"Essanda, I couldn't *bear* to lose you! It would destroy me."

She buried herself in his chest once more, her eyes overflowing.

"I'm so sorry, Steffan," she managed through her tears. "I never wanted you to worry about me. I just felt I couldn't let him do it—I couldn't let him destroy Will and everything you'd worked for."

"You wonderful girl. I'm not angry with you! I was very distressed, but I'm so proud of you. You're incredibly brave! And you saw the truth when I was blind to it."

"I didn't feel very brave. Seeing our men fighting and dying before my eyes—it was too much for me. I hadn't understood how terrible war is."

"It is terrible. But it's over now. And I'm so glad you're safe!"

She sighed her relief at his words, and hugged him tighter. "Please don't be angry with Gordy," she pleaded. "He feels so guilty, but it wasn't his fault."

"Hmmm. I'll have to see about that," he said with a half-hearted grumble. "Good did come of it in the end, I suppose."

He held her at arm's length and gazed seriously into her eyes. "No more escapades without discussing it with me first. Promise?"

"I promise," she said meekly, smiling as she wiped away her tears.

He tucked her under his arm and turned her toward the tent. "Come and see your father," he said with a happy smile.

THE NEXT DAY Will found Thomas sitting alone eating some food.

"What are your plans now, Thomas?" he asked.

"I'm planning to leave Hazelwood Ford as soon as I can. There were some pieces of the story that I left out," he said, a little shamefacedly.

"I thought as much," Will replied with a smile. "The stone?"

"Yes. I still have it. And it is working reliably again. There's quite a story behind that, too."

"I'll look forward to hearing it."

"And there's someone waiting for me, too."

Will raised his eyebrows. "Oh," he said. "That sounds like a tale worth hearing."

"The problem is that I'm not sure how to find her again."

"Tell me more," said Will.

Thomas briefly described his time in the forest. If he was vague in his description of Elena and her father, it was only because he felt at a loss to know how best to describe them.

Will listened for a while, then he smiled again. “This girl living alone with her father in the wilderness—did she appear at first glance to be an old hunchback dressed in black?”

Thomas was too astonished to reply. But he nodded his agreement.

“In that case, I think I can help you find them, because I suspect I met them myself when I was traveling to Stantony,” Will told him. “In fact, I can do better than that. I will accompany you. I need to visit somewhere very near there myself. I should warn you, though—it will be a few days before I’ll be able to leave.”

He explained his own connection with the mysterious pair. Thomas could only shake his head in amazement.

Will clearly had many demands on his time. Thomas was overwhelmed with gratitude for the help that his friend had promised, and told him so many times.

IN THE END a full week went by before Will was ready to set out. To the delight of Thomas, Rufe had announced he would be traveling with them as well.

A large party of mounted soldiers would also be accompanying them at the insistence of King Steffan. Will had tried to talk him out of it, but the king was unbending. He was not willing to take any risks with his two key leaders, for all that they were commoners.

On the last day before their departure from Hazelwood Ford, Nestor hosted a final farewell for the travelers. They ate their evening meal together, then relaxed in the cold evening air appreciating a magnificent sunset.

“I’ve decided to become a monk,” said Ander.

A loud guffaw immediately exploded from Nestor. He guffawed again, and before long all of them were laughing, Ander included. The mood of the moment took complete hold, and every one of them was soon held fast in the grip of uproarious merriment, weeping with laughter. Thomas knew it was excessive, but there had been so little to laugh about in recent days.

Finally they were able to calm themselves. Nestor shook his head. "You had me for a moment," he told Ander, a new chuckle rising up to threaten his equanimity once more.

"You've more than proven your mettle as a soldier and a leader," said Will. "We'll miss you."

Rufe nodded. "You'll be a huge loss to the army. But the world needs men like Brother Vangellis a lot more than it needs soldiers."

"Please don't compare me with Brother Vangellis," Ander protested. "I can't do more than aspire to be like him."

Nestor looked back and forth between them, a bewildered look on his face. "You're actually serious?" he asked.

"Of course," said Ander.

"But I don't get it."

Ander looked at him thoughtfully. "Do you understand what made him like he was?" he asked.

Nestor paused for a moment, then shook his head.

"Neither do I," said Ander. "But I intend to try to find out."

"Brother Vangellis would be pleased if he knew," said Thomas.

"He would," agreed Rufe.

THEY SET off from Hazelwood Ford early the next morning. King Steffan was there to see them off, with Queen Essanda at his side. Young as she was, she had already made a name for herself. It was the first glimpse for Thomas of his new queen, and he was impressed.

"Safe travels, Will! Take care of him, Rufe!" she called out in her clear high voice, a shy smile on her face.

Will bowed deeply in response. Thomas could see from his ready smile that she had won his affection as well as his admiration.

Once they were underway, Thomas looked back to see the young queen sending a final wave. Feeling unusually bold, he waved back.

They traveled along established roads whenever they could, and only set off across the fields when they needed to. They spent their first night under the stars. It was bitingly cold, but thankfully the worst of the winter weather was not upon them yet.

On the second day their scouts surprised a small group of men, who ran from them in fear. The soldiers spread out and rounded them up, bringing them to Will.

They were clearly Rogandan soldiers, and a miserable looking lot. The real question was whether they were defeated soldiers fleeing back to Rogand, or an armed rabble roaming the countryside looking for trouble. None of them were armed, but they might well have discarded their weapons when they were first discovered.

Will looked at them searchingly. Then he saw something that seemed to startle him. He pointed to one of the men, who shuffled forward unhappily. Will spoke to him in Rogandan. The man replied, and a long interaction ensued.

Will left the men and rode up to Thomas. He leaned forward, speaking in a low voice. "I need you to take a look at these men, Thomas. They claim they are simply on their way back to Rogand. I would like some verification."

Thomas surreptitiously reached for the stone, and surveyed the group. "They're harmless," he told Will.

"Including that one?" Will pointed out one of the men.

"He's weary and discouraged," Thomas told him. "He seems to have little to look forward to, and he certainly doesn't want to be a soldier. But there's nothing sinister about him at all."

Will nodded. He spoke to the men sternly before sending them on their way. He did, however, detain the one he had pointed out to Thomas.

He apparently asked the man his name.

"Haldek," was the reply.

Further conversation took place between them. Then Will asked for a spare horse. "This man will be joining us," he said.

The soldiers were clearly taken aback by Will's announcement. Rufe, who knew his commander too well to be surprised by anything he did, simply smiled.

Will swung Haldek in beside Thomas, asking him to keep an eye out for the Rogandan, and the column set off again. From the occasional glances Thomas directed at his new companion, the man seemed anxious and unhappy.

Thomas knew there was no reason to fear him, and he found himself recalling Elbruhe's initial reaction when she first joined them. The memory brought him a wave of compassion for his new companion. When Haldek next looked in his direction, he presented him with a friendly smile. The Rogandan looked slightly less miserable, and Thomas was willing to claim that as a success.

Over the next few days the two of them began teaching each other words in their own languages. Haldek proved the more able student. With little else to do as they rode, he concentrated hard on learning vocabulary, and soon was able to attempt very simple conversations. Thomas gradually discovered that he had a kind heart and an easy manner. Thomas could also see that Haldek was warming to him.

On one occasion Thomas found himself briefly alone with Will. "Why did you single out Haldek to join us?" he asked.

"He doesn't realize it, but he's saved me twice," Will replied.

"Another story for another time?" asked Thomas.

Will nodded, grinning.

SEVERAL DAYS HAD PASSED when Will finally drew Thomas aside. "We will soon be nearing the location where I expect to find your friend and her father," he told him.

Thomas felt his heart skip a beat. A flush flooded over his face. He had been so eager to see Elena, but now he felt unexpectedly shy. How should he behave when he saw her again? What if she had lost interest in him?

Will smiled at his confusion, but chose not to comment. "We don't need to take all of the soldiers with us," he said. "We can rejoin them later. I suggest we just take Rufe and Haldek."

Thomas was surprised at Will's inclusion of Haldek, but he decided not to question it. Will undoubtedly had his reasons.

When they set up camp that night Will told the soldiers that they should expect to be there for two or three days at the least. The smaller party set off in the morning after Will issued instructions for the soldiers to wait for his return.

Thomas did not recognize any landmarks, and Will could not identify the precise location of the cabin by the stream, either. So their search began without any clear idea of where to look.

Mid afternoon arrived with no apparent progress toward reaching their goal, and Thomas began to despair of ever finding Elena again. Then Rufe found a stream with a path beside it. Nothing about it was familiar to Thomas, but they decided to follow the path in one direction until it became dark. Will chose the direction, and they set off.

After a while Thomas began to suspect that they were retracing his path as he fled from the Rogandans. His excitement grew even as the light was failing. He became certain they were heading in the right direction. They picked up their pace and reached the cabin as the darkness deepened around them.

Thomas ran to the cabin and went in. It was deserted.

There was nothing they could do except wait until daylight came. They tethered their horses and bedded down near the cabin.

Thomas lay there in the dark, wide awake and deeply troubled. Where were Elena and Rubin? Had they been taken after all, in spite of his warning and his efforts to lead the Rogandans away?

He hadn't forgotten that he advised Elena to hide, though. Maybe she and her father had taken his advice and removed themselves to a different location. But she had asked him if he would come back for her. That made no sense if she wasn't going to be here anymore.

The night was far advanced before he finally surrendered to exhaustion and drifted off to sleep.

HE WOKE with a start to bright sunlight. The others were up already. Rufe spotted him and came to speak with him.

"Is this the right location, Thomas? The cabin hasn't been lived in for some time."

"Yes. This is where they were living. Where could they have gone?"

Will appeared from the direction of the stream. "I've found animal snares in the forest nearby—I'd say they were set not too long ago. And the garden beside the cabin appears to have been tended in the recent past."

Will's report restored a glimmer of hope to Thomas. There and then he decided that he would stay and wait, however long it took. He would remain there on his own if necessary.

His patience wasn't put to much of a test in the end. In the early afternoon a voice sounded tentatively from nearby. "Thomas, is that you?"

He looked up to see Rubin peering out cautiously from behind a tree.

Thomas ran to him with a joyful cry. "Rubin! Is Elena safe? Are you both well?"

"Yes, we are both safe and well."

Thomas's relief knew no bounds. "Where is she? Can I go to her?"

Hearing voices, the others gathered, and Rubin looked around him uncertainly.

Taking a deep breath, Thomas tried hard to calm himself. "Let me introduce my friends," he said. Restraining his eagerness with difficulty, he formally presented Will, Rufe, and Haldek to Rubin.

When the introductions were over, Rubin turned to Thomas. "I know you are anxious to see Elena, but I think it would be best if I break the news to her. It will be a very happy surprise, but still a shock. She understood why you needed to leave, but she has taken it hard as the days have gone by. She has greatly feared for your safety." He glanced around him. "I think, too, that she will be shy with so many people here."

Thomas was crestfallen, but he accepted that Rubin knew best.

"The Rogandans have been defeated," Will told Rubin. "They're leaving Arvenon. I think it is safe for the two of you to return to your cabin now."

Rubin nodded gratefully. “I don’t know you,” he said with a puzzled look on his face, “but there is something familiar about you.”

Will smiled. “I once accepted your hospitality for the night,” he replied. “It feels like a long time ago. I probably looked a little different back then as well.”

“Of course,” said Rubin, his face lighting up. “Elena told me that you faced some trouble after you left. I am glad you found a way through it.”

“That is largely why I am here,” Will replied. “It is time to end the folly that has forced you and your daughter into isolation from the world. The trouble has spread well beyond the two of you. You can continue to choose to live apart from other people if you wish, but the persecution must end.”

Rubin looked hesitant, but he nodded his understanding.

Will nodded toward Thomas. “My friend here seems barely able to contain himself,” he said with a smile. “Perhaps you could fetch your daughter.”

Rubin readily agreed and disappeared into the forest.

Little more than thirty minutes passed before Rubin reappeared, this time with a radiant Elena. Ignoring everyone else, she flew to Thomas and embraced him joyfully, tears of gladness flooding her cheeks.

After a few moments she drew back, noticing his arm bound tightly in the sling. “You’re hurt!” she cried, alarm in her voice.

“It’s nothing,” he told her happily, pulling her in once more with his good arm.

Will had been conferring quietly with Rubin, and he now called the others together. “We will spend the night here,” he said. “But in the morning we will travel together into Tallesford, a town that lies not far from here.”

Elena looked anxiously to her father, who gave her a nod and a reassuring smile.

Haldek took upon himself the task of preparing a meal. When he came to serve it, he bustled about cheerfully, paying special attention to Elena. It was very obvious that he had taken quite a shine to her.

Will taught him the Arvenian word for uncle, and he embraced it with a nod and a ready smile, speaking it aloud to practice his pronunciation.

Once they had eaten, they all lay down to sleep. Elena and her father re-established themselves in the cabin again, for this one night at least.

As Thomas lay quietly, waiting to drift off, he remembered his anxiety about how he should respond to Elena, and his uncertainty about whether she still cared for him. He smiled to himself, more amused than embarrassed at his own insecurity.

He did not think he had ever felt so content in his entire life.

24

The column of soldiers trooped into the town of Tallesford with Will and Rufe at their head. Rubin rode in the middle of the column, with Elena perched in front of him. Thomas had positioned his horse beside them.

As soon as it became known that the commander of the king's army had arrived, after defeating the Rogandans in a great battle, a large and enthusiastic crowd gathered to cheer them in. Hearing that the local baron had been sent for, and that he was on his way to greet them, they came to a halt in the market square.

Thomas knew that neither Rubin nor Elena felt at all comfortable in a crowd, and he hovered near them protectively.

The baron rode up and greeted them graciously, welcoming them officially to Tallesford. The nobleman was tall and dark and looked every inch a warrior. Thomas was gratified to see that he paid appropriate deference to Will, given his status as commander. Surprisingly, Will seemed uncharacteristically restless and distracted.

The baron invited them to join him and led them to a large building on the edge of the square. The soldiers remained outside with Haldek. The others began to file inside.

As they went in, a harsh voice called from the crowd, “The witch! The witch is with them.”

A couple of others took up the cry.

Will came to a halt and surveyed the crowd. It was impossible to tell who had spoken. Calling for the captain, he turned to Thomas. “Can you identify the people who said that?” he asked him quietly.

Thomas took the stone and scanned the crowd. The mental din was almost overwhelming, but he narrowed his focus and was soon able to pick out two women and an old man who still radiated hatred. Thomas pointed them out to the captain, and he disappeared into the crowd with several of his men.

Thomas followed the others inside, Will entering last of all.

Refreshments were being served, and Rufe was responding to the questions of the baron, delivering news of the king and the recent battle at Torbury Scarp. Pleasantries were exchanged, and the baron expressed gratification that no further incursions were to be expected from Rogandan invaders.

He explained that for many weeks he had been able to protect his lands from their scourge only with great difficulty and considerable loss of life. Then the Rogandans had all mysteriously disappeared. With the news of the recent battle, the reason for their exodus was now clear.

When the conversation slowed a little, Will addressed the nobleman. “My Lord Baron, could I please speak with you in private?”

The baron nodded his acquiescence, and ushered him into a small chamber off to one side of the main hall. Thomas watched them go with considerable interest. He suspected it had something to do with Elena, but he resisted the temptation to use the stone to discover Will’s intent in calling for the discussion.

“I HAVE two reasons for wishing to speak with you, My Lord.”

The baron nodded his permission to speak, all the while regarding him with obvious curiosity.

"The first concerns the young lady, Elena, who is traveling with us."

"She is very striking, to say the least," the baron acknowledged. "Does she live in this region? I wonder that I have not seen her before."

Will felt his eyes narrow. "She is spoken for, by another of my companions, the young man called Thomas. He also stands high in the king's regard, having played a key role in bringing down Lord Drettroth, the High Commander of the Rogandan army."

"Please, do not misunderstand my inquisitiveness!" protested the baron. "I have no interest in her for myself. I simply feel great sympathy for her father. It cannot be comfortable to have responsibility for a daughter with such beauty. I have a daughter myself, and I have more than once congratulated myself that she is merely attractive." He gave Will a rueful smile.

The nobleman seemed sincere. Will promised himself he would ask Thomas to confirm it.

"It is uncomfortable," Will continued, "and great harm has come from it already, thanks to superstitious minds and idle tongues. The truth, though, is that nothing about her or her father is at all unusual, apart from her remarkable appearance. They are common people who want nothing more than to live a quiet life. And they have already done great service to their king—I can attest to it personally.

"I wish to make a request on their behalf that they would never ask for themselves. I beg you to extend your protection over them. Even as we entered this hall some people in the crowd called her a witch. My men were able to identify those involved, and they have taken them aside in case you would like to examine their reasons for making such an accusation."

The baron frowned. "I will deal with this, and firmly." He pulled a cord, and a servant entered. He issued instructions to the man, and sent him away.

"I thank you," said Will, with a bow.

"You said that great harm has already come from this superstitious talk. Are you referring to some other wrong that has been done?"

Will felt himself color. "It is my turn to feel uncomfortable, My Lord. You and I have met before."

The baron looked surprised. "I have no memory of it."

"You were calling down curses on me as I rode away from you. I am the person who killed your son."

The nobleman's brows bristled.

"I was heading to Stantony on urgent business for the king. Elena and her father had sheltered me overnight and she gave me directions. Your son saw us parting, and tried to intercept me, believing that I had conspired with a witch. My business could not be delayed, even for an hour. I was forced to defend myself. To my lasting regret, I killed him. That was never my intention."

Will paused in an attempt to calm himself. "This is the second reason why I wished to speak with you. I felt it only right to give you the opportunity to confront your son's killer, and to take whatever action you deem necessary."

The baron regarded him silently for what seemed like an eternity. Then he spoke.

"I honor you, Will Prentis. You are a different kind of commander from anything I expected. I don't doubt that the king greatly values your obvious integrity. It cannot have been easy to face me in this way —I doubt that one man in a hundred would have been willing to attempt it.

"But you have punished yourself for no reason. My son is indeed dead, but you are not responsible for his passing. Yes, you did leave him gravely wounded. But he recovered. And I believe the encounter left him with a new appreciation for the value of a cool head and an even temper.

"My son died bravely, just three weeks ago, in battle against the Rogandans."

The eyes of the baron misted over, and he did not speak for a time. Finally he stood to his feet. "Your face is scarred, and you walk with a limp. No doubt you acquired these tokens in service to your king. I also carry a limp, and for the same reason. My face may not carry scars, but my heart certainly does. Will you walk with me?"

Will nodded, and he accompanied the baron out of a side door. Shoulder to shoulder the two veterans hobbled to a peaceful graveyard beside a large stone church. They stood together, silent before a cold stone tomb, mourning the death of a beloved son and grieving the departure of innocence from the world.

THOMAS HAD no need of the stone to discern the new sense of peace that radiated from Will when he returned with the baron. He followed his friend from the building as the baron led them to a different corner of the square where a crowd had gathered and hecklers could be heard calling loudly. The crowd parted as they approached to reveal two women and a man constrained in the stocks. It was obvious from the reaction of the bystanders that they were not popular.

The baron faced the crowd. "I will not tolerate accusations against this young woman," he said, pointing to Elena. "I am satisfied that she is no witch! If others of you are unable to control your envy, then keep your slurs to yourselves or pay the penalty."

Elena stood before the accused with a look of grief on her face. "I cannot bear for anyone to be punished on my account, My Lord," she said to the baron quietly. "Please release them! I forgive them freely."

"I will honor your request for mercy," he replied. "But they can bear their punishment for a while longer." He turned to his servants. "Release them before the sun goes down," he ordered.

The town no longer felt comfortable to Thomas, and he was relieved to learn that they were leaving immediately. The baron clasped hands warmly with Will, then bade them all farewell, and they departed.

Once clear of the town, Will drew his horse alongside Thomas. "Rufe and I have promised to return without unnecessary delay to rejoin the king. I am sure you will want to stay with Elena, though, Thomas."

"Yes, I have been planning to remain here," Thomas replied, trying not to sound too eager.

Will nodded. "After all that has happened, I suspect that such a course will be safest for you anyway.

"I have a request to make of you, though. Would you be willing to welcome Haldek among you? He has rescued me, twice, as I have told you, and you know better than anyone that there is no great harm in him.

"He has no family and no future back in Rogand. But I believe he might be helpful to you here. I have already spoken to Rubin and Elena, and they have given their consent. But I would not leave him here without your approval as well."

Thomas readily agreed, and Will went to Haldek to extend their offer. The Rogandan rode first to Rubin and Elena and then to Thomas to express his thanks. He probably could not have concealed his delight if he had tried, and even in his halting Arvenian he managed to be effusive.

The company parted well before they reached the forest refuge. Thomas had learned to value solitude almost as much as Elena and her father, and he looked forward eagerly to passing his time with them in the days to come. He nevertheless had a lump in his throat as he farewelled Will and Rufe and watched them ride away. It was hard to imagine a future devoid of them.

THE SMALLER GROUP of four reached the cabin before nightfall. After eating a simple meal they somehow all managed to stretch out on the floor inside, and in that way they spent their first night together as a small community.

In the morning Haldek was full of ideas for extending the cabin, and building a second beside it. He squatted down in the dirt and began drawing up rough plans, drawing a chuckle of appreciation from Rubin.

Thomas had lain awake for several hours, thinking about the future. He knew there were many things that he needed to tell Elena, so he sought and received Rubin's permission to spend the whole day with her.

They wandered slowly along the stream, remembering many previous happy afternoons spent in similar fashion. Then they sat down in Elena's favorite meadow, and Thomas made a beginning. The sun rose in the sky and passed its zenith as he laid out before her the whole of his history with the stone, hiding nothing, not even the most shameful of his memories. She remembered Brother Vangellis fondly from her earlier years, and she hung on every word as Thomas told her all they had experienced together. Her eagerness turned to shock when he revealed what the monk had done to protect her, and she became deeply distressed as he described the terrible consequences that had followed for him. Her discomfort began to ease as Thomas unfolded the events through which Brother Vangellis had found redemption. With great reluctance he relived the hours in Drettroth's prison room, and they wept together as he recounted the monk's final moments.

The daylight had almost faded by the time he finally finished. They returned to the cabin. Thomas was silent, lost in his memories. Elena had a faraway look in her eyes.

The following afternoon they set off together again.

Thomas was beginning to feel like a new person. His life in recent months had degenerated into a seemingly endless succession of crises, but he was daring to hope that the upheavals of the past might finally be behind him.

Elena had been thoughtful since his revelations, and it soon became clear that their conversation the previous day had left her with many questions. "Thomas, you said that for much of the time you had the stone it actually belonged to Simon."

"Yes. The stone didn't belong to me anymore once I lost it, although I didn't realize that at the time. Simon was the one who found it, so after that it belonged to him."

"If it belonged to him, why did it still occasionally work for you after you took it back?"

"I don't know."

"Didn't the scroll say that the stone would stop working if someone took it by force?"

"Yes, it did. I don't understand that, either. Maybe it was different in this case because the stone wasn't new to me. Perhaps I had adapted to it somehow. I'm only guessing, though. The scroll gave no hints about what might happen in that situation. There might have been answers in the section that was missing."

Elena nodded. "But it worked properly for Simon as soon as he had it in his hand again," she said. "So he suddenly understood all of Lord Drettroth's secrets. What about when he handed it to Lord Drettroth the first time, though? Why didn't the ownership change?"

"He put it into Drettroth's hand, but that's not the same as giving it to him." Thomas took out the stone and passed it to Elena. She examined it closely for a while with considerable interest, then returned it. He put it back in his pouch immediately. "The stone was still mine while you had it just then," Thomas told her, "because I was only letting you hold it and examine it. I didn't give it to you."

"Well, I'm glad you didn't give it to me, because I don't want it!" she said decidedly.

He wasn't surprised. In light of everything she now knew about the stone, he understood her reaction completely.

"I noticed you didn't look at me while you had the stone in your hand," she said.

"No. I've never used the stone to see into your mind, apart from the first time we met, when I thought you might be dangerous. You know about that already. And it wasn't working fully at the time, anyway. But I've never tried it on you or your father since, and I promise that I never will."

"Thank you, Thomas," she said with a smile and the faintest of blushes. "It would give you an unfair advantage."

Elena became thoughtful once again. "You said that Simon whispered something in Lord Drettroth's ear when he told Simon to call for the torturers," she continued. "What did Simon say to him? Was he telling Lord Drettroth he'd been poisoned?"

"No. He told Drettroth that he was freely and willingly giving him the stone. Simon could do that, because it was his to give away. And once he had the stone in his hand, he was soon able to get the full picture of how it worked from Drettroth and from me, especially since the stone was uppermost in both of our minds."

"Oh. So Simon gave Lord Drettroth the stone, and he was immediately able to read Simon's thoughts. Is that how he knew he'd been poisoned and was about to die?"

"Yes," said Thomas. "It must have been a huge shock to finally get what he wanted, only to discover it was all for nothing."

"And then Simon took the stone back after he'd killed Lord Drettroth. Did that make it his again?"

"No, he couldn't just take it back from Drettroth. He couldn't claim the stone after killing him. It didn't belong to anyone until Simon handed it to Brother Vangellis. As the next person who 'found' it, he became the new owner."

"Until he gave it to you again."

"Yes. And it's been mine since then."

"There's another thing I've been curious about," Elena said. "You told me that the scroll mentioned three stones, and that Lord Drettroth said he had knowledge of them. Where are the other two stones now?"

"I don't know," Thomas replied. "There's something I didn't tell you, and I wouldn't have mentioned it if you hadn't asked about the other stones. It occurred to me that Drettroth might already have the Stone of Authority, considering how powerful he had become. So I searched him before I left. Thoroughly, too.

"It wasn't because I wanted the other stones for myself. I didn't think it was safe to just leave them there. I thought the Stone of Authority would be safe with King Steffan. Or with Will, except that I don't think he needs it!

"Anyway, there was no sign of another stone. Either he didn't actually have the other stones yet, or one of his men had already searched him before abandoning the fortress. We'll probably never know."

Thomas became quiet for a moment, caught up in his memories.

"I also wondered if he might have had another copy of the scroll there with him," he continued. "Maybe even a complete copy, with a full description of all three stones and a more complete history of what has happened with them. I did see a few scrolls in one of the rooms in the fortress. But I couldn't tell what they said," he admitted. "I can't read."

"I can't read, either," she said. "Nor can my father."

"Perhaps I should have brought the scrolls with me, just in case. Will could have read them." He shrugged. "It's too late now, though."

They sat together quietly, absorbed in their thoughts.

Elena was first to break the silence, steering the conversation in a different direction. "What about your parents, Thomas?"

"Will expects to return to Arnost soon," he replied, "and he promised to let my father know that I'm safe. And now that the Rogandans have gone, I expect my mother will return to Arnost. So she'll find out the news as well."

"Do you want to go back to Arnost, to be with your parents?"

Thomas shook his head emphatically.

"Don't you think your mother would want to see you again?" she prodded gently.

"Yes, she would," he said. "I can't simply decide to move back to Arnost, though. I need to escape attention, even more than you do. After the Council meeting where Pisander was exposed, some of the nobles have probably guessed about the stone. It isn't safe for me there anymore."

He gazed at her earnestly. "But I very much want my mother to meet you. My father, too."

Thomas became thoughtful. "I learned something about my father from the stone. It came to me through Brother Vangellis, who caught a glimpse of Simon's thoughts, as you know. Simon seemed to think that my father was missing me. And that he blamed himself for driving me away. I didn't expect that." He fell silent, staring off into the distance.

"I know you and your father clashed at times," Elena said. "But from everything you've told me, I'm sure that he truly cares about you."

Thomas nodded. "I think you're right, although it's taken me a while to see that. I need to talk with him. I don't want things to stay the way they've been between us."

Elena nodded approvingly.

"This is my home now," he concluded, "and a part of me wishes I could just stay here and hide away from the world. But I know it's important to see my parents again. I'll find a way to do it somehow."

He paused, looking intently at Elena with a frown of concern. "I've been hoping I'll be safe here. But it does worry me to think that trouble might come to you because of me."

"I wish there was a way to escape trouble completely," she said with a wistful smile. "But it doesn't seem possible. I think what matters is how we behave when trouble comes."

She gazed up at him. "I'm so proud of you, Thomas!" she said.

"Why?" Her remark took him by surprise.

"Because of the way you stood up to Lord Drettroth. You thought it would lead to a horrible death, but you stood strong anyway."

Thomas would have been willing to bask in her esteem, but he wasn't entirely sure that he deserved it. He had defied Drettroth. But she didn't know how sorely tempted he had been to take the easy way out.

"I'm sure you've faced more trouble in the last few months than most people face in their entire lives. And you've been so brave!" She looked up at him, her face shining. "You risked your life to lead the Rogandans away from us. That was very selfless of you. And you were prepared to do it for a girl that you thought was deformed."

That at least was true. He knew he wasn't the same person who had left Arnost.

"I don't know if my father has told you, Thomas, but he missed you while you were away. He's come to depend on you in so many ways. Both of us have." A faint blush tinged her lovely cheeks.

Elena's words were gratifying. Nevertheless, Thomas couldn't manage to convince himself he was especially worthy of admiration.

He couldn't count the number of times in the last few months when he'd felt awkward or embarrassed. Or even completely out of his depth.

He thought about Brother Vangellis, and Will, and Rufe, and the other men he had come to know and respect. They were adults, and he knew he wasn't entirely there yet. He aspired to be like them, but he didn't know how to make it happen.

"Maybe trouble is behind us now. Maybe not," Elena continued. "But I'm not going to worry about what might happen in the future. There's so much to be grateful for, right here and right now." She got to her feet and spun slowly around with arms raised, taking in the peaceful meadow dotted with wildflowers, the sky with its flecks of blue among billowing white and gray clouds, and the deep greens and browns of the trees. The merry sound of the nearby stream provided a fitting accompaniment to her graceful movements.

He nodded slowly. She was right. He remembered Brother Vangellis saying that sometimes you had to let the future worry about itself.

Trouble would undoubtedly come calling again, sooner or later. But it didn't need to consume his thoughts or energy now. Every moment deserved to be lived to the full. And he felt like his life was only just beginning.

EPILOGUE

A face appeared tentatively in the opening among the rubble.

"It's safe to come out," Brother Dannel called. "They're gone."

The first of the monks emerged into the ruins of what had been the library, squinting and shielding his eyes from the bright sunlight. Another followed, and then another. Soon the ruined library building was dotted with robed figures picking their way through the rubble. Others stood motionless, dazed at the extent of the destruction. Brother Erastus sat on the remains of a wall, his head bent low and his hands covering his face.

The monks had huddled together in their bolt hole below the library for almost two days, while the Rogandans continued their rampage above. When everything had finally gone quiet, they waited another full day. Then Brother Dannel sent all of them except Brother Erastus to safety at the bottom of the winding stairway, while he went out through the secret entrance to explore the monastery. Once he was certain that the Rogandans had abandoned the plateau, he sent Brother Erastus down the stairs to fetch the others.

Brother Dannel called them together. "I found Brother Beneface over there," he said, pointing toward the fallen gates of the monastery. The monks followed him to a white-clad figure lying spreadeagled on the ground. Brother Dannel had known there was very little chance they would find their leader alive. Nevertheless, it had still been a source of great dismay to him when he discovered his body.

As they gathered around the earthly remains of their beloved abbot, Brother Dannel saw his own grief mirrored on the faces of others. The burden of leadership had fallen to him now, though, and he knew he needed to be strong for them all. He led the monks to a grassy meadow beyond the shattered outer wall of the monastery, and set them to work preparing a grave. They buried Brother Beneface there, in sight of the place that had been his home for so long.

When it was over Brother Dannel sent them out to see what could be retrieved from the ruins.

Lord Drettroth's men had been thorough. Everything had been destroyed. Not a single building remained standing. The piggery and goat pens had been broken down, and the ground around the pens was littered with the carcasses of goats, pigs, and chickens. Every single fruit tree had fallen to the ax, and even the plants in the cultivated strips of farm land had been torn up.

Late in the afternoon they gathered together outside the broken walls. It was a somber gathering. Brother Dannel led them in prayers. Then he invited questions.

"What will we do?" asked one of the monks in despair.

"We will rebuild," Brother Dannel replied. "If the Rogandans have been defeated and left Arvenon," he added.

"So we won't rebuild the monastery if they're still around?"

Brother Dannel shook his head. "No. If the Rogandans haven't gone, we'll be needed out there, among the people." He swept an arm across the lowlands surrounding the plateau. "And even if they are gone, people will still need our help for a while. Many other people will have been killed or injured, and farms and buildings destroyed."

He turned toward the shell of their home. "Tonight we will shelter here as best we can. Then tomorrow we will leave this place. If it is God's purpose, we will return in the spring and make a new beginning."

"WHAT DID you think about the conference, Essanda?" Steffan asked. His young wife had just accompanied him for the first time to a key meeting of the nobles, where plans and priorities for the future were under discussion.

Given the widespread destruction caused by the Rogandans, men had been sent throughout Arvenon to assess the state of the towns and villages and the preparedness of the people for winter. The first reports were just beginning to come in. Thankfully the weather had been unseasonably mild, and the first bitterly cold weather had yet to make an appearance.

Steffan had sent Ranauld back to Arnost with a strong contingent of soldiers. The Lords Dongan and Burtelen were about to head south and west, each with their own squads of soldiers. All of them were under instruction to provide assistance wherever it was needed.

Steffan would soon be returning to Arnost himself. His leadership was needed more than ever in the aftermath of a brutal invasion. Essanda would remain at the citadel for the moment, at least until Arnost had returned to some semblance of normality.

Inviting Essanda to the meeting was unconventional, but Steffan wanted sympathetic eyes and ears in the room, and he knew he would be able to debrief with her frankly.

She didn't respond immediately to his question. "It was interesting," she finally replied, a hesitant look on her face.

"What does that mean?"

"I don't think all of them were happy about having me there."

"Nonsense!" he exclaimed.

Her face fell, and she looked away.

"I'm sorry!" he said repentantly. "That came out much more harshly than I intended."

Her big round eyes reappeared slowly.

He sighed, raising his arms in resignation. "You're probably right, Essanda. When it comes to these things, you usually seem to be."

That won him the hint of a smile.

"As for you attending the meeting, I don't care what anyone else thinks," he told her. "I needed you there! And you've earned the right. You did far more to save our kingdoms than most of the self-important peacocks around the table."

Steffan paused long enough to regain his composure. Then he slowly reassessed the key points of the discussion, inviting her to comment. As usual, she asked thoughtful questions while offering few opinions. But she nevertheless managed to steer him in the direction of important insights he otherwise might have missed. He knew he was much too easily distracted by his annoyance at the blindness —sometimes the sheer stupidity—of many among the nobility.

Essanda had said nothing at all in the meeting, and most of the nobles probably thought that including her was a complete waste of time. They had no idea how keenly she had been observing them.

"I like Lord Burtelen," she told him. "He seems very wise. And he worked hard to get the archers—as well as Kuper and Rellan and Count Ranauld—to the battle on time."

"Yes. I'll have great need of Burtelen when I get back to Arnost. Capable and reliable noblemen like him are all too rare."

"I like Lord Karevis, too. I'm glad the Varasans are on our side now."

"I agree. Karevis impresses me. I'm pleased that he's able to remain in Castel for a while, now that he's returned the men we lent to Delmar. It was gratifying to hear him confirm that his country is firmly back under Varasan control again.

"Thankfully, neither Delmar nor Karevis has any illusions about the potential threat that Agon is likely to pose in the future, either. I'm willing to go to considerable lengths to strengthen our ties with Varas."

Essanda nodded. "That seems like a good idea."

She gazed up at him uncertainly. "It's nice that you wanted me at the meeting, Steffan. I didn't understand a lot of the things you were discussing, though. Have you thought about inviting Nestor instead? He has a lot more experience than me, and he's good at understanding why people behave the way they do. His opinions would be much more useful than mine."

He shook his head. "Impossible, I'm afraid. He's a commoner."

"Will is a commoner, and he was there."

"That's different."

She didn't look convinced. "Do the other nobles think it's different?"

"We just fought the greatest battle in Arvenon's history, and he was the commander who won it for us!"

She nodded. "That's the way I see it, too." She was silent for a moment. "Does everyone believe that he won it for us, though? In the meeting Will told everyone he doesn't deserve the credit. It looked like some of the nobles agreed with him."

Steffan felt his hackles rise at this latest reminder of the stubborn stupidity of the nobles, but he managed to keep himself in check. "Will was just being modest. There were other reasons for our victory, of course. We couldn't have won without Ranauld, and Kuper and Rellan, and especially the archers. Or without you, for that matter. But Torbury Scarp was fought against a vastly stronger enemy. No one else could have held the army together for so long in the way he did. None of the nobles with any military understanding—like Ranauld or Bottren—harbor any doubts about that. Nor anyone with common sense, like Burtelen!"

Essanda looked thoughtful again. "If it's such a problem that Will is a commoner, can't you make him a nobleman?" she asked.

Steffan was too surprised to respond immediately. "I'm not sure it would satisfy the nobles," he finally replied. "It might even make them more annoyed."

"It's been done before, in Castel at least. Did you know that Lord Eisgold's grandfather was born a commoner?"

"No, I didn't know! That's curious. Unfortunately, Eisgold isn't exactly an ideal example at the moment. But when I return to Arnost,

I will take a close look at Arvenian heraldry. There might be other precedents."

Steffan smiled warmly down at her, and she returned a smile of her own.

She was full of surprises, and had been from the beginning. Since his initial distress at discovering he had been deceived about her age, the surprises had been uniformly agreeable, serving only to highlight the astonishing depth of her character and her qualities. And the tiny seed of affection and respect planted at their first meeting had sprouted and grown prolifically. The truth was that she had won him over completely.

Essanda's presence at the conference had more than fulfilled Steffan's expectations. She had attended for his sake, and he decided to return the favor.

"Would you care to stroll with me, My Lady?"

She took the arm he offered with a pleased smile, and Steffan led her down to a sheltered garden just beyond the walls of the citadel. He looked on affectionately as she wandered among the winter blossoms—bright yellow pansies, carnations clad in white or dark red, and perfumed pink roses. Seeing the elegant grace of her movements, it might have been possible to mistake her for a woman.

But she was not a woman.

Steffan had married a bride who could not become his wife in full measure for a few more years at least. That had led to very real frustrations. He was a normal man with normal desires, and he couldn't pretend otherwise.

Even so, he valued her greatly, and he had high hopes for a future with her at his side. And in spite of his impatience, one thing had become clear to him. Even if he could magically revisit his decision to marry Essanda, he would not choose differently.

Whatever his frustrations in the short term, Steffan never doubted he would be thoroughly delighted with Essanda when she finally emerged into womanhood. He also recognized that it was no one's responsibility but his own to ensure that she emerged equally delighted with him.

WINTER WAS WELL ADVANCED, and a chill was in the air. A fresh layer of snow had dusted white the hut and everything that surrounded it. Nevertheless, each afternoon Thomas and Elena made their way to the meadow as they had done before.

They chatted happily about many things, but they didn't return to the past. By some kind of unspoken agreement, they had decided to make their home in the present.

Thomas had never felt so much at peace with the world. He was finding endless delight simply from being in Elena's presence. "There's nothing I want more than to be with you," he told her. "If I had to choose between the stone and you, I would give it up without a second thought."

He gazed into her face, a face that had been so long hidden from his sight. "I...I love you, Elena." He felt like he could drown in her eyes, and die happy. A sudden boldness filled him, and he spoke the words that rose unbidden to his tongue. "Would you marry me?"

Having said it, his heart skipped a beat. His own audacity took his breath away—even in his daydreams he had never dared to hope he could find the courage to ask her that question. If he had come to the meadow with any such plan, he knew he'd have frozen up long before he found a way to push the words past his lips. Somehow it had just happened, seemingly of its own accord.

How could he expect her to take such a question seriously, though? It wasn't unusual to marry at his age, and he didn't doubt that Elena was ready for such a step. But to seriously imagine that he was good enough for her? He felt a flush begin to creep up his forehead.

She gazed back at him. Slowly the smile faded from her face, and she regarded him seriously. "Yes, Thomas, I will marry you. I choose you, and I will bind myself to you. Whatever comes, for good or for ill, we will walk the journey together."

He felt dizzy with joy. Perhaps he didn't deserve her, but he was willing to spend a lifetime trying.

His heart overflowing, he took her hand, and they ran together back to the cabin to tell Rubin and Haldek.

The End

The saga continues in
The Stone of Authority Complete Set
(*The Stone Cycle Complete Sets Book 2*)

But first...

A NUMBER of important questions remain unanswered. How did Simon find his way to Lord Drettroth's fortress, what happened there before Brother Vangellis arrived, and what motivated Simon's actions?

The novelette that follows—*The Gamble*—answers these questions.

DOES the novelette also introduce a spoiler or two for the story that follows in *The Stone of Authority Complete Set*? Judge for yourself.

The Gamble picks up the story not long after Thomas departed from Arnost...

PART III

THE GAMBLE

A SEQUEL TO THE COST OF KNOWING

1

Simon stood motionless, hidden in the shadows near the gates of Arnost. The walls towered above him—thick, strong, and so far impervious to the Rogandan army besieging the capital of Arvenon.

As soon as night fell he had crept silently to the walls and taken up a concealed position near the gate, just as he had done every night for the past week. In all that time he had come no closer to finding an answer to his central problem—how to find a way out of the city.

From the moment he decided to leave Arnost, all of his attention had been focused on getting outside the walls, undetected and in one piece. He was no closer to a solution. In a siege the gates stayed shut. No one entered, and no one left. It was as simple as that.

As he watched in continued frustration, the guards emerged from the gatehouses on either side of the gates. The gatehouses held a dozen guards, more than enough to rouse the soldiers stationed nearby in case of an attack. Simon knew all this from close observation. The guards milled around, talking and laughing. He wasn't quite close enough to hear what they were saying. Then most of them looked around warily before heading off at a trot away from the walls. They obviously had plans—plans that didn't involve guard duties.

He frowned. Surely such behavior would be regarded as irresponsible at any time. It was reckless and dangerous in a siege.

Only two of their number remained. Once the others had left, these two began peering around them in the darkness. They appeared restless and impatient.

Before long he heard the sound of a horse approaching, and he shrank deeper into the shadows to stay out of sight. A rider approached the gate, and the pair of guards stepped forward to challenge him. The rider bent down and spoke to them in a low voice, before slipping off the horse's back and handing the reins to one of the guards. All three of them stepped back into the shadows on the far side of the gates and stood there quietly. If anything, they appeared even more anxious than before.

What could they be doing? Their behavior seemed very suspicious. His curiosity aroused, Simon crept closer, careful to stay out of sight, until he was standing immediately beside the left gate.

It occurred to him to wonder if he should be alerting someone in authority. Then he thought about the questions that might be asked. *Who are you, and what were you doing snooping around near the gates? What business did you have there?* With the kingdom at war, the city gates were off limits to anyone except the guards. He decided to take the sensible approach and stay where he was. Protecting the Arvenian capital was someone else's problem—he wasn't planning to be in the city for long anyway.

As he stood there wondering whether to retrace his steps and just slip away into the night, he heard the sound of footfalls. Someone was approaching, and at a rapid pace. He'd heard nothing until the person was almost upon him, giving him no opportunity at all to escape. Heart pounding, he crouched down in the shadows beside the gates, desperately trying to remain inconspicuous.

A figure hurried past him, and he caught a brief glimpse of a richly dressed man in late middle age, red in the face from exertion. Whoever it was had clearly not noticed him.

As the red faced man appeared at the gates, the three hidden figures stepped forward. A mumbled conversation took place. A bag, small but bulging, appeared in the hand of the newcomer. Simon heard the dull clink of coins as the bag was handed over to the person who had brought the horse. The reins of the horse were yielded up in exchange.

The man who had arrived with the horse climbed up onto the wall and peered out into the darkness. After a couple of minutes he called down softly to the men below. The two guards moved to the gates. They were so close to Simon that he didn't dare breathe. One by one the heavy bars were removed from the gates, the guards panting with the effort. Then the gates were pulled open.

The gates swung slowly inward until a wide gap had appeared. Hoof beats sounded as the horse raced abruptly through the opening, with the richly dressed man in the saddle. Once clear of the gates the horseman was soon out of sight.

"Hurry up!" a rough voice hissed. "There'll be hell to pay if these gates are still open when the others get back. Especially once the duke discovers that Pisander's gone missing!"

The Earl of Pisander? He was the red faced horseman? He must have somehow bribed his way out of the dungeons.

Simon had become very familiar with Pisander's name in recent days. Endless gossip had swirled around the disgraced nobleman after his treason had been laid bare. The information that leaked out had changed everything for Simon.

The two guards hurried into position and slowly began pushing the heavy gates shut. Simon stared wide-eyed at the steadily narrowing gap. His opportunity had arrived at last, if he could only find the courage to grasp it. With the opening continuing to shrink, Simon abandoned his agonizing and thrust aside his caution. Heart pounding, he darted forward into the gap.

The guards were taken completely by surprise. Before they could react he had sprinted through the gates and disappeared into the darkness.

"Hey! Come back!"

He ignored the soft call from the guards—he knew there was nothing they could do about his escape. They couldn't afford to waste time chasing him. And even if they had known who he was, they could hardly report him missing. That would require them to explain why the gates were open in the first place.

He could scarcely believe it—he was outside the walls.

Simon heard the sound of the bars being slid back into place. Then all went quiet.

He moved quickly away from the city, gradually putting distance between himself and the gates. Then he stopped and remained motionless, fully alert and listening for the slightest sound.

Everything was still and quiet. He crept on cautiously, not pausing until he was well out of bowshot range. A dip in the terrain appeared ahead of him. Once he reached it, he eased himself down into a sitting position. He was confident that he was no longer visible from the city walls.

He had done it. He was clear of the city.

What was he going to do now? He realized that all of his thinking and planning had been bent on finding a way out of Arnost undetected. He had expected that the next step would be obvious if he could achieve that. Now he wasn't so sure.

He shivered a little in the crisp night air, only partly because of the cold.

Huddling in the dark, an uncertain future before him, Simon thought back over the journey that had brought him here. So much had changed since the days in the stables when he had been happy. Even the faint recollection of that time—it seemed so long ago—caused a wave of anger to flood over him again.

It had felt like such a brief period. Years of humiliation and suffering had preceded it, and the experience of belonging had been exhilarating when it came. His jubilation had been short lived, though. It had all come crashing down when Thomas Stablehand—for reasons he still couldn't comprehend—had decided to make an enemy of him.

He hardened himself. He couldn't afford to be weak. Not now. Not tonight.

He began creeping forward, heading away from the city and

toward the Rogandan camp. He knew that his next move was extremely risky. Any Rogandan soldiers who stumbled upon him might simply decide to kill him.

His thoughts tumbled over each other, and he began to sweat. He tried to calm himself. He had a plan. He would demand to see Lord Drettroth. He couldn't speak Rogandan, but he had carefully memorized the name of the Rogandan army commander, and he felt certain it would carry weight.

He tried to remind himself that he had no reason for alarm. The reports he had heard about the letter found on the Earl of Pisander might have been fourth-hand, but they were surely close to the mark. If they were even vaguely accurate, Lord Drettroth would want to hear what he had to say. He would want to know about Thomas Stablehand. He would want to know everything Simon could tell him.

The very thought of his rival was enough to bring Simon back down to earth and renew his determination. He was doing this for a reason. After the Council meeting where the Earl of Pisander had been exposed, the news had spread like wildfire, but most of the attention had been focused on Pisander's treachery. It had taken Simon a while to piece together the information about the stone, and longer still to fully grasp what it meant.

Then his anger had slowly mounted as he began to realize that Thomas had used the stone—the same stone he had violently wrested from Simon in the stables—to selfishly carve out a reputation for himself. His use of the stone had allowed Thomas to mix with the likes of Will Prentis, the army commander, and the Duke of Erestor, who in the absence of King Steffan was the regent of the kingdom.

According to Pisander's letter, though, the stone actually belonged to the Rogandan lord.

Simon was doing the honorable thing by letting Lord Drettroth know who had his stone. He felt no compunction at all about exposing Thomas—the much vaunted army horse master fully deserved it.

It was unlikely that anything much would come of it, unfortunately. Thomas had long since left the city, and it was hard to imagine what the Rogandan lord could do to retrieve the stone. That wasn't Simon's problem, though. And it might give Thomas pause if he ever learned that the Rogandans were onto him.

Satisfying as it would be to avenge himself on Thomas, another matter had been working away in the back of his mind as he planned his escape from the city. The letter from Lord Drettroth had promised gold in return for the stone. Surely there would be some kind of reward for information. Maybe even a rich reward. He was, after all, able to identify the person who had the stone.

He had always been ignored and undervalued. Why should Thomas be the only one to benefit? He licked his lips involuntarily.

Simon peered ahead into the darkness. Campfires dimly flickered in the distance. He began to feel nervous again. He took another tentative step forward.

All of a sudden a dark figure loomed before him, and a harsh voice barked out words he could not understand. Then he heard a movement behind him. He opened his mouth to speak, but a sharp blow to the back of his head stunned him into silence. Pain flooded his consciousness. Then everything went dark.

A POUNDING headache greeted Simon when he woke. He opened his eyes to dazzling daylight, and immediately shut them again, trying to ease the pain in his head. His efforts were in vain. After a moment he cautiously squeezed his eyes open again and squinted around him. He was in some kind of animal pen with a few other men who looked like Arvenian farmers. He peered at them curiously. All of them looked thoroughly cowed—he could see no hope in their eyes. Rogandan soldiers surrounded them on every side, although they ignored their captives.

He groaned. The other prisoners turned to him, alarm on their faces. One of them put a finger to his lips.

So it wasn't safe to speak. Simon realized that he was thirsty and glanced around him. A small water trough sat within the enclosure, but he began wondering whether the water was fit to drink. He was even less certain if the prisoners were allowed to use the water without permission. He decided it was safest to wait and see.

His thirst became increasingly difficult to bear as the hours dragged slowly by. No one spoke, and the others barely moved. As the sun began to set, though, his fellow prisoners became visibly agitated. They watched the Rogandans anxiously, although Simon had no idea why. Clearly they were expecting something—something that filled them with dread.

Then two burly soldiers approached the enclosure. A few of his fellow captives began trembling uncontrollably, and Simon broke out in a cold sweat himself. The new arrivals barked orders that Simon could not understand, and other soldiers hurried to the enclosure. Pulling open a gate, they pushed into the enclosure and grabbed the first two prisoners who caught their eye.

One of the captives began struggling and crying out for mercy. They backhanded him, and he subsided to a fearful whimpering. The other man remained silent as they dragged him into the open. The soldiers closed the gate and bustled the two captives out of sight.

"Looks like we get to stay alive for another day," one of the other prisoners muttered. The words were spoken so quietly that Simon could barely make them out. The comment appeared to be addressed to no onc in particular.

A soldier arrived and threw some stale bread into the enclosure. One of the captives retrieved it. He broke it into pieces and handed them around. He didn't hesitate before giving Simon a share as well. The men all ate. The portions were small, and it didn't take long. Then each of them shuffled over to the water trough and knelt, scooping up water in their open hands and bending down to drink it. Simon copied them. The water tasted foul, but by then he was so thirsty that he didn't care.

As soon as darkness fell, Simon moved quietly to the person who had muttered aloud. "What's going to happen to us?" He spoke as quietly as he could.

The other man turned to him and shrugged. "Each day they come and take two of us," he whispered. "No one has ever come back, so it isn't hard to guess what happens."

"How did they capture you?" Simon asked.

"The filthy Rogandans stole my goats. I was trying to take one of them back. I have youngsters who need the milk. I would have gotten away with it, too, if the goat hadn't made such an infernal racket." He paused. "What about you?"

Simon didn't know what to say. It was already abundantly clear to him that he had made a colossal mistake. "I guess I was in the wrong place at the wrong time," he eventually managed.

The other man accepted his reply at face value. He nodded. "My name is Lennard. What's yours?"

"Simon."

Lennard studied him with a frown. "Someone as young as you shouldn't be in here. Maybe they'll take pity on you." He sounded doubtful.

DUSK FINALLY HERALDED the end of another anxious day. The soldiers came as before, and Simon cowered down, desperate to avoid their attention. His efforts proved futile. One of the soldiers headed straight for him, grabbing his arm and pulling him to his feet. As they dragged him outside he called out in desperation, "Drettroth! I must see Lord Drettroth!"

The soldiers paused, frowning. They exchanged a few words, then they both laughed—a cruel sound that filled Simon with fear. Calling to another soldier, they thrust Simon toward him. Then one of them re-entered the enclosure and to Simon's horror emerged with Lennard.

As he was dragged past Simon, the farmer aimed a look of surprise and disappointment at the youth. Simon opened his mouth to call out, to tell the farmer it wasn't as it appeared, that he had good reasons for his appeal to the Rogandan lord. But the words stuck in his throat.

Simon was held outside the enclosure in sight of his former fellow captives. They said nothing, but they peered at him grimly through the gloom. Darkness couldn't come soon enough for the youth. He sat in utter dejection, head in his hands, unable to think of anything except the farmer who had taken his place. Lennard's hungry children would never see their father again.

The sun was rising when a Rogandan soldier arrived who spoke a little Arvenian. "You seek Lord Drettroth? Why?" he asked bluntly.

Simon answered quietly, hoping the other captives wouldn't overhear their conversation. "He is looking for something—an heirloom. I have information about it."

"You want reward, no?" The soldier had an ugly smile on his face. "Maybe you lucky. Maybe he let you die quick."

The soldier looked critically at him for a long moment. Then he barked some commands, and the youth was bustled away toward some horses.

Simon had plenty of time to berate himself as the leagues rolled by under the hooves of their horses. What had possessed him to leave the safety of Arnost? He had thought to avenge himself against Thomas and enrich himself in the bargain. Having now experienced Arvenon's enemies up close for himself, his intentions seemed petty and absurd.

2

Simon's journey eventually ended at a stone fortress somewhere within Arvenon that the Rogandan commander had made his base. The youth was almost paralyzed with fear by the time he finally found himself in the presence of Lord Drettroth. The commander was tall with close cropped dark hair and an indefinable air of authority. Something about him radiated malice.

The Rogandan lord calmly looked him up and down. He didn't seem at all impressed with what he saw. Simon did not have the slightest doubt that his life would be over the instant that Drettroth lost interest in him. He began shivering uncontrollably.

"I am told you have information that might interest me." The nobleman spoke excellent Arvenian. He sounded bored.

"Y...y...yes. It's about your heirloom."

Lord Drettroth raised an eyebrow, then turned his head and gestured sharply to the guards who had brought Simon in. They bowed quickly and left the room, closing the door behind them.

"What do you know about this heirloom?"

"I heard about it," Simon said nervously. "From the letter you wrote to the Earl of Pisander."

The brow of Lord Drettroth darkened, and Simon belatedly regretted revealing that the letter had become public.

"I know who has the stone!" the youth blurted.

The Rogandan leaned close and narrowed his eyes. "Tell me everything you know," he said in a threatening growl. "Leave nothing out! I might even let you live if I decide your information is useful to me."

Simon swallowed convulsively. "Thomas Stablehand has it!"

"How do you know?"

Simon, thoroughly frightened, was on the brink of blurting out his entire history with Thomas and the stone. Then it occurred to him that it might not be wise to tell the whole story. Things might end badly for him if he appeared to be laying any kind of claim of his own to the stone.

A stream of answers spilled out. "I saw him with it once. I worked with him—in the royal stables. I didn't realize what it was. Not until later. Not until I heard the stories. About the meeting—where the Earl of Pisander was arrested." All of that was true enough.

"This Thomas Stablehand. Is he in Arnost?"

"No." He shook his head rapidly. "He left. Some time ago."

"On his own?"

"No. He went with some others."

"Where did he go?"

"I don't know."

"And he took the stone with him?"

"I think so." Then he nodded, vigorously, hoping to appear certain. "He wouldn't have left it behind."

The nobleman questioned Simon very closely. He gradually extracted everything the youth knew about the stone. The only thing Simon concealed was his fight with Thomas in the stables—he gave Drettroth no hint at all that the stone had ever been in his possession.

The Rogandan came away with a very detailed description of Thomas. To his shame, Simon also revealed that Will Prentis had departed Arnost with Thomas. He hadn't intended to say anything that might compromise the security of the capital. But Drettroth's questioning was relentless. Once the youth began answering questions, he couldn't find a way of stopping.

"So why have you told me all this? No doubt you heard about the reward I was offering."

He shook his head energetically. "No. I heard that the stone belonged to you. It seemed only right...to let you know what had become of it."

"So you abandoned your countrymen and sought out the commander of your enemies, all because of a moral obligation? Come now, Simon. Do you really think I am that naive? If you were so intent on doing the right thing, why have you turned so eagerly on the son of your mentor? And why have you willingly betrayed the commander of your own army?"

Drettroth stood tall, hands on his hips. "Perhaps you've invented this story because you're a coward. You'd do or say anything to save your skin, wouldn't you? Yes, I'm well aware of how eager you were for someone else to be taken away in your place after you were captured. A poor farmer, I'm told."

He gazed down at Simon with a condescending smile. Simon couldn't meet his eyes.

"Perhaps you think I should be grateful to you. But the truth is that you've told me little more than an entertaining tale. You claim that a Thomas Stablehand has the stone, but you offer no proof. You tell me he's left Arnost, but you can't say where he's gone. You don't even know if he took this supposed stone with him. You've given me no way to verify your fairy tale.

"It's obvious that you see this Thomas as an enemy. Perhaps you're simply making all this up in the hope that I will seek him out and kill him for you."

"No! I'm telling you the truth!"

"I think you were caught by my guards. You'd heard some rumors, about an heirloom I supposedly lost. So you thought of a clever way to save yourself. I'm impressed, Simon, really I am."

"That isn't how it happened! I came here by choice—to tell you about the stone!"

"So you chose to leave the safety of your city. And you decided to just walk up to my soldiers and give yourself up. Do you think I'm stupid?" Drettroth's eyes flashed dangerously.

The Rogandan commander called for the guards and spoke rapidly to them in their own language. "I will decide about you tomorrow," he told Simon in an offhand tone. "In the meantime, I hope you find your new accommodations to your liking." He aimed a mocking sneer at the youth, then turned away.

The guards dragged Simon out of the room. They led him for several minutes through a series of passageways and down multiple flights of steps. Eventually they came to a halt in front of a dank and gloomy cell. They shoved him inside and locked the door. No natural light penetrated into this dark place. The only illumination came from a single torch burning dimly somewhere down the passageway.

The cell held nothing except a hard bed with a single thin blanket. Simon sat down on the bed and buried his head in his hands.

FIVE SEEMINGLY ENDLESS days passed before Lord Drettroth called for Simon again. The youth had been fed once each day, and he felt certain that his ration could not sustain life for long. He was never given enough to drink, either. He was accustomed to cruelty growing up in the home of his uncle, but he had never gone hungry or thirsty. Now, hunger gnawed at him constantly throughout his waking hours, competing for attention with his thirst. He couldn't sleep for the cold, either. His mind churned over and over, the same thoughts spinning through his head as he constantly berated himself.

Simon could not summon up the resources to cope with his situation, and he soon began to abandon any hope of surviving his imprisonment.

When he was brought once again before Lord Drettroth, the nobleman assessed him critically for a long moment before speaking.

"You look tired, Simon. Haven't you found your quarters comfortable?" His words were accompanied by an ironic smile.

Simon didn't answer. Their previous interaction had drained his confidence as well as extinguishing his hope. He had delivered up the best information he had to offer, and it had failed to impress the Rogandan lord even a whit. He had nothing more to give.

"I have some good news for you. It seems I might be able to find a use for you after all."

Simon looked dully at his captor, unable to guess what might be coming next.

"You look hungry. Here, have some food and wine." The Rogandan nodded to a guard, who led the youth to a table laden with food.

The youth looked suspiciously at the food, then back at Drettroth.

"Go on," the Rogandan insisted, "help yourself! No need to hurry. Take your time."

Simon decided he had nothing to lose. And he was starving. He stretched out a trembling hand for some food, brought it to his mouth, and took a bite. He was convinced he had never eaten food that tasted so good. He ignored the wine and drank from an earthen cup filled with water, closing his eyes to fully savor the simple pleasure of slaking his thirst.

He stole a glance at Lord Drettroth. The Rogandan stood with arms folded across his chest, a self-satisfied smile playing across his lips. "Does it taste good?" he asked.

Simon nodded, stuffing more food into his mouth. He had no idea how long the nobleman's indulgence might last, and he decided to make the most of it.

"Try some of the wine. I insist! I'm told it's excellent."

He hesitated for a moment, then obediently sipped the wine. He had no doubt that it was the most expensive liquid he had ever glimpsed, much less consumed.

"Any strange aftertaste?" he was asked.

The youth stopped chewing, frowning in puzzlement.

"This food was prepared for me," Drettroth told him. "I'm interested to know if someone poisoned it."

Simon almost choked, gagging involuntarily. He felt the blood drain from his face, and he began to sweat.

Drettroth laughed contemptuously at his discomposure.

"My food taster always samples my food and drink before I eat," said the Rogandan. "He plays an important role—just yesterday he was able to save my life. It was, of course, necessary for him to sacrifice his own life to do so.

"But you'll be glad to know that he has been avenged. I personally supervised an investigation to find the fools responsible, and two of the kitchen hands along with one of my guards were executed early this morning. So I doubt that you need to concern yourself too much about being poisoned. Not on this occasion, at least.

"One can never be certain, though. For obvious reasons, I cannot afford to take any risks. So I find myself needing a new food taster.

"I pride myself on being a reliable judge of character, and it seems to me that you'll do very nicely," his captor concluded brightly. "You will oversee the preparation of my meals. Whenever food and drink are brought to me, I will select portions for you to eat. It will be strongly in your own interests to ensure that no one interferes with the food."

Simon wasn't asked if he was willing—he was not offered a choice. He began the job immediately.

The very first time he presented a meal to Drettroth, the Rogandan sniffed suspiciously at it before turning to Simon with fury on his face. "You spat in my food! Don't try to deny it! I'll have you strung up on the nearest tree!" He approached Simon threateningly, his eyes bulging wildly.

Simon was so taken aback he couldn't speak. He shrank back trembling with fear, his mouth agape.

Then Drettroth chortled, bursting into uproarious laughter. "Simon, you are invaluable! The village imbecile could not look more idiotic."

From that moment on, the nobleman went out of his way to devise creative ways of belittling his new food taster. Simon was familiar with abuse, but he had never been mocked so relentlessly. Nor did the Rogandan limit himself to verbal abuse. Whenever Drettroth was in a foul mood, he took it out on Simon. It was not uncommon for him to strike the youth multiple times each day for his supposed stupidity.

Simon's new job was not without its own set of risks, either. The quality of the food served to Drettroth was outstanding—uniformly so. No cook lived long enough to serve substandard food twice to his master. Quality made no difference if the food was poisoned, though.

On one occasion, sampling a truly delicious meal, Simon began to feel extremely ill. He was soon throwing up violently, feeling utterly miserable. Worst of all, he was convinced that he was about to die, certain that the food must have been poisoned.

His master stood by laughing raucously, apparently deriving considerable amusement from Simon's discomfort. "Absolutely delightful! You never disappoint me, my Simon." Drettroth belted him heartily on the back, prompting a further bout of vomiting.

Simon could not remember ever feeling so wretched.

"There's no need for alarm," Drettroth told him. "This isn't a surprise attack. I poisoned the food myself. Just a little joke of mine—not enough to kill you." He looked thoughtful for a moment. "At least I don't think it was enough to kill you. We'll have to wait and see." Then he burst out laughing again.

However good the food might be, Simon was never able to enjoy it again. He could never be sure that Drettroth hadn't arranged for it to be poisoned, simply to satisfy his depraved sense of humor.

Simon soon doubted that it was possible to loathe a person more than he did Drettroth. The Rogandan lord was at least evenhanded—he endlessly invented new ways of inflicting his brutishness on anyone unlucky enough to be around him. As his frequent companion, though, more often than not Simon bore the brunt of his petty hatefulness. The youth began to wonder if his predecessor might have welcomed death by poisoning.

IN SPITE of the bleakness of his situation, there were periods of time when Simon was almost happy. The food taster was not expected to accompany Lord Drettroth when he traveled beyond his fortress—

the nobleman apparently had other arrangements—so Simon occasionally enjoyed a temporary release from the torment visited upon him by his new master.

And he was not alone in his relief. When the commander departed, it almost felt as if the entire fortress heaved a sigh of contentment.

A senior Rogandan army officer was left in charge. The officer was terrifying, and Simon stayed well clear of him. But even so, Lord Drettroth's deputy seemed almost genial compared to the commander himself.

In this more relaxed environment, Simon was able to form a friendship with two of the kitchen maids. They were fluent in both Arvenian and Rogandan due to a mixed heritage.

Svea was quiet and gentle, a hard worker who rarely spoke, even when spoken to.

Ines, by contrast, was intense and passionate. Simon hadn't known her long before discovering that her waking hours were consumed with wild schemes and imaginings concerning the demise of her lord and master.

Hating the Rogandan overlord was one thing; talking about it openly in his own fortress was another, even using a foreign language. Simon didn't need to speak Rogandan to see that everyone around him hated Lord Drettroth almost as much as he did. But that didn't make it safe to be blatant about it in the way that Ines was. Most others rightly feared the nobleman even more than they hated him.

Simon worried at times that he might be putting himself at risk by associating with Ines. But it was hard to resist the gratification of hearing someone say openly what everyone else only dared to think.

LORD DRETTROTH HAD LEFT the fortress that morning, and no one seemed to have any idea when he might return. Simon took the opportunity to sit outside with the two maids, enjoying the afternoon sunshine.

Of late his secret thoughts had increasingly been wandering in the direction of Svea. Such idle fancies were by no means disagreeable, but they were still sufficiently unfamiliar to leave him feeling awkward. At that moment he sat quietly, trying not to be too obvious as he stole glances in her direction.

"I have a plan to get rid of Drettroth," Ines announced, tossing the hair restlessly from her face.

Simon looked at her skeptically.

"The plan depends on you," she told him.

He snorted, not feeling any need to take her seriously.

"Come with me," she said. "I have something to show you."

Simon wasn't sure whether to laugh at her or to be worried. He sat unmoving for a moment, then shrugged and got to his feet. Following Ines, he headed back into the castle. Svea trailed along quietly behind them.

Ines led the way to a small room adjacent to Drettroth's quarters. Normally it was guarded, but today the guards were nowhere to be seen. With their master absent, they were undoubtedly also appreciating the opportunity for a break.

The three of them slipped inside, and Ines pulled the door closed. The room, dimly lit from a high window, was filled with shelves covered with jars and pots, all labeled in Rogandan.

"These are all poisons collected by Drettroth," Ines told them. "I overheard some of the guards talking about it." She pointed to a particular jar. "This is the one we need."

"You're planning to poison him?" Simon couldn't believe she was serious. "You know what happened last time."

"The plan only failed last time because the food taster wasn't involved."

"How do you know that? No one can say for certain what went wrong. None of the plotters are still alive to ask!"

She tossed her head again. "We don't need to ask them. It's obvious."

He shook his head. "If you're planning to poison him, don't expect any help from me. Have you forgotten that I'm expected to eat and drink a portion of anything that's served to him?"

"Don't you want to see him gone?"

"Of course I do. But that doesn't mean I'm ready to poison myself."

"You won't need to. We won't poison all of his food. He loves leeks, so we'll poison them. When you sample his food, just make sure you don't eat any leeks."

Simon was aghast. "That's your plan? There's no way I'm going to be involved!"

"There's nothing to worry about! All you need to do is avoid eating the leeks."

Simon desperately wanted to be rid of Drettroth. But this wasn't the way.

The next few days were going to be extremely challenging. He knew from experience that once Ines got an idea in her head, she would never let it go.

3

"What's the matter, Simon? Is it possible that you're not pleased to have me back again?" Drettroth wore a condescending smile. He seemed to be watching Simon with unusual interest.

Simon's heart was racing, and he began to sweat. He said nothing, not trusting himself to respond.

"This food looks and smells delicious. Sadly, though, I find that I'm not at all hungry," Drettroth told him. "It would be a pity to waste such a fine meal. You can eat it, Simon." His eyes narrowed, and his voice took on a threatening tone. "All of it!" he commanded.

Simon began to shake uncontrollably.

The Rogandan lord began to smile, a pitiless leer that filled Simon with dread. He called in his guards and spoke to them rapidly in Rogandan. They left the room immediately.

"I have invited our cooks to join us," the nobleman explained. "The ones who prepared the meal."

Simon couldn't hide his dismay.

Soon Ines was dragged into the room, followed by Svea.

"I'm not hungry, and Simon seems to have lost his appetite as well. The two of you can eat the meal."

Ines shook her head.

"Eat it!" Drettroth roared.

The guards forced the two girls toward the plate. After a moment's hesitation, Ines grabbed the plate and began shoveling the food into her mouth, swallowing it whole without bothering to chew it.

When she had entirely consumed the food, she sat back, aiming a look of disdain at Simon. Then she turned her full attention to Lord Drettroth, making no attempt to hide the hatred on her face.

Svea watched on, pale and trembling.

Drettroth nodded in the direction of Ines. "She shows courage," he said, with reluctant admiration. He turned to his food taster. "Thankfully you are not equally bold, my Simon, or we might have been facing a different outcome." He fixed the youth with a look somewhere between a smile and a sneer. "Don't think I'm ungrateful, though. I can read you like a scroll. You're everything I hoped for in a food taster."

Drettroth fell silent, apparently content simply to wait. The minutes dragged painfully by. Then Ines abruptly began to spasm, her head snapping back and forth. Soon her entire body was convulsing violently. Lord Drettroth seemed to enjoy the spectacle, standing with arms folded across his chest and a tight smile of satisfaction on his face. Svea buried her face in her hands, unable to watch. Simon stood rooted to the spot, filled with horror.

After a few minutes even Drettroth seemed to have had enough. He spoke to his guards, and they carried Ines, still writhing, from the room. One of them grabbed Svea by the arm and bustled her out with them.

The Rogandan nobleman turned to Simon. "In recognition of the courage of your friend, I've decided to be more generous to her than she deserves. She will be executed immediately, along with her companion." Seeing the look of anguish on Simon's face, he growled, "Be grateful I didn't insist that all three of you take the same medicine."

For Simon, the execution of his friends signaled the passing of any remaining hope he might have had. From that hour, he plodded through life in a daze.

Once long ago he had caught a glimpse of a wind-swept hilltop where a twisted tree stood alone, bent and blasted by the elements. His life now seemed like that tree, stunted and shattered, solitary in the midst of a barren wasteland.

He no longer spent his free minutes with the kitchen hands. He felt too ashamed to show his face there now. He avoided human companionship entirely. Instead he haunted the deserted passageways of the fortress, passing through the shadows as silent as a ghost.

On one occasion Drettroth took him into the room with the poisons, pointing out the various substances and expanding on their origins.

"I've found these substances to be extremely useful at times," Drettroth boasted. "I've never made a secret of my research into poisons, and my enemies in Rogand have quickly learned to employ food tasters of their own. I've simply taken that as an encouragement to become more creative."

It was obvious that the Rogandan enjoyed any opportunity to gloat with an audience. Simon said nothing.

"You understand better than most," he continued. "You have some small experience of my prowess yourself." He laughed, a jarring sound that sent shivers down Simon's spine.

"You might wonder why I'm showing you this, Simon. I'm not at all concerned that you'll use these poisons against me. It should be obvious to you by now that I'll know immediately if you do. But I thought you might one day decide you need to take some of this yourself."

He lifted one of the jars from the shelf. "This is the poison that your friend tried to use on me. It's very effective—you witnessed the results first hand." He pointed to another jar. "This one is a better choice for you. Take some of this, and all your troubles will be over in a few short minutes."

Drettroth looked at him condescendingly. "Come and help yourself. Any time. I've already instructed my guards to let you in."

He gave Simon another of his mirthless smiles. "Taking poison would first require you to stop being a coward, of course. I simply can't imagine that ever happening." He threw his head back, and a harsh and mocking laugh echoed around the tiny space.

Simon was too dispirited to reply. He was aware that Drettroth was goading him, but he had no fight left in him. He was entirely powerless against Drettroth now. The Rogandan knew it, and he knew it as well.

It was on one of his wanderings that Simon first became aware that a monk was being held in the prison. The robed figure was being taken somewhere by the guards, and he spotted Simon and called out a greeting, using the language of Arvenon. Simon slipped out of sight without offering a response.

The youth could not easily put the monk out of his mind, though. Since the demise of his two friends, only Lord Drettroth was able to speak to him in his own language. And every minute Simon spent in the company of the nobleman felt like a punishment.

It wasn't long before a pressing need for less vicious human companionship led him to the cell of the monk. His first impressions were not encouraging. He quickly concluded that the prisoner had gone mad when he found him singing. And not just singing, but sounding forth with cheerful abandon.

The monk, who introduced himself as Brother Vangellis, wasn't crazy, though. It took no more than a brief conversation to confirm that.

"How did you come to be here?" Brother Vangellis had asked.

Simon squirmed inside. Every day he risked his life in service to a man that he hated and feared. Every day he endured countless humiliations, great and small. Yet none of it was necessary. He had left the safety of Arnost by his own choice. And for what purpose? He had long since abandoned any pretense that he had acted out of noble motives.

He knew now that he could never be free from the consequences of his folly. He had watched as Lennard was led away in his place. He had refused out of cowardice to eat Drettroth's poisoned food, then stood by while Ines ate it instead. He had witnessed silently the horror of the death throes of his friend, and made no protest as Svea was led away to be executed. His shame haunted his waking thoughts and tortured his dreams.

No one could be blamed but himself. His lot in life was to grovel each day before his master, and it was no more than he deserved.

"I made a mistake. Now my life is over."

The monk had shaken his head in denial. "Your life doesn't have to be over because of your mistakes."

No one who made such a statement could possibly fathom the ugly realities of life. "You're a monk. You wouldn't understand."

"I understand much better than you could imagine. I once thought like you do."

Simon had simply shrugged. How could a monk begin to understand the depths to which he had sunk? And even if he could somehow comprehend it, what use would that be?

"It makes no difference," he had said. "There is nothing I can do about my situation."

"There is always something you can do," the monk had insisted. "The choices before us may not seem obvious at times. But we always have choices."

Simon had not come to the cell with any intention of holding a serious conversation with this stranger. But he unexpectedly found himself engaging with someone who not only spoke the same language, but was a willing listener. He was soon drawn in, in spite of himself.

It didn't take long for his feelings about Drettroth to emerge. The stranger was Drettroth's prisoner, so it hadn't been difficult to believe he might be sympathetic. And as Simon's story began to spill out, the monk did not disappoint him.

Simon related the early part of his life, and how he had found his way to the royal stables at Arnost. "I was happy, working alongside Thomas Stablehand. For a while. But then he turned on me. I still don't know why."

"That must have been hard to take," the monk offered.

"It felt like a dagger to my heart. I was angry and upset, and I decided to get him back. I'd always been the victim before. This time I decided it was someone else's turn. My anger woke something in me—a burning desire for revenge; a passion I didn't know was there. I began scheming. I could see that the timing needed to be right, and somehow I found the patience to bide my time. I prepared my revenge, and when it came I savored it to the full."

"What did you do?"

"My first target was Ben, a mastiff that belonged to Thomas. That dog was the delight of his life. I convinced his father that the animal was dangerous and needed to be put down. Thomas didn't even see it coming.

"That was only the beginning, though. My main achievement—if you could call it that—was finding ways to get between Thomas and his father. That didn't turn out to be too difficult. Neither of them needed a lot of encouragement—they were already good at misunderstanding each other. His father eventually lost patience entirely with Thomas and preferred to work with me instead.

"But it was all for nothing in the end. After Thomas left Arnost, his father berated himself incessantly for driving his only son away, and became preoccupied with how upset Thomas's mother would be. He couldn't forgive himself for not doing things differently. It became obvious he cared very little about me."

"That must have upset you."

Simon nodded. "At the time I found it very frustrating. It's what finally convinced me to leave. Whether or not the Rogandans managed to capture the city, it was clear to me that I had no future in Arnost.

"I suppose I knew deep down that I deserved it, though. Maybe Thomas was entitled to some payback, but my revenge eventually went way beyond anything he'd done to me. When I look back now, I can see that I'd finally discovered something I was good at. Unfortunately for all of us, it wasn't anything useful or productive."

"Are you still angry with Thomas?"

"Yes, of course I am! I wouldn't be here now if he hadn't turned on me. But I know I can't blame him for my own responses. I did when I left Arnost. But not now. Drettroth constantly tells me that I'm worthless. And when I look back on everything I've done, I know he's right."

Brother Vangellis shook his head firmly. "You're not a hopeless case, Simon. Any more than I was."

The conversation ended soon after that. Simon knew he'd shown himself in a very bad light, and it was obvious that the monk had been distressed by what he'd heard. Yet for some reason Simon didn't feel judged by him.

IT WASN'T long before the youth was back, drawn almost compulsively to the cell of the monk.

Brother Vangellis began to unfold his own story, and Simon was quickly captivated. He listened intently as the monk told him about his early life, his fall and his slide into oblivion, and his eventual rehabilitation. He began to understand why the monk had been reluctant to pass judgment on him.

"There's something you need to know, Simon. You talked about Thomas, and, as it happens, I know him myself. We traveled together after he left Arnost. In fact, we were hiding together from the Rogandans at the time I was captured."

Simon couldn't hide his astonishment.

"And that's not all. Thomas talked to me about his history with you. You might be surprised to hear that he feels ashamed about the way he treated you. He largely blames himself for everything that happened as a result."

The monk's revelation astounded Simon. The youth said very little in response; he needed time to ponder this information.

Brother Vangellis made no mention of the stone as the days passed. Nevertheless, Simon guessed that he must know something of it. He imagined that the monk had his own reasons for choosing not to talk about it. The youth didn't care. The stone had loomed large in his thinking at the time he left Arnost, but it now seemed little more than a distraction to him. The stone wasn't his story. There were more important things he needed to think about.

The truth was that Simon's time with Brother Vangellis had increasingly unsettled him. He wasn't being dragged down further into despair. He wasn't exactly becoming more content, either. Something deep inside him was struggling to gain a foothold, and it refused to give up. The process left him feeling restless and troubled.

Brother Vangellis might not be crazy, but there was something very unusual about him. A mysterious quality oozed out of him, one that left him calm and peaceful in spite of his imprisonment and his uncertain future. It wasn't normal. Simon couldn't readily identify what this quality was, but it had begun to call to him. He increasingly caught himself longing for it, almost to the point of desperation.

He finally found a name for it—joyfulness. Given the monk's circumstances, both in the past and now in his prison cell, insanity might have seemed entirely understandable. It was much harder to account for him being joyful. Perhaps it had to do with Brother Vangellis successfully emerging from the depths of his own guilt and shame. And, strangest of all, the monk had said that in breaking free he encountered God as liberator, not as accuser. Simon was both baffled and intrigued.

Although the youth could not fully comprehend what he was experiencing, he eventually sought an opportunity to express in a practical way the changes stirring inside him. He had discovered another prisoner in the fortress—a nobleman who turned out to be King Delmar of Varas. Simon decided to free him.

He fully understood the risk he was taking, and he was in no doubt about the likely consequences once Lord Drettroth became aware of his actions. Nevertheless, he was eager for some kind of outlet.

Given the seismic shifts taking place within him, releasing the royal prisoner seemed to Simon little more than a token gesture. But his act of defiance proved to be more significant than he expected. It solidified what had been happening within him, and it also demonstrated that his master's hold over him was beginning to weaken.

His actions required a boldness that he would not previously have believed himself capable of. Yet he did it without hesitating.

He was rediscovering a quality he thought was lost to him forever —hope.

IF LORD DRETTROTH had perceived the tiniest portion of what was happening in the prison cells of his own fortress, he would have instantly disposed of both his food taster and the monk. As yet, though, the Rogandan lord was not privy to the secret thoughts of others. Without the Stone of Knowing he had no way to pry loose the hidden intents and imaginings of those around him.

4

"Come with me, Simon. I have a surprise for you." Lord Drettroth bared his teeth in a self-satisfied smirk.

Simon followed his master with considerable trepidation, a frown creasing his brow. Drettroth's surprises had never been pleasant, and he couldn't think of any possible reason why that might ever change.

Trailing along in the nobleman's wake, he entered a room where, to his intense alarm, he glimpsed Brother Vangellis chained to the wall. His friend did not appear to be injured, but attracting Lord Drettroth's close attention signaled extreme danger. It amounted to a death knell.

Then he saw Thomas Stablehand. He felt the blood drain from his face as he absorbed the shock. He had never imagined for a moment that they would meet again. But for it to happen here, under these circumstances?

His first emotion was one of overwhelming shame. Then he fully grasped the implications of Thomas's presence, and the completeness of Drettroth's victory began to dawn on him. Would his master's triumphs never end? An angry frown covered his face as he contemplated this latest setback for anything good in the world.

Thomas was chained not far from the monk, and he appeared to have injured his arm. He was clearly not at all pleased to see Simon.

"What a merry reunion this is!" said Drettroth. He turned to the monk. "I did promise that you would soon be reunited with your companion, did I not? And here he is."

Then he addressed Simon. "I understand you've become acquainted with the monk as well, my Simon. You seem to have been spending a lot of time with him lately." He watched their faces closely, then he laughed. "Surely you're not surprised. I make sure I know what's going on in my own fortress."

He scowled at Simon. "You've been playing some little games with another of my guests, too. Don't imagine there will not be consequences. I take it personally when people decide to cross me."

Simon did not flinch. He wasn't sure why, but the Rogandan lord no longer had the same hold over him.

Drettroth swung around to face Thomas. "It must have been quite some time since you last saw Simon. You must be delighted to find yourself reunited with him once again." Thomas did not speak, but the look on his face said plenty.

"I'm sure that's more than enough of pleasantries, though," said Drettroth, dismissing his guards. "We're all here for one reason. Simon, fetch the stone from Thomas."

Thomas resisted fiercely as Simon retrieved the stone, head butting him violently and screaming his rage. He inflicted pain on his former friend, but he was unable to prevent the removal of the stone from his pouch.

Simon squinted and rubbed his head, trying to ease the throbbing. Then, as he glanced down at Thomas with the stone in his hand, his eyes were opened.

He stood there, stupefied.

Thomas's fury battered him silently, washing over him with invisible force. Simon suddenly witnessed the extent of the damage his actions had caused. He saw the evidence of the Rogandans spreading out across Arvenon in their search for Thomas, leaving death and destruction in their wake. He saw the monks cowering beneath the ground while Drettroth's men demolished their beloved monastery. He saw Thomas fleeing downriver with his friend, and watched as a bound and helpless Brother Vangellis was beaten to the ground, felled by a heavy blow. He saw Thomas leading the Rogandans away from Elena and her father, and his injury and capture that had followed as a result.

Simon was responsible—for all of it. Lord Drettroth had not known who had the stone before Simon abandoned the safety and security of his life in Arnost to reveal it to him. The youth had acted out of a petty desire to wound Thomas, and the enormity of the consequences overwhelmed him.

Nor was that all. He glimpsed the origins of his quarrel with Thomas and perceived it to be little more than foolish immaturity on the part of the older youth. He saw that the monk had been right, and that Thomas regretted his behavior. And Simon witnessed for himself the magnitude by which his revenge had exceeded the wrongs that prompted it.

Now, experiencing the raw power of the stone, he immediately understood why Thomas had tried so desperately to keep it from Drettroth.

All this he grasped in no more than a few heartbeats. Seeking relief from the intensity of it, he spun on his heel and headed to Drettroth.

The moment his eyes fell upon the Rogandan nobleman, though, he was plunged into the vile turmoil of his master's inner being. He knew what Drettroth was like—every single day he had found himself on the sharp end of the nobleman's viciousness—but nothing prepared him for the assault on his own sanity that came with unrestricted access to Drettroth's mind. He blinked, and it all faded momentarily, then it flooded inexorably over him again.

Drettroth's full strategy for acquiring the stone was laid bare; his plans for Brother Vangellis and Thomas were instantly apparent. Simon inwardly recoiled from the horror of it. The barbarity planned for them was just the beginning, though. Once Drettroth commanded the Stone of Knowing, the world as Simon had known it would end.

He learned that there were other stones, too, and saw that the Rogandan would not rest until he possessed them all. Simon glimpsed, but could not entirely grasp, his machinations around securing a covenant with his Dark Gods. But he saw that Drettroth believed he could bargain with them to secure his longevity, and that he expected a heavy obligation in return. He would expunge this debt by means of human sacrifice on a grand scale. Tens of thousands of his captives would die—as many as it might take to achieve his purpose.

Simon was aware that he himself would not long survive. With the stone in the hand of his master, there would be little further need for a food taster. But the youth was not dismayed. He had no desire to live in the kind of world that Drettroth wanted to create.

Curiously, the recent infusion of hope into Simon's life had not come unaccompanied. Other qualities, arriving unannounced, had settled in at the same time. One of them was the willingness—whatever the cost—to take a stand when it genuinely mattered. Simon was not the same person who had hidden in the shadows when Brother Vangellis first called a greeting. He did not fully realize it yet, but he was no longer a coward.

Drettroth demanded the stone, and Simon briefly handed it over, before later returning it to Thomas's pouch. While Drettroth gloated aloud about the imminent glory of his future and the pointless futility of opposing him, the food taster's mind was working furiously. The youth only half heard the nobleman as he droned on. Before he was pushed from the room before his master, he knew exactly what he needed to do.

As the door closed behind them, the Rogandan lord strode off down the passageway, positively oozing with glee. "Wine, boy," he called back over his shoulder, "and be quick about it! All this talking is thirsty work."

Simon hurried away. He intended to do his master's bidding. But he had a twist of his own in store. First he went to his room and retrieved two small leather pouches, upending them to make sure they were empty. Then he set off for the poison room. His heart began to race as he saw the two guards standing alert in their usual position, but they made no attempt to interfere as he pushed past them into the room. They smirked knowingly at him, and he ignored them, closing the door behind him. Lifting down the two jars identified by Drettroth, he carefully emptied a generous amount of each poison into his pouches.

Scurrying down to the kitchen, he retrieved two silver chalices before making his way to the cellar. He knew the habits of his master well enough to anticipate that Drettroth would drain one chalice immediately, then demand the second later, most likely a few minutes before rejoining his prisoners. He filled the chalices with wine from the Rogandan commander's favorite barrel.

Finally, he returned to his room. Opening the pouches carefully, he chose the poison originally used by Ines. He had no idea how much would be needed, so he tipped a liberal dose into one of the cups. Then he glanced around the room, looking for something to stir it with.

A small piece of metal caught his eye—part of a horse's snaffle bit. To anyone else it was a useless piece of junk, but to him it was precious. He had been no more than a child, wide-eyed and eager at the stables, when the stable master had given it to him and told him he could keep it. The broken snaffle bit had been his most treasured possession ever since. It had traveled with him all the way from Arnost.

He picked it up and gazed at it for a long moment, allowing his mind to wander freely back to a simpler, happier time. Those days had vanished, like mist before the noonday sun. Soon even the memory of them would be gone forever.

For a moment his eyes brimmed, and the welling tears overflowed and rolled down his cheeks. Then he frowned, unwilling to allow himself the distraction of self indulgence. He wiped away the tears, choosing instead to embrace the starkness of his present reality.

Dipping the metal into the chalice, he slowly stirred the wine until all trace of the poison had disappeared.

Beside his bed lay a small wineskin, half filled with wine. He unstopped the wineskin and tipped the other pouch of poison into the opening—the entire dose. Sealing it again, he shook the wineskin vigorously before securing it under his belt.

He grasped the tainted chalice in his left hand and the normal chalice in his right hand, and set off to find Lord Drettroth.

Simon arrived flushed and agitated, working hard at trying to stay calm, and willing himself not to tremble. His master paced back and forth, awash with nervous energy. He failed even to spare a glance for his food taster.

Drettroth finally noticed him. "Where have you been? Give me my wine!"

Simon knew he had the opportunity to end it—once and for all—right here, right now. But he steadied himself. Brother Vangellis and Thomas should be allowed to witness the demise of their tormentor.

Sampling a generous portion from the untainted chalice, he passed it to his master. The nobleman drank greedily, wine spilling out around his cheeks. Having drained the cup, he cast it heedlessly aside, ignoring the clatter as it fell to the floor.

Drettroth seemed to forget that Simon was there. He continued to pace around the room, muttering loudly to himself in his own language.

Simon had set his course, and the pieces were all in place. He relaxed, finally allowing his thoughts to be drawn back to the stone. In spite of the overwhelming jumble of thoughts and impressions, so much now made sense. He felt that he understood Thomas for the first time. Even Lord Drettroth's single-mindedness no longer baffled him.

He wondered briefly what his life might have been like if Thomas had not wrested the stone away from him. But he had now seen the havoc wreaked by the stone on Thomas's life. What might it have done to his own? Simon had managed to do immense harm without the stone—he could only imagine the damage he might have unleashed if he had retained it. He quickly decided that he had been better off as he was.

"Wine, Simon!" Drettroth had snapped out of his reverie. The Rogandan lord had given Thomas one hour to make his decision, and soon the hour would be up.

The fateful moment had arrived.

Simon's heart began to thump. Bitter though his life had become, he didn't want to die. His hopes and dreams had been reawakened, and the greater part of his experiences and memories were still precious to him.

Everything would end with a single mouthful of the liquid. Could he bear it?

Simon blinked slowly and sucked in a breath.

He stood tall. *Ines, this is for you.*

Raising the chalice, he drank deeply from the poisoned wine.

Then he handed the cup to his master.

Lord Drettroth took it and drank.

The Rogandan grimaced briefly once, but continued swallowing until the chalice had been drained.

WHEN THEY RETURNED to the room, Drettroth called for the stone once again. Simon retrieved it, trying to ignore the overwhelming deluge that inundated his senses whenever he glanced at anyone. He handed it over with considerable relief.

The Rogandan overlord began talking again, but Simon had become restless, unable to concentrate. It was hard to believe that everything was about to end. He tried to remind himself that it was all for good reasons, but he couldn't seem to think straight.

Then Drettroth turned to him with a command, "Simon, call for my assistants!"

Simon snapped abruptly back to reality. The stone belonged to him—the unrestrained exhibition of its power confirmed it—and he had uncovered the principles that governed the way it worked. Everything he needed to know he had learned from the thoughts of both

Drettroth and Thomas. Instead of obeying the command, he leaned over to the nobleman and whispered in his ear. "The stone is yours—I'm giving it to you. Enjoy it while you can!" Then he stepped back, away from his tormentor.

Simon saw on the face of the Rogandan lord the dawning of full comprehension at last, as Drettroth finally attained his greatest prize. It was too late. "What have you done?" the overlord screamed, apoplectic with fury.

When Drettroth drew his sword and came for Simon, the youth made no attempt to flee. Knowing his end could not be long delayed anyway, he closed his eyes and waited for the blow to fall. It never happened. The Rogandan commander had instead triggered his own death throes.

Simon, unwilling to witness another agonizing death by poison, even if the victim was Drettroth, surprised himself by managing to dispatch the Rogandan with his own sword. Then he flung the weapon away.

He spoke to Brother Vangellis and Thomas in a detached way, explaining what had happened. But only part of his mind was engaged. The rest of his thoughts drifted aimlessly, remembering what had been, and imagining what might have been.

The monk and Thomas were still chained to the wall, and Simon had just enough presence of mind to retrieve both the stone and Drettroth's keys and to take them to Brother Vangellis. As he freed the monk, a profound sense of gratitude welled up within him. Leaning forward, he quietly whispered his heartfelt thanks. He dimly wondered how his life might have been if he had met the monk sooner. He handed Brother Vangellis the stone, and saw in his face the telltale signs of its revelations.

Then he turned to Thomas, intending to free him as well.

The poison got to him first, and he began to convulse. He tugged frantically at the wineskin under his belt, struggling to free it. Fumbling anxiously, he unstopped it, raised it to his lips, and gulped down the poisoned liquid.

As his life faded steadily away, his final thought was of something

Brother Vangellis had told him. He grasped hold of it tightly, just as a drowning man might snatch at a branch that floats unexpectedly within reach.

The end, when it came, found him at peace.

The saga continues in
The Stone of Authority Complete Set
(*The Stone Cycle Complete Sets Book* 2)

But first…

The Seer
A Prequel to The Stone of Knowing

PART IV

THE SEER

A PREQUEL TO THE STONE OF KNOWING

1

Kalvor bent low to the ground, studying the signs. To his practiced eye they were easy to read. Not just one person, but several had passed this way. Recently. The village must be nearby. His quarry was surely within reach at last.

For months he had searched for the woman. At first his efforts had been entirely in vain. Later he had little more to go on than hints and vague whispers. Kalvor had not been dismayed. There was a reason Lord Drettroth chose him for this kind of assignment.

The hunt had led him south beyond the borders of Rogand, deep into the northern forests of Lestanor. The woman he sought avoided towns and cities, choosing instead to live in lightly populated areas. But the entire region was filled with the rumor of her. Either she knew nothing about hiding herself effectively, or she didn't bother to try. She was foolish indeed if she didn't try.

Remaining hidden would have required her to stop using her special gift. Apparently that was a limitation she was unwilling to accept.

It still wasn't easy to find her. No one would tell him exactly where she was. The common people revered her and protected her, even at personal risk to themselves. A string of violent encounters had testified to that. Her talents were in demand, though, and her visitors left trails for those able to read them.

He wondered if she knew he was coming for her. Perhaps she would flee. He licked his lips involuntarily at the prospect—hunting was so much more satisfying when the rabbit decided to run. It wouldn't save her. He was no ordinary hunter—he was the best. And he never gave up.

THE SUN HAD BARELY RISEN when Kalvor finally reached the location he had been seeking. The village stood beside a small river, consisting of little more than a few rude huts. Between the huts and the river lay a cultivated patch protected from the river by a simple levee. He observed the village from a distance for the entire morning, staying out of sight. None of the villagers appeared to be armed—they were woefully unprepared for the arrival of someone like him.

He saw no sign of the woman. If she was in the village, though, it wasn't difficult to guess where she might be. One of the huts was attracting much more than its share of attention. People had come and gone constantly as he watched.

He waited until the sun had passed its zenith, then he simply walked into the village. He didn't doubt for a moment his ability to deal with whatever he might find there.

He went straight to the hut he had been watching. Without introduction or ceremony, he stooped down and stepped through the low entrance. A small group—an old man, a couple of children, and a woman—sat around a rough wooden table. He knew immediately she was the one Lord Drettroth wanted. There was an air about her, something indefinable that set her apart.

A frown creased the brow of the old man when Kalvor appeared. The children simply gazed up curiously at the newcomer. As for the woman, she didn't seem surprised by his arrival. Her face revealed no concern at all. She simply looked at him, studying him calmly without speaking.

He stared back at her. The woman was probably in her early thirties. She was almost certainly not Rogandan—she lacked the dark hair that characterized his race. She wasn't beautiful, although her brown curls fell attractively enough about her face, and there was something pleasing about the fullness of her lips. He registered all of this impassively—he had no interest in her as a person.

"Please join us," she said calmly, speaking to him in Rogandan, his mother tongue. She waved to an empty seat opposite her at the table. "We're about to share a simple meal together."

His lips curled back in a smile. Why not? His victims didn't usually feed him before he dragged them away, but he was hungry, and more than willing to make an exception.

She said a few words to the old man in the language of Lestanor. He nodded once, and left the table to fetch fresh milk, a loaf of bread, and a cluster of dates. Depositing them in the center of the table, he sat down once again, eyeing the newcomer suspiciously.

They ate together in silence. The old man looked troubled. The children stole curious glances in Kalvor's direction from time to time. The woman's eyes never left him.

When the food had almost been consumed, she broke the silence. "He never hated you," she said, addressing him once again in Rogandan.

Kalvor frowned in puzzlement. He had no idea what she was talking about.

"Your brother," she said. "He never hated you."

He scowled at her. She was a seer, of course—it was the one thing everyone agreed on. But he hadn't hunted her down so she could poke around in the dung heap of his past. Perhaps she was trying to put him on the defensive, to weaken him. If so, she was wasting her time.

"I didn't come here to talk about my brother," he told her curtly.

"No," she said quietly. "I know why you're here."

"Then it won't surprise you to know that I'm leaving, now, and you're coming with me." His hand moved to the hilt of his sword. "Do I need to explain why it will be better for your friends here if you don't argue?"

"No." She shook her head. "I fully understand what you're capable of."

"Good. Then you'll be sensible and come quietly."

The old man made to get out of his chair. He clearly had not understood the words they had spoken, but he seemed to grasp the general idea well enough. The woman addressed him rapidly in his own tongue. Kalvor knew a little of the language of Lestanor, but she spoke too quickly for him to catch it all. He thought she was telling him she couldn't stay there anyway.

The old man protested, but she shook her head firmly. Rising from the table, she embraced him briefly, then said goodbye to the children after kissing them both on the head.

"I'm ready," she announced. "Can I get a few things?"

"Make it quick. I'll come with you—I'm not letting you out of my sight."

He followed her around closely as she gathered some food and a few items of clothing and put them into a sack.

The moment she was ready he led her away from the village, avoiding established paths.

Once they had made a start, he found himself impatient to be away from there. They moved quickly, traveling until the afternoon was spent. Then he found a sheltered spot beside a stream and instructed her to sit. He didn't bother with a fire—he had nothing to cook, and they weren't lacking in warmth given the balmy weather.

The woman produced a loaf of bread from the bundle in her sack and broke it into two, handing him a piece. "My name is Sheylha," she said.

He took the bread with a grunt. He didn't offer his own name.

She watched him quietly again. Then she said, "Some men might come after me. If they do, please let me handle it. I can negotiate with them."

"I don't negotiate. If anyone comes, I'll deal with them my way."

Her brow furrowed. "Disagreeing with someone doesn't mean you need to kill them."

He snorted. “Disagreements should never be left to fester. I learned that the hard way.”

She fell silent.

“Who are these men?” he asked. “What do they want with you?” It didn’t hurt to be prepared.

She paused for a moment. “Their leader wants me, for my...gift.”

He didn’t respond.

“Your Lord Drettroth isn’t the only one who wants to control me,” she added.

So she knew who had sent him. The ambitious Rogandan lord must have had dealings with her in the past. Curiosity flickered briefly in his mind, but he stomped it down quickly. What difference did it make?

When night fell she lay down and was soon asleep. Kalvor sat silent in the darkness, brooding.

He trudged wearily back to the campsite. The woman sat there quietly, peering curiously at him in the early dawn light. She frowned. “Are you hurt?”

Stepping over to the stream he splashed the blood off his clothes. Then he found a patch of grass and cleaned his sword. He didn’t bother to answer.

“So they did come,” she said simply. “Three of them.”

Somehow she knew. She was a seer. “There will be more,” he told her.

“Yes, there will,” she said.

The day had only just begun, and already he felt tired. “Time we were going.”

Sheylha nodded. She stood and followed him away from the stream.

They had changed direction, heading directly away from the morning sun. “Where are we heading?” Sheylha asked curiously.

"West for a while. We're being tracked. I'm going to try to shake them off."

He left her late in the morning, heading back toward their pursuers. He expected to be gone for a while—a full day at least. It was possible she might try to run, but for some reason he didn't think so.

She'd been surprisingly cooperative. He couldn't account for it. It was almost as though she wanted to go with him. He pushed it from his mind, focusing instead on becoming the hunter rather than the hunted.

He located them early in the evening. There were twelve of them, and their numbers must have made them overconfident. They had stopped for the day and were making a lot of noise. They hadn't set sentries. He would teach them a valuable lesson that night.

Wild boar were foraging near their camp—Kalvor had seen their spoor. The creatures could be extremely dangerous when provoked, so he spent the next couple of hours locating a big one and provoking it. Then he let it chase him to the outskirts of the camp, swinging himself onto a low hanging tree branch at the last possible minute. The boar charged into the camp, causing instant chaos. When the confusion finally died down, two men lay seriously injured. The boar was responsible for that. Another three lay dead. He left the survivors to decide for themselves how that had happened.

Throughout the night Kalvor headed northeast, leaving a clear trail behind him. When he found a suitable opportunity, he doubled back. The trackers would eventually find that his trail had simply disappeared.

HE RETURNED to discover that Sheylha had indeed waited for him. They resumed their journey, heading west for three more days before swinging north. Crossing the border into Arvenon, they eventually made their way into the dense forests southeast of the town of Danford. Kalvor made camp with the intention of lying low for several days. He was confident that their new location in Arvenon would be extremely difficult to trace.

Having settled on a base, Kalvor addressed his attention to the problem of provisions. He set snares and gathered edible roots and wild berries.

Sheylha was both able and willing to assist with practicalities. He had never abducted anyone quite like her. She never descended into blubbering incapacity. She never even complained. She seemed to understand his moods better than he did himself, and knew when to speak and when to remain quiet.

A week stretched to two and then three, and still he did not resume their journey. He told himself he was simply being cautious. But it began to dawn on him that he might actually miss her company when the time came to hand her over to Drettroth. Alarmed at even the possibility of a sign of weakness, he determined to put her out of his mind entirely. Once it had become a conscious issue, though, the more he tried not to think about her the more impossible it became. Adopting the simplest solution of avoiding her, he took to spending large amounts of time away from their camp, testing a hunting bow and arrows he had recently fashioned.

One day he returned a little before noon to find Sheylha gone. A rapid inspection of the site revealed signs of a struggle. Furious with himself for his own foolishness, he immediately set out in pursuit. He quickly discovered he was tracking several men as well as the woman.

They were making no attempt to hide their tracks—they were in a race against time. His task would become much more difficult if he failed to reach them before darkness fell. Her captors would not stop when daylight ended, and he would be forced to wait until dawn to resume his tracking. By then they would be far away. He took comfort in the thought that however hard they drove her, the woman would still slow them down.

He could run through the forest like a deer, and follow a track from the faintest of signs. And he was angry now. He flew forward, passing through the trees like a breath of wind.

The sun was sinking low in the sky when he finally caught up with them. He counted six men, all part of the original group that had met the boar. They were more alert this time. Nevertheless, two of them went down with feathered arrows in their backs before they saw him. One remained with the woman, the other three attacked him together.

He threw down the bow and drew his sword. One came at him head on, while the other two closed in on each side. The location did not favor a group, though. They were attacking him among the trees, not in the open.

Kalvor lunged aggressively at the one in front, driving him back rapidly to keep him off balance. The defender soon stumbled onto a low shrub and lost his footing. Kalvor ran him through, then dived to the side as one of the remaining two tried to take advantage of his distraction. Both of them came at him at once. They clearly knew how to fight, and they were counting on overwhelming force to beat him down.

He had faced worse odds, though, and he was confident he was equal to the task. He was superbly fit, with rippling muscles and not an ounce of body fat, and his unusual height gave him superior reach. He settled into a familiar rhythm, allowing his arm to move his sword instinctively while he assessed their weaknesses.

"Kalvor, behind you!"

The warning shout shocked him into action. He feinted, then swung to one side, barely escaping a wild sword thrust from behind him. Sheylha's minder had joined the fight, and they came at him from all sides again. He ducked and weaved swiftly until he had placed a large tree at his back. Then he thrust forward, his sword flickering. He took the weakest of the three in the side, and the man crumpled with a cry. The others closed the gap and came at him together.

"Kalvor, behind you again!"

He registered—almost too late—that there were seven of them, not six. The seventh must have been scouting when he caught up with the main group.

Reversing his sword, he thrust it behind him. He got lucky, taking his new opponent by surprise. But while he was off guard, both of the others leaned forward and thrust at him together. One sword pierced his side and the other his right leg.

Searing pain overwhelmed his senses, and he almost blacked out. Grimacing, he somehow launched his sword at one of his two remaining attackers. The sword found its target, but Kalvor no longer had the strength to withdraw it. As the final attacker drew back his weapon for a killing thrust, Kalvor pulled his knife and threw it with the last of his failing energy. He pitched forward, his own blood spilling around him.

As blackness overtook him, his fading thought was one of wonder. Twice Sheylha's warning shout had saved him. Twice she had called him by name. And yet he had never told her what it was.

2

Pain engulfed his world. It blundered recklessly through his consciousness, competing for attention with the fever talk that inundated his head.

A voice was there, too, sometimes a murmur, sometimes comprehensible. It whispered soothingly. Occasionally it sang softly to him.

There were times when he could hear and think normally. Birds called in the forest, and the wind sighed in the treetops above. Before long he always slipped away again into blackness.

His past paraded itself before him, in all its aching beauty and excruciating agony. At times the torment of the memories eclipsed the physical pain. He saw again his bride, radiant and carefree, running to him with delight on her face. He saw his child, a perfect miniature of her mother, laughing as she played in the sunshine.

Through it all he watched as his brother turned away from their joy, anguish in his eyes. He felt himself shrugging helplessly once again. The decision had been neither his nor his brother's—she had made the choice.

He stumbled anew upon the murky trade in precious gems. He comprehended the risks, but could not ignore the dazzle of great reward. His wife's smile slowly faded as his secret hoard grew, but he willed himself not to notice. He told himself it was only temporary. Just until he could establish his fortune. Then he would leave it all behind.

But the greed had taken hold. The shadow of fear rarely left his wife's face now, though he no longer regarded it. His brother's bafflement did not move him—let his sibling remain a poor farmer if that made him content. Kalvor was destined for greater things.

His trade was perilous, and he soon controlled a network of ambitious, and often dangerous, men. He had become dangerous himself. He was not a man to be trifled with.

The business led him further from home. Long absences from his family became necessary and gradually ceased to trouble him. His wealth was growing rapidly. He kept telling himself that it wouldn't need to be for much longer.

And then it had all come crashing down.

He had returned home one day, calling for his wife and daughter, only to find their lifeless bodies sprawled on the ground. The two guards he had hired lay dead beside them. His hoard was bare—all of it gone. The robbers had surely forced the location of the hiding place from his wife. She would have volunteered it readily—she cared nothing for the money. Nevertheless, they had not been gentle with her.

Faced with the horrific consequences of his priorities, he understood too late the magnitude of his own folly.

He wasn't the only one who had loved his wife. His brother had loved her hopelessly from a distance, and Kalvor could not face him. Surely his sibling must hate him with a bitter passion. Kalvor became restless and agitated. He had to do something.

Grief had quickly turned to rage. He paused long enough to bury them, then he abandoned his trade and set out for revenge. It had taken many months to trace each of the killers, but he was single-minded. One by one he tracked them down and exacted payment from them in kind—blood for blood.

When it was finally over, he found himself restless and dissatisfied still. The aching void remained, and he had no idea where to turn.

He was offered a task to occupy him—the opportunity to avenge an acquaintance. Retribution was well deserved, and the job paid handsomely. He discovered he was good at it. Others soon heard of his capabilities and sought him out. One step at a time, and without conscious intent, he gradually underwent a transformation. He had always been tall and strong and relentless. Now he became an object of terror—a hired assassin, a killer without remorse. He wasn't above abductions if the fee was right.

None of it numbed the pain of his loss. In time he learned to force it out of his awareness, to push it far away where he had no need to deal with it.

THE VOICE SPOKE AGAIN in his memory. *He never hated you.* The voice was familiar to him now. *Your brother. He never hated you.*

He hadn't turned to his brother in his grief. Perhaps everything might have been different if he had.

But what did it matter? Even if his brother had somehow found it within him to offer comfort and support, Kalvor knew that his own stubbornness and pride would never have allowed him to receive it. Such support was entirely unearned and undeserved.

And it could never have satisfied him. His debt was too great to be so easily discharged. His wife and daughter had paid the ultimate price for his greed. There was no opportunity now to cast himself down before them and beg for their forgiveness. Where could he possibly turn for absolution?

Silent tears made tracks across his cheeks as he slid again into the blessed release of nothingness.

THE WOMAN—SHEYLHA—KNELT before a small fire, humming quietly to herself. He drank in the sight of her.

Turning in his direction, she noticed his attention and greeted him with a smile. "Welcome, Kalvor. So you have decided to rejoin the living?"

He did not try to speak. Her quiet movements captivated him, and he contented himself with watching her. She gazed at him for a long moment, a thoughtful look on her face. Then she turned aside, away from the intensity in his eyes, and continued with her chores.

He was too weary to watch for long. Sleep soon claimed him once more.

"Why?" It was the first word he had spoken, and all he could manage.

Nothing further was needed—she understood. "Why not?" she replied. "Do you think you weren't worth saving?"

He didn't respond. He just lay there, watching her and waiting.

"I had hope for you. In spite of everything." She regarded him frankly. "I had to dig deep to find it."

She softened her words with a smile. Approaching him, she examined his bandages, tending him with gentle and skillful fingers. It was hard to imagine a more considerate nurse—she seemed to sense what caused him pain the same moment he became aware of it.

"How?"

"How do I know things?" Her face clouded over for a moment. "You're not ready to hear that. Not now. Maybe not ever."

He wasn't offended in the least. He wasn't even sure if it was possible for her to offend him.

She sighed. Then she adopted a detached air. "We need meat. I'm going outside to check the traps. As for you, the thing you need to concentrate on is getting well again."

The day came when Kalvor was able to walk again. His injuries were not fully healed, but he was impatient to get back on his feet.

The weather was closing in, and decisions needed to be made while there was still time.

"I can build a shelter for the winter. I'll need to find the right place."

She nodded her agreement. "You can decide the location."

The next couple of weeks were hard work. He found a secluded site within the borders of Arvenon. It was deep within the forest, not far from a stream, and sheltered from the worst of the weather. Tall trees surrounded it on all sides, making it unlikely that smoke from their fire would be easy to detect.

It took him much longer to build the shelter than he expected. His recovering body still limited him frustratingly. With few tools at hand and restricted time he kept it simple. He managed to fashion a crude chimney, though, and gather a large pile of wood. They moved into the shelter before it began to snow in earnest.

He had abandoned any thought of his original mission. There was no longer any question of taking her to Lord Drettroth. Nor was there a need to inform her about the change in his intentions—she knew such things without needing to be told.

He asked a question that had long been on his mind. "The village in Lestanor—why did you need to leave it?"

"Those men you fought—they were sent by a person who believed he owned the entire region. Me included. You weren't the first person attacked by his thugs. None of the others gave back as good as they got, though. Not like you did.

"He was becoming very demanding. He wanted to use me to manipulate others. It would have ended badly—for me and for people I cared about."

"I'm not going to let anyone hurt you." His tone was matter-of-fact, but a resolve as unyielding as granite lay behind the words.

He had always needed a purpose in life—it had been true since he was a small child. His purpose now was to protect this woman. He owed it to her, and he had never been one to leave his debts unpaid.

She eyed him with a raised eyebrow. "You're in no state to fight anyone."

He shrugged. "Fighting doesn't seem to be necessary right now."

She laughed, a merry sound. "May it long continue to be true."

. . .

THE TWO OF them quickly became comfortable in each other's company. Kalvor could not complain about someone so understanding and accepting of his needs and his moods. For Sheylha's part, she seemed to very much appreciate a break from dealing with demanding people.

Kalvor was a man of few words, but Sheylha didn't seem to mind. He had long since accepted that she knew what he was thinking, so he saw little need to speak anyway. She somehow seemed able to reach into his mind to see his past, too. He wasn't entirely sure how he felt about that, but he trusted her completely. And he hadn't forgotten how much he owed her.

SHEYLHA'S favorite meal was fresh fish, and she never tired of idling away a few stray hours angling with a pole. Downstream, not far from their shelter, she had found a location frequented by trout. Kalvor often joined her there to fish. Whenever they enjoyed success they would squat together beside the stream to clean their catch, then they would return to the shelter and poach the fish in a pan over the fire.

With the onset of winter, the stream began to freeze over. Arriving one day at their favorite spot with hopes of fresh fish for dinner, they found it covered with ice. Before Kalvor could protest, Sheylha grabbed a fallen branch and stepped nimbly out onto the frozen surface of the stream. Alarmed at the risk she was taking, he called a warning.

"Don't worry! I've done this before," she called back cheerily.

Standing on the thicker ice near the bank, she began energetically laying into the ice around their fishing hole with the branch. He considered following her, but quickly decided that it would simply increase the risk of disaster.

The ice resisted at first, but soon began to splinter steadily under her blows. In a few short minutes she had almost cleared the fishing hole. She paused to rest.

An ominous cracking sound shattered the stillness.

"Get out of there!"

His cry of alarm came too late. The ice beneath her broke into pieces, and she was pitched headlong into the freezing water. The stream was not deep, and she pulled herself to her feet, shivering with the cold as icy water poured off her.

A broad sheet of ice still clung to the bank, preventing Kalvor from reaching her. She clambered onto the ice, trying to escape the stream. Her weight was more than the ice could bear, though, and a new piece broke away, dumping her back into the water. She struggled upright again, beginning to show signs of exhaustion.

Kalvor found a fallen branch and passed one end to her. She grasped hold of it, and he began to pull her in. Before she made it all the way across the remaining ice, though, her nerveless fingers lost their grip, and she slipped back into the water.

He grabbed a lump of wood and smashed away the ice that remained between Sheylha and the bank.

"Come to me," he called urgently.

She somehow found her feet once again and lurched forward. Stumbling suddenly upon something underfoot, she pitched forward into the water. This time she did not manage to stand upright again.

She had done enough, though. Kalvor grabbed hold of her clothing and dragged her out of the river by main force.

She was utterly spent. There was no question of her walking back to the shelter. He positioned himself in front of her, facing away. Kneeling down, he pulled her arms over his shoulders, clasping them tightly across his chest. Then he stood upright, lifting her with him, and set off for home.

By the time he reached the shelter he was soaking wet as well, and shivering with the cold. She was blue and barely seemed to be breathing. He stripped off her clothes, then tore off his own, letting the sodden garments lie where they fell. Then he dragged her into the warm shelter.

Grabbing a pile of furs, he spread them out before the fire, then lay down shivering on top of them before reaching for her, drawing her close to allow her body to absorb his own warmth. He shuddered with the shock as her icy cold body came into contact with his own. Covering them both with furs, he settled down to wait.

Eventually he slipped into an exhausted slumber. When he woke his own body temperature felt more normal. Some color had returned to her face as well. Locating some of her dry clothing, he pulled it onto her before settling her once again.

She slept through the hours of darkness without waking. He spent a tense night at her side, constantly checking her condition.

By the time the dawn came she was burning up with fever.

Thoroughly alarmed, he set out on a desperate hunt for feverwort, searching everywhere for any glimpse of its broad leaf and white flower. Feverwort was almost certainly growing somewhere nearby, but snow covered the ground, and he could find no sign of it.

He had no idea what to do, apart from trying to get her to swallow fluids.

As the day wore on her condition worsened. For the first time he began to fear that he might lose her. He couldn't bring himself to face even the possibility of such an outcome.

He went outside the shelter and cried aloud to the heavens, beseeching the mercy of the Dark Gods of Rogand—Malzakh the Destroyer and his fearsome sister, Nehrvina the Awful. He didn't doubt that turning to them for compassion was an exercise in futility, though, and he was soon casting about elsewhere in his search for hope. Sheylha had a softness for the god of Arvenon, and Kalvor tried to recall anything he'd heard about him. This deity had supposedly sacrificed himself for the sake of mortals. It sounded implausible, but he sent an earnest plea in his direction anyway. He would have pleaded with the gods of Lestanor, too, if he'd known anything of substance about them.

Sheylha clung to life throughout another sleepless night for Kalvor. She lingered on through the following day, then as the sun began to set, her fever finally broke.

By the morning she had opened her eyes. He trembled as he gazed at her, not certain if his unsteadiness was due to relief or fatigue. He fed her a vegetable broth he had prepared, and she managed to swallow some of it. Her dull eyes soon closed, though, and she slept.

Exhaustion overtook him, and he finally succumbed to sleep himself. When he eventually woke he discovered that he had slept through the entire day and the following night.

She lay silent among the furs, watching him. He leaped up, guilty at leaving her untended for so long.

"My clothes," she asked weakly. "Where are they?"

"You needn't worry—nothing happened," he assured her.

He immediately felt foolish. She, of all people, didn't need to be told such things.

"That isn't what I meant," she said. "I need the clothes I was wearing." She sounded surprisingly anxious.

He looked at her curiously. He didn't understand her request at all. "They're outside," he told her. "I can get them if you like."

"Please," she said simply, nodding.

He went outside and rummaged around in the snow until he found her garments. After brushing off as much loose snow as he could, he brought them inside.

"Could you please look away?"

That surprised him even more, but he complied with her request.

She went quiet for a time as she handled her garments. Then she spoke again. "Thank you." She sounded enormously relieved.

"You can look again now."

He turned back to her.

"I don't need these anymore." She was offering him all of the clothing except one undergarment. He regarded her with a puzzled frown, then he shrugged and took the clothes. He hung them inside in a place where they would eventually dry out.

Before the sun had set she was on her feet again.

By the time a couple more days had passed she seemed almost back to normal.

3

Outwardly life had resumed its normal rhythm. The reality, though, was that nothing could ever be the same again for either of them.

Kalvor looked back on their early weeks together as a time of innocence that had vanished forever. Sheylha's near death experience had stirred up intense emotions in him, and having suppressed his emotions for so long, he had no idea how to deal with them now.

Almost losing Sheylha had shaken Kalvor to the core. Crippling fear had gripped him as he watched her teeter on the brink of death. He had actually pleaded with the gods, an act he never imagined himself capable of.

He had kept her alive by lying with her skin to skin. There had been nothing sexual—much less romantic—about the experience. Nevertheless, it had awakened something in him. He had become aware of a hollow void within himself, and a nagging hunger for something more. He no longer knew how to be natural around her.

It hadn't previously bothered him that she knew his thoughts and his emotions, but now he felt exposed and uncomfortable. For the first time he wished he had similar insights into her.

He could have simply asked her what she was thinking and feeling, of course. But she knew what was on his mind, and she could have volunteered answers if she'd wanted to.

Once or twice he noticed her reaching out tentatively, as if to comfort him. But she had quickly withdrawn her hand and turned away.

They seemed to have reached an impasse, with neither of them willing to take the risk of crossing the divide.

KALVOR WAS out checking his traps when he was startled into alertness by a nearby sound. He looked up to find himself staring into an unfamiliar face. Instinctively he adopted a fighting stance. The stranger, who wore the robes of a monk, assessed Kalvor calmly, ignoring the implied threat.

With the monk showing no signs of aggression, Kalvor willed himself to relax. As he studied the cleric, an idea began to form in his mind. "Come with me, if you are willing," he said. "You will be welcome in our humble shelter. Please share a meal with us."

At the mention of food, the monk brightened visibly, readily accepting his invitation.

Sheylha was delighted to see the monk, and Kalvor busied himself preparing a meal while they conversed. As he worked, he consciously cleared his mind of anything apart from the task at hand.

Conversation between Sheylha and the visitor continued unabated throughout the meal. When all of them had finally satisfied their hunger, the monk sat back with a contented sigh.

Kalvor began watching Sheylha intently. The moment she glanced across at him, he locked eyes with her and opened himself to her probing. Her eyes widened. A deep blush covered her face as she read the question in his eyes. She sat unmoving for a long, lingering moment, then inclined her head, so slightly it was almost imperceptible. It was enough for him.

He turned to the monk. "I hope you enjoyed the meal."

"I did," the cleric confirmed. "Very much indeed."

"Would you be willing to do us a small favor in return?"

"Gladly, if it is within my power."

"Would you please marry us?"

THE MONK HAD GONE after pronouncing a blessing over them and their household. Having seen him off, Kalvor returned to the shelter and stepped inside.

Sheylha had arranged a bed of furs and laid herself down upon them. He offered her his thoughts without reserve, knowing that none of his hopes and dreams were hidden from her. She reached for him once more, and this time she did not draw back.

BY THE TIME winter had passed, Kalvor had recovered from his injuries. He scouted widely around their dwelling in every direction, and saw no sign that their refuge had been detected. Nor could he see any obvious reason why it might be detected in the future.

Kalvor's wounds might have healed, but he had yet to regain his full strength. In particular, he began to work hard to recapture his fighting edge. Sheylha always seemed willing to pause to admire her new husband as he put himself through his paces. Beyond that, she seemed content enough to spend the bulk of her time working away at the necessary chores of life.

He had a number of questions. He tried not to overwhelm her with them, though.

"Why did you agree to go with me in the village in Lestanor? You knew what I was intending to do."

"Yes, I knew," she agreed. "But I also saw things in you that you weren't able to see for yourself. You may not have realized it, but you were ripe for change. You just needed a nudge."

He wasn't sure what to say. He always needed time to absorb her revelations. She seemed to be in an answering mood, though, so he continued with another of his questions.

"Your gift—is that how you healed my wounds?"

She shook her head. "No. I can't use it to heal physical wounds. It helps, though, because I can see when someone is in pain. And when I'm tending wounds, I know if my actions are making the pain better or worse."

"You're the most gentle nurse I've ever known."

She smiled. She seemed to ponder for a long moment before continuing. Then her face became serious. "I think you're aware that I can see into the minds of other people," she told him. "That has the potential to be a very dangerous gift."

He simply nodded. Some people would stop at nothing to control such an ability.

"It reveals the past to you as well, doesn't it?" he said.

"Yes," she agreed. "You have seen evidence of that.

"At first I didn't know what to do with this gift," she told him. "I was terrified of it. Then I became inquisitive about people. I couldn't help myself—I pried into everything. It became very empty. Eventually I decided I would try to use the knowledge for good. I wanted to do whatever I could to heal people."

"But you said you can't heal wounds."

"I don't mean physical wounds. Many people are deeply wounded in their spirits. They can't easily see the roots of their own problems. With careful study, I usually can."

"So you saw that my brother's attitude was important to me. How could you be sure that he never hated me, though? You couldn't see into his mind, could you?"

"No, I couldn't. But I was able to witness your interactions with him, hidden away deep in your memory. Your conscious memory doesn't take you back that far anymore. At the time you agonized over what had happened, and you came to some conclusions about what your brother was thinking. Those conclusions are what you remember now. I was able to see these conclusions, as well as what originally took place between you and your brother. It became clear to me that your brother's attitude wasn't quite how you interpreted it."

"So I was about to take away your freedom and put your life in danger, and you were thinking about my brother?"

She shrugged. "I'm well acquainted with being in danger. And I've learned not to worry too much about the future. I'm no use to anyone, myself included, if I give in to that."

He gazed at her with renewed respect. Very few people seemed even vaguely capable of looking beyond their own self interest.

"So it somehow helps people if they learn to see their own past differently?"

She nodded. "People tell themselves things that aren't true. Setting it straight often changes them."

All this seemed like a foreign language to him. But apparently it made sense to her. "Are you sorry that you're not helping people anymore?"

She sighed. "It had become very tiring. I am grateful for a rest from it—a long rest."

He could see the point of helping others from time to time—even strangers. But people constantly coming at you, expecting you to somehow fix them? It would have driven him mad. "How many people came to see you?"

"I never counted. But it must have been hundreds."

He shook his head. She must have seemed a god-like figure to them. "I imagine they miss you."

"I'm sure that most of the common people miss me. They were grateful for my help, and they repaid me with love and respect. But others—too many others—lusted after my gift. Keeping them at bay became a constant struggle. I found it more and more exhausting. It's such a relief to be free of it."

It was very clear to him that she had badly needed to escape from the expectations and the strife. In time she might begin to miss it, though. "Do you think you will ever want to return to that life?"

"I don't know. It's hard to imagine hiding away for the rest of my days when there's so much need in the world. Perhaps if you were there to help me I could find a way to make it work. I'm in no hurry, though."

He sat silently, pondering all she had told him. To a stranger, the picture she had been painting would have seemed like no more than the ravings of a lunatic. But he had seen for himself the power and impact of her gifts.

"I've been very careful with what I say about this," she told him frankly. "No one else understands the full extent of what I'm able to see and do."

"Why are you willing to trust me with this information?"

She smiled, although there was no humor in it. "Remember that I can see into your mind. I trust you because I understand your intent. Perhaps better than you do."

THEY HAD CARVED out a simple but idyllic existence for themselves in the wilderness. More than three years had passed since Kalvor first built their shelter, and a sturdy cabin had taken its place. Three of them shared the cabin now—their daughter Ahnya was the delight of their lives, and she had just turned two.

They were acutely aware that nothing lasts forever, though.

The first hint of trouble came when Kalvor spotted a Rogandan soldier making his way stealthily through the trees, less than a day's march from their dwelling. Instantly alert, he began thoroughly scouting the whole region. Before he returned to report his discovery to his wife, he had established beyond doubt that the soldier was just one of many.

"We need to leave. Now." Kalvor moved quickly around the cabin, selectively choosing a few items and stuffing them into a sack.

Dismay showed clearly on Sheylha's face. "Are you sure this is necessary, Kal? They might not be looking for us."

"These are Drettroth's men, and they're searching for us. They're led by a man called Marek. I know him—he hasn't come here for a chat." He knew she could uncover the truth for herself in his mind, but saying it out loud somehow made it more solid.

"It must have been the monk," he said bitterly.

She opened her mouth to protest, but he forestalled her. "I don't mean he exposed us intentionally. It probably made a great fireside story—the monk stumbles upon a couple living together in the forest in unlikely innocence; he provides them with their happy ending. No one would forget such a tale."

He threw up his hands in frustration. "We should have moved. Far away from here."

Kalvor turned aside, moving quickly about the cabin. As soon as he had gathered a few essential supplies, he spoke to Sheylha urgently. "I have some preparations I need to make. I'll be gone, perhaps for an hour. Be ready to leave the moment I return." Then he vanished among the trees.

Sheylha was ready when he returned. She was only leaving with great reluctance, but she accepted it.

He led them rapidly away from their home. "We're heading to Arnost. The capital of the kingdom of Arvenon probably seems like an unlikely place to hide, so maybe they won't be expecting it. Either way, it's probably as good a destination as any when a large group of Rogandan soldiers is on your trail."

Just before nightfall he found a secluded spot for them to rest. "I'm going to do some hunting of my own. I'll be back before dawn. If I don't make it back by mid morning for any reason, keep heading west until you come to a main road. It leads to Arnost. Try to join a group of other travelers if you can."

She couldn't hide her anxiety. He ignored it. He lifted up their daughter and hugged her briefly before kissing Sheylha gently on the lips. Then he was gone.

HE RETURNED as dawn was breaking. Ahnya greeted him with a glad cry and he scooped her into his arms.

Sheylha could not contain her joy and relief at seeing him. She looked tired—he hadn't slept that night, and she probably hadn't, either.

He tried to cloud his mind. “Don’t try to see my thoughts,” he warned her. “You might find some distressing images there.”

She snatched her eyes away.

“It’s enough to say that I’ve long prepared against the possibility of this day. I had a warm welcome ready for them, and they didn’t miss any of it. While they were distracted I took the opportunity to further reduce their numbers.” He hung his head. “There are so many of them, though. They torched the cabin. I couldn’t prevent it.”

He hardened himself—he had a wife and child to consider. Not for the first time. This time he would not abandon his family for any reason. “I left a false trail to buy us some time.”

For her sake, he put the images of death and confusion from his mind, and resolutely set his thoughts on the future. He picked up their daughter and shouldered his sack, then he led them forward.

4

Kalvor glanced up at the sun, then across at Sheylha. The day had barely begun and already both of them were bone-weary. Traveling on foot with a small child meant frustratingly slow progress, and once again he berated himself for failing to acquire horses during their period of isolation.

In the hope of making up time, the little group made their way onto the main road. Noticing a caravan behind them traveling in the same direction, they paused to consider their options.

"Perhaps we should join them for a while," Sheylha suggested.

Kalvor didn't answer immediately. It would benefit them enormously if they could catch a ride. But they had no money to barter with, and exposing themselves would involve enormous risks.

The urgency of picking up the pace finally decided him. "Very well," he said reluctantly. "But not for long. And only while they're moving forward. We'll need to leave the minute they stop."

They quickly discovered that the caravan consisted of several Rogandan trading families. The traders readily welcomed Kalvor and his little family into their midst, and they soon found themselves riding on an open wagon in the middle of the column.

The bustle and noise of a caravan made for a dizzying change after the peace and quiet of the forest. Sheylha seemed to adjust immediately to the breathless pace of human interaction. Kalvor set his jaw and tried not to be noticed.

"What's your daughter's name? And how old is she?" asked one of the women.

"Her name is Ahnya," Sheylha replied with a smile. "She's two."

"She's so good at talking!"

It was true—Sheylha had assured him that Ahnya was unusually advanced. But how many children had a mother who always knew exactly what they were trying to communicate—a mother instantly able to help them find the right word?

"I see you have a little one too," Sheylha returned, nodding toward a screaming baby. "Is he unwell?"

"He's very unsettled. I simply can't understand what's wrong with him—it's so hard when they're too young to tell you."

"May I hold him?"

"Of course." The mother nodded to her older daughter, and she handed over the squawking infant.

Sheylha examined him silently for a couple of minutes. Then she tilted him this way and that before patting him firmly on the back a few times, first in one location, then in another. Several loud burps sounded, and the baby stopped crying.

The other woman looked at Sheylha with awe in her eyes. "Thank you! You're amazing! Do you know what makes him so upset?"

"It seems to be wind," she said, handing him back. "After each feed it might be helpful to spend some time getting rid of it."

"But I do! I've always burped my babies, but it's never seemed to fix the problem with him. I thought it was severe colic—or something much worse."

Sheylha smiled. "It's nothing serious. He just seems to be a lot more windy than your others were."

"How do you know so much about babies?"

She smiled again. "I've had some experience with them."

The conversation continued to flow without pause. Kalvor kept his head down, successfully managing to avoid attention.

The day had almost worn away by the time the wagons eventually came to a halt.

"Come and camp near us tonight," the woman suggested eagerly. "The caravan is going to pause for a couple of days before pushing on to Arnost."

Sheylha looked at Kalvor hopefully.

"We need to keep moving," he said regretfully, forcing a smile. "We're eager to reach Arnost as soon as possible."

"That's a shame. Happy travels, then. Thank you so much for your help with my baby!"

They said their farewells, and hurried off.

"WE COULDN'T HAVE STAYED for one night?"

He shook his head firmly. "If Drettroth's men found us, the traders couldn't have protected us. We needed to leave quickly. The men pursuing us will discover soon enough that we've been there."

They hurried along the road for a couple of hours after the sun disappeared below the horizon. Then they sought out a suitable location among the trees, well away from the road. They settled down to spend the night there.

"Just one more day of travel, and we should be in Arnost," he told her.

They were silent for a time, not speaking again until their daughter had drifted off to sleep.

"Kal, there's something I need to tell you."

He peered at her curiously.

"I've never told you where my gift came from."

"You were born with it, weren't you?"

"No. It isn't what you think. It isn't an ability I inherited at birth. All of the insight comes from a very simple source—just a small stone. It's colorful and attractive, but there isn't much else that's remarkable about it. And yet it allows me to see the thoughts of other people."

He looked at her in surprise. "A stone? Where did you get it from?"

"I found it when I was a young woman living in Lestanor. I was fishing, and I noticed it lying at the bottom of the stream. It was catching the sunlight. It looked attractive, so I waded in and picked it up.

"I have no idea how it came to be there. I haven't been able to learn anything at all about its origins or why it behaves as it does. It's a great mystery. It took me a very long time before I fully discovered what it was capable of."

"So this stone lets you see what a person is thinking? Any person?"

"It's only effective when I look at someone. And I have to be holding the stone at the time."

He gazed at her in puzzlement. "But you don't walk around all day holding a stone."

"No. I sewed it into one of my undergarments in such a way that it stays constantly in contact with my skin."

He frowned, trying to make sense of what she was telling him.

"After I nearly died of the cold after falling in the stream, do you remember that I asked you to bring me my clothes? I was anxious to get the undergarment that held the stone. I almost never take it off."

"Except when we're intimate."

A delicate blush covered her face. "That's true. There are times when I don't need distractions. I don't always want to be different. I want to be a normal woman, too—to have the same feelings and experiences as every other woman."

He looked into her eyes tenderly, filled with amazement once again that she had chosen him.

An intense look came across her face. "What I'm trying to tell you is that the stone's powers are not restricted to me. If someone else possesses the stone, they will receive all of these abilities with it."

Kalvor went cold inside. He was beginning to understand for the first time why Lord Drettroth had been so eager to have the seer in his clutches. "Drettroth made a strange comment," he recalled. "I didn't understand it at the time, but it's starting to make sense now."

"What did he say?" she asked.

"He said that hearing about you and your powers made him remember something he'd once seen in an old scroll. He said he needed to do more research, but he seemed very excited.

"I took no notice of it. He wanted a job done, he'd always paid well, and that's all I cared about."

"So he was never planning to manipulate other people through me," said Sheylha. "He'd heard of the stone and wanted to try it out for himself." She shook her head, frowning.

Kalvor shuddered involuntarily. "Drettroth mustn't be allowed to get his hands on it!"

"I've removed it from my clothing," she told him. "You're stronger than I am. In the morning when we set off again I'm going to ask you to take care of it."

"Will I be able to see into your thoughts when I'm holding it?"

She shook her head. "Not while it still belongs to me. It doesn't seem to work like that."

She took his hands and gazed earnestly into his eyes. "If anything happens to me, promise me you will hide the stone where it will never be found. I don't need to tell you what will happen if it falls into the hands of someone who will misuse its power. It's better that no one has it. Promise me!" she insisted.

"I promise."

He wanted to reassure her—to tell her that he would protect her, that he wouldn't allow anything bad to happen to her. But the words stuck in his throat. How could he give her such assurances when the future was not within his control?

Neither of them slept that night.

They set out before dawn, hurrying along the road toward the Arvenian capital. True to her word, she had given him the stone. It sat securely in the leather pouch at his belt.

He drove them forward relentlessly. Something told him they could not afford to delay even for a moment.

. . .

The city was in sight when they first caught a distant glimpse of horsemen behind them. Kalvor felt certain it was the Rogandans pursuing them. The gray stone towers of Arnost's castle were still far away, but they seemed to beckon, calling them to the safety of the walls that surrounded the city. They only needed to get to the river, cross the ford, and follow the road that wound its way through the foothills to the city gates. But they were on foot, and Drettroth's men were mounted.

"We're not going to reach Arnost in time," he said.

"Can't we hide in the forest?"

He shook his head. "They'll track us, and sooner or later they'll find us. On my own I might stand a chance, but not with the three of us. There are too many of them."

They were out of options. "We have to separate," he said. "It will be too easy for them if we stay together. You need to get Ahnya to safety!"

Tears filled her eyes, but she didn't argue.

"Take what's left of the food," he said, thrusting a small sack into her hand. "If I'm killed, stay hidden until they're gone. Then go far away from here. Search out a place where no one will find you—a place where Ahnya won't come to any harm."

She embraced him desperately. "I love you," she told him. "Thank you for three shining years."

He opened his thoughts to her, then abruptly remembered that she no longer had the stone. "You gave me back my life," he told her, "and you taught me how to truly love. Thank you!"

He reached down for Ahnya and drew her in close, rocking her back and forth.

The distant pursuers disappeared in a dip in the road. Kalvor pointed to a nearby slope covered with bushes, on the opposite side of the road to the forest. "You need to go! Up there! Get among the bushes and hide on the far side of the slope. You'll still be able to see the road. Hurry! I'll lead them away."

"But there are so many of them!"

"Let me worry about that."

"What about the stone? We need to hide it!"

"I'll dispose of it, right now. Before I do anything else. Whatever happens, keep our daughter safe! Don't come back down unless I call you. Promise me!"

After a moment's hesitation she returned a reluctant nod.

She reached out for their daughter. "Daddy, Daddy!" Ahnya cried, protesting tearfully as he handed her over. Kalvor kissed her tenderly on the forehead, hardening himself against the tears that rolled down his cheeks. He needed to be strong.

Sheylha bundled Ahnya into her arms and shouldered the sack with the food. Then she hurried off across the slope. She was fit and lean, and he soon lost sight of her among the foliage.

Kalvor looked back for any sign of the hunters. They were still out of sight. Now was the perfect moment to make good his promise about the stone.

Finding a place beside the road where the soil was soft, he used his knife to quickly dig a deep hole. Then he lifted the stone from his pouch and cast it in. Finally he filled the hole, scooping loose soil and stones over it until it was covered. Only a close examination would reveal any disturbance now.

If they all somehow made it to safety, they could come back for the stone later.

He stood up quickly and looked around. A quick scan of the surrounding area revealed no easily defensible location. Ahead of him the road was bisected by a river. He sprinted along the road until he reached the ford. Hurrying to the crossing, he waded quickly across the river and raced up the opposite bank to rejoin the road.

Beyond the river the road bent around in a broad sweep, and he hastened along it. A short distance ahead he spotted a rocky outcrop beside the road. It might offer a defensible position. He was an archer without peer—he would pick them off with arrows from behind cover.

The outcrop lay on the same side of the road as Sheylha's hiding place. She would be able to observe him from across the river.

The odds were stacked against him, but he would not sell himself cheaply. He cared only about drawing Drettroth's men away from his wife and daughter. And denying Drettroth the stone.

As he hurried forward, he glanced back over his shoulder. He caught a brief glimpse of his pursuers before the bend hid them from view. It would take no more than a few minutes before they reached the ford.

He ran until he was gasping for air, inhaling ragged breaths into heaving lungs. When he reached the outcrop he stole a glance behind and saw his pursuers crossing the river. Hastily he began laying out his arrows. He had at least thirty shafts. He intended to make them count.

The hunters rounded the bend at full gallop. He reacted without conscious effort, taking rapid aim with his bow and releasing arrows.

MAREK HAD BEEN RIDING HARD, followed closely by the twenty of his men who remained. If the traders in the caravan were to be believed, Kalvor was traveling not only with a woman—presumably the seer—but with their child. He spat. The hunter had gone soft.

A self-satisfied smirk covered his face when he caught a distant glimpse of two people on the road ahead. They were apparently heading in the direction of Arnost. They might try to hide in the forest, but if they did they'd be wasting their energy. It was only a matter of time now.

The fugitives were still far away, but his men were mounted and closing fast. The road dipped and for several minutes Marek lost sight of them entirely. As the terrain rose again he caught a brief glimpse of Kalvor before the warrior disappeared around a bend in the road. Even at a distance Marek recognized his huge frame.

The horses splashed across the ford and surged up the other side. When they rounded the bend in the road, no one was in sight. Then arrows flew toward them, and several of his men tumbled from the saddle. Marek belatedly spotted Kalvor, positioned behind some rocks.

He snorted. The renegade might have taken the searchers by surprise earlier among the trees, but not even Kalvor could overcome twenty men in the open without support.

Marek shouted instructions. Two of his men rode on toward Arnost, searching for the woman with her child.

The archers among them drew their bows and began to return the fire.

SHEYLHA WATCHED ANXIOUSLY from her hiding place on the ridge as their pursuers galloped past, entirely unaware of her presence above them. Having seen them, cold sweat broke out across her brow, and her heart began to pound. How could Kalvor possibly defeat so many?

If Drettroth's men succeeded in killing him they would begin searching for her next. Even if they caught her, though, she wouldn't be able to tell them where the stone was hidden. She hadn't actually seen Kalvor dispose of it, but she didn't doubt for a moment that he had fulfilled his promise. It wouldn't find its way into Drettroth's clutches.

Kalvor had seen the mounted men now, and he was firing arrows at them. Several of the men fell, but the rest quickly surrounded him. Her heart beat faster.

They were firing arrows back, but they didn't seem able to bring him down. Instead it was the attackers who were falling, one at a time.

Kalvor had single-handedly taken on an overwhelming force. Her eyes grew wider as she watched him gradually bring it down to size. It was only with great effort that she prevented herself from leaping to her feet and cheering out loud.

5

An arrow struck the rock beside Kalvor's head and skidded past his cheek, drawing blood. There was no point trying to dodge the arrows—they were coming in too fast. But he had chosen his location well. He could only trust to luck or providence now.

More of his arrows were finding their mark. He could see the frustration growing among his opponents. None of their archers were skillful enough to hit a partially protected target while shooting from horseback. And it wouldn't be helping their concentration to see men steadily falling all around them.

At first he targeted the bowmen. Then he realized that after the last archer was gone, the survivors would rush him. He couldn't hold all of them off. So he kept at the bowmen until just two of them remained, then he began picking off the others.

Marek was too canny to make himself an easy target. He hung back, contenting himself with yelling orders at the others. And he never stayed in one location for more than a moment.

The ground was littered with bodies now. Kalvor could see only Marek and three others still facing him. He had even managed to retrieve a couple of spent arrows they'd fired at him. For the first time he dared to hope.

MAREK GROUND his teeth in frustration as more of his men went down. He had expected his archers to finish it quickly, but they were worthless.

He knew of Kalvor's reputation, but until now he had never seen the man in action. He called down a bitter curse on the tall bowman.

Marek's options were diminishing rapidly, along with the men remaining to him. It had begun to dawn on him that Kalvor had chosen his location well. The bowman was taking full advantage of the only available cover, while his men were reduced to attacking in the open. He wondered briefly if Kalvor might have used a different strategy if he'd been leading the attack. He thrust such self doubts aside, screaming his frustration instead at the few men who remained.

The situation had become increasingly dire when a shaft caught Kalvor in the shoulder. The rain of arrows from the outcrop ceased instantly.

Seizing his opportunity, Marek spurred his horse in close, leaping off its back with his sword drawn.

His rival saw him coming. Gritting his teeth, he reached down for his own sword, struggling to draw it out. As he stepped into the open to give himself room, another arrow took him in the thigh. He hit the ground hard, writhing in agony.

Everything had changed, so abruptly and so completely.

Marek strode up to Kalvor, gloating at the sight of the mighty warrior lying prostrate and completely helpless before him. The renegade had caused him far too much trouble and accounted for far too many of his men. How could Marek possibly explain to Lord Drettroth that one man had taken out almost his entire squad? Lusting to repay the humiliation, he planted his foot on Kalvor's neck and ground his face into the dirt.

"Where's the seer?" he snarled.

"Somewhere you'll never find her," Kalvor gasped.

"Wrong answer, scum!" Marek reached down and twisted the arrow protruding from Kalvor's shoulder. His victim appeared to black out momentarily from the pain.

Marek kept enough pressure on Kalvor's neck that he could barely breathe. But the fool still had something to say. "Tell Drettroth," he wheezed, "he'll never find what he's looking for. She got rid of it. It wasn't worth the trouble."

With no useful answers on offer, Marek lost patience. He wasn't given to subtlety. Plunging his sword into Kalvor's back, he ended the conversation permanently.

The warrior breathed out a final whispered sigh, "Sheylha..." Then his body went limp.

Marek looked down at him contemptuously.

"That's a relief," said one of the other survivors shakily.

"The job's not finished," Marek growled. "Not until we have the woman. Lord Drettroth said to bring Kalvor in dead, but he wanted the woman alive. We'll all be served up as meat for Malzakh if we go back without her."

The other three paled visibly. They knew as well as he did that Drettroth would not hesitate to execute them all if he was unhappy enough. And Malzakh the Destroyer would be waiting hungrily to devour them in the afterlife.

At that moment the two riders returned.

"She got away. Into Arnost," one of them reported.

Marek spat. "How do you know it was her?"

"It was a woman carrying a child," the other replied. "Just like the traders said. We saw her hurrying through the gates."

"Idiots!" Marek sneered. "There must be hundreds of women with children going through those gates every day. We have to search for her."

He pointed to Kalvor's body. "Bind him up so he won't stink," he ordered. "Any of his loose belongings go into this sack. We were told to bring everything back untouched."

They tightly wrapped Kalvor's body and secured it over a horse. Then they dug a shallow grave and buried their dead. There were a lot of bodies, and it took a long time.

As soon as they'd completed their labors Marek gathered them together. "We need to find the woman. There are still six of us," he said. "We'll split up and search in pairs." He pointed at two of the men. "You two go back across the ford. If she didn't follow Kalvor to this side of the river, she'll have hidden back in the forest. Ride for an hour and start searching there." He pointed at two others. "You go back across the river as well. As soon as you reach the outskirts of the forest you can start searching in it. The two of us will search on this side of the river. We'll head toward Arnost."

He glanced up at the sky. The sun had passed its zenith, but a few hours of daylight remained. "We'll meet back here just before sunset."

"What if we don't find her?" one of the men asked. "She could be anywhere." He jerked a thumb toward the body of Kalvor. "If we go back to Lord Drettroth with nothing but him, we'll end up the same way."

"He's right!" agreed one of the others. "Lord Drettroth isn't known to be a reasonable man."

"So what do you propose?" sneered Marek.

"Why go back at all? Let him think we were all killed."

"He wouldn't just leave it at that, you halfwit!" Marek replied mockingly. "We all know he's searching for something. Whatever it is, he'll think we took it. He'll have us hunted down like dogs."

The other men went quiet.

"Just do as I told you," he snarled. "Get going!"

The first four men mounted their horses and headed for the river.

When Sheylha saw Kalvor drop his bow, her heart skipped a beat. He moved to the side, and the outcrop hid him from view. She couldn't tell what was happening. Her gut twisted into a tight knot. The tension became unbearable.

Sheylha didn't want to watch, but she couldn't tear her eyes away. She clutched her daughter to her helplessly. Not until Drettroth's men dragged Kalvor into the open and tightly wrapped him, completely covering his head, did Sheylha acknowledge to herself that he was dead. Then the tears blinded her as she sobbed her grief.

Her daughter began to wail loudly, no doubt responding to her mother's distress. Shocked out of her self-absorption, Sheylha pulled the child in close, shushing her frantically and desperately trying to muffle her cries. She looked up anxiously, but the men across the river seemed not to have heard.

Ahnya was her priority now. Sheylha managed to calm her, and in spite of her own agitation she somehow continued to comfort the child.

They would begin searching for her soon. But there were so few of them left. If she could only keep Ahnya quiet, they might not find her.

She saw the men separate into pairs. She watched anxiously as four of them crossed to her side of the river, riding in her direction. But they passed below her without looking up. Two of them rode on into the distance, back the way they had originally come.

The other two came to a halt not far beyond her hiding place. Would they come over to her side of the road and start searching the bushy slopes where she was hiding? Or would they turn away and search the forest? She looked on with heart pounding as they turned their backs on her, heading into the forest which lay on the opposite side of the road.

About an hour later they reappeared. They peered furtively back toward the ford, then they rode off at a gallop, following the two who had ridden that way earlier.

A LITTLE BEFORE sundown Marek and his companion returned to the rocky outcrop after spending the afternoon searching fruitlessly in the direction of Arnost.

They lit a fire, and sat down to wait. The sun sank lower in the sky and darkness fell. The clouds cleared, revealing a dazzling display of stars.

The minutes slipped away with no sign of the other four searchers.

Marek sat fuming. “Where are they?” he growled.

The other man watched him without speaking for a moment. Then he shrugged. “They’re not coming back,” he said.

“What are you talking about?”

He shrugged again. “They’re scared.”

Marek struggled to master his fury. “I’ll kill the cowards myself!”

He glared at the fire as it hissed and crackled.

“What are you going to do?” his companion asked.

“I’m going back to Drettroth, of course,” Marek replied. “I wasn’t exaggerating before. If I don’t return, Drettroth will have me hunted down.”

“What are you going to tell him?”

“I’ll tell him that Kalvor killed all the others. And that we saw the seer escape into Arnost. I’ll also tell him what Kalvor said—about her deciding to get rid of whatever it is he’s searching for.” It was his turn to shrug. “Then I’ll take my chances.”

“I’ll come with you,” the other replied.

“Let’s not waste any more time then,” said Marek. They kicked dirt onto the fire and mounted their horses. They towed the horse bearing Kalvor’s body behind them as they rode away.

The horses of their dead companions they left to wander wherever they would.

THROUGHOUT THE AFTERNOON Sheylha had cuddled her daughter, soothing her whenever she became distressed. Whenever she wanted to get up and wander around, Sheylha had sung to her softly or played quiet games with her. For the most part Ahnya was a placid child, and Sheylha never had more reason to be grateful for it.

When the sun sank low in the sky they shared a little food from the sack and drank water from a skin. As soon as it became dark, Ahnya settled into Sheylha's lap and went to sleep.

Sheylha had focused all her attention on keeping her daughter quiet and occupied. Once the last of Drettroth's men had disappeared into the distance, that burden finally lifted. Then the reality of Kalvor's death came crashing back in on her. How could she go on without him? How could she explain his absence to their daughter?

Tears welled up once more to flood her eyes, and sobs wracked her body. Ahnya woke and began to wail, and this time Sheylha made no attempt to restrain her. The two of them gave themselves over to their distress and howled together into the dark.

Eventually the tears dried up. With considerable effort, Sheylha managed to regain her composure. She recognized that this was a time to put the past behind her and face the future.

Everything would need to be different now. She had given up the stone willingly, and she had no desire to find it again. She was a seer no longer. The minds of others would forever be closed to her. She must find a new purpose in life.

Where could she go? She had no idea. But an opportunity of some kind would surely present itself. She was not without skills, and she was fluent in the languages of Arvenon, Rogand, and Lestanor. She would change her name and her identity and search out a way to provide for herself while she raised their daughter.

All that mattered now was Ahnya—she was precious beyond words. And she provided Sheylha with the only remaining link to her beloved husband.

Her immediate concern was to leave before any of their enemies decided to come back.

She glanced into the sack. There was probably enough food left in there for a couple of days. Shouldering the sack, she set Ahnya securely on her hip and made her way carefully back down the slope in the dark.

She headed along the road to the ford, intending to refill her skin in the river. A soft nickering caught her attention. Turning aside she found a horse, saddled and bridled. The animal nuzzled her, leaning in appreciatively as she stroked its head.

The opportunity was too good to miss. She lifted her daughter onto the horse, then climbed up behind her. Clicking her tongue, she guided the animal back onto the road, heading away from Arnost.

The outskirts of the forest soon appeared on her left. She rode on for a while before turning off the road, guiding her horse carefully among the trees. She didn't stop until she came to a meadow in a small clearing beside a stream. The meadow was secluded and well away from the road.

Overcome with exhaustion, she stopped the horse. Sliding from its back, she lifted her daughter down and set her in the meadow to rest among the wildflowers. She removed the horse's bridle and replaced it with a halter she found in a saddlebag. Then she secured the halter to a branch. Finally she lifted off its saddle.

Sheylha sat down in the dark beside Ahnya to find that the child had already fallen into a weary slumber.

With no pressing tasks to perform, Sheylha took a deep breath and willed her body to relax.

For a time she closed her eyes, remembering Kal and honoring him for who he was. She had loved him from the moment he stepped into her hut in Lestanor, cold and dangerous and wounded in spirit. She relived again the process by which he had received healing and had learned to appreciate life and goodness again. She remembered his quiet strength, their simple life in the forest, and the joy they had found together.

Then she exhaled slowly—a long shuddering sigh that rose up from the depths of her being. It began with murmurs of partings and bitter endings, of anguish beyond expression. It ended with soft whispers of hope, of peace that passes understanding.

She stilled herself once more, gazing up at the dark sky and the stars, listening to the call of the night birds and the burble of the water. Then she lay down beside Ahnya and slept.

In the morning Sheylha woke to find Ahnya stirring. She led her daughter to the stream. They both drank deeply, and she refilled the skin. Then she saddled and bridled the horse and they climbed once more into the saddle.

Turning their backs on all they had known, mother and daughter set their faces toward the vastness of the unpredictable world. Then they rode forward together.

They were soon lost to any certain knowledge.

EPILOGUE

The days gave way to months, and the months to years, and the Stone of Knowing lay hidden where Kalvor had buried it. Not even the wind and the rain disturbed it in its resting place.

It remained untouched until a day dawned when a burrowing animal chanced to unearth it. The animal dug energetically, scattering soil and debris everywhere. Having completed its labors, the creature scurried away.

The stone remained where it had fallen, exposed to the world once more.

A breeze sprang up and polished it clean, sweeping away any speck of dirt bold enough to linger on its surface.

Dazzling, alluring, and freely available once more, the stone gleamed brightly in the morning light.

It lay there unknowing, unaware of its influence, yet ready to capture the wandering glance of a new wide-eyed and unsuspecting guardian.

The End

The saga continues in
The Stone of Authority Complete Set
(The Stone Cycle Complete Sets Book 2)

AFTERWORD

The Stone of Knowing is not a children's story, but it did begin life as a bedtime tale I told our children when they were quite young.

In their early years all four children shared a single bedroom, and I began telling them stories before they went to sleep. The stories were mostly serial in nature and typically ran for a few days or weeks. The longest lasted about 18 months. I made them up as we went along, and we journeyed together wherever the creative mood of the moment took us. Usually two or three stories were active at a time, and the children took turns to decide which one they wanted to hear. This process of natural selection helped me discover the style and content that best pleased my audience. The stories were sometimes serious and sometimes silly. Occasionally they offered a useful way to convey a message. Mostly, though, the stories were simply intended to entertain and engage the listeners.

At some point I decided to turn one of the stories into a novel. I chose one of the longest running adventures and began the slow process of fleshing it out. I wrote in bursts, sometimes with long pauses that stretched into years. Life brought many distractions; during this period we moved as a family to the United States, and some years later returned to Australia. The story was placed on long-term hold while I authored a technical book, and further time passed before I found the energy to resume writing. When our children grew up, they embraced the emerging novel enthusiastically, and I returned to it largely because of their insistence that I finish it.

Most of the main characters in the novel appeared in the original story, and many of the major plot elements in both *The Stone of Knowing* and its sequel, *The Cost of Knowing*, also flowed from the same source. The bedtime tale came to an end before it reached the climax that unfolds in the sequel, although in many ways the developing plot anticipated the final outcome.

I never expected the journey to span 25 years. But I've enjoyed the opportunity to turn the spoken story—long forgotten by all of the children except our eldest—into something more solid and lasting. And it's helped me relive the days when a line of young faces were turned attentively to mine, as eager as I was to discover whatever might happen next.

Allan Packer
Adelaide, South Australia
2019

NOTE FROM THE AUTHOR

Thank you for reading *The Stone of Knowing Complete Set*—I hope you enjoyed it. Please consider leaving a review. Reviews make a huge difference to authors as well as benefiting other readers. I also very much appreciate feedback from my readers.

The saga of *The Stone of Knowing* continues in *The Stone of Authority Complete Set (The Stone Cycle Complete Sets Book 2), comprising The Stone of Authority (The Stone Cycle Book 3)* and *The Struggle for Authority* (*The Stone Cycle Book 4).* Both books are outlined below.

To be kept up to date on new releases, sign up to my mailing list at www.allanpacker.com. New subscribers will receive an exclusive bonus novelette, available in ebook and audiobook format. The novelette, *The Rending: A Prequel to The Cost of Knowing*, is described below.

But first, *The Stone of Authority (The Stone Cycle Book 3)* and *The Struggle for Authority* (*The Stone Cycle Book 4).*

The invasion is over, and the shattered Rogandan army has straggled home. The people of Arvenon and the surrounding kingdoms are at peace. Or so they believe.

Little do they know that a new stone of power has emerged, controlled by a cruel tyrant bent on destruction. But King Agon of Rogand lusts after much more than conquest. He will settle for nothing less than unending power.

No armies are massing at the border. The threat to the kingdom comes from within.

As chaos spreads, Will, Steffan, Essanda, and Arvenon's other key defenders are each confronted with crisis. If any one of them stumbles, the kingdom will fall.

Arvenon is controlled by a traitor. The kingdom of Castel teeters on the brink. With the unseen hand of King Agon of Rogand pulling the strings, a mantle of oppression is slowly settling over the four kingdoms.

Having recovered from the assassination attempt, King Steffan of Arvenon sets out to wrest back control of his kingdom, vigorously supported by Will, Rufe, Thomas, and familiar allies. Unlikely influences might ultimately tip the balance.

In a desperate attempt to block Agon, Will and Thomas set out for Rogand. What each of them encounters there will shake them to the core. The fate of four kingdoms will hinge upon the Stone of Authority.

To be kept up to date on new releases, sign up to my mailing list at allanpacker.com. New subscribers will receive an exclusive bonus novelette—a prequel to *The Cost of Knowing*. The novelette, The Rending: A Prequel to The Cost of Knowing, is a complete story four chapters (13,000 words) in length. It provides additional context to Anneka's story without introducing spoilers for other books in *The Stone Cycle* series. The novelette is described below.

Endings may be beginnings in disguise

Anneka is comfortable and confident, a noblewoman of consequence living a life of privilege. Until the day her world is torn apart.

After losing everything she most cares about, she must abandon her home and her way of life in an attempt to secure the future of those who depend on her.

No one, least of all Anneka, could anticipate a deeper significance to her struggle. Yet her journey will one day influence the fate of kingdoms.

ACKNOWLEDGMENTS

First and foremost, I would like to thank my wife and children for persisting in encouraging me to keep at the story, and for being willing beta readers at various stages of the journey. My son-in-law Ray also engaged enthusiastically with the story in the latter years of its development. My wife, Merilyn, was my most committed supporter throughout, and reliably provided worthwhile feedback whenever it was needed.

Special thanks to my beta readers, Merilyn, Stephen (who definitely wins the prize for the most completions of the early manuscript), Deborah, Melanie, James, Ray, Marc, Jen Neal, Brian Plush, Francie Hardy, Cherilyn White, Ali, and Llewelyn Hoy. Their feedback and suggestions led to improvements in a number of areas.

In the earliest stages I benefited from input and encouragement from a number of established authors. My father, Ken Packer, gave specific assistance in various technical aspects of writing. Roger and Sandra Carter also provided valuable feedback and urged me to keep going.

I am indebted to Brian Plush for the awesome map—he took my rough draft and created a work of art.

I would also like to express my appreciation to my developmental editor, Mary Novak. I received a great deal of valuable constructive criticism from her, all of which has improved the flow and polish of the story.

I am grateful to Deborah for her thorough proofreading, completed in spite of many worthy life distractions.

The responsibility for remaining flaws lies solely with me.

Thanks, too, to my daughter, Melanie Cellier, who drew upon her considerable experience as an author of young adult fantasy and fairy tale retellings to offer advice around presentation and release practicalities.

Final thanks go to God. I was emerging from a period of grief and loss when I wrote *The Cost of Knowing*, and the experience reminded me again that God is the one who sustains and nurtures me through the ongoing joys and trials of life. He has always provided purpose in living, comfort in times of sorrow, inspiration for creativity, and so much else besides.

ABOUT THE AUTHOR

Allan Packer writes epic fantasy, and the novels and novelettes of *The Stone Cycle* are his first published fiction.

Allan grew up surrounded by books and became an avid reader during his childhood. In his university years fantasy displaced science fiction as his favorite genre, thanks primarily to J. R. R. Tolkien. He later shared this love with his four children by reading *The Lord of the Rings* to them aloud—a three-month marathon he completed twice during their formative years.

Born in Australia, Allan has lived and worked on three continents, and spent one quarter of his working years abroad. Having worked as an IT professional throughout his career, he was first published as a technical author.

Today he lives with his wife in Adelaide, South Australia, near their children and a small but growing band of grandchildren.

Allan is currently working on his second epic fantasy series.

PART V

LIST OF CHARACTERS AND RESEARCH NOTES

THE STONE OF KNOWING

LIST OF CHARACTERS

- *Agon* - king of Rogand
- *Ander* - Arvenian soldier from Erestor; skilled swordsman and archer
- *Axel Stablehand* - master of the Arvenian royal stables at Arnost, and the father of Thomas
- *Beneface* - abbot of a high plateau monastery in Arvenon boasting an extensive library
- *Bottren* - high-ranking Arvenian nobleman and close confidante of King Steffan
- *Burtelen* - high-ranking Arvenian nobleman from Erestor and close confidante of King Steffan
- *Dannel* - monk at a high plateau monastery in Arvenon boasting an extensive library
- *Drettroth* - high-ranking Rogandan nobleman; commander of the Rogandan army
- *Duke of Erestor* - The uncle of King Steffan of Arvenon, and the regent during the king's absence; the senior member of the nobility in Erestor
- *Edgar* - greedy Arvenian soldier
- *Elbruhe* - young Rogandan woman; runaway slave

- *Elias* - abbot at the Monastery of St. Rodrig the Martyr where Brother Vangellis was hiding away
- *Erastus* - librarian at a high plateau monastery in Arvenon
- *Essanda* - Princess of Castel
- *Gordan* - Castelan nobleman and confidante of King Istel
- *Haldek* - Rogandan soldier; stronghold guard
- *Hann* - young monk at a high plateau monastery in Arvenon
- *Istel* - king of Castel, a neighboring kingdom to Arvenon
- *Kuper* - Arvenian soldier from Erestor; skilled swordsman and archer and twin brother to Rellan
- *Luzik* - Rogandan army commander
- *Marya* - wife of Axel Stablehand and mother of Thomas
- *Nestor* - Arvenian soldier from Arnost
- *Pisander* - Arvenian earl and head of King Steffan's foreign spy network; member of the nobility from Erestor
- *Ranauld* - Arvenian count; a confidante of King Steffan
- *Randolf of Clerbon* - author of an ancient scroll
- *Rellan* - Arvenian soldier from Erestor; skilled swordsman and archer and twin brother to Kuper
- *Rudungen* - a minor Arvenian baron
- *Rufe Sarjant* - respected and physically imposing Arvenian soldier; a close friend of Will Prentis
- *Simon* - boy who helps in the Arvenian royal stables
- *Steffan the Second* - king of Arvenon
- *Thomas Stablehand* - possessor of the Stone of Knowing; son of Axel, the Arvenian royal stable master, and Marya
- *Vangellis* - widely traveled Arvenian monk
- *Will Prentis* - young, ambitious, and unusually capable Arvenian soldier; fluent in Rogandan and widely traveled

THE COST OF KNOWING

LIST OF CHARACTERS

- *Agon* - king of Rogand
- *Ander* - Arvenian soldier from Erestor; skilled swordsman and archer; healed of severe wounds by Brother Vangellis
- *Anneka* - former noblewoman, Lady Neave; leader of a forest community near Erestor
- *Axel Stablehand* - master of the Arvenian royal stables at Arnost, and the father of Thomas
- *Beneface* - abbot of a high plateau monastery in Arvenon boasting an extensive library
- *Bottren* - high-ranking Arvenian nobleman and close confidante of King Steffan
- *Burtelen* - high-ranking Arvenian nobleman from Erestor and close confidante of King Steffan
- *Dannel* - monk at a high plateau monastery in Arvenon boasting an extensive library
- *Delmar* - king of Varas, a neighboring kingdom to Arvenon
- *Drettroth* - high-ranking Rogandan nobleman; commander of the Rogandan army
- *Duke of Erestor* - The uncle of King Steffan of Arvenon, and

the regent during the king's absence; the senior member of the nobility in Erestor

- *Eisgold* - influential Castelan nobleman; senior commander of the Castelan army
- *Elbruhe* - young Rogandan woman; runaway slave
- *Elena* - young woman living in hiding with her father Rubin in the forests of Arvenon
- *Erastus* - librarian at a high plateau monastery in Arvenon
- *Essanda* - Princess of Castel who marries King Steffan, becoming queen of Arvenon
- *Gordan* - Castelan nobleman; confidante of King Istel and Essanda
- *Grunsetz* - Rogandan ambassador to Varas
- *Haldek* - Rogandan soldier; stronghold guard
- *Hann* - young monk at a high plateau monastery in Arvenon
- *Hender* - young bowman living in Anneka's forest community
- *Istel* - king of Castel, a neighboring kingdom to Arvenon
- *Karevis* - Varasan nobleman; commander of the Varasan army
- *Kulzeike* - commander of the Rogandan army
- *Kuper* - Arvenian soldier from Erestor; skilled swordsman and archer and twin brother to Rellan
- *Luzik* - former Rogandan army commander
- *Marya* - wife of Axel Stablehand and mother of Thomas
- *Nestor* - Arvenian soldier from Arnost
- *Pisander* - Arvenian earl and head of King Steffan's foreign spy network; member of the nobility from Erestor
- *Ranauld* - Arvenian count; a confidante of King Steffan
- *Randolf of Clerbon* - author of an ancient scroll
- *Rellan* - Arvenian soldier from Erestor; skilled swordsman and archer and twin brother to Kuper
- *Rubin* - father of Elena
- *Rudungen* - a minor Arvenian baron

- *Rufe Sarjant* - respected and physically imposing Arvenian soldier; a close friend of Will Prentis
- *Simon* - boy who helped in the Arvenian royal stables
- *Steffan the Second* - king of Arvenon
- *Tarestel* - wealthy and influential Varasan nobleman
- *Thomas Stablehand* - possessor of the Stone of Knowing; son of Axel, the Arvenian royal stable master, and Marya
- *Vangellis* - widely traveled Arvenian monk
- *Will Prentis* - young, ambitious, and unusually capable Arvenian soldier; fluent in Rogandan and widely traveled
- *Yosef* - respected member of Anneka's forest community
- *Zornath* - senior Rogandan army liaison

THE STONE OF KNOWING
RESEARCH NOTES

Spoiler Alert!

The reader is advised to avoid this section before finishing *The Stone of Knowing*.

Mystery Plays

The guild-run mystery play / morality play in Chapter 9 was inspired by theatrical equivalents in medieval Europe.

From https://en.wikipedia.org/wiki/Mystery_play:

"By the end of the 15th century, the practice of acting these plays in cycles on festival days was established in several parts of Europe. Sometimes, each play was performed on a decorated pageant cart that moved about the city to allow different crowds to watch each play, and provided actors with a dressing room as well as a stage."

Delirium Tremens

Alcohol withdrawal, as experienced by Brother Vangellis, is today managed by drugs, but in the days before modern medicines the symptoms could be quite severe. The most severe form of with-drawal, sometimes referred to as Delirium tremens (DTs), usually occurs 24 to 72 hours after alcohol intake ceases. It can involve a range of symptoms including disorientation, tremors, and visual and auditory hallucinations. In the worst case, seizures can lead to death. For a discussion of signs and symptoms, refer to:

https://en.wikipedia.org/wiki/Alcohol_withdrawal_syndrome.

Encounters with wild bears

Some advisors recommend a vigorous defense should a bear decide to attack.

From http://www.bearsmart.com/about-bears/dispelling-myths/:

"If a bear attacks (particularly a black bear) in an offensive manner and physical contact is made, fight for your life. Kick, punch, hit the bear with rocks or sticks or any improvised weapon you can find."

The same site offers the following advice: "Warn bears of your presence by talking calmly and loudly or singing, especially in dense bush where visibility may be limited or around rivers or streams where bears have trouble hearing you coming. Your voice will help identify you as human and non-threatening."

I have personally heard a naturalist describe the beneficial effect of singing to a bear during an encounter in the wild.

Real-world religious elements

It isn't original in a fantasy story to include religious features that are recognizable from the real world—William Morris did the same in *The Well at the World's End*, published in 1896. It is, however, unusual in a modern fantasy, where religions are typically either absent or entirely invented.

Many of the religious elements in *The Stone of Knowing* stemmed from the original tale I told our children, and found their way into the written story for that reason. The end result may please some readers and disappoint others. Either way, it is worth noting that any religious components of the story, both recognizable and invented, are intended to be incidental. *The Stone of Knowing* is an epic fantasy adventure, not a religious allegory.

THE COST OF KNOWING

RESEARCH NOTES

Spoiler Alert!

The reader is advised to avoid this section before finishing *The Cost of Knowing*.

Poisons

Strychnine, ingested by both Lord Drettroth and Simon, has been used as a poison since ancient times. Its effects are described at:

https://en.wikipedia.org/wiki/Strychnine_poisoning.

Cyanide, used by Simon at the end, is another poison of long standing. It is said to have been the preferred poison of the Roman Emperor Nero. The effects of acute exposure to cyanide are described at:

https://en.wikipedia.org/wiki/Cyanide_poisoning.

www.ingramcontent.com/pod-product-compliance
Lightning Source LLC
Chambersburg PA
CBHW020533310726
48979CB00014B/2318/J

* 9 7 8 1 9 2 3 2 1 8 0 9 3 *